READER'S

DIGEST

CONDENSED

BOOKS

The Reader's Digest Association Ltd.
LONDON • NEW YORK • CAPE TOWN

....
With the exception of actual personages identified
as such, the characters and incidents in the fictional
selections in this volume are entirely the product of
the authors' imaginations and have no relation
to any person or event in real life.
....

THE READER'S DIGEST ASSOCIATION LIMITED
Berkeley Square House, London W1X 6AB
THE READER'S DIGEST ASSOCIATION
SOUTH AFRICA (PTY) LTD
Reader's Digest House, 130 Strand Street, Cape Town

Page make-up by Elite Typesetting Techniques,
Eastleigh, Hampshire
Separations by WACE Corporate Imaging, London
Printed by BPC Catalogues (East Kilbride) Ltd.
A MEMBER OF THE BRITISH PRINTING
COMPANY LTD
Bound by BPC Consumer Books Ltd, Aylesbury

CONTENTS

WHITE STAR
James Thayer

Owen Gray was once a legend, a sniper of outstanding skill. But it is many years since Gray was a serviceman, and killing is something he has vowed never to do again. Now, however, a sniper is stalking the streets of New York, apparently goading Owen Gray—once known as 'White Star'—into a duel. He has no choice but to summon every ounce of skill for a last pitched battle against a ruthless enemy.

COMING HOME
Rosamunde Pilcher

Porthkerris, Cornwall, in 1939. Judith Dunbar is on the brink of womanhood and life is full of promise—especially when she is invited to spend her summer holidays with the Carey-Lewis's at their large and sumptuous estate. New friendships are forged, romance is kindled. The only cloud on the horizon is the imminent prospect of war—a war that will leave no life unchanged.

IN THE SHADOW OF A RAINBOW
Robert Franklin Leslie

This is the extraordinary true story of Náhani, a silver-white timber wolf, whose pack is suspected not only of stealing from traps, but also of attacking humans. A price is placed on Náhani's head, and only one man can save her: a Chimmesyan Indian with a profound and sensitive knowledge of the she-wolf's territory, the rugged wilderness of British Columbia.

ENIGMA
Robert Harris

When German U-boat attacks on Allied shipping intensify, brilliant cryptanalyst, Tom Jericho, is summoned urgently to the government's codebreaking centre at Bletchley Park. As he toils round the clock to unravel the enemy's latest Enigma code, a second crisis hits: his colleague and ex-girlfriend, Claire, has disappeared, leaving a trail of evidence that points to a traitor within Bletchley's confines.

WHITE STAR

JAMES THAYER

WITH ILLUSTRATIONS BY STEVE EARLY

Long ago, Owen Gray was a sniper, capable of taking out an enemy with one clean shot at 1,300 yards. Now the ex-serviceman has a legal career, lives in a New York apartment with three adopted children, and just wants to live out his life in peace.

But there's a cold-blooded marksman stalking the city's streets, and the police need Gray's help. Only he can anticipate a fellow sniper's next move . . .

CHAPTER ONE

The star appeared in the void where none had been before, flickering as it struggled to life, sending forth delicate tendrils of light.

'Are you kidding me?' Anna Renthal whispered. 'Origami?'

Owen Gray looked down at his hand. The star rested in his palm. Startled, he flicked his fingers and it fell to the table where it lay lifeless and tiny.

She leaned along the prosecutors' table towards him, looking at the jury as it filed into the courtroom. 'It's a stupid hobby for a grown man, if you ask me.' She spoke almost without moving her lips.

'Damn it.' Pete Coates was also whispering. 'None of the jurors is looking at us. We've lost.'

'Number eight just smiled at Owen,' Anna Renthal insisted.

Coates said out of the side of his mouth, 'Number eight is in love with Owen. Sure she's going to grin.'

Anna Renthal asked, 'You OK, Owen?'

Gray looked again at the paper star. He had no recollection of folding it. The star often appeared at times of stress, emerging from whatever piece of paper was in front of him. He shook his head. 'Three years' work all boils down to whether a juror smiles at me.'

He had caught himself in a mirror that morning. He seemed to have aged five years during the trial. The new lines round his eyes looked permanent. His black hair still had tight waves, only there was less above his temples. Gray had a thin dagger of a nose and slate-grey eyes. A grin would have softened the sharp angles of his face, but in front of a jury his expression was always carefully deadpan.

The jurors moved slowly, taking their time, enjoying their portentous arrival. Gray glanced over his shoulder at the courtroom's gallery. There was not a seat to be had, and not one sound or movement from the spectators.

Carmine 'Chinaman' De Sallo had been charged with thirty-eight counts, everything from money laundering to hijacking to racketeering to conspiracy. The jury had deliberated eight days. De Sallo faced eighty-eight years in prison. 'He deserves life in the electric chair,' Anna Renthal had said.

The spectators were arranged as if at a wedding. De Sallo had packed the defendant's side of the courtroom day after day with his soldiers. Federal agents and New York City police sat on the other side, behind the prosecutors.

Detective Pete Coates was the NYPD case officer, allowed to sit at the prosecutors' table. He had tiny features—pinprick eyes and a splinter of a nose, so small that his head appeared to have swollen around his face. His hair was a dun colour and as short as a drill instructor's. His chest had the dimensions of an oil drum, and the sleeves of his sagging grey suit were two inches too short. His blue-rimmed spectacles were surprisingly stylish, given the faded look to the rest of him.

Also at the table, for the first time since the trial began, was Gray's boss, Frank Luca, the United States Attorney for the Southern District of New York. Newspaper columnists judged that Luca's senatorial ambitions depended on De Sallo's fate. But this was Owen Gray's case. He was an assistant US attorney and the chief prosecutor, the mastermind of the government's massive effort to put Carmine De Sallo into prison. Anna Renthal was his able co-prosecutor. Since the beginning of the trial she had worn her walnut-coloured hair pulled back in a severe bun. Today she was wearing a grey suit with a white cotton blouse buttoned to the neck.

As the last of the jurors filed in, Anna Renthal glanced behind her. Joseph 'Pots' Asperanti was in his usual position directly behind De Sallo. He wore glasses with amber lenses and a silk handkerchief in his suit pocket. Next to Pots was Danny Garbanto, known as the Boatman because it was thought he piloted the De Sallo runabout that dumped bodies into Jamaica Bay. But the star undoubtedly was Chinaman De Sallo, and he never let the limelight drift from him. Each day his measured gait and sanguine smile told his audience and jury that he fully expected an acquittal.

Chinaman was six foot four and weighed somewhere between 300 and 350 pounds. The US Attorney's office had a sweepstake on what his prison weigh-in would be. Gray had paid his five dollars, and if De Sallo flattened the scales at 342 pounds at the penitentiary medical, Gray would be $500 to the good.

The judge said, 'Mr Foreman, I understand you've reached a verdict.'

Gray turned back to the jury. His breath was shallow and he felt as if he were wearing a jacket three sizes too small.

The foreman, juror number three, replied, 'We have, Your Honour.'

'Please hand your verdict to the clerk.'

The clerk stepped towards the jury box. All eyes were on De Sallo as the clerk took the slip from the foreman, then stepped to the elevated dais. Judge Robert Kennelly reached across the bench for the paper, his face professionally impassive.

Count one was conspiracy, the easiest of the prosecution's burdens. If De Sallo walked on the conspiracy count, he'd walk on them all. Everyone in the courtroom knew it.

The accused and his attorneys rose from their chairs. De Sallo stood with his back as rigid as a poker. His expression was one of sublime confidence.

'Ah, damn,' Coates muttered. 'Number ten just winked at that piece-of-dirt Chinaman.'

'Contact-lens problems,' Gray whispered hopefully. 'She's had trouble before.'

The judge passed the slip back to the clerk. 'You may read the verdict.'

Gray glanced at his superior, Frank Luca. The attorney dipped his chin. Hell, Gray thought, he's watching me, not De Sallo.

'In the matter of the United States versus Carmine De Sallo,' the clerk intoned. 'On count one, we the jury find the defendant . . .'

Frank Luca inhaled sharply.

'. . . not guilty.'

Gasps filled the courtroom. Then dazed silence. Then the room erupted. De Sallo's supporters hooted and whistled and applauded. A defence lawyer raised his arms into the air like a sprinter first to the finish line. Journalists reached for their cellular phones.

Owen Gray sagged back into his chair.

Boatman Garbanto called out, 'Attaway, boss.'

Pots Asperanti blew a kiss at Gray, as he had every time he found Owen Gray looking in his direction during the trial.

The FBI agents and cops slumped as if in unison. Some leaned forward, arms on the seat-back ahead of them, some closed their eyes.

The judge pounded his gavel and after a moment a semblance of order settled on the courtroom. The clerk read, 'On count two, we find the defendant not guilty.'

Another smattering of applause. De Sallo brought his arm up to check his wristwatch as if he had other plans.

Next was the kidnapping charge. 'On count three, we find the defendant not guilty.'

A line of sweat formed on Gray's forehead and a hum of humiliation sounded in his ears. The clerk's voice seemed far away. 'Not guilty . . . not guilty . . .'

'Oh God,' Anna said miserably. Her face had gained a yellow hue. 'I think I'm going to vomit.'

When the acquittal on the last count was read, the judge said, 'I'm going to poll the jury. Juror number one, is that your verdict and the verdict of the jury?'

'Yes, Your Honour.'

Kennelly went through the jurors. Each affirmed the verdict. One of De Sallo's lawyers then said, 'Your Honour, I move to exonerate bail.'

'Granted. Mr De Sallo, you are released.' The judge thanked the jury, then dismissed court and disappeared into his chambers.

Gray squeezed Anna Renthal's hand. He put his notes into his briefcase, venturing a look sideways at the chair where his boss had been sitting. Frank Luca had slipped out of the courtroom.

Pete Coates had followed Gray's eyes. 'Luca wants to avoid the reporters. Smart guy.'

The detective patted Gray's shoulder, then joined the other cops and agents as they left the courtroom. Gray and Anna trailed after them. The paper star was left on the prosecutors' table.

The crowd was slowed by reporters who shoved their microphones into De Sallo's face the moment he reached the hallway. Camera flashes came as steadily as a strobe light. De Sallo pushed ahead, his troupe in tow.

'We'll wait two years, then indict him again,' Anna said with false cheer. 'We'll get him next time, Owen.'

'Yeah, you bet we will.' His voice was doubtful.

A bottleneck developed at the revolving door. Gray and Anna were the last to push through. Outside Gray saw a bank of microphones set up near the sidewalk. Furiously working their cameras, photographers flanked De Sallo as he descended the steps.

'This way, Chinaman,' some shouted. 'Just a few more.'

'He's usually camera-shy,' Anna said, descending the stairs next to Gray. She carried three volumes of the US Code under her arm.

Gray replied, 'This is his chance to make you and me and especially Frank look like dunces. He won't pass it up.'

De Sallo stepped down to the microphones. Reporters pushed their handheld recorders towards him. Questions were shouted until he held up both hands.

'I just got a couple of things to let you guys in on,' he said in his Brooklyn accent. 'Let me first say that America is a great country.'

A flock of pigeons lifted from Foley Square, passing over the Chambers Street subway station, then towards Federal Plaza.

De Sallo held forth magnificently. 'I would like to thank my beloved father, whose memory—'

At that instant the Chinaman's head ruptured in a spray of crimson. His body fell heavily against the microphone stand, streaking the steps red.

Screams and oaths filled the square. A dozen handguns appeared in the hands of agents and detectives. Pots Asperanti pulled out a .38 snub-nose, having somehow sneaked it in and out of the courthouse. Pots waved his pistol at imaginary targets, then nervously slid it back into his coat.

Spectators ran for cover, some up the steps into the courthouse, others towards the subway station. The agents scanned the crowd, the rooftops and windows. They had heard nothing, no shot. And now they saw nothing.

Asperanti rolled De Sallo's body over. A hole the size of a dime had been punched between the eyes.

Anna dropped to the steps, books falling from her arm. 'I'm going to be sick,' she said miserably.

Owen Gray bent to help her, but his gaze remained on the growing congregation around the body. He said quietly, 'I'm going to get Pots on a weapons charge. He's got no licence for that pistol.'

Anna looked up at him. 'Owen, a man just died. Murdered. And you're worried about a weapons charge on a two-bit hood?'

Gray's face was as cold as a carving, his eyes impassive and remote.

He said, 'Pots blew me a kiss once too often.'

She touched his sleeve. 'Owen. We've just witnessed a killing.' She swallowed repeatedly, fighting nausea. 'Doesn't it get to you?'

'Pots has a record, so he's looking at two years,' Gray said.

'Owen, listen to me,' she cried out. 'You … you're frightening me.'

'Anna, I'm not going to get misty-eyed over some mafioso getting shot, probably by some other hoodlum.' He gathered her books and helped her to her feet. 'Come on. We deserve a couple of beers.'

The wail of an ambulance trying to enter Foley Square resonated between the buildings. Gray and Anna moved down the steps towards Pearl Street, leaving the baffled assembly behind.

THE HAND-PRINTED SIGN on Owen Gray's apartment door read 'UN Security Council' and was stuck there by two *Sesame Street* Band-Aids, one of Big Bird and the other of the Count. Gray could hear the sparkling notes of a piano through the door.

He had spent the entire day at his desk replaying the Chinaman's trial in his mind, trying to alter yesterday's acquittal. He had been unable to leave his frustration at the office and had worn it home like a yoke, but at the piano's bright sounds it suddenly lifted.

He twisted a key in the lock. Pushing open the door, he called out, 'I'm home and, no, we aren't having a Security Council meeting.'

The twins slid off the piano bench and rushed to greet him. Gray dropped his briefcase and hugged one in each arm.

Carolyn giggled. 'We already had a vote.'

Julie added, 'And you lost three to one.'

They kissed him, Julie on the right cheek, Carolyn on the left.

'I want a recount,' he said.

'You lost fair and square,' Carolyn countered. 'We get the new piano.'

This lobbying had been going on a month. One piano apparently was not enough for four hands. The twins, twelve years old, practised with adult stamina on the old upright. Gray was tone-deaf, but even he could hear they were talented.

The twins were Korean, adopted by Gray eight years ago. They were identical and blossoming. Gray knew that in a few years he would be sweeping boys out of the apartment with a broom. The girls had wide cheekbones, teardrop eyes and sculpted lips. Their teeth were as white and even as the keys on their piano, and their smiles were glorious.

His son John always got the third hug, waiting until the girls were done. John smiled shyly from the kitchen doorway, half a cookie in his good hand.

Gray crossed the room to him. He lifted the boy so their noses touched and said accusingly, 'Did your sisters buy your Security Council vote with that cookie?'

John laughed wildly. 'Three cookies,' he crowed. 'I already ate two.'

'Does Mrs Orlando know you've been pigging out on those?'

The boy looked with transparent guilt towards the kitchen, then crammed the cookie into his mouth, shaking his head and laughing.

John was nine years old and of Vietnamese ancestry. Like his sisters he had been an orphan. When he was three he had found a shell in a pasture near the orphanage in the Dong Nai province and had hammered it with a stone. The explosion had ripped his hand from his arm. He had been brought to the United States by a Greenwich Village couple who somehow had not known that John's arm ended three inches below his elbow and who had changed their minds once they saw him.

Gray had been successful in adopting John because he persuaded

14

his landlord to temporarily switch apartments for the adoption-agency interview. The landlord's place had three bedrooms. Gray's had only two. The ruse worked. Now the girls occupied one bedroom, John the other, and Gray used a sofa bed in the living room.

Gray kissed the boy's forehead. His son had gaps between his front teeth, so Gray had just started writing cheques for startling amounts to an orthodontist. With John's braces and a clamp prosthesis where his hand should have been, the twins called him their Man of Steel. He loved it.

Julie began again: 'John's vote counts. Three to one.'

'This family is a monarchy.' Gray lowered the boy and removed his jacket. 'I'm the cruel king. You are serfs. The king scoffs at voting.'

'Aw, Dad,' Carolyn said.

John lifted the briefcase with his hook. He showed his braces in a smile and swung the case back and forth like a pendulum.

Mrs Orlando emerged from the kitchen and handed Gray a glass of iced tea. 'You must choose, Mr Gray. Me or the kimchi.'

'Three more days, Mrs Orlando,' Gray said. 'If I can stand it, so can you.'

'The smell.' She waved her hand up and down in front of her face. 'It is killing me.'

For nearly a week the apartment had smelt of kimchi. The twins had coaxed Mrs Orlando into buying a jar. They both gagged at their first taste of the fermented fish, cabbage, onions, garlic and horseradish; but in an attempt to savour Korean culture, they were determined to last a week of kimchi breakfasts.

The apartment was normally redolent of Mrs Orlando's Caribbean cooking. She was from Haiti. When Gray interviewed her for the job, he had asked to see her green card so he could fill out the immigration form. She had produced a photograph of her neighbourhood in Cap Haïtien showing a row of shacks on a dusty road, an abandoned clothes wringer on its side near a mound of rubbish, and two ragged chickens. She had said in her melodic accent, 'That's all the paper I've got.' It was enough for Gray.

Mrs Orlando was wearing her usual riotous colours. For Christmas, Gray had given her an ornate silver necklace with a dozen tiny bells hung among stylised fish and shells, and she had not taken it off since. Her skin was bronze and her eyes were set at a laughing cant. The children adored her. She was generous with her singing talent, and Gray credited her with instilling musical ability in the twins. She was patient and loving with John when the boy cried out against his missing hand. If she had a fault it was that she would occasionally miss an afternoon of work, always because she had met a new boyfriend, and would later claim that she had come down with Haitian pox, a little-known disease whose most distressing symptoms were an inability to work and a fuzziness of mind that precluded calling in sick.

Gray sank into an overstuffed chair next to the piano. 'Are you feeling better, Dad?' Carolyn asked.

He had been unable to hide from them his bitter disappointment over the De Sallo verdict. He balanced his glass of tea on the armrest.

'I feel great,' he sighed. He yanked on his tie, loosening it, revealing an unnatural ridge of purple skin on his neck. He leaned to the floor to pick up a schoolbook about the solar system. 'Pete Coates, the lead NYPD detective on the case, is coming over in a few minutes. Will you kids tidy up this place?'

'Are you going to talk about how you blew the case?' Julie teased.

'You are too kind.' Gray sipped the tea.

'John, stop swinging your father's briefcase,' Mrs Orlando ordered as she returned to the kitchen. 'You'll break something.'

The apartment was in Brooklyn, fifty minutes by subway from Gray's office in Manhattan. The living room was about the width of John's swing. The television, a twenty-five-inch monster purchased as the result of earlier lobbying by the twins, was the only item in the room not careworn, dented or frayed. The rug was a fine Sarouk that belonged to Gray's ex-wife, Cathryn. In a puerile fit, he had changed the lock before she remembered she had left the rug behind. She had also forgotten their framed wedding photo, and it remained on the end table. His family had never met Cathryn.

He said, 'John, the briefcase goes—'

The door buzzer interrupted him. He rose and crossed to the intercom. When Pete Coates identified himself, Gray pressed the lobby door button. He had no idea why Coates wanted to visit his apartment. It was unprecedented.

'Better warn Mrs Orlando,' Carolyn exclaimed, glancing into the kitchen. 'It's a cop.'

Julie laughed. 'Maybe she can make it down the fire escape.'

Gray waved them to silence and opened the door. Pete Coates climbed the last few stairs to the third floor. He was a large man, but his bulk was in his chest, not his belly. He was breathing easily, a man in shape.

As Coates entered the room, the twins were wide-eyed. A real police detective in their apartment. John stepped to his special corner beside Gray's chair.

'Nice-looking kids,' Coates said as he helped himself to the couch. 'Looks like you got your own Third World country here.'

Early in the De Sallo trial, Gray had learned that the tradeoff for Coates's legendary tenacity was his relentless unrefinement. At first

16

Gray thought the crassness was an act, part of the detective's tough-cop routine. But Coates was so persistent in his boorishness that Gray concluded he had brought it into the world with him like a birthmark.

Coates had proved himself again and again as a detective. And he had another quality Gray valued. He detested gangsters. His loathing of organised crime brought such an unbending moral principle to his police work that Gray gladly put up with him and had even become fond of him.

The detective kicked off a loafer and rubbed the ball of his left foot. 'It's good to get off my goddamn feet.'

John gasped at the profanity. The twins tittered and looked knowingly at each other. They were convinced they knew words their father had missed all his life.

Coates began. 'Owen, you're a cool customer. After the Chinaman went down, you left the scene like you had ice in your veins.'

Gray opened his hands in a vague gesture. Looking back on the scene later, he had been vexed and angered by his own callousness at the gruesome event. His long, exhausting journey back to normality—for years a harrowing day-to-day struggle—might not have succeeded. A healthy person would have reacted like Anna Renthal, sick at the abrupt and gory passage from life to death.

'Owen, remember that first day when you went to the gym with me and I saw your neck and asked about the scar there? You said you choked on a piece of ham and had to have a tracheotomy. Well, I recently was talking to a surgeon friend of mine. He said tracheotomies shouldn't leave much of a scar, not these days. So I got curious and did a little digging.'

The children were quiet, peering at the detective.

'If I showed initiative like this all the time I'd be mayor by now, I'll guarantee you that,' Coates said. 'You got a beer?'

Gray shook his head.

John called from his spot, 'We got Yoo Hoo chocolate drinks.'

'Who'd have figured it?' Coates asked. 'I read about that scar in your service file an FBI friend sent me. Made me queasy. No beer?'

'Pete, why were you interested in my service file?'

Carolyn asked, 'Why'd the scar make you queasy?'

'Just some blue and red and purple skin,' Julie chimed in.

The detective asked, 'Your dad ever tell you how he got that scar?'

'A leech,' Julie replied. 'Big deal. We Koreans eat them for breakfast.'

'You want that Yoo Hoo, mister?' John asked from his spot.

Gray said, 'My kids know I had an accident.'

'I'll say.' Coates put his shoe back on. 'One day out in the jungle you took a gulp from your canteen and swallowed a leech that had got inside when you were filling it.'

Carolyn made a production of shrugging. 'Wouldn't bother me.'

'And the thing got stuck in your throat. Your air was cut off and you started turning blue. Your spotter wasn't nearby, so he was no help.'

'What's a spotter?' Carolyn asked.

'So you took out your service knife and punched a hole in your own throat. Then you cut off a piece of bamboo and used it as a tube for air.'

John moved quickly from his corner. 'I'm going to ask Mrs Orlando for Yoo Hoos.'

'You were deep behind enemy lines and it took two days to get to an aid station and the leech was in your throat all that time.' Coates turned to the twins. 'Girls, I don't know about you, but a leech stuck in my craw could take the lustre off an otherwise fine day.'

The twins beamed. John marched back into the room carrying Yoo Hoos and straws. He handed a carton to the detective.

Coates sipped on the chocolate drink. 'It ain't a Guinness, but not bad.'

'What's a spotter?' Carolyn asked again.

'Your dad was with the 1st Battalion, 4th Marines, in a sniper-scout platoon.'

Gray quickly turned to his children. 'Girls, John, I need to talk to Detective Coates privately. Go to your rooms, please.'

They could tell he meant business. They disappeared without dawdling or argument.

The detective emptied the carton with a loud gurgle. 'You know, I'd be proud as hell if a rifle range down at Quantico was named after me.'

Gray replied tonelessly, 'I don't think you would, actually.'

The detective persisted. 'I made a phone call to a gunnery sergeant down there this afternoon. Sergeant Arlen Able, an old friend of yours. The sergeant called you a legend.'

Gray rubbed his chin. 'Yeah, well, I've left all that behind.'

The detective continued. 'The sergeant told me the Viet Cong called you White Star due to the little paper star you always left behind.'

In fact, the name had come first, then the paper star. The enemy began calling Gray White Star early in his tour because of the sniper's penchant for using twilight. All Marine snipers knew the sailors' rhyme, altered slightly: Red sky at night, sniper's delight. A lingering pink and red and purple dusk prompts the hunted to leave the safety of trees or hedges too early. First darkness is an illusion where the near foreground seems darker to the target than it is to a marksman viewing from a distance. The hunted may not suspect he can still be seen in the shooter's cross hairs. Gray's name

18

came from the first heavenly body visible at twilight, Venus, which Westerners call the evening star but which Vietnamese know as the white star.

Then one day in Vietnam in his hide, waiting, it turned out, thirty-six hours for the shot, Gray had idly begun folding a small piece of paper torn from his sniper's log. He folded and refolded, experimenting with a random design. Eventually his spotter, Corporal Allen Berkowitz, said, 'You've made a star. Just like your nickname.' After the kill, Gray left the star behind. From then on, he left a paper star behind at every firing site or, if he could get there, on the corpse.

'And the Viet Cong had a price on your head, the equivalent of five years' pay for a soldier.' Coates gurgled the dregs of the Yoo Hoo again. 'So how many of the enemy did you whack?'

Gray glanced at the wall over Coates's head. Several of John's crayon drawings had been taped there. 'A few.'

'I'll say.' Coates laughed, a peculiar clatter, like a stick dragged along a picket fence. 'Ninety-six is quite a few. More than any other sniper in American military history, the sergeant at Quantico told me. I asked why you left the service, but he didn't know or he wouldn't say, and your file wasn't too clear on the subject.'

Gray replied, 'Well, my tour was up—'

'Not quite,' the detective cut in. 'Your second tour was two months from being up when you flew back on a medevac plane.'

'Pete, why are we honoured with your visit tonight?' Gray asked.

'We need your expertise,' Coates said, crumpling the Yoo Hoo carton. 'De Sallo's killer was an ace with a rifle. And you know more about using a rifle than anyone else we can find.'

Gray knew it to be true.

Coates went on: 'De Sallo was killed thirty hours ago and we have only one hard piece of evidence—the bullet that passed through his head. We dug it out of the courthouse steps. The lab is looking at its contours and weight, and we'll hear from them shortly.'

He leaned forward, putting his elbows on his knees. 'My people have talked to thirty-five witnesses to the killing. Nobody saw anything. And, more puzzling, nobody heard anything. We thought of a silencer.' Coates dipped his chin at Gray as if testing him.

'Silencers louse up the aim,' Gray answered. 'A rifleman wouldn't use one if he was shooting from any distance.'

'That's what we thought, too.'

'There were television news cameras there,' Gray said. 'What's on their tapes?'

'We've got the tapes from all the TV stations. A fast-thinking cameraman turned his camera around to Foley Square just after the shooting. He did a slow sweep of the buildings. The tape showed quite a few open windows, and we checked them out. Nothing.'

Owen Gray reached round to a nearby drawer to pull out a map of Manhattan. He unfolded it carefully. 'You did all this checking since yesterday?' Gray said, examining the map, looking at the scale. 'You looked at every building with a view of the courthouse steps'—Gray traced a circle on the map—'all the way west to the Hudson River?'

Coates ran his tongue along his teeth. 'You think we didn't go out from the courthouse far enough?'

'A talented sniper could have fired from thirteen hundred yards.'

Coates corrected, 'Thirteen hundred feet, you mean.'

'Yards. Almost three-quarters of a mile.'

'Jeez!' Coates exclaimed while Gray studied the map.

'We've got another puzzle,' Coates said. 'We haven't heard anything on the street about the Chinaman's killing. Usually when these guys get thumped, gossip about it gets back to us. That's usually the point of the whole exercise, sending a message.'

Gray had often wondered at the NYPD's inexhaustible supply of synonyms for *killed*. The cops borrowed from sports ('The guy was dunked', or tagged out, beaned, or called out), the fashion industry (zipped, ironed, hung out to dry), the culinary arts (cored, fried, plucked, basted), pest control (zapped, flicked, swatted), and apparently nursery school (dinked, thwacked and boinged). There were a hundred others. Gray figured the police had a Department of Slang that issued a new word every few days.

'But this time we've heard nothing,' the detective concluded. 'Can you give us a hand tomorrow? If you can just find his firing station we'll take it from there.'

Gray folded the map. 'Yeah, well, I promised to take the kids—'

'You know about sniping. You'll save us days, maybe weeks.'

Gray wearily rubbed the side of his nose. 'All right, I'll go to Foley Square and look around.'

Coates rose. 'Tomorrow, eight in the morning. I'll meet you there.'

'Bring a spotting scope,' Gray said. 'A 20-power M49 if you've got one. And a tripod.'

Coates nodded. 'Thank your boy for the Yoo Hoo. Tell him I'll buy him a beer some day.' He laughed and started down the stairs.

Gray closed and bolted the door. Mrs Orlando immediately appeared from the kitchen.

'You've got calluses on your ear from the door, Mrs Orlando,' Gray chided.

'You told me you were trying to leave all that behind you,' she whispered, glancing towards a bedroom, expecting the children to appear. Faint Nintendo sounds came from John's room.

Except for his ex-wife and his psychiatrists, Mrs Orlando was the

20

only person in two decades Gray had spoken to about Vietnam. She had been a steady and devoted source of strength.

'Now you'll bring all those bad memories back,' she scolded.

'Just helping out a friend for a few hours.' Gray did not want to admit that during his conversation with Pete Coates his mouth had dried up and his chest had become tight

She clucked her tongue as she went into John's room.

Gray pulled' out a coffee-table book, *Manhattan On High*, that contained aerial photographs of the island. He sank into the chair and began leafing through it, studying Little Italy, Chinatown and other neighbourhoods near Foley Square. Ten minutes later Gray said to himself in a falsely composed voice, 'That guy was a passable marksman, I'll say that for him.'

CHAPTER TWO

'The Chinaman's killer must've been in one of those trees was our first thought.' Pete Coates pointed to the scraggly elms in the Foley Square traffic island. He and Gray were standing on the courthouse steps where Carmine De Sallo had met his maker. Gray was carrying a spotting-scope aluminium case. Coates held a collapsible tripod.

'The killer wouldn't have been able to see through the elm leaves,' the detective said. He was wearing the same grey suit as the day before and it looked as if he had slept in it. 'So we could rule out some of the distant buildings due west as his firing site.'

'That was your first mistake,' Gray replied. 'The further a rifleman is from foliage the easier he can see through it.'

Coates asked, 'What sense does that make?'

'I don't know the physics of it, but take my word for it. The killer probably could see through those sparse leaves to De Sallo even though we can't see in the other direction.' Gray turned to the steps, running his eyes left and right. 'There's his zero shot, that fracture in the riser of that step.'

The stone riser had a pocket dug out of it. A few chips of stone lay below the gouge.

'What's a zero shot?' Coates asked.

'The rifleman sighted his weapon by firing a practice round some time before he let loose at the Chinaman.' Gray bent down to stick his finger into the hole. 'The bullet isn't here. Probably bounced out and was kicked away by a pedestrian.'

Gray led the detective between parked cars and across Center Street towards the Court for International Trade. They walked west along Duane Street. Gray slowed his pace and looked skywards, up

21

the side of the twelve-storey Mardin Building. He narrowed his eyes, studying cornices above the street. He saw nothing of interest and moved along.

The detective walked beside him, his hands jammed into his pockets. 'You know, I would've made a pretty good sniper.'

Still looking skywards, this time towards a lamp fixture attached to the next building, Gray said, 'Sure.' He stared at the light bracket for a moment, then walked on.

Trying to follow Gray's gaze, the detective caught up. 'I'm serious. I'm pretty good at the NYPD firing range. I could've been a sniper.'

They approached Broadway. Gray was still peering above him. He said absently, 'You wouldn't have had a chance, Pete. The Marines don't let you become a sniper if you need glasses. Reflection off the lenses makes it too dangerous in the field.'

The detective said, 'Well, assuming I didn't wear glasses, I would've made a great sniper.'

'Not at all.' Gray's eyes were still looking skywards. His gaze moved in a measured grid pattern. He had done nothing like this for over two decades. A steady clicking—right, right, right, then back again, right, right, right, like a typewriter carriage, and shifting focus near to far, near to far. The skill had not been forgotten. 'You are left-handed. Lefties aren't allowed to become snipers because the movement required to operate the bolt over the top of the scope escalates the risk of detection.'

At the corner of Broadway and Duane they stepped round a band of street musicians playing a maraca, a cowbell, a conga drum, and a percussion instrument made of four crushed beer cans.

They crossed Broadway and continued west along Duane Street.

Coates tried again. 'Well, if I didn't wear glasses and wasn't left-handed, I would've made a great sniper.'

'Not even then, Pete.' Gray stopped abruptly at the Winlox Building, a grey fifteen-storey 1940s structure. Six storeys up, a flagpole was attached to a column between windows.

Eyeing the pole, Gray said, 'You need to have been a hunter or a wilderness guide to get into the sniper programme. You've only left New York a couple of times in your entire life and couldn't follow a bleeding coyote across fresh snow.'

'Well, hell—' Coates laughed.

Gray pointed to the flagpole. 'Your killer left some tracks. About halfway out the pole, there's a red streamer, cloth of some sort.'

'So?'

'It's his wind telltale, like on a sailboat. A sniper usually uses a strip of red cloth two feet long.'

He opened the spotting-scope case. 'Set up the tripod, will you?'

'How'd he get it out there?'

'The window near the pole is probably in a lavatory or an empty office that he got into.'

When the detective fumbled with the tripod, Gray tugged it out of his hands and pulled it open, then withdrew the scope from its case. He attached the scope to the stand and removed the eyepiece cover and lens cover. Bending over the eyepiece, he adjusted the focus.

He said, 'If the sniper could see that telltale we might be able to see his firing site from here.'

For twenty minutes Gray leaned over the scope, frequently looking up to relieve eyestrain. Coates kept a running count of the passers-by he chased away. 'Eight palmers, six jackets, five prunes and one mattress,' meaning beggars, mental cases, senior citizens and a hooker.

Finally Gray straightened to stare at an apartment building two blocks in the distance. He blinked several times, then lowered himself again to the scope. 'I've found it.'

Coates excitedly nudged Gray away from the eyepiece, but after a moment of squinting into it he said, 'What am I looking for?'

'A hole in that window. On the twenty-fifth or twenty-sixth floor. Your sniper was up there.'

Coates raised himself. He pulled back his jacket, reaching for his cellular phone. 'I'm going to call the crime-scene people.' He hesitated, scratching his chin. 'You positive that's his firing site?'

'It's where I would have fired from.'

PETE COATES FOLLOWED the building superintendent down the hallway. Gray was carrying the spotting scope and tripod.

As they hurried down the hall, Coates jabbed the superintendent's shoulder with a finger. 'You're telling me you thought this guy was into orgies?'

'Yes, sir.' The super wore washed-out jeans and his hair was tied in a short ponytail. 'What else was I to think? He had those mattresses delivered two and three at a time. Too many to sleep on, so I figure he's having a bunch of people over to party.'

'You ever see the guy?' Coates asked.

'It was just a month sublease. I handled the paperwork through the mail. He paid up-front.'

Coates drew a .38 Smith and Wesson revolver from inside his jacket as they neared the end of the hall.

Owen Gray stayed well back. 'The chance of this guy being in there is nil.'

'Then you stand with your belly in front of the door. Not me.'

The detective held his revolver near his chin. He reached across to

23

the door and hammered on it. After a moment he jerked a thumb at the superintendent. 'You open the door.'

'I don't plan on dying in a burst of gunfire.'

The detective took the super's keys, gingerly inserted one into the deadlock and turned it.

Coates lunged against the door. His bulk should have snapped it open. It gave only a few inches and he rebounded back into the hall. He charged again. With a soft scraping the door slowly opened. Both hands on his revolver, Coates rushed into the apartment.

'I'll be damned,' he said. His pistol in front of him, he walked through a door into a bedroom.

As he stepped into the apartment, Gray almost tripped on the first mattress. The floor was covered with them, as were the walls. A mattress had also been secured to the inside of the door. The only furniture in the room was a cane chair and a folding table. Stacked on the table were several bulky books next to a small television set.

Coates returned from the bedroom, moving unsteadily over the mattresses. 'Put your hands in your pockets, will you, Owen.'

'I'm not going to muck up your crime scene.'

'Not on purpose. But you might.'

Gray lowered his scope and tripod to a mattress, then shoved his hands into his pockets.

The detective added, 'Don't flush the toilet. Don't breathe on any surface. Don't scratch your head. Don't do anything.'

Gray glanced above him. 'He's even got mattresses on the ceiling.' A bulb on a wire hung between two mattresses. 'Twelve-inch screws, right through the mattresses into the ceiling.'

The living-room windows looked east down Duane Street. Mattresses leaned against them, blocking out the light. Only one window in the room had any exposed glass, an aperture a foot square, bordered on all sides by mattresses.

Coates asked, 'Why did he bother with the mattresses? He could've fired, then raced out of the building.'

'Yes, if he was only going to fire once. But he wanted the zero shot, probably an hour or two before the reporters arrived. He didn't want a lot of sound because he was going to hang around.'

A circular hole ten inches in diameter had been cut into the glass.

'The killer traced a pattern, maybe around a plate, with a glass cutter,' Coates explained. 'He was here awhile and kept himself company with that television set.'

Gray shook his head. 'The TV means he was probably working alone and didn't have a spotter.'

Coates looked at him.

'A rifleman can seldom see whether he hits his target,' Gray went on. 'The rifle kicks up and he can't quickly find the bull again. One of a spotter's jobs is to see if the target went down. The De Sallo courthouse-steps interview was run live on local TV stations, and the sniper would have known it. He fired the shot, then watched the results on his TV. Let me set up the tripod.'

The detective nodded at Gray. 'Watch your feet.'

Gray moved gingerly, sinking into the mattresses with each step. The opening in the window was at chest level. As he set up the tripod and attached the scope, Gray said, 'He sat at the table and balanced the rifle on the books. He fired with the rifle's barrel well inside the room. The mattresses muffled the noise of the shot in all directions.'

'How do you know the barrel was inside?' Coates asked.

'There are powder particles on the window around the hole. Those crusty specks.'

Coates high-stepped over a mattress to the spotting scope. 'So you can see the courthouse steps through the scope?'

'Take a look. When the wind moves the leaves, you'll see right where De Sallo stood.'

'He was firing between moving leaves?' the detective asked. 'You're right. I can see the steps.'

Gray resumed his position behind the spotting scope. He rotated the telescope a fraction of an inch, then said, 'Take another look.'

The detective again replaced Gray behind the telescope. 'I don't see anything interesting. A fire escape.' Coates raised his head to peer out of the window. He scratched his cheek. 'What am I looking for?'

'Another piece of red cloth.'

He went back to the eyepiece. 'Yeah, I see it.'

'De Sallo's killer tied the cloth strip to the fire escape to judge wind speed and direction, same as he did on that flagpole. There are probably a few more telltales between here and the courthouse. Let me see the print-out we looked at earlier.'

Coates lifted from his suit pocket a folded fax from the National Weather Service and passed it to Gray.

As he looked down a column of dot-matrix numbers, Gray said, 'At noon that day the wind was blowing a fairly steady twelve miles an hour out of the south. The humidity was close to one hundred per cent. The rifleman would have known that.'

'Why was the killer worried about humidity?' Coates asked.

'As humidity increases, air density increases, which slows the bullet and lowers its point of impact. The marksman would have compensated for the breeze and humidity by raising the rifle and aligning the barrel to his right.'

'How much off-target did he sight?' Coates asked.

'In a twelve-mile-an-hour wind over twelve hundred and fifty feet, about thirteen feet.'

Coates's chin came up. 'Thirteen feet? I was standing about that distance to De Sallo's left when he was killed.'

'That's right.' Gray smiled thinly. 'The killer probably had your head in his sights when he pulled the trigger.'

The detective was aghast. 'Maybe the killer was after me. I mean, maybe he knew nothing about wind and humidity. He just got my face in his cross hairs and pulled the trigger.'

'He had no interest in you,' Gray calmed him. 'Just De Sallo. From everything we've seen the guy was an artist.'

Coates laughed sharply. 'Is that how you snipers think of yourselves? Artists?'

'I don't think about it at all any more,' Gray said.

'You don't think about it?' Coates cackled. 'I can die happy now because I've heard everything.'

Coates padded round the room. After a moment he said with glee, 'Well, lookee here.' He pointed to the edge of the mattress covering the main window. A spent cartridge was balanced there.

Gray bent for a closer look. 'That's not the fatal bullet's cartridge. You can tell by looking at it.' With a finger, he indicated a narrow ring of red paint just above the cartridge's extractor recess.

Coates peered closely. 'Looks like nail polish. What's it doing on a shell?'

'It's the rifleman's sign. He leaves it behind as a signature.'

'Like your paper star? Any chance you know the rifleman? A sniper who leaves a painted cartridge?'

'Never heard of him,' Gray answered. 'But I've been out of the business awhile.' He looked at his watch. 'I'm going back to my kids. Maybe we'll get to the zoo yet today.'

FACES FLASHED IN THE CIRCLE, one after another, like cards dealt onto a pile. Children laughing and whooping at the end of the school day, a cascade of faces as boys and girls walked down the steps, each just a fleeting glimpse.

Red Army sniper scopes use a pointed aiming post rather than cross hairs. One face after another slid down the aiming post, gap-tooth grins, innocent eyes, skirts of wild colours, spilling into and out of the circular frame.

Hazel flecks on a green iris surrounding a flat black pupil. Frozen and unblinking, the eye behind the telescope might have been part of the scope's optics. The eye was locked in position as firmly as the scope was fixed to the rifle. Colours and smiles flickered before it.

Then a long swath of grey rippled down the circle. A trouser leg belonging to an adult. Owen Gray's face dropped into the circle. And now the scope moved fractionally, keeping Gray's face atop the aiming post. Owen Gray. White Star. The eye blinked, only once. Tight black curls, a few lines around the eyes, pale skin, a wise smile, Gray's face turned to speak to someone, the aiming post just under his nose, following him smoothly. White Star. Once more the eye blinked.

Owen Gray slid out of the ring. Next came a kaleidoscope of colours—green and red and yellow and blue, an exotic scarf round a woman's head. Her skin was brown and burnished. Bits of metal—a necklace—danced in the sunlight. The circle lingered on her a moment. Then the ring found the boy with one arm accompanying Gray and the black woman along the sidewalk.

The aiming post returned to Gray, his head in profile as he walked east. The circle went to black when the eyelid behind the scope slowly lowered and stayed closed. White Star.

GRAY MET PETE COATES at the Columbus Park Gym at the edge of Chinatown. The detective held a heavy bag from behind while Gray jabbed and crossed.

Early in the De Sallo investigation the detective had suggested that Gray join him at his gym for a workout. The gym was over the Three Musketeers pawnshop, up a narrow, squeaking flight of stairs to an ill-lit space where a boxing ring filled most of the room. Speed bags and heavy bags hung from frames on one wall and an assortment of free weights was along another. The gym was owned by Sam Owl, who was in his seventies, and the old man knew more about boxing than any man in New York.

The gym was last painted when Eisenhower was President. Paint chips and plaster regularly fell to the hardwood floor, and the equipment, from bags to ring ropes, was faded and frayed. The only bright spot was one wall decorated with floor-to-ceiling reproductions of some of boxing's most memorable prize fights.

Most of Sam Owl's clientele were club fighters with ring talents far superior to Gray's or Coates's. That first day, Gray had been ensnared by the rhythms of the workouts—the loud tattoos from the speed bags, scuffing of black shoes on the ring mats, and Sam Owl's incessant jabber at the boxers. He began appearing at the club almost every noon with Coates. The prosecutor and the detective had invariably briefed each other on the De Sallo investigation during their workouts.

'You've got to admit,' Coates shouted over the pounding of the bag, 'there're some mighty interesting things in your personnel files. Coming to New York after being raised in Nowhere, Idaho, for one.'

'Actually it was Hobart, Idaho.'

'How'd you end up out here?'

'After the service I got into NYU law school and met my wife there. She was from New York and loathed everywhere else, so I stayed. Tell me about the lab report on the cartridges.'

'You said that a sniper has to have hunting experience.' Coates's voice boomed over the staccato of the speed bags. 'Where'd you pick up yours?'

'My father owned a hunting lodge north of Ketchum. He'd take hunters into the mountains to find deer and goats and, in the early days, cougars. I learned from him and by the time I was thirteen I was leading four-man parties into the mountains.'

'You had a tough couple of years after you got out of the Marines.'

Gray began a new pattern on the bag, using fists and backhands. 'I'm not the only person in history to have a little clinical depression. Abraham Lincoln and Winston Churchill, for example.'

'But they both died.' Coates chuckled, but Gray wouldn't join in. 'The doctors didn't jolt you with electricity, did they?'

'My therapy consisted of counselling and a few medications.'

The detective left the speed bag and walked to a rack of equipment on a wall. He donned a headguard and shoved his hands into sixteen-ounce gloves. Gray did the same. Coates left his spectacles on the wooden bench. They bent through the ropes into the ring. They sparred lightly, bobbing and ducking. The big gloves resembled pillows, and the blows had little effect.

'You think it was your sniping that caused the depression?' The detective stepped back to wipe his forehead with the back of a glove.

'Hell, no.' Gray was too adamant. He sent a smooth combination at Coates, the left cross catching the detective. 'I was a soldier.'

'Ever been back to the hospital?'

'Not in ten years.' Gray grinned. 'But—the strangest thing—all my dreams are still seen through cross hairs.' Good effort, Gray thought. Making a small joke of the horror. He sounded fairly normal.

Coates came straight at Gray, throwing four jabs, then a right straight. Gray backstepped, his breath coming in gulps. 'You know, Pete, you're out of character this morning, what with all this chat. And this chat has a professional scent. You on the job right now?'

The detective said, 'I'm trying to learn how a sniper thinks. You're the only one I've ever met. Thank God.'

Sam Owl stepped to the ring. 'You two guys hurry up with your patty-cake. I want the ring free.'

Gray jabbed and said, 'I've got a plea-change hearing this afternoon and I want to hear the results of the lab work. Are you done interrogating me?'

Coates was huffing and dropping his guard, tiring. 'Is our killer married, you think?'

28

Gray spread his gloves. 'How would I know?'

'Is it possible for a woman to be married to a sniper?'

'It wasn't possible for Cathryn to be married to me.' Gray jabbed again lightly, catching Coates's forehead.

Sweat ran down Coates's face. 'So what happened?'

Gray moved in again, finding Coates's chin twice. 'I was carrying too much freight. That was her term. Too much freight.'

'From the sniping days?'

'I was up and down, a little wild maybe,' Gray replied. 'She thought it was an echo from the sniping.'

'You've been divorced ten years, but it doesn't sound like you've worked her out of your system.'

'Pete, if I want counselling I'll go back to the Veterans Hospital.'

'I quit,' Coates said, lowering his gloves. He slipped through the ropes. 'Looks like I win again. Do you still love her?'

Gray smiled wanly, stepping through the ropes. 'They don't teach questions like that at detective school.'

'One friend asking another.'

'I did when she left, but that didn't stop her from leaving. Couple of years ago Cathryn married a paediatrician. She now lives in the East Eighties. Has a maid and a weekend house in the Hamptons.'

'Ever hear from her?'

'Not in years.'

Gray pulled off his gloves and grabbed a towel from a table. He wiped his face, then added, 'But I've worked it out now. I've got a family. Three kids and Mrs Orlando.'

Coates laughed. 'I'll bet those kids scare off your girlfriends.'

'Yeah, something like that.'

'You got a girlfriend?' Coates asked bluntly.

Gray raised an eyebrow. 'You're not going to try to set me up with your sister, are you?'

'Just trying to fill in my file on you.' Coates stared at Gray a moment before changing the subject. 'The lab report. The colour on the red cartridge was indeed nail polish.'

Gray wiped his face again.

'No fingerprints on the television or anywhere else.' Coates pulled off his training shoes and rubbed his feet. 'But the guys at the scene found another shell, the killer cartridge. It was identical to the red shell but without the paint. Why would our sniper do something as stupid as leaving his spent cartridge behind?'

'Don't know.'

'You leave yours, Owen?'

'Only when I didn't have time to look for them.'

'The spent cartridge was informative,' Coates said. 'The lab has in its computers the characteristic markings from over three thousand models of firearms, markings from the mechanical action of loading, firing the round and ejecting the casing.'

'Out with it,' Gray demanded. 'What kind of weapon?'

'An M1891/30 Mosin-Nagant.'

'A Soviet sniper rifle.' Gray moved his mouth as if tasting the information. 'Why would the sniper use an inferior rifle when he could buy better equipment in any American gun shop?'

'Maybe he's a Russian and he likes his old rifle.'

'Why would a Russian kill an American gangster?' Gray asked.

'Maybe with Afghanistan and the Cold War over, he's freelancing. I've got no better guess, but I've been charged with finding out.'

'Keep me posted,' Gray said.

FORTY MINUTES LATER Gray met defence attorney Phil Hampton at the federal courthouse's alley door, where prisoners brought from Manhattan jails entered the building for court appearances.

Hampton's first words were, 'Frank Luca didn't waste any time, did he? One day you've got the hottest case in America and the next day you're prosecuting one of my grubby clients.' Hampton laughed. 'The mighty have done some serious falling.'

'Speculating on my career is something I can handle without your help, Phil. Let's do some business.'

'My guy is just so much chaff for your office, Owen. You don't need to stick him, do you?'

Phil Hampton resembled a pile of dirty laundry. His coat was askew on his shoulders. His tie had a splat of mustard near the knot. His shoes had been scuffed to the leather.

'I haven't studied the record yet, Phil.' Gray opened the file. 'Donald Bledsoe. A counterfeiter, it seems.'

'Nothing of the sort.' Hampton was carrying a battered briefcase. 'He's just an alleged passer. Hell, the cops found four bad bills on my guy. Just four bad hundreds.'

'We've got the change of plea in five minutes. I need a proffer.'

At a change-of-plea hearing the accused usually switches his plea from not guilty to guilty under the terms of a deal with the prosecutor.

Gray flipped to the second page—the last page—of the file. 'Detective Ames says Bledsoe is going to clam up. I'm not going to do a plea unless I get a proffer. Tell me all he knows.'

A van turned into the alley and approached slowly. A marshal was visible through the windshield and behind him a wire mesh partition.

Hampton said, 'My client is afraid. Can you get him protective custody?'

'For a lousy paper passer? I shall consider asking the court for something below the sentencing guidelines but only after I've heard what he has to say.'

The van stopped in front of Gray. A deputy US marshal climbed down and opened the van's rear door. He pulled Donald Bledsoe out then pushed him towards the alley door.

Bledsoe had spent fifteen of his forty years in assorted jails. He appeared only slightly relieved to see his attorney. His hands were cuffed to a chain belt round his waist. His hair was tossed and oily.

'What'm I going to do, Phil?' The prisoner's voice was fogged with self-pity.

Hampton put a hand on his client's shoulder. 'We don't know yet.' He stepped towards the door, moving his client along with him. The marshal had one of Bledsoe's elbows.

Two steps from the door, the marshal was abruptly pulled off-balance as the prisoner collapsed to the concrete. The side of Bledsoe's head was red pulp.

Owen Gray ducked behind the van, pulling the defence attorney after him. The marshal lunged for the protection of the courthouse door, drawing his pistol.

'What in hell happened?' he yelled. He was breathing as if someone had yanked his tie tight. 'You see anybody?'

A moment passed. The distant noise of traffic reached them. Holding the van's door handle, Gray rose unsteadily. He pushed Bledsoe's shoulder with his foot to roll him over.

The marshal made a show of squaring his coat. 'Who'd gun down a nobody like Donald Bledsoe? Stupid errand boy was all he was.'

Phil Hampton had crawled under the front axle of the van and showed no inclination to reappear. Bledsoe's blood snaked across the cement towards the defence attorney. Gray rubbed his temple, staring down the alley. There would be a window in a building—a sniper's hide— in the distance among the countless windows. Gray's hand on his head was trembling and he lowered it quickly.

He whispered to that distant window, to whoever might be peering back through a scope, 'Tell me who you are.'

CHAPTER THREE

From any distance the shooter resembled a clump of dried weeds, nothing but a mound of dusty vegetation wilting in the Virginia heat, attended only by two dragonflies that flashed iridescence among the leaves. But from the weeds protruded a rifle barrel, its unyielding horizontal plane at odds with the wafting thistle and bur.

The rifle barked, a flat crack that dissipated rapidly across the terrain. A smoking brass casing was ejected.

'It's a flier.' The voice came from another cluster of weeds, where a figure was nudged up against a tripod-mounted spotting scope.

'Missed entirely?' the shooter asked. 'Damn. My problem is I can't get my pulse rhythm.'

'Yeah, right.' The spotter laughed. 'Your problem is that your finger twitches like an old man's. You got to *squeeze* the trigger.'

Downrange a circular disc on a pole waved for five seconds, indicating the bullet had missed the target. The pole was held by a Marine in a concrete butt below ground level.

Sergeant Arlen Able called from behind the line, 'I can see your problem from here, Paley.' He walked to the two weed clumps, then bent to a knee. 'Part of your trigger finger is touching the side of the stock as you pull back, causing side pressure, rather than getting a straight front-to-rear movement. At a thousand yards you're going to bust a flier every time.'

'OK, Gunnery Sergeant.'

Calling Arlen Able just 'Sergeant' would have sufficed, but the students always tacked on 'Gunnery' as a mark of respect for their instructor. They knew Able's record.

Sergeant Able's face was tanned dirt-brown and lined like a cracked window. His eyes were canted as if always amused. He was small and graveyard-thin, with abrupt movements that broadcast enormous energy, a terrier of a man. He was wearing field khaki and a two-way radio on his belt.

'Trigger control is the hardest shooting skill to master, Paley. I want you to keep at it.'

The shooter nodded, wiggling the camouflage tassels hanging from his field cap. In his scope 1,000 yards downrange, was a twenty-inch ring target made watery by heat waves. Behind the firing line was a control tower, a miniature replica of one at an airport. The range master in the tower had binoculars at his eyes and wore a microphone mounted on a headset. He could speak over loudspeakers at the firing line or the four target butts, at 400, 700, 1,000 and 1,500 yards. On this range—the Sergeant Owen Gray Range at the Marine Corps Scout Sniper School near Quantico, Virginia—no targets were ever placed at less than 400 yards, because each Marine allowed into the advanced training unit could already hit perfect scores at anything under 400.

Shooting is only a fraction of sniping. At the Sergeant Owen Gray Range marksmanship is taught, but also camouflage and concealment, target detection, range estimation, intelligence collection, survival, evasion and escape. The Scout Sniper School is the first permanent facility of its kind in the US and the finest in the world.

It hopes to reverse a long trend in American soldiering. In the Great War, American infantrymen loosed 7,000 rounds for each enemy casualty. In World War Two the number rose to 25,000, and in the Korean War 50,000. In Vietnam the figure was a startling 300,000 rounds per casualty. Yet one Vietnam specialist, the American sniper, expended fewer than two shells per kill.

Before 1977, sniper instruction had been haphazard in the Marine Corps. That year the Corps determined that each Marine infantry battalion would have a sniper team. For a decade most of their marksmanship training had occurred at the Quantico training and competition ranges. Then the new range had opened, a dozen miles southeast of Quantico, hidden among gentle hills. The sniper for whom the range had been named had not responded to the invitation to the opening ceremony mailed to his New York address.

With only one firing line, the facility was small compared with other service rifle ranges. Other than the 1,500 yards of range ground the installation consisted of the control tower, a gun shed and a small headquarters building. The Marine Corps also owned the surrounding 1,400 acres of woodlands and meadows where snipers were instructed in fieldcraft. The facility was approached on a gravel road which led to a parking lot in front of the headquarters. Across from the lot was a hill spotted with pine trees, mountain laurel and a few wild rhododendrons.

'Cleared for firing, Paley,' the sergeant said. 'Get on with it.'

'Lay it in there, partner,' the spotter said.

The trigger had a three-pound pull. Knowing the target could be maintained precisely in the cross hairs for only an instant, the shooter applied pressure to the trigger until the slightest additional pull would be required to release the firing pin. He inhaled, then slowly let half of it out. He was so still that he could feel his pulse in his arms. He was waiting for that instant when two critical events occurred—the bull was quartered in the cross hairs at the same time as his heart was between pulses. Then he smoothly applied the last bit of pull.

The rifle spoke, leaving a diaphanous black cloud ten feet in front of the barrel. It dissipated quickly in the air currents.

A black disc waved above the butt, meaning the target had been struck. 'Finally,' Paley muttered.

A thousand yards downrange, the pit officer pulled the target, a 100-pound wooden rack on glides, down into the butt. A moment later it slid back up on its frame, a yellow triangle marking the hit.

'Cease firing,' crackled the loudspeaker. 'Civilian approaching.'

A tall man walked from around the headquarters building.

The sergeant stared hard as the civilian made his way towards the firing line. The visitor was wearing a madras shirt, casual slacks and a tentative smile. Something was familiar about him, maybe the way he held his head, at a slight angle as if favouring an eye, his scope eye.

Sergeant Able squinted, then leaned forward as if being an inch closer would make the intruder more readily recognisable. His face creased into a grin. 'Well, I'll be damned. It's Owen Gray.'

Gray returned the smile. 'I thought you'd find honest work some day, Arlen. Guess I was wrong.'

Sergeant Able shook Gray's hand, then bear-hugged him, almost lifting him off the ground. 'Man, it's good to see you, Owen. You've been hiding, seems like.'

The Marines left the firing line and gathered around at a respectful distance. The spotter cast his eyes at the sign above the headquarters door that read 'Sergeant Owen Gray Range', then looked back at Gray. The shooter cleared his throat, prompting the sergeant to make introductions.

'Have you kept up with the science, Owen?' the sergeant asked. 'Know anything about your range or our new equipment?'

'Haven't had much occasion.' Gray caught the sharp scent of Hoppe's No. 9 cleaning solvent.

When Able held out a hand, Paley passed him his rifle. 'Take a look. It's the M-40A1, developed especially for Marine snipers. This is a pressure-moulded fibreglass Remington Model 700 rifle receiver. Nothing alters the stock—rain, humidity, heat or cold.'

Sergeant Able patted the rifle proudly. 'Remember the trouble we had keeping the camouflage on the wood when it rained? This stock's colouring, the green and copper here, is pigment impregnated into the wood. We've got other rifles for snow and for the desert.'

Able attempted to pass the rifle to Gray, who involuntarily stepped back, unwilling to accept the weapon.

The sergeant retained the rifle and continued. 'The barrel has a diameter of almost an inch and it's free-floated. The rifle is chambered for 7.62 match ammo.'

'You got a moment, Arlen?' Gray asked. 'I've got a couple of questions for you.'

Able might not have heard him. He went on, 'Makes our Winchesters from the old days look like Model As.'

'I'm in a bit of a hurry, Arlen.'

With some force, Gray grabbed Sergeant Able's elbow to lead him towards the office. They left the sniper students and stepped towards the headquarters building, a grey clapboard one-storey portable unit.

'You were always a fanatic about sniping, Arlen,' Gray said in a pleasant voice.

'Sniping is my life,' the sergeant replied. 'I'm catching up with you, Owen. Three kills in Beirut and six in Iraq. I'm up to forty-eight.'

Gray avoided the invitation to discuss statistics.

'I've got some trouble with one of our old friends,' he said. 'Or one of our old enemies. I can't figure out which or who.'

They stepped into the building. The room was government issue, with a metal desk, a swivel chair, a bench, and clipboards hung on a wall. Two dozen framed photographs were on another wall, most showing a Marine receiving a trophy. Gray recognised himself, shaking the hand of Camp Perry's commandant after winning the national title.

Sergeant Able had made an avocation of studying snipers and this room was the repository of his collection, the result of a thirty-year search for the odds and ends of a singular profession. Rifles, scopes, sniper logs and other mementoes were mounted on the walls.

Able lifted a rifle from a display. 'Here is my museum's *pièce de résistance*. A Winchester Model 70 under an Unertl scope. Recognise it? Your old smoke pole.'

Gray took an uneasy step back. He breathed heavily, unable to remove his eyes from his old weapon.

'Brings back memories, I'll bet,' Able prompted.

Gray wiped his hand across his mouth. He was determined not to let this weapon regain an advantage over him. He knew this rifle intimately, knew every grain in the wood, every tiny pock on the barrel, every curve and hollow. The torturous memory of this heartless, soulless rifle was his constant companion, outlasting his military service, outlasting his marriage, living with him with unswerving and appalling fidelity.

But Owen Gray had rebuilt his sanity over the years, and he could beat this weapon. He had learned to suppress the memory, if only for short periods. He could do so now. Surely. With an effort, he turned and focused on the gunnery sergeant.

'You know about snipers.' Gray lowered himself to the bench. 'And you know stuff the Marine Corps doesn't tell the public.'

'Yeah,' Able said with satisfaction, leaning against a display case. 'Do you know that heart attacks are almost unheard of among ex-snipers? Type As can't last in the lonely bush, so they don't become shooters in the first place, I figure.'

'I wanted information, Arlen, but this isn't what I had in mind.'

'Then how about this?' the gunnery sergeant asked with undampened enthusiasm. 'Almost all snipers can routinely snatch mosquitoes and flies in midflight.'

Gray scratched the side of his nose. 'So?'

'Can you? Catch a buzzing fly right out of the air every time?'

'Sure.' He added hastily, 'Not that I do it much. What of it?'

'Owen, I'll bet you don't know that very, very few folks can do that. It's our phenomenal eye–hand coordination that makes such feats possible. Same thing that makes us great shooters.'

Gray sighed audibly. 'Arlen, have you ever heard of a sniper who left a cartridge with a red ring painted around it at his hides?'

Able looked at the ceiling. 'I haven't. He American?'

'Russian, maybe.'

'Is he the shooter who nailed your gangster up in New York? I saw it on TV. Sounded like a pro.'

Gray nodded. He told Sergeant Able about the killings of the Chinaman and Donald Bledsoe.

'Wish I could help you, Owen, but I've never heard of red shells.' He put the Winchester back on the wall. 'That all you want to know?'

'That's it.'

'How come you flew all the way down to Quantico to ask me one question, Owen? I mean, it's great to see you and all, but don't they have telephones in New York?'

Gray risked another glimpse at his Winchester. The years had recast the rifle in his mind. It was smaller and less malignant than he had remembered. Gray suffered the fleeting fancy that the Winchester was deliberately disguising its true lines, trying to woo him again, an old suitor returning with a placatory smile.

He shook off the notion. 'I'm not welcome at my office in New York. Too dangerous to be around, what with holes appearing in anybody I'm standing next to. So I had some time and I drove down in a rental car. Brought my kids and their nanny. They're at a motel swimming pool over in Quantico.'

Sergeant Able led Gray from the building. The Marines were still standing ten yards behind the firing line, an invitation to join them. Able gently placed his hand in the small of Gray's back lest his visitor escape to his car. The sun beat down, seeming to flatten the land under its weight, and the air rippled with heat.

Corporal Paley held his arms out and turned a circle. 'Anything wrong with my presentation, Mr Gray? Am I ready for the field? I mean, have I missed anything?'

'You look great,' Gray said quickly. 'You'll do fine. So long, Arlen.' He started for the parking lot.

Corporal Paley said, 'Advice from you could some day save my life, Mr Gray.'

Gray slowly turned back. 'Your dog tags.'

'Yeah?'

'I heard them click together when you got up from your firing position. Wrap some tape around them.'

Paley nodded, then asked, 'Want to show your stuff on this range, Mr Gray?' He held out his M-40A1.

'Go ahead, Owen,' Able said. 'Show these young pups what us old gummers can do.'

Able took the weapon from Paley and held it closer to Gray. With his other hand, he pointed downrange at the bull's-eye over half a mile away. 'You used to own the thousand-yard line. Let's see if you still do.'

'I hate to disillusion your men, but I detest weapons. I'm through with them for ever.'

'What in hell?' Able stared downrange.

A red disc was waving above the butt. A bullet had hit the bull's-eye. The distant sound of a rifle shot finally washed over them, softened by echoes and distance.

'Who fired that?' demanded the range master, his anger magnified by the metallic resonance of the loudspeakers. 'Take that name, Sergeant Able.' Then after a moment, 'There's nobody on the line. Who's shooting?'

Owen Gray knew. He spun round to search the hillside behind the parking lot. The shooter was there, amid the pines and grass and rhododendrons, made invisible by the contours and foliage.

The shooter moved, a short motion at odds with the timberland that hid him, a motion Gray sensed was designed to alert the watchers to his location.

'There he is,' Paley yelled.

The form stood out against the backdrop of greenery. A human head, maybe blond, but at too great a distance to be sure. Was that a flash of teeth, a smile? And a rifle. Then he was gone, again slipping into the vegetation to become one with the landscape.

'I can't make him out,' Sergeant Able said, shading his eyes. 'That's eerie. He's there, then he's not.'

'Your binoculars,' Gray demanded.

The spotter passed the glasses over. Gray held them up, scanning the hill, but he saw only pines and low bushes, tufts of bluegrass, and grey stone tinged by gold moss. Branches bent and released in the wind, rustling leaves and shifting shadows. The shooter had vanished.

Gunnery Sergeant Able whistled appreciatively. 'That target he hit is a good fifteen, sixteen hundred yards from his spot on that hill. And it was a bull's-eye. A pure, unconscious shot.'

Gray's eyes remained at the binoculars. He saw only the lovely east Virginia terrain.

'That was your shooter, you think?' Able asked. 'The one who leaves a red shell?'

Gray nodded.

'Looks like you've got a big problem.'

'MY DAD WAS AN UNDERTAKER,' Pete Coates said, rubbing the ball of his right foot. His black shoe was on the path next to the bench. 'I ever tell you that?'

Gray squinted against the sun and shook his head. When a jogger passed close to the bench he pulled in his legs.

'He owned a mortuary over in Brooklyn. I was working on bodies when I was twelve. Worst thing was the sore feet. You can't work on bodies sitting down, so I had aching feet all the time. I became a cop instead of a mortician. Shows what I know about anything.'

'Your father still around?'

'Gone fifteen years. Every time I see a body I think of him. How far did you run today?'

'Ten miles. It's quite a luxury, actually, not being allowed into my office because everyone is afraid to stand near me. I've got a lot of time on my hands.'

'You don't feel nervous, knowing there's a rifleman out there following you?'

'I'm the safest person in New York. He's had three clear chances to nail me so far and he hasn't. It's everybody else who should be worried.'

They were in Central Park. Gray had been jogging and his T-shirt was stuck to his chest with dampness. Coates was wearing a sports coat so frayed it looked as if he buffed his car with it. Their bench was in front of a granite outcropping and was surrounded by red maple, sycamore and birch trees. The path fed a stream of walkers, cyclists and baby strollers past them.

Gray glanced over his shoulder. 'This must be the only place in the park where you can't see a window or a building on Fifth or over on the West Side. We're completely enclosed by leaves and branches. Not by chance, I'd guess.'

'Sitting near you out in the open might open up my mind, literally.' Coates pulled a bag of peanuts from his pocket.

'You talk to the law-enforcement people in Virginia?'

'The Prince William County sheriff told me he had two dozen men looking for the shooter's tracks. They followed his trail for a quarter of a mile, but it ended at a roadside where he must have got into a car.'

Gray smiled at a parade of ten preschoolers as they passed the bench. A young woman led the troop.

Then Gray's hand moved so quickly the detective started. It was an abrupt blur that ended in a fist.

Gray held his balled hand at eye level and asked, 'Can you do that?'

'Do what?'

'Catch a fly in midflight like I just did?'

Coates regarded him narrowly. 'Is this one of your son's jokes?'

'I always thought snipers were made, not born,' Gray said. 'I'm not so sure now. Maybe I was destined to be a sniper.'

'Am I missing something?' Coates dug for another nut. 'What's catching a fly have to do with being a sniper.'

'My point is that I can snatch a dragonfly or a mosquito or a fly out of the air every time I try. I never realised before yesterday that few other people can. How could I have missed it?'

'Each and every time?' Coates stared at Gray's fist. 'Nobody can do that. I've got a beer that says you can't either.'

Gray smiled. He slowly opened his hand. The fly remained motionless on his palm for an instant, then shot angrily into the air towards the sun. But Gray was faster. He had to partly rise from the bench, his hand in the fly's wake. Gray's hand snapped shut. He lowered himself again to the bench and held his fist up to Coates's nose. 'It's in here again. You owe me a beer.'

'Mr Gray?' The new voice came from the south, ten yards away at a bend in the path. 'Are you Owen Gray?'

Gray jerked, wincing as if he had been caught smoking in the boys' lavatory. He quickly released the insect.

A woman in a rumpled maroon business suit and carrying an attaché case stared at him. 'After watching this little exhibition, I'm praying you aren't Owen Gray.'

'Then I've got some bad news for you,' Gray said.

'And you are Pete Coates?' She took a few tentative steps forward. 'Two grown men? Playing with bugs?'

'He's a policeman.' Gray pointed at Coates. 'He made me do it.' He smiled but she wouldn't return it.

She circled in front of the bench as if afraid to approach them. 'I worked my tail off in Moscow. An emergency, I was told. Then I fly five thousand miles, call your office to locate you and Detective Coates, and race here in a cab. And then I find you catching insects.' She watched them both with cold surmise. For an instant it appeared she might laugh. But she mastered herself. Her hair was crow-black. Her eyes were a glacial blue. 'I'm Adrian Wade.'

Coates quickly rose from the bench. 'You're the ace Don Shearson at the FBI told me about.'

'Shearson contacted me after it was determined your sniper's shell was Russian. I work for the Security Section of the State Department in Moscow.'

Rising to his feet, Gray offered his hand. A twist of distaste crossed her face.

'No need to look like a martyr,' Gray said lightly. 'The fly is gone.'

'It's not the fly,' she replied, lowering her briefcase to the path. 'It's your Marine Corps file. I've read it.'

Coates said hurriedly, 'Don said Adrian has learned as much about the Russian criminal investigative system as has ever been allowed an American.'

'Maybe you should've also learned about tact,' Gray said.

Earlier in his life Gray had decided he had seen too much and done too much to tolerate men or women who try to inflict their self-importance on others. His usual tactic was to remain silent, looking slightly bored, occasionally nodding in a woolly way. So vast was the difference in experience between Gray and almost everyone else that he also distrusted others' judgments about him. They hadn't looked through the scope. They didn't know and would never know.

'Adrian is a real Moscow gumshoe,' Coates forged ahead. 'At Shearson's request she took a crack at our puzzle of the red shell.' He turned to Wade. 'But we weren't expecting you to show up here.'

She sat at the far end of the bench. Her smile was wintry. 'After reading about your military service in Vietnam, Mr Gray, I had expected to meet a Jack the Ripper but with better technology. Instead I find a goof on a bench. I'm relieved.'

Gray rose from the bench. His voice was deliberately dry and bored. 'Pete, you can brief me later on whatever Ms Wade has to say. Suddenly I feel like I can run another ten miles.'

She smiled with the magnanimity of superior knowledge. 'Then you'll miss hearing the name of the sniper who leaves a red shell.'

Gray's mouth moved, trying to find the right words. Nothing came, so he returned to the bench, defeated.

'The name is Trusov,' she announced.

'Trusov?' Gray exclaimed. 'World War Two's Victor Trusov? He left a red shell? I never heard that before.'

She went on. 'I spent a week speaking with members of Russian police organisations. I must have set a world record for enduring patent lies, evasive answers and protect-your-butt responses.'

'And lewd propositions, I'll bet,' Coates said flatteringly.

'Thirteen by my conservative estimate.' She turned to give her smile only to the detective. 'Russian men view Western women as both naive and generous.'

Gray had no doubt about the number of propositions. Adrian Wade was a startling combination of pure colours. Her hair was so black it reflected light like obsidian. The fringe was swept to one side with apparent unconcern but the result was stylish. The contrast between her hair and the white skin of her face was almost shocking, and made her resemble a Victorian portrait. Her eyes were so blue they seemed lit from within. Her lips were painted a bold red that set off marble-white teeth. She used her smile to good effect, it seemed to Gray. One instant it was street smart, then cryptic and beguiling.

'Stop staring at me, Mr Gray.'

Gray scratched his nose, feeling ridiculous.

Adrian Wade said, 'I spent most of my time at the Red Army's Armed Forces Inspectorate, whose territory covers crimes by Russian soldiers. I met with Major General Georgi Kulikov, chief of the Inspectorate. He and his superiors decided that if there is indeed a renegade Russian soldier shooting Americans they'd better do all they can to try to catch him.'

A beggar dressed in a pea jacket and woollen cap encrusted with grime stopped in front of the bench. He held out his hand, almost under Adrian Wade's chin. Coates flashed his gold badge and the beggar shuffled on.

After what he thought was a respectable interlude, Gray again let his eyes settle on her, but guardedly. At first he had mistaken her wild colouring for youth, but he now saw that a fine pattern of lines—new and gentle lines—touched the corners of her eyes. A few strands of grey-white were lost in her black hair like shooting stars on a moonless night. Her voice had a knowing lilt and throatiness gained only with seasoning. Late thirties, Gray guessed.

She was saying, 'In the Red Army the left hand truly does not know what the right hand is doing. I think General Kulikov was being candid when he first said the army did not have a specialised sniper school. But he started to dig.'

'You speak Russian?' Coates asked.

She replied, 'I was an FBI special agent for ten years. Then I went to work for the Foreign Service in Moscow, where I've been for eight years. My job is to investigate crimes against United States citizens. I can't pass as a Russian, but I speak the language well enough.'

As she spoke, Adrian Wade flicked her head and the black hair jumped and rolled. This shiver of her head produced a fresh angle of her chin, as if she were renewing her presence and demanding the attention due to her. At some level of consciousness she knew of her glamour and its breath-catching effect on others.

She went on. 'General Kulikov was discomfited when he called me in again to say he had found the Red Army sniper school, something he had sworn the day before did not exist. He said that it was run by Spetsnaz, and then he nodded at me meaningfully, indicating that he could not have been expected to know anything about Spetsnaz. They are a highly trained elite. Most Russian boxers, marksmen and wrestlers who appear in the Olympics are actually active Spetsnaz soldiers.'

'The cheats,' Gray said genially. 'Small wonder the Soviet Union collapsed.'

She gave him the swiftest of glances, unsmiling, and turned to Pete Coates. 'The sniper school is five miles beyond the city of Kolomna. Kulikov and I spoke with three of the school's instructors. General Kulikov ordered them to speak candidly to me about a sniper whose signature was a red shell. One of the instructors quickly filled me in. Victor Trusov was with the 284th Division at Stalingrad in 1942, where in a three-day duel in the no-man's-land between Mamaev Hill and the Red October plant he killed a German—'

'It was Major Erwin König,' Gray interrupted.

'. . . who was the finest sharpshooter in the Reich and who had been brought to Stalingrad specifically to kill the Russian sniper.'

Gray added, 'Trusov was named a Hero of the Soviet Union for his eighty-two kills.'

'Russian schoolchildren are taught to recite Trusov's story,' she said. 'But what is omitted from their lessons is that Trusov left a red shell at his firing sites. Apparently'—she looked directly at Gray—'leaving something like a red shell was considered vulgar braggadocio that the masses could live without.'

'Trusov must be seventy-five or eighty years old,' Coates said. 'Could an old guy be our killer?'

With the angles of her face set with professional pride, she announced, 'We can ask him. He's a mile and a half from here at the Russian consulate.'

'Jeez, is he in custody?' the detective asked.

'He's recovering from heart surgery that he had two weeks ago,' she said. 'A Hero of the Soviet Union, or Russia as it is now called, is treated regally. Trusov came to the United States for surgery at Columbia Medical Center, then he was given a room in the consulate to recover. And I've just talked to the Russian consul general. We're free to interview him.'

Gray remarked, 'Doesn't sound like our man, red shell or no.'

'You asked me to find a Russian sniper who left a red shell,' she said in a strychnine voice. 'I have done so.'

They rose to their feet. Coates said, 'Let's go talk to him.'

'I need to check into my hotel. Can I meet you in an hour?'

Coates nodded. 'We'll meet at the consulate.'

After she had rounded an ash tree and disappeared, Gray said,

'You've just seen the perfect example of why I don't like people knowing about my experience in Vietnam. They conclude I'm loathsome without getting to know me. Adrian what's-her-name acted like I was an ogre. And I don't like being called a goof on a bench.'

Coates smiled. 'You know, other than Anna Renthal, I've never seen you interact with a woman.'

'So?'

'You're not very good at it.'

THE ASSISTANT CONSUL GENERAL pushed open a door on the Russian consulate's third floor. 'Please go right in,' he said in heavily accented English. 'I'll return in fifteen minutes.'

Adrian Wade asked, 'You aren't going to insist on being present for the interview?'

The assistant shrugged. 'This room is bugged. I'll listen while I eat my sandwich in the radio room.' He smiled.

Gray followed Coates and Adrian Wade into the room. His first impression was that it was a storehouse for old furniture. Antique pieces cluttered the room, seeming to spill into corners and wash up against the walls. The furnishings were opulent and overbearing. Along just one wall were an ebony dressing table inlaid with satinwood, a walnut cabinet, a globe that showed the Ottoman Empire and a leaded-glass china display case.

'Smells like my grandmother's attic,' Gray said softly. He wrinkled his nose against the odour of mildew, mothballs and old dust.

'I don't see anybody in here,' Coates said.

Gray caught his own reflection in a gilded wall mirror. His gaze moved to a pile of yellowed rags on top of the only comfortable item in the room, a reclining chair. 'There he is.'

The heap of rags turned out to be a man in a dowdy ochre bathrobe. Caught in a stark ray of sunlight from a window, his bald head shared the bathrobe's saffron colour. His face seemed made of transparent parchment, and spatulate cheekbones rose from the sunken skin. His nose was hooked and narrow, and his lips were thin and bloodless. He was asleep.

'Did he know we were coming?' Coates asked.

The old man started and cried out, a tenor chirp. His eyes rolled open. He blinked, then chuckled, a wheeze that sounded like paper being crumpled into a wad. '*Koshmar.*'

Adrian Wade translated. 'A nightmare. Maybe he has a lot of them, given his history.'

She stepped into the bath of sunlight at the foot of the chair and introduced herself in speedy Russian. The old man's jaw sagged open, presenting a hollow of bad teeth.

He held out a bony hand that resembled a vulture's talons and spoke for a moment in Russian, grinning and lifting his eyebrows invitingly. She laughed and replied, and he cackled appreciatively.

'What'd he say?' Coates asked.

'He asked me for a date.'

'And?'

'I told him a night with me would turn him into a mere husk of his former self.' She smiled. 'And now Mr Trusov and I are best friends.'

She made introductions, switching between Russian and English. Victor Trusov seemed delighted with the visit.

'*Zakuski?*' He pointed to a television table.

She translated: 'Hors d'oeuvres. Someone has provided Mr Trusov with *yobla*, a dried and salted fish, and this is *osyotr* caviar. It's not as rare as beluga, but it tastes as good.'

She lifted a blini from a plate and scooped a small portion of the black beads onto it. Gray noticed that she touched the caviar with her tongue before she bit into it, as if she wanted tactile pleasure as well as the taste. She was wearing a suit with stern lines but of a softening pale blue. On her lapel was a finely wrought silver brooch representing a bunch of grapes and curled vine leaves.

The old man spoke quickly, making small gestures with his hand. Adrian Wade said, 'He says the consulate is treating him like a *nachestvo*, one of the privileged.'

Owen Gray stepped forward. 'Tell Mr Trusov that I've long known about his heroism, and that I'm honoured to meet him,' he said.

Adrian translated and the old man's eyebrows came up. He eyed Gray closely, from head to toe, then said something directly to Gray. Adrian interpreted: 'Mr Trusov says, "We study each other, don't we?"'

Gray nodded.

'He asks, "What did you learn from me?"'

'The hat trick.'

For three glorious seconds on the rubble mound at Stalingrad, Wehrmacht Major Erwin König had thought his bullet had soared through Trusov's head. Then König was dead.

The old man waved his hand dismissively. Adrian translated: '"A stupid trick. It has galled me ever since that someone of König's stature fell for it. It cheapens my accomplishment."'

Gray said, 'But my favourite—'

'Favourite what?' she cut in. 'Favourite way of killing someone? Like your favourite pizza topping?'

Gray snapped, 'If I want moralising, I'll ask for it.' Then to the old man, 'My favourite of yours was the pine needles.'

Scowling, Adrian turned Gray's words to Russian.

'*Da, da, da,*' the old man chortled.

Gray explained for Coates's benefit. 'Mr Trusov could often smell an enemy's breath at a hundred yards.'

'"It was the sauerkraut,"' Adrian translated as Trusov spoke.

'Mr Trusov suspected the enemy might also be able to detect his breath. So before a mission he would chew pine needles. I learned that from him. Needles will kill any breath.'

Coates dipped into the caviar and asked, 'When is the last time you fired a rifle, Mr Trusov?'

After the translation, the old man pursed his lips. '"I suppose it's been two decades,"' Adrian interpreted. '"I passed along the torch long ago."'

Coates had been reaching for another blini, and his hand stopped abruptly. 'You passed along the torch? To whom?'

More translation, then a proud beam from the old man. '"To my boy Nikolai. He also served in the army."'

Coates glanced at Adrian. 'Know anything about Mr Trusov's son?'

'Nobody I spoke with ever mentioned him,' she replied. 'But I wouldn't be surprised. The Red Army is like an onion, and maybe I wasn't allowed to peel it back far enough. Perhaps even the instructors at the Spetsnaz school had never heard of him.'

'Could there be other sniper schools in Russia?' Gray asked.

'Not that I know about,' she answered. 'But maybe.'

The old man dipped a finger into the tin and brought a dab of caviar to his lips. After a moment he began speaking again.

'"My boy walked in my footsteps in Afghanistan. Seventy-eight confirmed kills,"' Adrian translated. '"Lots of turbans got ruined, thanks to my boy."'

He laughed heartily, which shook his frame like a leaf in a wind. '"He left a red shell at his firing sites, too."'

With that revelation, Adrian Wade found Gray's eyes. She smiled narrowly. The sun was edging lower in the sky, and rays reflected off the gilt on the mirror and Adrian's silver brooch.

The old man lifted a finger towards Owen Gray. '"Nikolai is about your age. Handsome boy, too, like you. His hair is lighter, though."'

'What's he doing now?' he asked.

The Russian squinted at the mantel clock. '"I don't know,"' Adrian translated. '"I haven't seen him since yesterday."' Then she blurted in Russian, 'You mean he's here in the United States?'

Trusov replied and Adrian turned it to English, '"He received an emergency visa and escorted me here for the surgery. He's having a good time in New York, he tells me."'

Gray mulled over this news. 'Does your son know me, Mr Trusov?' Gray asked.

The old man scooped the last of the caviar onto a finger. He spoke and Adrian interpreted. '"Nikolai didn't know anybody in the United States. Neither did I. But I've met a lot of nice people. My surgeons and nurses. You people aren't so bad as Khrushchev said."'

'When do you expect Nikolai to visit again?' the detective asked.

He chewed the caviar. Adrian echoed his words. '"He comes and goes. Brings me this caviar and *yobla*. He is a dutiful son."'

When the old man hesitated, Adrian nodded encouragement. Finally Trusov continued. '"My boy, I love him very much. But"'— he paused—'"but there is something missing from him. I was a sniper because of war. Nikolai is a sniper because that is all he can be. It is the centre of him."'

Coates said, 'We'll swamp the streets around here with my people. Nikolai won't be coming and going any more, not until we've talked to him.'

Adrian Wade thanked the old sniper. As they all moved towards the door, Adrian turned back and asked in Russian, then in English, 'Mr Trusov, do you ever catch flies out of the air?'

The old fellow narrowed his eyes. '"Why would I do that?"'

She looked at Gray with both censure and triumph.

'"But there was a time during the war when I caught bats. They were all I had to eat."'

As she translated, Adrian Wade's glare swept onto Gray. Reassessing him or dismissing him, Gray couldn't tell which. She said goodbye in Russian, then left the room. Coates followed.

Gray gave the sniper the thumbs-up salute. Trusov returned it.

'I know you can't understand me, Mr Trusov'—Gray laughed— 'but I owe you one for the bat story.'

CHAPTER FOUR

Gunnery Sergeant Arlen Able poured two fingers of Jim Beam into the range master's glass, then into his own. 'Can you believe I was ever that young, Bud?'

Sergeant Bud Blackman held up the photograph. 'You and Gray look like you should be carrying water pistols, not real guns.'

The photograph dated from 1969 and showed Arlen Able and Owen Gray kneeling on a dusty patch of ground, each holding a rifle, the barrels pointing to the sky. Both were wearing olive T-shirts and field pants. Their hair was shaved along the sides and cut short and flat on top. Both Marines' smiles were broad and engaging.

'Don't let the dummy grins fool you, Bud.' Able sipped his drink. 'We were already proven head-hunters.'

Sergeant Blackman had been in the range tower during Owen Gray's visit. Now he swirled the whisky, staring at the snapshot. He had seen it before. Early in any friendship, Arlen Able trotted out his photograph of himself kneeling next to the legend. Blackman said, 'He must've left it all behind in Vietnam. He looked like any other lawyer.'

'I ever tell you he saved my life?' Able asked.

'No, but I can't believe there is a story about Owen Gray you haven't told me.'

'Maybe I never mentioned it because it makes me look a little goofy,' Able said. 'Owen was an even better tracker than a shooter, if you can believe it.' He shook his head. 'Owen had a sixth sense about it. Sometimes the ground and the vegetation seemed to be speaking to him. Before he joined the Marines, he and his old man would often be asked by the county sheriff in Idaho to track lost hunters and climbers. He rescued me, too. One day in October 1969 near Tu Lun hill I took a mortar blast to the face.'

'That explains a lot of things.' Blackman chuckled.

'You laugh because it wasn't you. When a shell blew me down, I got right back up, climbed out of the hole, and moseyed into the field.'

'You were ordered forward?' Blackman asked.

'Hell, no. I was blacked out on my feet. Concussed. To this day I have no memory of it. I got up—shells landing all around—and strolled into the forest. It wasn't until dawn, after the firefight ended, that I was reported missing.'

'I gather you weren't killed by the enemy.' Blackman helped himself to another shot of whisky.

'Nobody could follow me, because I had wandered into North Vietnamese Army territory. But Owen Gray figures out two things: one, that I'm addled, and two, where he can find me.'

'I'll bite. How'd he figure them out?'

Sergeant Able leaned back and lifted his feet to the desktop. 'He knows nobody goes into the field in a firefight without a lot of equipment. If I'd been going anywhere with all my senses I'd have been carrying heavy armament and a pack and kit. But my footprint tells him my hands are empty and there's nothing on my back.'

'I'll bite again.'

Able said with satisfaction, 'A person carrying some weight rolls his foot out on the big-toe side as he walks. Plus, a walker carrying equipment takes shorter strides and has light heel pressure and a deep toe pushoff. I wasn't leaving any of these signs, so Owen knew I was out there damn near naked.'

'Which meant you were acting wacko.'

'Concussed, not wacko. Owen knew that if I survived I'd wander to a certain spot in the Vietnam wilderness. He knew that I would gradually circle to the right.'

'How?'

'Right-handed people who are lost and tired take a slightly larger step with their left foot. They walk in a big clockwise loop. By my bootprints Owen determined how fast I was ambling along, and then determined when I'd get to the half-circle point. He met me there.'

Blackman protested: 'He couldn't have known precisely where you'd show up.'

'He listened for me. Someone wandering in the wilderness makes a lot of noise. He took an antisapper parabolic listening dish to where his calculations suggested I'd appear. When he heard me thrashing around about a quarter of a mile away, he came and retrieved me.'

Sergeant Blackman threw back the last of his Jim Beam. 'If Gray's so smart, why didn't he wait until you had walked in a full circle right back to your foxhole?'

'That would have doubled the time I was out there, and the place was infested with NVA troops.'

'Gray would've saved himself a lot of trouble.' Blackman laughed.

Sergeant Able lowered the bottle into a drawer, then rose from his chair. 'I'll see you tomorrow bright and early.'

Blackman stepped towards the door. 'Bright and early is what the Marine Corps is all about.'

Pulling his ring of keys from a pocket, Sergeant Able snapped off the desk lamp. The room was shadowy, with only the last shards of daylight coming through the windows. He stepped towards the burglar-alarm control pad.

Able spun to the hollow sound of a blow, followed by a soft groan. A whirling blur swept in through the door, a man dressed in black and moving so quickly in the half-light that his image would not fully form in Able's mind. The club swept down again, and Able heard Blackman's other collarbone break.

Bud Blackman collapsed back into the room. He landed hard on the floor, his legs buckled under him.

It was a baseball bat. And it soared high as the intruder rushed towards Able. The dark demon under the bat was hidden behind a veil of dusky light and swift motion. Able reflexively raised a hand, a futile gesture against the bat that slammed into his nose.

His knees swayed and he blacked out before he hit the floor.

OWEN GRAY knew fifteen patterns on the speed bag, and he could blend them together in a lovely swirling and surging routine. His leather mitts were blurs producing a loud pounding rhythm as the bag struck the backboard. Knuckles, palms, elbows, even his chin, all were used to whip the bag around on its universal joint.

'This is your health club?' the tittering voice asked from the gym door. Gray lowered his fists and turned to see Mrs Orlando escorting the twins into the gym. She rolled her eyes to the ceiling. 'Looks like nothing but convicts in here.'

Mrs Orlando was wearing a flowing dress decorated with dozens of tiny red prints of Che Guevara's bearded face. Her necklace tinkled lightly as she guided Julie and Carolyn to the bench. 'Don't you girls talk to anyone here except maybe your father.'

Gray called his thanks to her. She retreated the way she had come, shaking her head.

The oldest twin—Carolyn by five minutes—wore a bulky sweater of a dozen colours and black leggings, while Julie had on jeans and a red denim jacket. They turned to watch two boxers spar in the ring.

Gray had asked Mrs Orlando to bring the girls to the gym because except for their apartment there were few venues now where Gray could spend time with his family. With the sniper at large, there were no visits to parks, no escorting them to school, nothing out of doors, and nothing indoors near windows. Sam Owl's windows looked across a narrow alley to a brown brick wall. That morning at breakfast Gray had offered to show them the speed bag if they would meet him at his gym, then had to explain what a speed bag was.

The twins seemed spellbound by the skipping, sparring and bag-punching. Gray decided to show off. 'Watch this, girls.'

Then Adrian Wade entered. Sound seemed abruptly sucked from the room. Sparrers lowered their gloves. Heavy bags swung loosely. The gymnasium became as still as a photograph.

Gray groaned when Adrian marched round the ring in his direction. In the steamy, tumble-down gymnasium she was wildly out of place, an electric flash of fierce colours. All eyes were on her, ogling and appreciating as she made her way to the speed bags. The slightest of smiles—perhaps one of mild cynicism—passed across her face like a breeze.

She was wearing a tight black skirt that ended two inches above her knees and a cedar-green jacket over a white silk blouse. Again Gray was startled by the contrast between her fire-red mouth, raven hair and blue eyes, immaculate colours setting off her bone-white face.

'It smells like old sweat socks in here,' she said to Gray.

'Yeah, it's great, isn't it?'

'I've got news, none of it good.'

'That bench is my new office. Come on over.'

The twins drew themselves up, awkwardly. Their father said briskly, 'Girls, I need to talk to this lady. Will you excuse me?'

'Your daughters?' Adrian asked. 'Introduce me.'

Carolyn and Julie seemed incapable of expression, their faces frozen by bafflement. They had never seen their father with a woman. Maybe a thankyou to a sales clerk or a quick word with a librarian. Mrs Orlando didn't count. This was a real woman, an attractive woman, someone their father's age. And—could it be?—she had come to visit their father. Their eyes mirrored their wonder. Gray missed it, but Adrian rapidly searched their faces and may have understood.

She stepped close to the twins and extended her hand to one, then the other. Her smile might have been given to long-lost loved ones. Her eyes engaged them fully and excluded all else in the gym, and certainly Gray. They flushed with the attention and fairly stammered their replies. After a few minutes, Adrian Wade had learned much about school and piano practice and Mrs Orlando.

Gray thought it a calculating inveiglement. She was entrancing them, doubtless to irk him. He scanned the room. The fighters were slowly returning to their workouts.

'We'd love to,' both girls said as one. They were bouncing with excitement.

'Give me a few minutes with your father, then off we'll go.'

Gray hadn't been listening. 'Off you go? Where?'

She looked at him. 'It's time for your girls to wear a little lipstick.'

'Looks like you've got plenty to spare,' he said, pleased with himself.

She ignored the jab. 'I'm going to show them a few things at Bloomingdale's cosmetics counters.'

'That place is the gate to hell. I don't want Carolyn and Julie anywhere near there.'

'Well, that's settled,' Adrian said, grinning at them. 'We'll catch a cab uptown in a minute, girls.'

The twins cheered.

'Am I just talking to a brick wall here?' Gray objected. 'Is anybody listening?'

She took him by an elbow and turned him to the bench. The girls moved to a corner near the water fountain but could not remove their eyes from her. 'Your friend Sergeant Able at Quantico has been hurt. So has Sergeant Blackman.'

Gray drew in a sharp breath.

She told him about the assault at the rifle range the night before. 'Sergeant Blackman will be all right, a week in the hospital and then physical therapy. Sergeant Able has a broken nose and was treated and released. The sergeants were hurt by someone who knew how to do it, someone fast and competent.'

'But what was he doing?'

She replied with gravity. 'The only thing taken was your sniper rifle from Vietnam. Your Winchester .30-06.'

Gray sank back against the chipped wall. He peeled off the mitts to wipe sweat from his forehead.

Until that revelation, a slight—admittedly exceedingly slight—chance had remained that the Russian sniper's actions were unconnected to Gray, that coincidence was playing a ghastly trick. No longer.

She pulled a photograph from the manila envelope she was holding. 'This is our man. Nikolai Trusov. General Kulikov wired his service ID photograph from Moscow this morning. There isn't a police department or FBI office on the east coast that doesn't have a copy by now. Kulikov also sent Trusov's fingerprints. The police have them, too, and the prints have already produced results.'

Gray stared at the photograph. 'I wouldn't want to run into this guy in a dark alley.'

With hard angles and sudden planes, Nikolai Trusov's face seemed chopped out of a log with an axe. It was overfeatured, with a broad and blunt nose and a jutting chin. His cheekbones were so rocky they threw shadows on the face below. Blond eyebrows were low and sunk deeply, and under them were flat, expressionless eyes. His forehead appeared too small because curly yellow hair was brushed forwards. Hair on the sides of his head was short. His mouth was crooked: the left side might have been about to smile while the right was set in a stiff line. It was a brawler's face, a dangerous face.

'What happened to him, do you think?' Adrian pointed at Nikolai Trusov's forehead. 'A meat cleaver, looks like.'

Trusov's forehead had a shallow trench in it, a furrow that ran from an inch above his right eye to disappear under the hairline. The groove was covered with puckered skin, darker than the rest of his face. Skin along the fracture was pleated from surgeon's stitches. The corrugated skin added to the dissonance of Trusov's face.

'This injury would've killed most people,' Gray said. 'Did General Kulikov give an explanation?'

'So far he has found only Trusov's Spetsnaz file.' She slid out a stack of paper from the envelope. 'These were also faxed to me this morning. It's Trusov's army record from 1977 when he joined the Spetsnaz to 1988 when he left it.'

'But he was in the Red Army before and after those dates, wasn't he?' Gray's wet shirt was clinging to his back, chilling him.

'He was already a sergeant when he entered Spetsnaz training, according to this,' she said.

She flipped through several pages of military forms. Gray could make out nothing from the mass of Russian letters.

She went on. 'In 1988 he was transferred from the Northwest Front to a Spetsnaz training brigade at Rostov. He was taught explosives, hand-to-hand combat, communications, parachuting, survival and the like. But he taught rifle marksmanship.'

'So he was already a shooter?'

She held up a page from the file. 'Trusov won a gold medal at the 1976 Olympics at Innsbruck in the biathlon. Shooting and skiing.'

Gray exhaled slowly. 'Where did he go after his training?'

'He was posted to Germany until after the Afghanistan invasion, when his company was transferred to the Turkestan Military District. He was in Afghanistan four years. That's where he killed the seventy-eight people.'

'They weren't people,' Gray corrected. 'They were enemy soldiers.'

'I see now why you went to law school,' she said with a schoolteacher's inflection. 'To learn to distinguish, which is what law school is all about. Not to understand, not to appreciate, but to distinguish. It is one of the lesser talents.'

'Were I to give it any thought at all,' he said with seeming indifference, 'I would conclude you are a bonebrain.'

Her face turned a gratifying pink. Then she said in the tone and cadence of a typewriter, 'I'm not going to get into kindergarten name-calling with you. I know Russians and you know sniping. You and I are going to concentrate on finding Nikolai Trusov.'

Gray had a good nose, a trained nose. It had saved his life more than once in Vietnam. Adrian was wearing a perfume that was somehow both faint and arresting. The fragrance was not flowery but was more veiled, maybe an exotic spice. It seemed to be dulling his senses. Calling her names, for God's sake!

She slid the photograph and file back into the envelope, and continued. 'I mentioned that the fingerprints have produced results. Pete Coates and I have been wondering how Trusov is funding himself. Soviet soldiers are usually penniless, and even the army sponsorship that sent his father and him here would not have given him enough money to rent an apartment and do the travelling he is doing.'

Gray rubbed the back of his neck. He never used to get stiff like this, not playing high-school football or in boot camp.

'Two weeks ago a cash machine near Great Neck was smashed and over ten thousand dollars was taken.'

'I read about it in the paper. The robber used a digger.'

'There was a pneumatic hammer drill installed on the hydraulic arm. A crew of electricians had been using it to tear up a road to install lines underground. Some time during that night he hotwired the digger and drove it to a First New York Bank cash machine. He used the drill to break into the front panel and spring the money cartridge, then rupture the cartridge.'

'Fingerprints?'

'The robber did nothing to hide his prints. They were all over the digger. This morning the FBI reported that Trusov is the cash-machine robber. So we know how he bankrolled himself.'

They sat for a moment. Then she demanded, 'How does this Nikolai Trusov know you?'

'I've thought of little else lately. I have no answer.'

'Maybe the only connection is that he heard of your reputation, and he can't stand the idea of someone being better at killing than he is. You had ninety-six kills, he had only seventy-eight. This town ain't big enough for the two of us, that kind of macho foolishness.'

Gray didn't feel like arguing. His workout had worn him down.

'You see that fellow over there?' he enquired obscurely. 'The black fighter working the heavy bag? He's a middleweight named Joe Leonard. Why don't you ask him for a boxing lesson?'

She rose from the bench. 'I don't need a lesson. I'm already tougher than him. And you.'

Gray prided himself on his ability to step back from a situation to assess it critically. But her adeptness at reducing him to childish responses bordered on the bizarre. He could not prevent himself from replying, 'You are not tough compared with me.'

Her smile could have melted paint from a Chevrolet. 'Let me show you something. Take a swing at me.'

Take a swing? Alarms went off inside Gray's head. He brought his eyes up to hers, but they were unreadable. Unfathomable.

'You mean hit you?' he asked.

She laughed brightly. Was this an awkward attempt at a truce? Gray thought.

'You don't have to actually hit me,' she said. 'Throw the punch but bring it up short.'

Gray pushed himself up from the bench. 'You know judo and I'm going to get hurt. Am I right?' he asked warily.

'If we are going to work together you need to learn to trust me. Throw a jab and I'll show you something. Trust me.'

She stepped closer, then tilted her head, presenting a target. Her hands were at her sides. Joe Leonard and the other fighters paused in their workouts to watch. The girls were smiling widely, perhaps thinking Adrian Wade was lifting her head for a kiss.

Gray brought his hands up in good imitation of Muhammad Ali, he thought. He gently—very gently—jabbed his left hand at her face, intending to stop well short of her chin.

She moved with a startling rapidity. Suddenly she was standing next to him, her black hair in his face, her hip dug into his thigh. Gray felt her leg sweep into the back of his legs, low on his calves. Her arms shot up. His feet left the ground, and he swung on the axis of her hip. He spun in a helpless cartwheel.

The gym's wooden floor must have been travelling at fifty miles an hour up at him. The entire length of his body slammed into the floor with a sickening crack. A surge of nausea rose from behind his breastbone. He tried to look up, but her foot was pinning his head to the floor.

Carolyn and Julie stared but did not move. Sam Owl was fond of Owen Gray, and was trying not to laugh, but with only limited success.

'You do have one tiny endearing element to your personality,' Adrian said from above him. 'You are delightfully naive.'

'Get your foot off my face.' Gray's words were muffled by her shoe against his lips. He was sprawled on the floor, one arm twisted painfully under his back.

She removed her foot. Gray found he could focus his eyes. She was wearing the same smile. The girls ventured over.

'You OK, Dad?' Carolyn asked.

'I'm fine,' Gray said weakly.

'He was showing me one of his moves,' Adrian deadpanned. 'How to make a gymnasium floor surrender.'

'You going to get up, Dad?' Julie asked.

'I want to lie here a minute.' He didn't trust his legs to get him up. 'You girls go with Ms Wade now. She'll take care of you.'

Adrian Wade led the twins away. Both girls glanced back at him several times until they disappeared through the gym's door.

Gray levered himself to standing. His legs seemed to work. Maybe nothing was broken. He wobbled in the direction of the shower.

'I DON'T LIKE IT, none of it,' Pete Coates said. 'But I can't talk the commissioner out of the plan.'

Gray was sitting across from the detective's desk. 'Did you level with him?'

'I told him the police department is in the business of arresting criminals, not whacking them. But he said Nikolai Trusov is never going to let himself be arrested, and he'll kill four or five policemen before he goes down. So your plan must go ahead. He says you are the only one who has a chance of beating Trusov.'

Coates's office had the dimensions of a closet. Gray had to sit rigidly upright because his knees were pressed against the front of Coates's desk. An interior window opened to a hallway and other offices. A hum of distant conversations and typing and telephone

ringing filled the area. There was no window to the outside.

The desk was covered with an inch of assorted documents, paper coffee cups, doughnut wrappers, a telephone. Coates turned from his computer monitor to Gray. 'So you think Nikolai Trusov will go for it?'

'He wants something from me. He'll strike again, because I haven't got his message yet. I don't have the slightest idea what he wants.'

Coates said, 'He hasn't had any targets in three days. You haven't been in the open near anybody.'

'So the Russian is probably hungry to deliver his message again. The super at a condo four blocks from my place reported a suspicious-looking character on the roof of the building next to his. The description fits Trusov.'

'We should just wait for him on that roof,' Coates said.

Gray adamantly shook his head. 'Pete, you don't realise who you're dealing with. The only way to get this guy is from a distance.'

When the telephone chirped, Coates snatched it and pressed it to his ear. He held the phone out for Gray. 'It's Adrian Wade.'

Gray made a face. He had told Coates about his free fall at Sam Owl's gym. 'Tell her I'm busy. Tell her an orthopaedic surgeon is putting my legs in casts.' But he reached for the telephone anyway.

With overwrought courtesy, he conversed a moment with Adrian, ending with 'I'll be there in about three hours.' He passed the phone to Coates and said, 'Mrs Orlando, our nanny, hasn't arrived at our place yet. She's late, and has undoubtedly found a new boyfriend. It's more romantic to walk along the Brooklyn Heights promenade than appear for work.'

'Dock her a day's pay,' Coates suggested.

'I might, depending on the cleverness of her excuse,' Gray laughed. 'But Adrian kidnapped my daughters at the gym, took them uptown and had a fine old time, then escorted them home in a cab. Now John has arrived back from his friend's. The girls have told Adrian that their father never leaves them in the apartment without adult supervision. So Adrian is stuck there with a bunch of hungry, tired kids.' He chortled again. 'She deserves it.'

'I did you a favour.' Coates lifted a sheaf of papers and wagged them at him. 'I asked a friend at the FBI to send me some information about Adrian Wade. When I'm working with people, I like to know what makes them breathe hard. Want to read it?'

Gray rebuked him. 'Pete, I'm surprised at you, thinking I'd stoop so low as to read someone's private file. Read it to me.'

'She's a widow, for one,' the detective said without missing a beat. 'Her husband was a pilot for Chesapeake Air Charter, and he went down in a De Havilland Beaver four years ago. She has studied judo for eight years, and was Northeast Judo Association senior champion two years running.'

Gray said dully, 'That news would have been more useful to me this morning.'

'Let's see.' The detective skimmed the pages. 'She was raised in Los Angeles. Her father and mother were professors at UCLA. She has a BA in psychology and an advanced degree in police science. She works sixty hours a week on average, real gung ho, and appears to be in line for a transfer back to Washington and a promotion.'

Gray shifted on the seat, pushing his knees to one side. 'Isn't there anything juicy in there?'

'How's this? Last November she was walking along Strelka Prospekt in Moscow and was attacked by a guy, who tried to yank her handbag away. She stabbed two fingers into his left eye socket, and the guy ran away screaming and bleeding and minus one eye.'

Gray bit his lip. 'Maybe I'd better try harder not to upset her.'

The door was opened by Gunnery Sergeant Arlen Able. The sergeant's nose was covered with black tape and the skin below his eyes had the texture of crepe paper, with touches of purple and yellow. He had a cardboard case painted in olive and buff camouflage in his hands.

Gray said, 'Judging from your face, Arlen, it looks like Nikolai Trusov is pretty good with a baseball bat.'

'If I laugh, my face will crack open and my brains will fall out.' The sergeant pulled a large scope from the box.

'How's Blackman?'

'He's got casts on him that make both hands stick out, so he's going to walk around like a mummy for two months, but he'll live. Have you used a starlight scope before?'

'Some,' Gray replied quietly.

'This is our new model, the AN/PVS-5. Battery-powered. Uses starlight and moonlight for target illumination and amplifies reflected ambient light to brighten the target.'

The starlight scope, which was about a foot long, resembled a bird-watcher's spotting scope, with an eyeshield on one end and a range-focus ring on the other.

'Can I remind you of a couple of things?' Able asked. 'Keep your eye tight against the eyeshield, or light from the eyepiece assembly will leak around the eyeshield and illuminate your face, make it a target.'

Gray nodded. 'What'll be the zero?'

'Eight hundred yards, the distance to that roof,' Able replied. 'Your eyes are out of practice. Eye fatigue will become a factor in about four minutes. So go easy.' Able returned the scope to the box, then brought up his wristwatch. 'The NYPD Special Weapons and Tactics team is going to let us use their rifle range. It's about forty minutes from here. You ready?'

Pete Coates responded, 'Give me a minute with Owen, will you, Sergeant?'

Able carried the scope from the office to disappear down the hall.

'So you are going to do this?' Coates asked. 'How do you know you've still got the talent? You haven't been practising.'

Gray thought for a moment. 'Ever since the Chinaman was killed I've been feeling the little skills coming back.'

'Little skills? Like what?'

'You had fish for dinner last night. Probably a saltwater fish, salmon or tuna. Not lake trout.'

A small moment passed, then Coates's features twisted. 'How do you know that?'

'The scent has come through your pores and is on your skin. I can smell it. Saltwater fish give off more odour than freshwater fish.'

'Is that another of your weird talents?'

'I was born with a good nose but it's mostly learned.'

'Maybe I should've changed my socks this week,' Coates said.

'Another thing. This past couple of days I've been incapable of looking at a distant building or tree without estimating its distance. Six hundred yards, eleven hundred, four hundred. My brain has been filled with an incessant flow of numbers.'

Coates sniffed his wrist, then pulled up his sleeve to smell his forearm. 'It was tuna, but I can't smell it.'

'And once again I've become acutely aware of motion at the periphery of my vision. I'm spinning to these vague movements to the right and left. These are little things, but they're flooding back.'

Coates asked earnestly, 'You've been sitting over there fidgeting, staring at the wall. How's your mental health?'

Gray pressed two fingers against his temple. 'What's worse for my mental health, knowing that anybody standing next to me may get an exploded head or me picking up a rifle again? I don't have a choice.'

He rose and walked down the hall towards the waiting Marine.

AT TEN O'CLOCK that evening Sixth Avenue in Brooklyn was still radiating the day's heat. Bricks and concrete seemed to shimmer. Not a whisper of wind touched the street, and air trapped between the buildings was heavy with the scents of auto exhaust, garlic and sewage.

Owen Gray's apartment was on the top floor of his building. The large window facing the street looked in on the twins' bedroom. The

58

sheer curtains were closed, but the shapes inside were visible—
though nebulous—through the translucent cloth.

Gray's bathrobe was a Black Watch plaid that Mrs Orlando had
given him for Christmas. 'Don't read too long tonight, girls.'

The words were wasted. The bundles in the two beds were
motionless. The room was a mad scramble of tossed clothing,
schoolbooks, old dolls and art equipment. Mrs Orlando insisted
that the room be orderly each night before bedtime, but she was still
out courting, and when that happened nothing taken out of closets
or from shelves got put back.

'You two must have had a big day. Adrian Wade wore you both
out?' A soft chuckle. 'She wears me out, too.'

Each form in the beds received a kiss. 'Good night, my girls. Sleep
tight and don't let the bedbugs bite.'

The bathrobe moved towards the door to the hallway.

If that instant could be expanded through some quirk of nature,
the first indication of order gone awry would be the dime-sized hole
appearing as if by sleight of hand in the curtain. The bullet breached
the room like a beam of light, ripping into the form in Carolyn's bed,
digging an appalling trench the length of the body to punch through
the headboard and bury itself in the wall.

Two seconds later, another bullet entered the room through the
curtain, this one plunging through the form in Julie's bed.

At the door, wearing Owen Gray's bathrobe, Pete Coates put the
two-way radio to his mouth. 'Now. He's done it.'

On the roof of the building, only his starlight binoculars visible
above the cornice, Sergeant Able barked, 'I just saw the flash. Zone
two, point three, ED four. They were right, that apartment roof.'

With those words, referring to zones and reference points and distances, Able informed the shooter of the target.

Owen Gray nudged the M-40A1 Marine Corps sniper rifle an inch
left. 'I have him.' Through the scope Gray saw the head, low behind
a roof cornice on a building four blocks away. A rifle was next to the
head, pointed at the air, perhaps coming down for another shot.

Gray inhaled, let half of it out. He had learned early in his sniping career that his vision—everyone's vision—blurred ever so
slightly with each pump of the heart. He waited a fraction of a
second for the target to clear between heartbeats. Then he brought
back the trigger. Two seconds had passed since Able had given him
the coordinates.

The rifle jumped back against his shoulder. His view through the
scope bounced to the sky.

Arlen Able cheered. 'You got him. He blew down. I saw his rifle
fall over, too.' He picked up the radio and pressed the send button.

'Pete, we can stick a fork in Trusov. Let's go gather the carcass.'

Below them, in the twins' room, Pete Coates muttered to himself, 'Thank God.' He stared down at the forms on the beds, forms made of artfully placed pillows. The bullets had spat up a few feathers. Julie and Carolyn and John were spending the night with Adrian at her hotel.

At the roof's door, Able turned back to Gray. 'Let's go dance a jig over this guy's body. I want to see you drop your paper star.'

Gray was slumped forward, leaning against the brick rail, blinking repeatedly and panting hoarsely. He had known he would pull the trigger. Of course he would. But the struggle to contain his disgust and confusion and to suppress burning memories had exhausted him. With an effort, one of the most arduous in his life, he pushed himself upright, gathered the rifle.

He stared out into the darkness towards his target. He had seen a head and a rifle. His shot had been clean, he was sure of it. But he whispered to himself, 'Something is wrong.'

Then he followed Sergeant Able.

Having shed the bathrobe, Pete Coates met them on the street, where an unmarked police car drove them to the sniper's lair, a five-storey apartment building on Tenth Avenue. They arrived a few minutes later. According to the sign above the mail slots, the apartment building was named the Zenith.

Coates leaned against the buzzer until the landlord appeared. The detective hung his gold badge in front of the man's eyes and pushed into the building, fairly dragging the landlord up the stairs. He pulled his .38 from his belt holster as he climbed the last flight and opened the door to the roof, Gray and Able right behind.

Heat-softened tar clung to their shoes. They walked round the stair house to the east cornice. The body was in a tight curl three feet from the edge of the roof. Gray's eyes had not fully adjusted to the darkness after the bright hallways, but he could tell the body lay in an unnaturally bent shape.

They drew close. 'What the hell?' Coates snapped.

The body was tied to a toppled chair. Strands of rope wound round the chest and waist and legs to secure the corpse to the chair.

A rifle had spilled to the roof. Able lifted the weapon. 'This is a Stevens .22. No sniper uses this. What's going on?'

Pete Coates lifted a red-rimmed cartridge that had been carefully set on its end near the chair. 'Here is Trusov's signature.'

Owen Gray bent to the body. He grasped its shoulder to turn the face towards him. Tiny bells jingled. The top of the head was missing, leaving a gaping cleft where her lustrous hair had been.

Mrs Orlando stared back at him in the sightless reproach of death.

CHAPTER FIVE

Owen Gray was going to ground. To the high country, to his old home. The land would gather him in and embrace him. The summer wind would let him breathe again, and he would find his footing among the granite and grass. Or he would die in these mountains.

He had finally figured out Nikolai Trusov's message. The Russian had wanted to chase Gray from the city to the wilderness, to a proper duelling ground. Trusov would have kept on killing until Gray complied. And now Trusov would follow Gray to these mountains. Gray was going to prepare for him as best he could. The Russian would quickly determine where Gray was. Time was short.

A thicket of kinnikinnick crowded the dirt road, the shrub in full white bloom. Gray engaged the rented Jeep's four-wheel drive for the last hundred yards up the incline towards the cabin. Rocks spat from under the wheels as they found purchase. The canyon of white fir and lodgepole pine opened in patches of sunlight.

He guided the Jeep round a stone outcropping to gain his first glimpse of the larch tree in the front yard. The larch was not common in the Sawtooth Range, and its trunk rose almost 250 feet, barren of foliage, until reaching a bushy top. This glorious spire had stood sentinel in front of the cabin for all of Gray's memory, and all of his father's and grandfather's.

Gray drove round the larch to the gravel patch that served to keep mud from the front door during the spring melt. When he opened the Jeep's door he was met with the stirring scents of mountain Idaho—the redolence of red cedar and bracken and columbine blooms and damp earth— scents that always filled Gray with a longing for times past and people gone.

He stepped towards the porch. Birthplace of three generations of Grays, the cabin was made of lodgepole pine. The building had outgrown its origins as a one-room hut with one grease-paper window hastily thrown up to keep the winter of 1903 at bay. Over the decades several rooms had been tacked on. Plumbing and electricity had been added, and a massive stone fireplace. Gray climbed the porch and opened the door with the key.

The air was thick with dust and mould and the scent of pine. Gray pulled aside window shutters to brighten the room. Memories rushed in with the light. The scene—every worn stick of furniture, every corner—was from his youth. The three-legged stool next to the iron fireplace tools, the pole and peg coat hanger, the couch covered with a red and purple Shoshone blanket, the cracked leather chair, the rag rug in front of the fireplace, the room was as it ever had been.

Gray had inherited the home and 500 acres from his father. He had returned to Idaho for the funeral, but not since. Gray's friend Jeff Moon, who lived in Ketchum, looked after the place. In return, Moon rented it to hunters during the season and kept the proceeds.

In the main room the fireplace almost made up the entire west wall. The mantel and hearth and fireback were washed river stone. The andirons and grate were made of mule-sled runners, bent into shape by a blacksmith. The dining area was at the rear of the main room, near the kitchen. Above the pine table was a moose-antler chandelier, a twisted horror lovingly fashioned by Gray's father. Three 1,400-pound moose had given their all to illuminate the Gray table, and each rack measured over fifty inches across. Six twenty-five-watt bulbs were attached to the antlers. The slightest draught would slowly swing the chandelier, sending gnarled and grasping shadows creeping across the table.

His parents' bedroom was off the main room, and Gray's was behind the kitchen. He passed the kitchen's wood stove and pulled open the door to his room. His grey and brown Shoshone blanket still covered the bed. His desk and chair were against a wall. A 1905 reprint of *The Original Journals of the Lewis and Clark Expedition*, all eight volumes, lined the top of the bookshelf. These books were the most influential reading of his youth.

Gray moved to the back of his room, to double-panel doors locked with a four-inch-square padlock. Here were items Gray didn't want the hunters who rented the cabin to take home accidentally or otherwise. He found the small key on his key ring and opened the door. He yanked the string of the overhead light.

The history of the Gray family in the Sawtooths could be traced by the contents of this closet. Gray's great-grandfather Mason had rushed into Idaho in 1878 when gold was discovered on Yankee Fork. Mason's placer pan, almost three feet across and worn to a high sheen by years of hope and backbreaking work, was on a ledge in the closet. Mason had died broke, the prospector's usual reward. His son George—Gray's grandfather—had turned to the forests and streams for his provender, harvesting a hundred salmon a day in the early years of the century. Later he tried sheep and then cattle. In a corner was his branding iron. George and his son Dalton—Gray's father—had supplemented their income by trapping wolves and coyotes for the government bounty. A dozen traps hung by their anchor chains from the closet's side wall.

It was a hardscrabble existence until Gray's father made a discovery that to his dying day he could scarcely credit: rich Californians would travel three days on a train to the Sawtooths to shoot game. In the mid-1940s, Dalton Gray began his career as a hunting guide.

He would help the outlanders kill anything they might like: blue grouse, moose, elk, bighorn sheep, and in the early days cougars, black bears and grizzlies.

A simple trick virtually guaranteed his clients would become repeat customers. During the hunts Dalton would always come across rattlesnakes, and while the Californians watched he would grab the snake by its tail, whirl it around, then crack it like a whip, snapping the snake's head off. He'd offer the head—inch-long fangs dripping poison—as a souvenir to the Californians. Every Gray for four generations had mastered this moronic stunt—Owen was no exception—but it never failed to leave the customer slack-jawed.

In the weapons rack on the closet's wall were a Remington 700 and a bolt-action .330 Weatherby Magnum with a muzzle brake Dalton Gray had made himself. When Owen was sixteen, his father had promised to purchase the Weatherby for him if Owen could spend one week in the mountains. 'That all I have to do?' Owen had asked. His father grinned. 'One week. You can take your bowie knife. Nothing else.' Gripping his knife, Owen had left the cabin that Sunday as naked as when he came into the world. He returned seven days later, only a few pounds lighter and wearing a mule deer's hide. The Weatherby and a handshake were waiting for him.

On the back wall, boxes of shotgun shells and rifle cartridges crowded the shelf. An axe, a two-man crosscut saw and a sledgehammer leaned against a wall. Gray lifted the axe and left the closet. He re-entered the kitchen and was startled not to find his mother standing at the counter, his eternal picture of her, wide and solid in her print dress, usually pounding dinner to tenderness, the fleshy thump-thump filling the house as her meat hammer rose and fell. His mother had died of stomach cancer six years ago. His father passed away a year later. His death certificate listed heart failure as the cause, but Owen Gray knew it had been loneliness and grief.

Carrying the axe, Gray left the cabin through the kitchen door. The screen slammed behind him. He crossed to the woodshed fifty feet behind the house. Hidden by a wall of choke-cherry and mountain maple and down a small ravine, Black Bear Creek gurgled and ran. Purple mountains rose above him in all directions.

The woodshed was a peaked and shingled roof on four posts. Two-by-four planks crisscrossed on three sides for lateral support. Gray stepped inside, picked up a length of wood and put it on the two-foot-high splitting block. The axe swung in a practised arc, and the blade sank in. Gray lifted the axe, wood clinging to the blade, and brought it down again. The halves toppled to the ground. He picked up one, and halved it again. Then he split the smallest piece with a well-aimed swing. Now he had kindling.

But he swung again, this time at the sticks on the ground. The blade bit through them and dug into the earth, the shattered halves flipping into the air. Gray grunted as he brought the axe round. This time the whistling blade missed wood entirely, and shot into the soft ground, sending chips skittering. Again and again and again the blade chewed up the ground.

The axe changed course, slamming into one of the shed's support posts. Splinters shot away. The axe slashed again, and the ancient wood fractured. Gray ferociously ripped the blade out of the wood and sent it soaring again into the post. He chopped maniacally, and the post began to sag under the roof's weight.

He swung at the toppling beam, a blind blow. The blade bounced off the wood and cut deeply into Gray's calf. The front of the shed drooped slowly to the ground, braces and posts cracking loudly. Still he swung, into the post, into the shingles, and chips burst from the wreckage. Blood flowed down his leg. His brow was damp with sweat and his cheeks shiny from tears. He swung savagely, the mad hiss-and-chop cadence filling the canyon. The old shed slumped further as the axe slashed into it.

Five minutes or an hour might have passed. When he finally dropped the axe his hands were bleeding from open blisters and his right trouser leg was damp and sticking to his calf. His breath ragged, he stumbled away from the wreckage.

Gray collapsed on the front porch. He gazed without seeing at the distant pinnacles. And again, for the thousandth time in two days, his mind produced the image of Mrs Orlando.

And with it came the black cloud, the unshakable agony of grief and guilt. This cabin, his family home, had always been his refuge and his cure. This time it had not been enough.

THE STOLEN STATION WAGON began to fail after 300 miles. With all its miles and years, it could not tolerate hour after hour of driving. First to go was the air conditioner. Then a left rear retread blew away and was replaced by a threadbare spare. The rods began to knock ominously. But only when a warning light came on did Nikolai Trusov pull off the highway to raise the hood. The fan belt had disappeared.

It was nearing one in the morning. He stepped round the car, picked up the nylon sports bag containing his rifle and walked west into the night.

HOBART IS UP THE VALLEY from Ketchum, about as far as an ore team can travel without collapsing in the harnesses, which is why the first white man settled there in 1891. The town is on the Big Wood

River at the confluence of Black Bear Creek. Only a handful of businesses remain, and one of them is the Right to Keep and Bear Arms Saloon, shortened to the Right Saloon by its patrons.

Owen Gray entered the saloon, and by instinct he stepped to one side until his eyes adjusted to the darkness. His bandaged calf ached where he had stitched the palm-sized flap of skin back to his leg with a needle and thread from his mother's sewing kit.

The saloon's east wall was dominated by a backbar of bevelled mirrors and topped by elaborate mouldings. Trophies hung from the walls—the heads of buffalo, moose, a mule deer. The trophies made the saloon seem crowded, even though the room was empty. The place smelt of cold cigarettes.

The bartender's doughy face first registered curiosity at a stranger having found the tavern, then surprise and pleasure. He stuck out his hand. 'I'll be damned, Owen. Welcome home.'

Gray tried not to wince as the bartender vigorously pumped his hand, blistered from the axe handle. He exchanged a few words with the bartender, Ray Miller, whom he had known all his life.

Miller said, 'I hope you're in the Tooths for a happier reason than last time, Owen.'

'A little R and R is all,' Gray replied. 'I stopped the phone service out at the place when Dad died, Ray. I need to use yours.'

Miller thumbed the payphone behind him. 'Let me post you to a beer when you're done.'

Gray punched in a number, and a few moments later Pete Coates was on the line. The detective asked, 'How you doing?'

'Better.'

'Anna Renthal asked about you. Wants to know when you'll be back.'

'Frank Luca gave me as much time off as I need,' Gray said. 'I don't know when I'll be back.'

'Where are your kids?' Coates asked.

'I'd trust you with my life, Pete, but the fewer people who know where they are, the better I feel.' The children were with Jeff Moon and his wife in Ketchum, dropped off on the drive from Boise Airport.

His eyes closed, Gray pinched the bridge of his nose. 'I thought we had him, Pete.' His voice trembled. 'Have you figured out how he got Mrs Orlando?'

'She was last seen a block from your apartment at a laundromat. We have no idea how he abducted her. Trusov is a cunning boy.'

Anger coloured Gray's words. 'Have you learned anything else, like why Nikolai Trusov is on my case?'

'That's Adrian Wade's department, and she's taking it seriously. She's in Kabul as we speak.'

'Afghanistan?'

'You know any other Kabul? General Kulikov found the name of Trusov's Afghan spotter. And the US consul in Kabul found the faction he fights for. His clan are now in the mountains. Adrian was on a plane ninety minutes after she got the news.'

'What's she after?'

'Anything that'll explain why Nikolai Trusov is hot for you.'

Gray's voice rose. 'I've got nothing to do with Afghanistan, or with Trusov.' He exhaled slowly. 'Your people surrounding the Russian embassy in Manhattan haven't had any luck, I take it.'

'Trusov never returned to the embassy and I found out why when I interviewed the old man again. Turns out the son called the father, and the old guy was delighted to tell his boy about the policemen visiting. And there's more news, Owen. We found where Trusov has been staying, a motel in Jersey City. We broke into the place. He's got a box of Owen Gray memorabilia.'

'Some of my stuff?'

'In a cardboard box in his closet we found a Hobart High School annual, class of 1967. There's a photo of young Owen Gray wearing a Beatles haircut and a narrow black tie. There's also some recent photos of you—one leaving your Brooklyn apartment leading your son down the steps, another showing you and me carrying gym bags into Sam Owl's place. There's one of Mrs Orlando.'

Gray rubbed his forehead. 'Damn, Pete, what's going on?'

'This guy isn't going to get out of New York,' the detective said. 'Trusov's got the police commissioner and the FBI director's full attention now. They've flooded this town with people. There isn't a bus station, train depot, airport or hotel where he can show up and not be spotted. The Russian's photo has been playing big on television and in the newspapers. It's just a matter of time.'

Gray hung up. He returned to the saloon's main floor and waved at Ray Miller on his way out.

CHAPTER SIX

Polk County Undersheriff Mel Schneider turned his patrol car off the road and into the Cat's Meow Café parking lot in the town of Mentor. He glanced at his wristwatch. He was meeting Deputy Mike Dickerson for lunch at the Cat's Meow, and Schneider was hungry. There were two open slots next to a silver Chevrolet Caprice. He pulled in next to the Chevy and set his parking brake. He'd wait a few moments for Dickerson before going into the café.

A silver Caprice. Schneider's head jerked left. He opened the car door, stepped five steps to the rear to read the Chevy's licence plate. He quickly returned to his car to punch the number into the computer. A few seconds later the screen blinked with the information.

'Aw, damn,' the undersheriff whispered as he read the screen.

The Caprice had been stolen in Brainerd, Minnesota. The auto's owner had seen a large man wearing a baseball cap low on his head drive by in the car while the owner was getting a haircut. The Caprice's owner had later identified Nikolai Trusov from a photo shown him by a Brainerd police detective.

A five-by-seven black and white photograph of Nikolai Trusov had been delivered to every airport, bus station, car rental agency and service station in every Midwestern state. The New York police had thought this man would never get out of their jurisdiction, and he was already halfway across the country. Earlier that morning a Mercury Cougar had been found in Brainerd that had been stolen just north of Minneapolis. The Russian's fingerprints were all over the vehicle.

Schneider peered through his windshield into the café. RayAnne Folger, the café owner, was putting a plate in front of the largest man at the counter. He was wearing a green baseball cap. He lifted a fork and bent to the plate. It had to be Trusov.

Schneider reached for his clipboard. On it was the bulletin given to every Minnesota law officer that morning. He read again about the Russian. 'I sure as hell don't want to do this.'

Deputy Mike Dickerson pulled his patrol car into the slot next to Schneider. When he saw that his boss was not getting out of the car, he squinted in puzzlement through the window, then opened the door and slid into the passenger seat.

'I got some bad news for our lunch plans,' Schneider began. 'You see that man at the counter, last one on the right?'

'Yeah,' Dickerson said. 'The big guy?'

'That's the Russian on the FBI bulletin we got this morning.'

Dickerson stared into the café. 'What're we going to do?'

'We're going to do what the taxpayers pay us for. Arrest him.'

'Shouldn't we call in reinforcements?' the deputy asked.

Schneider rubbed a temple. 'There's two of us. He's sitting peaceably at that counter. I'm going to walk right up to him and stick the Remington into his face and tell him he's under arrest. I don't need reinforcements for that.'

Dickerson wetted his lips. 'He's a commando. According to what I read, he's been at war for most of his life. He's probably pretty good at it.'

'Probably,' Schneider granted. 'Hell, what's he doing now?'

Nikolai Trusov was rising from the stool. He spoke a few words to

RayAnne, who pointed over her shoulder towards the rear of the café. He walked behind the other counter customers, then disappeared between the booths.

'He's going back to take a leak. Mike, as I recall, the window in the men's room might be big enough for a man to climb through. You go round the north side of the café and wait next to the window. I'm going in the front door.'

Dickerson nodded and unsnapped his holster.

The undersheriff laid a hand on Dickerson's arm. 'Mike, we only need to make an attempt to arrest this guy. If he looks sideways at you, shoot him. Don't give him a break. He won't give you one.'

Dickerson pulled his pistol from the holster as he exited the car, then disappeared round the north corner of the café. The undersheriff clicked the pump shotgun from its mount and entered the café.

A few customers turned towards him.

Acquaintances nodded, then stared at the shotgun. His eyes on the rest-room hallway, Schneider slowly walked down the aisle towards it. The customers followed him with their eyes, their burgers and fries forgotten. He held the shotgun in front of him like an infantryman, expecting the Russian to emerge from the rest room at any moment. The door remained closed.

Schneider paused in front of the door. He could feel his blood pump, and his tongue seemed stitched to the top of his mouth. He whispered hoarsely, 'God save me, I don't want to do this.'

But he did. The undersheriff lurched forward, his shoulder slamming into the door, which jumped back and banged against the wall. He charged into the room.

One hand on his belt and the other on his privates, the only man at the urinal stepped back, his mouth open.

Schneider ignored him. He turned a full circle. A knot formed between the undersheriff's eyebrows and he shook his head slowly.

He opened the rest-room door to return to the hall. Across from him was the door to the women's rest room. Then he understood.

Knowing he was too late, he bulled his way into the women's room. No one was inside. A breeze poured through the open window which exited south, the opposite side of the building from the deputy.

Schneider hurried from the room and sprinted down the aisle. 'How did the bastard spot us?' he said aloud.

He stopped in front of the stool where the Russian had been sitting. He stared across the counter to the backbar. Reflected in the stainless-steel coffee urn was the parking lot behind him, and his patrol car, clear as day. He moved by the stools and yanked the café's front door open. The Caprice was a block away and accelerating.

He yelled, 'Mike, hurry up.'

Undersheriff Schneider was going to give chase, but when he reached for his door handle he saw that the rear tyre had been slashed. Dickerson's car, too, had sunk to the wheel rim.

The deputy arrived panting, his pistol in his hand.

'He's gone, and we're stuck here.' Schneider waved a hand at the flat tyres.

Dickerson looked down the road, but the Caprice had already vanished. 'I can't say I'm disappointed to miss him.'

'Me, neither,' said Schneider, reaching for the radio handset.

'THE HAND OF GOD made these mountains.' Owen Gray's voice was soft with wonder at the panorama before them.

'It was glacial ice, not God.' Adrian stopped beside Gray on the bluff overlooking the valley. 'Those peaks are granite that crystallised below the earth's surface, then pushed through to create fault blocks. The granite crags were eroded by glaciers.'

Gray said wearily, 'And I'm telling you it was the hand of God.'

Below them, filling Gray's vision, were the narrow defiles of river canyons, topped with sharp ridges and peaks jutting forth at confused angles. Glacial gouges and horns gave the range an air of unyielding wildness. Near the peaks, blue and yellow lichen coloured the granite. When clouds passed overhead, the mountains changed hues, quickly purpling, then changing to grey, then lightening to blue and gold as the billows passed.

Gray pointed. 'Look, there's a bird called a Clark's nutcracker. If you hold out a sandwich, it'll only take him a few minutes to get the courage to land on your hand.'

The bird was perched on the low branch of a whitebark pine. Black wings rested against an ash-grey body. It peered at them intently, then hopped along its branch.

Gray looked at Adrian Wade. 'I was startled when Pete Coates told me you were in Afghanistan.'

'I was only gone two days. Even so, I'll bet you missed me.'

'Well, I feel safer when you're around.' He was deliberately cheery, not wanting to inflict his grief on her. 'I won't get mugged, anyway.'

She smiled quickly and he generated a grin in return. Then he lowered himself to his haunches. 'Look closely at the trail and tell me what you see.'

Adrian squinted at the ground. 'Dirt and twigs.'

'See these slight depressions in the surface of the path?' Gray traced them with a finger. 'They're paw prints. An hour or two ago a yellow-bellied marmot passed by this way.'

'What's a marmot?' Adrian asked.

'A big leaf-eating rodent.'

'How can you tell it's not a house cat lost in the mountains?'

Gray smiled. 'A marmot has four toes on its front feet and five on its back. A cat has four all around. And cats walk like babies crawl, moving diagonal limbs at the same time. But a marmot moves both legs on one side of its body at the same time, like skunks.'

'How do you know those tracks weren't made by a skunk?'

'A skunk has five toes in front. And we're too high for a skunk.'

Adrian was wearing a light blue jacket, jeans and climbing boots. She persisted. 'And how do you know the marmot came by here an hour or two ago, not yesterday?'

Gray could not resist showing off. 'The prints have just begun to deteriorate, with grains of dirt falling into the base of the tracks. There's a five-to-ten-mile-an-hour wind today, so I know from experience that an hour or two of loose grains have fallen into the paw print.'

Adrian pursed her lips. 'I'm stuck out in the wilderness with Mr Nature,' she said. 'I didn't come to Idaho to learn about rodents.'

Gray shrugged. 'So you found Nikolai Trusov's spotter?'

'Yakub Nadir worked as Trusov's spotter for almost two years. I found him in a hill town outside Kabul, one of the villages still controlled by his tribe.'

'He didn't mind talking to a Westerner?' Gray asked.

'I think he enjoyed it. Nadir is an educated man. He was studying to be an engineer when the Soviets invaded. He chose the wrong side, as he readily admits.'

'What did he say about Trusov?'

'Nadir said the Russian was a master of his craft. And he enjoyed it. Sometimes he would fire many shots at the same target, hitting a knee, then a hand, then a foot and so forth, taking care to place the shots where they wouldn't kill the target immediately. Nadir claims he saw Trusov fire twelve shots at a mujahideen, all hits, before the *coup de grâce*. Trusov told Nadir that his twelve shots before the kill must be a world record.'

'For God's sake, that's not soldiering.'

'Trusov knew about you.'

Gray's head came up.

'That same day, Trusov said to Nadir, "Not even the great American Owen Gray could place twelve non-lethal shots." ' Adrian Wade lowered herself onto a boulder. 'Trusov frequently talked about you.'

'Why? Did he tell his spotter he had ever met me?'

She shook her head. 'I questioned Nadir closely about this. Trusov never claimed any acquaintance with you. He knew of your reputation. He was envious of it.'

'How did he get the big scar on his head?'

'Nadir didn't know. He had it when they first teamed up in 1985.'

Adrian put her hand under her coat to adjust her holster, then continued. 'Nadir said Nikolai Trusov was crazy.'

'I already knew that.'

'He meant that while Trusov was a superb soldier during his first years in Afghanistan, he became increasingly unstable, erratic. But he was so valuable to the Soviet war effort that he was tolerated.'

A nutcracker landed at the other end of the boulder and dipped its beak at Adrian. Gray opened his backpack and brought out a peanut-butter sandwich wrapped in greaseproof paper. He tore off half the sandwich and tossed it to the bird. The nutcracker squawked and leapt onto the handout.

Adrian continued. 'The US immigration authorities are helping our investigation. They checked with their counterparts in Europe, and the Swiss came up with something. Victor Trusov could have had his operation three months earlier. The Swiss had given him and his son permission to enter a hospital in Geneva. But the Trusovs refused, apparently waiting for the US visa.'

'So Nikolai was willing to make his father wait for the surgery until things worked out. To come for me,' Gray said darkly.

'Yes, to come for you.'

'How did Trusov get his rifle into this country?'

She replied, 'Probably in a diplomatic pouch. A Hero of the Soviet Union would easily have found a Russian diplomat to help him get his rifle in.' Adrian leaned forward on the boulder and stared at him. 'It is impossible that no connection exists between you and Trusov.'

'I never said there wasn't,' Gray protested. 'I just don't know what it is.'

'You're hiding something from me. Something in your past connects you to Trusov. You might not know it, but it does. And I won't be able to make the connection unless you tell me everything.'

He nodded vaguely. 'You know everything important about me.'

'That's a lie.' She smiled to take some of the sting from her words. 'I've been a policewoman too long to buy that.'

'You and I are on the same side,' Gray said rather feebly. 'I'm not going to lie to you.'

Adrian brought her hands across her lap to fold her fingers. She gasped, then flicked her hand, her mouth beginning to curl in horror. She leapt up from the boulder. Her voice wavered. 'Have I hurt myself? There's blood all over me.'

Gray rose and hurried to her, reaching for her hand. A dark stain had spread along her right coat sleeve. Gray quickly undid the Velcro fastener and gently pushed back the fabric. None of the blood had seeped through onto her arm.

Gray said, 'The blood is from the rock you were sitting on.'

An edge of the granite slab was daubed with blood, and tinctures of the fluid darkened the moss on the stone.

'Where did it come from?'

'A wounded deer.' The corners of Gray's mouth turned down. 'A mule deer, probably.' He rubbed a finger along the rock, bringing a smear of blood to his eyes. 'It's been hit in the liver. You can tell from the dark colour of the blood.'

Gray knelt to look at the prints at the base of the boulder and found a hoofprint. 'The mule staggered against the rock, then took off again, uphill into that ravine.'

'Who shot him?'

'Some poacher. Deer are out of season.'

'Can we help the deer?' she asked.

'He can't survive this wound. There's nothing we can do.'

'Yes, there is. We can't just let him die.' Adrian started towards the ravine. 'I'm going to find him.'

'Damn it,' Gray muttered. He lifted his pack to follow her.

She led him along a trail through bushes whose flowers resembled white lilies. They reached a fork in the trail where the ravine branched. She slowed, then stopped. 'Which way did he go?'

Gray wetted his thumb and rubbed a leaf that appeared to be spotted with rust. It streaked. Blood. 'He went up the left ravine.'

'Why up?' she asked. 'Maybe he stopped and went back down.'

Gray shook his head. 'Confused, wounded deer always go uphill. And lost children usually walk uphill and lost adults go downhill. That's just how things work.'

They marched through pine trees, which gave way to an aspen grove. The soil was loose, almost a scree. A deep gurgling croak came from a ridge above Gray, followed by a roll of squawks and clacks, a riotous, unnerving sound in the high stillness. Ravens rose from behind the ridge, their enormous ebony wings beating the air.

'The mule deer is behind those rocks,' Gray called. 'The ravens are waiting for their dinner.'

They rounded the rocks. The ravens flew away, but not too far before landing on the scree to stare sullenly at the intruders. Adrian looked sadly at the wounded deer. The mule was lying on a blanket of grass, breathing raggedly, blowing pink blood from its nostrils. Blood trails mapped the animal's flanks and thighs.

Adrian said softly, 'He's going to die, isn't he? He looks bad.'

'It's a she. Yeah, she's in bad shape.'

'There must be something we can do.' Adrian Wade blinked back tears. 'The poor animal shouldn't have to die.'

Gray looked at her. Adrian had known loss, had been pushed to the brink by grief. Gray didn't want his small tour of his mountains to freshen those emotions. He said, 'Maybe I can dig the bullet out. You never know. She could make it.' He stepped across the lichens and stones. The deer raised one hoof, but did not have the strength to lever itself off the ground. 'Too many of us around will scare her. You head down the ravine. I'll catch up when I'm done.'

A tear trailed down Adrian's face. Her gaze went between the deer and Gray, then she turned back down the mountain. She looked back at Gray to see him draw the bowie knife from the scabbard. Gray waited until she was out of sight before he brought the blade to the mule's throat.

Three minutes later he caught up with Adrian. She glanced at the bowie knife, which was back on Gray's belt. 'That deer might live?'

'Maybe.' Gray stared down the valley.

He looked over his shoulder. The ravens had left their perch and were hidden by the crest of the ridge. It seemed to him their renewed croaking held a victorious note.

She said bitterly, 'I thought you weren't going to lie to me.'

After a moment he said, 'I won't. Mostly.'

ANDY ELLISON moved on his knees among the stalks, stopping at each one to sprinkle a small handful of fertiliser onto the dirt. He dragged the paper sack along with him as he went from plant to plant.

His marijuana patch was hidden in a black cottonwood glen in Jefferson County, Montana, in the low foothills of the Rocky Mountains, two miles north of the interstate highway. Marijuana plants favour sun, and it was Ellison's despair that he could offer only light dappled by the cottonwood branches overhead. Otherwise Drug Enforcement Agency planes would quickly find the crop.

Andy Ellison wanted no more to do with prison, being a three-time loser already. The next time the DEA found him tending his crop Ellison would surely face six to eight years. So he was careful. He limited each patch to twenty stalks, spending hours determining shadow patterns beneath the cottonwood boughs before he planted. He had fifteen patches at the edge of the Rocking R Ranch. The ranch's owner, a corporation based in Missoula, had rented a home-steader's shack and barn to Ellison. The corporation's concern was Herefords, and it was not too attentive to the perimeters of its grazing land.

Ellison crawled along the ground, dropping the fertiliser and mixing it in. A wren trilled in a cottonwood. A small breeze brushed the stalks, but even so it was warm. Sweat dropped from Ellison's forehead onto his spectacles. He took them off and wiped the lenses on his shirt. He had worn granny glasses since the sixties, and the spectacles and his sandals and tie-dyed T-shirts were his personal commemoration of the sixties, that apex of Andy Ellison's life, those shimmering years of innocence and incense.

The intervening years had hardened Ellison, at least his appearance. He wore a ponytail, but the hair came from the sides and back of his head because he had lost most on top. Ellison had always been thin, but lately his rib cage had begun to show. He made enough money growing dope to feed himself most of the time, but as harvest approached he was usually down to small change.

Ellison scratched his wrist, an ant bite. Then his head came up. He looked left and right between the stalks. Something was amiss. The wren had abruptly fallen silent. The buzz of insects had quietened. A prickly rash of fear crawled up Ellison's back. He was no longer alone in the cottonwood glen. Somebody was closing in on him. Surely the DEA.

Ellison rose quickly and turned south towards the house, his view blocked by the tall marijuana stalks. But surely his pursuers had come from the house. He dropped his paper bag and turned north, ducking below the top leaves of his plants. Still he heard and saw nobody. Sweat spread on his lenses, smearing his view. He turned left towards a brace of dwarf maples. Then a man appeared before him, forming out of the maple leaves. A huge man with a blond head.

The old hippie turned back, willing his legs to work, sprinting through the marijuana stalks. He missed his footing on a cottonwood root and fell to one knee. He rose, limping, pushing himself forwards.

The marijuana stalks ahead of him parted, and the big man was there. Ellison jerked his eyes over his shoulder. Were there two of them? How could he have moved so quickly? Ellison dodged right, towards a thimbleberry thicket, his feet churning the soil. His chest heaved, his breath rattled in his throat. He swatted aside vegetation and there the man was again, smiling slightly and raising a hand.

Panic almost closing his throat, Ellison turned again and flailed through the underbrush. Then he was on the ground, his face hard against the dirt, a rough hand at the back of his neck pinning him there. Helpless, he closed his eyes. Six to eight years this time.

The hand rolled Ellison over, gripped his arm and easily brought him to his feet.

'It's this scar, isn't it?' the intruder said.

Ellison was still blowing loudly, and he thought perhaps he hadn't heard the man. 'A scar?'

'It frightens people.' A clipped voice, unaccustomed to the language.

Ellison peeled off his glasses and wiped them on his shirtsleeve.

74

When he returned them to his nose, he wished he hadn't. Seen clearly, the intruder was even more frightening. Chopped face, gash of a mouth and a dent above his right eye that disappeared under the blond hair. The scar made everything on his face seem askew.

'I need a bed for the night.'

'A bed?' The slightest flutter of hope. 'You just want a bed?'

The stranger nodded.

'Thank you, God.' Ellison turned towards the shack. His confidence soared. 'I don't mind saying you scared the hell out of me.'

'I do that a lot.' The accent was strong. 'Sometimes on purpose, sometimes not.'

THE TRAILER was cramped and hot. Squeezed between banks of blinking red and green and yellow lights, dials and knobs and switches, Pete Coates drummed his fingers on a tiny metal table. 'Can't you hurry up?'

'I'll tell the pilot to rock back and forth in his seat to make his plane go faster,' the technician replied, not bothering to look at Coates.

The technician, an air force captain, was the master of the trailer, called a C3, for command, control and communications. The trailer, the captain and the reconnaissance planes were on loan to Coates and the FBI.

'You sure it's a car in there?' Coates had asked immediately after a ten-minute briefing on the trailer's communications systems. The captain had reviewed his evidence: an Army Beechcraft RC-12d had, with infrared equipment, detected heat coming from a dilapidated barn in Jefferson County. Within an hour, Coates's team had checked the farmstead against the county tax assessor's rolls and determined that there should not have been a heat source in the barn.

'A yellow Buick Regal is what I'm looking for,' Coates offered again. 'That's the last car Trusov stole, and we haven't found it abandoned, so he's still got it.'

The technician nodded. 'The second plane should be there by now. We'll see what shows up.'

A Grumman Mohawk from Fort Ord had been sent for a second flyby. The Mohawk was a multisensor tactical observation and reconnaissance platform equipped with an ESSWACS (electronic solid-state wide-angle camera system). A signal would be relayed to the trailer, and the picture reconstructed on the monitor.

'Still enough light, you think?' Coates asked.

The technician glanced at his wristwatch. 'It's only eight thirty. The sun sets late this time of year. There'll be enough light.'

Coates was counting on the tumbledown barn to be missing shingles. He rubbed his forehead with frustration. In front of the

76

technician, the monitor's screen turned to white, then ran through a palette of primary colours. Then an image appeared showing approximately a square mile of Jefferson County. Visible were a small stream, patches of forest, fence lines and two buildings.

'Here we go.' Pulling a mouse from behind the monitor, the technician clicked twice on a screen button. The image was instantly sectioned into twenty-five parts. The arrow then moved to the section containing the barn. More clicks, and that part was enlarged.

'Looks like you're right,' the technician said. 'Missing shingles. Look here, too. In the grass, the double lines of an automobile track. Abandoned barns usually don't have fresh track in front of them.'

Coates rose from the chair to lean towards the monitor. 'And beneath the roof in the gaps left by shingles . . .'

The captain pointed at a feature on the screen. 'Looks like there's some yellow in that barn.'

'Bright yellow,' Coates added. 'And shiny.' His voice was tight with excitement. 'It's a Buick Regal is what it is.' He slapped the captain on the shoulder and turned for the trailer's door.

'YOU CAUGHT THESE FISH?' Adrian asked, nodding at the two rainbow trout in the pan. The fish were cleaned but still had their heads and tails. 'Did you kill the pig, too?'

Gray ignored her. He had placed three strips of bacon into the frying pan and the trout and bacon sizzled together. On the other grill, steam rose from a pot containing brown rice in boiling water.

Adrian leaned against the post that separated the kitchen from the main room. She was wearing a white wool fisherman's sweater and jeans. Her arms were crossed and a glass of chardonnay was in one hand. Her mouth was pursed and her eyes moved back and forth. Gray thought she had the look of someone whose guard was up.

She turned her head at a distant plaintive tremolo that ended in a series of sharp barks. She raised an eyebrow at Gray.

'A coyote.' He used a spatula to turn the fish.

'I thought they only bayed at the moon.'

'They howl at anything. Maybe he's mad at the weather.'

Living in New York, Gray had become unused to monitoring the weather. Rain or snow or sun, by the time it reached Manhattan's streets it didn't make much difference. In the Sawtooths, Gray checked the barometer on the kitchen wall several times a day, just as his father had. That afternoon the mercury had dropped abruptly and the storm had swarmed into the mountains as night had come. Rain lashed against the roof in wind-driven waves. Windows rattled with the gusts, and the old cabin creaked and groaned.

Gray used the spatula to slide the fish onto two plates. With a spoon he retrieved spring peas from a steamer. He divided the rice onto the two plates, then carried them into the main room to the coffee table next to a wine bottle and two place settings.

He pushed aside the screen on the fireplace and lobbed two pieces of wood from the box onto the fire. The blaze roared and popped, filling the room with warmth and dancing light. He lowered himself to the couch, facing the fire.

Adrian Wade joined him, placing her glass on the table. 'You're not having wine?'

'Even one glass takes my edge off. I can't afford that now.'

Gray watched her eating the fish. The fire's hues played on her face and sweater. Golds and reds and blues painted her in reeling patterns, making her seem an illusion.

'You're staring at me again,' she said quietly.

He shifted his gaze to his plate.

'I still mind, but not so much.'

They ate in silence for a while. Gray had hoped for a comment about the fish, but none came. Trout was a meal he knew he cooked superbly, and this fish was tender and buttery.

She sipped her wine. Her lips left a slight red print on the glass. Gray stared at it for a moment. He wondered why such a common sight—lipstick on a wineglass—could be so suggestive.

She said, 'Your friend Pete Coates likes to look at the files of people he works with. Did he tell you a lot about me?'

'Nothing I'd call tantalising,' he answered.

'You know about my husband?'

'A pilot who died in a plane crash. Sad business.'

'I read once in a psychology text that for any given person in the United States there are sixty thousand other people that person could fall in love with. But I knew that statistic was sheer nonsense. There was one person for me. And I lost him.'

Gray raised a forkful of rice. He wondered where the conversation was going.

'I met Rick when I was in grade school. I don't remember when I didn't know him, and I always knew that I would one day marry him. It was just a given in my life.'

She was looking fully at him, so he thought there would be little risk of her snapping at him for staring if he turned to her to listen. Her eyes shimmered with reflected firelight.

Adrian went on, her voice a whisper above the fire and storm. 'When Rick died, I died, too, everything except my pulse. I became an empty shell with nothing inside.'

'It must have been hard.' About as inane a comment as possible, but he could think of no other.

'Do you know that I haven't dated anyone since he died? I doubt that little fact was in Pete's file.'

'In four years?' He wanted to add that it was a terrible waste, but thought better of it.

She smiled. 'It's a terrible waste, right? I've heard that before from guys trying to put the make on me.'

'But not from me.' He rubbed the side of his nose. 'I know what you're doing, Adrian.'

'Yes?'

'You are opening up to me, confiding your deepest wound and great secret. You believe that I have something hidden that will help your investigation. You think that if you bare your soul to me I'll reciprocate, that I'll reveal my past so you can clinically examine it.'

She grinned at him. 'It's working, isn't it?'

'Not at all.'

'Sure it is. The fire, this remote cabin, the storm outside, the delicious food, me. You are yearning to tell me your secret. The urge is overwhelming.'

'I don't feel any such urge.'

He abruptly rose and walked into the kitchen. He returned with a wineglass and filled it halfway. 'Half a glass and I'll still have all my reflexes.' He took a drink of the wine, then returned to the couch.

'Tell me your secret,' she demanded softly. She leaned back against the armrest as if expecting a long confession.

Gray swallowed more wine.

'A line of perspiration has appeared on your forehead, Owen.' She laughed lightly. 'You are sweating because you are about to break. You are desperate to tell me, someone who will understand.'

He waved his hand in dismissal. His throat was dry. The fire swayed and flashed, curling its tongues of flame around the logs and twining together and pulling apart. It was enticing him, beguiling him. Tendrils of her scent reached for him, a light gardenia.

'You've put something in my wine,' he protested feebly.

'It only feels like it. You were about to tell me.'

'I . . . can't.'

Her voice brushed him. 'Tell me.'

An age passed.

'That number.' The words at last escaped his mouth. 'Ninety-six.'

'The number of your kills in Vietnam.' She was utterly still, not wanting to derail Gray by a movement.

'That's the number that brought me fame in the Marine Corps, that got a rifle range named after me. My ex-wife and the army psychiatrists thought that number was the source of all my problems. The doctors talked about patriotism, a soldier doing his duty. My wife kept asking what it was like to look through cross hairs at ninety-six people.'

She lowered her chin slightly, a delicate encouragement.

'The number wasn't ninety-six.' He looked at her. 'It was ninety-seven.' He had said it. She had broken him.

'Ninety-seven,' she said, not a question.

He turned back to the fire. Blue flames curled around the bottom of the logs. 'My last shot in Vietnam. In Elephant Valley, that's what the Marines called it. My spotter Allen Berkowitz and I had been out for three days. We hadn't had any luck. I don't like to look back and think I was impatient and careless, but of course I was. Berkowitz didn't see them, but I did, the telltale white dots of a human in the brush, the face and two hands. And a flash of reflected light. We were in enemy territory. No friendlies anywhere near. So I aimed and fired as fast as I could, thinking the flash might be a scope and the enemy had me in it.' Gray's eyes dropped from the fire to the stone hearth.

'Go on,' Adrian whispered.

A moment passed, then he said, 'My kill fell out of the bush where he had been hiding.' Gray placed his glass on the table. His hands were trembling. 'He was an American. A Marine sniper.'

'Are you sure?' Adrian asked gently.

'He was wearing a Marine Corps field uniform and he was a Caucasian. The only whites operating in the area were Marine Corps snipers. We usually stay away from each other's territories, but somehow our signals got crossed.'

'Did you recognise him?'

'I didn't get close to him. I couldn't. A look through binoculars was enough, though. Blood and gore were all over his face as he lay there. He was as dead as I've seen anybody, and I saw a lot of dead people.'

'Was it someone from your unit?'

'We all were accounted for that evening. But there were other sniper companies in Elephant Valley.'

'And you didn't report this to your commander?'

Gray moved his head left and right, an almost imperceptible motion. 'I didn't have the courage. I never learned who my victim was.'

'Did Allen Berkowitz have trouble coping with this?'

'Berkowitz was killed by mortar fire two days after I left Vietnam.' Gray continued with his dinner, tasting nothing.

'What happened after the accident?' she asked.

'The old-fashioned term is a mental breakdown. My captain found me sobbing, sitting on an upside-down bucket near the latrine.

80

He hid me for several days, thinking I'd come out of it, but I didn't. So he drove me to the Division Hospital at Phu Bai. They locked me up in a padded ward. The kook cell.'

'You attempted suicide?'

'I don't remember it very well because of the medication the doctors were giving me. I took a couple of stabs at my wrist with a scalpel I stole from a surgery cart.'

Adrian reached for his left wrist. She pushed back his sleeve. Pink scars were only slightly visible. She said, 'These don't look too bad.'

She looked at his other arm. 'You only took the scalpel to one wrist?'

'It hurt too much. I quit after the first wrist.' He smiled weakly. 'You are the second person I've ever mentioned the ninety-seventh kill to. You and Mrs Orlando.'

'You didn't tell your ex-wife?'

'Cathryn couldn't handle ninety-six. No sense telling her about the last one.'

'Why did she marry you if she couldn't reconcile you with your past?'

Gray spread his hands. 'I lied to her at first. I told her I was an infantryman in Vietnam and only saw a little action. Two years into our marriage I figured Cathryn knew me well enough—knew I wasn't crazy, knew that it was behind me—that she could handle the news.'

'But she couldn't.'

Gray exhaled slowly. 'She couldn't come to grips with me peering through a scope at ninety-six human beings and pulling the trigger. I argued. Jeez, I argued. A war was on. They were the enemy. Made no difference to her.' Gray wetted his lower lip with his tongue. 'I'm not sure I blame her. It's a hard number, ninety-six. Tough to push it around and come up with anything redeeming.'

'Have you come to grips with it?'

'The first ninety-six, yes. But the last one—the American I left dead, and for ever left his family wondering—is something . . .' Gray hesitated. He measured his words. 'It's an inescapable pit of agony for me. That terrible moment is always present, day and night. You'd think a tough ex-Marine and federal prosecutor would be able to deal with it, but I never have.' His voice was barely audible.

They stared into the fire for a few moments. The fury of it had abated now and smoke twisted and rose up the chimney.

She gently patted his arm. 'I'm going to turn in. You'll talk about this more tomorrow, won't you? You won't clam up?'

'Feel free to interrogate me further. It's your job, after all.'

She smiled good night at him. She put her plate in the kitchen on her way to his parents' room, where he had made the bed earlier in the day. She closed the door behind her.

Owen Gray sat on the couch for another two hours, gazing at the fire. When he rose to go to his bedroom only blood-red embers remained.

'ARE YOU ON THE RUN?' Andy Ellison asked, bringing his cup of camomile tea to his lips. The hands shook uncontrollably and the tea splashed over the cup's sides. His voice was as steady as he could make it, the rush of confidence he had felt on learning this man was not a DEA agent having quickly evaporated.

'On the run?'

'A fugitive?' Ellison had quickly determined that the stranger knew no colloquialisms or slang, even common phrases. The foreigner had learned English from a book, probably an old book.

'Yes.'

Ellison sipped the tea, wishing he could control his hands. He was terrified of this big man with the dent in his head. The man's eyes were curiously flat, and they seemed to look through things rather than at them. His large nylon bag was on the floor near his feet.

'Who is looking for you?'

'US Immigration Service.'

'They want to send you back? To where?'

'To Russia.' The big man plunged a cleaning rod into the barrel of the Mosin-Nagant rifle. A scope was mounted on the rifle.

'You handle that weapon like you know what you're doing.' Ellison was determined to get this man to like him and therefore spare him.

The Russian said nothing, working the rod in and out.

His hands were busy with his weapon, but he was staring at the wall.

'You hungry?' Ellison asked. 'I've got dinner on the stove. There's enough for two.' He disappeared into the kitchen and returned with two soup bowls, spoons and a loaf of bread.

Trusov carefully placed the rifle across the table to accept the bowl. He dug into it with a spoon, turning the steaming contents over. Finally he asked, 'Where's the meat?'

With proud defiance Ellison replied, 'I don't eat meat.'

'What is this?'

'Rice and beans and corn in a tomato base.'

Trusov ate several spoonfuls, then pronounced, 'You are a hippie.'

Ellison beamed. 'Yes, I am. How do you know about hippies?'

'I read about them in Red Army school at Rostock. But I thought all hippies were gone many years ago.'

'Not many of us are still around,' Ellison conceded.

Trusov tore off a hunk of bread and used it to ladle the soup into his mouth. Ellison asked tentatively, 'Why did you come to the US?'

The Russian chewed. 'I need to stay here tonight. I will go in the morning.'

'Sure,' Ellison said quickly. He wasn't going to press for answers. But he was emboldened by the man's statement that he was journeying on after a night's sleep. His hands were calming. He ventured, 'Can I ask where are you going?'

'To your state of Idaho. I'm meeting someone in Idaho.'

'THREE MINUTES,' the pilot called over his shoulder. 'Check your safety harnesses.'

'You ever done this before?' shouted Ray Rafferty, the FBI agent next to Coates.

'All the time.'

The agent grinned. 'You don't look too comfortable in that flak jacket.'

Coates yelled above the scream of the engines, 'Don't worry about me, sonny. I'll do fine.'

Coates pulled his service pistol from under the jacket. He checked the load. It was hard to think in the belly of the Sikorsky Black Hawk. The engines roared and the blades pounded and the wind whipped by. Coates and three FBI agents sat in the waist. They wore bush coats over their Kevlar vests, green and brown camouflage colours. Their faces were blackened, and between their knees rested their M16s.

The helicopter was going to land a mile north of the farmhouse in a clearing, close enough to the farm to walk in but far enough away so the Russian would not hear the approach. Another copter was landing two miles south of the farmhouse. Yet more agents were hiking in from the highway. The Russian would be surrounded.

'Here we go,' yelled the pilot.

The helicopter sank and Coates's belly rose in his throat. The pink sky of dawn was visible through the portholes in the fuselage. Then the Black Hawk dipped into the trees. Dust and leaves blew up and the blades gained an even deeper throb. The pilot was skilled, and Coates did not know the helicopter was on the ground until Rafferty slid open the hatch.

The detective popped open his harness and crouched low to approach the pilot. 'Keep your engines idling.' He dropped through the hatch to the ground. He squinted against the swirling dust. The FBI team waited for Coates to lead off. This was his show.

'You ready, boys?'

Rafferty gave the stock of his assault rifle an affectionate squeeze. 'We're always ready.'

The detective brought up his wristwatch. 'The farmhouse is a mile south. We've got eighteen minutes to get there. Let's go.'

Coates led them away, the FBI agents running like infantrymen, their weapons across their chests. The pilot watched them cross the meadow in single file, heading for the trees. Special Agent Ward brought up the rear, occasionally glancing back, checking the avenue of retreat.

Dust blown up from the blades had coated the inside of the copter's windscreen. The pilot swatted a rag against the glass. Just as his eyes refocused through the windshield, a red halo abruptly formed round Ward's head. Mist and light swirled and flickered. Ward crumpled to the ground and was still.

The pilot squinted. The distance and the sun reflecting off his windshield made him unsure what he had just seen. All he could hear was the Black Hawk's turbines.

The three men ahead were unaware that Ward had fallen and continued to cross the field. With Ward down, the last man in the single file was Buddy Riggs. The pilot saw Riggs's head blur red. Riggs fell.

Coates and Rafferty marched ahead, the detective in the lead. The pilot leaned out of the hatch to scream a warning, but the sound was lost in the noise of the turbines.

Then Ray Rafferty's head flew apart and he collapsed onto the grass. The three shots had taken less than ten seconds.

Panting and oblivious, Coates reached the trees. He glanced at his watch, then turned to confer with the team.

And only then did he see the ghastly trail of bodies.

Coates dropped to the ground before he fully understood what had happened. His instinct saved his life, as a fourth bullet smacked into a lodgepole pine near where his head had been an instant before. Coates crawled behind a tree.

The pilot fought with himself. He might be able to help here on the ground, but all his training told him a helicopter was useless when idle. He decided he would get airborne, radio for help, try to extricate Coates. He engaged the rotors. The engines began to wind up. Twigs and grass and dirt whirled up.

The pilot yelped as the hot bore of a rifle was pressed into his neck. A voice from behind. 'Go up. Go west.' The words were slow and bent by an accent.

The killer had climbed into the fuselage. He must have been shooting from behind the helicopter.

Again the careful words, 'Go up. Go west. Listen to me.'

The Black Hawk lifted off quickly, then banked away from the sun. Trees and fields slipped by below.

Through the knee hatch the pilot saw a man running wildly across a field, legs and arms churning away. The man stumbled and fell. He gazed fearfully over his shoulder, then scrambled up again.

'Pick him up,' the man behind ordered.

The pilot narrowed his eyes. Perhaps it was a trick of the dawn light, but it appeared the runner below was wearing a tie-dyed T-shirt. He hadn't seen one in twenty years.

With the rifle barrel still against his neck, the pilot put the Black Hawk down near the runner, who crazily veered away, running and limping, in a panic. The gunman leaned out of the hatch, and when Ellison dared to look over his shoulder again, he saw the Russian signalling him. Ellison slowed, gritting his teeth with indecision. Grinning, the Russian waved again. Ellison bolted for the helicopter.

The gunman helped the hippie into the copter. His Mosin-Nagent on the pilot, the killer pointed skywards. The copter lifted off again.

Ellison slumped onto a jump seat. He was unable to catch his breath. He wiped his forehead with trembling hands.

He managed, 'The DEA. They were after me. Dozens of them.'

The Russian grinned. 'It is dangerous being around you marijuana farmers.'

Ellison barked a laugh of relief. 'Good God, yes. But it doesn't look like I'm going to prison. Today, anyway. Thanks to you.'

Trusov buckled himself in, the rifle still on the pilot. 'No, neither of us is going to prison.'

CHAPTER SEVEN

Owen Gray lowered the M-40A1 sniper rifle to the apple box. He picked up a bowl of cereal and shovelled flakes into his mouth with a spoon. He was sitting on the porch, his eyes on the big larch tree. The ground was damp from the rain, but a grey weeping dawn had given way to blue sky.

Adrian emerged from the cabin squinting at the morning light. She was wearing a white terry-cloth robe that had a red rose stitched over her heart. She was barefoot and wore no make-up. Gray thought she looked alluringly undone.

She stopped near him. 'Cereal? I thought you mountain men ate moose and moss for breakfast.'

He chewed a moment, then said, 'I told you I caught the trout we ate last night, but actually I bought the fish down in Ketchum.'

She raised a hand against the sun. 'Why the fib?'

'To see if you knew anything about the outdoors. You don't.'

'How could I have known you didn't catch the fish?' Her frown reflected her disapproval.

Gray dug the spoon into the cereal. 'The fins of a hatchery fish are worn down and nipped. Fins wear off on the concrete runways. And during feeding time the fish, in their frenzy, bite each other's fins. Wild fish are prettier, with full rays to their pectorals and dorsal fins. No outdoors person would mistake wild trout for farm-raised trout.'

'Well, golly,' she said in a broad hick's accent, 'I sure am dumb and you sure are smart.'

Gray wiped the corner of his mouth. 'I learned in Vietnam always to test my partners. I need to know what you know and make allowances for what you don't.'

'I don't know anything about the wilderness.' She walked behind him towards the south end of the porch. 'If you had simply asked, I would have admitted it.'

Gray mumbled round a mouthful of cereal, 'Don't get yourself bitten by a rattlesnake.'

'Thank you,' she replied. 'I won't.'

'Yes, you will, if you take three more steps.'

Adrian's hands came up as if someone had thrown her a basketball. Her mouth widened. She danced backwards, away from the rattlesnake lying half on and half off the edge of the porch, absorbing the early-morning sun. 'Damn it, Owen, you let me get too close.'

'You were perfectly safe. They crawl, they don't fly.'

'What's it going to do?' Adrian's voice carried a trace of fear unsuccessfully masked.

'It's going to sit there until the sun goes behind a tree or a mouse comes along, whichever happens first.'

'Get rid of it. Shoo it away. Look, it's staring at me.'

Gray lowered the bowl to the apple box. He cross the porch, passing Adrian. The snake's tail came up as its body contracted into a loose coil. 'Rattlers are less dangerous than people think,' Gray said. 'Watch this.'

The snake's rattles at the end of its tail trilled loudly, a relentless, sinister burr. Gray slowly moved his right hand away from his body. The snake's eyes followed the hand. Its forked tongue flashed in and out. While the snake's head was turning, Gray's other hand shot out and snatched the rattler just below its head. The reptile squirmed frantically as it wrapped itself round Gray's forearm. Adrian had stepped back as far as the door, her right hand at her mouth.

Gray stepped down from the porch, peeled the snake from round his arm and tossed it towards the remnants of the woodshed. The rattler crawled quickly under a pile of shingles.

Adrian exhaled loudly. 'What an incredible show-off you are.'

'But you have to admit you're impressed.'

After a moment, she grinned. 'A little.'

'THAT THING IS REACHING for me!' Pete Coates exclaimed, kicking his right foot. 'That hurts!'

'Watch where you're walking,' Gray said mildly. 'And it's only a wild blackberry vine. It won't kill you.'

'Damn it, it's torn my new pants. I just bought them last week.'

The blackberry had sharp spines, curved like talons. This plant had grown over a mountain maple, smothering it, and had reached along the path for more victims. It had found Coates, or rather Coates had found it.

'Is it any wonder I hate leaving New York?' With two fingers Coates prised the vine away from his leg. 'It's got my thumb now.' He flicked his hand. Blood oozed from his thumb.

'Looks like Central Park is about all the wilderness you can handle, Pete.'

Gray and the detective were walking downstream along Black Bear Creek 100 yards from the cabin. The trail was so narrow that they had to walk in single file. Boulders edged some of the stream, and dark pools of still water gathered behind them, lined with sword and maidenhair ferns. A willow trailed its branches in the water, the current tugging at its leaves.

They came to a pool ringed with small-leafed plants growing in patches as thick as a mat. The plants were anchored in the mud. Gray brought out a plastic bag from his backpack, stooped over the pool and tore bunches of the plant from the water.

'What is that?' the detective asked.

'Watercress.'

'It grows in streams?'

'Where did you think it came from?'

Coates shrugged. 'From grocery stores.'

He followed Gray along the path. The stream flowed through a ravine filled with hemlock and mountain laurel. Leaves were still damp from the storm the night before, but the strip of sky visible above was rinsed and smiling and lapis-blue.

Gray looked over his shoulder. 'You ever been out here before?'

'Never.'

'Did you bring any outdoor clothing?'

'I wear a tie when I'm on business.' Coates's grey sports jacket was dappled with water spots from the leaves. He wore a red tie and white shirt. His trouser cuffs were ragged from the vines. 'Aren't you supposed to put asphalt on these paths, and handrails?'

Gray had picked up Pete Coates at the Hailey airport two hours ago. During the drive, the detective had told Gray of the murder of the three FBI agents. Gray had never before seen the detective's hands tremble. Now, feeling each owed it to the other, both men were trying to generate a good humour neither felt.

'Watch the creek bank,' Gray said. 'It's soft here.'

'Where?' As Coates asked, the bank crumbled under his feet and his left leg plunged into the water to his knee. He flailed the air wildly before his hands seized a laurel branch to lever himself out.

'There,' Gray said.

He began climbing out of the ravine along a path he had known since he could walk, a trail so stitched into his memory that a growth of moss on a feldspar outcropping caught his eye as new, and a stretch of stones near the rim of the canyon was brighter than he remembered. Coates scrabbled up the path behind Gray, his damp trousers clinging to his leg. His glasses flashed in the dappled sunlight below the trees. The detective's leather shoes could not find purchase on the pebbles and loose dirt, and he churned his legs, slipping with each step. Gray grabbed his wrist and pulled him over the top.

Coates shook away Gray's hand and said with mock indignation, 'You think this gives you some sort of moral authority over me, don't you? Out here in the land time forgot, watching me cope.'

'Correct me if I'm wrong, but you asked for the tour of the property.'

Coates followed Gray towards the cabin. 'You are positively glowing, parading your knowledge. You know what the biggest difference is between you and me, Owen?'

'I'm afraid to ask.'

'It's this: I know crime and criminals. I know the underside of life, the rot of the big city, the vicious and the cruel, the complexity of urban life. And you know watercress.'

Gray laughed.

'What happened to this garage?'

'It was a rickety old woodshed. Wind probably blew it down.'

'Pretty violent storm, must've been, to hack out wood chips from the support poles just like an axe.'

'You don't miss much, do you, Pete?'

They approached the home. A panel truck was parked near the porch. The vehicle was unmarked, but Gray knew it belonged to the FBI. On the porch, Adrian Wade pointed directions to two technicians who carried a computer and a five-foot-diameter satellite dish into the house.

Gray muttered, 'She's going to make my place look like Houston Control.'

A police car was also parked on the gravel. The police officer was sitting on the car's hood watching the truck being unloaded, and watching Adrian in particular. When he saw Owen Gray, the man's face wrinkled into a grin and he crossed the gravel.

He pumped Gray's hand. 'Tell me you're moving back into the Sawtooths and that handsome woman is your bride.'

Gray smiled. 'Walt, I'm only here for a while.'

'And that's not your wife?'

'Lord, no. She's a combination Ninja assassin and Grand Inquisitor, and I'm not related to her in any way.' He introduced Coates to Hobart Police Chief Walt Durant.

Durant had a doughy, overfeatured face. His mouth was wide, and his nose was the size of a light bulb, lined with burst capillaries. With small gaps between every one of his teeth, his smile resembled a picket fence. He was bald except for a horseshoe of grey hair from temple to temple. Durant was wearing a tan uniform and above his badge were four citation plates awarded by the city council.

'You carry two shields, Chief?' Coates asked, pointing to Durant's shirt pocket.

Durant lifted the second badge from his pocket. It glittered gold in the sunlight. 'I'm also the Hobart fire chief. The badge I wear depends on the emergency. I'm also in charge of the Hobart sanitary landfill.' The police chief brightened. 'Another job I had once was a bounty counter.'

'A bounty hunter?' Coates asked.

'A counter. The federal government back in the early sixties offered a bounty for coyotes. You remember, Owen? You and your old man brought in two hundred and fifty coyotes in one month. Most ever, I'd bet. I'd pay ten dollars for every set of coyote ears you brung me.'

Durant had been Dalton Gray's closest friend, the first visitor to the house when Owen had been born. Decades later, as Dalton was being lowered into the ground in the Hobart cemetery, Durant had told Gray in a breaking voice, 'In the future, if you need anything from a father, you ask me, Owen.'

The police chief said, 'You haven't mentioned what brings you out here, Pete.'

While Coates told Chief Durant about Nikolai Trusov, Gray entered the cabin. He returned a few minutes later carrying sandwiches piled high on a plate. He stopped at the porch to hand some to Adrian Wade and the technicians.

'And what makes you think the Russian is coming to Hobart?' Durant asked Coates.

'We put two facts together. One, Trusov is heading west. And two, Owen is here.'

'So what are you proposing to do?' Durant asked.

'I tried to erect a series of concentric circles around Manhattan, circles of people looking for Trusov. But he got outside them all.

Now I'm going to put the same circles around Hobart, hoping I can spot Trusov coming in.'

From a coat pocket Coates removed a map of the area. The map had a 1:250,000 scale, with contours every hundred feet. The detective asked questions about the lie of the land, about the only paved road in and out of Hobart, about the small dirt roads that wandered up into the mountains, and about locations for highway checkpoints.

He finally summed up. 'It looks like I'm going to need two shifts of about eighty people each. I suppose you know most of the sheriffs and police chiefs around here.'

Durant nodded.

'Will they loan you their people?'

'As many as they can spare.' The police chief produced a can of beer from his pants pocket. He tapped the lid before opening it, then held the tin out. Coates declined.

'And I need some of your resources. What's the size of your department?'

'You're looking at it.'

'You? That's it?'

Durant put a back-country drawl into his voice. 'Hobart ain't Manhattan, Pete.'

'How about communications equipment?'

'I don't have much, because when I'm out of the office there's no one to call at the office, and when I'm in the office there's no one out on the road.'

The detective removed his glasses to scratch the side of his nose. 'Is there anything you can do to help me, Chief?'

'I'll call everyone in Hobart and tell them to keep their eye out. A stranger won't be able to belch in this town without me hearing of it.'

'Can you tell me by tonight how many people you can borrow?'

'You bet.'

Chief Durant returned to his car. He said he'd be in touch, and then he drove off down the road, disappearing down the hill.

'I USUALLY DON'T EAT things I can't lift.' Adrian Wade poked at her dinner.

Baked potatoes filled their plates, hanging over the edges. They had been opened and topped with spiced meat, cheese, olives, sour cream and chopped chives. Potatoes were the speciality of the Right to Keep and Bear Arms Saloon. Ray Miller hovered behind the bar wearing an expectant smile, waiting for Gray and his guests to begin their meal.

Adrian lifted a measure of potato. She chewed a moment, then beamed at Miller, who seemed to grow three or four inches with the

90

smile. When Gray had entered the saloon with Adrian Wade, Miller had gleefully whispered to him, 'And to think I worried about you.' Miller had been only slightly dampened when Pete Coates followed them. Coates was wearing a pea coat over a plaid shirt, jeans and hiking boots. Gray had loaned him the clothes, which were stretched to their limit over Coates's bulk.

The detective said, 'Chief Durant was as good as his word. Hobart is crawling with sheriffs' deputies and State Patrol. And the FBI will start arriving soon. Flights into Hailey will be full of them.'

Gray cut into his potato. He had eaten dozens of Miller's famous potatoes over the years.

'Adrian, you're all set up?' Coates asked round a mouthful of food.

'All in one corner of Owen's living room. I've got the communication capacity of the Manhattan FBI office.'

Ray Miller held up the telephone behind the counter. He called, 'Detective Coates, it's for you.'

Coates dropped his napkin on his seat and walked to the bar.

Gray said quietly, 'I suppose you've mentioned to Pete about my ninety-seventh shot.'

'Of course I told him. He's your friend and he's trying to figure out what's going on. Do you mind?'

Gray shook his head noncommittally.

Coates returned and said bleakly, 'Nikolai Trusov was spotted in Butte by a policeman an hour ago. Trusov was driving a pick-up truck, a red Dodge Ram. He had a passenger with him.'

'The policeman is positive it was Trusov?'

'No question. He tried to give pursuit but the pick-up disappeared. The Montana Highway Patrol found the truck in the western outskirts of Butte, abandoned. They speculate Trusov has another vehicle and is continuing west.' Coates lifted his beer glass. 'I'd sure like to know how Trusov figured out you are in Hobart.'

'Do you want to tell him?' Adrian asked, bringing her gaze round to Gray.

'Tell him what?'

Adrian said, 'You left him a message, Owen. I called your home telephone number in Brooklyn. On your recorder is the message "No one is home right now. If you are looking for Owen Gray, he is at his father's place on Black Bear Creek near Hobart, Idaho."'

The detective stared at Gray. 'You guessed Trusov would call your number, and you've told him where you are. You're intentionally setting up a duel between you and Trusov, is that it?'

Gray said nothing.

Coates put down his fork. 'Owen, this isn't the damn OK Corral. Trusov is a killer, and he's superb at it. And now you've decided to play a game with him, to meet him in the field. I thought you and I were working for the same thing, but I guess we no longer are.'

'I guess not,' Gray said quietly.

'I ought to throw you in jail for your own protection.' Coates's voice was lower. He was settling down.

'Pete, you might be the most skilled detective at the NYPD,' Gray said, 'but I don't believe you'll stop Trusov before he finds me.'

CHAPTER EIGHT

Owen Gray lay on his belly, the M-40A1 Marine Corps sniper rifle in front of him. His left hand was forward, with the palm against the stock ferrule swivel and the sling high on his arm. His wrist was straight and gently locked so the rifle rested on the heel of his hand. The wooden butt was firmly in the pocket of his right shoulder. Near his elbow was a box of match ammunition, so called because each bullet in the box had the identical serial number, indicating the bullets had been manufactured with the same batch of gunpowder on the same day, thereby eliminating vagaries in powder that might randomly change muzzle velocity.

He peered over the scope, reacquainting himself with the terrain. Shepherd's Bowl, so named because a Basque shepherd tried to raise sheep here in the early years, was spread out before him. Fed by a small spring, Black Bear Creek originated in the valley and exited at the eastern end to wander two miles to the Gray ranch and then on to the Big Wood River.

Gray was three-quarters up the north side of the bowl. The area was two miles long, running west–east, and a mile and a half across. The valley's centre was thick with trees and undergrowth. Also along the valley floor were a dozen patches of wild grass, each a half-acre to an acre, growing to the height of a man's waist. At this time of year the grass was yellow and dry.

Gray's hide was a small protrusion on the north slope, a cleft in the incline formed by stones and dirt sliding down and building up behind a boulder over the centuries. The ledge was just large enough to lie on. By taking an indirect route, ducking carefully through bushes and taking advantage of a few sparse trees on the slope, it was possible to climb to it without being seen from anywhere in the bowl. Apart from some dogbane growing around boulders, banks of broom, a few stunted lodgepole pines and clusters of rolling tumbleweed, the north slope was open and clear. It curved round like the stands of a football stadium.

Gray looked over the rifle to the other side of the bowl. The south side was hidden in shadows and was forested with pine and aspen and other trees. Gaps in the tree cover revealed green and flowering underbrush. So different were the north and south sides of Shepherd's Bowl that they could have been on different continents. Behind the bowl, jagged peaks were limned against the diamond-blue sky.

He lowered himself over the rifle's butt, stock and grip, which snipers call the furniture. Gray could not feel where his body ended and the rifle began. This firm weld would allow Gray's head, hand and rifle to absorb recoil as one unit. He brought his eye to a position behind the eyepiece, sighting on a knot in a pine near the valley's mouth. He kept his eye back from the lens to protect it from recoil. When he took a deep breath, the cross hairs moved down straight through the centre of the target, indicating he was well balanced over the rifle.

Gray had always credited a rifle scope with magical qualities. He well understood the optics. He knew that an object viewed from 600 yards through a 6X scope will have the same clarity as if viewed by the unaided eye from 100 yards. He knew that the magnesium-fluoride coating on his lens increased transmission of light from about 45 per cent to 86 per cent. But those same optics that magnified the view and flattened the perspective also dulled a hunter's humanity. In Vietnam when Gray peered through a scope, the image quartered by the cross hairs was not human but a target, nothing but a mathematical problem of windage and velocity and direction. The scope had a marvellous ability to eliminate sloppy moral issues. If it appeared through the scope, Gray could kill it.

The scope's magic survived time and tragedies, it seemed. He had accepted the rifle with stomach-churning trepidation, but even after the decades he had felt its supernatural power of simplification on the Brooklyn roof as he found the target. The ghastly outcome—the death of Mrs Orlando—had sickened him, left him exhausted with grief. Yet here he was on a perch high in a mountain bowl, ready again to pull the trigger, all the world's complexities filtered out by the rifle scope.

He lifted his head to avoid eyestrain. At the mouth of the valley, several low branches of a dogwood were rattling, whipping left and right. The only animals that would make such a commotion were a bear using the tree to scratch its back or an elk or moose trying to rid its horn of felt. Gray sighted in on the dogwood, not intending to pull the trigger. He narrowed his eye slightly. The rifle was dead calm in his hands, so still that a bead of mercury placed precisely on top of the barrel would have remained there.

Adrian Wade's face popped into the cross hairs. She had emerged

93

suddenly from under the tree, but now caught her jacket on a branch. She yanked on it and finally freed herself.

Gray jerked his eyes up from the scope. He pivoted the weapon aside and found her with his unaided eye. Her red coat and black hair stood out like a sailor's emergency dye on a calm sea. She was scanning the bowl, moving her head randomly, an amateur's search that would miss him entirely. He stood, removed his coat and waved it back and forth until she started in his direction.

She was hurrying. More than hurrying, she was frantically pedalling her legs. Gray brought up the binoculars to search the trees behind her, but she was not being chased. As he watched her ascend the bowl, he pulled an apple from his pack and ate it from the bottom up, consuming every part of it except the stem. He had learned to eat an apple that way in Vietnam because an apple core might be found by an enemy trying to follow him.

He liked watching Adrian Wade, Gray admitted to himself. She moved with the grace of an athlete, even though she was breathing heavily in this oxygen-weak altitude. She reached the loose scree just below his hide and used her hands to climb the last yards up to him.

She gasped. 'I don't suppose you could have met me halfway.'

'I was eating my lunch.' He flicked away the apple stem.

She collapsed on the soft soil and leaned back on her elbows. Gray handed her a canteen from his pack. 'What's going on?'

After a moment her breathing eased. She smiled and said majestically, 'I have your answer.'

Gray scratched his neck where a deerfly had bitten him. 'I have more questions than you have answers, I'll bet.'

She laughed and shook her head. 'Owen, you are going to grovel with thanks before me. You've spent years and years wandering in the dark, and now I'm going to lead you to the light.' She tilted her head back and laughed again, a victorious chortle.

The sun played with her hair. He had not seen the flecks of red and gold in it before, but the harsh high-altitude light found tiny glints of colour among the ebony. And the light made the shock-white skin of her face translucent.

Her mouth came together to say something but Gray beat her to it. 'I know. I'm staring. I'll stop.'

Her eyes were amused. 'Go ahead and stare.' Then another laugh. 'I'm going to blow you off this ledge with my news.'

'Stop crowing and tell me.'

'I don't want you to think it came easily.'

Surrounded by computer and communication equipment, Adrian Wade had spent hour after hour in her corner of the cabin's living room. Last night Pete Coates and Gray sat at the table under

94

the antler chandelier sipping coffee and watching her. She seldom rose from the monitor, and when she did it was to insert or retrieve a document from a fax machine. She would stare, pound the keyboard, then stare again, drumming the table, occasionally leafing through the pages of several ring binders. Or she would speak into the telephone, sometimes in English but usually in Russian. Once in a while she would say something aloud, but Gray doubted she was aware she was speaking. Things like 'Good for Captain Mason. I've got the patch-through.' And, 'I didn't even think Donetsk had telephones.' Coates and Gray would look at each other and shrug, not having the slightest idea what she was talking about. She had been at her station when they had turned in, and she was there when they got up in the morning. Gray did not know if she had slept.

She demanded, 'Give me a date between 1947 and half a year ago.'

'A game? I don't feel like playing games.'

'Any date.'

Gray pinched the bridge of his nose. 'December 6, 1975.'

'Trusov is in Olympic training at the Central Army Sports Club facility near Pervouralsk in the Ural Mountains. He is skiing forty miles a day, and is on a rifle range two hours a day.'

'August 12, 1987.'

'Trusov is operating near Safir Chir, a town about seventy-five miles north by northwest of Kabul. He is attached to the 1st Recon Company, 2nd Motor-Rifle Regiment, 15th Motor-Rifle Division.'

'I'm impressed,' Gray admitted.

'I've known all this for days. But there was a hole in my Nikolai Trusov calendar, and try as I might, I couldn't fill it in.'

'What dates?'

'July through November 1970. General Kulikov and his staff couldn't find anything. I began to wonder about the dedication Kulikov was bringing to his investigation. A chronicle of those five months of Trusov's military career had to exist somewhere.'

'So what did you do?'

She leaned back further on her elbows, and the scree rattled and shifted. 'At my request, FBI Assistant Director Robert Olin spoke with the Russian Republic's Vice-President Felix Ogarkov, whose main job is lobbying Western governments for aid for Russia. Olin spoke of how our government would view favourably any assistance General Kulikov might give to the investigation of Trusov. This was yesterday morning. As I understand it, Ogarkov immediately alerted General Kulikov that should he help in procuring American aid, a diplomatic position might open up for him in the US or Europe.'

'It worked?'

'Kulikov found what I was looking for. In the late 1960s a training brigade was formed that was so secret, it was under the command of General Bukharin, chief of the Main Political Directorate, rather than the ground-forces chief.'

'A training brigade that was secret?'

She let the question hang for a few seconds before delivering the punch line. 'The 1st Special Training Brigade was sent to Vietnam. The Pentagon has long known that Soviet pilots trained North Vietnamese pilots. It seems that the Soviets were training soldiers, also. Trusov taught marksmanship. And he did some shooting, too.'

A cable seemed to tighten round Gray's chest. 'He was in Vietnam?'

Another smile. 'He trained NVA and Viet Cong snipers. General Kulikov has now spoken to three other sniper instructors in the brigade. They all have clear memories of Nikolai Trusov, and they all remember his last day of active service in Vietnam.'

Owen Gray stopped breathing.

She said, 'The 1st Brigade instructors all knew of you, Owen. White Star was famous and feared. You and the other American snipers were the reason the 1st Brigade went to Vietnam. You had shown the devastating effect of a lone man and a high-powered rifle, and the Vietnamese were determined to counter you with their own snipers. So in came the Russian instructors.'

Gray willed his lungs to work. 'Where was Trusov in Vietnam?'

'He spent most of his five months at an NVA camp near Chu Lai until he left to travel south.'

Gray closed his eyes.

'He bragged to his 1st Brigade friends that he was the finest marksman in the world, and there was only one way to prove it. He was going to hunt you down. And so one day in November 1970 he took off, knowing you were somewhere in Elephant Valley.'

'The man I killed was an American.'

She shook her head. 'Nikolai Trusov was wearing a US Marine Corps field uniform and backpack. The NVA must've taken it off a dead American. He wore it to confuse you, knowing that at the very least you would hesitate a moment. That's all Trusov thought he needed, a moment of indecision on your part.'

Gray opened his eyes. Adrian was no longer smiling. He said, 'Even if what you say is true, I killed the man in Elephant Valley.'

'As hard as it is to admit for a sharpshooter like you, your bullet was high and wide. You put a trench in his head. It knocked him senseless and he bled profusely. You said yourself you only saw the downed target through your binoculars.'

Gray was staring at the scree behind Adrian, seeing nothing.

A small wind brushed her damp hair. 'I've been unable to discover who found Trusov in the valley, but we can presume it was an NVA patrol. But General Kulikov connected me with the medical officer who treated Trusov after he was carried back into the Chu Lai camp. The medical officer told me that the bullet had exposed Trusov's brain. He put a dressing on it, and Trusov was returned to the Soviet Union several days later, still out cold. Later he regained consciousness, and later still a metal plate was put in his head.'

Gray was still staring over her shoulder. He whispered, 'For all this time . . .'

Her news was seeping into him, impossible to absorb all at once. The central fact of his existence—the anchor secured to his mind and soul—had just vanished. It left a vacuum, and for the moment he was incapable of filling it with amazement or elation or gratitude.

'So you are back down to ninety-six.' Her grin was again in place.

He shook his head. 'Ninety-seven. Mrs Orlando.'

'I'm sorry,' she said in a diminished tone. 'But poor Mrs Orlando was different. You were tricked by an expert. You didn't kill Mrs Orlando. Trusov murdered her. You only pulled the trigger. You might as well blame the rifle's manufacturer as yourself.'

'I know all the rationalisations already,' Gray said.

'Much of your burden has been that you ran away in Elephant Valley. You've railed against yourself all these years, not so much because you thought an American soldier died by your hand but because you never reported it and left a family wondering. It was a bit of cowardice, and it has worked inside you like a worm ever since.'

Gray rubbed his temple.

'Nobody goes through life without an unflattering glimpse of himself or herself. You've had yours. You can fairly ascribe it to pressure of the field or youthful inexperience. But at least the hard fact of killing the American is gone, disappeared.'

He abruptly grinned. 'It has, hasn't it?'

The news was slowly sinking in. He felt lighter. And giddy. He breathed the sweet air. 'God, you have no idea . . .'

'So now all you have to worry about is Trusov.'

'Why has he waited all this time to come after me, do you think?' Gray asked.

She shrugged. 'Who knows? Maybe the desire for revenge took a long time to eat away at him. Or maybe he wasn't crazy enough yet.'

Gray nodded thoughtfully, his eyes on the distant rim of the bowl.

She stood up, staying well away from the rifle. 'I'm going back to the cabin.' She turned for her descent. Stones skidded in front of her as she sidestepped down.

After several moments Gray put the binoculars to his eyes to watch her. Watch her move. Watch her black hair and her hips and shoulders.

She must have known, because she suddenly turned to smile and wave. Gray flushed. She knew him better than he had supposed. She disappeared in the trees at the mouth of the valley.

'WHAT ARE YOU MAKING?' Ellison asked.

'A surprise.' Trusov poured nails onto a plate in front of him.

'Are you making a bomb?' Ellison nervously chewed on a lip. 'Don't you think that's a little . . . violent?'

Trusov shrugged. He used a knife to cut a stick of dynamite in half, then snipped off a length of tape to close off the dynamite's ends.

'Where'd you get all this stuff?' the hippie asked, pointing to the table and then to the green duffle bag on the floor next to Trusov.

'I find things. I'm good at finding things.'

'I mean, a person just doesn't find dynamite.'

'He does if he looks on a building site.' Trusov inserted a Madoz detonator into the half-stick, then placed the dynamite and detonator onto the plate. They were sitting in the kitchen of a two-storey house on the outskirts of Butte. The vacationing owners—the tiny placard under the doorbell identified them as the Robinsons—had stopped their newspapers, but it had taken the paperboy two days to figure it out. Trusov had found two old newspapers on the front step. He had broken in by a side window. The Russian had spread a newspaper below his work on the kitchen table. The rifle leaned against the wall.

Trusov put a second plate on top of the first and bound the plates together with duct tape. He held the thing up to show Ellison, turning it slowly. 'A mine.' He picked up yet another plate and ladled handfuls of nails onto it.

'Where did you learn English?'

'In prison. From a book.' Trusov's grin never touched his eyes. 'Now I ask you a question.'

'Shoot.' Ellison peeled back the wrapper on a chocolate bar, feeling safer now that the stranger was taking an interest.

'Why do you grow marijuana? Why not get a work?'

Ellison was offended. 'The word is "job", and that is my job. Growing weed is all I know how to do. And it's a matter of principle.'

Trusov fiddled with the detonator. 'You might not be as smart as I first thought,' he said.

Ellison hoped the big maul-faced man was joking. He ventured, 'I've tried to stop time, stop the clock. I stopped it in 1968.'

Trusov appeared uninterested, working on his second mine.

Ellison forged ahead. 'Do you ever wish you could stop time? Isn't there a time you wish you could return to?'

Trusov's eyes were blank. 'There is one day I would want to have back, yes.' Then he was silent and unblinking.

Andy Ellison generated cheer in his voice. 'But this'll soon be over. We'll shake them off.'

'Yes, we will soon be released.'

'The word is "free".'

The Russian looked at him. 'Yes. Free.'

THE MONITOR GLOWED with vibrant colours, blue and green and red and orange and yellow, wavy lines unreadable to Owen Gray.

Coates pointed at the blue. 'That's him. Heat shows as blue. He's in an upstairs bedroom.'

'What's this?' Gray raised a finger at a blue dot on the ground floor.

An FBI technician answered, 'He left a light on in the kitchen.'

The three men were in a delivery truck that read 'Big Sky Plumbing' on the side. They were parked fifty yards from the Robinson house. The infrared's sensor was in the passenger-side rearview mirror, and the apparatus was pointed at the house. The technician played with a dial. A row of blue shades appeared at the bottom of the screen, from ice-blue to dark purple.

The technician instructed, 'A person asleep has a different blue signature than one awake.' He pressed a finger below a light blue, then pointed at the figure in the middle of the monitor. 'See? Same colour. So he's asleep.'

'You sure it's Trusov?' Gray asked.

'A mailman on his way home from a softball game spotted Trusov entering the house about nine tonight.'

Every post office in the western US had a photograph of Trusov. Every newspaper had run photographs of the Russian. In Montana alone, three-quarters of a million people knew his face.

Coates carried a flashlight in his hand. 'And the county sheriff's department has been watching the house since about ten. No one has come or gone since then.'

'What about that dope grower Trusov forced the Black Hawk pilot to pick up?' Gray asked. 'That could be him asleep in there.'

'We don't know where he is. He's not in the house, because the heat detector sees only one body, and Trusov was seen going in.'

An hour ago Gray had arrived in Butte, flown from Hobart in the Black Hawk. After the disaster in Jefferson County, Coates had insisted Gray be present when next they cornered the Russian. Gray had the best chance of detecting a trap.

Coates ordered the technician, 'You tell me over the radio if Trusov gets up from that bed. You got that?'

The technician nodded. Coates pulled an earplug from his shirt pocket and pushed it into his ear. The plug was in fact the entire radio, with receiver, antenna, battery and speaker all in a package no larger than the tip of a finger.

Coates led Gray out of the van door. The night was still, the Montana night sky vast and painted. Six law-enforcement personnel waited at the back of the vehicle, and others were concealed 100 yards behind the house. The detective pulled his revolver from under his coat. 'We're going in.'

Gray flipped the safety off his M-40A1 and followed the detective along the road. An FBI agent followed, carrying a set of picks on a steel ring. He clasped the picks together so they would not jingle.

The three men neared the house. A slash of light was visible under venetian blinds at the kitchen window, the light seen on the monitor. At the picket fence Gray ran his free hand up and down the gate and over the latch. There were no booby traps.

They moved along a concrete walkway between beds of orange and red marigolds and stepped onto the porch. The FBI agent knelt at the door and worked his picks. Ten seconds later, Gray slowly nudged the door open three inches, then reached behind it to check the inside knob. He pushed the door a fraction and reached inside further, checking for string triggers.

When the door was open fully, Gray led Coates inside. Moving slowly to avoid sound, each step was deliberated before taken. Gray's eyes surveyed the walls and the rugs and the furniture. The room was dark except for light from the kitchen.

Coates tapped Gray on the shoulder, then put his lips at Gray's ear. The detective whispered, 'The earplug just said he's still lying on the bed. Hasn't moved.'

Gray's hand ran over the riser and the first step to the upper floor. As he climbed, he paused on each step, listening and feeling. He led Coates into the upstairs hallway.

When they reached the closed bedroom door, the detective tapped his earplug and gave the thumbs up. The tech had just reported Trusov was still asleep.

As slowly as he could, Gray turned the knob. His pistol was at his ear. His teeth were bared.

He inched the door open and slid his hand up and down the inside as far as he could reach in up to his elbow. No traps. He nodded at the detective.

Coates clicked on the flashlight and rushed the door. He swept into the room yelling, 'Hands up, you're under arrest!'

Gray followed, his rifle pointing at the bed. He almost slipped on the damp floor.

The detective aimed the flashlight. 'Damn.' He pointed the beam up and down the body. 'It's that hippie.'

Andy Ellison lay on the bed, his throat slit open from ear to ear.

OWEN GRAY SAT under the antlers in the dining room. The Marine Corps sniper rifle was on the table. Coates sat across from Gray and lifted the bottle of beer he had been nursing. A tray of cold cuts and a dish of apples were also on the table.

'The FBI has learned that his name was Andy Ellison,' the detective said. 'Why did the Russian go to all the trouble to pick him up in the helicopter, when all he was going to do was slit his throat?'

Gray replied, 'Maybe Trusov needed an audience for his cleverness, even some poor fellow he was going to murder.'

Coates nodded. 'Yeah, maybe.'

Behind Coates, Adrian Wade tapped at her computer keyboard. Lights in the room were low, but her hands and notes were illuminated by a nightstand light. The fire on the grate was crackling.

Coates looked across the table at his friend. 'Owen, are you holding up all right?'

Gray glanced over at Adrian, then back to the detective. 'No, I'm not.' He wiped his upper lip with a finger. 'My stomach feels like some farmer is turning it over with a mule and plough. Pete, my children have been orphans once and I'm afraid of leaving them orphans again. And I'm afraid for myself. I don't want a bullet to find me.'

Adrian flicked off her light and rose from her desk. She walked over, then lifted an apple from the basket. She must have been listening because she said, 'You don't need to be afraid yet, Owen.'

'The mad Russian isn't after you, so perhaps you aren't the best judge.' He smiled quickly to take offence from his words.

She said, 'Nikolai Trusov wants one thing in this life. Brick by brick, plank by plank, he is reconstructing the day you shot him.'

She took a bite of the apple and went on. 'Look at what he has done so far.' She brought up her other hand to count off with her fingers. 'First, he has chased you from the city into the wilderness. Idaho isn't Elephant Valley but it's still bush and forest. Second, he has forced you to return to sniping. Third, he has stolen your Vietnam rifle, and he is going to insist you use it.'

'What's he going to do with my old Winchester?' Gray asked.

'He is going to somehow present it to you. And that's what I mean when I say you don't need to be afraid yet. He won't begin the duel until you are using your Marine Corps sniper rifle. That's why he stole it from the museum. And we know that he is carrying a Mosin-Nagant sniper rifle, the one he used in Vietnam, or one identical to it. Trusov would import tropical birds and bamboo if he could. But he's going to settle for what he can get.'

'What if we don't follow his rules?' Coates asked.

'He'll continue to kill until Owen understands and agrees.'

When the telephone rang, the detective crossed the room to Adrian's desk. After a moment he dropped the handset. 'A sporting-goods store near Butte has been broken into. A smash-and-grab. Trusov left his prints again.'

'What'd he get?' Adrian asked.

'A .30-30 deer rifle and a .22 shotgun, ammunition, hunting knives, some climbing rope, baling wire and cold-weather clothing. What's he want with the rope and wire? And so many weapons?'

'Traps,' Gray answered. 'Protecting his routes with nasty surprises.'

The detective rubbed the back of his neck. 'Owen, tomorrow you'd better start teaching me the lie of the land so I can help you when the time comes.' He headed towards Gray's childhood bedroom. 'I've got the bottom bunk.' He disappeared through the door.

When Gray started to rise from his chair, Adrian's hand on his shoulder stopped him. She asked, 'Do you want to talk?'

'I'm out of talk.' Gray's voice was so soft it mixed with the sounds of the fire. 'Nikolai Trusov is reducing me to a rifle. Rifles don't have much to say.'

Her hand was still on his shoulder. 'We could talk about your plans after this is all over.'

He looked at her a long moment. Then he gently shook his head. 'For days I haven't been able to think of any future beyond Trusov.'

'You have a future, Owen. I'm interested in it.'

He stepped to the bedroom door, then glanced back. Searching for something to say, he found only 'I'm interested in your future, too.' He looked at her another moment, then continued into the bedroom.

CHAPTER NINE

The Civilian Conservation Corps built the fire tower in the late 1930s, and it had been repaired and upgraded over the years until the mid-1980s when it was abandoned, a victim of Forest Service cutbacks and satellite technology. The tower was on Fellows Mountain, a granite peak that offered a thirty-mile view of crests and cliffs and ridges in all directions. From the tower's height, man's feeble inroads into the wilderness—a few ranches, the town of Hobart, the occasional hunter's shack—were entirely hidden.

The tower was five miles east of Owen Gray's cabin. It straddled a sharp ridge, two of its support posts on the south slope and two on the north. Valleys fell away in both directions, steep walls of fractured granite that plunged to avalanche gullies below. Beyond the valleys the rim of Shepherd's Bowl was visible, the basin out of sight.

Gray and Coates parked the Jeep fifty yards from the tower and followed a trail to the south side of the ridge. The sun was a flat plate high overhead. The air was light and scentless.

'So you know where Trusov is?' Gray asked between deep breaths.

'You think I've been picking my nose all this time?'

'It means he crossed some hard country on foot.'

The detective said, 'The man's a machine. We learned a long time ago he could jog forty miles with a full pack over rough country. And he's done just that. But he's still twenty miles away. He hasn't made it over the Galena Pass yet. We're sure of that.'

The trail narrowed and curved round a boulder formation near the precipice. They carefully continued up the ridge. Gray was carrying the Marine Corps sniper rifle on a sling. In his hand was a rolled-up map.

The tower loomed above them. A shaky ladder attached to one post was connected to a closed trap door. Wooden planks framed all four sides, above which were picture windows. The roof was pitched sharply to allow snow to slide off.

Gray tested a rung with his weight, then began to climb. He pushed open the trap door and it fell back with a loud slap. He pulled himself up through the hole. Coates climbed after him.

The tower contained one room. Furniture and equipment had been removed long ago. Planks laid over sawhorses had served as a table and were still in the tower. Gray spread out the map. 'We are here.' He drew a finger across the map. 'This is north.'

'I know north,' Coates said testily.

'Your people shouldn't come anywhere inside this area.' Gray's finger traced a large circle round his house.

'I'm going to catch that bastard before he gets anywhere near your place. Owen, I've got three hundred people in the field.'

Gray might not have heard him. 'Once Trusov is loose inside this area, keep your people away. It'll be too dangerous to follow the Russian into the forest.'

'Three hundred skilled law-enforcement personnel—'

'They'll be ducks in a shooting gallery, Pete. Entirely outgunned and outwitted. Trusov will kill as many of them as he wants to. A dozen, two dozen.' Gray's voice rose a fraction. 'I'm telling you, keep your people away from him and me once this has begun.'

Coates stared at him.

'I'll have too much else to think about. I won't be able to keep them alive.' Gray pointed back to the map. 'Anybody in this circle is going to be a target. For Trusov and for me. I won't have the luxury of analysing targets. I'm going to fire at any human I see.'

Coates finally nodded. 'OK, nobody inside the circle.'

FINE OPTICS can make even clear air seem to ripple and bubble, giving substance to nothing. Those optics seem to enhance colour, and the small circle of pallid blue sky inside the metal band was sparkling blue. Inside the little disc of sky was a pointed post, a needle-sized metal twig sharpened at the top. The sky floated towards the top of the circle as the scope slowly lowered.

Rising from the bottom of the blue ring of sky was the tower roof. Nikolai Trusov lowered the rifle further. The Russian could make out slight warps in the glass of the window as wind brushed the tower. With steady motion, the barrel and scope glided lower. Owen Gray's head rose in the circle. Black hair, pale skin, a tall man. White Star.

Then the scene in the eyepiece lens drifted smoothly to the left. The shorter form slid into view. Barrel-chested, sandy hair. The aiming post came to rest on his nose, just below a pair of spectacles. Then it sidled down to the man's right arm. Eight hundred yards south and 100 yards below the tower, Trusov brought his trigger finger back. Slowly and slowly and slowly.

The Mosin-Nagant bucked back against his shoulder. Trusov instantly lowered the rifle to the boulder he was hiding behind and brought up his binoculars.

A black slash visible in the binocular lenses was Trusov's bullet, flickering through the air, then disappearing with distance. The tower window shimmered as a hole was punched into it.

BLOOD AND BONE and shards of glass filled the air and lashed against the tower's far window like wind-blown rain. Pete Coates spun and then collapsed.

Snipers are taught that if they are surrounded, the time to break out is now, before the enemy can regroup. All glass and plywood, the fire tower offered no protection from bullets. Coates groaned, blood spreading on the floor under his shattered elbow. Gray pushed him towards the hatch and without a word shoved him through. Coates landed heavily on the ground.

The rifle in one hand, Gray followed the detective through the hatch to the rocks below.

He landed hard on the incline and scrambled across the loose rocks to push Coates behind a boulder. The detective moaned. His jacket was soaking up the blood.

'Stay down,' Gray ordered.

A bullet slammed into the rock supporting Gray's right foot. His leg collapsed, and he slid down the incline, out into the blinding sun. He tightly gripped the rifle.

Hoping to find a foothold, he clawed at the rocks to slow himself. His slide stopped when his foot found a brace against a stone.

Blasting up a cloud of granite grit, another bullet kicked away that stone. Gray fell again. The side of the mountain gained in pitch and he slipped more quickly, his body bouncing painfully over the rocks. He tried to jam the stock of his gun against a boulder to stop himself, but the boulder ripped the weapon out of his hand.

Feet downwards he skidded, crashing down the incline. His fingers caught a branch. He stopped, perched precariously against the side of the mountain. Blood flowed from his legs where trousers and skin had been abraded.

A bullet coursed into his left arm, digging a half-inch trench in his triceps. His arm jerked and he lost his grip. Yet another bullet struck the heel of his boot, again sending him helplessly down the steep hill. His momentum flipped him to one side and he began to roll lengthways. Blue sky and grey stone spun over and over. His head banged into a rock, then another.

He came to rest at the bottom of the gully. He crawled behind a boulder that hid him from the south slope. His rifle was somewhere up the slope.

Gray heard more shots and the shattering of glass. Trusov was disabling the Jeep.

Five minutes passed before his vision lost the fuzziness at the edges and Gray could think clearly again. The Russian hadn't been out to kill him or he would have. All the pieces of that day in Vietnam weren't yet in place. Gray was safe, the Russian probably gone.

Limping and bleeding and aching, he crawled back up the slope.

THE COMPUTER MONITOR displayed the photographs one after another, all with the clarity of thirty-five-millimetre slides. Owen Gray at twelve months, a halo of dark hair, podgy cheeks, an open smile revealing four baby teeth. Owen Gray, eighth grade, shy grin. Owen Gray wearing a narrow black tie, his hair over his forehead in the new fashion imported from Liverpool, his high-school yearbook photo. Owen Gray's Marine Corps boot-camp ID photo, shaved head, stunned look. Another Marine photo of Gray, wearing a white dress cap and a single chevron.

Next was a snapshot of Gray from law school, then a photo from his first year as a prosecutor. Gray was ageing as the photos rolled by, a few wrinkles at the corners of his eyes, a slight rise in his hairline above the temples. The last, from six months ago, was taken at a federal prosecutors' dinner, showing Gray in black suit and a floral tie, wearing a confident but tired grin.

Adrian stared at the screen. Distant laughter from two troopers on the other side of the big larch tree did not distract her. She went through the photos of Gray, watching him grow and age.

She leaned back in her chair. Her work in the mountains was finished, her skills no longer needed. She should have been packing her things, readying for the journey back east, but her clothes remained on pegs in the bedroom. She idly tapped her fingers on the base of the keyboard. Outside, a song sparrow let loose three piping cheerful notes, followed by a rapid trill. Adrian lifted her wallet from the desk and pulled out her driver's licence. She held it up alongside the monitor. She stared at the small coloured photograph of herself, then her eyes shifted to the image on the screen.

She smiled knowingly and said to the screen, 'I know your future better than you do.'

The cabin's front door burst inwards with a splintering of wood. Adrian flinched, then spun out of her chair. The door wagged left and right, its top hinge dangling loose, and sunlight poured through the room. Her hand went inside her jacket.

Holding a deer rifle, Nikolai Trusov stepped to the door. He filled the frame and was backlit with rays of sun streaming off the black silhouette of his body like tiny searchlights.

He held out the rifle. His voice was guttural and entirely foreign. 'Give Gray his rifle. And this message—'

The Russian must have been astonished at her speed. Her Smith and Wesson Model 459 was small, yet it was a semiautomatic with a fourteen-shot staggered clip. It whipped out from under her jacket, its nickel finish gleaming. She fired six times, as rapidly as she could pull the trigger. The flat crack of the shots rattled the cabin's walls. Dust drifted down from the chandelier.

She lifted her finger from the trigger, the pistol still up and ready. Where she had expected to see a body there was nothing, just sunlight filling the doorway. The air smelt of burnt powder. She glanced through the door. One state patrolman was lying in front of a car, a slash of blood under an ear. The other officer was in the front seat, slumped forwards. Trusov had killed them both.

Adrian kicked the door shut and stepped quickly to her desk. She held the gun up with both hands, her back against the log wall. The room had too many windows. She would be safer in the back bedroom. She bent low to pass under the window that looked out onto the destroyed woodshed.

Trusov's arm lashed through the window, glass chips and shards followed the swinging arm into the cabin. The hand seized Adrian round the neck, yanked her upright, then through the shattered

window, dragging her over slivers of glass. A shard bit into her hand and she dropped her pistol.

Glass hung from her jacket and hair. A necklace of blood appeared on her neck. Trusov held her from behind, his hands like steel.

The Russian growled, 'Give him the rifle and this message—'

Adrian Wade had trained for years for this moment. She fiercely jerked her head back, cracking her skull into his nose. He grunted with pain. She abruptly shifted her weight and launched her elbow back at his groin. She caught him with full force.

He should have buckled over. He should have collapsed to the ground, vomiting and gasping. Instead he lifted her fully off the ground and caught a fistful of her black hair.

'Why do you Americans never listen?' he asked levelly, his voice a study in reason and courtesy. 'You are to give Gray the rifle and this message. I will be within eight kilometres of this house. He is to come into the field alone, with his rifle. Do you understand?'

He tugged her head back and forth, forcing her to nod. He tossed her against the wall of the cabin, a casual offhand motion. Her head hit the wall and she lay motionless as he retrieved the rifle from the porch. It was Gray's Winchester 70 with the mounted Unertl scope. He treated it more gently than he had Adrian, propping it up next to her, carefully so as to maintain the scope's alignment.

'I will be waiting for him.' The Russian disappeared round a corner of the cabin.

Only after several moments could Adrian push herself to a sitting position. She blinked. She was too dizzy to move, so there she waited for Owen Gray.

STEALTH OR SPEED? The dilemma had been an endless source of debate among Gray and his sniper friends in Vietnam. Hurry but risk detection? Or proceed carefully and risk losing the target? No satisfactory answer was ever produced, but now Gray settled on speed. He moved up Black Bear Creek Valley at a brisk walk, the rifle in both hands.

He was dead-tracking, moving faster than the man who had left the sign. Gray glanced at fresh footprints near the stream. Trusov's register indicated he had walked rather than trotted up the valley. He was doing nothing to hide his direction. Gray knew that at some point ahead, when Trusov decided it was time, the footprints would vanish.

Gray moved along the creek with unearthly quiet. His old skills had been slowly coming back to him since that day on the courthouse steps, but now he was enveloped in the armour of his Vietnam mind. The wound in his arm from Trusov's bullet should have been flooding him with pain, but Gray felt nothing. He hardly felt the scrapes and bruises from his mad slide. And he should have been frightened, but he was dead to fear. He was a coyote, with no ability to ruminate, considering nothing but the ground that carried him and the flora that hid him.

As Gray moved up the valley, Black Bear Creek was to his right. He looked at nothing and at everything, using a technique known as splatter vision, where he let his vision spread out. Rather than focus on any one object, his eyes gathered in all in front of them. His face and hands were covered with brown and olive and green greasepaint. He wore a field uniform that he had brought to the Sawtooths. Rawhide was tied round his ankles to keep the trousers from flapping. On his feet were his father's buckskin moccasins that were almost as quiet as bare feet. He wore a Marine Corps utility cap. Gray had put several short syringa branches into the webbing, and the leaves bobbed against his head as he walked. He had left his belt and watch behind because of the danger of reflection. A length of rope secured his trousers.

A Marine sniper in Vietnam travelled light, but even so his pack for a three-day mission contained over forty items, including tactical maps, plastic explosives, wire-cutters, extra bootlaces, blood coagulant, a strobe light, foot powder, a transistor radio, a Turkish battle-axe and more. Gray carried far less. In addition to the rifle and what snipers called the basic load—eighty-four rounds in a pouch—Gray had only a pair of binoculars, a Swiss army knife with screwdrivers for adjustments to the scope, a canteen, a pen and matchbooks. In his pocket was a small spiral notebook in which he hoped to record his kill, just as he had done for ninety-six other kills. Gray had no doubt Trusov also carried pen and paper. And a red shell.

The stream narrowed as it neared its source, and to avoid impenetrable brush thickets Gray jumped across the creek and back several times. As he neared Shepherd's Bowl, he began scanning, moving his eyes in abrupt and irregular movements, stopping for only an instant on any one thing. Scanning allows the viewer to catalogue and review an immense amount of information. Scanning seeks disturbances.

He had suspected Trusov would head to the bowl. It was four o'clock in the afternoon. A sniper's instinct is to get the sun behind him, and the bowl was west of the cabin. Trusov would want Gray staring into the setting sun not just because it would impair Gray at the instant of the shot but also because gazing towards the sun is highly fatiguing, and with weariness comes mistakes.

Shepherd's Bowl offered something else—a closed horizon, a self-contained duelling field. The bowl would fit Trusov's sense of order and would also limit the area he had to scout.

Because Trusov had put the Jeep out of action, Gray had used his belt as a tourniquet round Coates's shattered arm, and had left him at the fire tower to seek help. It had taken him two hours to hobble back to the cabin, where he had found Adrian. Another hour had passed while he waited for an ambulance to arrive for her. A helicopter was now on its way to the tower for Coates. So the Russian would have been in the bowl several hours before Gray could get there. In that time, Trusov would have learned all there was to know about the area.

The sky was narrowed by the valley walls and tall trees, but it was opening up ahead. Another 500 yards would put Gray at the mouth of Shepherd's Bowl. His options now were to travel faster or slower, but not at a walking pace. Nothing in the wilderness moves at a human's pace, and anything travelling at four miles an hour is always a target. He slowed, coasting over the ground. His feet melted to the earth's contours. Gray might have been invisible.

The memory of Adrian tried to push itself into his mind, and only with effort could he dismiss it, his eyes scanning. He had left her in the care of a physician and ambulance attendants. She had worn on her face most of the blood she had spilled, and looked worse than she was. Still, she would require stitches. The doctor said she might have a slight concussion, but she had been asking Gray questions, as always. Gray had gently chided her. He was relieved when she laughed. He had peeled her hand from his, then taken up the rifle to begin his journey to the bowl.

In shadows cast by the trees in front of him he ducked left and right, left and right. Nikolai Trusov was within two miles of him, Gray was certain. Through the trees he could see the sun lowering in the sky, sending out spokes of gold light.

Not far into the bowl was the small pool where the stream originated. As Gray moved forwards, the valley in front of him filled his vision. He stood behind a lodgepole pine and pulled his binoculars from the pack.

Shepherd's Bowl was a study in shifting greens and browns. Owen Gray moved the binoculars right to left, looking for agitation in the underbrush, looking for a too-straight line, the slightest of reflections, colour that was too lively, never focusing on one thing for too long. All he found was more green and brown.

Trusov's footprints went due west, entering the swath of trees along the creek. Following this long dell was the only way to enter the bowl unseen by anyone on the slopes, and this was the route of Trusov's prints. But to follow the Russian's path would most likely mean walking into a trap.

Gray moved west through the trees into the bowl, then took a dogleg route, south a few paces, then west again. He walked with exceeding care, following Trusov's route by a parallel course 100 feet from Trusov's trail. He watched the ground, avoiding dried foliage that might crackle underfoot. The Winchester was across his chest.

He approached a 100-yard expanse spotted by only a few trees. The spring and pool were to his left. Gray lowered himself and shimmied along the ground round a pine tree to two rotted logs, one fallen over the other. He crawled into the V formed by the logs then checked over his shoulder. From behind, he was protected by an upright pine. His hide was almost fully enclosed. He brought his backpack round and reached for his binoculars. Moving half an inch at a time, he rose to peer over the log.

Sound and pain rushed over him at the same instant. An explosion from above lanced his back from his shoulder to the base of his spine. Gray toppled sideways onto dry grass. He gasped with pain, then scrambled closer to a log, trying to tuck himself under it. He didn't know where the danger lay. He squeezed his eyes against the racking pain, then opened them to stare skywards.

Round the tree above him, about fifteen feet off the ground, was a circle of baling wire. Something had been attached to the tree. Gray's hand found fragments of pottery, portions of a plate, a littering of nails.

Gray knew then that the Russian had placed an impact mine above a likely hide. Trusov had somehow glimpsed Gray but had been unable to get him in his scope. Trusov had set off the explosive with a bullet fired from a long distance, causing the nails to blast down. The mine had not been meant to kill him. Trusov would want the purity of a bullet for that task.

Gray slowly brought a hand round to his back. Teeth clamped, he pulled out a protruding nail, then another. He ran his hand along his shirt and found more nails, gingerly pulling them out. His back was damp but there was less blood on the ground than he had feared. Gray decided he wasn't badly hurt. Several nails were still embedded where he couldn't reach, but this wasn't going to kill him.

He checked his canteen. No leaks. His binoculars were scratched, but the lenses were intact. His pack had holes in it but would carry his equipment. The Russian's mine had failed.

Gray concentrated on the best way to make it back to the thicket of trees near the bowl's mouth. He could not cross the glade, not with Trusov out in front of him—at least, that's where Gray thought the bullet had come from. He returned east the way he had come, this time more slowly, his head moving left and right.

He wanted to circle around Trusov, who he presumed was

somewhere in the middle of the bowl in dense trees. Because the north slope was mostly barren, Gray would have to do his circling on the south slope. But between him and that incline were tracts of grass, open killing ground, almost impossible to cross without being observed. The grass began under the trees where Gray now stood, and ran towards the south slope.

Gray slid his backpack round so that it hung on his left side. He hugged the rifle to his stomach with his left hand, then lowered himself to the ground. His back and buttocks yelped with pain.

Because lying on his belly would flatten more grass, Gray stretched out on his right side. Leaving the cover of the trees, he began a side crawl into the thick grass. He used his right hand to part the grass in front of him, pushing the stems to either side, careful not to snap the stalks. He moved slowly, like a worm, every part of his body in contact with the earth to push himself along. His motion resembled a swimmer's side stroke but more constricted. He travelled only a few inches a minute through the dry grass. With his toes he righted stems that did not spring back on their own. This would prevent shining, which occurs when the sun bounces off vegetation that has been pushed down, leaving a bright trail.

The crest of the grass was a foot above Gray's head. His nose was in the dirt. The raw scent of the earth, the hot puffs of an idle wind, the insistent drone of yellow jackets and bees, and the taste of his own sweat as it slid from his cheek were all magnified by his tiny horizon. Gray inched along.

There had been no choice between the M-40A1 sniper rifle and his old Winchester 70 that had been delivered by Nikolai Trusov. After the ambulance had carried Adrian away, Gray approached both weapons, both leaning upright against the log wall. The Winchester had seemed to leap into his hands like a lost dog. Even after all these years it felt like an extension of Gray's body. And now, rather than being inert wood and metal, the rifle helped Gray worm his way through the grass, bending and pushing. He pressed himself against the ground as he moved. Dirt and twigs kept finding their way into his mouth, and he quietly spat the bits out.

Each small and silent motion was an art. When the rhythm of the crawl came back to him after a while, he found he could pick up his pace a few feet an hour. The slightest mischance might send a bullet his way, so Gray constantly reined himself in. He desperately wanted the shelter of the trees. His clothes were sodden with perspiration. He was still leaking blood. Stray pieces of grass clung to him, and he began to resemble a scarecrow.

Two hours passed, all the while Gray knowing Trusov was in a hide somewhere, searching with his binoculars, occasionally raising his rifle to use the more powerful mounted scope.

Then the sound of a shot echoed round the bowl several times. Gray did not hear the bullet passing overhead or through the grass. He allowed himself the slightest smile of satisfaction. Trusov must be nervous. He had fired at a shadow or a bird. When a nail in his back brushed a nerve the smile vanished.

Gray dug his leading hand into the ground and pulled forwards, parting the grass. He could smell pine sap and knew he was drawing close to the trees. Maybe another sixty or seventy yards.

Then he smelt a scent entirely foreign in the bowl. For an instant all his nose could detect was some sort of chemical. And then he knew it was gasoline. Next he smelt fire.

Gray could not risk raising his head, but he could hear the fire ahead of him, spreading left and right, probably along a line of gasoline Trusov had poured. The Russian had no doubt left behind a partly filled can and had ignited the gas by firing into the can. Trusov must have suspected Gray was in the grass.

The fire quickly consumed the dry grass. Flames ate into the field, working east towards Gray. Smoke reached him, then tossing embers. Grasshoppers flicked by, fleeing the flames, then mice.

A wind-tossed bit of burning grass landed on Gray's back, but to swat at it would ruffle the grass that hid him. Trusov was surely scanning the field, hoping to put a bullet into him as he tried to escape. The fire was meant not to kill Gray but to flush him out. Only a bullet would do for the killing.

The heat reached for Gray, the first blushes rolling over him, then subsiding with a quirk of the wind. Then, more insistently, a pulse of heat that made him suck air. He looked forwards through the grass. Orange licks were sending waves of black smoke skywards. Not enough smoke was over him to cover him for a sprint. Gray had no choice but to lie there, his eyes two inches above the dirt. Bits of flaming grass rose and swirled, snapped and hissed. A new gust of wind sped the flames. The fire roared as it closed in.

CHAPTER TEN

Bite down. No trembling, no thinking. If he rose to flee he would die. If he made a sound he would die. He could feel the sweep of Trusov's binoculars, feel the Russian's eyes searching and searching.

To protect his weapon and ammunition from the heat, he slowly brought his backpack and rifle under his belly. Walls of heat rushed at him. He crammed his hands under him, squeezing the Winchester's stock, knowing he would need a grip on something.

Embers landed on Gray's shirt and trousers, burning through the cloth. The fire sounded like an animal tramping through the brush, closer and closer, cracking and bursting, homing in. Curls of flame came for his cap. The odour of burning fabric filled him.

He clamped his eyes shut and ground his mouth into the soil, filling it with dirt to dampen any scream. He tried to dig his face deeper, deeper into the cool soil. His head felt as if razors were being dragged across it, temple to temple.

The fire stitched its way down his neck to his shoulders. His shirt caught with hissing flame, and the fire line advanced past his shoulders and along his back, baking his skin. But the quickened wind pushed the flames. The fire ate but did not tarry. A cloud of smoke was above him now and he gasped for breath, and in the smoke was his salvation. He had cover.

Gray slowly drew his arms to his body with his elbows on the ground and pulled his right leg forwards. He rose by straightening his arms as if doing a pushup. Keeping his grip on the rifle, he dug his left foot into the soil and leapt up, willing his knees to work. He ran low to the ground.

The blaze leapt and twisted around him. He bolted along the fire line, the only place the smoke was thick enough to hide him, keeping a shroud of black around him. His burns were a straitjacket of pain, and every step squeezed him with agony.

Then the south slope and its trees appeared before him, blurred by the smoke. A trouser leg trailed fire, and Gray could feel flames chewing into his thigh. He sprinted into the woods, passing deeper into cover before he dropped the pack and collapsed at the base of a pine tree. He rolled on the ground, trying to extinguish the flames.

His cap was gone, and so was most of his hair. His mouth gaped open with the pain. Behind him, the fire continued across the field, smoke drifting slowly towards the bowl's mouth.

Gray brought his feet up and bent over into a foetal curl. His skull was a universe of suffering, his thoughts were dim pulses. He was safe in the trees, he knew, but he would have to move out. He had to push aside the agony from his head and shoulders and leg. He closed his eyes. Isolate the pain. Push it away. Survive.

He opened his eyes to survey himself. His left arm was burnt from the shoulder to the elbow. His belly had protected the skin below the elbow. The back of his shirt was gone, and Gray knew the skin there was scorched. Same with his shoulders. His left trouser leg had burned away, and the skin below was blistered and red.

He brought his hands to his face. He curled his trigger finger. Gray's hands were fine, and now he could focus his eyes. And he could run. He was still alive and could still work his rifle.

He whispered, 'I'm not done yet, you bastard.'

But his camouflage had gone. In the green and brown and grey bowl Gray's raw skin would stand out like a flare. He would have to improvise. Gray opened his pack to retrieve his canteen. He twisted off the cap and allowed himself two swallows. Then he crawled several feet to a flat patch of ground and poured the water from his canteen onto the soil, shaking the last drops from it. With his hands he worked the ground, kneading it, making a bed of mud.

Gray sat down and leaned back onto the mud. The pain was as if a knife was sinking into his back again and again. But he squirmed on the ground, rubbing his back into the mud and leaves. And when he thought he might pass out he forced himself to go on, to continue to writhe until the mud had caked his back.

He sat up shivering with agony, but before his resolve melted he scooped up handfuls of the remaining mud and dabbed it onto his leg and shoulders, then onto his face and skull. His teeth were clamped so tightly together his jaw ached. He bucked with agony and his hands faltered. But he pressed scoop after scoop of the mud mix on.

He gasped and breathed against the suffering, and again focused. He looked at his leg and hands and shoulders. He resembled a bog monster. After a moment he could bend down and put the empty canteen into the backpack. With the Winchester in one hand and the pack in the other, Gray walked unsteadily up into the deeper cover of the forested south slope.

NIKOLAI TRUSOV lowered his binoculars and rubbed his eyes. He had been scanning the grass from his hide behind a fallen and decayed pine trunk. His Mosin-Nagant rifle was at an elbow and his pack was near his feet.

He brought up the binoculars again, staring at the wild grass. He knew his mine had forced Gray to enter the bowl in the grass. But the field was broad, and he had not seen any movement. Trusov nodded, an acknowledgment of the skill required to move unnoticed through grass. But Trusov had known of Owen Gray's skills for decades.

The blaze was reaching the east end of the field. Yet Gray hadn't bolted. Where was he?

Trusov needed a closer look. He crawled from the hide, rose to a crouch and sped fifty yards down the gradual incline towards the blackened field. A perfect hide was ahead, a log topped with brush. He moved towards it.

Then he stalled. An animal was ahead of him. The creature's blunt nose and button eyes were followed by a mass of tan and black quills. The porcupine waddled towards Trusove, unconcerned, safe beneath its mantle of needle-sharp barbs. It stopped below the brush growing on top of the log.

Trusov had probably never seen anything like it. But he had no time to wonder about the strange animal. It was in his way. He brought out the knife from his belt and slashed down into the animal. The porcupine shivered its quills and caterwauled, then trotted away, leaving a trail of blood. Trusov wiped the blade on his leg and crawled into cover. He brought up his binoculars, but before he could place them against his eyes his nose came up. He had a scent. It was faint, there and gone. He sniffed the air. And the scent was there again.

He allowed himself a small smile, a terrible grin where the corners of his mouth turned down. He smelt burnt flesh. Gray was either dead or injured. Still wearing the rictus smile of a cadaver, Trusov began scanning the blackened grass.

GRAY HAD TO KEEP MOVING. He began a low crawl, keeping his body flat against the ground. His burns made it feel as if the ground was clawing at him with sharp talons.

He flinched and dug his head into the ground at the sound of a projectile soaring in at him and passing a few inches from his ear. He cursed himself. It was a hummingbird, curious and fearless, then bored and gone as quickly as it came.

He came to a halt behind a pine, his back to the tree. He swung his gaze along the trees uphill on the south slope. Nothing visible amid all the brush. Keeping his head close to the ground, pressing his cheek against the coarse bark of the tree, he brought an eye around.

His view was of much of the bowl, from the mouth off to his right to the high banks of the north wall. He brought out the binoculars. Nothing. The wind was slowly clearing the bowl of smoke.

Huckleberry and heath and sorrel offered low cover. Gray crawled from tree to tree, travelling 200 yards west, further into the bowl. Its snout forward, the Winchester urged him on.

Critical intelligence now poured into Gray. The sun's position, humidity, wind, ground cover, all were ever changing. Every few feet he had to assess entirely new conditions. He looked for unusual movement, he searched for untoward reflections, he listened for peculiar sounds. He moved quickly and quietly, but his skin howled with every motion. He was thirsty and knew that thirst, magnified by pain, would alter his judgment. He would need water soon.

He crawled forwards between a pine and a tree stump bracketed by a spiky gorse bush. He reached into his pack for the binoculars.

When he pressed the glasses against his face, his hand jumped. He swatted at his face, knocking a wasp away. He had been stung near

116

the corner of his left eye. Had his back and shoulders and leg not been in agony, Gray would have laughed. Fate had decided Gray just wasn't suffering enough, so it added a wasp sting to the mix. He touched his eye. The skin was already swelling. It should have smarted, but the pain was lost in the suffering of the burns. He looked skywards to find a nest the size of a basketball in the tree eight feet above the ground. A dozen wasps angrily patrolled near the nest's mouth. A wasp flitted down towards him. Gray resisted the instinct to swat at it because a sudden movement would alert Trusov if the Russian was surveying the area. The wasp moved away.

Gray started west through the trees. He slowed, then slowed again. He was not gathering information like he should. Pain was diverting his attention, numbing his senses. In this arena the slightest disadvantage might be lethal.

A rotting tree stump offered a spot where Gray could try to recuperate. When he neared the stump he saw a porcupine to one side, rocking back and forth. Not until he reached the stump did he notice the trail of blood the porcupine had been leaving. Gray quickly surveyed the view of the north slope, saw nothing, then looked more closely at the porcupine.

Blood was bubbling up from wounds in the creature's shoulder and back, wounds that could only have been made by a man with a knife. Trusov.

The blood trail showed the animal had come from the west. Trusov was to the west.

The animal was suffering and was clearly going to die. Gray whispered, 'Sorry, friend,' then brought his rifle barrel down sharply across the animal's only vulnerable spot, its snout. It collapsed instantly, a pile of sharp points.

Just as he was about to crawl on, a glint of light held him to the rotting tree trunk. The metallic shimmer was below him, a quarter of a mile away. The view was through a veil of vegetation, and Gray could make out no forms other than trees and undergrowth. He lifted his binoculars.

TWO HOURS LATER, in the failing light of evening, Gray's binoculars were still at his eyes. He had lowered them and brought them up again and again as he stared at the dot of light. All he knew was that the light was out of place in the wilderness. It came from a backpack buckle, a jacket button, a telescopic lens or a piece of litter.

Two hours' studying, all the while growing weaker and more thirsty. Although his stomach and chest and face had been spared by the fire, every inch of his skin seemed to emit pulses of pain. Gray slipped lower and lower against the stump. If only he could send a bullet at the light and end the waiting, but a wasted shot would alert the Russian to Gray's location.

The sinking sun was turning the little flash purple. The pinpoint of light had remained as motionless as a stone for two hours. No human could do that. He decided the light must be the reflection off a piece of litter, probably a chewing-gum wrapper. It was a fuzzy decision, and a terrible disappointment. He was now desperately thirsty and exhausted beyond his ability to make clear judgments.

He had to find the strength to move. Soon darkness would cloak him. But that maddening glimmer was worth one more look. With an effort he brought up the binoculars again.

AT THAT MOMENT Trusov caught Gray's scent again, the odour of burnt flesh. The wind had been shifting for much of the afternoon, but for several hours it had been steady from the south. Now the smell had found Trusov again. Gray had slowly moved west.

Trusov would move towards the still-pink sky in the west. Because daylight was fading quickly, he would not be able to watch his feet and would have to walk more slowly and softly.

When Trusov lifted his rifle the jaws of the earth seemed to open up, seize him and take him down its black throat. Trusov fell into the void, vaulting down into the black pool, and then he slammed against the bottom of the pit.

He found himself on his knees. Then a red sheet fell across his eyes, a veil of blood that blocked his view of the ground. He grabbed at the wound, a crease across his forehead a quarter of an inch deep.

Gray had shot him.

Blood spilled through his fingers, a torrent that filled his vision. He scrambled blindly downhill until he felt the resistance of a bush. He let himself fall to the ground and burrowed under the bush.

Again he felt his head. The slash was to the bone. Trusov's mouth contorted in rage and pain. Owen Gray's Vietnam shot had marred Trusov, and now the second had crossed the scar of the first. The Russian's head was marked by an X.

He pulled off his pack and pressed it against his forehead. Moments passed. The blood ebbed. He returned the sopping pack to his back. Shaking, he lifted his rifle and moved slowly west.

THE BOWL WAS LOST IN DARKNESS. Owen Gray had tried to find his target again, but Trusov had moved quickly. Sheer luck had given Gray a shot, and he had missed. The shard of light he had stared at had indeed been a piece of litter. Just as Gray had given up on that target, the Russian happened to walk into his field of vision. Gray had lifted his rifle and fired, quickly. Too quickly. The rifle had bucked up, and by the time he found the spot again in the scope, Trusov was gone.

Darkness providing cover, Gray walked downhill. The burns were rapidly sapping his strength. His thirst was an all-consuming craving and he would soon begin acting irrationally and dangerously.

He moved round boulders and trees, the rifle now a burden. He staggered but caught himself against a lodgepole pine. When his moccasin kicked a rock downhill he paused, listening, but could hear only the scrape of his throat as it tried to swallow. He stumbled on, turning east towards the mouth of the bowl.

The shallow pool was there, the small spring that was Black Bear Creek's headwater. Gray made his way towards it, brushing the undergrowth too loudly, letting his footfalls sound, all careless. He moved through a patch of field mustard and balsam root, and then in a giddy rush of sensation he could smell the water, almost feel the cool liquid on his lips and tongue. He heard the ripple of a thin stream rolling over rocks. Predators from frogs to cougars know to lie in wait at a pool of water, and Trusov was nothing if not a predator. Forty yards from the pool, Gray lowered himself to the ground and tried to focus on the surrounding brush.

He waited, searching and listening, the water all the while enticing him to come forward.

He whispered, 'It's OK, Dad.'

He clamped his jaw. His father's voice had just asked about the south fence. Was it in good repair after the storm? A voice Gray had not heard in years had spoken, as clear as if his father had been sitting beside him. Gray shut his eyes for a moment. He had begun hallucinating. He was now fighting both the Russian and his own mind.

He waited thirty minutes. He could no longer be certain of his own conclusions, but he did not think anyone was near the pool. He gripped his rifle and crawled towards the inky black water.

He planted his hands on the edge of the pool and lowered his head to drink. The water was cool and promising. But when he rubbed his finger and thumb together, his skin felt soapy. His jaw opened involuntarily. Despair made him sag, and his head almost went into the water before he could fight it back. He dipped a finger in and brought several drops to his mouth. The water stung his tongue, and he spat it out.

He knew what Trusov had done. Lye and fat are combined to make soap. Trusov had dumped lye into the pool, making it poison, not meant to kill, but to weaken him.

Gray gripped his rifle and backed away. Dampness clouded his vision, and he paused to wipe at his eye. His father spoke again. Owen Gray ignored him this time. He did not need his father to tell him he was not going to make it out alive.

CHAPTER ELEVEN

Nikolai Trusov stalked all night, travelling anticlockwise, making no more than fifty yards an hour. Several times he blotted away blood from his forehead. The shock of the wound was gone. His strength had returned. He used the night to try to cross Gray's trail.

He succeeded. He came to a stump that had dense spiked bushes on both sides and was protected uphill by a tree. The Russian knelt to peer at the ground. Even in the black of night he could see that the needles and leaves had recently been ruffled. Trusov felt the ground and brought up a leaf stained with dried blood. The American had been here. A good place to begin to stalk again at first light. He leaned against the stump to wait.

DURING THOSE HOURS Gray was lying on his belly near the pool. He had gathered handfuls of damp moss and held it above his mouth and had squeezed out precious drops of water. Then he lay on the stream bank and waited for the night to pass. He gripped his rifle fiercely as if that might compensate for his slipping mind.

He might have slept. He could not be sure. First light found him on the moss, his eyes and his mouth open. He tried to rise, but he felt nailed to the ground. He crawled forwards, away from the dead pool.

He heard a rough scrape. At first he thought it was his father again, clearing his throat for some new pronouncement. He heard it again, carried in the soft wind. He thought it was real.

Dawn had begun streaking the high rim of the bowl in faint purple. Gray turned to the south slope to face the sound. He wrestled his gun to his shoulder and put his eye to the scope.

TRUSOV HAD COUGHED in his sleep, and the ragged sound had brought him out of it. In the still bowl, a cough was the equivalent of a foghorn blast. But his position was well protected. Any shot fired from the centre or the opposite side of the bowl would sail over the stump he was leaning against.

Trusov recoiled when the sound of a shot reached him. Gray had fired. Trusov looked left and right. What had the American fired at?

A full-throated roar suddenly came from above Trusov. He looked skywards, to the uphill pine tree. A wasps' nest had a ragged hole through it, and bits of the nest were floating to the ground. And a black ball of wasps was growing in the air.

The nest blew apart as the second bullet sailed through it. The sound of the shot followed. As wasps streamed out of their fractured home the black ball of insects in the air grew and grew. Then the wasps found their enemy, the alien on the ground below.

Within five seconds of the second shot, fifty wasps were on Trusov, and within fifteen seconds there were more. The Russian dared not move from that spot. The wasps crawled angrily over him, working their stingers repeatedly.

His face was bunched against the pain, but he could do nothing lest Gray's third bullet find him. So he lay there, and he lay there. Wasps crawled along his neck, over his face. After several moments the wasps began to calm and to lift away. Trusov had been stung hundreds of times. The inhuman effort not to move or to scream seemed to have stilled the Russian. A moment passed before he opened his eyes.

Or tried to. His face had begun to swell. His eyelids and nose puffed up. His hands inflated to resemble mittens.

FOUR HUNDRED YARDS down the slope and east, Owen Gray was exhausted, desperate. But he grinned.

He moved out, in the direction of the wasps' nest, carrying his rifle. Progress was slow, but he travelled towards Trusov, one tree at a time, keeping himself covered. He came to the shattered nest. The insects still patrolled, but they paid no attention to Gray.

He lowered himself to his knees and began stalking Trusov. Despite his wounds, and revived by his small success with the wasps, Gray believed he was missing nothing. Perhaps the Russian had been in too much pain to disguise his obvious trail. But after fifty yards it became less so, as if Trusov was slowly gaining control of himself.

Gray slithered forwards. He came to a short whitebark pine with a thick and irregular trunk. Gray climbed, lifting his head, ducking branches, twisting his body up between the boughs without jiggling them. He brought up the binoculars. Nothing ahead.

Just as he was about to return to the ground, the slightest of motions caught the corner of his eye. Gray trusted his peripheral vision. Its best use was at dusk when objects that couldn't be seen directly might be observed at the edge of the eye. In daylight, side vision would pick up an oddity, some angle that did not fit into the wilderness pattern. Gray slowly brought his head round.

A moment passed before he located it. A rifle barrel at 150 yards. Only eighteen inches of it appeared above a fallen log, but when the bush behind it wafted gently in the breeze, the barrel stayed fixed. Then the barrel moved on its own. He could not see the Russian's head. Moving as slowly as if in molasses, Gray lifted the Winchester.

He found the Russian's rifle barrel through the Unertl scope. Gray lowered his rifle a hair. In the scope now was a brown woollen cap. Only the top few inches, but enough.

Gray was acutely aware he might be pulling down on a dummy position, an artful trap that would cause the shooter to reveal his position. But Gray could not wait. He was at the end of his resources.

Deep breath. Let half out. Hold. Cross hair once. Cross hair twice, softly, ever so softly, squeeze.

The Winchester bellowed and leapt back into Gray's shoulder. He quickly brought the rifle back down, searching through the scope for the target.

Gray's left hand vanished in a spray of blood that filled the air in front of him. He cried out and yanked himself to the ground and rolled onto his belly to flatten himself. Only then did he hear the distant roar of a rifle shot. The echo raced round the bowl's walls, washing over Gray again and again.

He frantically grabbed the Winchester and rolled out from under the pine, turning over and over like a child down a hill. He left a trail of blood. But a second shot did not come. Gray bumped into a tree. Only then did he look at his arm.

Trusov's bullet had blown out a third of his left palm. Several bones lay bare. A spear of agony flew up Gray's arm and his head snapped into the ground, jolted by the pain.

The day seemed to fade. Tiny dots of neon colours blinked on and off in front of Gray's eyes. He was growing faint with the loss of blood. Holding his breath, he reached into his pack and brought out one of the matchbooks. He bit off a match, then dropped the matchbook to the ground. He scraped the match against the score several times before his trembling hand could press down hard enough. When it sputtered to life he held the flame to the matchbook. It flared. Gray pinched the matchbook at the staple and held the flame under his wounded hand.

The fire crackled and hissed, turning the ragged gash brown, then black. Gray's teeth sank deeply into his tongue. Finally blood from the exposed artery stopped spurting. Gray dropped the matchbook and lowered a knee to extinguish it before pine needles and dry grass caught fire. He did not have the mental capacity to pray that Trusov had not seen the smoke. Gray coughed with agony. Every limb shook with suffering.

His thoughts careened to Pete Coates. Then to Mrs Orlando. He owed them. He reached for his rifle and began crawling again. He came to the cap and rifle that had fooled him. The hat was on a stick, and the weapon was balanced on a log with a length of twine between the stock and a nearby maple trunk. When the wind moved the maple, the trunk swayed and so did the rifle, just a little, making the rifle appear to move independently of the background foliage. A good ruse, he decided dimly.

122

TRUSOV GRIMACED as he ejected the smoking brass casing. He had fired too quickly. After the shot he had seen a fine mist of blood, so he had hit something. But he dared not waltz over to find out. Now he could see nothing but underbrush through his telescope. Then he detected again the smell of burnt flesh.

Tree to tree, Trusov moved downhill towards the bowl's centre. The Russian was a spectre flowing silently and smoothly, closing in on the American.

DOWN THE SLOPE, crawling, one hand on the wooden stock, the other useless, Gray scrabbled over stones and through barricades of thistle and wild raspberry. Because his ears rang with pain, he could not judge his own sound. He guessed he was making as much noise as a belled cow. He did not have long. His body and mind were moments from surrendering.

Gray glimpsed a patch of skin—maybe a cheek, maybe a wrist— off to his left 400 yards. Then it disappeared in the kaleidoscope of leaves and boughs. That fleeting patch was moving closer, in a round-about way. Gray could no longer care.

He came to the porcupine he had killed, its quills dully reflecting the morning sun. He tried to rise to his feet, but he toppled sideways into the dry grass, his hand brushing the porcupine's quills. His vision misted, then began to go dark.

THE TANTALISING SMELL of burnt flesh lingered in the bowl, an inescapable telltale. Trusov moved through a thick stand of pine, the smell growing stronger. Owen Gray had to be within 400 metres, dead ahead.

The Russian dropped to his knees. The trees offered thick cover. Because he was low, he could see only thirty or forty metres in any direction, and he was not presenting a target for a distant shot. Trusov pushed himself through the underbrush.

Then the woods opened slightly, and there on the ground was a body, partially obscured by trees and brush and just visible above bunches of wild grass. Gray's olive trouser leg and his khaki shirt, dappled by intervening syringa leaves. The clothes were charred.

The body lay still. Then it appeared to move. Trusov squinted. The movement might have been an illusion, caused by the sway of leaves. The body moved again.

Prone on the ground, Trusov positioned his Mosin-Nagant in front of him. His fingers were swollen from the wasp stings and his trigger finger barely fitted into the guard. He found the khaki shirt in his scope. A sure shot even through the waving leaves.

Trusov's exquisite moment was at hand. Decades in the making.

He nudged the rifle down for the trouser leg. A hair's width at a time, the trigger came back and back.

The rifle fired and snapped into Trusov's shoulder. The sound of the shot burst away and echoed in the bowl. He worked the bolt, sighted in and squeezed again, sending the projectile into the thigh. The body bounced as the bullet ripped into it.

The third shot was aimed at Gray's chest, the target mostly obscured by underbrush. The bullet flew true. Trusov sent two more bullets where he estimated Gray's head to be, hidden behind brush.

Nikolai Trusov rose to his feet. He touched the fresh wound on his forehead, then the deep gouge that had been with him since his first encounter with White Star. Now it was over. He walked towards the corpse of his enemy, a fresh shell in the breech.

The body lay still. As he drew near, Trusov could see two of his bullet holes, torn red gaps in the cloth. He could see burns on the cloth. He walked closer.

Five metres from the body, Trusov's mouth twisted with anticipation. And then he saw everything was wrong. The Russian was allowed three seconds of astonishment. The trouser leg was filled with grass. The burnt shirt covered the body of that animal Trusov had hacked with his knife the day before. Just behind the porcupine, a small fire had been ignited, using dry grass, and the fire had scorched the porcupine's body, providing the scent, Trusov's homing beacon. It was all wrong, shockingly wrong.

Trusov had time only to bring up his rifle a few inches.

His left foot danced when a bullet tore through his ankle. The Russian instinctively shifted his weight to save himself from falling. He desperately looked round and tried again to bring up his rifle.

Then his leg buckled, shot through the knee. A rifle's bellow came from uphill, somewhere in the pines. Trusov kept himself upright with his good leg and twisted round looking for a target. A third bullet streaked through his left elbow. Trusov screamed and began sliding to the ground, losing his grip on the rifle. He landed near the porcupine. He tried to squirm towards his rifle, but neither his legs nor arms worked, and he lay still, his eyes open. Waiting.

Owen Gray emerged from the trees, his reloaded Winchester on Trusov. The American was almost naked, with mud and pine needles and seeping burns covering his body. His mouth was open and his breath was a rasp. As he came for the Russian, he tottered, then found his footing again. His rifle waggled as if it was a bough in the wind.

Gray had only a meagre recollection of having surfaced from the blackout a few moments ago. From somewhere—from the depth of his training or from desperate need—he had found the strength to take off his trousers and stuff grass into the remaining leg. Then with a match he had ignited a handful of grass and had burned some of the porcupine's belly flesh, leaving a trail of scent for the Russian. He had draped his shirt over the animal and crawled away to wait.

Now Gray stepped across to the Russian. He had to balance himself after each step, fighting the blackness that wanted to take him.

The Russian stared at him. He coughed, inhaled raggedly. The red shell he had hoped to leave at Gray's body had fallen from his shirt pocket and lay beside him, insignificant in the grass.

With difficulty Gray bent to the porcupine, to his trousers. He pulled the spiral notebook from the pocket and ripped out a sheet. He fumbled with the paper but after a few seconds the white star emerged.

'This is from me.' Gray let the fabled white star float down to the Russian's chest. Trusov followed it with his eyes. It landed on his bloodstained shirt.

'You and I are even now.' Gray's voice was crabbed with pain. 'Our accounts are balanced. I'm done with you.' He took a few steps away.

Trusov sensed a reprieve. He asked weakly, 'You are done with me?'

A long moment passed. Gray turned back, as if with an afterthought. 'But then there's Mrs Orlando. Her account is still owing.'

Gray lowered the rifle, put its snout against Trusov's forehead and pulled the trigger. He managed only two steps away from Trusov's body before he sagged to the ground, unconscious.

THE TWO-MAN CROSSCUT saw creased the log, gliding across the pine, but it was a feeble effort. The twins pulled and pushed against each other, the saw wobbled and the log remained unscathed.

'Can we quit now?' Julie asked.

'You didn't give it much of a try,' Gray replied.

'Maybe you could take over for a bit?' Carolyn wiped her brow with histrionic embellishment.

'Can't. Doctor's orders.'

As Julie pulled again on the saw, her sister pulled at the same time, to no effect. The girls laid the saw on the ground.

The woodshed's four new corner posts were now set in concrete. Adrian had levelled the concrete with a trowel. Tools were spread around the construction site.

Gray was sitting on a stump. He lifted a canteen from his lap and took a long drink.

'The girls and I have made a pretty good start on your woodshed,' Adrian said. 'Are you going to be able to finish it after I've gone?'

'One way or another.'

'Will you have enough feeling return in your hand?' She sat next to Gray, taking the proffered canteen.

'Viable but flail. That's the surgeon's term.'

'What's that mean?'

'I'll keep all my fingers, but the little finger and ring finger aren't going to be of much use. In their charming terminology, the surgeons call such useless fingers flails.'

Two weeks had passed since the showdown with Trusov. Gray had been in hospital all that time, and had just returned to the Sawtooths. His arm was in a splint. Under his loose shirt, his back and shoulders were dressed with gauze. Same with his leg. The hair on his head was starting to grow back but still looked ragged. Stitches had closed the first wound Trusov had inflicted, on Gray's arm.

Adrian had taken care of the children at the cabin. But now Gray was back. Her bag was packed and on the porch.

'They took bone from my hip, a spare tendon from my wrist and a nerve from my leg, then put all of those assorted parts into my hand. I'll also need skin grafts.'

The girls had heard it before but they listened intently, adoration and worry on their faces.

Hobart's only police car pulled into the yard. Chief Durant was behind the wheel and Pete Coates was in the passenger seat. Durant had found Gray unconscious in Shepherd's Bowl that day and had brought him out. He waved, then looked at his watch. Time to get Adrian and Pete to the airport.

Adrian's forehead and neck were patched with small bandages. Her skin was so white the bandages seemed to blend in. She was wearing washed-out jeans and a denim shirt. She and Gray were silent a moment, watching the twins furtively observe them.

'Got it,' John yelled, pumping his arm. He was sitting on a patch of grass near his father. 'New record.' He beamed with Game Boy success. Gray gave him a thumbs up and the boy returned to the game.

Pete Coates climbed out of the car and walked towards them. His right arm was in a sling. He had been in the hospital bed next to Gray's for most of a week. His face was grey, and he had not figured out how to shave with his left hand, so his chin and a cheek were nicked.

Adrian watched him approach. She asked Gray, 'Why did Trusov have to shoot at Pete?'

'He knew we were partners. Maybe he wanted to make sure Pete wouldn't help me in the field. Or maybe he just couldn't help firing at him. He was like a crow that eats robin chicks. It was his nature.'

'How did Trusov know you and Pete would be at the fire tower?'

'He couldn't have. Trusov was travelling to the fire tower for the same reason we were, for a look at the land from a high point. We just happened onto him.'

The twins watched them, speculating.

Coates stopped in front of Gray. 'Owen, when are you coming back to Manhattan?'

'I don't know.'

Coates glanced at Adrian, then back to Gray. 'Are you coming back, Owen?'

'Most likely.'

'I mean, you proved to me you know sniping, but there's lots you don't know, I'll guarantee you that.' Coates smiled. 'Come back to Manhattan and I'll teach you the rest.'

He threw a kiss to the twins and patted John on the shoulder as he walked back to the police car. Chief Durant tapped his horn and held up his wristwatch, pointing to it.

Julie and Carolyn stood looking at each other as they always did, silently scheming, communicating with the slightest of expressions. Adrian smiled at them. They appeared to be working up their courage.

Finally Carolyn said, 'Have you asked Adrian, Dad?'

'Pardon? Asked her what?'

'You were going to ask her not to go back to Moscow, but to stay with us here in the Sawtooths. At least for a while.'

Julie was never one to let her sister carry all the load. 'At least to see if things worked out between you two.'

Gray protested, 'I never told you anything like that.'

'But we could tell by the way you always look at her,' Carolyn said.

Gray glanced at Adrian. She grinned and raised her eyebrows.

'I'm not that obvious,' he said.

Both girls said at once, 'Yes, you are.'

Carolyn raced on. 'And now Chief Durant is waiting to take Adrian to the airport. You've got to ask her now.'

Gray spread his hands in a gesture of reasonableness. 'Girls, you're making presumptions, and it's sweet of you but—'

'Ask her, Dad,' Carolyn demanded.

'Adrian will say yes if you ask her to stay,' Julie insisted. 'She told us she's got three weeks of vacation coming, and after that, who knows what might happen?'

'You're already hurt enough,' Carolyn added with an impish grin. 'If Adrian walks away, you'll have a broken heart, too.'

Gray's face warmed. He looked out of the corner of his eye. Adrian was still smiling, and there was a touch of colour to her cheeks.

He turned fully towards her. 'We haven't talked about these things.'

'Looks like we are now,' she said.

He cleared his throat. 'I don't like being brazen and I know—'

'Be brave, Owen,' she said, widening her grin. 'Show me some of the stuff you showed the Russian.'

He asked quickly, 'Will you stay, Adrian? For a while.'

'Yes. For a while.' Then she added, 'At least.'

The girls whooped and leaped and ran towards Chief Durant and Detective Coates to tell them Adrian wouldn't be going to the airport. As the twins ran past their brother, Carolyn yelled to him, 'Adrian is staying. She and Dad are together now.'

John didn't look up from his Game Boy. 'Cool.'

Adrian reached for Gray. They sat there holding hands and leaning towards each other while the twins danced and pointed back at them and happily speculated with the police chief and Pete Coates about the Gray family's future.

JAMES THAYER

James Thayer's study in his home in Seattle, Washington, is a room that any writer in the world might envy. Look in one direction and you get a 180-degree panorama of Puget Sound; look in the other, and you might catch a glimpse of three-year-old Annemarie or seven-year-old Alexandra coming through the door for a visit to Daddy. Both are pleasantly distracting for the author. So too are listening to the radio and playing computer games. 'Sometimes I just can't keep solitaire off that screen,' he confides. His wife, Patti, an information systems specialist, suggests that this mental 'down-time' is just part of the creative process. Jim doesn't agree. 'I hate every squandered minute,' he insists.

A typical working day begins at 6.30am, when James Thayer, a graduate of the University of Chicago law school, arrives at his office in Seattle. He practises maritime law until 11.30, then it's back home for an afternoon at the keyboard. To date, he has had six novels published, including *White Star*. 'If I haven't written a thousand words by dinnertime, I wonder what's wrong with me,' he remarks. He enjoys the contrast between his two careers—the solitariness and introversion of being a writer and the active, outgoing environment of the law. 'Being in the legal field makes me feel plugged in, a part of commerce. I once took some time off to do nothing but write, and pretty soon I felt cut off from the real world. Five in the afternoon came and I hadn't used my vocal chords.'

Thayer's interest in shooting began when he was boy. He was raised on his father's 2,200-acre wheat farm in Washington State. There was no other house within range of the ranch so 'my brothers and I, we'd just walk out there and plink at targets for a while.' Thayer is not a hunter, but he still enjoys an occasional afternoon at the shooting range—yet another distraction that he can resist when he needs to.

Coming Home

ROSAMUNDE PILCHER

WITH ILLUSTRATIONS BY JIM GRIFFIN

The narrow road wound and twisted, following the contours of meandering dry-stone walls, the boundaries of random farms, huddled against the wind. Gentle hills swept down to the cliffs and the dazzling, sun-speckled sea.

At last the road turned a final corner and the house stood revealed. It was of local granite, slate-roofed with long windows on the two floors and a line of dormer windows above these. Its eastern wall was smothered with clematis and climbing roses, and all about stretched green lawns and flowerbeds. In the distance was the blue horizon.

From that first moment, Judith fell in love with Nancherrow. Now she knew exactly why Loveday had run away from school and found her way back to this magical place . . .

PART ONE

1935

The Porthkerris Council School stood halfway up the steep hill which climbed from the heart of the little town to the empty moors beyond. It was a solid Victorian edifice, built of granite blocks, surrounded by a tall wrought-iron fence, and presented a forbidding face to the world. But on this late afternoon in December it stood ablaze with light, and from its doors streamed a flood of excited children, jostling, giggling and uttering shrieks of cheerful abuse at each other before finally dispersing and setting off for home.

It was the end of the winter term and there had been a school Christmas party. Singing games had been played and relay races won, and the children had eaten a tea of saffron buns and fizzy lemonade. Finally they had lined up and one by one had shaken the headmaster by the hand and been given a bag of sweets.

Gradually the noisy outflux of children was reduced to a trickle. Last of all, as the school clock chimed a quarter to five, there came through the open door two girls—Judith Dunbar and Heather Warren, both fourteen years old, both dressed in navy-blue coats and woollen hats. Judith was fair, with two stubby pigtails, freckles and pale blue eyes, while Heather had inherited her colouring from her father and, through him, back over the generations, from some Spanish sailor washed ashore on the Cornish coast after the destruction of the Armada. And so her skin was olive, her hair raven-black and her eyes dark and bright.

They were the last to depart because Judith was leaving Porthkerris School for ever and had had to say goodbye to all the teachers. But finally they were on their way through the gates. The overcast day had slipped early into darkness, and a thin drizzle fell, shimmering against glowing streetlamps. They began to walk, descending into the town. Judith sighed. 'Well, that's it. I never thought I'd feel sad to leave any school, but I do now.'

'It's not going to be the same without you.'

'It's not going to be the same without you either. But at least you've still got friends. I've got to start all over again, trying to find someone I like at St Ursula's. And I have to wear that uniform.'

Heather's silence was sympathetic. At Porthkerris everybody wore their own cheerful clothes, but St Ursula's was a private school. The girls wore green tweed overcoats, and hats and thick stockings guaranteed to make even the prettiest totally plain. But worst of all was the prospect of boarding. Heather could not imagine a worse fate than to be torn from her parents and her two brothers. It didn't matter that St Ursula's was in Penzance, only ten miles away. Ten miles was for ever if you had to live away from Mum and Dad.

However, poor Judith had no choice. Her father worked in Colombo, in Ceylon, and for four years Judith, her mother and her little sister had lived apart from him. Now Mrs Dunbar and Jess were returning to Ceylon and Judith was being left behind, with little idea of when she would see her mother again. Heather cast about for something cheerful to say. 'There'll be holidays. You can come over and we'll go down to the beach. Or go to the pictures.'

'It would be a sort of escape.'

'Oh, you,' Heather said. 'You make it sound like going to prison. What's your aunt's house like?'

'It's quite big, right up at the top of the golf course. I've got her best spare room, and there's even room for my desk.'

'Sounds all right to me. Why are you making such a fuss?'

'It's just not *home*. And it's so bleak and windy. The house is called Windyridge, and no wonder. There always seems to be a gale blowing. The other thing is, it's so far from everywhere, and the nearest bus-stop's two miles away. And Aunt Louise won't have time to drive me around because she's always playing golf.'

'What you need is a bike. Then you could go wherever you wanted. It's only three miles to Porthkerris over the top road.'

'You are brilliant. I never thought of a bike.'

'Get your mother to give you one for Christmas.'

'I've already asked for a jersey for Christmas. A polo neck.'

'Well, ask for a bike as well. She can scarcely say no, going away and not knowing when she's going to see you again.'

134

But Judith only said, 'I'll see.'

Their conversation had brought them down the hill to the centre of the town and the parting of their ways. Heather would carry on down cobbled lanes to the square granite house where the Warren family lived over Mr Warren's grocery shop, and Judith would climb another hill and head for the railway station.

They stood in the drizzle and faced each other. 'I suppose it's goodbye, then,' said Heather. 'You can write to me.'

'I'll do that.'

They had been friends for four years. It was a poignant moment. Abruptly Heather leaned forward and planted a kiss on Judith's rain-damp cheek. Then she turned and went running down the street. Judith, feeling bereft, continued on her way, climbing the narrow pavement between small shops brightly decorated for Christmas. The wind came in gusts, bringing the sound of breakers booming up on the beach below.

At the top of the hill she paused to lean her elbows on a low granite wall. She saw the blurred jumble of houses slipping away down to the dark harbour. The red and green riding lights of fishing boats were reflected in the inky water and, far out, the lighthouse flashed its warning to passing ships.

She shivered. Too cold to stand here. She began to run, her boot bag thumping against her side; came to a flight of granite steps and hurtled down them to the railway station. The little branch-line train was waiting at the platform.

Travelling to school in the little train was going to be one of the things that she was really going to miss, because the line ran for three miles along a spectacular stretch of coast: cliffs and deep cuttings, bays and beaches, and then the sand dunes and the huge lonely beach, which she had come to think of as her own.

Sometimes when people learned that Judith's father worked on the other side of the world for the prestigious shipping company Wilson-McKinnon, they were sorry for her. How awful to be without a father. But as with the children of every British India family, she had always known that long separations were inevitable.

Judith had been born in Ceylon and lived there until she was ten. During that time Colombo was home—the spacious bungalow on the Galle Road, with a verdant tropical garden, and always a fresh breeze blowing in off the ocean. But inevitably the day came when they had to say goodbye to the house and the garden. And to Dad. It was not until she and her mother were back in England that Judith was let into the secret that there was a new baby on the way.

Aunt Louise had located Riverview House for them and they had rented it as a furnished let. Soon after they took up residence, Jess was born. And now the time had come for Molly Dunbar and four-year-old Jess to return to Colombo. Judith envied them dreadfully.

At fourteen, Judith reckoned that she was mature enough to have really important decisions—those that were going to affect *her*—shared and discussed. But Mummy never discussed. She simply told.

I have had a letter from your father, and Jess and I are going to have to go back to Colombo. Which had been a bit of a bombshell.

But worse. *We have decided that you should go to St Ursula's as a boarder. It's all arranged for the January term*. As though she were a sort of parcel or a dog being put into a kennel.

But what about the holidays?

You'll stay with Aunt Louise. She's very kindly said that she'll take care of you and be your guardian while we're abroad.

Which was, perhaps, most daunting of all. During their sojourn in Penmarron, her father's sister, Aunt Louise, had never been anything but kind. It was just that she was all wrong. Old—at least fifty—and faintly intimidating; not cosy in the least. And Windyridge was an old person's house, orderly and quiet. Two sisters, Edna and Hilda, who worked for her as cook and parlour maid, were equally elderly, not a bit like darling Phyllis, who did everything for them all at Riverview House but still found time to play.

They would probably spend Christmas Day with Aunt Louise. They would go to church, and then there would be roast goose for lunch, and afterwards a brisk walk over the golf course. Not very exciting. Christmas ought to be as it was in books and on Christmas cards, but it never was. Mummy wasn't much good at decorating with holly or dressing a tree, anything like that in fact. As for St Ursula's, Judith hadn't even been to see the school, nor to meet the probably terrifying headmistress, Miss Catto.

The train ground to a hissing halt. She collected her bag and stepped out onto the platform. The tiny station stood opposite the bottom gate of the Riverview House garden. Emerging into an unlit lane, she crossed the road, opened the gate, and went up the steeply sloping path. At the top, the house loomed before her, with curtained windows glowing in friendly fashion. The lantern over the front door had been turned on, and in its light she saw an alien car parked on the gravel. Aunt Louise, no doubt, come for tea.

A big black Rover. Solid and dependable. But any person who ventured onto the narrow roads of Penmarron had reason to be wary of it. Aunt Louise, regular churchgoer and pillar of the golf club, underwent a sort of personality change the moment she got behind the wheel, roaring round blind corners at fifty miles an hour, the heel of her hand on the horn.

Judith did not want, instantly, to be faced by Aunt Louise. She made her way round to the back door, through the scullery, and so into the kitchen. Here she found Jess sitting at the scrubbed table with her crayons and colouring book, and Phyllis, in her muslin apron, dealing with a pile of ironing.

Phyllis smiled. 'Hello. What are you doing, sneaking in the back way?' She was a bony girl, pale, with mousy hair, but had the sweetest disposition of any person Judith had ever known.

'I saw Aunt Louise's car.'

'That's no reason. Have a good party, did you?'

'Yes.' She delved into her coat pocket. 'Here, Jess,' and she gave her little sister her bag of sweets.

Jess looked at them. 'What are they?' She was a beautiful child, chubby and silver-blonde, but dreadfully spoilt and babyish.

'Sweets, of course, silly.' Judith took off her coat and hat. 'I didn't know Aunt Louise was coming for tea.'

'Telephoned, she did, about two o'clock,' Phyllis said. 'And your Aunt Biddy called this morning.'

Judith perked up. Aunt Biddy was Mummy's own sister and a favourite of Judith's. 'What did she want?'

'I wasn't eavesdropping, was I? You'll have to ask your mum. You'd better go in. There's scones if you're hungry.'

Reluctantly Judith left the kitchen and crossed the hall. From the sitting room came the low murmur of voices. She opened the door.

They sat, Molly Dunbar and her sister-in-law, Louise Forrester, on either side of the hearth, with a tea table set up between them. This had been laid with a linen cloth and a plate of hot scones spread with cream and strawberry jam. A coal fire flickered in the grate. Because Riverview House was a furnished let, it was not especially well appointed. But Molly had brought from Ceylon her favourite bits and pieces, and these were set about the place: ornaments in jade and ivory and red lacquer, and family photographs in silver frames.

'You'll have such a lot to do,' Aunt Louise was saying. 'If I can help . . .' She leaned forward to place her cup and saucer on the table and glanced towards the door. 'Well, look who's here.'

Molly turned. 'Judith. I thought perhaps you'd missed the train.'

'No. I've been talking to Phyllis.' She closed the door and crossed the room to kiss Aunt Louise's proffered cheek. Aunt Louise accepted this but made no move to kiss Judith in return.

She was not one to show emotion. She sat there, a well-built woman in her early fifties, with surprisingly elegant legs and narrow feet in polished chestnut brogues. She wore a tweed coat and skirt, and her short grey hair was deeply marcel-waved.

A handsome woman, but never beautiful. Indeed, when she was twenty-three and still unspoken for, her parents had packed her off to

India to stay with army relations. There she met Major Jack Forrester, who shared her love of tennis and golf. It was a sound marriage, and when Jack retired they returned to England and settled in Penmarron to be near the golf course. Most fine days saw them out together on the fairways. After Jack died, every day still saw Louise on the golf course.

Now she asked Judith, 'How did the Christmas party go?'

'It was all right. There were saffron buns'—Judith eyed the tea table—'but I'm still hungry.'

'Well, we've left plenty,' said Molly. Judith pulled up a low stool and reached for a plate and a scone.

'Did you say goodbye to all your friends?'

'Yes. And then I walked down the hill with Heather—'

'Who is Heather?' asked Aunt Louise.

'Heather Warren. She's my special friend.'

'You know,' said Molly, 'Mr Warren, the grocer in Porthkerris.'

'*Oh!*' Aunt Louise raised her eyebrows. 'The dashing Spaniard. Such a good-looking man.'

They were obviously in a good mood. Judith decided that this was the right moment to broach the subject of the bicycle.

'Actually, Heather had the most frightfully good idea—that I ought to have a bicycle.'

'A *bicycle*?' Molly said.

'Mummy, you sound as though I'm asking for a car or a pony. I think it's a really good idea. Windyridge is miles from the bus-stop. With a bicycle I can get myself about; Aunt Louise won't have to drive me. *Then* she can get on with her golf.'

Aunt Louise laughed. 'You've certainly thought of everything.'

Molly found her voice. 'But, Judith, isn't a bicycle dreadfully expensive?'

'I thought you could give it to me for Christmas.'

'But I've already got your Christmas present. Besides, you'll have to go on the main roads. You might have an accident—'

Here Aunt Louise intervened. 'Oh, Molly, don't fuss. What harm can the child come to? I'll stand you a bicycle, Judith.'

'Really? Aunt Louise, you are a brick. When can we buy it?'

'What about Christmas Eve?'

Molly said faintly, 'Oh, no.'

Louise frowned. 'What's the matter *now*?' Judith thought Aunt Louise was often impatient with Molly, treating her more like an idiot girl than a sister-in-law. 'Thought of more objections?'

'No . . . It's just that we won't be here. I haven't told you, Louise.' She turned to Judith. 'Aunt Biddy rang. She's asked us to spend Christmas with them in Plymouth. You and me and Jess.'

Christmas with Aunt Biddy! If Aunt Louise hadn't been there,

138

Judith would have jumped up and down and danced round the room in her excitement.

'In that case,' Aunt Louise said, 'we'll buy the bicycle after Christmas. In fact, I was going to ask you all to spend Christmas with me, but it looks as though Biddy's saved me the trouble.'

'Oh, Louise, I'm sorry. Now I feel I've let you down.'

'Rubbish. Better for us all to have a bit of a change. Will Biddy's boy be there?'

'Ned? Unfortunately, no. He's going to Zermatt to ski with some of his term at Dartmouth Naval College.'

Aunt Louise raised her eyebrows, not approving of extravagant gallivanting. 'Pity,' was all she said. 'He would have been a companion for Judith.'

'Aunt Louise, Ned's sixteen! He wouldn't take any notice of me at all. I expect I shall enjoy myself much more without him there.'

'You're probably right. And, knowing Biddy, you'll have a high old time.'

'What will you do for Christmas, Louise? I do hope you won't feel abandoned.'

'Heavens, no. I'll maybe ask Billy Fawcett over for a drink and then we'll go down to the club for lunch.'

Molly frowned. 'Billy Fawcett? I don't think I know him.'

'No. You wouldn't. Old friend from the Quetta days. Retired now, and thought he'd give Cornwall a try. He's rented a bungalow down my road. Keen golfer, so I've put him up for the club.'

'That's nice for you, Louise, having an old friend nearby. And a golfer too. Not that you're ever short of a partner.'

But Louise was not about to commit herself. 'It depends,' she said, 'on what sort of handicap he gets.' She looked at her watch. 'Heavens, is that the time?' She pulled herself out of her chair, and Molly and Judith rose to their feet. 'Tell Phyllis, a delicious tea. If I don't see you before Christmas, Molly, have a ripping time. And Judith, we'll buy the bicycle at half-term.'

1936

The morning was so cold that, slowly waking, Judith felt as if her nose were frozen to her face. She reached to turn on the bedside light. Her new clock—from Uncle Bob, and one of her best presents—said seven forty-five. She felt a bit depressed. Their Christmas holiday was over and today they were going home.

A short time before Christmas the temperature had dropped alarmingly, which was unfortunate because Aunt Biddy and Uncle

Bob lived in what had to be the coldest house in Christendom. The house went with Uncle Bob's job, which was captain in charge of the Royal Naval Engineering College at Keyham.

Despite the freezing cold, this had been a truly magical Christmas. Biddy, who never did things by halves, had dressed the entire house. Her Christmas tree, filling the hall with lights and tinsel and the smell of spruce, was the most magnificent that Judith had ever seen. Other rooms were just as festive, with swags of holly and ribbon, and in the drawing room great coal fires burned nonstop. And there had been so much to do, so much going on. Luncheon and dinner parties, and friends dropping in for tea or for drinks.

Being with Uncle Bob was the high spot of the holiday. In his study he had shown her his photograph albums and let her play records on his gramophone. He had introduced her to classical music, and she felt as if she were being transported into another land. They had all gone ice-skating, and it was he who had helped her round the rink until she found what he called her sea legs. And at parties he introduced her to guests, just as though she were a grown-up.

Dad, although dear and missed, had never been such fun. Admitting this to herself, Judith had felt a bit guilty, because over the last couple of weeks she had scarcely thought of him. It was not easy to go on missing a person after so long without him.

The new clock now pointed to eight o'clock. Time to get up. She hopped out of bed and, as swiftly as she could, got dressed and packed her case. Breakfast would be waiting, and she was hungry.

BIDDY SOMERVILLE sat at the end of her dining-room table, drank black coffee and tried to ignore the fact that she had a slight headache. Bob sat at the other end of the table reading *The Times*. She was wearing a housecoat over her nightdress, but he was fully dressed in uniform because today he returned to work. The rest of their little house party had not yet appeared.

The Dunbars were leaving today, and Biddy found herself feeling quite sorry that the time had come to say goodbye. Molly was Biddy's only sister, and there was no knowing when they would see each other again. As well, Biddy felt a bit guilty; she hadn't done enough for them during their last four years here. Finally she had asked them over for the holidays.

It had all been a surprising success. Molly, it was true, had wilted from time to time, defeated by the social whirl, and Jess was a spoilt brat, dreadfully indulged. But Judith had proved the sort of girl Biddy would have liked as a daughter of her own—entertaining herself if necessary, and enthusiastic about any diversion. She was also,

Biddy thought, extraordinarily pretty. The rapport she had struck up with Bob was a bonus. He liked her for her good manners and the way she spoke up and looked you in the eye; but, as well, there was a natural attraction, a father-daughter affection.

Perhaps they should have had daughters. But there was only Ned, packed off to prep school when he was eight and then to Dartmouth Naval College. The years flew by so fast. Now he was sixteen and soon he'd be done with his studies and sent to sea. He'd get married and produce a family of his own. Biddy sighed. Being a grandmother did not appeal to her.

Bob lowered his paper, folded it, and slapped it down on the table. 'Time I was off.' He pushed back his chair and stood up, a tall and squarely built man, his bulk made yet more impressive by the dark, double-breasted, gold-buttoned naval jacket. His face, clean-shaven and craggy, was shadowed by bushy eyebrows, and his thick hair, iron-grey, lay smooth on his head.

He looked at the empty table. 'What time is their train?'

'This afternoon. It's the "Cornish Riviera".'

'Say goodbye for me. Say goodbye to Judith.'

'You'll miss her.'

'I . . .' A man who did not show his emotions, he searched for words. 'I don't like her being abandoned. Left on her own.'

'She won't be on her own. Louise is there.'

'She needs more than Louise is able to offer. Maybe you could ask her here during the holidays. Or would that be a bore for you?'

'No, not at all. I'll suggest it.'

He came to drop a kiss on the top of her unruly head. 'See you this evening, then.'

'Bye, darling.'

He went. She finished her coffee and poured another. Then she leafed through her mail. There was a letter from Devon, where her father was the incumbent of a tiny parish and her mother had struggled all her life with genteel poverty. It was a miracle, thought Biddy, that she and Molly had managed to escape the vicarage in which they had been brought up.

Neither had been prepared for life. Neither had trained as a nurse, nor gone to university, nor learned how to type. If Molly hadn't been invited to that tennis party with the Luscombes and there met Bruce Dunbar, home on his first long leave from Colombo and searching desperately for a wife, heaven alone knew what might have happened to the poor girl. A lifetime of spinsterhood, probably.

Biddy was different. From an early age she saw clearly that if she was going to have any sort of life, she was going to have to take care of herself. At school her best friend was the daughter of a naval commander, living in a large house near Dartmouth. As the girl had brothers, Biddy decided this was fertile ground, and managed to wangle an invitation to stay for the weekend. She was, as she had every intention of being, a social success. She was attractive, with long legs and bright dark eyes and a mop of curly brown hair, and she had a sure instinct as to when to be polite, when to be charming, how to flirt with men. But when she was twenty-one, she had married serious Bob Somerville, and had never regretted it. They had had good times, for she loved to travel and was never unwilling to up sticks and join Bob wherever he was sent. No, she had been very fortunate.

The clock on the dining-room mantelpiece struck half past eight, and Biddy scooped up Bob's newspaper. It did not make cheerful reading. Spain seemed headed for a civil war, Herr Hitler was making noisy speeches about the remilitarisation of the Rhineland, and Mussolini boasted of his growing naval strength in the Mediterranean. It was all a bit frightening, and she tried not to think about Ned, committed to the Royal Navy, ripe for combat. Then the door opened and Molly came in.

'I'm sorry I'm late,' she said.

'Not late at all. Did you sleep well?'

'Not really. I was up and down all night. Jess had dreadful nightmares. She's still asleep, poor pet. Judith's not appeared either?'

'She's probably packing. Get something to eat.'

Molly went to the sideboard, lifted the lid of the sausage dish and hesitated.

'I think I'll just have a bit of toast.'

Molly Dunbar's claim to beauty lay in her extraordinarily girlish appearance—the fluffy fair hair, the rounded cheeks, the eyes which reflected a sort of bewildered innocence. Men were apt to find this charming, because it made them feel protective. Now, however, Biddy experienced a certain concern. There were dark shadows beneath Molly's eyes, and her cheeks were unusually pale.

'Are you feeling all right?'

Molly poured coffee. 'Oh, I don't know. It's all the things that have to be done when I get home. Organising everything—closing the house, trying to help Phyllis find a new job. I'd put it all out of my mind while I was here with you. Now I've got to start being sensible again.' She hesitated and then said quite violently, 'The awful thing is that right now I think I'd give anything not to be going. I hate leaving Judith. I hate us all being torn apart.'

Her voice cracked. For a dreadful moment Biddy feared that she was about to burst into tears. 'Oh, Molly, you're just tired. Not sleeping. It makes one depressed.'

'Yes.' Molly sighed. She drank coffee, laid down her cup. 'But still

I can't help wishing that Bruce worked in England so that we could be together. I know you think I'm being silly.'

'No, I do understand. When Bob and I went to Malta, I simply hated leaving Ned. But there it is. We can't be everywhere at once. The thing to be certain about is that you're leaving Judith at a school that is sympathetic. You're happy with the school?'

'Oh, yes. Even if I hadn't been going back, I think I should have sent Judith to St Ursula's. The Porthkerris School is excellent academically, but the children there are a pretty mixed bunch.'

Biddy had to laugh. 'Honestly, Molly, you always were the most appalling snob.'

'I'm not a snob. But people matter.'

'Yes, they certainly do.'

'What are you getting at now?'

'Louise. I wouldn't want to spend my holidays with her.'

This threw Molly into a state of instant agitation. 'Oh, Biddy, *please* don't start raising objections. It's all been arranged.'

'She's such a tough old bird,' Biddy protested. 'So boring with her endless golf and her bridge games.'

'Actually, she's very kind. She's been a tower of strength to me. But most important, she's reliable. She'll give Judith security.'

'Perhaps Judith needs more than security. She'll soon be fifteen. She'll need to spread her wings. You don't want her to be bored stiff.'

'It's too late now. She's going to Louise.'

Biddy managed to control her rising impatience. 'But wouldn't it be fun for her to come to us from time to time? No, don't look so horrified; it was Bob's idea. It would be a nice break for her.'

'I—I don't want to upset Louise . . . rock the boat. Oh, please understand, Biddy. Perhaps later on.'

'There may not be a later on.'

'What do you mean?' Molly demanded in evident alarm.

'Read the papers. Bob doesn't trust Herr Hitler further than he could throw him. And the same goes for fat old Mussolini.'

'You mean'—Molly swallowed—'a war?'

'Oh, I don't know. But I don't think we should fritter around with our private lives, because, perhaps very soon, we won't have any. You think I'm a bad influence on Judith, I suppose. All those wicked parties and young lieutenants coming to call. That's it, isn't it?'

'It isn't that! You know it isn't.'

It had turned into a row, with both of them raising their voices.

'Let's just forget it.' And with this, Biddy, exasperated, reached for *The Times*, snapped its pages open, and retreated behind it.

Silence. Molly sat in a state of trembling agitation. Finally she pushed back the cuff of her cardigan and looked at her watch.

'Where is Judith?' She stood abruptly and went to the door to call for her tardy daughter. But Judith was already there, just across the hall, sitting at the foot of the staircase.

'What *are* you doing?'

'Tying my shoelace.'

She did not meet her mother's eyes, and Molly realised that her daughter had heard every word of the acrimonious exchange.

It was Jess who came to her rescue. 'Mummy!' Molly looked up and saw her younger child peering at her through the banister rail. Jess, still in her nightdress and with her curls awry. 'Mummy!'

'I'm coming, darling.' She crossed the hall and went upstairs.

Judith waited until she was gone, then went into the dining room. Aunt Biddy looked at her bleakly. 'Oh, dear. Sorry about that.'

'It's all right.' Judith was not used to having grown-ups apologise to her. She got herself a sausage and sat down. 'I shall be all right with Aunt Louise, you know,' she said after a bit.

'I know that. It isn't that I'm worried about your well-being, just the fact that quite possibly it won't be much fun.'

Judith said, 'I've never had proper grown-up fun before. Not before this Christmas. I would love to come back.' She picked up her knife and fork and cut the sausage in two. 'If I came to visit, would you still be in this house?'

'I don't know. Keyham's a two-year appointment and we're due to move this summer. Bob wants to go back to sea. If he does, I shall try to buy a little house of our own. We've always lived in quarters, but it would be nice to have a permanent base. I thought Devon.'

Judith popped a bit of sausage into her mouth and chewed thoughtfully. 'What I really hate is being treated as though I were the same age as Jess. I'm never *asked* about things or *told* about things.'

'I know. But you mustn't be too hard on your mother. At the moment she's in a state of upheaval, and who can blame her if she does start twittering around like a wet hen?' She laughed and was rewarded by the beginnings of a smile from Judith.

'Now'—Biddy got to her feet—'I can hear your mother and Jess on their way downstairs. I must go and put some clothes on.'

Before she reached the door, Molly and Jess had come into the room, Jess now dressed in a little smock and white socks. Biddy paused to drop an airy kiss onto Molly's cheek. 'Don't bother about a thing,' she said, which was the nearest she could get to an apology; then she was gone, running up the stairs to her bedroom.

AND SO THE QUARREL was swept away. Judith was relieved that the air was clear between her mother and aunt, and it was only when they were at the station, waiting for the 'Riviera', that she had time to regret the absence of Uncle Bob. She wanted to thank him for so much, and thanks were never the same written in a letter.

Her feet were frozen. She tried to stamp some life into them, while Aunt Biddy and Mother chatted and Jess sat on a trolley, hugging her golliwog, a revolting toy she took with her everywhere.

And then something really good happened. Aunt Biddy stopped chattering and said, 'Oh, look. There's Bob.'

Judith swung round. Frozen feet were forgotten. There he was, a huge, unmistakable figure coming down the platform, with a great grin on his craggy features. 'Had a moment or two to spare, decided to come and see our little party on board.' He looked down at Judith. 'I couldn't let you go without saying goodbye properly.'

She beamed up at him. She said, 'I'm glad you came. I wanted to thank you for everything. Especially for the clock.'

'You'll have to remember to wind it.' Then Uncle Bob cocked his head, listening. 'I think that's the train now.'

And indeed the railway lines were humming and Judith saw the huge green and black engine surge into view. It crept alongside the platform and, with a hiss of steam, stopped, dead on time.

The porter heaved their suitcases on board and went in search of seats, Uncle Bob following to make sure the job was done in a proper fashion. Molly lifted Jess into her arms and kissed her sister goodbye. 'We've had a wonderful Christmas. Wave goodbye to Aunt Biddy, Jess.'

Jess, still clutching Golly, flapped a little white-furred paw.

Aunt Biddy turned to Judith. 'Goodbye, dear child. You've been a little brick.' She stooped and kissed her. 'Don't forget. I'm always here. Up you get now.'

On board, Judith gave a final wave and then plunged down the corridor after the others. A compartment had been found containing only one young man, who sat with an open book on his knee while the porter piled luggage in the racks over his head. When all was stowed, Uncle Bob tipped the porter and sent him on his way.

'Goodbye, Judith,' he smiled down at her. Then he was gone. A moment later the train moved off.

The other occupant of the carriage sat by the door, and so they settled themselves in the window seats. It was very warm, so gloves and coats were removed and stowed in the rack. Jess knelt on the prickly plush and pressed her nose against the smutty window. Judith sat opposite and her mother sank down beside Jess. She began to fan her face with her hand.

'Goodness, it's hot,' she said to nobody in particular. 'I wonder...' Now she was addressing the young man whose privacy they had disturbed. He looked up from his book, and she smiled disarmingly.

'Would you mind if we opened the window a chink?'

'Of course.' He was very polite. He laid aside his book and moved to the window. Judith tucked her legs out of the way and watched as he let the window down an inch. 'How's that?'

'Perfect.'

He went back to his seat and picked up his book again. Covertly, Judith studied him. His book looked large and dull, and she wondered why it so absorbed his interest; he did not strike her as a studious type, being broad-shouldered and solidly built. He was dressed in corduroys and a tweed jacket, and draped round his neck was a long, striped woollen scarf. He wore horn-rimmed spectacles and there was a deep cleft in the middle of his chin. She wondered how old he was and decided about twenty-five.

She turned back to the window. In a moment they would be going over the Saltash Bridge, and she didn't want to miss the sight of all the naval men-of-war at anchor in the harbour. But Jess was already bored, and she began scrambling down off the seat in order to scramble up again. Her shoe kicked Judith's shin painfully.

'Oh, sit *still*, Jess.'

Jess responded by flinging Golly at her sister and howling.

'Oh, *Judith*.' Mother took Jess on her knee and then apologised to the young man. 'I'm sorry. We've disturbed your peace.'

He looked up from his book and smiled. It was a particularly charming smile, revealing even white teeth, and it lit up his plain features so that suddenly he was almost good-looking.

'Not at all,' he reassured her.

'Have you come from London?' Molly asked conversationally.

'Yes. I was working over Christmas and the New Year. I'm taking my holiday now.'

'Goodness, what a shame. Fancy having to work over Christmas. What do you do?'

Judith thought she was being rather nosy, but the young man looked quite happy to talk. 'I'm a houseman at St Thomas's.'

'Oh, a *doctor*!'

Judith thought he looked much too young to be a doctor, but it explained the reason for his heavy book. He was probably studying some obscure disease.

'Not a very amusing Christmas for you. Now you're going home?'

'Yes. To Truro. My parents live there.'

'We're going further than that. We've been staying with my sister and her husband. He's a captain at the engineering college.'

It sounded a little as though she were bragging. To divert attention, Judith said, 'Here's the bridge coming now.'

To her surprise the young man seemed as excited about this as she was. 'I must have a look,' he said, and he came to stand beside her, steadying himself with a hand on the window's edge. He smiled down at her, and she saw that his eyes were neither brown nor green, but speckled, like a trout. 'It's too good to miss, isn't it?'

The wheels were slowing. The iron girders clanked past, and far below gleamed cold winter water, crammed with sleek grey cruisers and destroyers and pinnaces, all flying the white ensign.

She said, 'I think it's a special bridge.'

'Brunel's masterpiece, designed for the Great Western Railway. The wonder of the day. Still wonderful, for that matter.' They fell silent. He stayed there until the train had crossed the bridge and steamed into Saltash, on the Cornish side of the Tamar, and then he went back to his seat and picked up his book again.

Judith, gazing out into the gathering twilight, decided that, after all, it had not been such a bad day. It had started a bit gloomily, with her mother and Aunt Biddy having that row, but out of it had come the knowledge that Aunt Biddy and Uncle Bob actually liked her enough to want to have her to stay again. Another good thing had been Uncle Bob's appearing at the station to see them off. And finally, talking to the young doctor. It occurred to her that he was the sort of person one would like to have as a brother.

Eventually the train steamed into Truro, and their fellow passenger stood and said goodbye. Through the window, Judith watched him make his way down the lamplit platform. Then he was gone.

After that it was a bit dull, but there wasn't far to go. At the Porthkerris junction, they crossed to the other platform and piled into the small train, and minutes later they were piling out again onto the platform at Penmarron Halt.

Jess had fallen asleep, and Molly had to carry her across the dark road and up the shadowed path. As they came to the house, the door opened and Phyllis was there to welcome them.

'Look who's here, turned up like a lot of bad pennies.' She hurried down the steps. 'Here, give me the child, madam. You must be tired. Now come along, let's get you all in. There's a nice fire in the sitting room and a boiled fowl for your supper.'

Phyllis bore Jess upstairs to put her to bed. Judith followed, chattering. 'I got a clock from Uncle Bob, Phyllis. It's in a leather case . . .'

With the journey behind her, Molly all at once felt totally exhausted. She gathered up the post on the hall table and went into the sitting room. The coal fire burned brightly, and she stood in front of it and leafed through her letters. There was one from Bruce, but before opening it she would pour herself a large whisky and soda. Settled in her chair by the fire, she took a delicious, warming mouthful, then reached for her husband's letter.

In her bedroom, Judith unpacked her night things, then her Christmas loot. She laid her gifts out on her desk, and once Phyllis had finished with Jess she came in to have a look.

'Yours was the best gift, Phyllis. It was kind of you.'

'At least you won't come asking me for scissors all the time. And thank you for the bath salts. I like Evening in Paris best.'

Phyllis had to inspect everything and marvel at its splendour. 'Feel that jumper. So soft. And the little clock! No excuse for being late for breakfast now. What did you get from your dad?'

'I asked for a cedarwood box, but it hasn't arrived yet.' Then Judith told her all about Aunt Biddy's house, and about skating, and about Uncle Bob and his gramophone, and about the parties and the Christmas tree and the decorations.

'Aw.' Phyllis let out a sigh of envy. 'It sounds *lovely*.'

Judith was sure that Phyllis's Christmas had been a fairly thin one. Phyllis, whose father was a tin miner out St Just way, was the eldest of five children, and how they all squeezed into their tiny stone house was a conundrum.

'What did *you* do, Phyllis? Did you get a Christmas present?'

'Yes. A blouse from Mum and a box of hankies from Cyril.'

Cyril Eddy was Phyllis's young man, another tin miner.

'What did you give him?'

'A collar for his whippet. He was some pleased.' A coy expression came into her face. 'You meet any nice young men, did you?'

'Oh, Phyllis, of course not. Aunt Biddy's friends are grown-up. Except on the last night two young lieutenants came in after dinner for a drink. But,' she added, 'they were far too busy being amused by Aunt Biddy to look at me.'

'That's your age. Couple of years, you'll have boys round you like flies round a honeypot.' Phyllis smiled. 'You never fancy a boy?'

'I don't know any. Except...' She hesitated.

'Go on. Tell Phyllis.'

'There was this man on the train. A young doctor. He was really nice. I wouldn't mind meeting somebody like that.'

'Perhaps you will.'

'Not at St Ursula's.'

'You don't go to a place like that to meet boys. You go to get educated. And don't turn up your nose at that. I had to leave school to go into service. I can't do much more than read and write.'

'I suppose you didn't have time to look for another job?'

'Didn't have the heart, somehow. Never mind. Madam said she'd give me a good reference.' She rose. 'I'd better see to the potatoes.'

When she was gone, Judith combed her hair and went downstairs to the sitting room. Something was terribly wrong. Her mother sat in her armchair by the fire, her face swollen with weeping. On the floor at her feet were the pages of a letter.

'Mummy!' She rushed to her mother's side. 'Whatever is it?'

'Oh, *Judith*. It's a letter from Dad. I can't bear it.'

'What's happened to him?'

'Nothing.' Molly dabbed at her face with a sodden handkerchief. 'It's just that . . . he's got a new job. We have to go to Singapore. It's *another* move, to somewhere strange. And I shan't know anybody. And I'm so tired, and there's so—'

Her tears flowed anew. Judith kissed her, feeling almost as distraught as her mother. But one of them had to be strong. She took a deep breath and composed herself. 'May I read the letter?'

'Of course.' Molly handed it over.

Dearest Molly,

By the time you get this, Christmas will be over. I hope you and the girls had an enjoyable time. I have fairly momentous news. The chairman called me into his office yesterday and told me that they want me to move to Singapore, as company manager. It is a promotion, and I hope you will be as pleased as I am. The new job does not commence until the month after you and Jess arrive here, so the three of us will sail to Singapore together. I know you will miss Colombo, as I will, but we shall travel together, and be together when we set up in our new home.

Judith did not need to read any more. She folded the pages and gave them to her mother. 'It sounds quite exciting.'

'I don't *want* to be excited. I want a *home*, not moving all the time. And everybody telling me I do things all wrong.'

'But you *don't*!'

Molly blew her nose and smiled a bit sheepishly. She said, 'I'm sorry about this morning. That silly row, about Biddy asking you to stay and me being so uncooperative. It's just that Louise, well, she doesn't approve of Biddy, and it just seemed another complication to deal with. Perhaps I didn't handle it very well.'

Judith said truthfully, 'I don't mind about any of that.'

'And I feel so guilty, because I have made plans for you without discussing them. School and Aunt Louise. And now there's so much to do.' She was off again. 'I haven't even bought your uniform.'

Judith felt, all at once, enormously protective. She said, 'I'll help. We'll do it together. Why don't we get the uniform tomorrow? We'll go to Medways, in Penzance. We'll take the car, and we won't come back until we've got every single thing.'

Molly looked instantly more cheerful. 'All right. We'll leave Jess with Phyllis and we'll have lunch at the Mitre Hotel, for a treat.'

'And then we'll drive to St Ursula's and look at the place. Now I'll go and tell Phyllis that we're ready to eat.'

Her mother leaned forward and kissed her. 'Thank you. You've made me feel quite different.'

MOLLY OPENED her eyes at half past seven. It was scarcely light, but she felt refreshed, ready for whatever the day had to bring.

She got out of bed and drew the curtains. The sky was clear. Perhaps, Molly thought, it would turn into one of those days that spring steals from a Cornish winter. She would keep it separate, an entity on its own, a single day spent with her elder daughter. Remembered, it would be sharp-edged and vivid, like a photograph.

Over breakfast she spooned boiled egg into Jess's mouth and broke the news that she was to be abandoned for the day.

Jess said, 'I don't want to.' Her bottom lip stuck out like a shelf.

'Of course you do. You and Phyllis can take Golly for a walk.'

'Don't *want* to.' Tears poured down Jess's face and her mouth went square. But just then Phyllis came in with hot toast in a rack. She scooped Jess up into her arms and bore her firmly out of the room. By the time she reached the kitchen, the wails had started to subside.

'Thank goodness,' said Judith.

Half an hour later they were ready to go, Molly armed with the school's clothes list and her handbag and chequebook. They climbed into the little Austin Seven and set off.

In town, they parked the car in the Greenmarket and headed for Medways, an old-fashioned shop, with plate-glass windows displaying outdoor wear—tweeds, woollens, hats and raincoats. Inside, all was fitted in dark wood and smelt of rubber waterproofs and fusty assistants. An elderly woman who approached them wore a sad black dress and walked as though her feet hurt.

'Good morning, madam. Want some help, do you?'

'Yes, we do.' Molly fished in her bag for the clothes list. 'The St Ursula's uniform. For my daughter.'

Two bentwood chairs were produced and Molly, drawing off her gloves, settled down.

'Where would you like to begin, madam?'

'At the top of the list, I think. One green tweed overcoat.'

'Lovely material, the overcoats are. And I'll bring the jacket and skirt as well. For Sundays, they are. For church.'

Judith, sitting down, found her attention caught by something on the other side of the department—a second mother and her daughter also shopping together. Their shop lady was young and jolly-looking, and a lot of chat and laughter seemed to be taking place. Which was extraordinary, because they too were buying the entire St

Ursula's uniform, and piles of garments, most in that deadly bottle green, were being packed into large boxes and tied up with string.

'I could have them delivered, Mrs Carey-Lewis.'

'No. We'll take them. I've got the car. I'll just need some kindly body to help me down.'

'I'll fetch young Will from the stockroom.'

Judith saw that the girl across the room was about thirteen, very thin, and long-legged and flat-chested as a boy. She wore scuffed sandals and knee stockings, a pleated tartan skirt and a dreadfully shabby navy-blue sweater that looked as though it had once belonged to some large male relation. But she was sensationally pretty, with a long, slender neck and curly dark hair cut quite short. Her eyes, beneath strong dark brows, were violet-blue, her skin the colour of honey, and when she smiled it was a wicked urchin's grin.

She sat leaning her elbows on the counter, her spindly legs wound round the legs of the chair, until the last knot was tied, the string cut with scissors. 'How will you be paying, Mrs Carey-Lewis?'

'Oh, put it on my account. That's the simplest.'

'*Mummy!* You know Pops said you had to pay right away because you always throw bills into the wastepaper basket.'

Much laughter. 'Darling, you mustn't give my secrets away.'

Mrs Carey-Lewis's voice was deep and ripe with amusement, and it was difficult to come to terms with the fact that she was anybody's mother. She looked like a film star. Fine-boned and slender, her face was made up to porcelain paleness, with arched eyebrows and a scarlet mouth. Her hair was corn-gold and silky straight, cut in a simple bob that had nothing to do with fashion and everything to do with style. She wore—and this was particularly outré—grey flannel trousers. Slacks, they were called. Over her shoulders was a short brown fur jacket. A red-tipped hand dangled by her side, holding the loop of a scarlet leather leash, the other end of which was attached to a motionless, furry, cream-coloured cushion.

'Well, that's it.' She slid her arms into the sleeves of her jacket and, in doing so, dropped the leash. 'Come along, darling, we'll go and have coffee and I'll buy you an ice cream or something.'

The furry cushion on the floor came to life, pulled itself onto four velvety feet and proceeded with much dignity across the carpet towards Judith, trailing the red leash like a royal train.

A dog. Judith adored dogs but had never been allowed one. A Pekingese. Irresistible. She crouched to greet him. 'Hello.' She laid her hand on the soft domed head, and it was like stroking cashmere.

'Pekoe! What are you up to?' His mistress came after him and Judith straightened up. Mrs Carey-Lewis stooped and picked up the leash, and Judith caught a drift of her perfume—sweet and heavy as the scent of remembered flowers in the gardens of Colombo. 'Thank you for being kind to him. Do you like Pekes?'

'I like all dogs.'

'He's very special. A lion dog. Aren't you, my darling?'

Her eyes were mesmerising, so brilliantly blue and unblinking that Judith could only stare. Mrs Carey-Lewis smiled, as though understanding, and turned to go, moving away like a queen, with her dog and her daughter and the shop assistant, beneath the pile of boxes, forming a procession behind her. As she passed Molly, she paused.

'Are you kitting your child up for St Ursula's as well?'

Molly, caught unawares, seemed taken aback. 'Yes. Yes, I am.'

'Have you *ever*, in *all* your life, seen so many hideous garments?' She was laughing. She raised her arm in a vague gesture of farewell and led her little party down the stairs.

They watched her go. For a moment nobody said anything. Their departure left behind an extraordinary vacuum, as though a light had been turned off or the sun lost behind a cloud.

Molly cleared her throat. 'Who was that?'

'That's Mrs Carey-Lewis, of Nancherrow,' said the lady in the sad black dress. 'Out beyond Rosemullion, on the Land's End road.'

'And is that her daughter?'

'Yes. That's Loveday. Her baby. She's got two older children, a girl and a boy.' Loveday. She was called Loveday Carey-Lewis. It was a marvellous name. You couldn't miss with a name like that.

'Is she going to St Ursula's as a boarder?' Judith asked.

'Weekly boarder, I believe. Going home at weekends. Apparently Colonel and Mrs Carey-Lewis sent her to a school in Hampshire, but she ran away. Got herself home on the train and said she wasn't going back, because she missed Cornwall. So they're sending her to St Ursula's instead.'

'She sounds,' said Molly, 'a little spoilt.'

'Being the baby, she's had her own way all her life.'

'Yes.' Molly looked a bit uncomfortable. 'I see ... Now, Judith, go into the fitting room and try on this gym tunic.'

By eleven o'clock they were done with Medways, and the piles of uniform were folded and boxed. For them there was no offer to carry their purchases to their car. And so, laden like a couple of packhorses, they went back to the Austin.

They still had the shoe shop and the sports shop to visit, and the saddler for an attaché case. By then it was half past twelve, so they walked down Chapel Street to the Mitre and there lunched splendidly on roast beef and apple charlotte with Cornish cream.

Afterwards they drove to the other side of town. At the top of a hill they came to a pair of gates. A sign said ST URSULA'S SCHOOL.

They turned in through the gates and onto a driveway bordered by stands of rhododendron. The house stood at the end, with a gravel sweep in front of the imposing front door. It was holiday time and there didn't seem to be anybody about.

'Do you think we should ring?' Molly asked.

'Don't let's,' Judith said. She saw that the main part of the house was quite old, with stone windowsills and Virginia creeper clambering up granite walls. Beyond this original building lay a modern wing and, at the far end, a stone archway leading into a small quadrangle.

'Let's explore the garden,' Judith said. They followed a wandering path through shrubberies. After a bit they came upon a cobbled sun trap with a bench, and it seemed a good place to sit for a moment. They faced a view of the bay, framed by eucalyptus trees.

Molly leaned back, turned her face up to the sun, closed her eyes. She said, 'What do you think?'

'It's a beautiful garden.'

Molly opened her eyes and smiled. 'Is that a comfort?'

'If you have to be shut up somewhere, it helps if it's beautiful.'

'Oh, don't say that. It makes me feel as though I were abandoning you in some sort of prison. And I don't want to leave you anywhere. I want to take you with me.'

'I'll be all right.'

'If—if you want to go to Biddy at any time, you can, you know. I'll speak to Louise. All I really want is for you to be happy.'

'I do too, but it doesn't always happen.'

'You must make it happen.'

'So must you. You mustn't be in such a state about going to Singapore. You'll probably love it. It's like going to some party. The ones you dread very often turn out to be the best fun of all.'

'Yes,' Molly sighed. 'I have to think of it as an adventure.'

A vapour, too fine to be called a cloud, drifted over the face of the sun. Judith shivered. 'I'm getting cold. Let's move.'

They strolled back to the Austin and set off for home. It had been a good day, Molly decided. Not just because they had achieved so much but because it had been done so companionably. Somehow she had crossed a difficult bridge in the relationship with her elder daughter. Perhaps she had left it rather late, but at least it was done.

OVER THE FOLLOWING days at Riverview House there seemed to be crates and boxes everywhere. Molly found another position for Phyllis, in Porthkerris, and spent much time on the telephone, speaking to the shipping company, the bank, Louise and Biddy.

'What was that about?' Judith asked, coming in on the tail end of one conversation.

153

'Oh, I think I've fixed everything. After I've taken you to St Ursula's, I'll close this house and Jess and I will spend the last night with Louise. She's promised to drive us to the station in her car.'

'How are we going to get to St Ursula's?' Judith asked. The Austin Seven had been sold to the man who ran the village filling station.

'We'll order a taxi. And it can bring Jess and me home again.'

'I don't actually want Jess to come. She'll just be a nuisance. Cry or something. And if she cries, then you will, and me too.'

'Oh, Judith. It seems a little unfair.'

'I think it's kind. Anyway, I don't suppose she'll even notice.'

But Jess was not a stupid child, and she witnessed the dismemberment of her home with considerable alarm. She had no idea what was happening; only that she liked none of it.

On the last day, they had lunch in the kitchen, the four of them sitting round Phyllis's scrubbed table. Afterwards Jess was given a tiny packet of fruit gums, which occupied her attention while her mother and Judith disappeared upstairs.

Phyllis was in the scullery, scouring saucepans, when Jess saw the strange black car turn in at the gate. Cheeks bulging with sweets, she went to tell Phyllis, who dried her hands. 'That'll be the taxi.'

Jess went with her into the hall and they let the man into the house. Luggage was piled at the foot of the stairs—the brassbound trunk, suitcases and bags. He went to and fro, manhandling everything out to his taxi. Jess stood and stared.

And then Mummy and Judith came downstairs, and Mummy had her coat and hat on, and Judith was wearing a green suit that Jess had never seen before. It was so frighteningly strange that Jess burst into hysterical weeping, clinging to her mother's coat.

It was Judith who stepped forward and picked her up and hugged her very tight, and Jess put her arms round Judith's neck and sobbed, 'Where you *going*?'

Judith had never imagined anything so dreadful would happen. 'Oh, Jess, it'll be all right. Mummy will be back very quickly.'

'I want to *come*.'

Her fat little arms and legs were unbearably soft and dear. She smelt of soap and her hair was silky as floss. It was no use recalling all the times that Judith had been cross with her. All that was important was that they were saying goodbye and that Judith loved her. She pressed kisses onto Jess's cheeks.

'You mustn't cry,' she implored. 'I'll write you letters, and you must send me lovely drawings and pictures. And just think. When I see you again, you'll be nearly as tall as I am.' Judith kissed her again and then handed her to Phyllis.

'You take care of Golly, now. Goodbye, Phyllis. I'll write.'

They embraced, but Phyllis didn't seem to be able to say anything much except, 'Good luck.'

They all trooped out of the house. Her mother dropped a kiss on Jess's damp cheek. 'I'll be back,' she promised, 'in a little while. You be a good girl for Phyllis.' Then they got into the taxi.

'Wave goodbye, Jess,' Phyllis told her, and they saw Judith's face pressed against the back window, and Judith was waving too, until the taxi trundled out of sight.

Halfway to Penzance, Judith announced that she wanted their goodbyes to be quick. She could manage, she said. She did not want her mother to go into the school with her.

And so it only took moments. A porter dealt with her trunk and her suitcases. There were other children there in their green uniforms, and all at once Judith was one of them. Molly looked into her face and saw there the promise of a beauty which would be evident when they were together again. They kissed and hugged, promised to write, and then Judith was gone, walking away, up the steps and through the open door. She didn't look back.

THE HEAD GIRL of St Ursula's was a strapping creature named Deirdre Ledingham, who took her responsibilities with great seriousness: ringing bells, escorting the long, straggly line of girls, weekly, to church, and each day standing behind a large oak table in the main hall handing out the mail.

'Emily Backhouse. Joan Betworthy.'

A large, heavy parcel, plastered in foreign stamps. 'Judith Dunbar?'

'She's not here,' somebody said.

'Well, someone fetch her. Who's in her dorm?'

'I am.'

The girl who had spoken was Loveday Carey-Lewis. Deirdre frowned. She had decided that this newcomer was altogether too big for her boots, and a small penance seemed to be in order. 'No, you'd better take it to her. Mind you don't drop it.'

Loveday moved forward, gathered up the enormous parcel and set off up the wide staircase. Her burden became heavier with each step. What on earth could be in it? She reached the landing, went to the door of her dormitory and staggered in.

Judith was there, washing ink off her hands in the single basin which the six girls in the dorm shared. 'I've found you,' said Loveday, and she tipped the parcel onto Judith's bed and collapsed beside it.

Her unexpected appearance, bouncing in like a jack-in-the-box, caused Judith to be overcome by a painful shyness. From that moment in Medways when she had first set eyes on the Carey-Lewis mother and daughter, she had thought Loveday fascinating and

155

longed to get to know her. But during their first few weeks at St Ursula's, Loveday had totally ignored her presence, leaving Judith with the sad conviction that she was such a nonentity that Loveday did not even recognise her. Now she was here.

'You weren't at Letters. Deirdre told me to bring you this. It weighs a ton. Do come and open it; I want to know what's inside.'

Judith reached for a towel. 'I think it's a Christmas present.'

'Christmas present! But it's February.'

'I know. It's taken ages.' She joined Loveday on the bed, the impressive package between them. She saw the stamps and smiled. 'It's come from Ceylon. My father works there.'

'What about your mother? Where is she?'

'She's just gone back to be with him. She's taken my little sister, Jess, with her.'

'You mean you're all *alone*? Goodness, that's awful. I didn't know. When I saw you in the shop—'

'So you *did* see me?'

'Yes, of course. Do you think I'm blind?'

'No. It's just that you didn't talk to me. I thought you hadn't recognised me.'

'Well, you haven't talked to *me*,' Loveday mocked, her vivid face alight with amusement. 'Anyway, we're talking now.' She laid her hand on the parcel. 'Do open it. I'm bursting to see what's inside.'

But Judith couldn't open the present in a hurry. She had waited so long for the cedarwood box, and now it was here, and she wanted to keep the excitement alive.

'There's no time now. I'll do it later. We'll open it together before supper. It'll be something lovely to look forward to all afternoon.'

'Oh, all right.' Loveday was persuaded, but obviously against her will. 'How you can be so strong-minded I can't imagine.'

'It just makes it last longer.'

'Have you got a photo of your dad?' Loveday's eyes moved to Judith's white-painted chest of drawers, identical to the other five around the dormitory.

'Yes.' She reached for it and handed it to Loveday.

'He looks quite nice. And is this your mother? Yes, of course, I recognise her. Would you like to see my photographs?'

'Oh, yes, please.'

They got up from the bed and went to Loveday's end of the dormitory. The school rule was that you were allowed two photographs, but Loveday had about six.

'This is Mummy, all dressed up in her white fox furs. And this is Pops...Isn't he heaven? And Tiger, his labrador. And this is my sister Athena and my brother Edward.'

Judith had never imagined anyone could have such a handsome, glamorous lot of relations, all looking as though they had stepped from the pages of a society magazine. 'How old is Athena?'

'She's eighteen. She had her London season last year and then went off to Switzerland to learn French. She's still there.'

'What will she do when she comes back?'

'Stay in London probably. Mummy's got a little house in Cadogan Mews. Athena's got strings of boyfriends, and she's always going away for the weekend and things.'

It sounded an enviable existence. 'She looks like a film star,' Judith said a little wistfully. 'And your brother?'

'Edward? He's sixteen. He's at Harrow.'

The building was suddenly rent by the clangour of the lunch bell. 'Oh, bother,' said Judith. 'We'd better go. We'll open the parcel later.'

'I can't wait.'

AFTER THAT, it felt as if the whole colour of the day had miraculously changed. She got eight out of ten for her French verb test, and when it was time for games she even enjoyed hockey, whacking the leather ball with effortless precision. And then it was tea, and then prep, and, at last, time to change for supper. She fled upstairs, two at a time, to the dormitory and tore off her clothes. She managed to grab a bathroom before anyone else got there, but even so, by the time she returned to the dormitory, Loveday was waiting, sitting on Judith's bed dressed in the green gabardine frock which was their regulation garb for evenings.

'Gosh, you've been quick!' Judith exclaimed.

'Hurry up. I've got my nail scissors here to cut the string.'

Judith flung on her dress, slapped a brush over her hair and was ready. She cut the string, then had to pick away at the coarse stitches with which the heavy outer wrapping had been sewn into place. Then there was a thick wadding of newspaper covered with strange Eastern characters. Everything smelt spicy and foreign. The last wrapping was shiny white paper. This was torn away and, at last, the Christmas gift was revealed. They sat and gazed at it.

'It's divine,' Loveday breathed.

It was indeed more splendid than Judith had dared to hope. The wood was the colour of honey, smooth as satin and intricately carved. Its ornamental latch was silver, embossed in a flowerlike design, and a Chinese lock slipped into this like a little padlock. The key was fastened by a strip of glued paper to the lid of the box. With it, Judith opened the padlock, and then she raised the lid to reveal two miniature chests of drawers. The scent of cedar filled the air.

Loveday said, 'Did you *know* it was going to be like this?'

'Something like this. My mother had one in Colombo, but not

nearly as lovely.' She opened one of the little drawers. It slid smoothly, revealing a gleaming red-lacquer finish within.

'What a place to keep your treasures! Goodness, you're lucky. Let's close it up again and then I can have a go with the key...'

They might have played with it for ever had not Matron come bouncing into the dormitory. She heard their voices and flung back the cubicle curtains. Startled, they looked up to see her glaring at them. 'What are you two doing, whispering away? You know you're not allowed in cubicles together.'

Judith opened her mouth to apologise, but Loveday, not frightened of anybody, said, 'Look, Matron, isn't it gorgeous? Judith got it from her father in Ceylon. Do look, it's got darling little drawers.' She opened one to show Matron in such a beguiling manner that Matron's fury abated and she even took a step forward to peer through her spectacles at the object.

'I must say,' she admitted, 'that's a pretty thing, but where on earth are you going to keep it, Judith? There's no space in your locker.'

'I suppose I could take it to Aunt Louise's at half-term.'

'Haven't *you* got somewhere safe, Matron?' Loveday cajoled. 'In a sickroom cupboard, maybe? Just for the time being?'

'Well, I'll see. Meanwhile, clear up that mess before the supper bell goes. And back you go to your own cubicle, Loveday.'

'Thank you, Matron.' Loveday smiled sweetly and Matron turned and stalked off. They kept straight faces until she was out of earshot, and then dissolved into giggles.

MATRON TOOK the box and put it in the bottom of the first-aid cupboard. That Sunday, Judith wrote to thank her father. On Wednesday of the following week, when she presented herself to collect her mail, she was told by Deirdre Ledingham that Miss Catto wanted to see her right away.

Judith's heart dropped. Eyes turned towards her as though she had done something dreadfully wicked. She did a quick dig-around in her conscience and came up with nothing. Terrified, she went off.

Miss Catto, the headmistress, was held in much respect by the girls, and when she made an entrance, black academic gown flowing behind her, at prayers or meals in the dining room, the entire school fell silent and rose to its collective feet.

Miss Catto's study stood at the end of a long corridor. Dry-mouthed, Judith rapped on the door and heard, 'Come in.'

Miss Catto sat behind her desk. 'Oh, Judith. Come, sit down.'

Judith closed the door, went into the room and sat down. It was a bright morning, the study flooded with sunlight. There was a jug of wild primroses on Miss Catto's desk.

'Stop looking so agonised, Judith. I just want to have a word.' She leaned back in her chair. 'How are you getting on?'

'All right, thank you, Miss Catto.'

For all her elevated position, Miss Catto was comparatively young—not yet forty—with a fresh complexion and clear blue eyes. She smiled. 'Have you heard from your mother?'

'Yes. I got a letter that was posted in Gibraltar.'

'I'm glad. Now, you seem to have made friends with Loveday Carey-Lewis?'

Did Miss Catto miss nothing? 'Yes.'

'What's happened is that Mrs Carey-Lewis phoned me. Loveday wants to take you home for a weekend. Would you like to go?'

'Like to?' Judith could scarcely believe her ears. 'Oh, Miss Catto, I'd love to.'

'You must understand that it's a great privilege, because officially half-term is the only weekend that boarders are allowed away. But in the circumstances I think it might be good for you.'

'Oh, thank you.'

'You'll go with Loveday on Saturday morning. I'll telephone your Aunt Louise. As your legal guardian, she must know. So . . .' Her smile was a dismissal. She rose to her feet, and Judith scrambled to hers. 'I'll let Mrs Carey-Lewis know. Off you go now.'

'Yes, Miss Catto, and thank you so much.'

She ran Loveday to earth in her classroom, waiting for the luncheon bell. 'You beast, Loveday! You brute!'

But Loveday saw her rosy, ecstatic face and shrieked with glee. 'She said *yes!*' They clung to each other, leapt up and down in a wild dance of delight. 'I never thought she would.'

'But you never told me that you'd asked your mother.'

'I promised I wouldn't, because we were afraid Miss Catto would refuse permission. And I've nearly burst keeping it secret. Oh, I can't wait . . . What are you suddenly looking so gloomy about?'

'I've just remembered. I haven't any home clothes. All my things are at Aunt Louise's.'

'Oh, heavens, that doesn't matter. You can borrow some.'

There was no time for more as the bell began to clang.

'The best thing about going home,' said Loveday in her loud and carrying voice, 'is that there are no bloody bells,' which earned her an order mark from her shocked form prefect.

AT TEN O'CLOCK on Saturday morning they were both packed and ready to leave. They had even rescued the cedarwood box from a disapproving Matron. With Judith carrying her new treasure, and Loveday an overnight bag in each hand, out of the door they went.

It was a wonderful day, cold and windy, with great white clouds scudding across the starch-blue sky. The car was already there, with Mrs Carey-Lewis behind the wheel. It was a new Bentley, navy blue, and Mrs Carey-Lewis had let the top down.

She raised an arm as they appeared. 'There you are, darlings.'

'Mummy, this is Judith.'

'Hello, Judith. Lovely to see you. Heavens, that box looks heavy. Put it all on the back seat. Now, everybody settled?' She switched on the ignition, the engine purred and they were off.

Judith settled back in the padded leather seat and heaved a great secret sigh of pleasure. As they swept out through the school gates, Loveday chattered. 'We decided at the last moment to bring the box, and Matron was livid, wasn't she, Judith? I don't think she likes us much. Mummy, who's home this weekend? Anybody exciting?'

'Not really. Only Tommy Mortimer, down from London.'

'Oho! Tommy *Mortimer*. He's Mummy's boyfriend,' Loveday explained to Judith. 'He brings her gorgeous chocolates.'

'Oh, Loveday, you are ridiculous.' But her mother didn't sound annoyed, simply amused. 'You mustn't believe a word this child says, Judith, but you've probably found that out already.'

'It's true! Athena says he's been swooning over you for years; that's why he never married. Have you had a letter from Athena?'

'Oh, darling, you know she's hopeless at letters. But we did have a scrawl from Edward to tell us that he's in the second pair for rackets. And Jeremy Wells turned up this morning. He and Pops and Tommy have disappeared into the woods to shoot pigeons.'

'Jeremy. Oh, good. I haven't seen him for ages.' To Judith she said, 'He used to be Edward's tutor when he was trying to get into Harrow. His father is our doctor. Pops simply loves Jeremy.'

Judith was beginning to be a bit nervous. So many people and so much going on, and all so worldly, so alien to anything she had ever experienced. She hoped that during the next two days she would not commit some gauche social blunder and so embarrass everybody, especially herself. As for Loveday, she had never heard any child speak to her mother in such a way, gossiping, teasing her about a boyfriend. Tommy Mortimer. He, more than anybody, was a source of wonder. The mothers Judith knew simply did not have boyfriends. It was all going to be extremely interesting.

By now they had left the town behind them, driven through a small fishing village and climbed a steep hill onto the empty country which lay beyond. The narrow road wound and twisted, following the contours of meandering dry-stone walls, the boundaries of random farms, the buildings of which could be glimpsed, low-roofed and ancient, huddled against the wind. Gentle hills swept down to the cliffs and the dazzling sun-speckled sea. It was very different from the other side of Cornwall. Judith said, 'It's so beautiful.'

Mrs Carey-Lewis smiled. 'It's not far from Penmarron. Nowhere in Cornwall is very far from anywhere else.'

'It is if you haven't got a car.'

'Didn't your mother have a car?'

'Yes. An Austin Seven. But she wasn't very fond of driving it.'

Mrs Carey-Lewis was silent for a moment and then, 'What do you call your mother?' Which was, thought Judith, a fairly odd question.

'Mummy.'

'And what are you going to call me?'

'Mrs Carey-Lewis.'

'Very right and proper too. But I simply hate being called Mrs Carey-Lewis. I always think people are talking to my mother-in-law.' Judith could think of absolutely nothing to say to this, but Mrs Carey-Lewis just went on talking. 'I really like being called Diana.' She turned her head to smile at Judith. 'So let's start as we mean to go on. Say my name now, aloud.'

'Diana.'

'Shout it to the world.'

'Diana!'

'Much better. Now all together . . .'

'Diana!'

Their voices were blown away by the wind. The road, a grey ribbon, wound ahead of them, and they were all laughing.

After another ten miles or so they were in a district of running streams and deep wooded valleys. Rosemullion lay ahead, a cluster of whitewashed cottages, a pub and an ancient church. Then the road climbed steeply again, and at the crest of the hill it levelled off and the impressive gateway came into view—curved walls enclosing tall wrought-iron gates which framed a long wooded drive. The Bentley swung in through the entrance. 'This is it. Nancherrow,' said Diana.

As the road wound on, Judith fell silent. Everything was a bit overpowering. She began to suspect that Nancherrow was not a house at all, but a castle. 'It's such a long drive,' she finally said.

Diana laughed. 'Yes. The old house burnt down in 1910. My father-in-law built another—larger and much more convenient. Just the most wonderful home that we all adore.'

At last the road turned a final corner and the house stood revealed. It was of local granite, slate-roofed like any traditional farmhouse, with long windows on the two floors and a line of dormer windows above these. Its eastern wall was smothered with clematis and climbing roses, and all about stretched green lawns and ornamental flowerbeds. At the front of the house these lawns took the form of terraces, with flights of stone steps. In the distance could be glimpsed the blue horizon and the sea.

For all its splendour it wasn't frightening in any way. From that first moment Judith fell in love with Nancherrow. Now she knew exactly why Loveday had run away from school in Hampshire and found her way back to this magical place.

The Bentley drew to a halt outside the front door. They piled out, gathering up possessions, and filed indoors, Judith bringing up the rear. Up stone steps they went, through a flagged porch and into the central hallway. It all seemed enormous, but the immediate impression was of a family house, friendly and unpretentious.

The walls of the hallway were panelled in wood, and polished floors were scattered with worn Persian rugs. The wide staircase rose in three straight flights to the upper landing. In the middle of the hall was a round table, on which stood a tureen with white narcissi, a dog lead or two and a stack of mail.

Diana paused at the table. 'Off you go, then, Loveday, and take care of Judith. I think Mary's in the nursery. The men are coming in for lunch at one, so don't be late.' And with that she picked up her letters and was on her way, walking down the long, wide hallway furnished with antique furniture and ornate mirrors.

'Come on. Let's find Mary. She's my old nanny.'

Loveday headed up the stairs, lugging their overnight bags. Judith followed with her box. At the top of the stairs was another long passage. Loveday broke into a run. 'Mary!'

'Here I am, pet!'

The Nancherrow nursery was a large, sun-filled sitting room, with a great bay window and a view of the garden and that distant sparkling horizon. It had bookcases, sofas and chairs with flowery loose covers, and a round table covered with a blue cloth. Other delights stood all about: cheerful pictures, a radio, a fireplace, a basket of knitting. The only concessions to nursery life were a battered rocking horse and an ironing board.

This board was set up, and at it Mary Millyway had been hard at work. 'Well, here you are.' Mary set down her iron and opened her arms to Loveday, who flung herself into them for a huge hug. 'There's my wicked baby.' Releasing Loveday, Mary said, 'So this is your friend. What's this you've brought with you?'

'It's my cedarwood box.'

'It looks as though it weighs a ton. Put it on the table, for goodness' sake.' Which Judith gratefully did.

Loveday explained. 'We wanted to show it to Mummy. Judith got it for Christmas. This is Judith, Mary.'

Mary Millyway. A tall and rawboned Cornishwoman no more

than thirty-five, with coarse fair hair and a freckled face, and wearing a grey tweed skirt and a white cotton blouse.

'Hello, Judith. You look older than I thought you'd be.'

'I'm fourteen.'

'She's in a form above me,' Loveday explained, 'but we're in the same dormitory. And, Mary, she hasn't got any home clothes and mine will be too small for her. Is there something of Athena's she can borrow? Something she doesn't want any more.'

'There certainly is. Never known such a girl for wearing things once and then throwing them away. I'll tell you what—you take Judith and show her where she's sleeping. The pink room. And when I've finished my ironing I'll see what I can find.'

'All right.' Loveday grinned at Judith. 'Come on,' and she was off. Judith, pausing only to grab up her bag, had to run to keep up. At the far end the passage took a turn to the right, and another rambling wing was revealed. 'It's all so big,' Judith said in wonder.

'I know, it's huge, isn't it? But it has to be because there are always people coming to stay. This is the guest wing.'

They reached the last door, and like every other room in this delectable house it was panelled in wood. It had two windows, hung in a chintz of toile de Jouy. The carpet was pink, and there was a high brass bed and a huge Victorian wardrobe.

'Do you like it?'

'It's lovely.'

Judith saw a kidney-shaped skirted dressing table with a triple mirror and a proper armchair with pink cushions.

'And this is your bathroom.'

Quite overwhelming. She went to inspect it and saw the black-and-white-checked floor, the huge bath, immense white towels.

Loveday returned to the bedroom to fling wide a window. 'And this is your view, but you have to peer a bit to see the sea.'

Judith joined her, and they stood side by side, feeling the wind on their faces. Below them was a large cobbled courtyard, in the middle of which stood a dovecote. White pigeons flew about, to fill the air with their satisfied cooing. Beyond the courtyard was a gravelled road and then mown grass, rolling away to a line of trees.

Judith leaned out a little further. 'Is that a stable?'

'No. You can't see the stables from here. But I'll take you after lunch to meet my pony, Tinkerbell. You can ride her if you like.'

'I've never ridden a horse,' Judith admitted, not admitting at the same time that she was frightened of horses.

'Tinkerbell's adorable, and she never bites or bucks.' Loveday paused. 'It's Saturday, so maybe Walter will be there.'

'Who's Walter?'

'Walter Mudge. His father farms Lidgey—that's the home farm. Walter's really nice. He's sixteen. He sometimes comes at weekends to muck out the horses.' Abruptly Loveday withdrew her head. 'I'm getting cold. Come on. Let's do your unpacking.'

There wasn't very much to unpack. When they had finished, Loveday kicked the empty bag under the bed. 'Now let's go and see if Mary dug up something for you to wear.'

And she was off again, racing away back to the nursery.

They found Mary kneeling in front of a tall armoire, with the deep bottom drawer opened and various garments set around her.

Loveday couldn't wait. 'What have you found? Mary, this is a new jersey. Athena got it last hols. What's it doing in this drawer?'

'You may well ask. She caught the elbow on a bit of barbed wire. I mended it, but would she wear it? Not her, the little madam.'

'Here . . .' Loveday tossed it to Judith, who caught it, and it was like catching thistledown, so weightless and soft was the wool. Cashmere. And holly-red, one of her favourite colours.

'Now, here's a nice gingham blouse. And a pair of shorts.' The shorts were navy flannel, pleated like a little skirt.

Loveday approved. 'Those'll do, won't they, Judith? Go and put them on, because I want to show you everything else.'

Back in her bedroom, Judith took off her uniform and dressed in Athena Carey-Lewis's castoffs. She brushed her hair, tying it back with a fresh navy-blue ribbon, and inspected herself in the long mirror set in the wardrobe door. And it was amazing, because she looked so different, almost grown-up. She could not help smiling.

The door burst open. Loveday had pulled on a disreputable pair of jodhpurs, which were already too short for her skinny shins, and a shapeless sweater of dark purple, which had darns in the elbows. 'Are you ready?' she demanded. 'Goodness, you look nice. It must be something to do with Athena. She always looks sensational. Perhaps she magics everything she wears. Now let's explore the house, and then you'll know your way around. You've seen the guest wing, so we'll start with Mummy's room.'

'Are we allowed?'

'Oh, yes. She doesn't mind, provided we don't fiddle and squirt all her scent.' She opened the door and pranced ahead of Judith. 'Isn't it gorgeous?'

Wordless, Judith gazed about. She had never seen such a bedroom. The walls were pale, neither white nor pink nor peach. There were thick swagged draperies smothered in roses, and inside these a drift of filmy white curtains. The bed was draped in the same filmy white, with a canopy over it, like a bed in which a princess might sleep.

A thought occurred to Judith about the sweet-scented, flowery bedroom. 'Where does your father put his things?'

'Oh, Pops has got his own bedroom because he snores and keeps everybody awake. Come on, I'll show you more.'

After a tour of the other family bedrooms they went downstairs.

'This is Pops's study. And in here the billiard room; sometimes the men come here after dinner and play. And the dining room, all laid for lunch, as you can see. Come and meet Mrs Nettlebed.'

'Who's that?'

'Our cook, and she's married to Mr Nettlebed, our butler. They have a little flat over the garage.'

A butler. It was all becoming grander and grander.

And so they came at last to the kitchen. This was the same as most Cornish kitchens, except that it was much larger. There was the familiar rack for airing clothes, hoisted high to the ceiling, the dresser loaded with china, the table in the middle of the floor.

At this stood Mrs Nettlebed, arranging bits of glacé fruit onto the top of a trifle. She was a small, dumpy lady in a white apron and cap. When Loveday burst in, Mrs Nettlebed's round cheeks bunched up into a besotted expression of pure delight. Loveday, it was instantly obvious, was her treasure and her joy.

'My dear life. There's my baby!' She held her sticky hands wide and leaned forward for the kiss which Loveday pressed upon her cheek. 'Look at you! Soon be taller than me. This is your friend?'

'She's called Judith.'

'Pleased to meet you, Judith. Come for the weekend? Up to high jinks you'll be with this little tinker.'

'What's for lunch, Mrs Nettlebed?'

'Shooter's stew and boiled cabbage. I just heard the men in the yard. Shouldn't be more than ten minutes.'

'Ten minutes.' Loveday made a face. 'I'm starving. Come on, Judith. Let's go and find Mummy.'

They found Diana in the drawing room, curled up in the corner of a vast cream sofa, reading a novel. She raised her head to smile a welcome. 'Darlings, there you are. What do you want to drink?'

A mirrored table stood against one wall, neatly arranged with bottles and glasses. Loveday went to inspect its offerings. She said, 'I really feel like Orange Corona, but there isn't any.'

'That dreadful stuff that turns your mouth orange? Ring for Nettlebed, and we'll find out if he has a bottle tucked away.'

Loveday pressed a bell in the wall above the table. Diana asked Judith, 'What do you think of my darling house?'

'It's beautiful. But I'm not sure that this room isn't the nicest of all.' With a parquet floor scattered with rugs, it was filled with sunlight and exotic hothouse blooms, all purple and white and fuchsia.

The curtains and loose covers were cream brocade, the sofas and chairs filled with cushions in pale greens and pinks and blues.

The door behind them quietly opened and a deep voice was heard. 'You rang, madam?'

Loveday had not prepared Judith for Mr Nettlebed's awesome appearance. He was tall, white-haired and quite handsome in a gloomy way. Judith wondered how anybody plucked up the nerve to ask him to do anything, let alone give him an order.

'Oh, Nettlebed, thank you,' said Diana. 'Loveday wants some Orange Corona. Would you see if there is any in the pantry?'

'Certainly,' said Nettlebed. 'I shall go and ascertain.'

He went, closing the door behind him. Loveday grimaced. 'He's a pompous old—'

'*Loveday,*' Diana interrupted. Her voice had turned icy.

Judith felt awkward, but Loveday was undismayed. She went to lean over the back of the sofa, her curly dark head almost touching her mother's sleek golden one. 'What are you reading?'

'A novel.'

'What's it about?'

'Love. Unhappy love.'

'I thought all love was happy.'

'Oh, darling. Not every woman is lucky.' She reached for her drink, a little triangular cocktail glass filled with silvery liquid. As she took a sip, the door of the drawing room opened once more.

'Pops!' Loveday left her mother's side and fled into his arms.

'Hello, my baby.' They hugged and kissed, he stooping to her. 'We've missed you.' He ruffled her hair, smiling down at his youngest child. So loved was Loveday by everybody that Judith found it hard not to feel a small pang of envy.

'Diana'—he crossed over to kiss his wife—'are we late?'

She tilted her head to smile up into his face. 'Not at all. Did you have a good morning?'

'Splendid. Tommy's on his way, and Jeremy's cleaning my gun.'

Standing on the sidelines, Judith assumed a bland expression, hiding her shock at his appearance. For Colonel Carey-Lewis was so much older than in the photo she had seen that he looked more like Diana's father than her husband. True, he held himself with the stance of a soldier, but his hair was white, his nose long and beaky, and his eyes, deep in his lined face, were the faded blue of some ancient countryman. He was tall and spare, dressed in venerable tweeds and moleskin knickerbockers.

He turned to Judith. 'And you must be Loveday's friend?'

She looked up into his eyes and saw them both watchful and kindly. Then he smiled. 'How very pleasant that you could come,' he said, and they shook hands formally. She realised instinctively that he was just as shy as she felt. This made her like him very much.

At this moment they were interrupted by the appearance of a second gentleman with Nettlebed hard on his heels.

'Diana, are we all in disgrace for taking so long?'

'Oh, darling Tommy, don't be silly. Had a good morning?'

'Great fun.' Tommy Mortimer stood for an instant rubbing his hands together, as though grateful to be out of the cold. He too was dressed for shooting, in elegant tweeds and a canary-coloured waistcoat. His face was boyish and good-humoured, his whole manner theatrical. *Here I am*, it seemed to say. *Now we can all start having a wonderful time.*

He crossed the room to drop a kiss on Diana's cheek, then turned to Loveday. 'Hello there, wicked one! Got a kiss for your honorary uncle? How's school? Have they turned you into a lady yet?'

'Oh, Tommy, don't ask such stupid questions. This is Judith Dunbar, and this, ta-ra, ta-ra, is Tommy Mortimer.'

Tommy laughed, amused by her impudence. The Colonel by now had had enough of formalities. It was time for a drink. Nettlebed poured a dry martini for Mr Mortimer, beer for the Colonel, Orange Corona for the girls. Tommy came to sit on the sofa beside Diana, with an arm gracefully disposed along the back of the cushions. Judith wondered if he was an actor.

As she sipped her Orange Corona, she did not notice the last member of the shooting party enter the room: a much younger man, bespectacled, dressed in corduroys and a hefty sweater. Judith looked up and saw him watching her. For an instant they stared, and then he smiled. 'It is you, isn't it? The girl on the train?'

He came across the room to her side. Judith was so delighted that she was unable to speak, so she simply nodded.

'What an extraordinary coincidence. Are you Loveday's friend?'

She smiled and nodded again. 'I'm Judith Dunbar.'

'Jeremy Wells.'

'Jeremy!' From the sofa, Diana had spied him. 'You must have tiptoed in. Are you introducing yourself to Judith?'

He laughed. 'We've already met. On the train.'

Everybody was suitably amazed by the coincidence and wanted to hear all the details of how they had shared the compartment and gazed from the Saltash Bridge at the naval men-of-war.

'How's your little sister?' Jeremy asked.

'She's gone back to Colombo with my mother. And then they're moving to Singapore. My father's got a new job.'

'Will you be joining them?'

'No. Not for years.'

It was lovely. It was like being a grown-up—dressed in Athena's clothes, and sipping a drink, and having everybody delighted because she had a friend of her own. She remembered telling Phyllis about him and saying, *I wouldn't mind meeting somebody like that.* And now he was here. It had really happened.

From the hall, the gong for luncheon rang out. Diana handed her empty glass to Tommy Mortimer, rose to her feet, and led the way to the dining room.

THE COLONEL SAT at the head of the long dining table, with Loveday and Judith placed on either side. Diana was at the far end, with Tommy on her left and Jeremy on her right. Mary Millyway, who had appeared as they all settled down, had taken her seat and was talking to Jeremy—whom she had obviously known for ever—being brought up to date on his work at the hospital.

The meal was delicious. The stew was dark and rich, with a winy sauce, and the cabbage, lightly dusted with grated nutmeg, was green and sweet. Having handed round the plates, Nettlebed had withdrawn from the room, to Judith's relief. His chilling presence was enough to make anybody knock over a glass of water or use the wrong fork. Now, however, she was beginning to enjoy herself. The Colonel was being very courteous, making her feel at home.

Pudding was treacle tart and bottled plums and Cornish cream. Judith spooned cream over her treacle tart and heard Tommy Mortimer and Diana laying plans for London—for the Chelsea Flower Show, and Wimbledon and Henley and Ascot.

All at once, Diana became aware of Judith. She smiled. 'I'm sorry. We're being boring. And this is your day. Tell me, what do you want to do this afternoon?' She raised her voice slightly. 'What does everybody want to do this afternoon?'

Loveday said, 'I want to ride Tinkerbell.'

'Darling, what about Judith? Perhaps it would be kind to do something that she wants to do.'

'I don't mind,' Judith said, fearing some sort of argument, but Loveday didn't seem to care about arguments or rows.

'Oh, Mummy, I really want to ride Tinkerbell. And it's not good for her not being regularly exercised.'

'I don't want you going out on your own.'

'She won't be on her own,' the Colonel told her. 'Young Walter's down at the stables this afternoon. I'll send word to him to have the horses saddled up and ready.'

Down the table he indulgently regarded his wife. 'How are you going to spend the rest of the day? I've letters to write.'

'Oh, Tommy and I are all arranged for. I've asked the Parker-Browns over for bridge. But that still doesn't solve the problem of our guest.'

Judith felt dreadfully embarrassed, a tiresome nuisance. Then Jeremy Wells said, 'Why don't I do something with Judith? We'll all go down to the stables, and she and I will take the dogs on down to the cove.' He smiled at Judith, and she was filled with gratitude because he had come to her rescue. 'Would you like to do that?'

'Yes, I'd love it.'

Diana beamed. 'Well, isn't that splendid? Everything settled. Judith, you'll adore the cove, our own little beach. Now, why don't we go to the drawing room and have coffee?'

The two girls stayed in the dining room to help Mary and Nettlebed clear the table and then went upstairs to prepare for their expeditions. Mary produced extra pullovers for them and said, 'Off with you now. And when you get back I'll have tea ready here.'

Like puppies escaping, they galloped downstairs to the drawing room. Loveday opened the door. 'Jeremy! We're ready.'

'I'll meet you in the gunroom. In one minute.'

They went on their way. The back passage led to the gunroom, which smelt pleasantly of linseed oil and old mackintoshes and dog. Tiger was there, ready for a bit of exercise. He was a huge black labrador, with a tail that wagged like a piston.

'Hello, darling Tiger. Are you going to come for a lovely walk?'

'Of course he is,' said Jeremy, coming in with Pekoe.

Loveday said, 'Come on, then. Walter will be waiting.'

The stables lay a little way from the house, screened from sight by a coppice of young oak trees. They approached the yard, where two mounts were saddled up and tethered to iron rings set in the wall: Tinkerbell and Ranger. Tinkerbell was a charming little grey pony, but Ranger, the Colonel's hunter, was a great bay, seeming, to the wary Judith, the size of an elephant.

A young man stood with the animals, tightening the girth strap of the little grey. 'Hello, Walter,' Loveday called. 'This is my friend, Judith Dunbar.'

Walter nodded at Judith. He said, 'Hello.'

He was extraordinarily good-looking—slim and dark and sunburnt as a gypsy, with black hair that covered his head in curls and eyes dark as coffee beans. He wore corduroy breeches, a thick shirt striped in blue, and a leather waistcoat. He made Judith think of Heathcliff in *Wuthering Heights*, and she could see why Loveday was so keen to go riding. Even Judith could understand the lure of the horse if one was to have the dashing companionship of Walter Mudge.

Judith and Jeremy stood and watched them mount. Walter swung himself up into the saddle with an effortless grace that suggested that he might, just slightly, be showing off.

'Have fun,' Judith told Loveday.

She raised her crop. 'You too.'

As the entourage disappeared round the oak coppice, Judith asked, 'Where will they go?'

'Probably up to the moor. Come on. It's too cold to stand.'

They went the way that the riders had taken and then turned off to the right, where the path sloped down through the gardens. The dogs shot ahead and were soon lost to view. 'They won't get lost, will they?' Judith, feeling responsible for their well-being, was anxious, but Jeremy reassured her.

'They know this walk as well as anybody. By the time we've reached the cove, they'll be there.'

He led the way and she followed, along a winding gravelled path which led to the sea. The formal lawns and flowerbeds were left behind them as they passed through a small wrought-iron gate. Then the path narrowed and plunged downwards into a jungle of semitropical vegetation—camellias, lush thickets of bamboo and

tall-stemmed palms. A stream appeared from the undergrowth and tumbled its way down a rocky bed. The path where they walked crossed and recrossed the stream by means of ornamental wooden bridges that were vaguely oriental in design.

Over the last bridge, Jeremy paused, waiting for Judith to catch up. 'How are you doing?'

'All right.'

'Well done. Now we come to the tunnel.'

Judith saw that, ahead, the sloping path plunged into a cavern of prickly-stemmed plants with leaves as large as umbrellas. She ducked her head and followed her guide into the tunnel. It was like being under water, so damp was everything, so aqueous and green.

Moments later they emerged from the primeval gloom and stood once more in the bright winter afternoon. The air smelt of seaweed and she knew that they were close to the beach. They climbed a grassy bank and then jumped down onto a narrow farm road. On the far side of this was a dry-stone wall and then there were there

were the cliffs and the sea—intensely blue, flecked with whitecaps.

As Jeremy had promised, the dogs were already there. Otherwise there was no living soul to be seen.

'Does anybody ever come here?' Judith asked.

'No. I think most people don't even realise that the cove exists.'

Jeremy climbed down to a wide shelf of rock overhanging the sand, and she followed. He smiled at her. 'It's such a perfect place. This rock is where we have picnics. Let's sit down for a moment.'

Shifting about to find a perch on the hard rock, Judith was warmed by the dazzling sunshine and the easy presence of her companion.

She said, 'I'm glad you brought me to see it. But I hope you don't feel that you had to.'

'Don't worry. I wanted to come. I like it here.' He sat with his elbows on his knees, squinting out to sea through his spectacles.

They fell silent. Judith thought of Loveday and Walter, probably cantering over the moors, but the tiny twinge of envy she had known was gone. Better to be here, and with this nice man.

After a bit she said, 'You know it all so well here, don't you? I mean Nancherrow. As though it were your own home.'

Jeremy leaned back on his elbows. 'I've been coming here for years. I got to know the Carey-Lewises because of my father being their family doctor. Then as I grew older, the Colonel sort of took me under his wing, began to ask me to shoot with him.'

'And Athena and Edward? Are they your friends too?'

'They're a good deal younger than me, but yes. When Athena was first going to dances, I used to be given the responsibility of being her partner—not that she ever danced with me, but I was considered reliable enough to get her home in one piece.'

'She's very beautiful, isn't she?'

'Ravishing. Like her mother. Men fall about her like ninepins.'

'And Edward?'

'Edward I got to know very well, because when I was a medical student I was perpetually short of cash, so the Colonel offered me a holiday job when Edward needed extra coaching to get into Harrow. So I spent a good deal of time around and about.'

'I see why you seem to be part of the family.'

'One becomes absorbed. And you? Had you any idea what to expect when you were invited to Nancherrow?'

'Not really.'

'The first impression is something of an experience. But I don't think you've been overwhelmed.'

'No.' She thought about this. 'But only because they're all so nice. If they weren't, it would be a bit frightening. I mean, butlers and ponies and nannies. Is Colonel Carey-Lewis frightfully rich?'

172

'The money is Diana's. She was the only child of an immensely wealthy gentleman called Lord Awliscombe. When he died, she was well provided for.'

Diana, it seemed, had been blessed with everything. 'She must have had a very special fairy godmother. To be so beautiful and wealthy and charming. And still so young.'

'She was only seventeen when she married Edgar. He's much older than Diana, of course, but he adored her all her life and finally won her. And it's been a great marriage.'

'If he loves her so, doesn't he mind about Tommy Mortimer?'

Jeremy laughed. 'Do you think he should mind?'

She was embarrassed, as though she had sounded like some dreadful prig. 'No, of course not. It just seems...' She floundered. 'I wondered if he was an actor.'

'All those expansive gestures and the mellifluous voice? An easy mistake to make. No. He's a jeweller. His family owns Mortimer's, in Regent Street. His great cry is that he loves only Diana, but I think he enjoys being a bachelor and playing the field. He looks after Diana when she disappears up to London, and he comes down here when he feels in need of a spot of fresh air.'

It was still difficult to understand. 'Doesn't the Colonel *mind*?'

'I don't think so. They've worked out their own lives. Diana has this little mews house in London, and she needs to escape to the city from time to time. Edgar hates London. His life is Nancherrow and the farm and the estate. A busy man.'

At this juncture the dogs, having had enough of sand and sea, came scrabbling up over the rocks. At the same time, the wind turned cold. The time had come to move on.

They got back to the house by five o'clock. 'Mary'll be expecting us, with her kettle on the boil,' Jeremy said. 'I want to wash my hands. I'll meet you in the nursery.'

Judith went upstairs to her room. But it felt different now. She was returning to Nancherrow, not seeing it for the first time. She pulled off the cashmere sweater and went into the bathroom to wash her hands with scented soap. Her face in the mirror was rosy with exercise and fresh air. She turned off the light and went in search of tea.

Jeremy was already there, sitting at the table with Mary and Loveday and buttering himself a hot scone. 'Did you love the cove, Judith?' Loveday asked.

'It was beautiful. And did you have a good ride?'

Yes, Loveday had had a perfect afternoon, with plenty of adventure. Tinkerbell had jumped a four-barred gate and Ranger had been spooked by an old sack blowing on a thorn hedge, but Walter had been brilliant and managed to calm him down. And on the top of the moor they had galloped for miles, and it had been absolute heaven.

Jeremy leaned back in his chair and stretched. 'If I don't go now, I shan't be home in time for supper.' He pulled himself to his feet, and as he did so, the door opened and Diana appeared.

'Well, here you all are, gorging. Jeremy, you look as though you're about to leave us.'

'I'm afraid so. Thank you for the lunch and everything.' He said his goodbyes to everyone, went to the door and was gone.

Diana came to settle herself on the sofa. 'Judith, what about that beautiful box you brought with you? You promised you'd show it to me. Bring it over here and we'll look at it now.'

And so the next ten minutes or so were spent in Judith's displaying the charms of the cedarwood box. Diana was gratifyingly enchanted, opening and shutting the tiny drawers. 'Where will you keep it?'

'I suppose at Aunt Louise's. I'll take it at half-term.'

'Why don't you leave it here,' Diana said, 'in your bedroom. So every time you come to stay it will be waiting for you.'

'Here? But . . .' She was going to be invited to return. That was all she could think.

'And you must bring some clothes and leave them here as well. Then you won't have to wander around in Athena's castoffs.'

'I've loved wearing them. I've never had a cashmere pullover.'

'Then we'll hang it in your cupboard. The beginning of your Nancherrow wardrobe.'

IT WAS SUNDAY MORNING. On the other side of the village of Rosemullion, Lavinia Boscawen lay in her bed and watched the night sky lighten with the dawn. The curtains were drawn back as far as they could go because she had always believed the outdoors, with its scents and sounds, was too precious to be shut away.

The curtains were very old—not as old as Mrs Boscawen herself, but as old as the nearly fifty years she had lived in the Dower House. Sunshine and wear had faded and shredded them. No matter. Once they had been pretty, and they would see her out.

This morning it was not raining. For that she was grateful. Although at eighty-five she had stopped striding up and down to the village, it was still pleasant to be able to spend an hour or two pottering about in the garden.

Today her nephew Edgar and dear Diana were arriving for luncheon, bringing Loveday and Tommy Mortimer and Loveday's schoolfriend. It would be interesting to discover what sort of a girl that wayward child would choose to bring home for the weekend.

For luncheon there would be a pair of ducklings, fresh vegetables, a lemon soufflé and bottled nectarines. The luncheon would mean a lot of work for Isobel.

Isobel. In old age Lavinia had very few worries. But Isobel was a bit of a worry. Ten years younger than Lavinia, she was getting beyond all the cooking and the caring which had been her life for forty years. Yet whenever Lavinia brought the conversation round to the subject of Isobel's retirement, Isobel would become huffy.

Downstairs a door opened and shut. Lavinia turned to reach for her spectacles on the bedside table. She looked at the time: seven thirty. She could hear the stairs creak, footsteps across the landing. A cursory knock and Isobel appeared bearing on a tray Lavinia's early-morning glass of hot water, in which floated a slice of lemon.

Isobel said, 'Morning. Some cold it is.' She set down the tray on the table with hands that were gnarled and reddened.

'Oh, thank you, Isobel.' Then on impulse Lavinia said, 'I do hope you're not going to have to do too much today. Perhaps we should stop having luncheon parties.'

'Now don't start that again.' Isobel fussily tugged at the curtains. 'Anyway, it's all on the road. Table laid, all the vegetables done. Like a fried egg for your breakfast?'

'Thank you. That would be a treat.'

Isobel departed. Her footsteps faded, treading cautiously down the staircase. Lavinia drank her hot lemon water, thought about the lunch party and decided that she would wear her new blue dress.

LOVEDAY'S BEHAVIOUR that morning made it clear that Great-aunt Lavinia was one of the few people capable of exerting any influence on her wayward personality. She dressed without the slightest objection in the clothes which Mary Millyway had set out for her—a checked woollen dress with shining white collar and cuffs, white kneesocks and black patent-leather shoes.

Finding Loveday looking so unusually smart, Judith started to worry about her own appearance. 'I can't go out for luncheon in *shorts*, can I?' she appealed to Mary.

'I'll find you a nice skirt and I'll polish up your shoes for you. Then you'll be bright as a new penny.'

The skirt, purloined from Athena's cupboard, was a tartan kilt. Mary wrapped it round Judith's waist and fixed the leather straps. 'There. Perfect.' She smiled. 'Lovely, you look. As though you wouldn't call the king your cousin.'

By the time the nursery party put in its appearance at breakfast the others were already there. Diana wore a pale grey flannel coat and skirt, so immaculately cut that it rendered her slender as a wand.

The Colonel and Tommy Mortimer were equally formal, wearing suits with waistcoats.

Later in the morning they drove to Rosemullion, all five of them in the Colonel's Daimler, for morning service at the tiny church. Afterwards the Colonel decided they would leave the car and walk to the Dower House. They took the narrow, winding road up the hill from the village. Ten minutes later they reached their destination, an open gateway in the wall on the right, where a narrow drive curved away between neat hedges. The little party followed the drive.

And then the Dower House stood before them. It was not large, but possessed a dignity that at once impressed. A square house, tucked into the shelter of the hill, whitewashed, with Gothic windows, a grey slate roof and a stone porch smothered in clematis.

As they approached, an elderly woman emerged onto the porch.

'Good morning, Isobel.'

'Morning, Mrs Carey-Lewis. Lovely, isn't it, but chilly yet. Come along in. Take your coats, shall I?'

Judith, unbuttoning her school coat, looked covertly about her. The Dower House was like stepping back in time. So old, so perfectly proportioned, so quiet that over the murmur of voices the slow ticking of the grandfather clock was clearly audible.

Diana led the way through an opened door into the drawing room. 'Aunt Lavinia!' Her voice was warm with genuine pleasure. 'You are a saint to tolerate such an invasion.'

As Lavinia Boscawen greeted her guests, Judith hung back, not because she was shy but because there was so much to look at. A pale room, flooded with sunshine which streamed through tall windows. A long bookcase crammed with leather-bound volumes, an ornate Venetian mirror over the mantelpiece.

'Judith.'

She realised with a start that Diana had said her name.

'Come and say how do you do. Aunt Lavinia, this is Loveday's friend, Judith Dunbar.'

Mrs Boscawen waited, sitting very upright in a chair, her blue woollen dress flowing to her ankles. She was old. Wonderfully old. Her cheeks were netted with wrinkles but her faded blue eyes sparked with interest.

'My dear.' She took Judith's hand in her own. 'How delightful that you were able to come. I do love meeting new friends. Now come and find somewhere to sit. Edgar, will you see that everybody has some sherry? Diana, my dear, what news of Athena?'

At the base of the window was a long cushion. With attention elsewhere, Judith went to kneel upon it, to look out over the deep, roofed verandah to the sloping garden. At the foot of the lawn stood

176

a coppice of pines and, beyond it, the distant blue line of the sea. It was as though they had all been magically transported to some Italian villa high above the Mediterranean.

'Do you like gardens?' Again the old lady was addressing her.

'I like this one especially,' Judith told her.

'You are a child after my own heart. After luncheon we shall put on coats and go out and look around.'

'*I'm* not going to,' Loveday interrupted. 'It's far too cold.'

'I don't suppose anyone else will want to,' Aunt Lavinia observed gently. 'But that won't stop Judith and me enjoying a walk. We can get to know each other. Ah, my sherry. Thank you, Edgar.' She raised her glass. 'And thank you all, so much, for being here.'

Judith sat with her back to the window and reached to take a tumbler of lemonade from the Colonel. Opposite, Loveday caught her eye and her urchin face broke into a wicked grin. Judith's heart brimmed with affection for her. And gratitude too, because Loveday had already shared so much with her, and now, because of Loveday, she was here.

AUNT LAVINIA had not forgotten her promise and, when lunch was over, brought Judith out of doors for a little tour. She had put on a pair of stout gardening boots and an immense tweed cape. An ebony cane kept her steady and was useful for pointing.

'As you can see, my land slopes all the way down the hill. When we came here, I wanted a garden in compartments, each with its own character. So we planted privet hedges and trained the gateways into arches. You see?' They passed beneath the first archway. 'My rose garden. All old-fashioned roses.'

'How long have you lived here?'

Aunt Lavinia paused, and Judith decided that it was pleasant to be in the company of a grown-up who seemed to be in no hurry and happy to chat. 'Nearly fifty years now. But my home, when I was a child, was Nancherrow, and this was the Dower House for Nancherrow. My grandmother lived here when she was as old as I am. We rented it for years, and when my husband retired we were able to buy it. We were very happy here. Now... Next we come to the children's garden. Has Loveday told you about the Hut?'

Judith, bewildered, shook her head.

'No, I don't suppose she would. The Hut was never hers the way it was Athena's and Edward's. I suppose because she was younger than they and didn't have a sibling to share it with. Athena and Edward used to spend whole days here and, when they were older, were allowed to sleep out—so much more fun than a tent. Come along.'

She led the way, down a flight of stone steps into a little orchard of apple and pear trees. Across the orchard, tucked in a sheltered corner, stood the Hut. It was like a log cabin, with a shingle roof and two windows on either side of a blue door. At the front was a porch with wooden steps and a fretwork rail. It wasn't a child-size house, but a proper place, where grown-ups could come and go without ducking their heads.

'No one comes here now,' Aunt Lavinia said. 'But I keep it aired, and each year it gets a good coat of creosote. Here's the key. Go and open the door.'

Judith walked up the two steps to the porch. She opened the door. Inside, she saw two bunks, one on either side beneath the slope of the roof; a table and two chairs; a rag rug. The windows were hung with blue-checked curtains, and there were blue blankets and cushions on the bunks. Above her head a hurricane lamp hung from a hook. She imagined the Hut in darkness, with the lamp lit and the blue curtains drawn, and the thought occurred to her, rather sadly, that perhaps at fourteen she should be too old for such innocent joys.

'So what do you think of it?'

Judith turned, and Aunt Lavinia stood in the open doorway.

'Perfect.'

'I thought you would be charmed.' The old lady peered about her. 'Poor little house. It needs company. We need babies, don't we? A new generation.' She smiled. 'Perhaps it's time to return. I am glad you are Loveday's friend. I think you are a good influence.'

TWO WEEKS LATER Judith was standing at the window of her bedroom at Windyridge, staring out at the view of the golf course, but not able to see anything very clearly because her eyes kept filling with childish and stupid tears. It was half-term and she was suffering, quite suddenly, from the most acute homesickness. She wanted Riverview, and Mummy and Jess and Phyllis.

She thought of sunny Nancherrow, wishing she were there with Loveday instead of at Aunt Louise's soulless house, with only her aunt and the cook and the housemaid for company.

At ten o'clock that Friday morning the boarders had streamed out to the waiting cars. Aunt Louise was there in her old Rover. On the journey through the rain, sitting beside Aunt Louise as she had clashed her gears and pressed hard upon the accelerator, Judith had closed her eyes and expected instant death. But somehow they had reached Penmarron, and Windyridge, the house rearing up through mist.

Hilda, the maid, had come to the door to help carry suitcases upstairs, and Judith followed her. Staring out of her bedroom window now, she tried to think of cheerful things. The new bicycle, to be bought in Porthkerris. Four days of freedom from school. She

178

would cycle to the beach and walk on the sand. She would telephone Heather and make some plans. The prospect of seeing Heather again cheered her up. Gradually her misery dissipated. She tied her hair back and went downstairs in search of Aunt Louise.

After lunch, which was chops and stewed apples, they drove to the Porthkerris bicycle shop. They agreed on a dark green Raleigh with a black saddle, three speeds and its own pump for blowing up the tyres. The rain had, obligingly, stopped, and when they returned to Windyridge Aunt Louise watched Judith mount the bike and do a couple of turns round the path which circled the lawn.

'Well,' said Aunt Louise, 'and how's that?'

'It's absolutely perfect. Oh, thank you, Aunt Louise.' Hanging on to the handlebars, she planted a kiss on Aunt Louise's unreceptive cheek. 'I'm going for a ride now. Round the village.'

'Off you go, then. Enjoy yourself.' And with that she went indoors to her knitting.

IT WAS HEAVEN, like flying. Spinning down the hill and through the village, she sailed past the shops, the post office and the pub, and cycled on. The air was sweet, the tyres of the bicycle skimmed over the bumps and puddles, and she felt as though she could have travelled to the ends of the earth.

But the afternoon was fading and it was time to head for home. The road ran uphill, with fields on one side and the golf links on the other. Pedalling furiously, she discovered that it was much steeper than she had imagined. Alongside the clubhouse she dismounted, resigning herself to pushing the bicycle.

'Hello there!' Judith stopped and turned to see who had called. A man was coming through the clubhouse gate. He was dressed for golf, in baggy plus fours and a yellow pullover, and wore a tweed cap at a rakish angle. 'You must be Judith.'

'Yes, I am,' said Judith, without any idea who he could be.

'Your aunt told me you'd be here for the weekend.' He had a florid complexion, a moustache, and a pair of bright and knowing blue eyes. 'I'm Colonel Fawcett. Billy Fawcett. Old friend of Louise's, from India. Now I'm her next-door neighbour.'

Recognition dawned. 'Oh, yes. She told Mummy and me about you. You were a friend of Uncle Jack's.'

'That's right. Same regiment.' He eyed the bicycle. 'That's a handsome piece of kit. Walking, are you? I'll walk with you, if I may.'

It was rather annoying to have her solitude disturbed, but she said, 'Yes, of course,' and they set off, talking in a polite but stilted fashion. At the gate of Windyridge she paused, expecting him to say his goodbyes. But Colonel Fawcett made great play of squinting at his wristwatch. 'Quarter past five. Well, I've a few moments to spare, so why don't I come in with you and pay my respects to Louise?'

Judith could think up no objection to this and so together they went up the gravelled path. At the front door, 'I have to put my bicycle in the garage,' she told him.

'Don't worry. I'll let myself in,' and without even knocking, he opened the door and went inside.

Judith made a private grimace at his retreating back. She did not approve of his highhanded behaviour. But perhaps Aunt Louise was fond of him and did not object to his bursting in uninvited. Thoughtfully she wheeled the bicycle into the garage.

In the sitting room she found him already settled by the fire. Aunt Louise had poured him a drink and picked up her knitting.

'And how are you going to spend your weekend, Louise?' He was cradling the glass in his stubby fingers. 'Made plans?'

'I'm playing golf on Sunday with Polly and John Richards and a friend they've got staying.'

'So how are you going to spend your day?' Billy Fawcett cocked an eye at Judith. 'Can't have you kicking your heels on your own.'

'I'll probably visit a friend in Porthkerris.'

Colonel Fawcett laid down his tumbler and reached into his pocket for a cigarette. He lit up, and Judith saw that his fingers were stained with tobacco. His moustache looked a bit frizzled too.

'How about a visit to the pictures?' he suddenly suggested. 'They're showing *Top Hat* at the Porthkerris cinema. Fred Astaire and Ginger Rogers. Why don't you let me take you both? Tomorrow evening. My treat, of course.'

Aunt Louise seemed a bit taken aback. 'That's very good of you, Billy. What about you, Judith? Or perhaps you've already seen it?'

Judith had been wanting to see *Top Hat* for ages. But she would have preferred to go with Heather; together they could have swooned contentedly over the glamorous pair gliding over the dance floor. It wouldn't be quite the same with Aunt Louise and Billy Fawcett.

'No. I haven't seen it.'

'Would you like to go?' asked Aunt Louise.

'Yes.' There wasn't much else to say. 'Yes, I'd love it.'

'Splendid.' Billy Fawcett slapped his tweeded knee. 'When shall we go? Six o'clock show? I'm afraid you'll have to be the chauffeur, Louise. My old banger's coughing a bit.'

'Very well. If you come here at five thirty, we'll all go together. It's very kind of you.'

'A pleasure. Two lovely ladies to escort.' He reached for his tumbler, drained the whisky and sat on, empty glass in his hand.

Aunt Louise raised her eyebrows. 'The other half, Billy?'

'Well.' He gazed into the empty glass, as though surprised to see it in such a sad state. 'Well, if you insist.'

'Help yourself.'

So he heaved himself to his feet and went to the drinks tray. Watching him, Judith thought he looked quite frighteningly at home. She wondered about his bungalow and decided it was probably cheerless and cold. Perhaps he was dreadfully poor. Perhaps that was why he seemed to be insinuating himself into Aunt Louise's well-ordered life. Perhaps, horror of horrors, he was *courting* Aunt Louise, with marriage in mind.

Judith decided to forget her instinctive fears. Aunt Louise was far too sensible to make any rash commitment. But the idea, once planted, had taken root and there was no way of ignoring it.

THE NEXT MORNING she rang Heather.

'Judith! What are you doing?'

'It's half-term weekend. I'm with Aunt Louise. I wondered if I could see you tomorrow. Could I come over?'

'Oh, darn it. We're going up Bodmin for the weekend to visit my gran. We're leaving in about five minutes. I didn't know you'd be home. What's school like? Made any friends?'

'Yes. It's not bad.'

'And your mum? Had a letter yet?'

'Yes. Lots. And they're all right, and Jess is all right.'

'Look, I'll see you Easter holidays. Ring me up and we'll fix something. I've got to go, Judith. Dad's tooting the horn. Don't forget. Ring me.'

She went, feeling flat, to tell Aunt Louise the bad news.

'Oh dear. Never mind. With a bit of luck, tomorrow will be fine and dry and you can go out on your bicycle. Perhaps up to Veglos Hill. All the wild primroses are out up there. You can bring me back the first bunch of the season.'

'Yes. I suppose so.' But it was still disappointing.

Billy Fawcett presented himself at the door at half past five, eager and ready for the night out. They piled into the Rover, Billy in the front with Aunt Louise.

They coasted down the hill into town as the last rays of the setting sun washed the old grey stone houses with a golden-pink light. Aunt Louise parked the car and they crossed to the cinema. Billy Fawcett lined up at the ticket office to pay for the seats, while Aunt Louise and Judith gazed at the shiny black and white photographs which advertised the film. A thrill of anticipation shivered down Judith's spine.

The inside of the cinema was cramped and stuffy. Judith was

about to edge her way into a row but Billy Fawcett intervened. 'Ladies first, Judith. Let's see your aunt comfortably settled.' Which meant that Judith sat between them.

The lights dimmed. They watched trailers for the next show. Then there was the news—Herr Hitler strutting around, reviewing some parade. And then, at last, *Top Hat*.

Settled deep in her seat, her eyes glued to the screen, Judith was caught up in the sight and sound of the story being told. And before long there was Fred Astaire on a stage, twirling and tapping his way through the 'Top Hat' number. The plot thickened, and he met Ginger Rogers and pursued her and sang, 'Isn't This a Lovely Day to Be Caught in the Rain?' and then they danced together.

It was at this juncture that Judith became aware that Billy Fawcett was shifting around. She changed her position slightly to give his legs more space and, as she did so, felt something on her knee. The something was Billy Fawcett's hand, heavy and warm.

The shock of this destroyed all concentration. She continued to stare at the screen, but saw nothing as she grappled with this alarming crisis. What was she meant to do? Did he know that his hand was on her knee? Did he perhaps think it rested on the narrow arm which divided the cramped velvet seats? Should she tell him?

But then his fingers tightened and gripped, and she knew that his intrusion was no accident. His hand moved higher, up her thigh. In the darkness she sat in terrified horror, wondering where he would stop and how she could possibly alert Aunt Louise.

Up on the screen something amusing had taken place. The audience burst into peals of laughter. Under cover of this sound, Judith pretended she had dropped something, slid out of her seat and landed on her knees, jammed between the two rows of seats.

'What on earth,' Aunt Louise demanded, 'are you doing?'

'I've lost my hair-slide.'

'Leave it, then, and we'll find it at the end of the film.'

'Shh! Quiet!' came a furious whisper from the row behind.

'Sorry.' With some difficulty she wriggled back into her seat, this time squeezed so close to Aunt Louise that the armrest dug into her rib cage. Surely now he would leave her alone.

But no. Another five minutes and the hand was there again. Fondling, moving, creeping upwards...

She sprang to her feet.

Aunt Louise became exasperated. 'Judith, for heaven's *sake*.'

'I have to go to the lavatory,' Judith hissed. 'Sorry.'

She went clambering past Aunt Louise and all the other irritated people in their row. She sped up the dark aisle and into the ladies' cloakroom, where she sat and nearly cried with disgust and despair.

That horrible man. Why did he have to touch her? The idea of going back into the cinema gave her the shivers. She just wanted to go home and never, ever have to see him again.

She had thought Billy Fawcett rather pathetic and ridiculous. Now she felt ridiculous too, and demeaned as well. So demeaned that she knew she could never bring herself to tell Aunt Louise what had happened. The mere idea of looking her in the eye and saying 'Billy Fawcett tried to put his hand up my knickers' was enough to make her burn with shame.

One thing was for sure: she would go back into the cinema and would not budge until her aunt took Judith's seat beside Billy Fawcett and let Judith take her own place. Billy Fawcett was Aunt Louise's friend, and *she* could jolly well sit next to him.

THE MARCH SKY, which had been clear, with a brilliant full moon, suddenly darkened and a wind sprang up from nowhere, howling about the house on the hill. She lay in bed, terrified, and stared at the window, waiting for what was inevitably going to happen. Over the sound of the wind, she heard footsteps on the gravel and then a thump as the top of a ladder was set against the windowsill. She lay still. There was nothing else to do. He was coming, with his manically twinkling eyes and his hot and fumbling fingers. And then his head came over the windowsill, and he was smiling.

Billy Fawcett.

Judith sat up in bed and screamed and screamed, but it was daylight now, she was awake, and the terrible image mercifully faded. There was only her own window and the morning light beyond.

A dream. Her heart thudded like a drum. She was trembling. And the dream was gone, but the problem of Billy Fawcett remained.

Aunt Louise had been very good about the disaster at the cinema, saying no word until she and Judith were back at Windyridge alone. After the film was finished, they had piled into the Rover and returned to Penmarron, Billy Fawcett keeping up a perky conversation all the way. As they approached the gates of Windyridge, he said, 'Drop me here, Louise my dear, and I'll make my own way home. Splendid of you to drive us.'

'We enjoyed ourselves, Billy. Didn't we, Judith?' The car halted and he clambered out. 'Thank you for our treat.'

'A pleasure, my dear. Bye, Judith.' And he had the effrontery to wink at her. Then he was on his way.

At the house, Aunt Louise had not been really angry, simply at a loss to know what on earth had got into Judith. 'Hopping about like that, and all the fuss about sitting in *my* seat.'

Judith apologised. 'I am sorry about everything.'

'I was quite enjoying the film too. I didn't think I would, but it was amusing.'

'I thought it was funny too,' Judith fibbed. In fact, from when the fumbling started, she couldn't remember anything about it at all.

Now, the morning after, Judith felt not only tired but grubby. Contaminated by the unspeakable Billy Fawcett and his prowling hand. She flung back the rumpled sheets and went across the landing to have a bath and wash her hair. Then, feeling marginally better, she put on clean clothes and went downstairs.

Aunt Louise, dressed for golf, was sipping coffee, cheerfully looking forward to her game. 'How did you sleep? Did you dream of Fred Astaire?'

'No. No, I didn't.' Judith helped herself to bacon and eggs.

Her aunt glanced out of the window. 'It looks quite a promising day. Do you want to go off on your bicycle, or is there something else you'd like to do?'

'No. I think I *will* go up Veglos and look for primroses for you.'

'I'll get Edna to make a sandwich and pack it in a haversack. And maybe a bottle of ginger beer. She and Hilda are off at ten today.'

Later, with her clubs stowed on the back seat of the Rover, Aunt Louise departed for the club. In the kitchen, Judith's picnic had been assembled on the table. The spectre of Billy Fawcett, lurking just down the road, knowing she was alone, meant that there was no time to hang about. With the haversack slung across her shoulder, Judith wheeled her bicycle out of the garage and sped away.

It was a bit like escaping. Furtive, swift and secret. But the awful thing was that as long as Billy Fawcett was around, this was how it was going to be.

THE FOLLOWING AFTERNOON Aunt Louise drove Judith back to St Ursula's, dressed once more in school uniform.

'Hope you've enjoyed yourself.'

'Very much, thank you. I really like my bike.'

'I'll keep an eye on it for you.'

Judith couldn't think of anything else to say, because the bike was really the only good thing about the weekend. All she wanted now was to get back to the familiar surroundings of school.

DEIRDRE LEDINGHAM opened the library door. 'So *there* you are.'

Judith looked up. It was an afternoon in late March and she had come to the library to do some reading for an English essay.

'Miss Catto wants to see you in her study. Better not keep her waiting,' she added bossily.

After that first interview Judith was no longer terrified of Miss

Catto. Now, having neatened herself up and only slightly apprehensive, she went to the study.

Miss Catto was there, behind her desk, just as before. 'Judith. Come and sit down.'

She complied, and Miss Catto came straight to the point. 'I am afraid this is going to come as something of a shock, so I want you to prepare yourself. It's your Aunt Louise...'

Judith stopped listening. She knew instantly what Miss Catto was about to tell her. Aunt Louise was going to marry Billy Fawcett. The palms of her hands went clammy and the blood drained from her cheeks. The nightmare was going to come true.

Miss Catto's voice continued. Judith tried to concentrate on what her headmistress was saying. Something about last night. '...driving home from a bridge game at about eleven o'clock...'

The truth dawned. She was talking about Aunt Louise and her car. Nothing to do with Billy Fawcett.

'An accident. A terrible collision.' Miss Catto paused. 'Are you all right, Judith? You understand what I'm trying to tell you?'

She nodded. Aunt Louise had had a car smash. That was it. Aunt Louise driving too fast, as always. 'She's all right?'

'Judith, no. I'm afraid she's not. She was killed instantly.'

Judith stared at Miss Catto, her face filled with disbelief, because she knew that something so violent and final simply couldn't be true. Then saw the compassion in Miss Catto's eyes and knew that it was.

Dead. Aunt Louise. She heard herself take a deep breath that sounded like a shudder. She said calmly, 'Where did it happen?'

'Up on the road that goes over the moor. A truck had broken down, been abandoned. No lights. She drove into the back of it.'

Aunt Louise driving home in the darkness. 'Who told you?'

'Mr Baines. He's your aunt's solicitor in Penzance. I believe he has sent your father a telegram. He will, naturally, follow this up with a letter. And I will write to your mother.'

'Will there be a funeral?'

'Yes, of course. And I shall come with you.'

'I've never been to a funeral.'

Miss Catto rose to her feet, crossed to the window and gazed out. 'Funerals are a part of death, Judith, as death is part of life. That is a desolate thing for someone of your age to come to terms with, but you're not alone. I am here to help you through it. You are being very brave, but don't feel constrained. Don't be afraid to cry.'

But tears, with their easing, had never seemed further away.

'I'm all right.'

'Good girl. I think it would be nice to have a cup of tea. Would you like that?'

Judith nodded. Miss Catto rang for a housemaid, then settled herself in an armchair by the hearth. She said, 'I only met your aunt a couple of times, but I liked her so much. There was no nonsense about her. I felt quite at ease knowing you were in her charge.'

Which brought the conversation to the vital question. Judith made her voice as casual as she could. 'Where will I go now?'

'We must talk about that.'

'I have Aunt Biddy.'

'Of course. Mrs Somerville, in Plymouth. Your mother gave me the address and telephone number. I will contact her.'

A knock sounded on the door and one of the housemaids put her head into the room. 'Oh, Edith, could you bring us a tea tray?'

The girl withdrew and Miss Catto continued. 'Would you like to spend your holidays with your Aunt Biddy?'

'Yes. I love her and Uncle Bob. They're really nice and fun.'

'Well, we'll work something out. Just remember that you are surrounded by friends. Now come and sit here by the fire.'

SUNDAY, APRIL 5, 1936

Dear Mummy and Dad,

I know that you have got telegrams and that Mr Baines is writing to you. It was dreadfully sad about Aunt Louise and I shall miss her very much, because she was so kind.

As for me, please don't worry. I could have gone to Aunt Biddy for the Easter holidays, but she is very occupied just now with a new house which she has bought in Devon. But I am sure that I can stay with the Warrens in Porthkerris for a bit. And then I can go to Aunt Biddy in the summer.

The funeral was last Thursday. The service was in Penmarron church and there were lots of people there and a great many flowers everywhere.

Here Judith became stuck. Memories of the funeral were blurry. Known faces had swum into her vision from time to time; it was hard to put names to them. But Billy Fawcett had been there. She had spied him standing at the back of the church looking at her and, with a new courage bolstered by the presence of her headmistress, she met his eye and stared him down. Before he turned away, she saw on his face an expression of pure hatred.

He was not among the mourners at the graveside, and for this small mercy Judith felt grateful. But his was a recurring spectre, still haunting her dreams. Shivering in the wind, she had wished that it was *he* they were about to inter in this grave and not Aunt Louise. It was all so dreadfully unfair. Why should Aunt Louise be snatched away to eternity while that gruesome old groper lived on?

But no time for brooding, because she had to finish her letter.

> *Tomorrow afternoon Mr Baines is coming to school to talk to me about what he calls family affairs. I have no idea what this means, but I just hope he is able to help Edna and Hilda get another position. And I hope you are all well, and that Dad isn't too unhappy about Aunt Louise. Miss Catto says she died so quickly she never knew what happened, but this isn't much comfort when you were so fond of each other. Please don't worry about me.*
> *Lots of love,*
> *Judith*

MR BAINES HAD ESTABLISHED himself behind Miss Catto's desk and littered it with a lot of documents. He was a very tall man with brindled hair and in his tweed suit and checked shirt he looked the very epitome of a successful country solicitor. When Judith entered the room he came out from behind the desk and brought forward a chair for her. Then he returned once more to his papers.

'First I want to set your mind at rest about Edna and Hilda. I have found a position for them with an old client of mine who lives up near Truro. A single lady, pleasant working conditions.' He smiled.

'Oh, thank you.' Judith felt most grateful. 'It sounds perfect.'

Mr Baines opened a folder. 'Now, down to business. Before she died, your aunt drew up a comprehensive will. Generous annuities have been arranged for Hilda and Edna. Everything else, her entire estate, she has left to you.'

Judith gazed at him. 'It sounds an awful lot.'

'It is a lot,' said Mr Baines gently.

'But...' Mr Baines was being very patient, watching her. 'Why me? Why not Dad? He's her brother.'

'Your father has a sound job, a career, and future security. And your Aunt Louise was very fond of you. She wanted you to have the freedom to make your own choices.'

'But...I see.' It sounded overwhelming. Worrying, even.

'She has left you her house and everything in it. And most important, her capital investments.'

'But what would I do with her house?'

'I think it should be put on the market and the resultant sum of money invested.' He leaned forward, his arms on the desk. 'You have to understand that your Aunt Louise was a very wealthy lady. She has left you substantially provided for.'

It was all very puzzling. 'The Dunbars were never rich. Mummy and Dad were forever talking about economising.'

'Mrs Forrester's fortune was not Dunbar money. Jack Forrester was a man of considerable private means. Everything he had he left to his wife. Your aunt. She, in turn, hands it on to you.'

'It's hard to imagine, exactly, what it all means.' She frowned.

'Don't be alarmed. For the time being, the inheritance will be administered by trustees. I shall be one of them, and I thought we should ask Captain Somerville to join the team.'

'Uncle Bob?' Mr Baines had done his homework. 'Yes.'

'I'll get something drawn up. And meantime, I'll arrange an allowance for you. You'll need to buy clothes, books, all the small expenditures that parents or guardians normally deal with.'

'Thank you very much.'

'You'll be able to go shopping. I'm sure there must be something that you've been yearning for.'

'Well, I'm saving up for a gramophone, but I haven't got far.'

'You can buy a gramophone,' Mr Baines told her. 'And a stack of records. Perhaps there is something of Mrs Forrester's that you would like to keep?'

'No. There's nothing I want.'

'Right.' He started to gather together his documents. 'That's it, then. We'll have another meeting and I'll fill in any details—'

At this moment the door opened and they were joined by Miss Catto. 'Not interrupting, am I? Given you enough time?'

Judith rose to her feet. Mr Baines, too, stood. 'Plenty of time. And thank you for letting us have the use of your study.'

He packed his briefcase and came round from behind the desk. 'Goodbye, then, Judith.' He beamed benevolently down on her and loped from the room.

Judith turned to face her headmistress. There was a moment's pause, and then Miss Catto said, 'Well? How does it feel?'

'I never knew Aunt Louise was wealthy.'

'It was one of her greatest assets—a total lack of pretension. And I think your aunt has paid you a great compliment.'

'Mr Baines says I can buy a gramophone. And a collection of records like Uncle Bob's.'

She smiled at that. 'I have more news for you. I have had a long chat on the telephone with Mrs Carey-Lewis. She was deeply distressed to hear about Mrs Forrester's death. And she says that of course you must go to Nancherrow for the Easter holidays.' She paused. 'You look astonished. Are you pleased?'

'*Yes.*' Nancherrow. A month at Nancherrow. It was like being offered a holiday in paradise. 'I . . . Yes, I would like to go.'

'Then I'll accept, conditionally, on your behalf. I must get your mother's permission. But I can send a cable.'

'I'm sure she'll say yes. But all my things are at Aunt Louise's.'

'That can be taken care of. Mrs Carey-Lewis told me that there is plenty of space for everything in your room at Nancherrow.'

'I don't know how anybody can be so kind.'

'People are kind. There's just one more thing to remember: to talk of money, the excess or lack of it, is vulgar in the extreme. Do you understand what I am saying?'

'Yes, Miss Catto.'

'Good girl. Now, I've got history essays to correct, and you must be on your way.'

SHE WALKED OUT of the study thinking of Nancherrow, and the best thing was knowing that she was going to stay for the whole of the Easter holidays. She would go back to the pink bedroom, where the window looked down onto the courtyard and the doves and where her cedarwood box awaited her.

She thought about Aunt Louise and tried to feel grateful, though sad, but was incapable of feeling anything very much. She thought about being very wealthy. So what did she want above all else? A car? A house? Roots perhaps. A home and a family and a place to go to that was for ever. Belonging. All the money in the world couldn't buy roots. She knew that.

She tried to sort out the momentous confusion of the day. Maybe for now it was simply going to have to be a case of taking one thing at a time. Easter holidays and then back to school. School for four years and, after that, with a bit of luck, a voyage to Singapore. The family once more—Mummy and Dad and Jess. After Singapore, perhaps England again. Oxford or Cambridge.

She found herself yawning. She was weary. Tired of being a grown-up, with all a grown-up's decisions and dilemmas. She wanted to giggle and whisper with Loveday and to concoct plans for their time together at Nancherrow.

SATURDAY, APRIL 11

Dear Mummy and Dad,

Thank you for sending the cable to Miss Catto and saying that I can spend Easter with the Carey-Lewises. This is the first day of the holidays and someone from Nancherrow is going to come and collect me. The reason I didn't go home yesterday, with Loveday, is because Mr Baines wanted to take me shopping in Truro to buy a gramophone. I'd never been there before and it's very beautiful and old.

'Judith!' Matron, in her usual bossy fluster. 'For heaven's sake, what are you doing? The Nancherrow car is here.'

Judith sprang to her feet, gathering up the pages of her letter and bundling them into her attaché case. By the time she had pulled on her coat and jammed on her hat, Matron was on her way, a bustle of starched apron, down the corridor.

Outside, it was a beautiful morning, with a blue sky and sailing clouds. Judith's luggage had already been stowed, and beside the car, leaning against the hood and yarning companionably, stood two male figures. One was Palmer, the Nancherrow chauffeur. The other was a stranger, young and blond, dressed in a white pullover and a pair of corduroys. When he saw Judith emerge through the door, he came across the drive to meet her. 'Hello there.' He held out his hand. 'You're Judith. How do you do. I'm Edward.'

Loveday's brother. He had his mother's blue eyes, and strong, chunky features. Though full-grown and broad-shouldered, he still wore the youthful face of a boy—smooth and fresh-complexioned— and his friendly grin was a flash of even white teeth. Despite the informality of his clothes, his appearance was so glamorously adult that Judith wished she had taken time to comb her hair.

Politely she shook his hand. 'Hello.'

'We're early, I know, but we've got some things to do in Penzance. Now, are you ready?'

'Yes, of course.'

Edward smoothly ushered Judith into the car with a touch of his hand on her back. As they rolled down the drive, Judith settled herself in her seat and pulled off her hat.

'Sorry it's us come to fetch you, but Pops has got some meeting and Ma's taken Loveday to a rally.' A lock of fair hair fell across his forehead and he put up his hand to push it back. 'Do you like horses?'

'Not particularly.'

'Thank heavens. One in the family's quite enough. I personally could never be doing with them. One end bites, the other end kicks, and they're uncomfortable in the middle. Anyway, that's why Palmer and I are here. Incidentally, I've got to go to Medways to get measured for a new tweed. Do you mind hanging around for a bit?'

'No.' In fact, she felt quite pleased, because hanging around meant time spent in the company of this engaging young man.

'It won't take long. And Pops said I could give you lunch at the Mitre, but it's such a stuffy old place.' He leaned forward. 'Palmer, what's that pub called in Lower Lane?'

'You can't take the young lady into a pub. She's under age.'

'We can pretend she's older.'

'Not in that uniform.'

Edward looked at Judith. She hoped that she wouldn't blush. He said, 'No, I suppose not. Well, we'll find somewhere splendid that isn't the Mitre.'

Judith said nothing to this. The Mitre had always been her idea of a really special place to be taken for lunch. But now, it seemed, it was stuffy and Edward had more lively ideas. Wherever they went, she hoped she would be able to deal with it all, and order the right sort of drink, and not drop her napkin. Despite these private anxieties, it was impossible not to feel rather excited.

By now they were in the middle of the town, heading towards the Greenmarket. 'This is perfect, Palmer. Drop us here. And perhaps pick us up in a couple of hours.'

He leaned across Judith and opened the door. She got out, and he followed, and they walked together down the sunny, crowded pavement in the direction of Medways.

They strolled casually into the shop and a tailor emerged from a back room with his tape measure slung round his neck.

'Good morning, Edward.'

'Morning, Mr Tuckett.' He and Edward shook hands.

'Tweeds for shooting, the Colonel said. Shall we get on with measuring you up? If you'll come this way.'

'You'll be OK, Judith?'

'Yes. I'll wait.' She found a chair and settled down.

Eventually Edward and Mr Tuckett reappeared from beyond the curtain, Edward hauling his sweater back over his head. Now came the choice of tweed, and thick books of samples were produced. Was it to be Harris tweed or Yorkshire tweed, dogtooth or herringbone? Finally Edward made his choice, a Scottish thornproof in a sludgy green, with a faint red and fawn overcheck.

Mr Tuckett said, 'I shall order it immediately,' and he saw them to the door with as much flourish as Nettlebed himself.

On the pavement, Edward let out a sigh of relief. 'Phew. That's over. Let's go and find a drink and something to eat.' And he put a hand beneath her elbow and steered her across the road.

What he found was a pub with a small garden, so Judith didn't need to go into the bar. There were tables dotted about, and over a low stone wall a good view of the harbour. Judith said she would have Orange Corona to drink, and he laughed and went indoors, ducking his head under the low doorway. Presently he came out again, with her orange and a tankard of beer and a luncheon menu.

'Sausages and mash. Cornish pasties. Let's go for the pasties.'

'All right.'

A woman in a pinafore came out to take their order. Edward gave it, his lordly manner belying his sixteen years. He was really, Judith marvelled, extraordinarily sophisticated. She sipped her drink. It was fun to sit in the open air, with the wheeling, gliding gulls making their endless racket around the fishing boats.

'I didn't realise that you were back from school already.'

He smiled. 'Why should you?'

'I thought Loveday might have told me.'

'Some hope. She thinks of nothing but that wretched pony.'

Across the wooden table his smile faded. Suddenly serious, he said, 'Ma told me about your aunt being killed. Ghastly. I'm sorry. It must have been the hell of a shock.'

'Yes, it was. But I'm afraid she never drove very carefully.'

He said, 'I went to her house. Palmer and I were detailed to bring back your stuff. Mary Millyway has probably unpacked your clothes by now. Ma told me firmly that the pink bedroom is yours.'

'She's been so kind. Everybody has been.'

'No skin off her nose. And she likes a mass of people around.' He looked up. 'Oh, hurray, here come our pasties. I was beginning to feel faint with hunger.'

The pasties were enormous, steaming and fragrant. When Judith cut hers in two, bubbling morsels of steak and potato slipped out. A breeze gusted from the sea and blew her hair over her face. She pushed it back and smiled at her companion. 'I'm so glad,' she told him in a burst of contentment, 'that we didn't go to the Mitre.'

BACK AT NANCHERROW, Judith settled into the pink bedroom, feeling it was really hers now because all her things were there. Mary Millyway had made space for her books and had unpacked all her clothes. It was six o'clock and a beautiful evening, and beyond the window Judith could hear the doves in the courtyard. Loveday and Diana weren't back from the Pony Club yet, so Judith sat down to finish the letter to her parents: *Please write soon and tell me everything you are doing. Or tell Dad to take some snaps so that I can see if Jess is growing. Everything is changing so quickly that sometimes it is quite difficult to keep up. I wish I could be with you and talk about it all. I suppose growing up is always a bit lonely. Lots of love, and please don't worry. I'm all right. Judith.*

1938

In Singapore, in her Orchard Road bungalow, Molly Dunbar awoke with a start, in a sweat of panic, consumed by some nameless fear. Ridiculous, she said to herself. It was not even dark, but midafternoon. Siesta. No ghouls, snakes or intruders. A nightmare perhaps.

After a little the terror evaporated. Just her own imaginings flying in all directions, as usual, even as she rested, safe in her own bedroom, with her husband beside her.

She looked at her watch. Three o'clock on an April afternoon and the heat almost unbearable. On the far side of the bed, Bruce was snoring lightly. Cautiously, so as not to wake him, she got up, drawing a thin wrapper about her. Treading softly, she went through the slatted doors onto the wide, shady verandah.

It was immensely quiet. Jess, servants, dogs still slept. Molly sank into a long rattan chair and picked up Bruce's three-week-old copy of the London *Times* from the cane table beside her. The date was March 15, and the headlines leapt at her, for on March 12 Nazi Germany had occupied Austria.

Old news now, of course. They had heard it on the wireless almost as soon as the shocking event had taken place. Bruce, though grim-faced, had not talked about it very much, and Molly had simply pushed it out of her mind. There was a photograph. Hitler, driving in state through the streets of Vienna, his car flanked by German troops. If this, she asked herself, had been allowed to happen, then what on earth was going to happen next?

In London, in Parliament, the mood was grave. Winston Churchill had stood to speak and his warnings tolled like a death knell: *Europe is confronted with a programme of aggression...only choice open...to submit or take effective measures.*

She folded the newspaper and dropped it to the floor. Effective measures meant war. If there was a war in Europe, if England was involved, then what would happen to Judith? Should they not send for her right away? Bring her out to Singapore? War would never touch them here.

But even as the idea occurred to her, she was sure that Bruce would not agree to it. He could not imagine England in mortal danger. Judith would be perfectly safe. Ridiculous to panic.

She knew this because she had heard it all before. When Louise had been killed, and Molly was all for getting the first passage home to be with her daughter, Bruce had insisted that there was no point in taking impulsive action. Judith was at boarding school, Miss Catto was in command, and Biddy close to hand if needed.

Molly had done her best to come to terms with the situation. And in the end Bruce had been maddeningly right. All the problems had sorted themselves out, and the void left by the death of Louise was filled by this benevolent family called Carey-Lewis.

She remembered that day in Medways when she had seen Diana Carey-Lewis for the first and only time. Their lives had touched only for a moment, but she still retained a vivid image of the beautiful youthful mother and the bright-faced ragamuffin child. Molly was grateful that Mrs Carey-Lewis had taken Judith into her home. Now it was two years later—Judith would be seventeen in June—and in all that time scarcely a week had passed without the arrival of a long letter, with all the news a mother would want to hear. The earliest letters were of school, life at Windyridge, the shock of Louise's death and Judith's astonishing inheritance. Then the visits to Nancherrow and Judith's gradual absorption into the Carey-Lewis clan. Later there was news of a Christmas with Biddy and Bob in their new house in Devon; a half-term with Heather and the Warrens in Porthkerris; a trip to London with Diana Carey-Lewis and Loveday to stay with Athena at Cadogan Mews and to go on a round of shopping and luncheons culminating in an evening at Covent Garden to see the Russian Ballet.

All the trials and treats of a girl growing up. And Molly, her mother, was missing it all. It was so unfair, she told herself on a surge of resentment. It was all wrong. She sighed. Behind her, indoors, the bungalow was stirring. She heard the amah's soft voice from Jess's bedroom, rousing the child from sleep. Jess, now six, had grown tall and slender. Soon Bruce would emerge, neatly turned out for the office, and later it would be time for afternoon tea: the silver teapot, the cucumber sandwiches.

She must pull herself together, shower and dress, and then present herself once more as a respectable memsahib.

AT SEVENTEEN Judith was as excited about Christmas as a small child, counting the days until the end of term. From Loveday she had gleaned scraps of information concerning plans laid and guests to be invited to Nancherrow.

'We're going to be the most enormous houseful. Mary Millyway is counting sheets like a maniac, and Mrs Nettlebed is up to the eyes in mincemeat. Athena's coming from London, and Edward's going to Arosa to ski, but he's promised he'll be back in time.'

Which caused Judith a tremor of anxiety. How awful if Edward didn't make it home. He was grown-up now, had done his first term at Cambridge, and seeing him again was a big part of her excitement. His presence added such glamour and life to any occasion that it was hard to imagine any celebration being complete without him.

At last it was the final morning of term, the annual carol service in the chapel, and then home. Judith and Loveday escaped out into the bitter cold. Palmer was there, and they were soon away.

At Nancherrow, they found a huge spruce erected in the hall. As they came in through the front door, Diana hurried down the stairs to meet them with a long festoon of tinsel in her hands. 'Oh, darlings, there you are. Judith, heaven to see you.'

'Who's here?' Loveday asked.

'Only Athena so far, and not a cheep yet from Edward. Pops and

Walter Mudge have taken the tractor and gone to find me masses of holly. And Athena's writing Christmas cards.

'Now, what was I doing?' Diana gazed, as though for inspiration, at her tinsel. 'Decking halls, I think. Why don't you go and find Mary?' Already she was drifting off in the direction of the drawing room. 'See you at lunch.'

Alone in her pink bedroom, the first thing Judith did was to change out of her uniform and put on comfortable clothes. She was rummaging in her suitcase for a hairbrush when she heard Athena calling her name. 'I'm here,' Judith said.

The next instant Athena came in. 'Just popped along to say hello.' She flopped languidly down on Judith's bed. 'How's everything?'

Judith sat back on her heels. 'Fine.'

Of all the Carey-Lewis family, Athena was the one she knew least well, and consequently Judith was always a bit shy. It wasn't that Athena wasn't friendly or funny or easy-going, because she was all those things. She was just so sensationally glamorous and fashionable and sophisticated that the impact of her presence was apt to stun. She didn't have a proper job and, done with Switzerland, she now spent most of her time in London, leading a life of pleasure. Men buzzed about her, and whenever she was at Nancherrow she spent much time on the telephone, placating lovelorn swains.

In a way, Judith thought, it must be a terrible responsibility to be possessed of such beauty. Athena was as tall as her mother, slender and long-legged, with long blonde hair, flawless skin and enormous blue eyes fringed with black lashes. Despite all this, she was sweet and generous and not in the least swollen-headed.

Now she curled up her legs and settled herself comfortably for a chat. 'How's school? Aren't you sick of it? I nearly went mad with boredom when I was seventeen. All those ghastly rules. Edward said he never realised how stultifying Harrow was until he left.'

'Have—have you seen him lately?'

'Yes. He spent a night in London with me before setting off for Arosa. We had a lovely time, lots of catching up on news. He's joined the University Flying Club, and he's learning to fly an aeroplane. Don't you think that's frightfully brave?'

'Yes, I do,' Judith said with total truthfulness.

'What are you going to wear for Christmas feasties? Have you got something new?'

'Well, yes. It's made out of a sari. Mummy sent me one for my birthday, and your mother helped me draw a picture, and her dressmaker made it.' It felt very companionable, discussing clothes with Athena. Loveday never talked about clothes, because she didn't care how she looked.

'Sounds sensational. Can I see it?'

Judith went to open the wardrobe and reach for the padded hanger on which hung the precious dress. She held it in front of her, spreading the skirts to reveal their width. So fine was the silk that it all felt light as air. Around the deep hem the gold key pattern of the sari's border glittered with reflected light.

Athena's jaw dropped. 'It's divine. And what a colour. Not turquoise and not blue. Utterly perfect.' Judith felt warm with delight. It was reassuring to have Athena so genuinely enthusiastic. 'And you must wear gold earrings. I'll lend you some.'

She looked at her wristwatch. 'Goody. It's a quarter to one. I'm starving. Let's go down before Nettlebed starts banging his gong.' She rose from the bed. 'Isn't it heavenly to know it's holidays and you've got days and days? All the time in the world.'

JUDITH WAS WOKEN by the wind, a gale which had risen during the night, howling in from the sea. The morning had not yet started to lighten, so she lay in bed thinking of the day ahead.

Although parcels were already piling up under the tree, Judith had not yet got a single present for anybody. She brooded about this for a bit, then got up and made a list. Only three days in hand. Swiftly she got dressed and went downstairs.

It was now eight o'clock. Breakfast started at half past eight, but she knew that Colonel Carey-Lewis was always early. She opened the dining-room door and he lowered his paper and looked up.

'I know I'm interrupting you,' she said, 'but I've got a problem,' and she explained about the Christmas presents.

He smiled and immediately offered her a lift into town. He planned to go to the bank there anyway and then on to his club. Then they could meet for lunch at the Mitre at about twelve thirty.

'Oh, I am so grateful,' she told him.

IN PENZANCE that morning the streets ran with water, gutters overflowed and beleaguered shoppers struggled with umbrellas, only to have them blown inside out. Bundled up in boots, a black oilskin and a woollen hat, Judith fought her way from shop to shop, gradually becoming laden with parcels.

At half past eleven she found herself in the stationer's, having bought presents for everybody except Edward. She thought about it, then plunged once more out into the rain and set off for Medways.

Even this old-fashioned shop was touched by seasonal cheer. Paper bells hung from the lights, and there were more customers than usual. An elderly salesman approached her and Judith said, 'A scarf. Something bright. Red perhaps.'

'We've got some lovely tartan scarves. They're cashmere, though, and quite pricey.'

Cashmere. A tartan cashmere scarf. She imagined Edward with such a luxury knotted casually round his neck. She said, 'I don't mind if it's a bit expensive.'

'Well, let's have a look, then, shall we?'

She chose the brightest—red and green with a dash of yellow—and the salesman retreated to wrap it. Standing there, waiting, she looked about her with affection, for this fuddy-duddy old shop had been the unlikely venue for momentous memories.

'There you are now, miss.' He had wrapped the scarf in holly paper. 'And this is your bill.'

Judith wrote her cheque, and as she handed it over, somewhere from behind her a voice said her name. She turned and found herself face to face with Edward.

The shock lasted an instant, to be replaced by a joyous leaping of her heart. '*Edward!* I thought you were still in Arosa.'

'Got back this morning, on the night train from London.' He laid a hand on her arm. 'We can't talk here. Let's go to the Mitre.' He was already gathering up her packages, making his way towards the door, and she hurried after him. Then they were out in the rain-driven streets, crossing the road to the Mitre Hotel.

In the lounge there was a welcome fire and no other people to disturb them. Edward piled her packages on the floor, and Judith took off her oilskin and hat and tried to do something about her hair. There was a mirror over the mantelpiece and she saw her face, cheeks rosy from the wind and eyes bright as stars. Happiness shows, she thought, and she turned to face him. He looked very tanned and fit. He had divested himself of his sodden ski jacket and beneath it wore corduroys and a navy rollneck sweater. She said, 'You look wonderful.'

'So do you.'

'We didn't know when you were coming home.'

'I wouldn't miss Christmas for all the skiing in the world.' He smiled at her. 'Got in at seven o'clock. It seemed a bit early to start ringing home and demanding transport, so I left my stuff at the station and walked up to Pops's club and beat on the door until somebody let me in. I spun a sob story. Told them I'd been travelling for two days. So they let me have a bath, and then some kind lady cooked breakfast.'

'Edward, what a nerve you've got.'

He grinned mischievously. 'And just as I was finishing breakfast, who should walk in but Pops.'

'Was he as astonished as I was?'

'Just about. And he told me he'd brought you into town and was meeting you here at twelve thirty. So I came to look for you.'

The very thought of him, in this appalling weather, trudging round Penzance in search of her filled Judith with a warm glow.

He said, 'What have you been doing with yourself?'

'Nothing much. Just school. I only got back from St Ursula's yesterday. But tell me about Arosa.'

'Terrific,' he told her. 'Fantastic snow. We skied all day and danced most of the night. There's a new bar, Die Drei Husaren, where everybody goes. We were usually swept out at four in the morning.'

We. Judith suppressed an unworthy pang of envy. 'Athena told me you're learning to fly.'

'I've learned. I've got my pilot's licence. It's bliss. Easy as driving a car and a million times more fascinating.'

'I think you're dreadfully brave.'

'Of course,' he teased her, 'the original intrepid birdman.' He checked his watch. 'It's a quarter past twelve. Pops will be here before long. The sun's over the yardarm, so let's have a glass of bubbly.'

'Champagne?'

'Why not? You don't hate it, do you?'

'I've never drunk it.'

'Then now is a good time to start. What better way is there for you and me to start Christmas?'

JUDITH SAT at her dressing table, leaned anxiously towards the mirror and for the first time applied mascara to her eyelashes. Athena's Christmas present to her had been a beautiful casket of cosmetics, and the least she could do was to try them. She checked her reflection now; it was wonderfully improved.

It was seven o'clock on Christmas evening, and she was dressing for the climax of the holiday, Christmas dinner. She brushed out her hair and coaxed the ends under into a gleaming pageboy. Now, the dress. She went to her bed, where she had laid out the butterfly-blue concoction. She lifted it, weightless as gossamer, over her head, felt the thin silk settle over her body. Next the gold earrings which Athena had lent her. The new lipstick—Coral Rose—the new scent, and she was ready.

She surveyed herself in the long mirror. It was marvellous. She looked really grown-up. Eighteen at least. And the dress was a dream. She turned, and the skirts floated out around her, just like Ginger Rogers's, just the way they would float if Edward asked her to dance after dinner. She prayed that he would.

She turned off the lights and went along the passage, down the backstairs, and so to the drawing-room door. She took a deep breath and went through, and it felt a bit like walking onto the stage in a school play. The huge room danced with firelight and glittering

Christmas baubles. She saw Aunt Lavinia, majestic in black velvet, ensconced in an armchair by the fireside, with the Colonel and Tommy Mortimer and Edward standing grouped about her. Aunt Lavinia raised her hand in a little gesture of welcome, and the three men turned.

For an instant there was silence. 'Judith!' The Colonel shook his head in wonderment. 'My dear, I hardly recognised you.'

'What a gorgeous apparition!' That was Tommy Mortimer.

'I don't know why you're all so surprised,' Aunt Lavinia scolded them. 'Of course she looks beautiful . . . And that colour, Judith! Just like a kingfisher.'

But Edward didn't say anything. He crossed the room and took Judith's hand in his own. She looked up into his face and knew that he didn't have to say anything, because his eyes said it all.

At last he spoke. 'We're drinking champagne,' he told her.

'*Again?*' she teased him, and he laughed.

IN YEARS TO COME, whenever Judith recalled that Christmas dinner at Nancherrow in 1938, it was a bit like looking at an Impressionist painting: all the sharp edges blurred by the softness of candlelight and the muzziness of a little too much champagne. The fire flamed, but the panelled walls retreated to become no more than a shadowed backdrop for the festive table. Silver candelabra marched down the centre of this, with, all about, sprigs of holly, scarlet crackers, dishes of nuts and chocolates. The dark mahogany was set with white linen place mats and napkins, the most elaborate of the family silver, and crystal glasses fine and clear as soap bubbles.

The men were dressed in formal evening wear—dinner jackets, white shirts and black bow ties. Edward sat opposite Judith, and whenever she looked up and caught his eye, he would smile as though they shared some splendid secret and raise his wineglass to her.

Alongside Edward was his younger sister. Loveday at sixteen was still on the cusp of becoming an adult. Clothes were still unimportant to her. She still lived for her riding and spent much of her days down at the stables, mucking out in the company of Walter Mudge. Tonight her dark curls were artless, as always, and her vivid face, with those amazing violet eyes, innocent of make-up. But her dress—her first long dress, chosen by Diana—was sheer enchantment: green organdie cut low over Loveday's shoulders and deeply ruffled at neck and hem. Even Loveday had been seduced by it, and dressed herself up without a complaint.

At the far end of the table Diana's slinky satin dress was the colour of steel. With it she wore pearls and diamonds, the only dash of colour her scarlet nails and lipstick. Beside her sat Tommy

Mortimer and Athena, looking like a summer goddess in white.

Conversation buzzed, voices rising as the wine and delicious feast went down. First, paper-thin slices of smoked salmon, then turkey, roast potatoes, buttered sprouts and carrots, bread sauce, cranberry jelly, dark gravy rich with wine. There followed Mrs Nettlebed's Christmas pudding, her brandy butter, mince pies, and dishes of thick Cornish cream. Then nuts to be shelled and little tangerines to be peeled.

Finally the ladies rose from the table and withdrew, headed for the drawing room and coffee. As Diana led the way, she paused to stoop and kiss her husband. 'Ten minutes,' she told him. 'That's all the time you're allowed to drink your port.'

And by the time the men did join the ladies, Diana had the sofas and chairs pushed aside, the rugs rolled back and the gramophone stacked with her favourite dance records.

The music was another thing Judith was always to remember, the tunes of that year: 'Smoke Gets in Your Eyes' and 'You're the Cream

in My Coffee' and 'Deep Purple'. She danced that one with Tommy Mortimer, who was so expert that she didn't even have to think about what her feet were doing. Dancing was a thirsty business, and at the end of the song, Judith went to pour herself an orange juice. She turned from the sideboard to find Edward at her side. 'I've left the best till the last,' he told her. 'Done my duty to all friends and relations. Now come and dance with me.'

She laid down the glass and went into his arms.

> *I took one look at you,*
> *That's all I had to do,*
> *And then my heart stood still.*

But her heart wasn't standing still. It was thumping so hard she was sure that he must feel its beat. He held her very close and sang the words of the song softly into her ear, and she wished the music would never end. But finally it did, and they drew apart.

There was a bit of a lull, and everybody was grateful for a

breather. Aunt Lavinia was preparing to go home and saying good night to everybody. And when she was gone Diana waited for a moment, then turned to her guests. 'What shall we do now?' She smiled. 'I know. Let's play sardines.'

Athena let out a groan. 'Oh, *Mummy*. Grow up!'

'Why not sardines? We haven't played for ages. Everybody knows how to play, don't they?'

Edward explained. 'We turn off all the lights. One person hides. The others wait here. We count a hundred and then all go off in search. If you find the hider, don't say anything. Just sneak in and hide alongside, until everybody's crammed into a laundry basket or a wardrobe or wherever. Last one in is the booby.'

They drew cards to see who would hide first. 'Spades are high,' Diana explained. Judith turned her card over. The ace of spades. She said, 'It's me.'

Loveday was dispatched by Diana to switch off all the lights. 'But not the upstairs landing. Otherwise there'll be people falling downstairs. Quickly, off you run.'

'Now'—Edward took charge—'we'll give you a count of a hundred, Judith, and then we'll come after you.'

'Anywhere out of bounds?'

'The kitchen, I think. I don't suppose the Nettlebeds are finished in there yet. Otherwise you've got a free rein.'

Loveday returned. 'It's really dark and spooky,' she announced with some satisfaction. 'You can scarcely see a *thing*.'

Judith was gripped by a tremor of fear. It was ridiculous, but she wished that the high card had been picked by one of the others. However, there was nothing to be done except to brave it out.

They started counting before she was even through the door. 'One, two, three . . .' She closed the door behind her and was overwhelmed by inky blackness. She shivered, searching in her mind for some bolt hole. As her eyes became used to the dark, she was able to see, at the far end of the hall, the faint gleam from an upstairs light.

She went forward uncertainly. On the right the small sitting room and then, further on, the dining room. She moved to the left, bumped into a table, felt the cold brush of leaves against her bare arm, then the upright of a doorway. Fingers fumbled across the panelling, found the handle, and she slipped inside.

The billiard room. Black-dark now. Softly she shut the door behind her. Her feet made no sound on the thick rug.

The tall windows in this room had a deep sill, where sometimes she and Loveday perched, watching a game in progress. She gathered her long skirts and scrambled up onto the sill, then swiftly drew the curtain across.

Far off, a door opened. A raised voice. 'We're *coming*! Ready or not!' They were on the hunt.

The wait seemed to last for ever. More voices. Footsteps. Laughter. Minutes passed. And then, very softly, the billiard-room door opened and was closed again. She held her breath. Then the curtain was gently drawn back and Edward whispered, 'Judith?'

'Oh.' An involuntary sigh of relief that the waiting and the tension were over. 'I'm here,' she whispered back.

He vaulted lightly up onto the deep windowsill and drew the curtain behind him. He stood there, tall and very close. And warm.

'Do you know how I found you? I smelt you.'

She stifled a nervous giggle. 'How horrible.'

'No. Lovely. Your scent.'

'I'm freezing.'

'Here.' He drew her towards him and began to rub her arms briskly. 'You *are* frozen. How's that? Is that better?'

'Yes. Better.'

And with that, he put his arms round her, pulled her close, and kissed her. She had always imagined that being kissed for the first time, properly, would be terrifying and strange, but Edward's kiss was not strange in the least, just wonderfully comforting and, obscurely, what she had been dreaming of for months.

He stopped kissing her, but continued to hold her, pressed to his shirtfront, nuzzling her ear. 'I've been wanting to do this all evening. Ever since you came through the door looking like—what was it Aunt Lavinia said?—a beautiful kingfisher.'

He drew away and looked down at her. 'How could such a funny little cygnet grow into such a beautiful swan?' There was enough light to see his smile. She felt his warm hand move from her shoulder, down her back, caressing her waist and her hips through the thin folds of the dress. He kissed her again, and now his hand was kneading her soft flesh . . .

And it all came back. The horror returned. She was in the dark, grubby little cinema, and Billy Fawcett's hand was on her knee, groping, violating . . .

Her panic was totally instinctive. What had been pleasurable became all at once menacing, and it was no good telling herself that this was *Edward*, because it didn't matter. She could not have stopped herself had she wanted to, but sharply brought up her arms and shoved hard against Edward's chest.

'*No!*'

'Judith?' She heard the bewilderment in his voice as he let her go. For a moment neither of them spoke. Gradually Judith's panic died away and she felt her racing heart settle down to its normal beat.

What have I done? she asked herself, and was filled with shame because she had behaved like a flustered idiot. Billy Fawcett. She suddenly wanted to scream with rage at herself. She thought about trying to explain it all to Edward, and knew that she could not.

She said at last, 'I'm sorry.' It sounded pathetically inadequate.

'Don't you like being kissed?' Clearly, Edward was confused. Edward Carey-Lewis, that privileged, gilded youth, had probably never in all his life had any person say no to him. 'I thought that was what you wanted.'

'I did . . . I mean . . . It's *nothing* to do with you.'

'But—' He stopped. Turned his head to listen. The billiard-room door was opened and gently closed. Discovery was close at hand. Too late now to make amends. In some despair Judith gazed up at Edward's profile and told herself that she had lost him for ever.

The curtain twitched aside.

'I thought you might be here,' whispered Loveday, and Edward stooped to hoist her up to join them.

THAT NIGHT the old dream returned. The nightmare that she had thought buried for ever. Her bedroom at Windyridge and Billy Fawcett climbing up his ladder. And then she was jerking awake in a sweat of fear, her mouth open in a silent scream.

It was as though he had won. He had spoilt everything, because in some ghastly, gruesome way Edward's hands had become Billy Fawcett's hands and all her inhibitions had leapt into life. She lay in her darkened bedroom and wept into the pillow, because she loved Edward so much and she had ruined everything.

But in the morning she heard a soft knock and her door open. 'Judith?' She sat up, blinking and confused.

Edward. She stared at him stupidly. 'What is it?'

'Don't look so alarmed.' He came to settle himself on the side of the bed and he said, 'We have to talk.'

'Oh, Edward.' She felt as though she were about to cry.

'Here.' He stooped and retrieved her dressing gown from the rug. 'Put this on, or you'll die of cold.' She took it, shoving her arms into the sleeves. 'Now look, what happened last night—'

'It was my fault.'

'It wasn't anybody's fault. Perhaps I misjudged the situation. Certainly forgot how young you still are. Dressed up and looking so glamorous, it seemed to me that you'd grown up in a minute. But of course nobody can do that.'

'No.' Judith looked down at her fingers pleating the edge of the sheet. She said, 'I did want you to kiss me. And then I spoilt it all.'

'But you don't hate me?'

She looked up into his blue eyes. 'No,' she told him. 'I'm much too fond of you to hate you.'

'In that case, we can wipe the slate clean. I just wanted to be certain that we understood each other. We're all going to be together for a few days, and nothing would be more uncomfortable than any tension between us. Do you understand what I'm saying?'

'Yes, Edward.'

'My mother is as sharp as a needle when it comes to other people's relationships. I don't want her sending you quizzical looks or asking me loaded questions. So you won't droop around, will you, doing an imitation of the Lady of Shalott?'

'No, Edward.' But Judith was churning with mixed emotions. Relief was uppermost. Relief that Edward wasn't going to despise her. And she found herself touched by Edward's good sense, prompted by concern for his mother and her house party, but surely, too, he had been thinking a little bit of her.

'So'—he smiled—'family loyalties?'

Which filled her with love for him. She pulled him close and kissed his smooth cheek. The nightmare of Billy Fawcett had flown again, chased off by Edward and the clear light of morning.

He got off the bed. 'I'll go down to breakfast. See you later.'

1939

Speech day at St Ursula's took place during the last week of July, the end of the school year. It was an occasion of great ceremony, following a time-honoured pattern—assembly of parents and girls in the great hall, a prayer, a speech or two, prize-giving, the school hymn, a blessing from the bishop, and then afternoon tea.

By ten to two the hall was packed with humanity and extremely warm, for outdoors bloomed a perfect summer day. Mothers sported garden-party hats and white gloves and flowered silk frocks. Fathers were in dark suits, except that here and there stood a man in service uniform. Edgar and Diana Carey-Lewis were part of this throng, as were the solicitor Mr Baines and his wife.

The front of the hall was filled with girls in their regulation party frocks of heavy cream silk and black silk stockings. Judith, sitting in the very back row of the school party, looked at her watch. Speech day was always an ordeal, and being eighteen and knowing that this was the very end of school somehow didn't make it any more bearable. To divert her thoughts from her discomfort, she began to make a mental list of cheering events that were about to happen.

The most important was that Miss Catto had started to make arrangements for Judith to go to Oxford University. But that wouldn't be for another year, because passage had already been booked for October on a P&O boat bound for Singapore. She was going to spend ten months, at least, reunited with her family. She could hardly wait to see them all.

More immediately, there were the summer holidays. Two weeks in August to be spent with Heather Warren and her parents and, later on, a visit to Aunt Biddy. Uncle Bob was at sea, and Ned had joined the *Royal Oak*, so she would be happy to have a bit of company.

Otherwise, Nancherrow. Which meant Edward.

She sat in the stuffy hall suffused with blissful anticipation. The events of Christmas had tipped the scales in Judith's relationship with Edward, and she had fallen totally in love. Because of him the incident at the party had slipped away unnoticed, and she could not imagine how any man so attractive and desirable could be, as well, so understanding.

Judith had not seen Edward since January. He had spent Easter on a ranch in Colorado, invited by a fellow Cambridge undergraduate, a young American. Edward had sent Judith a couple of postcards, with pictures of the Rocky Mountains. These treasured mementos she kept. Now he was in the South of France with a party of friends, but he'd be home later in the summer. Anticipation—looking forward to seeing Edward again—was all part of the joy.

Another exciting thing was that Mr Baines had said that Judith could buy a little car. She had learned how to drive and had passed her test first go. It occurred to her now that with luck she would get the car before she went to stay with the Warrens and would be able to drive herself to Porthkerris. Loveday had been invited as well to join the cheerful household over the grocer's shop for a few days. At seventeen, she too was leaving St Ursula's for ever, having made it perfectly clear to her long-suffering parents that without Judith St Ursula's would be unbearable.

Two o'clock, and at last the ceremony was under way. The bishop delivered his short prayer, followed by speeches and then prize-giving. For Judith the English Prize, and also the History Prize—a bonus because that had not been remotely expected. Then, finally, the school hymn. The music mistress crashed out a chord on her piano and eight hundred voices just about raised the roof.

The power of the music affected Judith deeply. Now she had come to the end of an era, and knew that she would remember every detail of the moment. The hot summer afternoon, the great surge of voices. It was hard to decide whether she felt happy or sad.

Happy. She was happy. As she sang, her spirits soared.

IT WAS A WET MONDAY morning in August. Summer rain, soft and drenching, streamed down upon Nancherrow. Wearing gumboots and an old raincoat, Loveday set off in the direction of Lidgey Farm with Tiger at her heels.

She took the road up onto the moors. The big black labrador ran ahead and she quickened her pace to keep up. She couldn't see much, but it didn't matter, because she knew all of Nancherrow, the farm and the estate, like the back of her hand.

At last Lidgey farmhouse loomed out of the murk. Loveday climbed the gate and crossed slippery cobbles to the door. Here she toed off her boots and let herself in.

The ceiling was low, the little hall dim. She pushed open the kitchen door to be assailed by the warm smell of cooking. Vegetable broth and warm bread. 'Mrs Mudge?'

Mrs Mudge was standing at her sink peeling potatoes. Because the kitchen was the living room as well, one end of the table was piled with newspapers, seed catalogues and bills waiting to be paid. Uncleaned boots stood by the range. There was a dresser, painted blue, its shelves crammed not only with mismatched china but curling postcards, dog leads and a basket of eggs waiting to be washed.

The Lidgey kitchen always looked this way, and Loveday liked it. It was somehow cosy. And Mrs Mudge was comfortably grubby as well, standing there flanked by all the unwashed crocks and bowls of her morning's labour. Mrs Mudge turned from her sink. 'Loveday!' As always, she looked delighted. There was nothing she enjoyed so much as an excuse to put the kettle on, make a pot of tea and gossip. 'Well, this is some nice surprise. Want a cup of tea, do you?'

Loveday said yes, because drinking tea with Mrs Mudge was part of tradition. 'Where's Walter?'

'Up the top field with his father.' Mrs Mudge abandoned her potatoes and filled her kettle. 'What did you want him for?'

'Would you tell him I'm going away tomorrow to Porthkerris for a week, so he'll have to see to everything for the horses. But there's plenty of hay, and I cleaned all the tack last night.'

'I'll make sure he don't forget.' Mrs Mudge took her tea caddy from a shelf. 'Why are you off to Porthkerris?'

'I'm going to stay with the Warrens, with Judith. And you'll never believe this, Mrs Mudge. Judith and I are going to drive ourselves! Judith's gone off today with Mr Baines, the solicitor, and he's going to help her buy a car for herself.'

Mrs Mudge, clattering cups and saucers, paused. 'A car of her own! You can hardly believe it, can you? What else is going on down at the house? Full up yet, are you?'

'The very opposite. Pops and Judith and I are the only ones there.

Athena's in London and Edward's in the South of France.'

'What about your mother?'

Loveday made a face. 'She went off yesterday to London. Between you and me, Mrs Mudge, I think she got a bit depressed. She needed to get away. I suppose she wanted a change.'

Mrs Mudge poured the tea and settled down in her chair. 'What does she want a change for, then?'

'Well, everything is a bit depressing, isn't it? I mean, everybody talking about war, and Edward's joined the Royal Air Force Reserve, and I think that frightens her. And Pops is a bit down in the mouth as well, and insists on listening to all the news bulletins full blast. So she just packed a suitcase and went.'

'It's not a good time for any of us. Except I don't suppose Walter will have to go. Farming's a reserved occupation.'

When Loveday had finished her tea, she looked at her watch. 'I'd better be getting back. Come on, Tiger. We've got to go home.'

The rain had eased off a little. She went back across the farmyard and climbed the gate, then sat for a bit on the top rail.

Walter. She thought of Walter and the coming war, and felt grateful that he would not be leaving Nancherrow to be a soldier. She was very fond of him. For all his wild ways she found him enormously attractive. He was rough and foul-mouthed, but still, he was a constant in her existence and one of the few young men with whom she felt at ease. Ever since prep school Edward had been bringing friends home to stay, but they seemed to come from a different world. While Loveday mucked out the stables or rode with Walter, they lay about in deck chairs or played not very energetic tennis.

Walter. She thought about war. Every evening they all listened to the nine o'clock news, and every evening world events seemed to be worsening. Loveday could not begin to imagine war. Would there be bombs dropping? Would the German Army land somewhere and march across the country? If they came, what would happen?

Tiger, impatient, was whining at her. She sighed and climbed down from the gate and set off. To cheer herself up, she thought about tomorrow and going to Porthkerris. And by the time she reached home her spirits were quite restored.

AUGUST 9, 1939

Dear Mummy and Dad,

I am sorry I have not written for such a long time. I am at Porthkerris with the Warrens, and Loveday has come too. The weather is absolutely gorgeous. Heather has left school, and she's going to do a secretarial course.

Mr Baines and Uncle Bob have let me buy a car of my very

own. It is a little dark blue Morris with four seats, and too sweet.
It meant that Loveday and I were able to come here under our
own steam. I can't tell you what fun it was, driving ourselves, and
just as soon as I can, I'm off to see Phyllis. She is married now
and is living in Pendeen and even has a baby.

I must go. Loveday and Heather want to go to the beach, and
Mrs Warren has packed us a picnic.

My love to you as always.

Judith

LOVEDAY STAYED a week, and it was a constant source of wonder to
Judith the way she fitted into life in the crowded house over the
grocer's shop. But ever since her first visit, when they were both still
at school, Loveday had been entranced by the Warrens and by the
novelty of living bang in the middle of a busy little town. Most of all
she enjoyed the beach, the sands bright with striped tents and cheerful holidaymakers. And so slender and tanned and dazzlingly pretty
was Loveday that she inevitably drew admiring glances.

But the time flew by and soon Palmer, the chauffeur, turned up
from Nancherrow, and Loveday's suitcases were loaded, and everybody emerged onto the pavement to see her off with kisses and hugs
and promises that she would come again.

At first it felt a bit strange without Loveday. But it was nice, too,
to have just Heather for company and to talk about the old days.

They sat at the kitchen table and drank tea and discussed how they
would spend the day. They decided to go off to Treen to swim and to
picnic. The cliffs would be lovely on a day like this.

At Treen, they parked the car by the pub and, with picnics in
haversacks on their backs, made the descent along the precipitous
path to the sandy cove. When they finally reached the sands it was
like being abandoned on a desert island, for there was not another
person to be seen.

Sunbathing on the rocks, they talked. Heather confessed that she
now had a boyfriend, one Charlie Lanyon, the son of a prosperous
timber merchant. Judith deliberated as to whether to tell Heather
about Edward, but decided against it. What she felt for Edward was
too precious, too tenuous to share with anyone, even Heather.

'Are you going to get engaged?'

'No. What's the point? If there's a war, he'll be called up and we
shan't see each other for years. Besides, I don't want to get married
and be lumbered with kids. Not yet.'

'So what do you want? A job in London?'

'Eventually. Have my own little flat, a proper salary. I want to see
the world. I'd like to go abroad.'

They spent all that day on the rocks and the sand and in the water. When it was time to go, Heather turned to look at the sea, a deep aquamarine blue. She said, 'You know, it won't ever be like this again. Not ever. Just you and me, and this place and this time.'

Judith understood. 'I know. It can never be quite the same.'

BY SIX THEY WERE BACK in Porthkerris, sunburnt and exhausted. The shop was closed, but Mr Warren was in his little office and had a message for Judith. 'You had a phone call about an hour ago.' He searched around on his desk and handed a scrap of paper over. On it were two words: *Ring Edward.*

Heather was agog, but Judith hesitated. The telephone on the desk was the only one in the house. Mr Warren caught her hesitation. 'I'm going upstairs to have a beer.'

Heather, her black eyes sparkling, said, 'I'll come and pour.'

Judith watched them go, then took Mr Warren's seat behind his desk, lifted the receiver of the old-fashioned telephone and gave the operator the Nancherrow number.

'Hello.' It was Edward.

She said, 'It's me. Mr Warren gave me your message. I thought you were still in France.'

'No. I got home to a practically empty house. No Ma, no Judith. Pops and I have been leading a bachelor existence.'

'Did you have a good time in France?'

'Amazing. I want to tell you about it. How about this evening? I thought I might drive over to Porthkerris and take you out for a drink. Would the Warrens mind?'

'No, of course they wouldn't mind.'

'Well, say eight o'clock. How do I find you?'

'It's just behind the old marketplace—Warren's Grocery. A bright blue door with a brass handle.'

'Unmissable.' She could hear the smile in his voice. 'Eight o'clock. I'll see you.' And he rang off.

She sat for a little, dreamy and smiling. He was coming. He wanted to see her. She must change, bath, wash her hair. She sprang from the chair and ran up the stairs two at a time.

AT EIGHT O'CLOCK she was in her bedroom applying lipstick when she heard a car draw to a halt outside the grocery. She went to the open window and saw a dark blue Triumph, Edward clambering out of it. 'Edward! I won't be a moment.'

She collected her shoulder bag, took a last glance at her reflection, then ran downstairs. Edward held out his arms, and she went to him and they kissed on the cheek. He was very brown, his hair bleached

210

by the Mediterranean sun. She said, 'You look wonderful.'

'You too,' he said. 'So where shall we go? Which is the fashionable nightspot this season?'

'I suppose we could try the Sliding Tackle.'

'What a good idea.' So they set off, strolling down the narrow street to the water, and turned along the harbour road. It was a fine golden evening, and summer visitors were ambling along the quay. Outside the Sliding Tackle a noisy young group sat at a wooden table downing their beer.

Edward led the way inside, ducking beneath the crooked lintel of the doorway. Judith stepped into semidarkness and was assailed by the reek of beer and the din of convivial voices. 'Dreadfully crowded,' Edward observed. 'You grab that table under the window. I'll get you a shandy.' He shouldered his way towards the bar.

Judith eased herself onto the narrow wooden bench and when he returned he set down their drinks and slid down beside her.

'I never realised the Sliding Tackle was so small.'

'Tiny.' Edward raised his glass. 'Cheers. It's good to see you again. It's been so long.'

'Since Christmas. Tell me about France. Where did you go?'

'To a villa up in the hills behind Cannes. Very rural. Surrounded by vineyards and olive groves. And the villa had a terrace wreathed in vines where we had all our meals. Heaven.'

'What about the drive? Was it beautiful?'

'It was great going south, but not so much fun coming back. After Paris the roads to Calais were choked with traffic. Panic. War nerves. All the British families on holiday suddenly deciding to scuttle for home.'

'What did they think was going to happen?'

'I don't know. I suppose the German Army suddenly bursting through the Maginot Line and invading France. Or something.'

'Are things *really* as bad as that, Edward?'

'Pretty bad, I reckon. Poor Pops is racked with apprehension.'

'I know. I think that's why your mother ran away to London.'

'She's never been much use at facing up to cruel facts. She telephoned last night, just to make sure we were all surviving without her and to give us the London news. Athena's got a new boyfriend. He's called Rupert Rycroft and he's in the Royal Dragoon Guards.'

'Goodness, how smart.'

'Pops and I have got bets on how long it will last. A fiver each way. I'm going to get another beer. How about you?'

'I'm all right. I've not finished this yet.'

He left her to fight his way back to the bar, and Judith looked about her. Two old men, clearly locals, sat firmly established on the benches which flanked the fireplace. And there was a rather grand group of people, probably staying at one of the big hotels up on the hill, making this foray to see how the natives lived. They were finishing their drinks and preparing to leave.

Their going created a gap, and Judith was left with a clear view across the room to the far end. A man sat there alone, a half-filled tumbler on the table before him. He was watching her. Staring. She saw the pale unblinking eyes, the nicotine-stained moustache, the tweed cap low on his brow. She reached for her shandy, then quickly laid the glass down because her hand had started to shake.

Billy Fawcett.

She had neither seen him nor heard news of him since the day of Aunt Louise's funeral. As the years passed, her girlhood trauma had gradually faded, but never totally disappeared. Older and better informed, she had even tried to find some sympathy for his pathetic sexual aberrations, but it was impossible. The memory of him had almost destroyed her relationship with Edward.

And he was here, staring at her, his eyes like two pebbles in his florid face. She looked for Edward, but he was jammed in at the bar. Come back quickly, she begged silently.

Now Billy Fawcett was making his way to where she sat, petrified. His cheeks were flushed and netted with purple veins.

'Judith.' He was steadying himself with his knotted old hand on the back of a chair. 'Mind if I join you?' He pulled the chair from the table and cautiously lowered himself onto it. 'Saw you,' he told her. 'Recognised you the moment you came through the door.' His breath stank of old tobacco and whisky.

Edward was on his way. She looked up, her eyes a mute appeal for help. He said politely, 'Hello there,' but there was not much friendliness in his voice and his expression was wary.

'My dear boy, I apologise . . .' The word took a bit of saying, so Billy Fawcett tried again. 'Apologise for interrupting, but Judith and I are old friends. Had to have a word. Fawcett's the name. Billy Fawcett. Ex-colonel, Indian Army. I don't think we've had the pleasure . . .' His voice trailed away.

'Edward Carey-Lewis.' Edward did not put out his hand.

'Delighted to meet you.' Billy Fawcett took a slug of whisky, then slapped the glass back on the table. 'I suppose, Edward, you wouldn't have a cigarette on you? Seem to have run out.'

Silently, Edward offered his packet of Players to Billy Fawcett. Fawcett extricated one and lit up. He took a long drag, coughed, and settled his elbows on the table as though he intended to stay for ever.

'Judith used to live next door to me,' he told Edward. 'With her Aunt Louise. Wonderful woman, Louise. My best friend. You know,

Judith, if you hadn't turned up, I'd have probably married Louise. She had a lot of time for me before you turned up. Good friends. Miss her like hell. Never felt so alone. Abandoned.'

His voice shook. He had reached the maudlin stage of drunkenness, wallowing in self-pity. Judith stared into her shandy, appalled.

Billy Fawcett rambled on. 'You didn't do too badly, did you? Scooped the lot.' He brooded on this injustice for a bit and then fired his broadside at Judith. 'Conniving little bitch.'

Edward rose unhurriedly to his feet, towering over the old drunk. 'I think you'd better go,' he told him quietly.

Fawcett's apoplectic face, wearing an expression of disbelief, stared up. 'Go? I'll go when I'm ready, and I've not done yet.'

'Yes, you are. You're finished. Finished with drinking and finished with insulting Judith.'

'Go to hell,' said Billy Fawcett.

Edward's response was to take hold of the collar of Billy Fawcett's sagging jacket and yank him to his feet. Despite his protests, Edward propelled him away from the table, across the threshold and out of the door. He dumped him on the cobbled pavement, where Billy Fawcett collapsed into the gutter.

'Don't come back here,' Edward told him. 'Don't ever show your face in this place again.'

Edward strode back into the bar. Judith was white as a sheet. She took a deep breath, determined not to shake or cry.

Sitting down at the table Edward said, 'Tell me, was that old toad really a friend of your aunt's?'

'Yes.'

'She must have been mad.'

'No, not really. Just kindhearted. I hated him.'

'Poor Judith. How horrible.'

'And he...' She thought about Billy Fawcett's hand creeping up her leg and wondered how on earth she could possibly explain to Edward and make him understand.

For a bit nothing was said. Edward lit a cigarette. 'I think you need to talk, don't you?' he said at last. She simply sat, staring at her hands. 'You hated him. Surely not just because he was a bit of a boozer?'

She began to tell him about the cinema, and once she had started it wasn't as difficult as she thought it was going to be. At the end she said, 'I was fourteen, Edward. I hadn't got the faintest idea what he was up to. I panicked.'

'Did you tell Aunt Louise?'

'I couldn't. I just couldn't. Afterwards I had nightmares about him. I still have sometimes. I know it's childish, but my psyche jumps every time I'm reminded of him.'

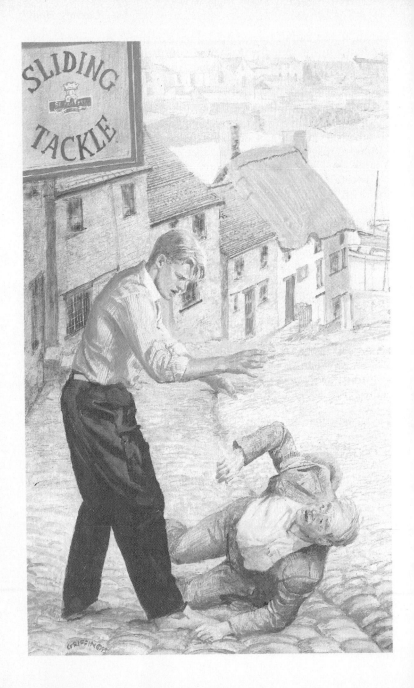

'Is that what happened at Christmas when I kissed you?'

She was so embarrassed by Edward's even mentioning the incident that she could feel the blush, like fire, creeping into her cheeks. 'It wasn't a bit like Billy Fawcett, Edward. It was just that when you . . . touched me . . . it all went wrong.'

'I think you have a trauma.'

She turned to him, almost in tears of despair. 'But why can't I be shed of it? I'm still frightened of him. At Aunt Louise's funeral he looked as though he would like to kill me.'

'If looks could kill, we'd all be dead.' Now Edward smiled and bent to kiss her cheek. 'Darling Judith. You will get over this, you know. Something will happen. You mustn't let one unhappy memory come between you and love. You are far too sweet for that.'

'Oh, Edward, I'm so sorry.'

'There's nothing to be sorry about. And now I think I should take you home. When are you coming back to Nancherrow?'

'Sunday, next week.'

'We'll be waiting for you.'

He got to his feet and stood until she had extricated herself from the bench. Outside, the sun had slipped behind the sea. There were a few people still around, relishing the twilit warmth, but Billy Fawcett had gone.

EDWARD TELEPHONED the next morning. 'Judith, good morning. I wanted to ask if you'd slept well.'

'I did. I'm sorry about last night. Did you get back all right?'

'Yes, I got back, but . . .' He hesitated. 'This is the other reason I phoned. There's a slight panic on here. Aunt Lavinia took ill last night. She's got pneumonia, and everybody's a bit worried.'

'Oh, Edward, I can't bear it.' Aunt Lavinia, so seemingly indestructible. 'Is your mother home?'

'Pops phoned her last night. She's driving back today. But Athena took off for Scotland with Rupert Rycroft at the beginning of the week. Pops put a call through to some remote glen or other, but all he could do was leave a message.'

'And Loveday? Is she all right?'

'A bit tearful, but Mary Millyway's a motherly comfort.'

'I'll come back to Nancherrow today if it would help.'

'That's what you mustn't do. I only told you because I thought you'd be upset if you weren't told. But don't cut short your holiday. We'll see you next Sunday. And incidentally, a friend of mine, Gus Callender, will be here as well. There was a message when I got back last night. He's driving down from Scotland today.'

'Oh, *Edward*. What an inopportune time. Can you put him off?'

'I don't know where he is. It'll be all right. He's an easy guest.'
'Well, send my love to everybody. And love to you.'
'The same, by return. Bye, Judith.'

GUS CALLENDER, behind the wheel of his dark green Lagonda, had finally reached Cornwall, the last leg of his journey. After Scotland the changing colours of the sun-washed landscape had caught his painter's eye, and he longed to stop then and there to capture on his sketch pad this place and this light for ever. But he was expected at Nancherrow, and painting must wait. He had come a long way, he thought as he entered Truro. Perhaps longer than anyone realised.

It was Edward Carey-Lewis who had first started to call him Gus. Before that, he had been Angus, the only child of two elderly parents. His father, Duncan Callender, was an astute Aberdeen businessman who had pulled himself up from humble beginnings and amassed a tidy fortune. Accordingly, when Angus was seven, the family moved from a town house in Aberdeen to an enormous Victorian mansion on the banks of the River Dee, where the neighbours were old noble families who occupied huge estates. Duncan was determined to raise his son a gentleman.

Angus was dispatched to an expensive preparatory school. He came top of his class and very soon his Aberdeen accent was a thing of the past. Duncan Callender was delighted.

Finished with prep school, Angus went on to Rugby School, where he discovered his ability to draw and paint. With the encouragement of a sympathetic art master he began filling a sketchbook with pencil drawings. Then one day, leafing through a copy of *The Studio*, he read an article on the Cornish painters—the Newlyn School. Illustrating this was a coloured plate of a work by Laura Knight: a girl standing on a rock and watching the sea. The sea was peacock-blue, and the girl's hair was copper-red, in a single plait which fell across one shoulder. For some reason it set his imagination ablaze. Cornwall. Perhaps he would become a professional artist, settle in Cornwall, wear bizarre paint-stained clothes, grow his hair; and there would always be some beautiful, devoted girl to live with him in his fisherman's cottage.

The illusion was so real that he almost felt the warmth of the sun, smelt the sea wind scented with wild flowers. A schoolboy's fantasy. He could never be a professional painter; he was already committed to Cambridge and a degree in engineering. But he carefully removed the colourplate and, suppressing his conscience, spirited it away. Later he framed it, and the unknown girl by the Cornish sea was hung on the wall of his study.

In other directions as well, Rugby widened his experience. Too self-contained to make close friends, he was nevertheless popular, and from time to time invitations were proffered to spend part of the holidays in country houses in Yorkshire or Wiltshire or Hampshire. These he accepted, and was kindly received. But it all seemed a bit like play-acting, and the thought occurred to him that since he was seven and the family had left Aberdeen he could remember no place where he'd felt comfortably at home. However much he enjoyed himself, he always felt that he was standing apart and watching others. And he wanted to belong.

Cambridge, for Angus, came as a revelation and a release. He thought it the loveliest city he had ever seen and the college buildings a dream of architecture. Soon his sketchbook was filled with swift pencilled impressions—punts on the willow-fringed river, the Bridge of Sighs, the twin towers of King's College silhouetted against the sky.

His college was Pembroke, as was Edward Carey-Lewis's. They had arrived as freshmen in 1937, but it was not until their second year that they got to know each other. Almost immediately Edward had begun to call him Gus. And such was Edward's influence that he was never again called anything else.

LOVEDAY WAS PICKING raspberries. It was good to have something to do outside because anxiety for Aunt Lavinia pervaded the house like a cloud. Her father spent all his time on the telephone, talking to the doctor and arranging for nurses to be at the Dower House. It was Loveday's first experience of possibly mortal illness. People died, of course. But not Aunt Lavinia.

She moved down the line of canes, picking the sweet red fruit and dropping them into a basket which she had slung, by a piece of string, round her waist. It was a bright afternoon, but a nippy wind blew in from the sea. She had pulled on an old yellowed cricket sweater of Edward's. It was far too long, drooping down over her cotton skirt, but she was grateful for its brotherly comfort.

She was on her own because after lunch her father and Edward and Mary Millyway had all gone up to the Dower House. They would see the doctor, then sit in Isobel's kitchen and drink tea. Isobel, perhaps, needed comforting more than any of them.

'How about you, my darling?' her father had said to Loveday. 'Do you want to come as well?'

And she had put her arms round him and, weeping, told him no. If the worst happened, she wanted to remember Aunt Lavinia the way she had been, alert and gracious, not sickly and bedridden, slipping away from them.

So Loveday had stayed at home and picked raspberries for Mrs Nettlebed. Now, carrying the heavy basket, she made her way along to the kitchen. She found Mrs Nettlebed icing a cake and dumped the basket onto the table. 'Do you want me to help you make jam?'

'Haven't time now. Do it later, I will. And you've better things to do because the visitor's arrived.'

'The visitor?' Loveday had forgotten about Edward's wretched friend. 'Is he here already? Bother. What's he like?'

'No idea. Nettlebed let him in, took him up to his room. You'd better go up and say how do you do.'

Reluctantly, Loveday went. Up the backstairs and down the guest-room passage. His door stood open. He was standing with his back to her, staring out of the open window, and she realised that he was unaware of her presence. She said, 'Hello.'

Startled, he swung round. For an instant they faced each other across the room, and then he smiled. 'Hello.'

Loveday found herself disconcerted. What she had expected was a clone of the various youths Edward had brought home during his schooldays. But here was a different breed altogether. He looked older than Edward, more mature. Dark and thin, rather serious. Up to now Walter Mudge had been her yardstick for the sort of man she found attractive. Gus Callender had the same dark hair and dark eyes, but he was taller, less stockily built, and when he smiled his whole face changed and he didn't look serious any longer.

'You're Gus Callender.'

'That's right. And you must be Loveday.'

'I'm sorry there's nobody here but me.'

'That's all right. Your butler made me welcome.'

Loveday looked at his luggage, still standing at the foot of the bed. 'You don't seem to have done much unpacking.'

'No. To be truthful, I was wondering whether I should. Mr Nettlebed led me to believe that there are some problems. An illness in the family. Perhaps I should tactfully take myself off.'

'Oh, you *mustn't* do that. Edward would be so disappointed. He'll be back for tea soon. What time is it now?'

He looked at his wristwatch, heavy gold and leather-strapped to his sinewy wrist. 'Just on three o'clock.'

'Well.' She considered. 'What would you like to do?' She was not very good at being hostessy. 'We could go down to the cove. It's rather a steep path to the sea, so have you got rubbery shoes on? And a pullover? It might be a bit nippy on the cliffs.'

He smiled at her bossiness. 'OK on both counts.' He slipped on a dark blue Shetland sweater. 'Lead the way.'

She took him down the stairs and out of the front door. The wind pounced upon them, chill and salty, as they went across the terraced lawns and onto the path, down towards the sea. Loveday went speeding ahead, so that it took Gus a good deal of effort to keep up with her. But he cantered along, ducking through the hedge, slipping and sliding down the precipitous steps and over the gate; a farm lane, a stone stile and, finally, the cliffs.

She was waiting for him, standing on grassy turf. The wind tore at her cotton skirt and sent it ballooning about her long tanned legs, and her violet eyes were brimming with laughter.

'I thought I was going for a walk, not a marathon run.'

'But worth it. You must admit, worth it.'

And Gus looked, and saw the dark turquoise sea, the scrap of beach, and the mammoth breakers hurling themselves against rocks at the foot of the cliffs. Spray, in rainbow-shot explosions, sprang twenty feet into the air. It was spectacular.

They found shelter from the wind behind a huge boulder, yellow with lichen and stonecrop. Loveday settled herself, snuggling into her sweater for warmth. Gus lay beside her, legs outstretched.

She turned her face up to the sun. 'That's better,' she said. 'Warmer now. You live in Scotland, don't you?'

'Yes. Aberdeenshire. On Deeside.'

'Are you near the sea?'

'No. Just the river.'

Loveday thought about this. 'I don't think I could live away from the sea. It'd be torture.'

He smiled. 'As bad as that?'

'Yes. And I know, because when I was twelve I was sent off to boarding school in Hampshire and I nearly expired. I lasted half a term and then I came home. I've been here ever since.'

'I see.'

She brooded for a bit, and then, 'Do you think there's going to be a war?' she asked.

'Probably.'

'What will happen to you?'

'I'll be called up. I'm in the Territorial Army. The Gordon Highlanders. It's like being a part-time soldier. I joined in 1938, after Hitler walked into Czechoslovakia.'

'Edward's going into the Royal Air Force.'

'I know. I suppose we both saw the writing on the wall.'

'What about Cambridge?'

'If the balloon does go up, our final exams will have to wait.'

Loveday sighed. 'What a waste.' She fell silent for a while, then said, 'What time is it?'

'Half past four. Someone should buy you a watch.'

'They do, but I always lose them. Perhaps we should go back.' She unfolded her long legs and abruptly stood up, impatient to be off. 'The others should be home before long.'

He pulled himself to his feet and felt the smack of the wind. 'This time how about keeping to a reasonable pace?' He spoke lightheartedly, but Loveday wasn't listening. She had paused, turned away from him, as though reluctant to leave the sea. And in that moment Gus saw not Loveday, but the Laura Knight girl, the picture that he had stealthily removed, so long ago, from the pages of *The Studio*. Even her clothes—the worn tennis shoes, the striped cotton skirt, the aged cricket sweater—were the same. Only the hair was different. No russet plait lying like a heavy rope over one shoulder: instead, Loveday's mop of dark, shining curls, ruffled by the wind.

They retraced their steps, and by the time the house appeared above them Gus was warm with exertion. He stopped to shed his sweater and Loveday smiled. 'On a really hot day, by the time you've got this far, all you want is another swim.'

Just then, Gus heard the sound of an approaching car and saw a stately Daimler cross the gravel to halt by the side of the house.

'They're back.' Loveday seemed filled with apprehension. 'Pops and Edward . . .' And she raced across the grass, calling to them. 'What's happening? Is everything all right?'

Gus followed slowly, all at once wishing that he were anywhere but here. This was not the time to be an unknown guest.

But it was too late now. He climbed the wide stone stairway which bisected the top terrace and stepped onto level ground. The Daimler stood there, its occupants forming a little group.

Edward, seeing Gus, came forward. 'Gus! Great to see you.' And so warm was his welcome that all reservations vanished.

THE FOLLOWING MORNING Edward rang Judith at the Warrens'.

'Hello?' Her voice was thin with anxiety. 'Edward? What news?'

'Aunt Lavinia seems to have pulled through. Apparently she woke up this morning, asked the night nurse what on earth she was doing sitting by her bed and demanded a cup of tea. If she's fit for visitors, I'll take you to see her on Sunday. Meanwhile, everybody's flying back from all points of the compass to be here. Ma arrived last night, and Athena and Rupert are on their way from Scotland. The whole thing has turned into a complete circus.'

'Wish I was with you all.'

'Don't wish too hard. It's a bit like living in the middle of Piccadilly Circus. But I miss you. There's a hole in the house without you.'

'Oh, Edward.'

'See you Sunday morning.'

IT WAS NOT until the final day of her stay in Porthkerris that Judith set off to see Phyllis. Just beyond Pendeen she drove past the tin mine where Phyllis's husband, Cyril, was working a weekend shift. The countryside was bleak, primeval, forbidding.

As Judith pulled up to the cottage, Phyllis came running to greet her with the baby in her arms. 'Judith!' she cried, and they hugged.

She had changed. Not aged exactly, but lost weight and, with it, some of her bloom. But nothing could stop her smile.

The cottage was dismal, a two-room affair with a washhouse tacked onto the back. It had one cold-water tap. All was clean as a bleached bone, of course, but just about as cheerful.

Judith had brought small presents and Phyllis was thrilled with them: some chocolates and lavender soap for her, and a coat for little Anna. After Phyllis had put the baby in her pram, they settled down to tea.

Over the years they had always kept in touch by means of letters and Christmas cards, but still there was much to talk about and details to be filled in. 'How is Mrs Somerville?' Phyllis asked. 'She always made me laugh, she did, with her funny ways.'

'As far as I know they're all in splendid form. They've got a dear little house near Bovey Tracey. I've been to stay there two or three times. But mostly I'm with the Carey-Lewises at Nancherrow.'

'Sounds lovely,' Phyllis said. 'By this time it must feel like they're your own family. How's that young doctor you met on the train? The one you wrote to me about. Still around, is he?'

'You mean Jeremy Wells? We scarcely see him now. He went into practice with his father in Truro, so now he's a busy country doctor with little time for socialising.'

Judith had brought with her a wallet of recent snapshots of Singapore taken by her father. 'It must be a wonderful place,' Phyllis said, leafing through the pictures. 'And now you've finished school you'll be joining them. When are you going?'

'I've got a passage booked in October.' Judith sighed. 'But I don't know what I'll do if there's a war.'

'Terrible, isn't it?' said Phyllis. 'Everything so uncertain. Why can't that Hitler leave people alone?'

All at once she sounded desolate, and Judith tried to cheer her. 'But *you'll* be all right, Phyllis. Mining's bound to be a reserved occupation. Cyril won't have to go and be a soldier.'

'Some hope,' Phyllis told her. 'Made up his mind, he has. Reserved occupation or not, if war breaks out he's going to join the navy. He's wanted to go to sea ever since he was a little boy.'

'But what about you? And the baby?'

'I dunno. The mine company owns this house. We don't have to pay rent; it's like a tied cottage. But if Cyril goes in the navy, we'd have to get out. I'd go back to Mum's, I suppose.'

They fell silent for a while, then Phyllis sat back in her chair and suddenly grinned. 'I don't know what we're doing,' she said, 'sitting here like two old men at a funeral. Why don't I put the kettle on again and we'll have a fresh pot of tea?'

It was late in the afternoon before Judith said her goodbyes and set off on the drive back to Porthkerris. She found it painful to tear herself away and leave Phyllis in that unlovely cottage which spoke of little money and hard times. It was all grossly unfair.

And if there was a war, then Cyril would be going, leaving Phyllis and her baby behind. *I'd go back to Mum's, I suppose*. If only there was some way of helping. But it would just be interfering, and Phyllis had her dignity. All Judith could do was keep in touch and visit as often as she could.

THE NANCHERROW KITCHEN on Sunday mornings was a cauldron of furious activity. Nine in the dining room and five in the kitchen to feed. No, not nine in the dining room, Mrs Nettlebed corrected herself, eight, because Mrs Carey-Lewis had taken to her bed and would probably have to be taken a tray.

Mrs Nettlebed stood at her kitchen table preparing vegetables. In the oven a twelve-pound sirloin of beef on the bone was simmering away and the aroma was of rich meaty juices mingled with the scent of onion.

The kitchen door opened. Mrs Nettlebed, imagining that it was her husband, did not raise her head but said, 'Do you think we should have whipped cream with the soufflé?'

'Sounds delicious,' said a man who was not Mr Nettlebed. She jerked round and saw none other than Jeremy Wells.

'Dr Wells!' She stood there beaming. 'You're some stranger. Did the Colonel send for you?'

Jeremy closed the door. 'Why should he send for me?'

'Mrs Carey-Lewis is poorly.' She frowned. 'If the Colonel didn't send for you, then why are you here?'

'Just to see you all. Where is everybody?'

'All gone to church. Except Mrs Carey-Lewis.'

'Perhaps I should pop up and see her. Have you got a houseful?'

'Bulging, we are. Athena brought her young man, Captain Rycroft, and Edward's got a friend staying too. And Judith's coming back from Porthkerris this morning.'

'Is there enough lunch for me?'

'Enough and over, I would say. Now why don't you go up and see Mrs Carey-Lewis?'

JEREMY FOUND DIANA propped up on downy pillows and wearing a lace-trimmed voile bed jacket.

'Jeremy, what are you doing here? Edgar didn't summon you, did he?'

'No, he didn't call.' He came to sit on the edge of the bed. She looked washed out, pale as paper. 'So what have you been up to, to get yourself in this state?'

'Oh, Lavinia's been so ill, and there's too much to do. Mary and I have got to buy thousands of yards of horrible black cotton and make curtains for every window in the house. The truth is, I'm tired and depressed and I've run out of energy. So I came to bed.'

'Are you worrying about Mrs Boscawen?'

'Yes, a bit. Lavinia's not out of the wood yet. And I was frazzled anyway, after bolting home from London to find everybody bringing people to stay.' She smiled at him wryly. 'This young man of Athena's wants to marry her. He's called Rupert. Terribly sweet. Royal Dragoons. Rather conventional and totally unexpected.'

'That sounds rather cheering news.'

'Well, it is, in a way, but how can anything be joyful when the papers are full of such gloom and doom and everything gets worse every day? Edgar makes me listen to the news each night with him, and sometimes I think I'm going to be sick with terror.'

Her voice shook, and for the first time Jeremy felt real concern. He laid his hand over hers. 'You mustn't be afraid, Diana. You're never afraid of anything.'

'I've been like an ostrich all this year, burying my head in the sand and pretending that it's not going to happen. But it isn't any good deceiving oneself. There isn't going to be a miracle. Just another terrible war.' To his horror Jeremy saw her eyes well with tears, and she made no effort to brush them away. 'After the Armistice in 1918, we told ourselves that it would never happen again. A whole generation of young men wiped out in the trenches. All my friends gone. And do you know what I did? I stopped thinking about it. I stopped remembering. But now, only twenty years later, it's all starting again, and I can't help remembering. Dreadful things. Going to Victoria Station to say goodbye, and all the boys in khaki, and then the pages and pages of casualty lists.'

She was weeping now, dabbing at her streaming cheeks with a scrap of handkerchief. 'I'm talking too much, aren't I?'

'It seems to me you need to talk, and I am here to listen.'

'Oh, darling Jeremy, you are the dearest man. And actually, I know there has to be a war. Somebody has to stop Hitler, and I suppose it has to be us.' She smiled at him wryly, and it was like a watery beam of sunshine on a wet day. 'Now, I'm not going to moan any more. It's so lovely to see you. But I still can't think why you're here. Why aren't you mixing potions and telling people to say "Aah"?'

'As a matter of fact, I am no longer a partner in the practice. I volunteered to join the navy. Surgeon Lieutenant-Commander Jeremy Wells, RNVR. How does that sound to you?'

'Oh, Jeremy. Terribly impressive but frightfully frightening and brave. Do you really have to do this?'

'I've done it. I have to report to Devonport Barracks next Thursday. I wanted to see you all to say goodbye.'

'You'll stay, of course.'

'If there's a bed.'

'Oh, darling boy, there's always a bed for you. Did Mrs Nettlebed tell you about Gus Callender, Edward's chum? He's rather interesting. Loveday, I fear, is besotted.'

'Loveday?'

'Isn't it astonishing? You know how offhand she's always been with Edward's friends. Giving them dreadful nicknames and mimicking their voices. Well, this is quite a different cup of tea.'

Jeremy found himself amused. 'Why is he so interesting?'

'I don't know. Reserved, I suppose. And he's an artist. Amazingly good. Anyway, we all seem to have entered a tacit agreement not to tease. Even Edward's being tactful. After all, we sometimes forget that our wicked baby is nearly eighteen. Perhaps it's time she fell in love with something that doesn't have four legs and a tail. And I must say, he's very sweet with her.'

Suddenly she yawned and fell back on her pillows. 'I wish I didn't feel so tired. All I really want to do is sleep.'

'Then sleep.'

'It's made me feel so much better, just talking to you. Tell Mary you're staying. She'll find a room for you.'

'Right.' He stood. 'I'll come and see you later on.'

HE LEFT HER, closing the door behind him. For a moment he hesitated, hearing the sound of music coming from Judith's room. She had returned from Porthkerris and had put a record on her gramophone for companionship while she unpacked.

It was Bach: 'Jesu, Joy of Man's Desiring'.

He stood there and listened. After a bit he went down the passage, his footsteps muffled by the thick carpet. Judith's door stood ajar. He pushed it gently open. Suitcases and bags stood about the floor, apparently abandoned, for she sat at her desk writing a letter. Her profile was framed by the open window, and he remembered the little girl in the railway carriage. Now, with her honey-coloured hair falling across one cheek, he saw that she was in the full flower of womanhood. Her concentration, her unawareness of his presence rendered her so vulnerable, so lovely, that Jeremy found himself wanting the moment to last for ever.

The music of Bach came to its stately conclusion. 'Judith.'

She looked up and saw him, and he watched her face pale with apprehension. She said, 'Diana's ill.'

'Not a bit,' he told her instantly. 'Just tired out.'

'Oh.' She dropped her pen and leaned back in her chair. 'What a *relief*. Come and sit down. I haven't seen you for months.'

So he stepped into the room and lowered himself into a little arm-chair. 'Did you have a good time in Porthkerris?'

'Yes. It's always fun there.' Then she smiled. 'You know, Jeremy, you are extraordinary. You never change. You look just the same as you did when I first saw you, in the train from Plymouth.'

'I don't know quite how to take that. I always thought there was room for improvement.'

She laughed. 'It was meant as a compliment. Have you got the day off or something?'

He said, 'I'm on leave. Embarkation leave, I suppose you call it. I've joined the navy. I report to Devonport next Thursday.'

'Oh, *Jeremy*. We'll miss you. Will you go to sea?'

'With a bit of luck. Now'—he heaved himself out of the little chair—'I must go and find Mary and be given a billet.'

Standing in the open doorway, he paused, listening. From down-stairs could be heard voices, footsteps, slamming doors. 'The church party would appear to have returned. See you later.'

THEY HAD ALL COME BACK, flooding into the house: the family and the two strangers whom Judith had yet to meet. And Edward. Her heart began to beat with scarcely suppressed excitement. As she put on a splash of scent, Loveday appeared in the doorway.

'Judith! What are you doing? You've got to come down and see everybody...Gosh, you look super.'

'So do you! Where did you get that heavenly jacket?'

'It's Athena's. She lent it to me. It's Schiaparelli. Isn't it divine? Oh, Judith, I have to tell you about Gus before you meet him. He's simply the most wonderful person I've ever met in my life, and we've done lots and lots together, and he never seems to be the least bit bored with me or anything like that.'

Her face, as she imparted this riveting information, shone with a sort of inner happiness that Judith had never seen before. She had always been pretty, but now she looked sensational. Falling in love, Judith decided, suited Loveday well.

'Oh, Loveday, why should he be bored with you? Nobody's ever been bored with you in all your life. Tell me, what sort of things have you been doing together?'

'Oh, *everything*. Swimming, and showing him the farm, and taking him places so that he can do his painting. He's a frightfully clever artist. But do come down. Everybody's having drinks in the garden.'

Following Loveday down, stepping outdoors, Judith was dazzled by light. The garden shimmered and flickered in the noonday sun. In the breeze the leaves of the eucalyptus shivered, and the thick white fringe of Diana's garden umbrella, speared through the centre hole of an ornate cast-iron table, jigged in the wind.

Beyond the dark shadow of the umbrella, canvas chairs had been set up and tartan car rugs spread upon the grass. Judith looked for Edward, but he was not there. Only three figures waited for them, gracefully arranged, as though they had been posed. This impression of a canvas was so strong that Judith found herself regarding the scene as though appraising a painting, a brilliant oil, framed in gold: *Before Lunch, Nancherrow, 1939*. A work that one would long to own, be impelled to buy, and keep for ever.

Three figures. Athena lay on a rug, propped up on her elbows. Two men had drawn up chairs facing her. One was very dark, the other fair. They had shucked off their jackets and ties and rolled up their shirtsleeves. Gus Callender and Rupert Rycroft. So which of them had captured the wayward Loveday's heart?

Loveday ran to join them. 'Where is everybody?' she demanded as the two young men rose from their chairs. Judith followed her across the grass, momentarily suffused with shyness. Both men, she saw, were tall, but the fair one was exceptionally lanky and thin.

Athena turned her dark glasses onto Judith. 'Hello, darling. Heaven to see you. You haven't met Gus and Rupert. Chaps, this is Judith, our surrogate sister. The house always seems half empty when she isn't here.' They all shook hands.

Rupert was the very tall one, Athena's friend, unmistakably army with his neat moustache and relentless haircut. But Gus was not unmistakably anything. His eyes were as black as coffee, his skin was olive and his demeanour was one of a man strangely contained, even shy perhaps.

'Where is everybody?' Loveday asked again.

Athena told her as they all settled down. 'Pops has gone up to see Mummy, and Edward's hunting up something to drink.'

Gus had laid his jacket on the grass beside him. Now he reached to pick it up, feeling in his pocket for his cigarettes. As he did this, an object slipped from an inner pocket and fell upon the grass alongside Judith's chair. Loveday, sitting at his feet, pounced upon it. 'Your sketch pad. You mustn't lose that.'

He looked embarrassed and put out a hand to take it, but Loveday hung on. 'Oh, do let me show Judith. You wouldn't mind. I want her to see. Please.'

Judith felt a pang of pity. She said, 'Loveday, perhaps he doesn't want us all gawping.' She looked at Gus. 'Do you carry a sketchbook with you always?'

'Yes.' He smiled at her, and suddenly his solemn features were transformed. 'Some people take photographs, but I'm better at drawing.'

He took the book from Loveday and tossed it into Judith's lap. 'Feel free. Just pencil sketches—nothing very good.'

But Loveday intervened, coming to kneel at Judith's side, turning the pages and keeping up a running commentary. 'And this is the cove. Isn't it lovely? Gus did it in a moment. Here's Mrs Mudge's barn, with the hens on the steps.'

As the pages were slowly turned, Judith found herself filled with wonder. Each small sketch had been set down with the detail of an architect's drawing, and he had tinted them with pale washes of watercolour. The colours were totally original, observed by a true artist's eye, so that an old tin-mine stack stood lilac in the evening light, a slated roof was blue as hyacinths.

Halfway through the book, Loveday announced, 'This is the last. The rest is blank.' She turned the final page with a flourish. 'Ta-ra ta-ra, it's me. Gus did a painting of *me*.'

But there was no need to be told. Loveday, sitting on some cliff-top and silhouetted against the sea, wearing a faded pink cotton dress, the wind ruffling her dark curls. And Judith saw that Gus had captured the very essence of Loveday, at her most vulnerable, her sweetest. This was a miniature portrait painted with love.

She looked up and saw that Gus was watching her. For a split second she experienced an intense rapport with him. *You understand. I know that you know. Don't say anything*. He had said nothing, but the words came through like a telepathic message. She smiled at him and tossed the sketchbook over. 'Really brilliant. Thank you for letting me look.'

'Not at all.' He turned to reach for his jacket and the spell was broken, the moment over. 'It's just a hobby.'

Now, from the open French windows, Edward and Jeremy emerged, both bearing trays of bottles and glasses. Judith watched them, treading across the sunlit summer lawn, laughing together over some unheard joke, and just seeing Edward made her heart lift. She knew that this was the instant of total certainty, that she loved him beyond all else, had always loved him and always would.

The trays were set down with a thankful thump. Edward came to stand between Judith and the sun. She looked up into his face, saw his blue eyes and his lock of fair hair. He stooped, supporting himself on the struts of her deck chair, to give her a kiss. He said, 'You got home safely.'

'About an hour ago.'

He smiled and straightened up. And it was enough.

The drinks were dispensed, and with everybody finally settled they discussed plans for after lunch.

'We're definitely going to the cove,' Loveday announced. 'Anyway, Gus and I are going, whatever anybody else wants. The tide's high at five o'clock and it'll be quite perfect.'

'I wouldn't miss it for anything,' said Athena. 'We'll all go. And we must have a picnic—tea and lemonade and biscuits.'

'It sounds a bit like a military expedition,' said Rupert.

Athena slapped his knee playfully. 'Oh, don't be silly.'

Edward frowned. 'Judith and I aren't coming. We're going up to the Dower House to see Aunt Lavinia. Just for a little while. She hasn't seen Judith since she was ill.'

'Oh, well.' Athena shrugged. 'If it's only for a while you can join us later. We'll leave one of the tea baskets for you to lug down, so don't not come or we'll be short of food. Talking of which...'

At that point Colonel Carey-Lewis made his appearance, stalking across the lawn towards them. 'How very comfortable you all look,' he said. 'But Nettlebed asks me to tell you that luncheon is served.'

RIGHT AFTER LUNCH Edward drove with Judith to the Dower House. Aunt Lavinia, her bedroom filled with sunshine and flowers, lay in bed, propped up by snowy pillows, her shoulders wrapped in a Shetland shawl, her white hair neatly dressed.

'Oh, my darlings, I've been so looking forward to this. Judith, I haven't seen you for far too long.'

She had lost a lot of weight, but those eyes were as bright as ever. Judith stooped to kiss her.

'And Edward, dear boy. Come and sit down. Now'—Judith had drawn up a chair, and Aunt Lavinia reached for her hand—'how was Porthkerris? And tell me all about Athena's young man.'

They stayed for half an hour, and they talked and laughed and brought Aunt Lavinia up to date on every single thing that had happened, including Rupert, Jeremy and Gus. Finally, discreetly, Edward glanced at his watch. 'I think perhaps we should be on our way, Aunt Lavinia. We don't want to tire you out. Is there anything you want?'

'No. I have everything.' And then she remembered. 'Yes. There is something you can do for me.'

Aunt Lavinia let go of Judith's hand and turned to the drawer of her bedside table. She groped inside and withdrew, attached to a crumpled label, a key. She said, 'The Hut,' and held it out to Edward. 'It has been sadly neglected since I fell ill. Before you go, will you and Judith check that everything is all right?'

Edward laughed. 'Aunt Lavinia, you're a constant surprise. The last thing you need to worry about is the Hut. But rest assured, if there is so much as a mouse or a beetle, we will send it on its way.'

Outside, Edward led the way along the path through the rose garden and down to the orchard. The Hut, tucked into its sheltered corner, basked in sunshine. Edward fitted the key in the lock and Judith followed him inside.

They stood, very close, in the small space between the two bunks. It still smelt pleasantly of creosote but was musty with imprisoned heat. A huge bluebottle buzzed round the hurricane lamp, and in a corner was an enormous cobweb studded with dead flies.

Edward went to open the windows and the bluebottle buzzed away into the open air. He delved into a cupboard and came up with a small brush and dustpan. She watched while he neatly disposed of the cobweb and its victims, then went out and shook the contents onto the grass. 'What else needs to be done?' he asked her.

'I think that's all. Perhaps the windows need cleaning.'

'That'll be a nice job for you, one day when you've nothing better to do.' He stowed the dustpan and brush, then settled himself on the edge of one of the bunks. 'You can play house.'

She sat too, on the other bunk, facing him. He was so close she could have reached out and touched his cheek. Their eyes met. He said, 'Dear Judith. You've become so lovely. Did you know that? And I did miss you.'

'Oh, Edward.'

He put his hands on her shoulders, and leaned forward across the little space and kissed her. A gentle kiss that swiftly became passionate, but this time she neither drew away nor rejected him, because her entire body seemed to leap into life.

He stood and lifted her, and laid her down on the bunk. He sat at her side and stroked her hair from her face, and then, gently, began to undo the small pearl buttons of her cotton dress.

'Edward . . .' Her voice was a whisper. 'I've never—'

'I know you haven't. I shall show you the way.' He gently pushed her dress down from her shoulders. And she wasn't frightened, just peaceful and excited all at the same time. She took his head between her hands and gazed into his face.

'I love you, Edward.' And after that there was no need to say anything more.

A BUZZING SOUND. Judith opened her eyes and watched an enormous bumblebee settle on one of the dusty windowpanes.

Beside her, on the narrow bunk, Edward lay, his arm beneath her. She turned her head, and his brilliant eyes were open and startlingly close. He said very quietly, 'All right?'

She smiled and nodded. 'What time is it?'

He raised his arm to look at his watch. 'Half past three.' He sighed deeply. 'Perhaps we should stir ourselves. We have to show up at the picnic, otherwise a thousand questions will be asked.'

'Yes. I suppose.' He kissed her. Then he sat up and, with his back to her, pulled on his trousers. Beyond the opened door the breeze stirred the apple trees. Edward left her then and went through the door, reaching in his pocket for cigarettes. Judith watched him lean a shoulder against the wooden post of the small verandah, a bit dishevelled and deliciously decadent, with his bare feet and his tousled hair.

She could feel the smile creep into her face. Now they had taken the final step, and he had been wonderfully sweet, claiming her for his own in the most complete of ways. They were a couple. Some time, somewhere, they would be married and together for ever.

She yawned and sat up and reached for her own clothes, then slipped on her dress. Edward, finished with his cigarette, came back to her and sat down once more. They faced each other, just as they had done before, an hour ago, an age ago, a world ago.

She did not speak. After a bit he said, 'We really should go.'

But there was so much to say. 'I do love you, Edward.' That was the most important. 'I suppose I always have.' It was wonderful to be able to say the words, not to have to be secretive any longer. 'I can't imagine, ever, loving anybody else.'

He said, 'But you will.'

'Oh, no. I never could.'

He repeated himself. 'Yes. You will.' He spoke very kindly. 'You're grown-up now. Eighteen. With the whole of your life ahead of you. This is just the beginning.'

'I know. Of being with you. Belonging with you.'

He shook his head. 'No. Not with me.'

Confusion. 'But—'

'Just listen. What I'm saying doesn't mean I'm not enormously fond of you. Protective. Tender. All the right emotions. But they belong to now. This moment, this afternoon. Not for always.'

She listened and was stunned with disbelief. He didn't know what he was saying. She felt the warm certainty of being loved drain slowly from her heart. How could he not realise what she knew beyond all doubt? That they belonged to each other.

She searched frantically for reasons for his excuses. 'I know what it is. It's the war. You're going to have to go and fight with the RAF, and you might be killed—'

He interrupted her. 'The war has nothing to do with it. I'm not twenty-one yet. I have a whole life to live before I commit myself. Maybe I will marry some day, but not until I'm at least thirty-five, and by then you will have gone your own way and made your own decisions and be living happily ever after.'

He sounded like a grown-up trying to coax a sulky child into a good humour. She lost her patience and rounded on him. 'Edward, what you're saying is that you don't love me.'

'I do.'

'Not the way I love you.'

'Perhaps not. Like I said, I feel ridiculously protective about you, as though I were in some way responsible for your happiness. I've watched you growing up, and you've been part of Nancherrow all these years. That incident with the wretched Billy Fawcett brought it all home to me. It made my flesh creep to think of you being traumatised by that bloody man. I wanted to lay his ghost to rest for ever. It had to be me, not some lusty lout giving you a miserable time, destroying all the joy.'

She began to understand. 'So you were doing me a kindness. You were sorry for me.' Her head was starting to ache. She could feel the pain throbbing in her temples. 'A good turn,' she finished bitterly.

'Darling Judith, never think that.' She looked down, away from his eyes. She said, 'I seem to have made a terrible fool of myself.'

'Never. It's not foolish to love. It's just that I'm not right for you. You need somebody quite different—an older man who'll give you all the wonderful things you deserve.'

'I wish you'd said all this before.'

'You're angry.'

'Well, what do you *expect* me to be?' Her aching eyes were hot with unshed tears. 'So what happens now?'

He shrugged. 'We're friends. Nothing changes that.'

'We just carry on? Being tactful and not upsetting Diana? I don't know if I can do that, Edward.'

He stayed silent. After a bit he stood and went to the door, waiting for her to go out before him. As she did so, he stopped her and turned her to face him. 'Try to understand. Nothing's changed.'

Which Judith thought was perhaps the most stupid, untrue thing she had ever heard any man say. She pulled away and plunged out into the orchard, running, willing herself not to burst into tears.

They returned to Nancherrow in silence. As they approached the house, Judith took a deep breath. 'I don't think I want to come to the cove. I've got a terrible headache.'

'Oh, *Judith.*' He clearly thought this was some excuse, and he turned to look at her. 'I say, you do look pale. I am sorry. When we get in, why don't you lie down for a bit? We can go to the cove later.'

'Yes.' She thought with longing of her own quiet room, a space of time in which to gather up her dignity and lick her wounds. 'Perhaps I will. You mustn't wait for me.'

When they got out of the car and went into the house, there on the table in the hall stood the picnic basket. Beside it was a note: *Come right away. No hanging about. X. Athena.*

Judith said, 'You'd better go.'

But he clearly felt guilty about leaving her. He gazed down into her face. 'Are you sure you'll be all right?'

'Of course. Just go, Edward.'

Still he lingered. 'Am I forgiven?' He was like a small boy, needing reassurance that all was right with his world.

'Oh, Edward. It was just as much my fault as yours.' Which was true, but so shame-making it was unpleasant to think about.

It was, however, enough for Edward. He smiled. 'I couldn't bear the thought of us not being friends.' He lifted the heavy basket and turned. 'I shall be waiting for you,' he told her.

Judith could feel the tears again swimming up into her eyes and it was not possible to speak. So she nodded, and he walked away through the open door and was gone.

She went towards the staircase, sank down at the bottom, and leaned her forehead against the cool wood of the banister. The tears now were flowing and she was weeping like a child. It was a relief to give way to her misery and let it all pour out.

At that moment she heard footsteps at the top of the staircase. 'Judith?' It was Mary Millyway. But Judith, frantically mopping at tears, was not capable of speaking.

Mary was coming downstairs. 'I thought you'd gone to the cove.'

Judith shook her head. 'No.'

'So what are all the tears about?' Mary sat beside Judith and laid an arm round her shoulders. 'Tell Mary. What is it?'

'Nothing. I've—I've just got a headache. I didn't want to go to the cove.' Only then did she turn her face to Mary. 'You haven't got a handkerchief, have you?'

One was produced and Judith blew her nose.

'Now, what are we to do about this headache? How about coming up with me and I'll find something in my medicine cupboard?'

The comfort of her presence, her aura of normality and good sense were like a balm. She helped Judith to her feet and led her upstairs to the nursery, settled her in a corner of the sofa. Then she disappeared and returned with a glass of water and a couple of tablets. 'Take those now and just sit quiet, and I'll make tea.'

Judith dutifully took the tablets. She lay back and, with her hand clenched round Mary's handkerchief, closed her eyes.

Presently Mary returned, bearing teapot and cups on a little tray. 'There's nothing like a cup of tea when you're feeling a bit down.'

Judith took the steaming tea from Mary. 'Thank you, Mary. You are a saint.'

'I don't think,' said Mary, 'that I've ever seen you cry like that before. Something happened, didn't it?'

Judith glanced up, but Mary was concentrating on pouring tea for herself. 'Why do you say that?'

'Because I'm not a fool. I know you children like I know the back of my hand. You wouldn't be in tears for nothing, sobbing your heart out as though you'd lost the world. It's Edward, isn't it?'

Judith saw in Mary's face neither curiosity nor disapproval. She was simply stating a fact. She would neither judge nor blame.

She said, 'Yes, it's Edward.' The relief of admitting it, saying it out loud, was immense.

'Fallen in love with him, have you?'

'It was almost impossible not to.'

'Had a row?'

'No. Just a sort of misunderstanding. You see, I thought it was all right to tell him how I felt. But I was wrong, and at the end of it all, I made a complete fool of myself.'

'Edward's a lovely man, and he'd charm the birds out of the trees, but he's no thought for others, nor for the future. Skims over life like a dragonfly.'

'I know. I suppose I've always known . . . I told Edward I might go down to the cove later. But I don't want to face them all, asking questions, wondering. I wish I could just disappear.'

She waited for Mary to say, 'Don't be so silly; no point in running away.' Instead, she said, 'I don't think that's such a bad idea.'

Judith looked at her in amazement.

'Where's Mrs Somerville now?' Mary asked.

'Aunt Biddy? In Devon. I'm going to stay with her later.'

'I think you should go now. This very afternoon.'

'But I couldn't just go.'

'Now listen, my dear. Someone has to say this, and there's nobody but me to do it. I've watched you growing up, seen you being absorbed by this family, and a wonderful thing it's been. But it's dangerous too. Because they're *not* your family, and if you're not very careful you're in danger of losing your own identity. You're eighteen. It's time to break loose and go your own way.'

'How long have you thought this, Mary?'

'Since last Christmas. I guessed then that you were getting involved with Edward. I prayed you wouldn't, because I knew how it would end. You've landed yourself in a bit of an emotional mess, but the best thing to do is to take the initiative. If for no other reason, to shore up your own dignity.'

'How can I just leave, without any sort of excuse? It would be *too* ill-mannered.'

'Well, the first thing to do is to telephone your aunt. Ask if she'd mind if you turned up this evening. And then we'll make *her* the reason for your going. Say she's unwell, all alone, needs nursing. When the others get back, I'll say she rang you, and it sounded so urgent you just got into your car and went.'

'So you mean—'

'You don't need to see anyone, not until you're strong enough, and ready. Now it's time to get moving.'

JUDITH HAD FETCHED her car from the garage and Mary stowed her suitcase in the back. Then they hugged. 'So. That's it. Don't grieve for Edward,' Mary said. 'Don't look back, nor let your heart be broken. You're too young and too lovely for that.'

'I'll be all right.'

Judith got in behind the wheel and started the engine. It was agony not crying, but she managed not to. She told herself, 'It's not for ever,' but it felt like that. The car rolled forward. In her side-view mirror she saw the reflection of Nancherrow, washed in sunlight, receding away. And she knew that she would come back, but Nancherrow, as she'd known it, would never ever be quite the same again.

P A R T   T W O

1939

Biddy Somerville's house, perched on the hill above the little town of Bovey Tracey, was called Upper Bickley. Its date was carved into the lintel above the front door, 1820, so it was quite old, solidly built of whitewashed stone. On the ground floor were kitchen, dining room, sitting room and hall. Upstairs were three bedrooms and a bathroom, and up again a musty loft packed with sea chests, old photographs and Ned's long-abandoned toys.

The house was reached by a steep, winding Devon lane, and the entrance was a farm gate which always stood open. Behind the house was a garden with a stone boundary wall, and beyond that was the beginning of Dartmoor.

It was the first house the Somervilles had ever owned, and very different from living in naval quarters, but before long they were taken up by a number of county families whose hospitality was generous. They were invited to formal dinner parties, less formal race meetings and cheerful, family-orientated tennis afternoons. In no time at all they were accepted, and the only cloud on Biddy's horizon was the darkening threat of war.

On Sunday evening at nine Biddy was at the window of her sitting room waiting anxiously for Judith. Bob had been home for the weekend but after tea had set off back to the base at Devonport. In these tense times he was never away from his office for more than a day.

Biddy was not alone, because a dog was lying at her feet—a border collie, with a thick coat and an engaging face, that Ned had found wandering round the dockside at Scapa Flow. Ned had brought her home two months before, and now Biddy could scarcely imagine life without Morag.

Hearing the car coming up the hill, Biddy hurried to the hall, and watched the little Morris drive through the open gate. The car door opened and Judith emerged. 'Oh, darling, what a relief.' They hugged. 'Did you have a dreadful journey?'

'Not too bad. Just long. I'm sorry for springing myself on you.'

'Oh, don't be ridiculous. We always love it when you come.'

Biddy carried Judith's case inside and dumped it on the bottom stair. In the glare of the hallway light they stood and looked at each other. Judith seemed a bit pale and much thinner than when Biddy had last seen her.

'Where's Uncle Bob?'

'Went back to Devonport after tea. You'll see him next weekend. Now, what would you like? Food? Drink?'

Judith shook her head. 'Just bed. I'm exhausted.'

'Up you go, then. And in the morning I'll bring you a cup of tea.'

AT NINE O'CLOCK Biddy woke Judith, bearing the promised cup of tea. My first day without Edward, Judith thought, and wished that it hadn't had to start so soon.

'It's a bit misty, but I think it's going to be fine. How did you sleep?'

One step at a time: that was the only way to get through such an unbearably miserable vacuum. Judith made a huge effort and sat up. 'Like a log,' she said as she reached for her tea.

'You looked drained.' Biddy came to sit on the bed. She wore linen trousers and a checked shirt, and though she had put on a bit of weight, her face was just the same—lipstick and laughter lines and bright eyes.

She waited for a moment and then said, 'Do you want to talk?'

Judith's heart sank. She tried stalling. 'What about?'

'Oh, darling, I'm not a dimwit. Something's happened. Nervous silences are not in character for you, nor making impulsive decisions. So tell. Whatever it is, I shall understand.'

Judith, trying to marshal her thoughts, met Biddy's eyes. Biddy was really family, not just pretend. Being here with her felt right. She put down the teacup and said, 'It's just that I've made the most awful fool of myself.'

'How?' Judith told her just about everything, starting at the beginning, when Edward came to pick her up from school for those first spring holidays, and ending yesterday, when she had told him she loved him, only to suffer the terrible humiliation of his rejection. 'It was Mary Millyway who suggested that I come to you. I'd like to stay. Just till I've had time to pull myself together.'

'I hope it takes ages, because I love to have you here.' And Biddy put her arms round Judith and hugged her. 'And don't feel you have to be cheerful all the time. The great thing is to keep busy. I've got blackout curtains to cut out and sew, and a great list of stuff that Bob says we've got to lay in, in case the war starts and there's an instant shortage. Why don't you have a bath and get dressed?'

Biddy was right. Occupation was all-important. After breakfast they sat at the kitchen table and made shopping lists. Candles and electric light bulbs. Petrol. Tins of soup. Spools of black thread for making the curtains. Then they drove down the hill into the little town.

That afternoon they started on the blackout curtains. While Judith set up the old sewing machine on the dining-room table, Biddy measured the windows and cut the lengths of cloth. As soon as the first curtain was finished, they hung it and stood back to survey the result. Biddy sighed. 'I've never made anything so unattractive or so disagreeable. All afternoon, and we've only made *one*. The whole house is going to take us for ever.'

'Well, just be grateful you don't live at Nancherrow.'

After supper they talked, and then it was time for the news: Nazi troops on the march; Anthony Eden flying somewhere with a fresh missive from the government; mobilisation of reservists imminent. Biddy, unable to bear this gloom, turned the knob of the wireless to Radio Luxembourg, and all at once the room was filled with music.

And Judith was back with Edward, dancing, and it was last Christmas at Nancherrow. I've survived one day, she told herself. One day without him. It felt like the first step of a thousand-mile journey.

BY THE TIME Bob Somerville returned to Upper Bickley on the following Saturday morning, a number of events—some quite alarming—had taken place. Morag had disappeared, to hunt on the moor, and returned with fourteen ticks embedded in her thick coat, all of which had to be painstakingly removed. In Austria, Herr Hitler, orating at his generals, announced that the destruction of Poland would commence within days. Then the sinister news broke upon the world that the Nazis and the Russians had signed a non-aggression pact. It seemed that nothing now could avert war. Local people had to present themselves at the school hall and were duly issued with gas masks. Biddy and Judith carried theirs home, stowed them under the hall table and devoutly prayed that they would never have cause to wear them.

By the weekend Judith had completed the mammoth task of stitching the curtains. Bob had driven from Devonport, arriving just before midday on Saturday. Biddy went out to meet him. 'I feared you mightn't make it,' she said. 'I thought there might be some panic on.'

'There is. It's nonstop. But I did want to see you both.'

That evening, Biddy gave a small drinks party for old friends. The next morning Judith and Bob, with Morag bounding at their heels, climbed five miles up a moorland track to Haytor. They paused to sit companionably in the shelter of a handy boulder where the view was immense: a sweep of Dartmoor, and villages, tiny as toys spread upon a carpet, and in the distance the glimmering silver sea.

Judith plucked a blade of grass and began to shred it with her thumbnail. She said, 'Uncle Bob, do you think we could talk?'

He had taken out his pipe and was filling the bowl. 'Of course. You can always talk to me.'

'It's about something rather difficult. I've decided not to go to Singapore. More than anything I want to see Mummy and Dad and Jess again.' Judith took a deep breath. 'But it's the war. Everybody's going to be in the thick of it. If I go to Singapore, I'll feel like a rat deserting a sinking ship. I mean, it would feel like running away.'

Bob was puffing on his pipe. He said, 'If you join your parents, I'm convinced no one will think the worse of you. You've all been apart for too long. And if you don't go . . . you must realise that it's going to be rough. However, it's your life. What about university?'

'Well, that would have to wait. What I'd like to do is join one of the services, but there's not much point joining up unless I've got some sort of a qualification. Heather Warren, my friend in Porthkerris—she's learning shorthand and typing. Perhaps I could go back to Porthkerris and do it with her.'

'But why not do that from here? Go to Exeter or Plymouth. Biddy misses Ned, and she likes having you around. You'll be able to keep each other company.'

'But you've said yourself that the first thing to be rationed is petrol. I wouldn't be able to use my car and there's only one bus a day out of Bovey Tracey.'

Uncle Bob began to laugh. 'What a girl you are for details. You'll make an excellent petty officer. I'll work something out. Just be with Biddy for a bit.'

She was suddenly filled with love for him. She said, 'All right,' and leaned forward and kissed his weather-beaten cheek.

It was nearly half past two before they started home. As they made their way through the garden, they heard a car climbing the hill. They stood waiting until the car appeared, a dark Royal Navy staff vehicle with an officer at the wheel. Bob frowned. 'My signal officer,' and he went to meet him.

The young man, a lieutenant, stepped out of the car and saluted. 'Captain Somerville, sir. A signal. It came through an hour ago.'

Bob Somerville read the message. After a bit he looked up. 'Yes,' he said. 'Well done, Whitaker. I'll need fifteen minutes. I must have a word with my wife, and pack.'

'Right, sir.'

Uncle Bob went indoors and Judith knew that he would want to be alone with Biddy. She felt fearfully apprehensive, her imagination leaping ahead to imminent invasion or dire news of Ned. 'What is happening?' she asked.

'It's a special appointment,' the lieutenant told her. 'The Commander in Chief, Home Fleet, has requested Captain Somerville to join his staff at Scapa Flow. With all convenient speed.'

Exactly fifteen minutes later Bob reappeared, with Biddy at his side. Back in uniform, back in charge, he looked distinguished.

Lieutenant Whitaker relieved him of his luggage, and Bob turned to embrace his wife. 'Send Ned my love,' she said.

It was Judith's turn. 'Goodbye, Uncle Bob,' and they hugged.

He got into the passenger seat, and then he was gone. Biddy and Judith listened until they could hear the car no longer.

Afterwards Judith was always to think of that August Sunday afternoon, and Uncle Bob's going, as the moment when the war really started. The events of the following week—the German invasion of Poland and Mr Chamberlain's speech declaring war—became in retrospect simply the final formalities preceding a mortal struggle that was to continue for nearly six years.

SEPTEMBER 13, 1939

Dear Diana,
   I am so sorry I haven't written to you before, but somehow there hasn't been time. It was horrid leaving you all at such short notice, but I know that you understood.
   Aunt Biddy is much better now. But Uncle Bob has gone to

Scapa Flow to take up the post of engineer captain on the staff
of the Commander in Chief, Home Fleet. Biddy can't go with
him, and for the time being I am staying here with her.

I decided, before Uncle Bob left us, that I must learn shorthand
and typing. It turns out that Biddy has a friend called Hester
Lang, a retired civil servant in Bovey Tracey, who has said she'll
teach me. Once I've got that under my belt, I think I might join
the services. The Women's Royal Naval Service, probably.

I do hope all is well. Please give my love to Colonel Carey-
Lewis and everybody.

THE REPLY TO JUDITH'S missive arrived at Upper Bickley in an envelope addressed in Loveday's childish scrawl. Judith curled up on the
sitting-room sofa and slit the envelope.

September 22

Darling Judith,

We loved getting your letter and Mummy's asked me to write.

Tremendous news about your uncle. He must be frightfully
efficient and clever. I had to look Scapa Flow up in the atlas. It's
practically in the Arctic Circle.

Here, things are happening. Palmer has gone off to join the
infantry. Mary's been making blackout curtains. Mummy held a
Red Cross meeting here, and Pops is putting buckets of water
everywhere in case we catch fire. When winter comes we are going
to dustsheet the drawing room and live in the little sitting room.
Pops says we must conserve fuel.

After you went, we all missed you dreadfully, but the others
followed pretty sharpish. Jeremy was the first to go, and then
Rupert shot off to Edinburgh. Edward is at some training base,
but we don't know where, because his address is Somewhere in
England. I expect he's having the time of his life, flying around
and drinking beer in the mess. And Gus went to Aberdeen, the
HQ of the Gordon Highlanders. It was simply ghastly saying
goodbye to him. It's so mean, meeting the only man one could
ever possibly fall in love with and then having him whisked away.
I cried buckets.

Three days after Rupert left, Athena announced that she was
going to Edinburgh too, and she got into a train and went. Isn't
she the end? She's living in the Caledonian Hotel. She says that
Edinburgh is bitterly cold, but it doesn't matter because every
now and then she can see Rupert.

As for me, I am staying put. Mummy is going to get masses of
hens and they will be my war work, and Walter Mudge says he'll

teach me how I can help on the farm. I'm longing to see you
again. Come back as soon as you can.

Lots of love, love, love,
Loveday

P.S.—STOP PRESS! Too exciting. A moment ago, a telephone
call from Edinburgh. Athena and Rupert got married in a regis-
ter office there. Mummy and Pops are torn between delight and
fury that they missed the ceremony. It can't be much fun being
married and living all by yourself in the Caledonian Hotel.

Judith folded the letter and put it back in its envelope. She gazed
from the window and thought about Nancherrow. And Edward.
Somewhere in England. Training. He's having the time of his life,
flying around and drinking beer.

It was still impossible to remember him dispassionately, the sound
of his voice, and the lock of hair that fell across his forehead. But
remembering him did not make her want to cry any longer, so perhaps things were getting a little better. She pulled herself out of the
sofa and went to find her aunt to share the news.

BY MID-OCTOBER, six weeks into the war, nothing very much had
happened: no invasion, nor bombing, nor battles in France. But the
horrors of the destruction of Poland kept everybody glued to the
wireless. It was beginning to get colder and Judith looked forward to
the long, dark months ahead without enthusiasm. At least she had
her typing and shorthand lessons to keep her occupied.

On Saturday, October 14, Judith and Biddy were in the kitchen,
discussing how they were going to spend their day. Judith had to go
down to Bovey Tracey to return a book borrowed from Hester Lang,
and so she would do the shopping. As Biddy began to compose the
inevitable list, the phone rang.

It was Uncle Bob. Last night a German submarine had breached
the defences of Scapa Flow. The *Royal Oak* was in the harbour.
She'd been torpedoed and sunk.

Ned's ship. Ned Somerville was dead.

UNCLE BOB GOT HOME for a couple of days, trying to comfort Biddy,
feeling all the time just as lost and bereft as she. Then he went back
to Scapa Flow, and Judith and Biddy were on their own again.

It was a shattering time, but Biddy was grateful for letters, including a kind note from Colonel Carey-Lewis. And Judith had another
letter from Loveday, with news of Nancherrow. Athena was home
and was going to have a baby. Rupert had gone to Palestine with his
regiment and their horses. Gus was in France with the Highland

240

Division, and Edward had one of the new planes called Spitfires. Jeremy Wells was bucketing to and fro across the Atlantic in a destroyer escorting merchant-ship convoys. It sounded pretty rough. Mr Nettlebed had become an air-raid warden. And they were all so terribly sad about Judith's cousin, Ned.

Towards the end of the year it got bitterly cold, and there was snow all over Dartmoor and down the road in Bovey Tracey. Uncle Bob got home for four days over Christmas, then was gone again. Without Ned they tried to treat Christmas just like an ordinary day.

Now Judith sat in the kitchen writing to her parents. She paused and blew on her chilled fingers, then went on with her letter:

> *Biddy is still not able to cope with much. She doesn't want to do anything or see anybody yet. It will be better when she gets interested in Red Cross work or something. She is too energetic a person to be doing nothing for the war effort.*
>
> *I miss you all dreadfully, and sometimes wish I were with you, but now I know I made the right decision. How worried we would have been to think of Biddy on her own.*

1940

By the end of March, after the coldest winter that people could remember, the worst of the snow had finally disappeared and in the garden of Upper Bickley the first of the daffodils tossed their yellow heads in the breeze.

The telephone rang, and Judith went to answer it. 'Judith, it's Athena. Mummy wanted me to call you. I'm afraid it's very sad news. Aunt Lavinia died on Monday night. She just went to sleep, and didn't wake up.'

Judith, stunned, said, 'I am so dreadfully sorry. She was such a special person. You must all feel devastated.'

'Yes. Judith, would you come to the funeral? Next Tuesday, the sixteenth. It would mean a lot to us all if you did.'

Judith hesitated. 'Will—will you all be there?'

'Of course. Not Edward, though. He's incarcerated on his airfield.'

'I'll—I'll have to have a word with Biddy.'

'Surely she'll be all right. Besides, it's time we all saw you again. Come on Sunday. Jump on the train. I'll meet you at Penzance. Must fly, darling. See you then.'

Judith sought out Biddy and explained the situation.

'Of course you must go. What a sadness.' Biddy eyed Judith, standing there chewing her lip. 'Will Edward be there?'

Judith shook her head. 'No. He can't get leave. If he was going, I'd probably make some excuse.'

'Darling, all that happened half a year ago. You can't languish over him for the rest of your life. So off you go.'

But Judith remained doubtful. To all outward appearances Biddy was recovered. She had joined the Red Cross and had started seeing friends again. But Judith knew that with Ned's death something of Biddy had died as well. Some days a flicker of her old liveliness returned; other days a depression fell upon her, and she lay in bed and refused to get up. Judith said, 'I don't like to leave you alone.'

'I shall have Hester down the road and all my nice Red Cross ladies. Besides, now that you have finished with the shorthand and typing, there's really no reason for you to stay. I don't want you to go, of course, but let's face it—I must be independent. A few days without you will give me practice.'

So Judith said, 'All right,' and all at once looked forward to returning to Nancherrow. It was going to be dreadfully sad, but she would be *there*, returned to her own pink bedroom, her loved possessions. She thought of being with Loveday, Athena, Mary, Diana and the Colonel, and she knew that it was the next best thing to coming home.

AFTERWARDS, WHEN IT WAS all over, everybody decided that Lavinia Boscawen's funeral was so exactly right that she might have arranged it herself: a sweet spring afternoon, Rosemullion church filled with flowers, and the narrow pews crammed with people from all parts of the country and all walks of life. Isobel was there, and the solicitor Mr Baines, and Jeremy's parents, Dr and Mrs Wells. The Nancherrow party occupied the first two pews. All of them were decked out in inky black except Athena, who wore a flowing maternity dress of cream crepe and looked like a serene angel.

They sang a hymn or two and Colonel Carey-Lewis read a passage from the Bible, and then there was a prayer. The coffin was borne out into the sunlit graveyard and the congregation followed.

Judith, tactfully distanced from the family, watched the ritual of burial. *Ashes to ashes, dust to dust.* And then she found herself wishing that Edward, for his sake, could have been here to help send Aunt Lavinia on her way.

The wake took place in the Nancherrow dining room. The great table had been set out with Mrs Nettlebed's tarts and scones, tiny cucumber sandwiches and iced fairy cakes.

Judith helped Loveday hand round cakes, pausing now and then to chat. She was headed for the sideboard when she found herself, midpassage, face to face with the solicitor.

'Mr Baines. How good of you to come.'

'Judith, I want to talk to you. Could we remove ourselves for five minutes or so? The Colonel says we may use his study.'

'Of course.' She eased her way from the room, and with Mr Baines she went down the passage to the study. She sank into a sagging leather armchair. 'What did you want to talk to me about?'

'A number of things. But first, how are you?'

She shrugged. 'All right.'

'Colonel Carey-Lewis told me of your cousin's death. Tragic.'

'Yes, it was. He was only twenty. It's terribly young to die, isn't it?'

Mr Baines sat down. 'He told me, too, that you'd decided not to join your family but to stay in this country.'

Judith smiled. 'You seem to have caught up on everything that's happened.'

'I see the Colonel from time to time at the Penzance Club. I like to keep tabs on my clients.' Judith watched as he took off his spectacles and gave them a polish with his silk handkerchief. 'Now, it is perhaps a little precipitant, but I wanted to have a word before you departed for Devon. It's about Mrs Boscawen's house.'

'The Dower House?'

'Exactly so. I wonder what your response would be if I suggested that you should buy it.'

Judith stared at him as if he had taken leave of his senses. 'The last thing in the world that I need just now is a *house*. I'll probably join the services and be away for years. Besides, isn't it part of the Nancherrow estate? Won't Colonel Carey-Lewis want it?'

'I have discussed it with him, and apparently not. Let me explain. As one of your trustees, I consider that property is probably the best investment you can make. And this is a good time to buy because house prices have dropped, as they always do in wartime. I know the future is filled with uncertainties, but we must look ahead. Whatever happens, you would have a home. Another consideration is your family. Owning the Dower House would mean a base for them to return to when their time in Singapore is over.'

Judith fell silent. All at once there was a great deal to think about. The Dower House. Her own home. Roots. Leaning back in the armchair, she gazed at the empty fireplace and let her imagination lead her through the quiet old house. She thought of the drawing room, sparkling with sunlight and firelight, the time-stopped atmosphere that never failed to enchant. She saw the terraces down to the orchard, Edward's hut. Would it be possible to deal with so many memories?

She said, 'I've always dreamt of having a house of my own. But if I can't live in it, what is the point?'

'It needn't stand empty,' Mr Baines pointed out. 'Isobel will go, of course. She's made plans to live with her brother and his wife. The house could be rented, perhaps to some London family anxious to evacuate to the country. Or we could find some person grateful for a roof over their head who would care for it . . .' He talked on, but Judith had stopped listening.

A person grateful for a roof over their head, a person who would care for the house. She said, 'Phyllis.'

Halted midstream, Mr Baines frowned. 'Sorry?'

'Phyllis could caretake.' Alight with excitement, she sat up, leaning forward. 'She used to work for us at Riverview.'

And she went on to explain about Phyllis, who had had to return to her mother's overcrowded house in St Just because her husband had joined the navy. 'Phyllis could look after the Dower House for us. Wouldn't that be the most perfect arrangement?'

'Judith, you're not buying a home for Phyllis. You're making an investment for yourself.'

'But it's *you* who wants me to buy it, and *you* suggested a caretaker. And I've come up with the perfect answer.'

He accepted this. 'Fair enough, but this is a big step we're considering, and an expensive one. You have to be certain.'

'How much will we have to pay?'

'I would guess in the region of two thousand pounds. There will be repairs and renovations, but the bulk of those will have to wait until the war is over.'

'Two thousand pounds. It seems a lot of money.'

Mr Baines allowed himself a small smile. 'But a sum that the trust can easily afford.'

'In that case, let's go ahead.'

They talked for a little, laying plans. 'I'll call you in Devon when I have any news,' Mr Baines promised. ' Then you should come back to Cornwall and we'll complete the arrangements.'

'I can't wait. Is it wrong to feel so excited on Aunt Lavinia's funeral day?'

'I think,' said Mr Baines, 'that the reason for your excitement would afford her nothing but pleasure.'

A MONTH HAD PASSED at Upper Bickley before the telephone call came through from Mr Baines. It was a Thursday morning. Biddy had taken herself off to her Red Cross ladies and Judith was in the garden when the telephone rang.

'Judith, Roger Baines here. The Dower House has all been arranged. All we need is your presence and a few signatures. Unfortunately, the surveyor's report is not that good.'

'Never mind,' she said. 'Some day we'll mend the defects. The most important thing is that we've got it. I'll come to Cornwall on Monday. I hope that's soon enough. Goodbye. And thank you.'

She hung up the receiver and stood there, smiling in an idiotic fashion for a moment or two. She'd take Biddy with her.

By noon on Monday they were in Penzance, where the newsagent's placards were black with the morning's news—GERMANS REACH THE BELGIAN COAST.

She walked to the offices of Tregarthen, Opie & Baines. Inside, Mr Baines stood up from behind his desk. 'Judith! Right on time too. Is Mrs Somerville with you?'

'Yes, and the dog. We're all settled in at the Mitre. She's taken Morag for a run on the beach, but I said I'd be back for a late lunch. I hope you can join us.'

'What a nice idea. Well, let's not waste any time.'

It didn't take very long. When the papers were signed, Judith filled out the cheque and pushed it across the desk to Mr Baines, who attached it neatly to the rest of the documents.

He leaned back in his chair. 'The Dower House is, actually, ready for habitation. All Mrs Boscawen's personal effects have been disposed of and Isobel leaves this afternoon. Her brother is coming to pick her up.'

'Is she terribly distressed? I'd like to see her before she goes.'

'In truth, I think she's quite excited starting out on her new life. And she has spent the last two weeks scouring every nook and cranny so that you will find no speck of dust.' He smiled. 'We'll go to Rosemullion after lunch. Then she can hand over the keys.'

'What about the furniture?'

'The Carey-Lewises want you to have it.'

'Oh, but—'

Mr Baines overrode Judith's protestations. 'None of it is particularly valuable, but it is perfectly usable and will do splendidly until you acquire some bits and pieces for yourself.'

AFTER A CHEERFUL luncheon with Biddy they all got into Mr Baines's car and set off for Rosemullion. Isobel was waiting at the Dower House when they arrived, dressed in her best black coat and skirt. She was ready for departure, but she took them round, basking modestly in their admiration for the labour she had put in washing curtains, polishing floors, cleaning windows.

They were walking downstairs again as Isobel's brother arrived at the front door. Her luggage was loaded into the car, then Isobel shook hands with all three of them and was driven away without, as Mr Baines observed, so much as a backward glance.

'I'm glad,' said Judith. 'Wouldn't it have been awful if she'd got all emotional? I'd have felt as though I was throwing her out. Let's put the kettle on and we can have a cup of tea.'

Because it was a warm afternoon they took their tea on the sheltered verandah. A breeze rustled the branches of a deep pink prunus, and somewhere a thrush sang. While they drank from Aunt Lavinia's rose-entwined bone-china cups, Morag went exploring.

Presently Biddy lay back in her chair and closed her eyes. Mr Baines and Judith left her and went on another tour of the house, this time with a beady eye for defects that needed attention—a damp patch in the attic, a dripping kitchen tap. Mr Baines then went outside to eye gutters and downpipes. Judith, her presence now unnecessary, returned to Biddy. On her way through the kitchen she took, from its hook, the key of the Hut. Biddy turned to her. 'Mrs Boscawen must have been a very tranquil lady.'

'Why do you say that?'

'Because I don't remember ever having been in such a tranquil place. It's like another country. Already Devon seems so far away.'

'Is that a good thing?'

'Yes. Upper Bickley is too full of memories. I wake in the night and think I hear Ned. I go into his bedroom and bury my face in his blanket and weep with desolation. It's been such a terrible winter. Without you I couldn't have endured it.'

Judith said, 'It's over now.'

'I still have to go back. Face up to reality. I know that.'

'You don't have to go back. We can move in here tomorrow.'

'But my poor little house in Devon! I can't just *abandon* it.'

'You can let it, furnished. Some naval family would jump at it, it's so handy for Plymouth. Staying here will be a lovely holiday for you, and you can help me sort things out.'

Biddy laughed. 'That won't be much of a holiday.' But Judith could see the growing excitement in her expression.

'Come on, Biddy, say yes. Now the sale is completed, I'm going to ask Phyllis and her baby to live here, so even if I do go off to be a Wren or something, the three of you can be here together. And I'll take you to Nancherrow, and once you've met all of them you won't feel a bit lonely. Don't you see? It all works out perfectly.'

'But how about Bob? I must be there if he has leave.'

'It's only a little further than Devon. Please don't think of any more objections.'

Finally Biddy succumbed. 'All right. We'll give it a try.'

'Now come and let me show you the garden.'

So together they stepped out across the grass to the rose garden, and then to the orchard. Biddy breathed the scented air.

'What's that little house?'

'Oh. That's the Hut. It was built for Athena and Edward.'

She went ahead of Biddy, climbed the wooden steps and smelt the warm odour of creosote. She unlocked the door. Saw the bunk where she had found and lost her love. And her eyes filled with tears.

'Judith.' Biddy was behind her.

She brushed the tears away and turned. She said, 'So stupid.'

'You and Edward?'

'I haven't been here since. I had to come today.'

Biddy said, 'This is yours now. You can fill it with new memories. And failing all, you can always use it as an extra spare room. For, possibly, guests who snore?'

All at once the tears receded and they were laughing. Biddy gave Judith a hug and shooed her out through the door. And they hurried back through the orchard and up through the garden to tell Mr Baines of the plans that they had laid.

THE DOWER HOUSE
Saturday, May 25

Dear Mummy and Dad,

Once more, ages since I have written. I am so sorry, but so much is happening. As you can see, we've moved in. Biddy and her dog and me, and Biddy loves it.

On Thursday, Biddy and I drove to St Just to see Phyllis, and we invited her to bring Anna and come and live here. Phyllis burst into tears, she was so overcome with delight. She and Anna will sleep in our attic, where Isobel used to sleep.

On Friday I took Biddy for lunch at Nancherrow. She and Diana were gassing away in no time and shrieking with laughter at silly jokes, and Biddy is going to join Diana's Red Cross group.

I really want to go and join up with the Wrens. The war news is ghastly. The Allies have fallen back to Dunkirk. But Mr Baines is utterly certain that we're going to win the war, so I have decided to be certain, too.

Lots of love,
Judith

THE NINE DAYS' WONDER—the evacuation of the British troops trapped at Dunkirk—began. The first men were brought home on the night of May 26, but Dunkirk was ablaze, and the jetties and harbours destroyed. And so what was left of the British Expeditionary Force gathered on the beaches to wait for rescue.

Troopships and naval destroyers, under constant gunfire and air attack, lay offshore, but there was no way that the beleaguered troops could reach them. Word went out, and the following night, from Dover, a fleet of small boats began to flow across the English Channel: yachts and barges, tugs and dinghies. The men who skippered these craft were old men and young boys, bank managers and fishermen—any person, sufficiently resolute, who had spent his peacetime summers in boats. Unarmed, raked by enemy fire, they delivered the troops from the beaches to the waiting troopships. On June 3 the operation ceased. Over three hundred thousand troops had been ferried home to England.

The 51st Highland was not at Dunkirk. This division remained in France to fight on alongside a disheartened French Army. It was a losing battle. The German advance continued until this last courageous remnant of the British Army was driven to the coast. Finally, at St-Valéry-en-Caux, they were surrounded by the German divisions, and all that remained of the Highlanders were marched into captivity. The Black Watch, the Argylls, the Seaforths, the Camerons, the Gordons. Gus.

During those dark days Judith existed on tenterhooks of anxiety and suspense. Gradually, in dribs and drabs, came news of who had been rescued and who had been left behind as prisoners of war. Palmer, the Nancherrow chauffeur, had made it. As had Edward Carey-Lewis, his fighter squadron having flown successive patrols over the mayhem of Dunkirk, driving German bombers away from the beaches. Mrs Mudge's nephew, from St Veryan, was posted missing, presumed killed.

After St-Valéry all hope was lost for Gus. They all prayed that he was alive and had been taken prisoner, but so many had been killed during the ferocious fighting that it seemed unlikely. Loveday refused to be comforted.

'THE THING TO DO,' said Mrs Mudge, 'is to keep busy. Least that's what people say, but how can I say that to my poor sister, worrying herself sick over whether her boy's dead or alive?'

Loveday had never seen Mrs Mudge so down.

'I feel I should go to St Veryan and be with her for a few days. For company there isn't nothing like a sister, is there?'

'Then why don't you go, Mrs Mudge?'

'How can I? Got the cows to milk and the dairy to see to.'

It was half past ten in the morning, and they were sitting at the kitchen table at Lidgey and drinking tea. Helping Walter and his father on the farm, feeding poultry and pigs, Loveday spent much of her day at Lidgey. Lately, since the black tidings of St-Valéry, she had taken to escaping here on the smallest excuse. For some reason she found the down-to-earth company of Mrs Mudge comforting. While trying to come to terms with the idea that Gus was dead, all she wanted to do was talk about him as though he were still alive. Mrs Mudge was good at this. Over and over she would say, 'Mind you, he might have been taken prisoner.'

Mrs Mudge pulled herself wearily to her feet and went to the range to pour herself another cup of tea. Loveday looked at her and thought that something must be done. By the time Mrs Mudge sat down again, Loveday had made up her mind. She said firmly, 'You must go to St Veryan. Today. For a week if necessary. Walter can help me, and I'll do the milking.'

EACH MORNING, after she had taken the full churns up to the end of the lane, delivered them to the milk-marketing lorry and brought back the empty churns to the dairy, Loveday walked back to Nancherrow, ravenously hungry for breakfast. Mrs Mudge had been away for a week and was returning to Lidgey. In a way, Loveday felt rather sorry. Coping with the milking had proved to be tremendously hard work. At first she had been slow and clumsy, but Walter, alternately swearing at her or handing out a bit of foul-mouthed encouragement, had been uncharacteristically cooperative and had seen her through.

Loveday was not sure if he had been told about Gus. Whatever, Walter said nothing. When Gus was staying at Nancherrow, the two young men had met one morning down at the stables and Loveday had introduced them, but Walter had been at his most offhand and mannerless. It had occurred to Loveday at the time that perhaps he was jealous, but the idea was so preposterous that she put it out of her mind.

The last cow had been milked and the little herd turned out into the fields again. Loveday crossed the farmyard and climbed the gate that led into the lane and sat there on top of the rail. This was one of her favourite views, and this morning the distant moors and fields looked particularly bright and sparkling.

Her mind, curiously, emptied. She thought about nothing for ages, and it felt rather pleasant, like floating in space. And then, gradually, mindlessness was filled with the image of Gus, striding up the lane towards her, with his painting gear slung in a knapsack over his shoulder. His presence came across so strongly that all at once she was consumed with the irrefutable conviction that he was still alive and thinking about her. She closed her eyes and sat clinging to the rail. And when she opened her eyes again, everything was different, and the world was brimful with the possibility of happiness.

She jumped off the gate and ran all the way to the house and through the back door.

'Take your boots off, Loveday. They're caked with dirt.'

'Sorry, Mrs Nettlebed.' In socked feet she came into the kitchen. She wanted to ask if there had been any news. But until there came some confirmation of Gus's safety, Loveday was not going to whisper a word of her new hope.

She said, 'What's for breakfast? I'm ravenous.'

'Fried eggs and tomatoes. On the hot plate in the dining room. Everyone else has finished already. You'd better hurry along.'

So Loveday washed her hands in the scullery, then went down the passage to the dining room. She was about to go in when the telephone began to ring. She stopped dead and waited and, when nobody answered, picked up the telephone.

'Nancherrow.' For some reason her mouth had gone dry.

Click, click went the telephone. 'Hello?' *Click, click.* 'Who's that?' A man's voice, blurred and distant.

'Loveday,' she said.

'Loveday, it's me. It's Gus.'

Her legs, literally, turned to water. She collapsed onto the floor, taking the telephone with her. 'Gus, where are you?'

'In hospital. Southampton. I'm OK. Being shipped home tomorrow. I tried to ring before, but there aren't enough telephones.'

'What—what happened? Are you badly hurt?'

'Just my leg. I'm on crutches, but all right. There's no time for more. I just wanted to speak to you. I'll write.'

'I'll write too. What's your address?'

But the line went dead. 'Gus? Gus?' She jiggled the hook on the receiver and tried again. 'Gus?' He was gone.

Still sitting on the carpet in her father's study, she laid her head against the cool dark wood of her father's desk and tears streamed quietly down her cheeks. She said aloud, 'I knew you were alive.'

And after a bit she got up, calling for her mother, and fled up the stairs to share the incredible news.

LOVEDAY RECEIVED two letters from Gus at the end of June. They came in the same envelope. One was a long account of his escape from France, the other a little note on a single sheet. The note said:

> *I thought your father might like to read the enclosed account, but this little note is just for you. It was so wonderful to hear your voice answering the telephone. I thought about you all the time I was waiting to get on that hellhole of a beach, determined that I was going to make it. Write to me and tell me everything you are doing.*
> *With all my love,*
> *Gus*

ON JULY 24, at two o'clock in the morning, Athena had her baby at Nancherrow, with old Dr Wells in attendance. She was called Clementina Lavinia Rycroft. The Colonel immediately sent a cable to Palestine letting Rupert know.

That evening Judith went to Nancherrow to see the new arrival. Old Dr Wells dropped in again to check on mother and child, and also to tell them that Jeremy was in a naval hospital near Liverpool. His destroyer had been sunk by a U-boat in the Atlantic, and he and three other men were in the sea, hanging on to a raft for a day and a night before they were picked up by a merchantman. He was suffering from exposure as well as burns from the explosion, and Mrs Wells had gone up to Liverpool to sit at his bedside.

Meanwhile, invasion fever had swept the country. Aluminium pots and pans were being collected and melted down and made into Spitfires. The Colonel was back in uniform, now as commanding officer of Rosemullion's defence volunteers—the Home Guard—with Nettlebed as his sergeant. In the air battles over the Channel young fighter pilots were doing brilliantly.

At the Dower House, little Anna was thriving. Cyril was in the Mediterranean and had been made a leading seaman. He'd sent Phyllis a photograph of himself, looking very brown and well. Phyllis thought she was in heaven, for after the dismal little house in Pendeen and then her mother's overcrowded cottage, the Dower House seemed the very height of luxury.

It was a Monday in July, washday, and outside in the washing green, a space between the garage and the back door, Judith and Phyllis were pegging out the laundry to dry. They paused as a car came up the gravel approach to the house and stopped. 'Know who it is?' said Phyllis.

'Yes.' Judith could feel the smile spread across her face. 'It's Jeremy Wells.' And she went across the grass to meet him.

Over the washing line Phyllis watched. She'd waited a long time to set eyes on the young doctor Judith had met all those years ago on the train. Only fourteen she'd been then, but she'd fancied him, no doubt about that. Then she'd met him again at Nancherrow, and Phyllis decided that it was written in the stars.

Judith, of course, pretended that there was nothing in it. But she'd been distressed enough when she heard that he'd been blown up in his ship. And now here he was, looking right as rain as far as Phyllis could see, and they were talking away nineteen to the dozen, grinning like Cheshire cats.

Judith called to her, and she crossed the crunchy gravel.

'This is Phyllis Eddy, Jeremy. Her husband's in the navy too.'

'Leading seaman,' Phyllis was able to tell him proudly.

'That's terrific. He must be doing well.'

Judith said, 'Jeremy's on his way to stay at Nancherrow.'

'Lovely,' said Phyllis. He wasn't actually good-looking, and he wore spectacles, but he had the nicest smile she'd ever seen.

He said, 'I'm not expected until lunchtime, and I couldn't drive through Rosemullion without coming to see you.'

Phyllis smiled to herself. 'Why don't you take Dr Wells inside, Judith? I'll get the last of the washing on the line.'

THERE WAS A GREAT deal to talk about, news to catch up on. It was eleven months since they had been together—that hot August Sunday that had ended so disastrously with Judith's precipitous flight from Nancherrow. Now, she thought, the months of war at sea had hardened Jeremy, honed him down, and there were lines on his face that had never been there before.

They talked about Athena and Rupert and baby Clementina. 'We all thought Athena would hand her straight over to Mary Millyway, but in fact she's frightfully maternal. And Loveday's become a total land girl. She works like a beaver and has dozens of hens.'

Jeremy had heard the story of Gus Callender's miraculous escape from St-Valéry. Judith told him of Gus's secondment to the Gordon Highlanders overseas. 'Gus and Loveday write to each other a lot.'

He asked about her family in Singapore, and she was telling him their latest news when Phyllis appeared with a coffee tray. She set it down and with a faintly coy smile went on her way. Judith, hoping that Jeremy had not noticed, handed him a cup of coffee. She said, 'We've talked about everybody but you. Your ship being torpedoed and everything.' She saw the expression on his face and added quickly, 'But perhaps you don't want to talk about it.'

'It doesn't matter.'

'Your father said you had burns.'

'Yes. My shoulder and back. Not too gruesome. No skin grafts.'

'What happens next? Another ship?'

'I devoutly hope so.'

'But aren't you frightened at the thought of going back?'

'Of course. But you learn to pretend you're not afraid.'

It was all very depressing. Judith sighed. 'So many battles.'

'And Edward's in the thick of it. Have you heard from him?'

'Only family news.'

'Doesn't he write to you?'

Judith shook her head. 'No.'

'What happened?'

She looked at him. 'Nothing.' But she was useless at lying.

'You loved Edward.'

Judith dropped her eyes. When she stayed silent, he spoke again.

'I know how it was. I knew, that last Sunday, when you were all in the garden at Nancherrow before lunch. Edward and I brought the drinks out. Then he went over to speak to you, and it was as if some magic, glittering ring enclosed the pair of you... held you apart from the rest of us.'

She found it almost unbearable to be reminded. She said, 'Perhaps that's what I wanted you all to think.'

'In the afternoon you left Nancherrow abruptly. Something happened, didn't it?'

There was little point in denial. 'Yes. I always loved Edward, Jeremy, right from the moment I met him. I imagined that he felt the same about me. But, of course, he didn't. He was not taken with the idea of a permanent commitment.'

'And you let that end all friendship?'

'I'd gone too far, said too much. I had to leave Nancherrow. I couldn't stay, not seeing him every day.'

'Are you still in love with him?'

'I try not to be. But I suppose you never fall out of love with the man who was the first love of your life.'

'How old are you?'

'Nineteen. Just.'

'So young.' Jeremy smiled, understanding. 'I'm sorry to have pried. It's just that I know Edward so well, his good points and his faults, and I was concerned. Afraid that he'd hurt you.'

'It's over now. And I don't mind *you* knowing.'

'Good.' He finished his coffee. 'Now, before I have to be on my way, will you show me round your property?'

So after a tour of inspection, which started at the top with the new attic nursery and ended in the kitchen, Judith went with him to his car. 'Will I see you at Nancherrow?' she asked.

'Of course. Tell you what, why don't you come down this afternoon, about three, and we'll walk down to the cove? We could swim.'

It was an inviting idea. She hadn't been to the cove for too long. 'All right. I'll bike over.'

THE LONG DRIVE was lined with hydrangeas in full flower. Judith had changed into shorts, and in her bicycle basket was her bathing suit rolled in a towel. As she cycled out of the trees, the windows of Nancherrow blinked in the sunshine. Judith parked her bike, leaning it against the house, and turned to go indoors. But she suddenly jumped nearly out of her skin because Jeremy had appeared from nowhere and was standing right behind her.

'Oh! You brute. What a fright! I never heard you!'

He put his hands on her arms, holding her still. 'Don't go in.'

His face was taut and, under his tan, very pale. Judith stood bewildered. 'Why?'

'A telephone call. Half an hour ago. Edward's dead.'

She was grateful that he held her so steadily, for her knees were trembling and she felt a terrible panic. She shook her head in passionate denial. 'No. Not *Edward*.'

'He was killed this morning. His commanding officer rang up to break the news. He spoke to the Colonel.'

Edward. She looked up into Jeremy's face and saw, behind the spectacles, that his eyes shone with unshed tears. And she thought, We all loved Edward, in different ways. Each one of us, every person who ever knew him, is going to be left with a great hole in his life.

'How did it happen?' she wanted to know.

'There was a tremendous enemy raid on the shipping in the harbour at Dover. Stukas and Messerschmitts. The RAF fighters got twelve German planes but lost three of their own. Edward's Spitfire was one of them.'

Shock had drained her. Now she found herself suffused with rage. 'How do they *know* he's dead? How can they be *sure*?'

'Another Spitfire pilot saw it happen. A direct hit from one of the Stukas. His plane exploded. No ejection. No parachute.'

She listened in silence, and hope died. Then Jeremy took her in his arms. She put her arms round his waist, and thus they did their best to comfort each other, her cheek pressed against his shoulder, feeling the warmth of his body. She thought of the family indoors, and the grief that had invaded the happy, sun-filled house. How were they going to come to terms with the agonising loss? All that was certain was that she, Judith, had no part in this private desolation.

She drew away from Jeremy. 'We shouldn't be here, you and I.'

'You go if you want to. But I must stay. The Colonel's anxious for Diana. There might be something I can do to help.'

'Oh, Jeremy, I wish I could be like you—strong. But at the moment I just want to escape. Go home. Is that awful?'

'No. Not awful at all.'

'Tell Diana I'll be back. Give her my love. Explain.'

He nodded. She got on her bicycle and pedalled slowly away.

Afterwards Judith had little recollection of that journey from Nancherrow to the Dower House. Her brain felt numb. She went inside, into the flagged hall, where the only sound was the slow ticktock of the grandfather clock.

'Phyllis!'

Silence. She went out onto the verandah. In the garden she saw Phyllis, sitting on a rug with Anna and some toys. 'Judith! We

weren't expecting you back so soon. Didn't you go swimming?'

'No.' Reaching Phyllis's side, Judith sank down on the rug beside her. 'Phyllis, I have to ask you something. If I go away, will you take care of Aunt Biddy for me?'

Phyllis frowned. 'What are you talking about?'

'I'm going tomorrow to Devonport. I'll sign on there, in the Women's Royal Naval Service. Of course, I'll come home again; I shouldn't get my orders for at least two weeks. And then I'll go for good. But you won't leave Biddy, will you, Phyllis? Promise me.'

She was, Phyllis realised, working herself into a state. But why? She laid a hand on Judith's shoulder. 'Of course I shan't. But what's this all about? I know you've been thinking for months about joining up. But why all at once? Has something happened?'

Judith took a deep breath and said it. 'Edward Carey-Lewis has been killed.'

'Oh, God.'

'Jeremy just told me. That's why I came home.' Suddenly her face crumpled like a child's, and Phyllis pulled her roughly into her arms and rocked her as though she were a baby. 'I don't think I can bear it, Phyllis.'

'Shh . . . There now.' Then all at once Phyllis understood. It was young Carey-Lewis to whom Judith had given her heart.

Life was so cruel, she thought, and war was worse.

THREE DAYS PASSED before Judith returned to Nancherrow. She propped her bicycle by the front door and went in. The old Nancherrow perambulator was parked in the hall and on the table was the usual pile of letters. Down the passage, the door of the small sitting room stood open and she saw Diana at her desk.

The desk was littered with correspondence, but Diana was simply gazing out of the window. She looked thin and pale.

Judith said her name, and she turned. She held out an arm. 'Darling, you've come.' Judith swiftly crossed the room and stooped to embrace her.

'Oh, Diana. I'm so sorry.'

'Darling, you mustn't say things like that, otherwise I go to pieces. You've just got to talk ordinarily to me. Did you bike over? Sit down for a moment.'

'I'm not disturbing you?'

'Yes, you are, but I want to be disturbed; writing letters was never my strong point, and so many people have written to us about Edward, and I simply have to answer them. And when I read the letters, even the most banal of condolences fill me with pride.'

'How is the Colonel holding up?'

'Shattered, lost. But trying not to show it too much. I keep think-ing of Biddy, when her Ned was killed. How terrible for her to have no other children to keep her going. *You* must have saved her life.'

'Diana, I've signed on with the Wrens.'

'Oh, darling.'

'I knew I had to go sometime. Biddy and Phyllis and Anna are set-tled at the Dower House, and there, I imagine, they'll stay for the duration. Perhaps you can keep an eye on them.'

'Of course. What are you going to do in the Wrens? Something frightfully glamorous?'

'No. Shorthand and typing. They call it being a writer.'

Diana sighed deeply. 'I can't bear the thought of you going, but I suppose you must. I couldn't bear saying goodbye to Jeremy either, when he left. And that reminds me.' She turned to her desk, opened a drawer. 'If you're going to leave us, you must have a key.'

'A key?'

'Yes. To my house in Cadogan Mews. When war broke out, I had half a dozen spares cut. Rupert's got one. Athena, of course. And Jeremy. And Edward had one . . . Oh, here it is.' She tossed it across and Judith caught it.

A small brass latchkey. 'But why are you giving me this?'

'Oh, darling, you never know. In wartime everybody goes to and fro through London, and it could be a place to lay your head for a night. Are you going to stay for lunch? It's rabbit pie.'

'No. I think another day. I only wanted to see you.'

Diana understood. 'All right.' She smiled. 'Another day.'

EACH MORNING Edgar Carey-Lewis made it his business to collect the post from the hall table, take it into the privacy of his study and go through all the condolence letters before handing them over to Diana. He read each one, filtering out well-meant but clumsy efforts which might upset his wife. These he answered himself.

This morning there was a large buff envelope, with an Aberdeen postmark. He sat at his desk and slit the envelope with his paper-knife. From it he withdrew a letter and a sheet of cardboard folded in two. The letter was signed 'Gus', and he felt touched that another of Edward's Cambridge friends had taken the trouble to write.

Gus wrote of Edward's charm, his boundless capacity for friend-ship, and his generosity of spirit. And then:

Looking through my Cambridge sketchbook I came upon this drawing I did of him. At a college cricket match, as he stood by the pavilion, padded up and waiting to go in. If you wish, toss it into the wastebasket, but I thought that you might like to have it.

257

Edgar laid the letter aside and took up the makeshift folder. Inside was a sheet of paper, the top edge rough where it had been torn from Gus's sketchbook.

His son. Sketched in pencil, later washed in colour. Edward, dressed for cricket, in white shirt and flannels. Face half turned, smiling, that stubborn lock of hair falling across his forehead. In a moment he was going to put up a hand and push it aside.

Edward.

All at once he couldn't see it properly because his vision was blurred by tears. Caught unawares, disarmed, he was weeping.

1942

The Wrens' quarters, where Judith had lived for eighteen months, was an uncomfortable block of flats in the North End of Portsmouth. Ten girls occupied each small flat, sleeping in double-decker naval-issue bunks. There was no heating, for reasons of fuel economy, and the cold of winter was so extreme as to be painful.

It was a relief to be going to London, even for a single night. Judith was looking forward to meeting Heather Warren, whom she hadn't seen since the beginning of the war. Heather was working for the Foreign Office now, somewhere very secret. And so, bundled up in her greatcoat and carrying her overnight bag, Judith stepped forth into the bitter January morning to catch a bus to the railway station.

The train was blissfully overheated. She took off her coat and hat and settled by the grimy window with her newspaper. It was then she became aware of an uncomfortable tickle at the back of her throat, the classic start to one of her miserable colds. Since joining the Wrens, she had endured at least three. I shall ignore you, she told the tickle. I've got two days' leave and you're not going to ruin it.

The train would soon be on its way. She unfolded her *Daily Telegraph*: JAPANESE ADVANCE THREATENS SINGAPORE was the headline. Filled with apprehension, she thought of her family. And of Gus Callender, now with the 2nd Gordons in Singapore. Judith had heard nothing from her family for weeks, and she prayed that by now they had left Singapore and gone to Sumatra or Java. Anywhere. Somewhere safe.

DIANA'S PROPERTY in London had been converted, years earlier, from two coachman's dwellings with stabling for horses beneath. The front door stood in the middle, with garage on one side and kitchen on the other. A narrow staircase led straight to a spacious upper floor, with a sitting room, two bedrooms and a bathroom.

Miraculously, the house had survived the Blitz. Judith took out her key and let herself in. She glanced into the kitchen, saw the fridge, empty and open, so closed its door and turned on the switch. Before the corner shop closed she would buy some rations.

Carrying her grip, she went up the stairs to the sitting room. She had been to Cadogan Mews several times and was always assailed by the comforting sensation of coming home. It was a bit like a miniature Nancherrow, comfortably appointed with cream curtains and thick beige carpeting, relieved here and there by Persian rugs. There were pictures and mirrors and even family photographs.

Judith looked at her watch. Half past twelve. No time to change. Now her throat felt rough as emery boards, and she went into the bathroom to take a couple of aspirin. Then she fixed her hair, put on some make-up, and left. Already she was running late for her rendezvous with Heather.

In Sloane Street she got a bus to Piccadilly Circus. The streets of London were battered and dirty, houses bombed and store windows boarded up. It was a city at war, and every other person seemed to be in uniform.

She got off the bus and walked to Swan & Edgar's. Heather was there, instantly visible with her dark, shining hair, and wearing an enviable scarlet overcoat and long suede boots.

'Heather! I'm sorry. Ten minutes late. No, don't hug me. I'm getting a cold, and I don't want to pass on any germs.'

'Oh, I don't give a damn for germs.' So they hugged anyway, laughing, because it was so wonderful to be together again.

'You're looking terrific, Heather.'

'You too. I like the uniform. It suits you.'

'How long have you got?' Judith asked.

'Just today. I've got to be back this evening. I'm starving. Let's eat lunch. Now, where to?'

Judith suggested the Berkeley, which was frightfully grand, and they set off to walk the short distance. Going inside, they were injected into a world of comfort. There were a great many people about—elegant women, staff colonels, Free French officers, all talking and drinking and laughing. When they were seated, a waiter came forward and Heather ordered champagne.

Judith muttered, 'Shades of Porthkerris Council School,' and they began to giggle.

The champagne was poured, and they raised their glasses and drank. Almost at once Judith felt better. She said, 'I must remember, champagne is the remedy for colds.'

It was a lovely lunch, the pretty restaurant so different from the battered streets beyond. They ate oysters, chicken and ice cream. They talked, catching up on the months since they had seen each other.

'Are there any nice chaps where you're working, Heather?'

She laughed. 'Most of them are so bright they're just about barmy. They're interesting, very cultured. But weird.'

'What do you do with the Foreign Office? What's your job?'

Heather shrugged, reached for a cigarette, and Judith knew that she didn't want to talk about it. 'Let's talk about you,' Heather said, blowing out a cloud of smoke. 'What's your job?'

'Not very exciting. I'm at Whale Island, the gunnery school. I work for the training-development officer.'

'Got a boyfriend?'

Judith smiled. 'Lots.'

'No one in particular?'

'No. Not after Edward. I don't want to go through that again.'

'I'm sorry.'

'It's over now.'

'Have you heard from your family? I read about Singapore in the paper this morning.'

'Not for too long. I just hope they've been evacuated. But I wish I could find out what's happening.' She looked at Heather. 'You—you couldn't find anything out, could you?'

Heather stubbed out her cigarette. 'No. We only deal with Europe.' She sighed. 'It's a bloody war, isn't it?'

They drank the coffee the waiter had brought to them, then paid the bill and plunged out into the bitter cold.

Heather had two tickets to a concert at the Albert Hall—Walton's Violin Concerto and Rachmaninov's Second Piano Concerto—given to her by the man she worked for. It was wonderful, everything that Judith had hoped for, but finally it was all over and time to go.

Heather said, 'It's been great. A wonderful day.'

'I adored every moment.'

'Goodbye, love.' A quick hug and a kiss, and she was gone.

JUDITH PROCEEDED back to Cadogan Mews, stopping at the corner store for groceries. Armed with her emergency ration card, she bought bread and eggs, margarine and milk and a jar of jam. Back at the house, she put the groceries in the fridge. She filled a hot-water bottle, went upstairs and put the bottle between the sheets.

She took more aspirin and looked in the bathroom mirror. Her face seemed peaky and pinched, and she drew a deep scalding bath and soaked in scented steam. Dried, she put on her nightgown and an old Shetland sweater and climbed into bed. Within moments she succumbed to exhaustion and closed her eyes. Almost at once, or so it seemed, she opened them again.

A sound. The front door opening and softly being closed. Some person had come into the house. Petrified, she lay rigid, unable to move, and then flung herself out of the bed and ran to the head of the stairs.

The newcomer was halfway up already, muffled in a heavy overcoat, gold lace gleaming on epaulettes. She saw him and felt weak with relief. Not an intruder breaking in. Instead, the one person— had she been given the choice—she would have really wanted it to be.

'Jeremy.'

He paused and looked up. 'Good heavens, it's Judith.'

'I thought you were at sea. What are you doing here?'

'I could ask the same question.' He came on up the stairs, dumped his canvas sailing bag and stooped to kiss her cheek. 'And why are you receiving gentlemen in your nightgown?'

'I was in bed, of course. I've got a rotten cold.'

'Then get back into bed right away.'

'No. I want to talk to you. How long are you staying?'

'Just till morning.' He placed his cap on the top of the newel post and draped the greatcoat over the banister. 'I had a couple of days' leave and went to Cornwall to spend them with my parents.'

'I haven't seen you for ages. Years.' She suddenly thought of something. 'There's nothing much to eat here. Are you starving?'

He was laughing. 'Don't worry. My mother packed me a nosebag.' He heaved up the canvas bag. 'Come, I'll show you.'

He led the way downstairs to the little kitchen and unloaded the bag. To Judith it was like watching somebody open a Christmas stocking. A bottle of whisky. Gordon's gin. Two lemons. An orange. A pound of farm butter. Last of all, a sinister bloodstained parcel.

'What's in there?' Judith asked. 'A severed head?'

'Steaks.'

'Where did you get steaks from? And farm butter? Your mother isn't dabbling in the black market, is she?'

'Grateful patients.' He opened the fridge and laid the butter and the bloody parcel alongside the meagre rations Judith had placed there. 'A whisky would do that cold good. Whisky and soda?'

He poured two whiskies, squirted in some soda. The drinks fizzed deliciously and he handed Judith one of the tall tumblers.

They went upstairs and made themselves comfortable by the gas fire, Jeremy settling in one of the armchairs and Judith curling up on the hearth-rug. She said, 'Tell me about you. What's been happening?'

'I had to come to London to see their lordships at the Admiralty. I'm getting a promotion. Surgeon commander.'

'Oh, Jeremy.' She was delighted. 'Well done. You'll get your brass hat. What else?'

'I'm joining a new ship. A cruiser, HMS *Sutherland*.'

'Still in the Atlantic?'

He shrugged. He was being cagey. He said, 'Have you heard from your family?'

'Not since the beginning of the month. All at once they're in so much danger. I wish now I'd gone to Singapore when I finished school. At least we'd all be together.'

To her horror her voice had started to shake. She took another sip of whisky. 'I'm all right. It's just that this evening I'm not feeling well. I'm sorry. I'm not very good company.'

'I like you just the way you are. However you are. My only regret is that I have to leave early in the morning. Now'—he got to his feet—'what we both need is a good hot meal and perhaps a little music. You get back into bed and I'll take charge of the galley.' He switched on the wireless. It was dance music, the distinctive strains of Carroll Gibbons relayed live from the Savoy Hotel. She imagined the diners crowding onto the floor.

He pulled her to her feet. 'Bed,' he said, and propelled her towards the bedroom. She went through the door and heard him go downstairs. She sat at the dressing table and gazed at her pallid reflection in the mirror. She combed her hair and put on a bit of lipstick and wished that she had a beautiful frilly bed jacket—the kind Diana wore. The old sweater was scarcely romantic. But this was Jeremy, so did she want to look romantic? The question caught her unawares, but there didn't seem to be any answer, and so she got into bed again, savouring the delicious smells emanating from downstairs.

Presently Jeremy appeared at the door, carrying a tray. He had taken off his jacket and wore an apron over his dark blue sweater. He set the tray on the bed beside her. The steaks were still sizzling, served with tinned peas—even gravy. There were, as well, two replenished drinks.

'Eat the steak before it gets cold,' he said.

It was all delicious and immediately restoring. And her steak was so tender that it slipped easily down her painful throat.

Finally she told him, 'I'm completely stuffed,' and she lay back on the pillows in total satisfaction. 'Thank you, Jeremy. You never cease to surprise me. I didn't know you could cook.'

'Any man who's ever sailed a boat can cook, even if only to fry a mackerel.'

Carroll Gibbons and his orchestra were playing their sign-off tune. A second or two of silence, and then the chimes of Big Ben tolled out, slow and sonorous. 'This is London. The nine o'clock news.' Jeremy looked at Judith enquiringly, and she nodded. However dire or grave, she must listen, and she would be able to cope, simply because Jeremy was there, strong and companionable.

The news was bad. The Japanese were closing in. Singapore had suffered its second day of bombing . . . trenches and fortifications being dug . . . fierce fighting on the Muar River.

Jeremy went to the sitting room and switched the wireless off. Presently he returned. 'Doesn't sound too good, does it?'

'Gus Callender's there too. With the Second Gordons. Poor Loveday. Poor Gus.'

'Poor you.' He leaned down and kissed her cheek. 'I'll take the tray away and tidy up the kitchen. Then I'll bring you a pill. I brought some back from America. They look like small bombs, but they usually do the trick. You'll be all right in the morning.'

He went, and Judith was left alone in the warm, downy bed. It was strangely quiet. Quite suddenly, without meaning to, she started to think about her mother. Not as she was now, half a world away, in mortal danger and probably terrified, but as she *had* been. As Judith remembered her last, at Riverview.

Riverview. She remembered getting off the train after school and climbing the path to the house, bursting in through the door, calling 'Mummy!' And she was always there. In her pretty sitting room, with tea ready on the table. She heard her voice, reading to Jess before bedtime. Day had slipped into day without much excitement. But nothing bad had ever happened either.

There was, of course, the other side of the coin. Molly Dunbar, sweet and pliant, had been an ineffectual mother. Change had always alarmed her. War, disaster, brought out the best in some women— steadfast courage, enterprise, determination. But Molly Dunbar was barren of such resources. She would be defeated. Destroyed.

'No.' Judith heard herself speak the word, an anguished refutation of her own fears. As though it were possible to shut out despair, she turned and buried her face in the pillow. She heard Jeremy coming back up the staircase, across the sitting room.

His voice. 'Did you call me?'

Still muffled in pillows, she shook her head.

'I've brought the magic pill. And a glass of water.' He sat on the edge of the bed beside her. 'Judith!'

Furious with weeping, she flung herself onto her back and stared up at him with tear-sodden eyes. 'I don't want pills,' she told him. 'I just want to be with my mother. I *hate* myself for not being with her.'

He said nothing to this, just held out the pill, which did indeed look like a tiny bomb. 'Swallow this, and then we'll talk.'

With an effort she raised herself onto one elbow, took the pill, and sank gratefully back onto the pillows. Jeremy smiled. 'Do you want to try to sleep?'

'No.' She sighed. 'It's so *stupid*, not to be able to stop thinking. So *stupid*. I'm twenty years old and I want my mother. I want to hold her and touch her and know she's safe.'

Tears filled her eyes again, and she felt too weak to control them. 'It's six years since we were together. And now I just want a letter. Something. So that I know where they *are*.'

'You mustn't give up hope. Even now they may be en route to somewhere safer. Communications at a time like this are bound to fall apart. Try not to be too despondent.'

Judith thought about this for a bit. Then she said, 'My mother isn't strong. She has no confidence, and I fear for her.'

The tears returned, streaming down her cheeks. Jeremy could scarcely bear it. She seemed so despairing that he did what he'd been longing to do all evening. He took her into his arms and drew her near. She lay passive, grateful.

Her hand came up to touch the thick wool of his sweater, and her fingers closed upon it, clinging to him.

She took a long breath. 'Jeremy, when you were clinging to that raft in the middle of the Atlantic, what did you think about?'

'Staying afloat. Staying alive.'

'Didn't you remember things? Lovely places? Good times?'

'I tried to.'

'What in particular?'

It was clearly important to her, and so Jeremy, trying to ignore the physical arousal of his body, dug into his memory for the images that still had the power to delight him. 'Autumn Sundays in Truro, and the bells of the cathedral ringing out for evensong. Being at Nancherrow. Early-morning swims with Edward and, walking back, knowing that we'd be eating the most tremendous breakfast. Music. "Jesu, Joy of Man's Desiring", and knowing that you had come back to Nancherrow.'

'Music's good, isn't it? It lifts you up, away from the world.'

He said, 'That's me. It's your turn now.'

She sighed. 'All right. My house. My own home. The way it feels, and the clock ticking in the hall, and the view of the sea. Knowing that I can go back one day and never leave it again.'

He smiled. 'You hang on to that,' he told her. He looked down at her face, at the long lashes against the pale cheeks, at the shape of her mouth. He leaned down and kissed her forehead. 'You're tired, and I've got an early start. I think we should call it a day.'

At once her eyes flew open in alarm and her grip on his sweater tightened. Jeremy, telling himself to be resolute, began to ease away. 'You mustn't go,' she said. 'Please. Don't leave me.'

'Judith—'

'No, don't go.' And she added, 'It's a double bed. There's masses of space. I'll be all right if you stay. Please.'

Torn between desire and his inbred good sense, Jeremy hesitated. 'Is that a good idea?' he asked. 'If I spend the night with you, I shall, in all probability, make love to you.'

She was neither shocked nor seemed particularly surprised. 'That doesn't matter.'

'What do you mean, it doesn't *matter*?'

'I mean, if you want to, I would like you to make love to me.' Suddenly she smiled. He had scarcely seen her smile all evening, and he felt his heart turn over. 'It's all right, Jeremy. I want you to hold me and make me feel safe.'

'I can't make love to you with all my clothes on.'

'Then go and take them off.'

'I can't. You've got hold of my sweater.'

She smiled again, and her hold on him loosened.

'JUDITH.'

She stirred and put out a hand to touch him, but the bed was empty. She dragged open her eyes. Jeremy was sitting beside her, dressed and shaved. 'I've brought you a cup of tea.'

A cup of tea. 'What time is it?'

'Half past five in the morning. I'm on my way.'

She stretched and yawned and pulled herself into a sitting position, and he handed her the steaming cup. 'I just wanted to say goodbye. I wanted to say thank you.'

'Oh, Jeremy, I'm the one who should be grateful.'

'It was lovely. Perfect. A memory.'

Suddenly Judith felt shy. She lowered her eyes.

'Try not to worry too much,' he said. 'And take care of yourself. I'll write. I'll write and try to say all the things I wish I'd said last night. On paper I'll probably make a much better job of it.'

'You didn't do too badly last night. But I'd love a letter.'

'Goodbye, darling Judith.'

'If you take this tea away from me, I'll say goodbye properly.'

And he laughed and relieved her of the cup and saucer, and they embraced and kissed like the friends they had always been, but now like lovers too. 'Don't get blown up again, Jeremy.'

'I'll do my best not to.' Then he drew away from her and Judith heard the door close behind him. Almost instantly she was asleep.

It was ten o'clock before she woke again. She thought of Jeremy, smiling to herself, remembering their lovemaking. An interlude of magic unexpectedness, and even joy. Everything was changed now.

Meantime, she realised that she was recovered. The cold was gone.

How much of this was due to Jeremy, rather than his professional medications and a good night's sleep, it was impossible to say. Whatever, she was herself again, filled with energy.

She didn't have to report back to quarters until evening, but at the back of her mind there lurked the possibility of a letter from Singapore, and all at once it became important to return without delay. She flung back the covers and sprang out of bed.

By two o'clock in the afternoon she was back at the Wrens' quarters, signing herself in. She went to the wooden grid of mailboxes, and under 'D' there was a thin blue envelope with her mother's writing. Judith took it to her flat. Because it was Sunday there was nobody around. She sat on a bunk, still in her greatcoat, and slit the envelope.

Orchard Road, Singapore
January 16, 1942

Dearest Judith,

I haven't much time, so this will be rather short. Tomorrow Jess and I sail on the Rajah of Sarawak *for Australia. Kuala Lumpur fell to the Japanese four days ago, and they are advancing like a tide towards Singapore. Dad has to stay here, as he is responsible for the company office and the staff, and if it wasn't for Jess I would stay and take my chance, but what can I do? When we get to Australia, I shall send you a cable to let you know that we have arrived. Please tell Biddy, as I haven't time to write to her.*

If anything should happen to Dad and me, you will look after Jess, won't you? I love you so much. I think about you all the time, darling Judith.

Mummy

It was the last letter from her mother. Four weeks later, on Sunday, February 15, Singapore was surrendered to the Japanese.

IT WAS NEARLY a month since Jeremy had said goodbye to Judith. He was in New York, where HMS *Sutherland* was having a refit. For the Royal Navy, New York was open house, and Jeremy had never experienced such hospitality.

At a cocktail party a delightful couple called Eliza and Dave Barmann had invited him to 'weekend' with them on Long Island. Now, in their large old clapboard house on the water's edge, he sat at a desk writing to Judith.

Jeremy laid down his pen, his eye deflected by the sight of a ferry-boat chugging across Long Island Sound. He had been putting this letter off because it was so personal, and so important, that he feared he would not be able to find the right words. He watched the boat disappear from view, then he picked up his pen again.

Finding you at Diana's house was one of the best and most unexpected of bonuses. I am so grateful that I was there when you were feeling unwell and so worried. Being with you that night has become, in retrospect, like a small miracle, and I shall never forget your sweetness.

The truth is that I love you very much. I suppose always have done. But I didn't realise it until that day you came back to Nancherrow, and I heard 'Jesu, Joy of Man's Desiring' from your room, and knew that you were home again. In that moment I finally understood how important you were to me.

One day the war will end, and with a bit of luck we'll all come through it, and we'll go back to Cornwall and pick up the threads of our lives. When that happens, I would like us to be together again, because I cannot contemplate a future without you.

Here he stopped once more, assailed by self-doubt. He wanted, more than anything, to marry Judith, but was it fair even to suggest such a thing? At over thirty, so much older than she, he wasn't much of a catch—a country GP short on worldly goods, while Judith, thanks to her late aunt, was a girl of wealth and property. And she had grown so lovely, so desirable, that it was obvious that men were going to fall in love with her. Was it being desperately selfish, at this moment in time, to ask her to marry him?

He simply didn't know, but he ploughed on.

We have always been friends, and I don't want to say anything that might spoil our good relationship for ever. But please write to me as soon as you can, and let me know whether in time you might consider our spending the rest of our lives together.

I love you so deeply. Please *write and set my mind at rest.*

Finished. He threw down his pen for the last time, then sat gazing despondently at the pages which had taken him all morning to compose. Perhaps he shouldn't have wasted his time. Perhaps he should tear them up, forget it all.

'Jeremy.'

His hostess appeared through the open door. She said, 'We're taking you to the club for lunch. Did you get your letter finished?'

'Just about.'

'Do you want to mail it?'

'No. No, I might want to add something later. I'll post it when I get back to the ship. I'll just go and tidy myself up.'

AT THE END OF APRIL, at the end of a long day, Judith finished typing a final letter for Lieutenant-Commander Crombie. It was nearly six.

The two Wrens who shared the office had already packed up and gone, and now Judith left too. It was a golden spring evening and she cycled out onto the main road, heading back to quarters. She was tired. Pedalling along, she thought about putting in for leave, going back to Cornwall. Just for a few days; that was all she needed.

A terrible void had been left by the loss of contact with her family. For nearly seven years she had lived with the pleasurable anticipation of a regular envelope filled with trivial, precious news from Singapore. But now each time she returned to quarters, she had to remind herself that there would be nothing to look for in the pigeon-hole labelled 'D'.

Not even a letter from Jeremy. Over two months had passed since they had said goodbye in London. *I'll write*, he had promised, but nothing had come. As the weeks slipped by, there dawned the uncomfortable suspicion that Jeremy had made love to her for much the same reason that Edward had. After all, it had been she, unwell and deeply upset, who had begged him to stay with her. *Darling Judith*, he had called her. All that she could imagine was that he had had second thoughts. Their love in London had simply been an interlude, charming but lightweight. She felt dreadfully hurt.

These not very cheerful reflections lasted all the way back to quarters. She went to the mailboxes and found a scrap of signal pad: *Wren Dunbar. 1630 hours. Telephone call from Loveday Carey-Lewis. Please ring back.*

Loveday. What was Loveday wanting?

She went in search of a free telephone, dialled the number for Nancherrow and dropped some coins in. Loveday answered.

'*Judith!* Sweet of you to ring back. Look, I'll be terribly quick. Mummy and I are coming to London this weekend, staying at the mews. Please come up too. Can you?' She sounded frantic.

'Well, I could try for a short weekend.'

'Oh, do. Say it's dreadfully important. Life and death. Mummy and I are going up in the train. How soon can you be with us?'

'I don't know. Saturday at the earliest.'

'Perfect. Make any old excuse. Anything. Byeee.' *Click*.

Judith, in some puzzlement, replaced the receiver. What on earth was Loveday up to now? The only thing that was perfectly clear was that tomorrow morning somehow she must persuade First Officer to sign a weekend pass.

SATURDAY WAS A BEAUTIFUL April morning, without a cloud in the sky. In the warm spring sunshine London looked surprisingly lovely. Carrying her overnight bag, Judith walked the cobbled length of the mews to Diana's house and opened the door.

268

Loveday was at the head of the stairs. 'Hello. I was terrified you wouldn't make it. Did you have to tell frightful lies to get permission?'

'No. Just bow and scrape a bit.' Judith climbed the staircase. She dumped her bag and they hugged. 'Where's Diana?'

'Shopping, needless to say. We're meeting her at the Ritz for lunch.'

Judith flopped down on one of the ample sofas and sighed with pleasure. 'When did you get here?'

'Thursday, on the train.' Loveday had curled up in one of the big armchairs. 'Everybody sends their love—Pops, Athena, Mary Millyway, the Nettlebeds.'

'What news of Rupert?'

'Battling it out in North Africa. But he writes long letters to Athena.' She fell silent. Across the room they faced each other, and the laughter died from Loveday's face. 'At least she hears from him. Nothing, I suppose, from your family?'

Judith shook her head. 'Not a word. It's like a shutter's come down. But the boat Mummy and Jess were on never got to Australia. The *Rajah of Sarawak* was probably torpedoed, but there's been no official confirmation.'

'And your father?'

She shook her head again. 'Nothing.' Then, 'And Gus?'

For a moment Loveday sat, eyes downcast, her fingers picking at the braid of the armchair. Then abruptly she sprang to her feet and went to stare out of the window. After a bit she said, 'Gus is dead.'

Judith felt cold with shock. 'Then you've had news?'

'No. But I know.'

'*How* can you know he's dead?'

Loveday shrugged. 'I just know.' And then she turned to face Judith. 'I would know if he was alive. Like I did after St-Valéry. Then, it was like a message, but without any words. And I was right. He was safe. But after Singapore fell, every day I sat on the gate by the Lidgey farmyard and thought and thought about Gus, and tried to get a message to him, and to get him to send one to me. There's nothing there but darkness and silence. He's gone.'

Judith was horrified. 'But, Loveday, you mustn't give up hope. Just because it happened once, that telepathy thing, it doesn't mean it's bound to happen again.'

Loveday was immovable, stubborn as she had always been once she had set her mind on something. 'I would know if he was alive. And I know, I *know*, that he's been killed.'

'Oh, Loveday.' Judith sighed. 'Is this what you had to tell me? Is this why you wanted me to come to London?'

'That. And other things.' Then Loveday dropped her bombshell. 'I'm going to get married. I'm going to marry Walter.'

'*Walter*. Walter Mudge?' The whole idea was inconceivable. 'But what has got into you that you want to marry Walter? You love Gus—'

Loveday rounded on her. 'Gus is dead,' she shouted, 'so I'll never marry Gus. And don't tell me to wait for him, because what is the use of waiting for a man who's never coming back to me?'

Judith, prudently, made no answer to this. She changed her tack. 'Look, you're only nineteen. Even if you're right about Gus, there are thousands of other men in the world just waiting to come into your life. I understand about you and Walter. You work together, and you see him all the time. But, Loveday, what have you got in common with Walter Mudge?'

Loveday threw her eyes to heaven. 'Oh, Lord, we're onto that. Lower-class, ill-educated farmworker. Marrying beneath me—'

'I don't think that.'

'I've heard it all, particularly from Mary Millyway. But Walter's my friend, Judith. I like working with him. We're the same sort of people. Besides, he's masculine, attractive. I thought you'd understand. Back me up.'

Judith shook her head. 'You know I'd back you up to the ends of the earth. It's just that I'm not able to sit and watch you making such a mess of your life. After all, you don't *have* to marry him.'

'Yes, I do. I'm going to have a baby.'

'Oh, *Loveda*y. When did . . . I mean—'

'Don't try to put it delicately. If you're asking when was the baby conceived, I'm happy to tell you. At the end of February, in the hayloft over the stables, and I'm not in the least ashamed.'

'You thought Gus was dead?'

'I knew he was. I was so lonely, so unhappy. And Walter and I were seeing to the horses and suddenly I started to cry, and I told him about Gus and he took me in his arms and kissed away my tears. It was the most comforting thing that had ever happened to me.' She was silent for a little and then said, 'It didn't seem wrong at all.'

'Does your mother know?'

'Of course. I told her as soon as I was sure. And Pops too.'

'What did they say?'

'A bit astonished, but sweet. Said I didn't have to marry him if I didn't want to. Another baby in the nursery wouldn't make any difference. And when I said I *did* want to marry Walter, they bucked slightly but said that it was my decision. Besides, with Edward gone, at least they know I'll always be around.'

All of which, knowing the Carey-Lewises, was perfectly understandable. In their charmed, upper-class fashion they had always been a law unto themselves. Their children's happiness came before everything else, and their loyalty to those children would always override social mores. Diana and the Colonel, shoulder to shoulder, were clearly making the best of the situation. The most sensible thing that Judith could do was join their ranks and gracefully accept the inevitable.

Suddenly she was smiling, despite the prick of tears behind her eyes. She pulled herself off the sofa.

'Oh, Loveday, I'm sorry. I had no right to be so difficult.' And Loveday came to her, and they were both laughing and hugging. 'I was just a bit surprised. Forget everything I said. You and Walter will be fine. When's the wedding?'

'Next month. You'll come, won't you?'

'I wouldn't miss it for anything. I'll fix a week's leave right away. Where are you going to live, you and Walter?'

'There's an old cottage on Lidgey. Pops is going to do it up for us, add on a proper bathroom. It's only two rooms, but it'll do for now.'

'A real little love nest. What about a honeymoon?'

'Haven't really thought about it. Look'—Loveday peered at her watch—'it's midday. We'll have to set off for the Ritz in a moment. Let's have a drink to celebrate.' She headed for the stairs and then turned. She was grinning like the wicked little girl Judith remembered from schooldays. 'Thank heavens we're grown-up. I never thought it would be much fun, but it is fun, isn't it?'

Fun. Loveday's high spirits were infectious, and Judith felt the lift of her own heart. The dark tides of war, with all its anxieties and anguish, receded, and she was filled with the reasonless happiness of childhood; something she had not experienced for a long time. After all, they were young and pretty, the sun was shining and the air filled with the scent of spring flowers. Loveday was going to be married and she herself would be going home on leave for the wedding. She smiled. 'Yes. Yes, it's fun.'

> THE DOWER HOUSE
> *Sunday, May 31*

My darling Bob,

Well, the wedding is over, and the happy pair are on a three-day honeymoon at the Castle Hotel in Porthkerris. Goodness, I wished you had been there. But I said a little prayer for you, stuck up there in Scapa Flow.

Today I'm on my own. Judith, Phyllis and Anna have taken a picnic down to Nancherrow cove, so I am able to sit down and write to you all about the wedding while it is still fresh in my mind.

On Thursday, Judith arrived home, and she behaved exactly

like a small girl back for the school holidays, i.e., tore off her uniform and put on old clothes, and then went from room to room checking every detail of her little domain.

On Friday she went off on her bike to Nancherrow to inspect Loveday's new house, which is now just about finished. The afternoon was spent gathering wild flowers with which to decorate the church, and we spent Friday evening decorating—Athena and Diana and Mary Millyway and myself.

Saturday was the most perfect day for a wedding. We all got into our rather outworn finery and walked down the hill to the church.

I have to admit the church looked really lovely, lacy with cow parsley and garlands of honeysuckle. The place was packed. Diana looked a dream in pale turquoise silk, and the Colonel immensely distinguished in a grey frock coat. Little Clementina Rycroft was a fairly inefficient bridesmaid, removing her shoes and socks before she walked down the aisle and ending up on Mary Millyway's knee sucking jujubes.

As for the bride and groom, they made an extraordinarily attractive couple. Loveday looked enchanting in white voile, white stockings, and white ballet slippers. No veil. Just a wreath of marguerite daisies on her shining dark head.

Then we piled into carts the Colonel had hired. Nancherrow was looking suitably festive, with flowers everywhere and long tables all set for luncheon in the courtyard. Even with rationing, it really was a feast. There was cold salmon and roast pork, and wonderful puddings coated with cream.

The meal took quite a long time, but by five o'clock the bride and groom were on their way. Loveday flung her bouquet at Judith, and then they got into Mr Mudge's old car and rattled off to Porthkerris.

It's been such a special time. I think it's done us all good to put depressing news out of our minds, just for a little, and simply enjoy ourselves. As well, it has given me cause to think ahead. If the worst happens, and Molly and Bruce and Jess never return to us, then I think that you and I and Judith must make every effort to stay together after the war.

Perhaps it would be a good idea for us to find somewhere near Rosemullion. In truth, I don't want to go back to Upper Bickley. The house is too full of memories. Here I have made a new life. This is a place where I would like to stay. Would you mind, my darling Bob?

My love. Take care of yourself.
Biddy

1945

Trincomalee, Ceylon. HMS *Adelaide*, her steel decks simmering in the heat, was the depot ship for the Fourth Submarine Flotilla. Her permanent berth was Smeaton's Cove, a deep inlet enclosed by two jungly promontories. The commanding officer was Captain Spiros, and each day two Wren writers were ferried on board the ship to work in his office. One of these was a languid girl called Penny Wailes. The other was Judith Dunbar.

Judith had been here about a year. In September 1944, after D-day, she had volunteered to go overseas, and the next thing she knew she was on a ship sailing through the Indian Ocean with a small detachment of Wrens towards Trincomalee. Now, with the war in Europe over, more ships of the Royal Navy arrived daily, and in the haven of the harbour lay battleships, cruisers, destroyers and frigates—sufficient might to strike terror into the most aggressive of enemies.

At the end of another long, broiling day Judith and Penny stepped ashore at the naval headquarters jetty and set off to walk wearily up the dusty white road to the Wrens' quarters. A long palm-thatched building was the mess and the recreation room.

In the mess hall Sinhalese stewards were serving an early supper, and Judith helped herself to a glass of lime juice, then went out onto the terrace. A path led to the far side of the camp, where sleeping bandas—thatched huts—were grouped beneath trees for shade.

At this time of day there were always a good many Wrens about. Those who worked ashore finished at four o'clock and so had plenty of time for a game of tennis or a swim. They wandered about in bathing suits, pegged underwear to washing lines, or had already changed into the khaki slacks and long-sleeved shirts which were regulation evening wear in this area of malarial mosquitoes.

Judith reached her own banda and went in. Twelve beds stood on either side, not unlike a school dormitory, and wooden fans, high in the palm-thatched ceiling, stirred the air into some semblance of coolness. Over each bed hung a white mosquito net.

Girls lay reading books, perusing mail, blancoing shoes. One had put a Bing Crosby record on her portable gramophone: '*When the deep purple falls, Over sleepy garden walls . . .*'

Judith flopped down on her bed, her hands linked beneath her head. It was strange how things happened. Days passed when she didn't even think of Cornwall, the Dower House and Nancherrow. There was little opportunity for brooding, and old times, old friends were all an age away. But now, hearing 'Deep Purple', precipitated a flood of recollections that had lain dormant for months. That record was inextricably entwined with those last days before the war because Athena had brought it down from London.

She thought of the group. The picture that had never been painted but remained in her imagination: *Before Lunch, Nancherrow, 1939*. The green lawns, the blue sky, the sea, the breeze skittering the fringe of Diana's sun umbrella, the dark shadow cast upon the grass. And the figures who sat about in deck chairs or on tartan rugs.

Edward, the golden charmer, loved by all. Shot out of the sky during the Battle of Britain. Athena, shining blonde head, bare arms the colour of dark honey. Then not even engaged to Rupert Rycroft. Now she was twenty-seven and Clementina was five, and Clementina had scarcely ever seen her father. Rupert, the archetypal Guards officer. He had survived the North African campaign and then Sicily, only to be nigh mortally wounded in Germany. The doctors had amputated his right leg.

Gus Callender, the dark, reserved young Scot. The engineering student, the artist, the soldier, who had slipped so briefly into their lives, only to disappear in the mayhem of Singapore. *He is dead*, Loveday had insisted. And Loveday was now a farmer's wife and the mother of Nathaniel. Gus's name was no longer mentioned.

Finally, Jeremy Wells. News of him had filtered out to Judith via letters from home. He had come through the Battle of the Atlantic and had been posted to the Mediterranean, but that was all she knew. Since the night with him in London, she had received no message, no letter. She told herself that he was out of her life, but sometimes she yearned to see his face again, to talk. And yet, what would they have to say to each other after all the years? Time had healed the hurt that he had inflicted, but the wound had left her wary.

'Is Judith Dunbar in here?' A Wren was making her way down the banda towards Judith's bed.

'Yes, I'm here.' She sat up.

'Sorry to burst in, but I just looked through my mail and I got one of your letters by mistake. Thought I'd better bring it.'

She handed it over. Judith saw Loveday's writing and experienced a spooky nudge of coincidence. 'Deep Purple', and now a letter from Loveday. She hadn't had one from her in months. She leaned back, slitting the envelope with her thumbnail.

Lidgey
July 22, 1945

Darling Judith,
Nat and I have just been for tea at the Dower House, and I missed you so much that I thought I would write. Nat is asleep and Walter's gone to the pub to have a jar with his mates. Nat's

274

two and a half now, and the biggest thing you've ever seen.

Biddy told me that your Uncle Bob has been posted to Colombo. Funny that you have both ended up there. I wonder if you've seen him yet. I looked on the map, and it's the other side of the island from Trincomalee.

News of Nancherrow. About two months ago Athena and Clementina left, to go and live in Gloucestershire with Rupert. He was brought home and was in hospital for ages, and then in a rehabilitation place learning to walk with a tin leg. So he has been invalided out, and he and Athena are living in a farmhouse on his father's estate, and he's going to learn all about running the place.

The war being over is a great relief, but everyday life hasn't changed much, still only a trickle of petrol, and food as tight as ever. But we can always slay a hen, and there are still eggs. One of the bottom fields of Lidgey is now a vegetable garden, and Walter's father and Nettlebed work it together. Mrs Mudge is still slaving away in the dairy. She adores Nat and spoils him dreadfully.

Now I suppose I must wash up the supper things, which are all over the place. Do write back. It seems funny walking down to Nancherrow and having to tell myself that you aren't there.

Love, love,
Loveday

ON A MONDAY in August came news about the bomb dropped on Hiroshima. Then, three days later, came news of Nagasaki. After a few more tense days the Japanese finally surrendered.

All the ships of the fleet held thanksgiving services, and the Royal Marine buglers played the last post in memory of all the men who had been killed. There were great celebrations that night, the whole East Indies Fleet lit up with flares and searchlights, rockets exploding and hooters hooting.

It was wonderful, but at the same time Judith felt a bit scared. She knew that sooner or later somebody would tell her what had become of Mummy and Dad and Jess.

SHE WAITED FOR NEWS. Life continued, travelling each morning to HMS *Adelaide*. Long, sweltering hours spent typing. Back to quarters each evening.

Perhaps now, she would tell herself. Perhaps today.

Her anxieties were compounded by the driblets of information trickling in from the first of the Japanese prison camps—atrocities, slave labour, starvation, disease. Everyone in the captain's office was thoughtful and kind, and each evening as they made the return journey Penny remained at Judith's side until they had passed through the Regulating Office and confirmed that there was still no news.

And then at six o'clock one evening Judith was in her banda after a swim, combing her wet hair, when one of the leading Wrens from the Regulating Office came in search of her.

'Dunbar. Message for you. You're to go and see First Officer tomorrow morning. Ten thirty. She's fixed it with Captain Spiros.'

'Fine. Thanks,' she heard herself say quite calmly.

The next morning she blancoed her shoes and her cap, put on a fresh white uniform and walked out into the dazzling sun, down the road that led to NHQ.

THE MORNING WAS almost unbearably hot. Even the fan churning overhead did little to cool the air, and First Officer Beresford's cotton shirt was already damp and sticking to her neck.

The relevant papers lay on her desk and she began to read, although, already, she knew them by heart. A knock at the door. Outwardly composed, she raised her head as Judith entered. 'Dunbar. Pull up a chair and make yourself comfortable. Would you like a cup of tea?'

'No, thank you, ma'am.'

The chair was a plain wooden one, and not particularly comfortable. Judith sat facing the officer across the desk. Their eyes met. First Officer looked down, busying herself by neatening the papers. Then, 'I'm afraid it's not very good news, Dunbar. I am sorry.'

'It's about my family, isn't it?'

'Yes. We heard through the Red Cross. I—I have to tell you that your father is dead. He died in Changi Prison, of dysentery, a year after the fall of Singapore. Others with him did all they could to care for him, but there were no medicines and little food. But he had friends around him. Try not to think of him dying alone.'

'I see.' Judith's mouth was suddenly so dry that she could scarcely speak the words, and they came out in a sort of whisper. 'And my mother? And Jess?'

'So far we only know that their ship, the *Rajah of Sarawak*, was torpedoed in the Java Sea, a few days out of Singapore. She was grossly overcrowded in the first place, and she went down almost instantly. The official verdict seems to be that if there were survivors, there could have been no more than a handful.'

'Have they found anyone who did survive?'

First Officer shook her head. 'No. I think, my dear, that you shouldn't hold out any hope.'

The fans circled overhead. From beyond the open window came

the sound of a boat's engine approaching the jetty. Somewhere a man was hammering. They were gone. They were all dead. Years of waiting and hoping, and now this.

Out of the long silence she heard First Officer say, 'Dunbar? Are you all right?'

'Yes, I'm all right,' she said, and was astonished to hear her voice so expressionless and calm. 'I knew something had happened to the ship. But still, I told myself they would have got themselves into a lifeboat, been picked up . . . But I don't suppose they had a chance. Jess was little. And my mother had never been much of a swimmer.'

First Officer again glanced down at the papers on her desk, which Judith now realised were her own service record. 'I see that Captain and Mrs Somerville are your next of kin.'

'Yes. He's Rear-Admiral Somerville now, over in Colombo, in charge of the dockyard. Biddy Somerville is my mother's sister. '

'I think you should take some leave. Get away from Trincomalee. Why not go to Colombo and spend some time with Rear-Admiral Somerville?'

Uncle Bob. At this bleak watershed of her life Judith knew that there was no man in the world she would rather be with. 'When could I go?'

'Right away. You're due two weeks' leave, but we'll add compassionate leave onto that. Which would give you a month.'

A month. A whole month with Uncle Bob. Colombo again. She remembered the house where she had lived for the first ten years of her life. She remembered her mother sitting on the verandah sewing, and the cool winds blowing in from the Indian Ocean.

First Officer was waiting patiently. Judith looked up, and all she could say was, 'You've been so kind to me.'

COLOMBO
Tuesday, August 28, 1945

Darling Biddy,

Thank you for the cable in response to mine. It made me feel much better, knowing that, although we are worlds apart, we are thinking the same sad thoughts, perhaps comforting each other. The worst is knowing that they died so long ago and we never knew. The conditions in Changi were unspeakable. Poor Dad. As for Mummy and Jess, I simply pray they were killed instantly when the Rajah of Sarawak *was torpedoed.*

As for me, I am safely here with Bob. (Not Uncle any more; he says I am too old.) When I first arrived in Colombo, he simply took me in his arms and hugged me, and didn't say a word. It was at that moment that I fell to pieces and bawled like a baby. It was such a relief to know that I didn't have to be brave on my own any longer.

His house is a bungalow but enormous. The butler is a lovely man, a Tamil called Thomas. He is tall and has a lot of gold teeth, and always wears a flower behind one ear. Bob also has his own car with a driver called Azid.

I didn't do anything for days, just slept. In the evenings we talked a lot. Bob told me that he's laying plans to leave the navy and that you've been thinking of selling up in Devon and moving to Cornwall. I can think of nothing that would be more wonderful for me.

On my third evening Bob took me to a cocktail party on board a visiting cruiser. Lots of new faces, civilians and military. Afterwards about eight of us went ashore and had dinner. I am going to have *to do something about my wardrobe. Colombo ladies are very chic, and my washed-out garments make me look like a poor relation.*

It's funny, but I'm just beginning to realise how heavy was that load of uncertainty, never knowing what had happened to Dad and Mummy and Jess. Now, at least, I don't have to lug it around any more. The void left by their going is unfillable, but some sort of a future is starting to be possible again. Getting back to England and picking up the threads will be a bit like starting all over again, at the beginning. The beginning of what, I haven't worked out. However, I suppose I will.

IT WAS SEVEN IN THE MORNING—pearly and still, the coolest hour of the day. Barefoot, wrapped in a thin robe, Judith emerged from her bedroom and made her way out onto the verandah. She found Bob breakfasting in peaceful solitude and asked if she could borrow his car to go shopping. 'Of course,' he said. 'I'll tell Azid.'

That morning she asked Azid to take her to Whiteaway & Laidlaw, the store that Molly used to patronise. Judith found her way to the ladies' department, where she was confronted by an overwhelming profusion of clothes.

In a curtained changing room she slipped on dress after dress. Silks and cottons and fine voiles, peacock shades and pastels. It was agony to have to choose. In the end she bought a ball gown of pink sari silk, and three cocktail dresses, including an irresistible black dress of mousseline de soie, and three day dresses. Then accessories: sandals and pumps and handbags. And, finally, a luxurious assortment of cosmetics.

That evening she donned the irresistible black dress and went dancing with her new friends. After that, the days slipped by so fast that they turned into a week and then another. Swimming, tennis, cocktails, dinner and dancing. Now it was mid-September, and it would soon be time to journey back to Trincomalee.

AT HALF PAST FIVE in the evening Bob Somerville, still in uniform, was on the verandah having afternoon tea when Judith appeared. 'Pull up a chair,' he said. 'Thomas has conjured up some cucumber sandwiches. How was tennis?' he asked.

'Good game. Serious stuff.'

'Before I forget, I've fixed that lift for you. A car, next Saturday morning. They'll pick you up at eight o'clock.'

Judith screwed up her face like a child. 'I don't want to go.'

'Don't want you to go. But there it is. Duty calls. And talking of duty, Chief Officer Wrens rang me this afternoon. Asked if you'd be available to help tomorrow morning.'

'Help do what?' Judith asked cautiously.

'Go and be welcoming to a lot of chaps who deserve it. There's a ship stopping off en route for England. The *Orion*. A hospital ship. The first batch of prisoners of war from the Burma Railway. They're being allowed ashore here for a few hours, their first step back to civilisation. There's going to be a reception for them at the fort. Chief Officer's rounding up some Wrens to act as hostesses.'

'What did you tell her?'

'Told her I'd have to discuss it with you. I explained that your father died in Changi and perhaps meeting up with a lot of emaciated prisoners would be a bit close to home.'

Judith nodded. From the Burma Railway. At the end of the war the labour camps had been opened and their horrors exposed. Thousands of men had died. Those who survived had laboured in the steaming jungle for as long as eighteen hours a day despite hunger, exhaustion, malaria. Now they were coming home.

She sighed. 'I'll *have* to go. If I don't, I shan't be able to look myself in the eye for the rest of my life. What do I have to do?'

'Muster at nine o'clock, the Galle Road Wrennery.'

'Right.'

THE NEXT MORNING, in uniform and feeling apprehensive, Judith reported to the Wrens' quarters. A lorry was parked outside, and when the Wrens had all assembled they trooped aboard. A moment later they were lurching up the Galle Road.

Judith and another Wren sat side by side at the back. The girl looked at Judith. 'I don't know you, do I? I'm Sarah Sudlow.'

'Judith Dunbar.'

Behind them the Galle Road streamed dustily away between tall palm trees. Judith thought of her father driving this way day after day to and from his office. She thought of him dying in the filth and hopeless misery that had been Changi. Dad, I'm doing this for you, she thought. Don't let me be too useless.

Beside her Sarah Sudlow shifted on the seat. 'It's a bit of a facer, isn't it? I mean, drumming up things to *say*.' She considered the problem. 'Tell you what, much easier if we do it in pairs. Then if one of us runs out of chat, the other can chip in. What do you say? Shall we stick together?'

'Yes, please,' said Judith instantly, and at once felt better.

The lorry rumbled across a bridge, then past the fort and on to the harbour. And in position at a jetty, immaculately ranked, was a Sikh pipe band in khaki shorts and tunics and magnificent turbans.

The Wrens climbed down from the lorry. Others were there before them: officers from the garrison and naval headquarters, two ambulances and some naval nursing sisters. On the grassy expanse of Gordon's Green could be seen army tents strung with bunting, and at the head of a tall flagpole flew the Union Jack.

Orion lay at anchor about a mile offshore. 'Looks a bit like a prewar liner on a pleasure cruise,' Sarah observed. 'Ironic to know that most of her passengers are too sick to make the trip ashore. Oh, goodness, they're actually coming.'

Judith looked and saw three tenders headed for the jetty, each packed with men. Suddenly the drums rolled and the Sikh pipers hoisted their instruments and began to play an old Scottish air: *Speed, bonny boat, like a bird on the wing...*

'Oh, no,' said Sarah. 'I hope I'm not going to blub.'

The tenders drew closer, and the men who had survived hell were returning to the world again. What a way to make their landfall, greeted by the sound of the pipes—some person, Judith decided, had been inspired. The wild music streaming out into the wind sent shivers down her back, and she, like Sarah, felt tears behind her eyes.

Judith said in as steady a voice as possible, 'Why are they playing Scottish tunes?'

'Most of the prisoners are Durham Light Infantry, but I think there are some Gordon Highlanders as well.'

All Judith's senses pricked. 'I once knew a Gordon Highlander. He was killed at Singapore.'

'Maybe you'll meet up with some of his chums.'

The first tender had come alongside, and her passengers, in orderly fashion, began to climb up onto the jetty. Sarah squared her shoulders. 'Come on. Nice smiles and a cheerful manner.'

But after all their apprehension it wasn't difficult at all. They were ordinary young men, and as soon as Judith heard them speak, in the accents of Northumberland, Cumberland and Tyneside, she lost all her reservations. Bone-thin, still wearing the pallor of sickness and malnutrition, they all came down the jetty looking neat and clean, kitted out in jungle-green battledress. They approached slowly, as though not certain what to expect, but as the white-clad Wrens mingled among them, their shyness melted away.

'Hello. I'm Judith.'

'I'm Sarah. Welcome to Colombo.'

Soon each girl had gathered about her a number of men, all of them clearly relieved to be told what they had to do.

'We're going to take you up to Gordon's Green, where the tents are. We've plenty of transport if anyone wants a lift.'

But Judith's group, now swelled to about twenty men, said that they would walk, and they set off at an unhurried pace, up the gentle slope that rose from the shore.

Long afterwards Judith remembered the official reception for the returned prisoners of war. The Royal Marine band playing out on the green. The visiting dignitaries come to pay their respects. Inside the tent, trestle tables were loaded with sandwiches and cakes, iced coffee and lemonade. Having safely delivered their charges, Judith and Sarah were pressed into duty making sure that every man got his share of the feast. At last the assembled company, sated, drifted out to lie on the grass, smoke cigarettes and listen to the band.

By half past eleven the stewards had begun clearing away the detritus of the party. So Judith left the tent and stood observing the peaceful scene of random groups of relaxing men. And then her eye was caught by a single man, who stood with his back to her, apparently intent upon the music. She noticed him because he was different. Lanky and fleshless as the others, but not wearing a jungle-green uniform and canvas gym shoes. Instead, a pair of battered desert boots. On his dark head was a Gordon glengarry, ribbons fluttering in the breeze. A worn khaki shirt, the sleeves rolled up to his elbows. And a Gordon kilt—ragged and faded, the pleats stitched down with twine. But still, a kilt.

For an instant she thought it might be Gus, and then knew at once that it wasn't, because Gus was dead. But perhaps he had *known* Gus. She walked across the grass towards him. She said, 'Hello.'

Startled, he swung round, and she was looking up into his face: dark eyes, thick brows, cheeks cadaverous. She experienced an extraordinary sensation, as if for an instant she was frozen in time.

It was he who broke the silence. 'Good God. Judith.'

Oh, Loveday. You were wrong. You were wrong all the time.

'Gus.'

He isn't dead. He's here. With me. Alive.

281

She said, 'You're alive.'

'Did you think I wasn't?'

'Yes. I've thought for years you were dead. Ever since Singapore. We all did.'

'Do I look like a corpse?'

'No. You look wonderful.' And she meant it. 'The boots and the kilt and the glengarry. How on earth did you hang on to them?'

'Only the kilt and the bonnet. I stole the boots.'

'Oh, Gus.' She took a step towards him, put her arms round his waist and pressed her face into the worn cotton of the shirt. She could feel his ribs and could hear the beating of his heart. His arms came round her and they simply stood there, very close. After a bit they drew apart. 'I never saw you in the tent,' she told him.

'I was only there for a little while.'

'When do you have to be back on board?'

'Tenders at three o'clock.'

'We could go back to the Galle Road, where I'm staying. Have a drink or some lunch. There's time.'

'What I would really like,' said Gus, 'is to go to the Galle Face Hotel. I've got a sort of date there. But I couldn't go on my own, because I haven't any money.'

'I've got money. I'll come with you. We'll get a taxi up on the road.' So they slipped away.

In the taxi, she said, 'My parents were in Singapore, about the same time as you. And my little sister. They didn't survive.'

'Oh, God. I *am* sorry.'

The taxi was driving along the edge of the Galle Face Green. Gus was saying, 'It's not exactly in the same league, but my parents have died as well.' He turned to face her. 'They were elderly. I was the only child. Perhaps they too thought I was dead.'

'At Singapore couldn't you send word to *anyone*?'

'I tried to smuggle a letter out, but I don't suppose it worked.'

The taxi turned into the forecourt of the hotel. Judith paid the driver and they went inside.

'Gus, you said you had a date. Who with?'

'Wait and see.' Behind the reception desk stood a Sinhalese clerk. 'Does Kuttan still work here?'

'But of course, sir. He is in charge of the restaurant.'

'I wonder if I could have a word. I'm Captain Callender. A friend of Colonel Cameron's. Gordon Highlanders.'

'Very good, sir. Would you like to wait out on the terrace?'

They walked out, Gus choosing a table, arranging the cane chairs. She wondered at his coolness, his detachment, his air of authority despite his rags of uniform. There was an inner strength that was palpable. She found this a little daunting. Sooner or later she was going to have to tell him about Loveday.

Drinks were brought to them on the terrace. Children, with amahs in attendance, were swimming in the pool. The breeze rattled the palms. Gus said, 'It's just the same. It hasn't changed.'

'You were here?'

'Yes, on our way out to Singapore. Our troopship stopped off here for four days. It was a particularly riotous time. Parties and pretty girls.' He said again, 'A good time.'

'Captain Callender.'

They had not heard him come, but now Gus rose to his feet. 'Kuttan.' The man stood, beaming, his white tunic embellished with red silk epaulettes. He held a silver tray on which stood a bottle of Black & White whisky.

'I could not believe my ears when I was told that you were here. God is very good. This is Colonel Cameron's bottle of Black and White that he asked me to keep for him.' He looked about him. 'Colonel Cameron is not with you?'

'He died, Kuttan.'

The old man stared with sad dark eyes. 'A fine gentleman.' He looked at the whisky bottle. 'He paid for this that last night. He said, "Kuttan, we will celebrate on our way home." And now he is not coming.' He set the bottle on the table. 'So you must take it.'

Gus held out his hand in thanks. 'Goodbye, old friend.' They shook hands. And then Kuttan stepped back, placed his palms together, and salaamed with affection and respect.

When he had gone, Gus sat down and looked at the bottle. He said, 'I shall have to find some sort of bag to put it in. I can scarcely be observed carrying it on board.'

'We'll find something,' Judith promised him. 'You can take it back to Scotland. What will happen when you get home?'

'Report to HQ in Aberdeen, I suppose. Medical checkups.'

'Were you very ill?'

'No more than anyone else. Beriberi. Dysentery. They reckon about sixteen thousand Brits died.'

'Do you hate to talk?'

'What about?'

'Singapore. I had a last letter from my mother... but it didn't really tell me anything, except confusion and chaos.'

'That was pretty much it. After the Japanese invaded Malaya, Singapore was doomed. We were sent to do rearguard action at the causeway onto the island. We held our positions for three or four days. Then the Japanese reached the reservoirs that supplied all the fresh water. They turned off the taps. That was it. Capitulation.'

'What happened to you then?'

'We were put into Changi. I got put in a working party, sent out into the streets to repair bomb damage. I got quite good at scrounging supplies. I even sold my watch for Singapore dollars and used them to bribe one of the guards into posting a letter to my mother and father, but I don't know if he did. As well, he brought me paper and pencils, a drawing block, and I managed to keep them filled and hidden for the next three and a half years. A sort of record. But not one for human consumption.'

'What happened next, Gus?'

'Well, after six months in Changi we were put in steel cattle trucks and taken to Bangkok. It was ghastly. For five days and nights we had one cupful of rice each and one cup of water a day. At Bangkok we all fell out of the trucks, weak with relief that the ordeal was over. What we didn't know was that it was only just beginning.'

Gus downed the last of his drink. 'That's all,' he said. 'No more about me.' Across the table he sent her the ghost of a smile. 'I want to hear about you. When did you join the Wrens?'

'The day after Edward was killed.'

'That was grim. I wrote to the Carey-Lewises. I was in Aberdeen then, after St-Valéry.' He frowned, remembering. 'You bought Mrs Boscawen's house, didn't you?'

'Yes. After she died.'

She waited. He said, 'And Nancherrow? Diana, the Colonel?'

'Just the same.'

'And Loveday?'

He was watching her. She said, 'Loveday's married, Gus.'

'Married?' His expression became one of total incredulity. 'Loveday? Whom did she marry?'

'Walter Mudge.'

'But . . . *why*?'

'She thought you were dead. She was utterly convinced that you'd been killed. I don't know if I can explain. But after St-Valéry she had this premonition that you were alive. And you were. It made her believe that there was some sort of telepathy between the two of you. After Singapore she tried again, thinking about you, waiting for some sign or message from you. And none came.'

'I could scarcely ring up on the telephone.'

'Oh, Gus, you know Loveday. Once she's got an idea in her head, she's immovable. In some strange way she convinced us all.'

'Is she happy?'

'I think so, though I haven't seen her for quite a long time. Oh, Gus, I'm sorry. I've been dreading telling you. But—'

He said, 'I thought she would wait for me.'

All at once he looked desperately worn and tired. He rubbed a hand over his eyes. She thought of him going home, back to Scotland, to nothing. No family. No Loveday.

She said, 'Gus, whatever happens, we *must* keep in touch. You must give me your address so that I can write to you. I'll go and get some paper and a pen. I shan't be a moment.'

She went back indoors, paid the bill and was given a hefty brown paper bag in which to conceal the Black & White. After that, she found writing paper and a pencil. When she returned to Gus, he sat as she had left him, his eyes fixed on the horizon.

'Here.' She handed over the paper and pencil. 'Your address.' He wrote, then pushed them back to her. 'Gus, if I write, will you promise to answer? We haven't, either of us, got much left. So we must sustain each other. It's important.'

'Yes. Important. Judith ... I must go. I mustn't miss the boat.'

'I'll come with you.'

'No. I'd rather go alone.'

'We'll find a taxi. Here ... Money for the fare.'

'I feel like a kept man.'

'No, not kept. Just pretty special.'

They went out through the foyer and the doorman called a taxi. 'Goodbye, Judith.' And then he said, 'Just one thing. When you tell them at Nancherrow about today, tell them I'm OK.'

'Oh, Gus.' She reached up and kissed him on both cheeks. He got into the taxi and was driven away. Judith watched him go. *Keep in touch*, she thought. *You mustn't disappear again.*

'Can I get a taxi for you?'

She turned and looked at the doorman. No point in returning to the fort. She would go home now. 'Yes. Thank you.'

The Galle Road once more, but now driving in the opposite direction. Soon the taxi was slowing down. She saw the familiar gates, the sentry. She got out and paid the driver. And then the doors of Bob's bungalow stood open and he was running down the steps to meet her.

'Where have you *been*?' He sounded distraught.

'I—I—' Completely knocked off course by his outburst, she could scarcely find the words to explain. 'I met someone. I'm sorry.'

'Don't be sorry.' He put his hands on her shoulders. 'Just listen. I got a telephone call from Trincomalee. A signal's come through. Jess survived ... Java ... the *Rajah of Sarawak* ... a lifeboat ... a young Australian nurse ... internment camp ...'

She watched his craggy face, his eyes keen with excitement, his mouth making words that she scarcely understood. 'Tomorrow. RAF ... Jakarta to Ratmalana. She'll be here.'

It finally sank in. He was telling her that little Jess was alive. Safe. 'Jess?' It took an enormous effort even to say her name.

Bob pulled her into his arms. 'Yes,' and there was a break in his voice that he didn't even try to conceal. 'She's coming back to you!'

'PRETTY EXCITING day for you. Your sister, isn't it?'

'Yes.' It was five o'clock in the afternoon. Judith and Bob had presented themselves at the RAF station, Ratmalana. The plane from Jakarta would be landing soon. They walked across the dusty parade ground towards the control tower—Bob Somerville and Judith, a group captain and an aide. Outwardly cool, Judith was trembling inside with nerves. Shading her eyes, she stared into the sky.

And then she saw the plane floating out of the distance. It touched down in a blast of thundering noise, then came taxiing back to the control tower. At last the doors opened and the passengers alighted: a group of American pilots, two soldiers...

Finally she was there, clambering down the steps. Skinny and brown, wearing shorts and a faded green shirt, with sun-bleached hair clipped in a crop. A fourteen-year-old girl with a small canvas rucksack slung over one shoulder. She paused, clearly a bit lost, apprehensive. Then bravely she set out after the others.

Jess. At that moment they might have been the only two people in the world. Judith moved to meet her, searching that bony little face for some trace of the chubby child, the sweetly weeping four-year-old to whom she had said goodbye all those years ago. Jess saw her and stopped dead.

'Judith?' She had to ask, because she couldn't be sure.

'Yes. Judith.'

She held out her arms. Jess hesitated for an instant, then flung herself forward into Judith's embrace. She was so tall now that the top of her head reached Judith's chin, and holding her felt like grasping something very brittle, like a starved bird. Judith buried her face in Jess's rough hair, and it smelt of disinfectant, and she felt Jess's skinny arms latch tight round her waist.

When they joined the three men, they were met with great kindness and tact. Bob did not kiss Jess, simply rumpled her hair with a gentle hand. She didn't say much, didn't smile. But she was all right.

The group captain walked with them to where the car waited, then saluted smartly as the car moved away. 'Now'—Bob smiled down at his small niece—'you're *really* on your way.'

She sat between them in the back of the huge car. Judith couldn't stop looking at her. There were scars on her right leg, and her hair looked as though it had been chopped off with a carving knife. But she was beautiful.

Jess gazed with some interest from the windows as they bowled northwards to the city. 'Where are we going?'

'To my house,' Bob told her. 'Judith's been staying with me.'

'Is it a big house?'

'Big enough.'

'Will I have a room by myself?'

'If that's what you'd like.'

Judith said, 'I've got two beds in my room. You could sleep with me if you'd rather.'

But Jess did not commit herself. 'I'll think about it.' And then, 'Could I change places with you so I can see out of the window?'

After that, she simply sat with her back to Bob and Judith, intent on all that passed them by. Little farms, then wayside shops and filling stations. Finally they entered the Galle Road, and it was only when the car swung in through the gate that she spoke again.

'There's a guard on the gate.' She sounded alarmed.

'Yes. A sentry,' Bob said. 'He's not there to stop us getting out, just to make certain no unwelcome guests come in. I have a gardener too, and a cook, and a butler called Thomas. He cannot wait to meet you.' The car drew up and stopped. 'In fact, there he is.'

Thomas was down the steps and opening the car door, a hibiscus blossom tucked behind his ear. Beaming with delight, he helped Jess out. He gathered up her rucksack and led her indoors, with an arm about her thin shoulders. 'You have had a good journey? You are hungry, yes? You would like refreshment?'

But Jess, looking a bit overwhelmed, said that what she really wanted was to go to the lavatory, so Judith retrieved the rucksack and led her down the passage to the quiet of her bedroom.

'You mustn't mind Thomas. He's been so excited ever since we knew you were coming. The bathroom's in here.'

Jess stood in the open door and simply looked at the polished taps, the gleaming white porcelain. 'Is this all for you?' she asked.

'You and me.'

'There were only two lavs in the whole camp at Asulu. They stank. Ruth used to clean them.'

'That can't have been very nice.' Which was inadequate but the only comment she could think of.

'Was Ruth the girl who looked after you?' Judith asked.

'Yeah. She was great. In my bag I've got a letter for you from her. She wrote it yesterday.'

Jess reached for her rucksack and from its depths produced a toothbrush and a comb. Then she withdrew a wad of yellow lined paper. 'This is for you. From Ruth.'

Judith took it. 'Do you want me to read it now?'

Jess shrugged her shoulders. 'Doesn't matter.'

'I'll keep it for later.' And she put it on her dressing table.

She showed Jess how to work the shower and left her to it. When Jess emerged again, she smelt of rose-geranium soap. They spent time choosing clothes, deciding on a pair of Judith's white tennis shorts and a blue silk shirt. Tomorrow they'd go and buy a new wardrobe for her. Jess took up her comb and flattened her damp hair.

'You look perfect. Feel comfortable?'

'Yeah. I'd forgotten about silk. Mummy used to wear silk dresses. I thought you'd look like Mummy, but you don't.'

Judith turned. 'I'm sorry.'

'No. Just different. She never wore lipstick.' Jess looked at her. 'Will we stay together? You and me?'

'Yes. Together. No more being apart.'

'Where shall we go?'

'Cornwall. To my house. Now'—she looked at her watch—'I must change for dinner. It's early tonight. We thought you might be tired.'

'I'm going to go and find Uncle Bob.'

'You do that.'

It was good, for a moment, just to be alone. Judith was exhausted by emotion. Ten years was too long for love to survive; too much had happened to Jess. But it would be all right if they took their time rebuilding a relationship. Jess was back. It was a beginning.

She showered and dressed in thin trousers and a sleeveless shirt, then picked up the yellow pages of the Australian girl's letter.

Jakarta
September 19, 1945

Dear Judith,

My name is Ruth Mulaney. I am twenty-five years old. I am an Australian. In 1941 I finished my nurse's training in Sydney and went to Singapore to stay with friends. When the Japs invaded Malaya, I managed to get a passage on the Rajah of Sarawak.

We were torpedoed six days out in the Java Sea at about five in the evening. Jess's mother had gone below for a moment and asked me to keep an eye on Jess. The ship sank very quickly. There was a lot of screaming and confusion. I grabbed Jess and a life jacket and we jumped overboard. I was able to hang on to her, and then a lifeboat came and we managed to get into it.

We were adrift the next day and another night. The next morning we were sighted by an Indonesian fishing boat and taken in tow to their village in Java. I wanted to go to Jakarta to try to get another boat to take us to Australia, but Jess was ill. She had cut her leg somehow, and it was septic and she ran a fever. So the other survivors went on, but we stayed in the village. I thought Jess was going to die, but she's a strong little tyke and managed to pull through. By the time she was fit to be moved, Japanese planes were appearing in the sky. Finally we got a ride in a bullock cart to Jakarta. But the Japanese were there, and they picked us up and put us in a camp at Bandung.

Bandung was the first of four camps. The last, at Asulu, was the worst of all, a labour camp, and all of us women were made to work in the rice fields or clean latrines. We were always hungry and sometimes starving. Jess was never really ill again, but suffered boils, which have left some scars.

Around the end of August we were told that Allied forces would be landing in Java. After that, the guards disappeared, but we stayed in the camp because there wasn't anywhere else to go.

Finally the British came. I think they were pretty shocked when they saw the state we were in.

Over these three and a half years Jess has witnessed some terrible events, atrocities and deaths. But she's a very courageous little person. During this time we have become very close to each other. She is miserable about saying goodbye. To make things easier, I've said that one day she must come to Australia and stay with me and my family. I'd be grateful if, when she is a bit older, you'd let her make the trip. Take care of our little sister.

Regards,
Ruth Mulaney

Take care of our little sister. For three and a half years Ruth had been Jess's security, however tenuous. This was where her love and her loyalty lay. And she had had to leave it all behind.

Judith got up and went out in search of Jess. She found her alone on the lamplit verandah, turning the pages of Bob's old photograph album. Jess glanced up. 'Come and see these. They're so funny. Mummy and Dad. Ages ago. Looking so young.'

Judith settled herself beside Jess on the cane settee and laid an arm round her shoulders. 'Where's Uncle Bob?'

'He's gone to change. He gave me this to look at. This is when they lived right here in Colombo. And here's one of you in a terrible hat.' She turned another page.

Judith said, 'I read the letter. Ruth sounds a special person.'

'She was. And she was brave. Never frightened, not of anything.'

'She says you were pretty brave too.' Jess elaborately shrugged. 'She says when you're a bit older she wants you to go to Australia and stay with her. I think it's a great idea.'

Jess's head shot up and she looked into Judith's face.

'*Could* I? Could I go?'

'Of course. Absolutely.'

'That was the worst thing about saying goodbye. Thinking I'd never, ever see her again. I thought you'd say I wouldn't be able to go. Australia's such a long way from England... Can I write to her and tell her?'

'Certainly. It's important to have something to look forward to. But...' She hesitated. 'Meanwhile, perhaps you and I should begin to make more immediate plans. I think it's time we went home.'

JUDITH WAS PACKING, a chore made more complicated by the fact that there were two to pack for and only four items of baggage. The great shopping expedition had taken most of a day, and Judith had cast prudence aside.

She knew that in England clothes rationing was tighter than ever, and once they got home there wouldn't be a hope of buying anything very much. So for Jess they had bought a complete wardrobe: shirts, sweaters, skirts, woollen knee stockings, pyjamas, shoes, a thick dressing gown, and a sensible raincoat. All this lay on Jess's bed in neat folded bundles.

It helped having a rear-admiral as a relation. Bob had pulled strings and fixed them berths on a troopship heading home, and Judith was now on indefinite leave pending a compassionate discharge. In three weeks' time she and Jess would be in England.

> *THE DOWER HOUSE*
> *Rosemullion*
> *Cornwall*
> *Sunday, October 21*

My darling Bob,

They're home. Safe and sound. I hired a huge taxi and went on Friday to scoop them off the train at Penzance. Both are looking well, if tired. Jess has talked a lot about you and the time she spent in Colombo.

The most touching thing was when she saw Phyllis again. As the taxi arrived at the Dower House, Phyllis and little Anna came out to meet us. Jess took one look and was out of the taxi before it had even stopped, to cast herself into Phyllis's arms.

This morning I went to church and said thank you.

In the house, we are a bit of a squash, but managing comfortably. I think the time has come for me to fly this nest, though. I saw a lovely house in Portscatho, looking over the sea. I shall put in an offer for it. I want to be settled in for when you come home.

As for Phyllis, the great news is that Cyril has decided to stay

in the navy. He is now a petty officer, with a DSM for gallantry.
So that's about it. Darling Bob, how lucky we are.
My love as for ever,
Biddy

AS THEY TRUDGED up the Nancherrow drive, it looked a bit unkempt, with potholes and puddles. The hydrangeas were long over, their flower heads browned and sagging with the rain.

Round the last curve of the drive, and the house stood before them. They stopped for a moment. Jess said, 'It's really big.'

'They needed a big house,' said Judith. 'They had three children and lots of friends always coming to stay.'

They reached the sanctuary of the front door. There they shed raincoats, toed off their boots, then went into the hall. It was unchanged. Flowers stood on the round table, where still lay the dog leads, the stack of mail.

'Judith.' Mary Millyway, a bit greyer now, came down the stairs. 'I can't believe you're really here. And this is Jess? Lovely to meet you. Oh, you're both soaking. Walk down, did you?'

'Yes. I don't yet have a petrol ration for my car, and we've only one bike. Where's Loveday?'

'She'll be here directly. Walking down from Lidgey. Let's tell Mrs Carey-Lewis you're here.' She led them to the small sitting room.

And there they were, sitting on either side of the fireplace—Diana with a tapestry and the Colonel with the *Sunday Times*. At his feet old Tiger lay asleep, but Pekoe, who had been dozing on the sofa, let loose a cacophony of barks. Diana sprang to her feet.

'It's Judith. Oh, darling, it's been a thousand years. Come and let me hug you.' She was as lovely as ever, despite the fact that her corn-coloured hair had faded to silver. 'You're looking utterly wonderful! And Jess. We've heard so much about you.'

Released from Diana's embrace, Judith turned to the Colonel, who was now standing, awaiting his turn.

'My dear.' Formal, as always, a little shy. She took his hands in hers and they kissed. 'How pleased we are to have you home again.' Then he smiled at Jess. 'What do you think of Cornwall, eh? Doesn't rain like this *all* the time.'

Jess said, 'I actually remember Cornwall.'

'Do you, by Jove? Why don't we sit down, and you can tell me about it? Here, on this stool by the fire.'

Diana sank back into her chair. Judith sat on the end of the sofa.

'Darling, what a time you've had. You look thin. And little Jess! Such experiences. Biddy telephoned the moment she got the cable from Bob. And so dreadfully sad about your parents. Was it heaven to get back to the Dower House? Isn't the garden looking pretty?'

Brittle with excitement, she chattered on and Judith tried to listen, but she was thinking about Gus Callender. Was now the moment to tell them that Gus was alive? No, she decided. The first person to be told, and in private, was Loveday.

'And what plans have you made for Jess?'

'First a bicycle,' Judith smiled. 'Then I suppose I'll go and see if Miss Catto will take her at St Ursula's.'

'But, my darling, of course she will. Oh, isn't it too extraordinary how life goes full circle. Oh, I haven't told you about Athena. She's going to have another baby. In the spring. I can't tell you how we missed them when they went. The house was empty without a child.'

No sooner were the words out of her mouth than could be heard the piercing tones of Nathaniel Mudge, on his way from the kitchen and in full spate of argument with his mother.

'I don't want to take my boots off.'

'You've got to. They're covered in mud. Now come here.'

A howl. Loveday had clearly caught him and was forcibly removing his boots. Diana said faintly, 'Oh dear.'

A moment later the door burst open and her grandson catapulted into the room, his cheeks scarlet with indignation.

Judith got up from the sofa as Loveday appeared in the open doorway. Looking exactly the way she always had—a ragamuffin teenager in trousers and an old pullover.

They simply stood there, grinning at each other. Then, 'Well, look who's here,' said Loveday. They met and hugged and kissed perfunctorily, just the way they always used to. 'Sorry we're late, but—Nat, don't put your fingers near Pekoe's eye.'

Nat glared at his mother, and Judith, for all her good intentions, dissolved into laughter. 'You seem to have met your match.'

'Oh, he's a horror. Aren't you, Nat? Very sweet but a horror.'

He set about clambering onto the sofa and commencing to bounce, but then Mary bustled in to tell them that tea was on the table and scooped Nat out of the air to bear him, shrieking with what one hoped was glee, in the direction of the dining room.

'She's the only person,' said Loveday with a sort of hopeless pride, 'who can do a thing with him. Come on. Let's eat.'

So they trooped through to the dining room, where the tea table had been set with all the remembered nursery treats—jam sandwiches, chocolate biscuits and a fruit-cake baked in a ring.

By the time tea was finished the afternoon had faded into darkness. Yet nobody stood to draw the heavy curtains. 'Such bliss,' said Diana. 'No blackout. I still haven't got used to it. Mary, don't start clattering about with the teacups; we'll wash them up. Take Nat up to the nursery and give Loveday a few moments to herself.' She turned to Jess. 'Perhaps Jess would like to go too. There are lots of books and jigsaw puzzles.'

'What a sweet girl,' Diana said when they had gone. 'No tears? No nightmares? No ill effects?'

'I don't think so.'

'Perhaps a check-over by a doctor might be a good idea. Talking of which, old Dr Wells popped in the other day. Jeremy is hoping to come home for a bit. He hasn't had leave for about two years.'

Judith said, 'I should think he'd be demobbed soon,' and was delighted with the casualness of her voice.

Loveday helped herself to a slice of cake. 'I can't see him settling down in Truro after all that bobbing about on the high seas.'

'I can,' said Diana. 'The perfect country GP.' She surveyed the shambles of the table. 'I suppose we'd better wash up.'

'Don't worry, Mummy,' Loveday said. 'Judith and I will do it.'

And they went to the kitchen, where Judith filled the old clay sink with scalding water from the brass tap and put in the first pile of plates. She said, 'How's Walter?'

'He's all right.'

'How's the farm going?'

'Fine.'

Her answers were so laconic, so disinterested that Judith's heart chilled. She said, 'What do you do when he's not working? I mean, do you go to the cinema or picnics or down to the pub?'

'I used to go to the pub sometimes, but to be truthful, I'm not all that keen on pubs. So Walter goes alone.'

'Oh, *Loveday*, it doesn't sound much fun. What about the horses? Do you still ride together?'

'Not much.' She had found a tea towel and was taking the plates from a rack and drying them very slowly, then setting them down in a stack on the scullery table.

'Are you happy, Loveday?'

Loveday took another plate out of the rack. 'Who was it who said that marriage was a summer birdcage set out in a garden? All the birds of the air wanted to get in, and all the caged birds wanted to get out. You're a bird of the air. Free. You can fly anywhere.'

'No, I can't. I've got Jess.'

'Not wanting to get into the summer birdcage? No lovelorn sailor? I can't believe it.' She wiped another plate. 'I always thought that Jeremy was in love with you.'

Judith said, 'I think you were probably wrong.'

The last plate and Judith pulled out the plug and the suds seeped away. She turned, leaning against the sink. 'Loveday—'

'You will come and see me, won't you? At Lidgey.' Loveday put the plate on the stack. 'You never saw my funny little house when it was finished. I love the farm and the animals. And I love Nat too, even though he's such a holy terror.'

She looked at her watch. 'I must go. I've got to get Walter's tea and get Nat to bed.'

Judith said, 'Don't go. I have something to tell you.'

Loveday looked a bit taken aback. 'What?'

'It's about Gus.'

Loveday froze. The only sound was the hum of the refrigerator.

'What about Gus?'

Judith told her.

'SO THEN HE SAID it was time he went back to the hospital ship, and we got a taxi for him and said goodbye. And he went. End of story.'

Loveday asked, motionless as a statue, 'Is he all right?'

'I don't know. He looked amazing, considering all he'd gone through. Thin and a bit worn.'

'I was so certain he was dead. It was like being certain with every bone of my body. A sort of emptiness. A void.'

'I know, Loveday. You mustn't blame yourself.'

'Did he believe that I would wait for him?'

'Yes.' There wasn't any other answer.

'Oh, God.' Her face under the cold overhead light was shadowed and pinched, her violet eyes empty of expression.

'I'm sorry, Loveday. I hated telling you.'

'He's alive. I should be rejoicing. Not sitting here looking like a wet weekend.' She fell silent for a moment and then said, 'Do Mummy and Pops know?'

'No. I wanted to tell you first of all. If you like, I'll go and tell them now.'

'No. I will. It's better that way. Then I must go home.'

THE NEXT MORNING Diana came to the Dower House. The little household had dispersed after breakfast, leaving Judith alone in the kitchen making soup. She heard a car draw up outside the house and saw Diana getting out of the battered little fishmonger's van, which had been bought to conserve petrol at the beginning of the war. Judith went to the door.

Diana carried a large, old-fashioned marketing basket on her arm. 'Oh, darling, not interrupting, am I? I've brought you some vegetables and fresh eggs. And I wanted to have a word.'

'Come in. I'll make you a cup of coffee.'

In the kitchen, Diana put the basket on the table and sat down.

Judith went to fill the kettle and then set it on the range. 'Do you mind if I go on chopping?'

'Not a bit.' She loosened the knot of the silk scarf draped about her throat. 'Loveday told us about Gus.'

'Yes. She said she was going to.'

'We were so fond of him, Edgar and I . . .' Her voice trailed away. She sighed. 'Do you blame me?'

'Blame you?'

'For letting Loveday marry Walter?'

'You could scarcely stop her. She wanted to marry him.'

'Yes. And we didn't just *let* her; in a way we encouraged her. Edward was gone, and I couldn't face losing Loveday as well. Marrying Walter meant she stayed near us. And we'd always liked him, despite his lack of polish. He'd always been so fond of her. He was her friend. I've always thought that the most important thing when you get married is to marry a friend. Passionate love cools down after a time, but friendship lasts for ever. I believed they were right for each other.'

'Is there any reason to suppose that they're not?'

Diana sighed again. 'No. Not really, I suppose. But she was only nineteen. Perhaps we should have told her to wait.'

'Diana, if you'd argued, she'd have just become more determined to get her own way. That's the way she's made. I tried to argue when she told me, and I got my head bitten off.'

The coffee was ready and Judith poured two mugs. Diana said, 'I really thought it would work. It worked for me.'

'I don't understand.'

'Edgar was always my friend. I knew him from when I was a little girl. He was a friend of my parents'. And then the war started—the First War. I was sixteen and wildly in love with a young man I'd met. He was in the Coldstream Guards, and he went off to France. And then he came home on leave. But of course he had to go back to France, and he was killed in the trenches. By then I was seventeen. And I was pregnant.'

Diana's voice never changed. She said all these things, evoking who knew what memories, and continued to sound as inconsequential as though she were describing a ravishing new hat.

'Pregnant?'

'Yes. Too careless, darling, but we weren't very worldly-wise in those days. I couldn't tell my parents, so I told Edgar. And Edgar said that he was going to marry me and be the father of my little baby, and that I would never, ever have to be worried or troubled for the rest of my life.'

'And the baby?'

'Athena.'

'But...' But there was nothing to say.

'Oh, darling, you're not shocked, are you? It was just another sort of love. I never felt I was *using* Edgar. And after all the turmoil and passion and despair, being with him was like slipping into a peaceful harbour, knowing that nothing could ever harm one again. And that's how it's stayed.'

'Does Athena know?'

'No, of course she doesn't. Why should she? Edgar's her father. He always has been. It's odd. I haven't thought about it all for years. In fact, I'm not quite sure why I'm telling you now. I've never told anyone else.'

'I would never breathe a word.'

'I know you wouldn't. What I'm trying to say is, Edgar is my life. I expect you used to wonder about Tommy Mortimer, but he was never my lover. Just a person I needed. And Edgar let me have him. Because Edgar is the dearest, most generous man in the world. And has made me so happy. You see, it really *worked* for me. That's why I thought it was right for Loveday to turn to a friend.'

'Diana, it was Loveday's decision. Not yours.'

At this moment, perhaps fortuitously, they were interrupted. The door burst open and Jess appeared, looking tousled and cobwebby. She caught sight of Diana. 'I'm sorry. I didn't know you were here.'

'Oh, darling Jess, don't be sorry. What *have* you been doing?'

'Cleaning the Hut. When the summer comes, I'm going to sleep out there. All the time.'

Diana smiled. 'Won't you be lonely?'

'I shall take Morag with me for company.' To Judith she said, 'Did you ring St Ursula's?'

'Yes. And we've got an appointment with Miss Catto tomorrow.'

IT WAS FOUR O'CLOCK in the afternoon and Judith sat in Miss Catto's study. The headmistress, now in her late forties, looked a good deal older. But her eyes were just the same, wise and kindly.

Jess, clearly, had taken to Miss Catto. At first a bit overawed and nervous, she had answered questions with no more than monosyllables, but it hadn't taken long for her to lose her shyness, and the interview had turned into a chatty conversation. After a bit a senior girl called Elizabeth had come to show Jess round the school. They had not yet returned.

'I suppose we'll have to have a clothes list?' said Judith.

Miss Catto smiled. 'You'll be delighted to know that it has been considerably reduced. The girls all go about in their own cheerful clothes. Now each one is very much her own person.'

Across the desk they looked at each other. 'I promise you, my dear, that I will do my best to make sure that Jess is happy. Now, how about a cup of tea?'

'I DON'T WANT you to come in, Judith. I want to say goodbye on the front doorstep. If you come in, it will just go on for longer.'

'You'll be all right?'

Judith recalled saying exactly the same thing to her mother on their way to St Ursula's.

'Yes. That nice girl, Elizabeth, said she'd be there to show me my dormitory and everything.'

'That was kind of her.'

They were nearly there. Judith turned the car up the hill and through the school gates. It was half past two and raining, a steady mizzle of a sea mist gently drenching the bare trees.

As she had promised, the senior girl was at the main door, waiting for them. 'Hello. I'll take your suitcase. Can you manage the rest?'

Everything was duly carted indoors. On the step, in the drizzling rain, Judith and Jess faced each other. Given the smallest encouragement, Judith knew she might behave like the most sentimental of mothers and start brimming at the eyes.

'Bye, Jess. Love you.'

They kissed. Jess gave her a grin, turned away and was gone.

Judith wept a bit in the car going home. It was hard not to feel rather empty and bereft. Trundling back across the mist-driven moor, she decided that what she needed was company, and so she would go and see Loveday. She hadn't been to Lidgey yet, simply because all her time lately had been taken up with Jess.

She drove past the gates of Nancherrow to the turning to the farm. Half a mile down the bumpy lane stood the low stone cottage that the Colonel had had renovated when Loveday and Walter were married. Judith got out of the car, walked up the path and opened a paint-scarred door.

'Loveday!' Judith was in a tiny hall hung with old coats and mud-stained waterproofs. She opened a second door.

Kitchen, living room, all in one. Almost a replica of Mrs Mudge's. A Cornish range, clothes hung on a pulley high overhead, flagged floors, a few rugs; the clay sink, the pig bucket, the dresser laden with odds and ends. Nat lay on the sagging sofa, fast asleep. The wireless, perched on the dresser, burbled away to itself: '*We'll meet again, don't know where, don't know when ...*' Loveday was ironing.

'Well, where have you turned up from?'

'St Ursula's. Just left Jess there.'

'Is she all right?'

'She was amazing. No tears. The one who's feeling really blue is me, so I've come for a bit of cheering.'

'I'm not sure if you've come to the right place. But take your coat off. Sling it down somewhere.'

Which Judith did. She went over to the sofa and gazed down at Nat. His cheeks were bright red and he clutched an old blanket. 'Does he always sleep in the afternoon?'

'Not usually. But he didn't get to sleep till two this morning.' Loveday filled the kettle and put it on the range. '*But I know we'll meet again some sunny day,*' mooned the wireless. She went to the dresser and switched it off. 'Soppy tune.'

She dumped herself down on the sofa beside her sleeping son. 'Hey, Nat. Wake up. We're going to have tea.' She laid a hand on his round stomach and bent to kiss him. Judith thought she looked terrible. She seemed tired out, with dark rings under her eyes.

Nat's eyes opened. Loveday set him on her knee and cuddled him, talking to him until he was properly awake. Staring about, he spied Judith. 'Who that lady?'

'That's Judith. You met her at Granny's. And she's come to see you.' She set him down on the floor, found a little truck for him to play with and left him to his own devices.

The kettle was boiling. She reached for the teapot. 'If you want to help, you can lay the table. There's saffron cake in the bread bin.'

Between them they pushed some old newspapers to one side to make space at the table. Loveday said, 'I'm sorry about the mess.'

'Don't be silly. Where's Walter?'

'Oh, somewhere. Up the top field, I think. He'll be back soon for the milking.'

'You're looking tired, Loveday.'

'So would you if you hadn't got to sleep until two.'

Loveday fell silent, and to her dismay Judith saw that her eyes shone with seeping tears.

'Oh, Loveday.'

Loveday shook her head. 'I'm just tired.' A tear dribbled down her cheek. She put up a hand and roughly brushed it away.

'Is it you and Walter?' It took some courage to say, because Judith knew she was liable to have her head bitten off. But Loveday hadn't flown at her. 'Is there something wrong between you?'

Loveday muttered, 'Another woman. He's got another woman.'

Judith felt herself go weak. Carefully she laid her mug on the table. 'How do you know?'

'I know. He's been seeing her. Evenings, at the pub. Mrs Mudge told me.'

'*Mrs Mudge?*'

'Yes. The word got through to her from the village. She told me because, she said, I ought to know. Have it out with Walter.'

'Who is this woman?'

'She came down to Porthkerris during the summer. Turned up with some phoney painter or other. She lived with him for a bit and then moved out. She's in a caravan up the back of Veglos Hill.'

'What's her name?'

'You're not going to believe this—Arabella Lumb.'

'It can't be true.' Suddenly, incredibly, they were both laughing.

'Arabella Lumb.' The name, on repetition, sounded even more unlikely. 'Have you ever seen her?' Judith asked.

'Yes, once, when I went for a beer with Walter. She sat in the corner by the bar all evening eyeing him. She looks like a great bosomy tinker. You know, mother-earth stuff. Bangles and beads and sandals and green varnish on her toenails.'

'She sounds ghastly.'

'I have a horrid feeling that Walter is besotted.' Loveday sat back in her chair. 'And I don't know what to do.'

'Take Mrs Mudge's advice. Have it out with him.'

'I tried last night. Walter got home at eleven o'clock, and he'd been drinking. We had the most terrible row and he said he'd do what he bloody pleased and see who he bloody wanted. And he said it was all my fault anyway, because I was such a bloody useless wife and mother.'

'That's unkind and unfair.'

'And there's another thing. He doesn't like me taking Nat down to Nancherrow. Says I'm trying to turn Nat into a little sissy.'

It was all understandable, but bewildering too. 'I'm not being much help, am I?' said Judith.

'Yes, you are. Just being able to talk about it helps. Mummy and Pops would'—she searched for the word—'*explode* if they knew.'

Nat had been lying on his stomach, intent on his toy. Now he scrambled to his feet. 'I want somefin to eat.'

Loveday hoisted him up onto her knee. With her arms encircling him, she buttered a slice of bread and gave it to him.

By the time tea was over, it was past five o'clock. Judith said, 'I must go. Phyllis will be wondering what's happened to me.'

'It was lovely seeing you. Judith, you won't say anything, will you? About what I've told you.'

'Of course not. But you must keep talking to me.'

'I'll do that.'

They came to the door to see Judith away. Outside, the mist had thickened. Judith turned up the collar of her coat and prepared to dash for the car, but Loveday said, 'Have you heard from Gus?'

Judith shook her head. 'Not a word.'

And she drove home through the dark, dismal evening.

By now she had written to Gus three times. As the days went by with no message from him, her anxiety grew. Instincts told her loud and clear that all was not well.

AS CHRISTMAS LOOMED, the weather deteriorated. Judith, battling with a recipe for a wartime Christmas pudding, broke an egg into the flour mixture and began to stir. In the hall the telephone rang. Phyllis, cleaning in the attic, did not hear it, so Judith went to take the call.

'Dower House.'

'Judith, it's Diana. Darling, I've got such exciting news. Jeremy Wells is home. On leave. And the best is, he's going to be demobbed and come home for good...Judith? Are you there?'

'Yes. Yes, I'm here. It's wonderful. When—when did you hear?'

'He rang me this morning. He's coming to Nancherrow to spend a few days. So we thought we'd have a coming-home party on Wednesday evening. You will come, won't you?'

'Of course. I'd love to.'

'About a quarter to eight? Such heaven to have you all with me again. Good news of Jess?'

'Yes, good news. She's a star at hockey, and she's doing well in her studies.'

'Clever little thing. And Biddy?'

'Biddy's in Devon. She phoned on Saturday. Sold the house, so now she can pay for the new one. But she'll be here for Christmas.'

'Send her my love when she rings again. See you Wednesday.'

Judith put down the telephone. Jeremy. Back. Demobbed. No longer safely far away in the Mediterranean, but home for good. She told herself that she was neither sorry nor glad. She only knew that before they could resume any sort of an easy relationship all must be brought out into the open and she must face him with the hurt and disappointment that he had caused her. Jeremy had given a promise and broken it. Thoughtfully, she walked back to the kitchen.

IT WAS RUPERT RYCROFT, ex-major, the Royals, who found Gus Callender again. Rupert had stepped from the portals of Harrods at twelve thirty on a bitterly cold December day, and he decided to go to his club for lunch. When a taxi appeared at last, he hailed it by raising his walking stick like a flag. The driver drew alongside. 'Where to, sir?'

'Cavalry Club, please.'

As Rupert opened the door he noticed, among the stream of

oncoming pedestrians, a young man walking towards him—tall, vaguely familiar, painfully thin, in a battered leather jacket. Rupert called to him. 'Gus!' The young man stopped dead and turned.

'Gus. Rupert Rycroft.'

'I know. I remember.' Close up, his appearance was even less encouraging. He was unshaven and gaunt and looked like a down-and-out. And Rupert suddenly knew that if he let Gus out of his sight he would never find him again. 'Gus, how about lunch?'

'Thanks, but no. I'd disgrace you. Haven't shaved.'

But Rupert persisted. 'I've all day. Why don't we go back to your place and you can clean up and then we'll go to a pub?'

Still Gus hesitated. 'It's a pretty crummy place.'

'No matter.' Rupert opened the taxi door wider and stood aside. 'Come on, old boy. Get in.'

AT HOME THAT NIGHT Rupert told the story to Athena. Gus's flat on the Fulham Road was down at heel, cold and dreary. Rupert waited while Gus shaved and combed his hair, and then they went down the road to a pub, whose interior was dark and comforting, with a lot of mahogany and brass.

There, over lunch, Rupert asked Gus straight off how he had got himself into this situation. Gus explained that it had not been much of a homecoming when he got back to Aberdeen. He had expected to have enough family money to start life over again. But with the hospital costs for his elderly parents and the drop in the property market, the capital had dribbled away.

Even worse, the desire to draw seemed to have left him. In fact, he'd been in a psychiatric hospital in Dumfries for the past seven weeks. The doctors had put him there because he'd had a sort of breakdown.

Listening to all this, Rupert was appalled. He urged Gus to return home with him, but Gus firmly refused. After that, there didn't seem to be much else to say, and each went on his separate way.

That evening, after talking it over with Athena, Rupert put through a call to the Dower House to give Judith the alarming news.

As she listened, she realised she was shivering. Her worst fears about Gus had been confirmed, and when Rupert asked if she'd help she said, 'Give me his address.' She would drive to London tomorrow, spend the night at the mews and find Gus the next morning. Perhaps she could convince him to return to Cornwall with her.

She suddenly realised she would miss the party for Jeremy. With a sigh she dialled Nancherrow and explained everything to Diana. 'If Gus comes back with me, I don't think we should tell Loveday.'

'But she's bound to find out sooner or later.'

'Yes, but not immediately. From what Rupert said, it doesn't sound as if Gus is in any state for emotional confrontations.'

For a moment Diana was silent. Judith held her breath. Then Diana said, 'Yes. You're right, of course.'

'I'm sorry about spoiling your party.'

'I think darling Jeremy will be sorry too.'

JEREMY HAD BEEN GIVEN his old, familiar bedroom, and found his own way upstairs, lugging the battered green naval-issue suitcase. It was so long since he had been at Nancherrow that he didn't immediately unpack, but went to open the window and gaze out at the courtyard. He found he had to remind himself that the war was over and he was really back in Cornwall.

Presently he heard swift footsteps in the passage outside and the voice of his hostess.

'Jeremy!' She was there, wearing grey flannel trousers and a pale blue mohair sweater. 'Goodness, you do look wonderful. Mediterranean tan. Now listen. I've got so much to tell you I don't know where to start.'

She told him all that had happened to Gus and how Rupert had found him. And Judith had gone to London today to see if she could do anything to help.

'It's all a bit depressing, because this evening I'd planned a lovely coming-home party for *you*, and Nettlebed had plucked pheasants, and Edgar was blissful, down in the cellar choosing a wine. But then Judith rang last night, and Loveday telephoned to say that Walter couldn't make it either, so we've decided to forget about it for the time being. It's too disappointing.'

'Don't worry,' Jeremy assured her bravely. 'It was sweet of you even to think of it.'

She left him with his mind in something of a turmoil. This new peacetime life seemed to be beset by problems, decisions to be made. A colleague in the navy had approached him with an idea that Jeremy found attractive. He could not commit himself, however, until he had spoken to Judith.

He longed to see her again and, at the same time, dreaded a confrontation that might end for ever his long-cherished dreams. Over the years since that night in London he had constantly thought of her. From the mid-Atlantic, Gibraltar, Malta, he had started letters that were never finished. Time after time he had run out of words and crumpled up the pages, telling himself that by now she would have found someone else.

But she wasn't married. He knew that much. Now, the fact that she had opted out of the coming-home party and gone to be with

302

Gus Callender filled him with disquiet. Perhaps her compassion had turned to a deeper emotion. Love. He didn't know. He had not known anything for far too long.

IT WAS NINE O'CLOCK on Thursday morning and still only half-light. In Cadogan Mews lights still burned inside the little houses. Judith heaved her overnight bag into the car and got in behind the wheel.

She followed Rupert's directions and found the building on the Fulham Road. When the door finally opened, Gus didn't look nearly as awful as she had feared: dreadfully thin and pale, of course, but shaved and neatly dressed. Using all her powers of persuasion, she tried to convince him to come back to Cornwall, to the Dower House, with her. Politely he refused.

She argued, begged, cajoled—all with no result. At last, exasperated, she said, 'I'm not *asking* you to come with me. I'm *telling* you. And I shall stay here and nag at you until you do.'

For the first time Gus smiled. 'Just give me five minutes.'

It was a long drive, and by the time they reached the Dower House it was dark. Gus rolled down the window and took a huge breath of fresh air. He said, 'You know, I can smell the sea.'

'Me too.'

He closed the window. 'Judith.'

'What is it?'

'Thank you.'

The next morning she let Gus sleep late while she went into Penzance. There she bought a range of art supplies, hoping that in time he would feel like painting again.

ELEVEN O'CLOCK on Friday night, and still Walter had not returned. Loveday, curled up on the sofa, sat and watched the clock, the slow minutes ticking by. Since the afternoon that Judith had come for tea, relations between Loveday and Walter had deteriorated at an alarming rate. She was beginning to believe that he actually hated her. He hadn't spoken kindly to Nat for days, and if they did all sit down to a meal together, Walter endured it in silence. Lately she hadn't even tried to break through his sullen antipathy.

Restless, Loveday got off the sofa and switched on the wireless. She thought about Gus. Most of the time she didn't think about him, because memories of what she had done filled her with such anguish and regret. She now realised that at nineteen she had been childishly set on getting her own way, refusing to countenance the fact that perhaps she was mistaken in her conviction that Gus had died in Singapore; grabbing at the first straw which came her drowning way, which happened to be Walter. She knew now that Arabella Lumb was simply a catalyst. If it hadn't been her it would have been something, or someone, else bringing everything to a head.

From the bedroom she heard Nat crying. She went through and picked him up out of his cot, bundled in a big blanket, and brought him back to the sofa. Presently he quietened, and she switched off the wireless and lay down beside him.

When she woke at seven, the electric light was still on, and she knew at once that Walter had not been back. Nat was slumbering peacefully, and cautiously she slid off the sofa.

Outside, it was dark and stormy. She went to the range and riddled out the ashes and made up the fire. The range, simmering gently, was set for another day. That was all she was going to do. Her husband's welfare was no longer of any concern.

In the hall, she took her thick raincoat from its peg and tied a woollen scarf round her head. Then she gathered Nat into her arms, swaddling him into his blanket. Carrying Nat, Loveday set out on the long walk home to Nancherrow.

IN THE MORNING Nettlebed was the first down, and his routine was changeless. Drawing back curtains, opening windows a chink to let the fresh air in. Then a kettle on the Aga for the Colonel's tea. As he reached for the tea caddy, he heard the scullery door fly open. Startled, he called, 'Who's there?'

'Only me, Nettlebed.' Loveday kicked the door shut behind her, her arms filled with a blanketed bundle that could only be young Nat. 'I've just walked down from Lidgey.'

He was horrified. 'Carrying Nat?'

'Yes. I'm exhausted.' She laid Nat carefully on the huge scrubbed table, making a pillow with a corner of the blanket.

Nettlebed watched, heavy-hearted. He had known for some time that there was trouble afoot at Lidgey. It was his custom a couple of evenings a week to take himself down to the Rosemullion pub. He had noticed Walter with that woman, Arabella Lumb. It was obvious that they had not met by chance.

Loveday asked, 'Where's Mrs Nettlebed?'

'Upstairs in the flat. She's taking the morning off. Everything all right, Loveday?'

'No, Nettlebed. Not all right. All wrong. Walter never came home last night.' Biting her lip, she met his sad gaze. 'You know, don't you? Arabella Lumb.'

'Yes.' He sighed. 'I guessed.'

'It's all over. Me and Walter, I mean. Right from the beginning it was one huge, horrible mistake. And I'm not going back.'

'What about young Nat? He's Walter's boy.'

'I don't know. I haven't had time to think it through.' She frowned. 'I have to get it all clear in my head before I face them all—Pops and Mummy and Mary. What I would really like is to be on my own for a bit. Go for a walk.'

As he listened to her steady voice, watched her, it occurred to Nettlebed that this was a Loveday he had never known before. No tears, no tantrums. Simply a stoic acceptance of a miserable situation. Perhaps, he told himself, she has finally grown up.

He said, 'I could take young Nat up to our flat. Mrs Nettlebed will keep an eye on him for the time being.'

'Oh, Nettlebed, you are kind. You won't say anything, will you?'

'Breakfast's at half past eight. I'll keep mum till you're back.'

'Thank you.' She gathered up the sleeping Nat and handed him over. Nettlebed carried the child up the backstairs to his quarters. When he returned, having left Nat in the care of his astounded wife, Loveday had gone, and taken Tiger with her.

GUS OPENED HIS EYES. From downstairs he heard the gentle chimes of the grandfather clock softly striking seven o'clock. He could not remember when he had last slept so soundly.

He thought back to yesterday, a day of ordered tranquillity, exercise and fresh air. In the evening he and Judith had played piquet, and when it was time for bed, Phyllis had made him hot milk and honey, laced with a teaspoonful of whisky. Perhaps this potion had knocked him out; more likely it was the extraordinary healing quality of Lavinia Boscawen's old house. A sanctuary.

He was now filled with a long-forgotten energy. He got up, went to the open window and leaned out, smelling the cold air and the tang of the sea. He thought of the new day ahead, the first rays of dawn streaking the skies with pink. And he was once again obsessed by the old desire to set it all down, to capture it with brushstrokes and washes of colour.

He stepped back. On the dressing table were the drawing book, pencils, paints and brushes Judith had bought for him. He looked at them and told them, *Later. When there is light in the sky and shadows on grass; then we shall get to work.*

He swiftly dressed in his cords, a heavy sweater, his leather jacket and made his way down the stairs, through the kitchen and out into the cold.

He remembered the length of the Nancherrow drive. It was too far to walk and he was impatient to be there. So he opened the door of the garage and wheeled Judith's bicycle out onto the gravel.

The bicycle was far too small for him, but he swung his leg over it and set off, spinning down the hill and through Rosemullion. Then up the hill and through the Nancherrow gates.

Out of the trees, and the house loomed—a pale bulk. By the front door he propped the bicycle against the wall. He cautiously made his way round the house and finally stepped onto the grass.

The sky was lightening. There was the smell of damp earth, and all was clean, pristine and pure. He went down the slope of the lawns and plunged down the path through the woods and to the cliff.

The tide was out, and the beach, a grey sickle of sand, was rimmed by seaweed. The sun was up now and long shadows lay on the clifftop. And he remembered that August afternoon, the summer before the war, when Loveday had brought him to the cove. They had sat, sheltered from the wind, and it had felt like being with a person whom he had known for the whole of his life.

He looked for that rock where they had been together. And then he saw her, and screwed up his eyes in disbelief. She sat with her back to him, crouched against the rock, the dog close against her side. For a second he thought that he had gone mad again. But then, sensing his presence, Tiger raised his head, heaved himself to his feet, and came lumbering up over the boulder-strewn grass, tail thumping, as fast as his arthritic legs would carry him.

He reached Gus's side and Gus stooped to fondle his head. 'Hello, Tiger. Hello, old boy.'

And then he straightened, and she was standing there with her back to the sea. The woollen muffler had slipped off her head, and he saw her dark curls, lit from behind by the sun, like an aureole.

Loveday. He had found her again. And it was almost as though she had known he would come and had been waiting for him.

He heard her call his name. 'Gus,' and the wind caught the word and sent it flying inland, over the winter fields. 'Oh, *Gus*.' And she was running up the slope, and he went to meet her.

JEREMY WELLS had overslept. Not by much, but breakfast at eight thirty was a Nancherrow rule and he didn't get downstairs until a quarter to nine. In the dining room he found Diana and the Colonel now onto second cups of coffee.

He apologised. 'I am sorry.'

'Oh, darling, it doesn't matter a bit.' Diana was opening her mail and the Colonel was deep in *The Times*. At Nancherrow, conversation at breakfast had never been encouraged. Jeremy took a boiled egg from the sideboard and went to sit at the table.

In the kitchen, Nettlebed was starting to get edgy because Loveday still had not returned. He now regretted his collusion and simply wished that she would come back before he was forced to break the news to the Colonel. Preoccupied, he wandered to the window. There wasn't a sign of the wretched girl.

At ten to nine he let himself out of the scullery door and walked out to the back drive. There was nobody on the path from the woods, but he could see that one of the garage doors stood open. The little van was gone. In something of a state he returned to the house. In the gunroom, he found Tiger, fast asleep in his basket. And then as Nettlebed went back to the kitchen, he heard, from his flat upstairs, unmistakable roars of rage from Nathaniel Mudge.

Time's come, he told himself. He went into the dining room, cleared his throat. 'Could I have a word, sir?'

The Colonel looked up from his paper. 'Of course.'

'It's . . . rather delicate, sir. It's Loveday. She turned up in my kitchen this morning, sir, at half past seven. With young Nat.' He cleared his throat again. 'There seems to have been some trouble. Between Walter and her.'

Mrs Carey-Lewis said, 'But what's *happened*?'

'I think, madam, that Walter's eye has been caught by another young woman. He never came home last night.'

The three of them were staring at him in apparent total astonishment. The Colonel spoke. 'Where is she now?'

'That's it, sir. She went off for a walk, to be on her own. Said she'd be back for breakfast And she's not back, sir. And the small van has gone from the garage.'

'The poor precious.' Mrs Carey-Lewis sounded despairing.

Then Jeremy Wells spoke. 'You're certain she's not down on the cliff? Do you think I should go and look?'

The Colonel considered this. 'Just to set our minds at rest.' He stood up, folded his newspaper and laid it neatly by his plate. 'And *I* must make my way to Lidgey and find out what the hell is going on.'

WITHIN HALF AN HOUR Jeremy had jogged down to the cliff and back. He found them all in the kitchen—Diana and Mary Millyway, Nettlebed and young Nat, finally placated by a serious breakfast. As Jeremy went into the room, they all turned to look at him. He shook his head. 'Not a sign.'

Diana gazed forlornly at him. 'I do wish Edgar were back.'

Just then they heard a door slam, and the next moment he was there, his expression as angry as Jeremy had ever seen it. 'Mary, take the boy away,' the Colonel said. And when she had whisked Nat out of the kitchen, he told them the sorry saga as Mrs Mudge had vociferously given it to him.

Walter had not returned in time to see to the milking, and his parents had finally done it themselves. Not until they were finished did their errant son appear, looking much the worse for wear. He had shown no remorse. He had told the Mudges that he had had it up to here with Nancherrow, with Lidgey, with serfdom. He was getting out. He'd been offered a job in a garage and he was going to live up Veglos Hill with Arabella Lumb.

'So that's the situation. The first person to be enlightened must be our solicitor, Roger Baines. I shall telephone him from my study.' He looked about him, from one grave face to another. Then his gaze alighted on his wife, and his steely expression softened. 'My darling Diana, you were about to say something.'

'It's just that . . . Loveday might have gone to Judith. Judith would be just the person she would turn to.'

'It's an idea. Do you want to ring up the Dower House?'

'No,' said Diana. 'Telephone calls can be distressing. I think somebody should go to her and explain the situation.' She smiled persuasively. 'Jeremy would go for us, I'm sure.'

'Of course.' He wondered if she knew what she was doing to him. Or, perhaps, for him. He said, 'I'll go now.'

JUDITH, FOR ONCE, was on her own. It being a Saturday, there was no school for Anna, and Phyllis had taken her to St Just for the day. Now it was past ten o'clock, and the other occupant of the Dower House, Gus, had not appeared. The door of his room remained closed, and Judith was pleased that he was having a good rest.

She had decided that this was a good opportunity to do what she had been meaning to for ages—measure the drawing-room windows for new curtains. And so she was balanced on top of a stepladder when she heard the front door open and shut. Footsteps crossed the hall, and then Jeremy walked into the room.

He was wearing a thick, tweedy sweater and had a scarlet muffler round his neck. Her first thought was that he looked so exactly the same that the years that had flown by since their last encounter might never have happened. And the second thought was identical to her reaction that night in London: had she been given the choice, he was the only person she would have really wanted to see.

Which was unexpected and rather annoying, because it left her defenceless and she had intended being quite cool with him.

He said, 'What are you doing?'

'Measuring the window. I'm going to have new curtains.'

He smiled. 'Can you come down? I want to talk to you, and if you stay up there I'll get a crick in my neck.'

So she descended and he came to give her a hand. When she reached the floor, he kissed her cheek and said, 'It's wonderful to see you again. Are you on your own? Loveday's not here?'

'Loveday?' Judith looked into his face and realised then that something was amiss. 'Why should Loveday be here?'

'She's disappeared. She's left Walter. Or rather, Walter's walked out on her. Look, why don't we sit down and I'll explain.'

They sat on the wide window seat and Jeremy told her all that had happened. Judith listened in growing dismay, unable to think of anything to say except, 'Poor Loveday.'

'Is Gus about?'

'Yes. He's upstairs. He's still asleep.'

'Are you sure?'

Judith frowned. 'Perhaps I'd better go and look.' She got up and went up the staircase.

'Gus?' No response. She opened the door of the room, to be met with the sight of the empty bed.

Bewildered, she went downstairs again. 'He's not there,' she told Jeremy. 'He must have got up early.'

Jeremy said, 'I have a feeling he's with Loveday. We must call Nancherrow.'

As he said this, the telephone started to ring. Judith went out into the hall, and Jeremy followed so that he was by her side when she picked up the receiver. 'Dower House.'

'Judith.' It was Gus.

'Gus. Where are you?'

'I'm in Porthkerris. Telephoning from your friends, the Warrens. Loveday wants to talk to you.'

'She's with you? Has she spoken to her mother and father?'

'Yes. Just this moment. They were first, you're second. Look, before I put her on there are three things I have to say. One is that I stole your bicycle, and it's at Nancherrow, sitting by the front door. The second thing is that I'm taking your advice and I'm going to be a painter. Or try to be.'

It was almost too much to begin to understand. 'But—'

'There's a last thing. I've said it once, but I have to say it again. Thank you.'

'Oh, Gus...'

But he was gone and, instead, she was hearing Loveday's voice, high with excitement, gabbling away as she used to, when they were children. And Judith was so relieved to be speaking to her that she forgot all about being cross.

'Loveday, you are the *end*.'

'Oh, Judith, don't fuss. You don't need to worry any more. I went down to the cliffs, just to work out what to say to everybody, and I took darling Tiger with me, and we were sitting brooding and watching the sun come up, and the next thing I knew there was Gus. And I didn't even know he'd come *back* to Cornwall. I didn't even know he was with *you*. And suddenly he was *there*, exactly at the moment when I was wanting him most.'

'Loveday, I'm so happy for you. So what did you do?'

'We talked and talked. And then we went back to the house, and I put Tiger back into the gunroom, and then Gus started up the fishmonger's van, and we drove over the moor to Porthkerris.'

'Why Porthkerris?'

'To find a studio for darling Gus, to work in and live in. I knew Mr Warren would be able to tell us who to go and see, so we came here. And they were utterly adorable, as always, and Mr Warren's been blasting away on the telephone and we're all going to look at a flat on the North Beach. It's got what's known as a kitchenette.'

She might have wittered on for ever, but Judith decided that the time had come to interrupt. 'When are you coming home?'

'Oh, this evening. We haven't *eloped* or anything like that. We're just being together. Planning things.'

'What about Walter?'

'Walter's gone. Arabella Lumb has won the day, and good luck to her. Pops spoke to Mr Baines and they reckon I can keep Nat. And Gus says he thinks it's quite a good idea to start married life with a ready-made family.' She fell silent for a moment, then said in a different voice, 'I always loved him, Judith. Even when I was sure he was dead. When you said he'd come back from Burma, it was the worst and the best thing I'd ever been told. I know I've been impossible.'

'Oh, Loveday, if you weren't impossible you wouldn't be you. That's why we all love you so much.'

'Come tonight,' said Loveday. 'Come to Nancherrow. Let's all be together. Just like it used to be. Only Edward gone. But I think he'll be there too, don't you? He'll be around somewhere, drinking our health.'

Judith said, through her tears, 'He wouldn't miss it for all the world. Good luck, Loveday.' She put down the receiver and was in floods. 'Have you got a handkerchief?'

Jeremy fished one from his pocket and gave it to her, and she wiped away the tears. 'I gather,' said Jeremy, 'that all is well.'

'Blissful. They're together. He's going to paint and live in a studio in Porthkerris. With a kitchenette.'

She smiled at him, and all at once there were just the two of them. No other diversions. And for the first time a certain shyness. 'Would you like a cup of coffee?' Judith asked.

'No, I don't want coffee. I want you and me. It's time to talk.'

They went back into the drawing room, and the deep window seat. Judith said, 'Where do we start?'

'At the beginning. Why did you never answer my letter?'

310

She frowned. 'But you never wrote.'

'I did. From Long Island.'

'I never got a letter. I waited and waited. And I decided you'd simply changed your mind, got cold feet, decided that you didn't want to keep in touch.'

'Oh, Judith.' He let out a sigh that sounded more like a groan. 'All these years.' He took her hand in his. 'I did write. I just about tore myself to pieces trying to get the right words down. I sent it off by service mail from New York.'

'So what happened?'

'I imagine a ship was sunk. The Battle of the Atlantic was at its peak. My letter may have ended up at the bottom of the ocean.'

She shook her head. 'What did the letter say?'

'It said a lot of things. It said that I would never forget that night we spent together in London. And it told you how much I loved you. How much I'd always loved you, from the moment of finding you again at Nancherrow and hearing the sound of "Jesu, Joy of Man's Desiring" come from your bedroom. And at the end I asked you to marry me. Because I couldn't imagine a future without you. I asked you to write. To say yes or no and to set my mind at rest.'

'But you got no answer. Didn't that strike you as odd?'

'Not really. I never considered myself much of a catch. And you had youth and beauty and financial independence. So when I received no reply, I didn't think it odd. Just the end of everything.'

Judith said, 'Edward made love to me because he was sorry for me. I was so afraid that your motives were the same.'

'Never that, my darling.'

'I see now. But I was younger then. Not all that sure of myself.' She looked at him. 'There's something we haven't talked about—Jess. She's part of me now. My responsibility. Whatever happens to me happens to Jess as well.'

'Would she mind if I happened to you? Because I would like very much for all three of us to be together. I always remember her in the train, being terribly naughty. I can't wait to see her again.'

'She's fourteen now. And when we get married—'

'Did you really say that? *When* we get married?'

'I believe I did.'

'I've got grey hairs now.'

'I know. I've seen them, but I'm much too polite to remark.'

Suddenly she was laughing, and he kissed her, and the thought flashed through his mind that it would be a brilliant idea to gather her in his arms and make long and passionate love to her. But common sense told him that now was not the right moment.

Gently he let her go, putting up a hand to smooth honey-coloured hair away from her face. He said, 'Shall we, for the moment, pull ourselves together and try to plan for our future? Except that I haven't decided anything for myself yet, let alone you and Jess.'

'Are you going back to Truro to take over from your father?'

'Is that what you would like?'

Judith was honest. She said, 'No. I'm sorry, but I never want to leave this house. It's so special. It's been a haven, a sanctuary, for so many people. Do you understand?'

'Completely. So cross Truro off the list. I have an old naval colleague, a good friend. A surgeon commander, RNVR, called Bill Whatley. He put an idea to me a couple of months ago, when we were both in Malta. Supposing the two of us started up a new practice right here? In Penzance.'

Judith, scarcely daring to hope, stared at Jeremy. 'Could you?'

'Why not? Bill's a Londoner, but he wants to settle his family in the country, preferably by the sea. We talked it over, but I didn't want to commit myself. I didn't want to come blundering back into your life if you didn't want me around. A bit embarrassing, having a lovesick old flame on your doorstep.'

'Penzance is scarcely my doorstep. And if you're a GP in Penzance, it's too far away to live *here*. Night calls and things like that.'

'There'll be two of us in the practice. I can commute. We shall build a beautiful modern surgery, with a flat for night shifts.'

'With kitchenette?'

'Of course.' Jeremy was laughing. 'You know something, my darling? We're crossing bridges we haven't even come to.' He looked at his watch. 'It's a quarter to twelve. I suppose I ought to get back to Nancherrow, or Diana will think that I've joined the club and eloped as well. Will you come with me, my darling Judith?'

'If you want.'

'I do.'

'Shall we tell them all? About you and me?'

'Why not?'

For some reason the prospect was a bit daunting. 'What *are* they going to say?'

'Why don't we go and find out?'

ROSAMUNDE PILCHER

Because so many of Rosamunde Pilcher's books are set in Cornwall, many people imagine the author lives or was born there. In fact, she is of pure Scottish blood (her father was related to the great nineteenth century novelist Sir Walter Scott) and lives with her husband, Graham, near Dundee, in a home filled with flowers, dogs and visiting grandchildren. 'I've been very lucky,' she says. 'I've been married for nearly fifty years and lived in only two houses. That suits me very well.'

It was in her childhood years that Rosamunde Pilcher came to know and love Cornwall. 'Like my heroine in *Coming Home*, I grew up there, and my father, just like hers, was posted abroad—to Burma. It was an accepted situation then. Mothers had to choose whether they stayed with their husbands or their children. My mother chose to stay with us; whenever she went to Burma we would be dumped on somebody, but never for more than six months. You always felt different, though. However kind and loving people were, it wasn't the same as having your own home. We became a bit withdrawn.'

The outbreak of war meant that the author had to grow up 'in rather a rush'. She left school at sixteen, joined the Wrens, then married young and raised four children. Not having gone to university is something she still regrets. She has, however, written stories for as long as she can remember, and had her first one published when she was just eighteen, and serving as a submarine spotter in Ceylon. After the war, she wrote for *Good Housekeeping* and Mills and Boon. 'Gradually,' she explains, 'my writing matured and became less predictable.' The first major breakthrough came with *The Shell Seekers*, which topped best-seller lists in Britain and America. 'It was a great thrill. I felt at last [she was then sixty-two] that I really had been a writer all those years.'

Now in her early seventies, Rosamunde Pilcher is contemplating retirement. 'I've been working since I was eighteen, and this is the first time in my life when I haven't had to think, "Oh my golly, I've got to get started again." It's a rather good feeling.'

In the Shadow of a Rainbow

Robert Franklin Leslie

WITH ILLUSTRATIONS BY ADAM HOOK

Greg tingled from head to foot when the wolf stepped slowly out of the darkness and strode deliberately into the circle of camp-fire light. Something clicked between them when their eyes finally met . . . an irresistible friendship. The understanding between them would later grow: a bond, shaky at first, that would bridge the communication chasm between man and wolf.

Robert Franklin Leslie tells the remarkable true story of Náhani, a timber wolf, and the man who chose to protect her at all costs.

Author's Note

Late one afternoon in the summer of 1970, a young Indian beached his canoe near my Babine Lake campsite in the backwoods of British Columbia. The young man introduced himself as Gregory Tah-Kloma, and told me he was a Chimmesyan of the Tsimshian band. That evening Greg sat by my campfire and grilled salmon fillets for us.

During the weeks that followed, Greg and I became staunch friends. I learned that he had worked in various mills and mines to pay his way through college. He was a graduate student in mineralogy, and spent his summers at placer gold deposits along drainage systems footing British Columbia watersheds. We were both on the way to prospect Babine tributaries when we met.

Night after night we sat by the campfire and talked. Gradually Greg told me the remarkable story of his devotion to a threatened pack of timber wolves, a story that included his search to relocate the amazing female wolf-pack leader, known as Náhani, whose unusual company he had first enjoyed in the summer of 1964. His compelling drive to find the wolf and her pack before trappers and bounty hunters could destroy them reached unique proportions.

I asked Greg's permission to write down his story, and he agreed. He had kept a log in which he listed events in chronological order, and a diary in which he entered his personal feelings and reactions. He allowed me to draw freely on both.

In order to protect the privacy of living individuals and to protect Náhani certain place names and locations have been changed. However, the facts of Gregory Tah-Kloma's adventures with Náhani and her wolf pack are as he told them to me.

Robert Franklin Leslie
March, 1974

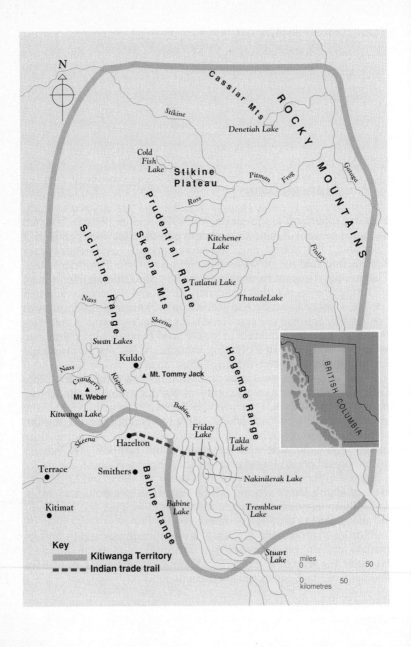

1. Náhani of Nakinilerak

Along the southern belly of British Columbia's north-central wilderness stretches the lake country. Narrow troughs of water up to 130 miles long wind through the canyonlands and resemble wide, gentian-blue belts.

The longest of these 'belly' lakes, Babine and Takla, lie in trenches between the Babine Range to the west and the Hogem Range to the east. An ancient Indian trade trail through the Babine-Takla region connects several primitive mountain settlements, often fifty miles apart. The route skirts the upper beach of Friday Lake, northernmost of five basin tarns. Of a winter the trail serves aged Carrier Indian trappers. Of a summer, possibly half a dozen die-hard prospectors may dream their way along this obsolete footpath.

Seven miles south of this trail lies Nakinilerak Lake, a wilderness gem five miles long, half a mile wide.

In a clump of Sitka spruce and quaking aspens, Gregory Tah-Kloma's campsite straddled a breezy, bug-free peninsula near the lake's intake flume. The year was 1964. About two months remained before a late September or early October snowstorm would hurl him back over the archaic trade route to the totem-pole settlement of Hazelton, where he had left his station wagon with a friend. Prospectors cursed that sixty-mile trek between Friday Lake and Hazelton as a backbreaker, full of deadfalls, icy fords and landslides. But much of the route would skim downhill, paralleling the right bank of the Suskwa River.

During the first ten days of July, Greg had panned the stream bed between his campsite and Friday Lake. Thousands of years ago receding Ice Age glaciers had deposited pockets of gold nuggets the size of pinheads—and smaller—along the bedrock riffles.

One morning shortly after breakfast, Greg sat rocking back and forth on a log near his campfire. He liked to finger the two pounds of 'dust' he had accumulated during his stay—a bonanza to supplement his winter salary at the refinery near Prince George. If gold came in any other colour, he reflected, nobody would prize the metal half as much. Chimmesyans say, 'Gold is sunshine stored in a rock.'

As he zippered his loot into a rucksack side pocket, he noticed a man trudging up the beach from Nakinilerak's southern end.

From a distance the stranger appeared to be middle-aged. Probably a Carrier, Greg surmised, by the way the Indian stooped under a tumpline basket pack, supported by a strap across his forehead.

Plainly bushed after his long cross-country journey, he leaned heavily upon an alpenstock every four or five steps. With a carbine balanced and clutched at the breech, the man's left arm swung like the shank of a pendulum.

'GOOD MORNING, SIR!' the stranger said as he shuffled up to the smoky campfire. His bucktoothed smile reminded Greg of cartoons depicting friendly beavers. 'My name is Eugene Charley. You have been here long?'

'I came before the Moon-of-Walking-Thunder,' Greg said. To an Indian that meant early July, four or five weeks ago. 'I'm Chimmesyan—part Haida, part Tsimshian.'

'You must be gulch-happy. What about Náhani? Have you seen her?' As Eugene Charley pronounced the name, he raised his upper lip like a nickering mule. He lowered the lever of his Winchester to check the chamber. The sun shot a brassy glint off a breached cartridge rim.

Greg urged the man to sit down on the log and remove his heavy pack. He grinned when Greg offered him a cup of coffee and a pipe stoked with India House tobacco.

'Who is Náhani?' Greg asked.

Charley spat into the fire. 'The great silver she-wolf. Queen bitch of the deadliest wolf pack in all Canada. They den somewhere near here. I've studied them for a year or more, ever since a sweet price was put on Náhani's head. Those wolves are hunting somewhere south of here. I wish to hell I knew where. When they come back, they'll gnaw your Chimmesyan bones. Nakinilerak is where they winter.' With a speculative squint he probed Greg for a reaction.

'Why should anybody be afraid of wolves?'

'Are you armed?'

Perhaps Eugene Charley suspected a rich 'poke' of gold. While he smoked, his glance kept shuttling between Greg's gold pan and trench shovel.

'I'm prepared to defend myself,' Greg said without admitting that he carried no firearms. He considered everyone trustworthy until proven otherwise, but this Eugene Charley somehow seemed to speak from two faces. 'Tell me more about your Náhani.'

'Náhani means "one who shines". Carriers call her Silver Skin. Colour, you know. She's too damned big for a timber wolf. Eight, maybe ten years old. She leads twenty, maybe thirty killers. Who knows? Nobody ever gets a shot at that pack. She can smell a gun a mile away. Livestock killed, traps emptied, and now lately *people* have disappeared. When they raise the bounty enough, I'll bring her down. You'll see.'

Greg concealed his relief when Eugene Charley declined an invitation to rest the day and night. He was headed for Pendleton Bay on Babine Lake. Carriers had to hurry, otherwise the lumber mill would hire Tsimshians to manhandle summer-felled logs into the dog-chain lifts. Instead of following the trade trail, Charley was cutting through the brush in order to save time 'and maybe bring in a skin'.

'I'll guarantee you a horrible death if you stay here,' he said as the two men shook hands. 'Náhani's phantoms will eat you alive!'

'Weasel words!' Greg said aloud. To himself he thought: small-bore talk from a bounty hunter with a forked tongue who builds bad reputations in order to get local authorities to hike the rewards.

NEVERTHELESS, EUGENE CHARLEY'S brief visit set in motion an exciting trend of thought. Greg's past experience with wolves attested that Náhani and her 'phantoms', if they existed other than in rum-soaked Carrier imaginations, weren't as dangerous as Charley claimed—unless, of course, they were infected with sylvatic rabies. He remembered that a Canadian newspaper had for years offered a substantial cash payment for any documented record of a wolf having attacked a human being without provocation. No one ever claimed the money. That thought was consoling on a dark and rainy night, for Greg was alone and unarmed and an organised pack of timber wolves comprised the most audacious legion of carnivores on earth.

On the third night following Eugene Charley's visit, Greg squatted near the campfire's orange plumes in order to inhale the fragrance of sweet balsam and cascara bark. An hour after moonset he had watched Ursa Major cross the northern zenith. Not the slightest breeze stirred the forest. For some intuitive reason—certainly not because of any sound or movement—he looked up into the wall of darkness on the other side of the campfire. Barely within the outer perimeter of light stood the largest, most patrician wolf he had ever seen. From Charley's description, it had to be Náhani. Her coat glistened like burnished silver. She stared back at him intently for several moments, then retreated into the dark aisles of spruce and aspen— disappeared as silently as an owl.

Despite certain fears and momentary shock, Greg recognised that the wolf had held her head and bushy tail high—nonaggressive positions. Her black muzzle and chaps had remained closed. She seemed to be alone, although this would be highly unlikely.

Greg retired to his sleeping-bag. At midnight a wolf chorus began a series of songs at lakeside. He slipped out and hurried towards the beach in hope of glimpsing the pack. But the wolves heard his approach and dashed into dense forest. At greylight they sang again, this time from a headland palisade a mile east of the lake. Náhani and her troop had apparently resumed residence on that hillside. Greg hoped his presence wouldn't interfere with their privacy.

From sunrise until dark the next day the wolves studied every move the young man made. Without so much as snapping a twig or stepping on a dry leaf, they crept like ghosts through the timber, peered from behind shrubs and boulders. Greg felt their piercing gaze, saw the occasional blur of a movement, but was unable to locate one flesh-and-blood wolf. So he squandered the day, crouching on the beach or straddling the camp log—in plain sight at all times. When he considered it necessary to move about, he did so on all fours, a Chimmesyan technique often employed to make friends with predator mammals. When he tried to mimic their sporadic calls, they replied with chomps and snarls—not hostile, but not friendly. His harmonica tunes and deep-chested chants froze them in rigid listening silence, but they manifested no real interest in man-made music.

That evening Greg decided upon a rash course. Beyond one mile, the beach along the lake's eastern shore line narrowed and disappeared into rocky, brushy impasses; but since the wolves favoured the hill and forest on that side, he hoped that they would allow him to get closer to them in the owl-light if he walked there. A feeling of wild ecstasy gripped him as he stepped through the moving moon shadows towards the lake. He had walked less than half a mile when a speeding body crashed recklessly through forest debris across the hillside forty feet above the beach. From size and colour there could be no mistake. She was the big wolf he had seen the night before. Although she allowed him only glimpses as she flashed between covering shrubs, she was the most spectacular animal he had ever seen. In spruce-filled moonlight her coat shone like sterling silver.

At last Greg turned to retrace his steps towards camp. The wolf also dashed in that direction, a little closer perhaps but as yet unwilling to risk any gesture that might be interpreted as friendly or trusting. On the other hand, the young man detected no hint of enmity. He saw many of his own tracks half obliterated by wolf prints, yet he had been unaware of being closely followed down the beach.

The lake was a chilled sapphire. A slip of a breeze rocked the forest shadows and waterfowl in cradlelike motion. The closer Greg drew to camp the more conscious he became of large converging masses in the thicket—huge ghosts that made delicate swishing sounds as they moved through dense vine maple and dry scrub willow. No wonder Carriers venerated the pack as 'phantoms'!

If an attack had been planned, Greg assumed it would have

happened before he returned to camp. But the wolves simply van-ished into the hillside forest. Back in his kitchen area shortly before moondown, he stirred up the smouldering embers in the fire pit, then crossed his legs on the spongy sward, leaned back against the old driftwood spruce log, and smoked his pipe. Eugene Charley had spoken with a forked tongue.

On the following morning he sensed a change. From the big hill-side east of the lake, the wolves came down—no closer to camp, but they made no further effort to hide. An atmosphere of relaxation seemed to surround the pack, but Greg decided not to continue his prospecting. Veteran woodsman that he was, he still felt concern in the close presence of possibly two dozen timber wolves.

From then on, the wolves ignored him by day. They appeared non-chalant as long as he went about camp on all fours, but the moment he resumed the upright position, they assumed a defensive attitude. Older pairs began to relax on the meadow between his camp and the creek, while the younger wolves ventured to romp on the beach or to swim in the lake. Most of the pack swam every day.

Four days later, Náhani sat for more than an hour on a sparsely covered ridge of the hill. It was the first time Greg had seen her in daylight. He observed her through binoculars.

For a week Greg continued to walk down the east beach at night, and on each occasion six to twelve wolves crept silently through the forest adjacent to the strand. At length, Náhani and four adult males walked to within fifteen yards when he sat down a mile from camp and tossed pebbles into the lake. To Greg, they seemed to be probing for a possibility of trust.

Occasionally snorting, whining, snarling, they followed him back until he crossed the flume and returned to his campsite. Footprints here and there revealed cabalistic inspections of his equipment during his absence. Nothing had been touched.

Given that he half expected her on the seventh night, Greg tingled and shivered from head to foot when the long-legged queen wolf stepped slowly out of the darkness and strode deliberately into the circle of campfire light. She sniffed the sweat-laden air, walked to the opposite end of the log, faced the crackling flames, and haunched. Small campfires have always fascinated wolves, and outdoorsmen have often misinterpreted lupine curiosity for aggression. Except for deeply rhythmic breathing, she sat as motionless as a mounted museum specimen.

There is no doubt that something clicked between that wolf and Gregory when their eyes finally met; an irresistible friendship had begun. As an unmated female—as monarch of the pack—Náhani, he felt, was an entity apart from her kind, aloof, alone and lonely.

Each time their eyes met, further understanding seemed to grow; a bond, shaky at first, began to bridge the communication chasm between man and wolf.

Greg made no move to get closer to her that night. After an hour of silent communication, she stood up mechanically and without turning her head walked slowly towards the hill east of the lake. On all fours Greg followed at her heels until she leapt across the creek and disappeared into the forest.

The next evening, Greg and Náhani sat by the log—almost within touching distance—and listened to the wide-awake wilderness: a bull moose's trumpet, a great grey owl's flute, the reedy babel of geese feuding on the lake. Their gaze often met as they followed shooting star trajectories behind thin veils of aurora borealis. They watched night itself roll before the amber flood of foredawn, which occurred at 4.00am in late August. There is no calm like summer dawn in the lake country of British Columbia.

Silently Náhani leapt from camp when a team member began an amberlight song. Greg wriggled into his sleeping-bag and slept until noon in firm belief that the seeds of trust had sprouted.

2. To Know A Wolf

When Náhani bounced into camp on the third night, the big silver female's mood of jubilation found expression in tail-wagging and barking, and she attempted to communicate a mysterious enthusiasm. She trotted round the campfire, head and tail high, muzzle open between utterances, toes spread wide apart. Greg thought her behaviour strange until it occurred to him that her elation was not intended for *him*.

Eight dark-haired males, each about two stones lighter than Náhani, paced restlessly back and forth over the meadow between Greg's camp and the lake's intake. They gruffed, yelped and whined like chained hounds, impatiently pleading with Náhani for something Greg could not understand at that time. Unexpectedly, she placed her front paws on the log and issued a single high-pitched command. Silently, instantly obedient, the eight males bounded in single file up the game trail towards Friday Lake.

Náhani haunched within eighteen inches of where Greg sat smoking his pipe next to the log. She remained until the males returned an hour before sunrise, at which time she bounded up the trail with about a dozen of her troop.

That afternoon when Greg went on all fours to the creek, six adult wolves and three subyearlings sprawled along the sunny lake shore. After a quick identifying glimpse, they ignored his presence among them. Every belly was gorged, which seemed to answer the question of the night before. The eight males comprised a hunting squad. They had brought down game somewhere between Nakinilerak and Friday lakes.

Except during the Indian's moonlight hikes along the lake shore, Náhani had not appeared in camp before eleven o'clock of an evening. However, on the afternoon following the night of the hunt, she entered camp for an early visit. From belly dimensions it was plain that she, too, had feasted.

In his diary, Greg described the manner in which Náhani projected monarchy over her entourage from the moment she stepped on the beach.

'She must weigh at least two stones more than her biggest lieutenant. In animal societies, weight, speed and guts count for most. Add brains and you come up with leadership. Náhani has all four. Every wolf awakes and springs to attention when she shows up. After a quick round of rear-end smelling—to make sure no stranger has joined the pack—she starts browbeating the other females, to make sure they remember who is boss. She kowtows to no special male. And that means she either lost a mate or never had one. It is plain funny the way she about-faces and showers affection on every wolf in her pack—after she chomps hell out of a few. Lifts her hind leg and pees on rocks and stumps just like a male.'

Given that any adult pack member could cover seventy-five miles or more in four hours, Greg assumed that before the wolves had reoccupied their denning complex scouts had reconnoitred his camp at times and then reported back to Náhani wherever the pack had holed up along their runway. He considered it conceivable that Náhani herself had studied his habits long before moving her charges back to Nakinilerak. One point was clear. The wolves had reoccupied their quarters only after observations of the man camped near what may have been their ancestral whelping dens.

When the pack more or less accepted human presence near their hillside, Greg resumed most activities, including panning, on foot rather than on all fours. Although the pack quickly tolerated his presence, one old pair of black, heavily mantled individuals always scooted away with parted lips and chomping teeth if he approached except on all fours. Both black wolves limped. When those two slept on the sand or the sward, Greg continued to respect their preference. He discontinued all panning when he discovered that the work disquieted the entire pack.

Náhani was first to accept the man-walk position. One evening she trotted into camp after Greg had finished ash-baking a sockeye-salmon dinner. On several occasions she had refused offers of raw fish but gobbled it baked or fried. She accepted a second fish and took it to the hillside beyond the creek, which meant she was probably succouring an incapacitated associate in a den.

She returned immediately to camp. Haunched by the log, she eyed a number of activities that Greg deliberately performed on foot. Quite suddenly she jumped squarely in front of him and blocked passage. At first her act appeared a protest at his upright position, but finally she reared up on her hind legs, then placed her forepaws on his shoulders. The shock of her 140 pounds almost bowled him backwards into the fire, but more than the physical shock, that huge head twelve inches wide, maw open, two-inch daggerlike fangs so close to his face, caught him unprepared. She simply licked his nose, gently shoved him, and backed away. He was to learn that her head-long acts revealed a complex of deep-seated emotions that often surfaced without prior announcement.

In addition to her sensitivity, Náhani's every physical characteristic struck Greg as beautiful and satisfying: her extraordinary silver coat; her bicycle-pedalling gait that broke into an effortless canter like that of a thoroughbred horse; her wide-set, greenish-amber eyes; the heavy, foxlike tail whose position and hackles expressed her every whim and mood. To Greg, of course, her comeliest attribute was the new routine she often employed—that of placing her forepaws on his shoulders and licking his face.

During his first three weeks of association with the wolf, Greg made no move to soft-hand Náhani, not even when she came to lean against him near the campfire after long runs down the beach. He considered it unsuitable to touch any wild creature until positive the gesture would not be misinterpreted.

Some days before he began petting Náhani, she developed a nuisance habit. She took his arms, hands or feet into her mouth and chewed. The action probably demonstrated affection, but it may have been to deposit her own salivary scent, thus proclaiming dominion or ownership. As pack matriarch, she never engaged in frivolous play. When moulting hair caused her skin to itch, Greg seized the opportunity to run his fingers through her coat—to curry loose hair, to rub her head, back and belly. Under those circumstances she learned that *unchewed* hands and arms performed better services, because her friend refused to comb and scratch when she insisted upon chewing human extremities.

Repeatedly six to ten subordinates stood fifteen lengths from the log and eyed the combing and rubbing. They had seen her place paws on

Greg's shoulders and lick his face. They had never been far away when the two walked or raced along the lake shore. Yet, on the surface at least, Náhani was the only wolf in the pack interested in Greg's company. At first it annoyed him, because he had tried to make friends with several more approachable wolves. Then he recognised that Náhani herself, through the scent of her urine, saliva and paw sweat had forbidden the others to have anything to do with him.

Apparently satisfied that combing and rubbing would do their queen no harm, the other wolves retired to the open beach to chant solos or sing in chorus. Greg was unable to associate their songs with any form of lupine communication other than an emotional expression of the moment. They never bayed at the moon. Baying appeared to be a kind of family excitement and nothing more. The true wolf song was in no way related to hunting, mating, calling or 'mooning'. To Greg it seemed the purest animal music in all nature.

At times the colony was an anthill of laudable activity. Náhani coerced all wolves without young to feed, protect and train other pack members' cubs. Apparently each adult did regular sentry duty. Clean-up committees periodically removed bones, fur and ordure from the dens. The matriarch assigned special guards and helpers at the den of any sick or disabled wolf. Her chieftainship was perhaps most conspicuous each time she assembled her hunting squad and either led them or sent them towards the scent of game, having drilled and timed each member's duties for offence, defence or escape.

The wolves demonstrated wide individual differences in intelligence and disposition. When they were 'off duty' they evidenced tender affection and loyalty towards one another throughout the several generations represented in the pack. There was neither petulance nor fighting among the several families. In play they adhered strictly to the 'pecking order' principle.

Late one afternoon Náhani and Greg went berrying along the stream between Friday and Nakinilerak lakes. When they returned, twelve members of the pack were on their way to escort them back to camp. They were obviously in a state of agitation. As they led the way a solitary, sorrowful voice drifted down—a tremulous wail. Greg ran after Náhani as she jumped across the creek and loped up the steep, spruce-crowded slope east of the lake. When Greg arrived at the summit, he was gasping for breath. The wolves were baying in a state of high-pitched rage, lunging and slashing at a huge grizzly bear—in Chimmesyan dialect, Ozilenka.

The 800-pound giant had stalked and killed a truant wolf cub. The mother's moan had signalled the crisis. Erect on his hind legs, the bear stood nine feet tall as he swung at fifteen wolves who had just seen their sanctuary outraged by their only natural enemy.

Like an Indian chieftain, Náhani commanded each organised charge. Twice the bear's deft right hook intercepted her lunge, but she allowed herself to fall limp into a heath cover of button willow. The bear, of course, recognised her as the leader. He knew that her offer of herself as the target spearhead for each attack was to distract him long enough for pincer wolves to move in on both sides. Although outwitted in strategy, the bear was fast enough and strong enough to extricate himself from each of Náhani's manoeuvres.

Her guttural baying goaded the pack to furious attacks at the grizzly's loins and shoulders, but his tough skin and dense hair easily resisted their vicelike jaws and dagger fangs.

The wolves lost a measure of fury when the bear hammered two of their number to the ground—one with a broken neck, one with a crushed skull. Finally the panting pack bayed as one voice and paced a wide circle round their foe.

Expecting the wolves to back him up at this point, Greg seized two baseball-sized rocks and bounced them off the bear. At the same time he yelled a tribal war whoop that frightened not only the bear but the wolves. He had already estimated the distance to the last timber-line spruce in case the bear charged him. He depended upon the ancient precept: adult grizzlies don't climb trees.

The bear dropped to all fours, locked his jaws round the dead cub, and lumbered down the hillside. Every wolf slashed at the retreating grizzly's hind quarters. The noisy melee disappeared among moorland boulders too distant for Greg to follow.

AT NIGHTFALL NÁHANI dragged into camp and dropped at Greg's feet, panting and whining. He lifted her head to his lap and combed the dried blood and saliva from her coat. He found no wounds other than bear-claw welts along her sides and neck—welts the size of shrew runs. She was plainly exhausted but continued to rumble with the fire of hatred. Her lieutenants moaned, yipped and yowled round the campsite. Greg recognised at once that they were begging for leadership to pursue that grizzly and resume combat.

For days following the tragic episode, Náhani drilled her fighting team along the ridge where the grizzly had been. She divided her forces into two squads that practised brutally against one another.

After the battle with Ozilenka, the pack regarded Greg with less suspicion, but no wolf dared violate what the queen-leader had pre-empted. His friendship with Náhani flourished exclusively on the wild terms of its inception—uncompromising independence and trust. In order to keep that trust, Greg gave up further attempts to cultivate friendly relationships with other wolves.

At no time did he require of Náhani any form of obedience. In deep humility he honestly admitted his obedience to the wolf. When she chewed his boots, gobbled his food, destroyed his only bath towel and urinated on every item of his equipment, he was careful to allow no resentment to enter his expression.

Day or night, only one bark was needed to bring him to her on the run, to follow her along the shore line, or over the rocky ridge to sniff for fresh bear tracks. When she craved a salmon dinner—and ordered it by bringing fishbones to his camp—he fished and cooked for her. Once he had memorised her physical signals, the communication was generally obvious. In a sense, Greg became one of Náhani's subjects. He felt a bond that defied analysis.

WHEN ANY LIVING BEING is threatened with premature death, the Chimmesyan believes that the individual has stumbled into the shadow of a spear. Thus, when Ozilenka the grizzly bear returned, killed a second cub, maimed an adult wolf, and went away unscathed, Greg foresaw disaster for the pack. To compound the problem, on September 5 an icy blizzard from the Beaufort Sea drenched and frosted central British Columbia. Balsam poplars, maples, aspens, dogwoods and alders changed into autumn dress and storm shadows intensified the conifers' sombre green.

On the night of the eighteenth, Náhani's entire pack assembled round the perimeter of Greg's camp, squinted into the frost-heavy wind, raised their throats, and sang to the grumbling clouds overhead.

At first Greg interpreted the serenade as a statement of friendship, but better judgment warned him that the song was a medley of command calls. He and Náhani huddled for hours in the lee of a tarpaulin lean-to and watched snowflakes sizzle on campfire embers. When the great white wolf finally turned her face, Greg saw a faraway expression come into her eyes.

The queen wolf had reached her inevitable decision, her inevitable response to those calls. After one swift lick across Greg's face, she sprang to her feet and leapt into the stormy darkness. She yelped for her pack to follow.

'Náhani!' the young Chimmesyan called several times, but she had no understanding of what the word meant—even if she could have heard him above the wind and the baying of the pack. *Náhani* was man tongue. Greg had never used the name in her presence.

·The wolves skirted Friday Lake and headed up the pass into the Nilkitkwa basin. They had scented woodland caribou herds migrating to their winter quarters.

By October's Fallen-Leaf-Moon, Náhani and her legion had not returned. Greg had no more food and he broke camp. Soon the deep snows would bury the only route out of the wilderness.

330

3. An Awesome Journey

Greg returned to Nakinilerak Lake under the June Moon-of-the-Moose-Child, 1965, to prospect for gold and to renew association with the wolves. Gold he found, but Náhani and her team did not return. During the autumn and winter moons Greg questioned Babine, Beaver, Sekane and Carrier Indians about the Silver Skin. They all assured him that Skeena bandsmen had reported sighting the 'phantom clan' on the Stikine Plateau to the north.

To the Ancient Ones—the aborigines—this isolated region, walled against human trespass on the west by the Coastal Mountains and on the east by the towering Rocky Mountains, had long been known as the Kitiwanga. To all but a few woodland Skeenas, Tsimshians and Chimmesyans, the word has lost its historical meaning—'not for man'.

In the short span of two years, Náhani had become a legend among northwoods Indians. For alleged crimes against the Dominion—mushrooming tales disseminated by bounty hunters like Eugene Charley—there was a growing price on her head.

Greg consulted aerial survey maps. After weighing the hardship, expense and massive odds against ever finding the silver wolf in a pathless wilderness, he returned to his job in Prince George. When not at work he constructed specialised backpacking equipment and dreamed of renewing his search.

ON JUNE 10, 1966, Greg arrived at the auto repair shop of his boy-hood friend Rocky Longspear in the Tsimshian village of Hazelton. It was almost twenty months after he had last seen Náhani and her wolf pack. During that time there had been many reported sightings on the Stikine Plateau south of the Skeena River. At last the great Kitiwanga snows of two consecutive severe winters had melted, and Greg could now begin his search for the wolf. Rocky garaged Greg's station wagon.

Two seasoned Tsimshian guides who were lounging around the auto repair shop eagerly offered their services until Greg revealed the object of his trip. To prove he was 'off his rocker', they took him to Trapper-Dan Tall-Totem's cabin on the Kispiox River road. Dan had trapped along the Skeena River during the preceding ten winters. When the trapper answered the knock at his door, Greg at once interpreted the apathetic expression and bloodshot eyes as danger signals—here was a combustible man. One of the guides explained the reasons for disturbing the trapper.

'You gotta be nuts!' Dan growled with an unmistakable tone of hostility. 'For two seasons your big Náhani and her pack destroyed every trapped skin north of Kimolith Creek. They dug and chewed out the trap sets and run off with 'em. Three strings I lost.'

He revealed a recent meeting with Tlingit and Skeena bandsmen from the Stikine River country. They had experienced identical misfortunes. The trappers' association had upped the reward for Náhani's hide to $800.

'By the end of Moon-of-Walking-Thunder, Mr Wolf-man,' Dan said as he pointed a shaky finger towards Greg's face, 'you can kiss your playmates goodbye. We all heard that damn yarn about you buddy-buddying with the wolf bitch at Nakinilerak. Every trapper in the Kitiwanga meets at Kimolith Creek in July. We won't sleep till Náhani is dead and skinned.'

'How do you know where she is?' Greg asked.

'We'll get there before you do, wherever she is. There ain't no trails in the Kitiwanga. But we know that country like the palms of our hands. You don't. That's all.' He backed inside and closed the door.

News that the 'wolf-man' was a guest of Rocky Longspear the local mechanic spread throughout the totem-pole-lined village within minutes. Feelings and superstitions concerning Náhani and her pack ran high. Most of the six hundred inhabitants depended on 'the goods of the woods' for a living.

'Get out of town as soon as possible, Greg,' Rocky warned. 'You are best off not to trust Trapper-Dan.'

'I've got to find her now, Rocky,' Greg said. 'I have to get her further north if possible. With that reward dangling in front of their noses—and these blockheads gobbling up everything they hear...'

A WET CHINOOK blew in from the coast. For the next two days Greg sloshed through wind-driven rain until he waded into the sudsy mud at the settlement of Kuldo. All but one of the cedar-planked shacks on the mighty Skeena's right bank were deserted. A wrinkled, toothless squaw who called herself Moiso invited him to spend the night in her one-room hovel.

The roof leaked, the only window had been nailed shut, and a stewpan half full of overaged venison liver gurgled on a smoky cast-iron stove in one corner. Despite the rank atmosphere, Moiso's hospitality kept the young man from bolting back into the rainstorm. She explained that Kuldo villagers had packed out to swap winter pelts for staples at the trading post in Smithers.

'Pelts?' he asked. 'I thought Náhani had destroyed the trap sets.'

Moiso all but choked on the hunk of liver she had been gumming. After an adequate burp she whispered, 'Crow talk!'

'You know about Náhani?'

'She came to Kuldo last winter.'

'Trapper-Dan Tall-Totem said his clan aims to kill her under the Moon-of-Walking-Thunder.'

'So they plan. They may kill her. Trapper-Dan killed plenty renegade wolves. But Náhani runs further and faster than any man ... or any wolf before.'

Later that evening Moiso directed Greg to follow the Skeena's right bank until the river flowed round Mount Tommy Jack's northernmost shoulder. If he was determined to commit suicide, she declared, he should camp at Tatlatui Lake, headwaters of the Finlay River, and wait there for Náhani. Moiso had camped there with her father when she was a girl, and claimed to have seen many white wolves at Tatlatui. According to Moiso, *Tatlatui-meh-Náhani* meant 'home of the shining white wolves'. All silver skins came from and returned to that region.

As soon as greylight opened the trail, Greg gave the old squaw a dollar and started up the wide Skeena River gorge. Ten miles beyond Kuldo the teeming Kitiwanga game herds began to appear. Mountain goats and bighorn sheep trotted to the riverbank and ogled when they saw the young Indian. Beyond the big bend, where the Skeena flowed northwest through a gap in the Sicintine Range, he overtook moose, wapiti, deer and tagtail coyotes.

The river flowed in a deep, unveering trench for about forty miles, the first half of which demanded four and a half days, twelve to fourteen hours a day, of complicated trail blazing. Because of clifflike banks, Greg often considered himself lucky to walk fifty yards at the water's edge. Then the only way through was to scramble to heights 2,000 feet above the timber line. Fearing a fractured bone, even a serious sprain in that remote jungle, Greg slackened his pace even though he knew he was losing valuable time.

Low-skirted spruce, branching almost to the level of forest debris, further impeded his progress. Despite mosquito clouds, deadfalls, low branches and steep terrain he felt intense fascination for the savage Kitiwanga territory with its radiant life forms. And always there was the goal of finding Náhani before the trappers and bounty hunters reached her.

It was all but impossible to get lost as long as he followed the narrowing Skeena River canyon. He might have cost himself an extra twenty-five miles, however, had he failed to leave the big river gorge at Iceberg Creek. The insignificant little waterway, he discovered, joined the Skeena under woven willow and alder overhang, as if intentionally screened from right-bank view. But Moiso had instructed him well.

At the Iceberg confluence the resounding Skeena, fifty yards wide, cackled through a quarter-mile of braided rapids—fast, deep, cold, and deadly. No possible ford. Greg sat by the campfire that night and played his harmonica, trying in vain to get that river crossing off his mind. There seemed to be no choice but to continue up the right bank.

The next day he had walked less than half a mile alongside the frothing stream when he came upon a mass of driftwood logs. A raft! He spent the morning extricating suitable lengths and lashing them together with the nylon rope he carried for animal-proofing his food at night. He cut a living spruce sapling to provide a ten-foot drag-brake pole for slowing the raft in swift water.

After tying his clothing and pack rack to the forward end, Greg eased the raft into the current. It submerged immediately when he got aboard, so he decided to walk it across. Fifteen feet out from shore line the raft collided with the first whitecaps. The water was ten feet deep. All Greg could do was float downstream and hang on to the hindmost. At the first cataract the raft became wedged between two underwater boulders so abruptly that Greg's breath was knocked away and his chest scraped.

At length, with the drag pole, he pried the raft over the rocks. The clumsy mass no sooner refloated than a spouting current spun it immediately out of Greg's control. A side eddy beached the raft within twenty feet of his previous night's campsite.

His body was too cold to feel the sting from a scraped chest, but he broke out in a rash of itchy welts. He untied the logs. With the rope he strung his food over a limb, then built a bonfire to restore his blood to normal circulation.

Greg recognised his navigational mistake. Instead of attempting to cross what he misjudged as shallow rapids, he should have towed the logs along the shore line to quiet water. At that point he could swim behind the raft and push it across the Skeena with only the inconvenience of half freeezing.

That night he slept soundly from dark to daylight. Shortly after breakfast he reassembled the raft and swam it to the left bank in less than half an hour.

Impatient to reach Tatlatui Lake after the delay, Greg began the long slog up the obstacle-filled canyon of Iceberg Creek. He had considered the first ninety miles beyond Kuldo among the most difficult terrain he had ever encountered. The route between the Skeena River and the lake was to prove even more exacting. The distance, less than thirty miles, required six and a half suns, so dense was the forest, so rough the terrain.

At Tatlatui Lake, Greg installed a base camp in a cove at the upper end. Grayling, squaw fish and char seized every lure that moved. Bitterns, coots and loons fluted night and day from reedy inlets. Moose, elk, goats and deer jostled through the campsite as if the presence of man posed no threat. On regular night-time feeding circuits, lynx, bears, foxes, coyotes and cougars glided between camp and the glassy, moonlit countenance of the lake.

Wolves were the only missing creatures. Recalling what had happened at Nakinilerak Lake—and old Moiso's prophetic words—Greg simply sat tight, hoping Náhani would come to him. For four days he hiked along the lake front. A kind of pre-wolf silence pervaded.

He waited.

Then one morning at sunrise as he was about to light himself a breakfast fire, he sprang to his feet. The easterly breeze brought to his nostrils the unmistakable smell of coffee and sizzling sow belly. Someone had camped near the outlet flume. With a flood of apprehension, Greg realised that Trapper-Dan and the bounty hunters had arrived.

4. Trapper-Dan

Greg scooped up his binoculars, slipped on his side-knife scabbard, and began the five-mile trek towards the source of his concern.

He ran along the first three miles of beach, blaming himself for the number of footprints he had left. Trapper-Dan was well known as the smoothest tracker in the province. He would deal harshly with any man who tried to stand between him and the reward for the queen wolf's pelt. But the reward was a side issue as compared to the glory he would receive after bringing in the skin of Náhani.

Trapper-Dan was an opportunist. He had no tribal tradition, no religious belief, no conscience. He regarded the taking of human life with the same lack of concern he showed for a trapped fur-bearer—less, because he could sell the skin of a fur-bearer.

A mile from where he could see the campfire smoke that curled into the morning breeze, Greg climbed to a ridge. One look through binoculars confirmed his worst fears. There, sipping coffee, smoking, and polishing rifles, sat five men—Trapper-Dan, three white strangers and the beaver-faced Eugene Charley.

Even more disconcerting was the float plane beached near the lake's outlet flume. How could an airplane land on that lake, Greg wondered, without his having heard it? Perhaps the pilot had cut the engine long before the approach, hoping to surprise the predators if they were in residence.

After a one-minute study of the situation, Greg carefully retraced his steps to his own camp. He packed quickly, then obliterated as many traces as possible of his having camped there. For two miles during his retreat into the range south of Tatlatui Lake, he erased his every footprint.

There was no visible pass through the range, and the perpendicular limestone cliffs along the entire north face prevented further advance. Greg could see a gulch that ran east, but that would take him back within two miles of the Tatlatui outlet. Although he dared not risk an encounter with Trapper-Dan, the only choice was to drift carefully down the narrow ravine.

At sunset he walked into the gap formed by the Finlay River. Stepping on solidly packed glacial gravel, he experienced a momentary sense of comfort, but as the gorge deepened, thick shore-line growth often forced him to slosh along up to his knees in water. He struggled into a box canyon for the night. Still too near the enemy camp to risk a fire, he ate dried fruit and a candy bar before retiring for a long night's sleep.

Two days dragged by before he splashed abruptly into the riverlike Thutade Creek. At this point he left the Finlay and climbed seven miles to the debris-jammed outlet of one of the most resplendent bodies of water in Canada. Thutade Lake is about three miles wide and winds for thirty-seven miles through spectacular forest and mountain palisades.

The narrow collar of beach near the outlet was uniformly imprinted with fresh spoor from an extensive wolf pack. The largest set of prints revealed that two toes were missing from the right front paw. Either Náhani had met with mutilating misfortune or Greg was

fruitlessly endeavouring to overtake a different wolf pack whose leader's paw print measured six inches in length. He had seen only one wolf print six inches long.

Greg wove an Indian broom of willow canes and brushed out every track, including his own, for more than a mile. Because there was no unobstructed passage from one end of the lake to the other, he quickly pegged and tied together eight dry logs for a raft he could pole along the shore. Two days of downpour and two of bludgeoning gale increased the amount of daily effort required for poling. To achieve the lake's brushy west end, Greg paid a ridiculous price: ten days of devastating labour.

At a level, timbered cove, he set up base camp for an indefinite bivouac. The site afforded an unimpaired view of the lake and surrounding mountains and it would be difficult—but not impossible—for an airplane to enter the area without being seen.

Fresh spoor, including the set with the missing toes, imprinted every damp surface of sand and soil.

On the morning following his arrival, Greg sat scanning the brushy ridge that formed an amphitheatre round the entire west end of the basin. A pack of timber wolves, trying to outflank the wind, raced single file over the ridge, but the leader had already disappeared by the time Greg first saw them. He had only one clue to associate the group with Náhani: two limping, solid black individuals with thick mantles. They resembled the pair that had always spooked when Greg walked upright near them at Nakinilerak Lake.

He rushed towards the hill. With all his strength he hurdled through knee-deep subshrubs, sphagnum and fallen timber to the

337

stony ridge, but the wolves had disappeared. Tracking northwest, he jogged up and down ridge after ridge along what appeared to be an established runway until the spoor drove a straight line towards a pass in the limestone range immediately south of Tatlatui Lake. There was no way for an Indian afoot to overtake a fleeing pack of wolves.

Hoping the troop was not Náhani's, he turned towards camp. Along the way he found a urine-marked shrub to which he tied a per-spiration-soaked bandanna. He told himself that the wolves would surely double back when Náhani got a whiff of firearms and air-plane at Tatlatui Lake. She would recognise Greg's sweat signature and sniff his footprints into camp.

That night Greg kept a small campfire burning until the morning star cleared the treetops. He crawled down the beach on all fours, threw stones into the bay, rattled cooking utensils and whistled, but in the end finally concluded that such antics frightened away more wildlife than they attracted.

Before falling into a deep sleep, discouraged, he wondered: 'Have I gone and chased Náhani square into Trapper-Dan's gunsights?'

FOR TEN DAYS following the sighting, during the early part of August, Greg neither saw nor heard a wolf. His disappointment made him recognise—more than he had been willing to admit—the profound fascination he had sustained for Náhani. Hatred was an emotion previously foreign to Gregory Tah-Kloma, but subcon-sciously he was beginning to hate Náhani's persecutors.

The desire to have another look at Trapper-Dan's camp became an obsession with him. On the eleventh day he packed his gear and left. First, he began the onerous trek along the ridge where he had sighted the wolves. His excitement grew when he reached the shrub where he had tied the bandanna. It had been removed, but a thundershower had erased all tracks. By maintaining the same direction in which the wolves had disappeared, he walked straight to the buckhorn pass, a practical foot route through the precipitous range. At the end of two days, he reached the upper shore line of Tatlatui Lake.

It took no expert woodsmanship to determine that Trapper-Dan—and the wolves—had discovered his earlier campsite. Boot prints and wolf tracks were everywhere, including those of the two-toed member. Almost in panic, he counted seven widely scattered empty Magnum cartridges—all fired from the same rifle.

In Greg's reconstruction of what took place, Trapper-Dan and his men had either stalked or surprised the busy wolves in the act of exploring the campsite. The decaying carcass of a female wolf, skinned, lay on the open forest floor 150 yards up the hillside behind the campsite—mute tribute to the lethal accuracy of the rifleman. One of the Indians had driven a pointed sapling pole into the sward where Greg's sleeping-bag had flattened the grass . . . to put him 'in the shadow of the spear'.

When he reached the lower end of the lake, Greg's suspicions were confirmed. The plane had taken off. The trappers' fire pit was buried.

Fatigued, tense, and threatened by heavy storm clouds, Greg stretched his rubberised nylon ground cloth over a double-A frame of sapling-spruce poles. Although he needed the rest enforced by the three-day storm that ensued, Greg begrudged the loss of time and the bite into his food supplies. Prompted by an impulse the moment the wind changed direction, he started north even before the rain clouds broke apart.

At Kitchener Lake he examined the tracks of a large wolf pack. Careful inspection of the distinctively broad lead prints confirmed earlier observations—two toes were missing from the right front paw.

FOR NINE DAYS GREG DRIFTED in the wake of northbound paw prints. On several occasions he lost the trail for as much as six hours. Did the pack sense a pursuer and purposely lead him over terrain in which even the sharpest-toed animals left no print? In any case, a large pack of twenty or more wolves left other signs for the Indian tracker: a turned pebble here, a clawed lichen there, scats, the smell of urine on 'boundary posts' along the runway, the remains of prey.

In the Prudential Range there were nights when songs of distant wolves floated faintly through the air. If he camped more than one night where he heard the serenades, either they sang no more or moved further northwards . . .

Softly one night he played the harmonica. He felt at peace. Even if he failed to overtake his enchanting Náhani—provided it was indeed Náhani's trail he followed—he *had* succeeded in hounding her north of Trapper-Dan's and Eugene Charley's sphere of slaughter.

Then, high above the alpine lakelets of the Prudential Range, Greg received a disappointing answer to one of his questions. A pack of eighteen wolves of mixed age circled within fifty feet of his campsite one evening shortly before sunset. Their coats all bore the same family trait: bright brindled-grey. The keenly curious troop sniffed, whined, then single-filed away without changing gait or speed.

Náhani had thrown him off her trail. Little doubt remained that she had led him into the established runway of the brindled wolves. At some point along the way, she had turned her group over traprock for a short distance, and then disappeared.

5. The Náhani Mystique

Although Greg carried a boot-repair kit, his footgear was worn beyond safety. No modern woodsman goes further than his shoes. Therefore, when the Moon-of-Painted-Leaves brought the first colour to broad-leaved foliage, he set a left-bank course down the familiar Skeena River canyon. When he arrived at Hazelton, shortly before midnight, he went directly to his friend, Rocky Longspear.

Before going to bed he told Rocky what he had seen at Tatlatui Lake. 'I have to spend the winter around here,' he concluded. 'If Náhani crosses the Skeena this winter, she'll get it sure as hell. I think I know the route she'll take if she comes down this way. Maybe I can rent a cabin from the Kuldo people.'

'She'll get shot if she goes to Kuldo again,' Rocky said. 'They'll be waiting for her this year. Like everybody else.'

'Then what about a trapper's cabin? Do you know of one I could rent? A wilderness cabin, north of here?'

'Only one. On Kitwanga Lake. Owned by Trapper-Dan Tall-Totem. He won't be using it. He'll be working all winter at the smelter in Kitimat.'

The next morning Greg took a decisive, if unimaginable, step. He went directly to Trapper-Dan's cabin where greetings were exchanged in the form of invectives. Dan's two wives interceded before a fist fight could break out. They pulled both men into the cabin by their hair and stood between them. When the two agreed to sit and smoke in peace, the women said they would prepare a meal of grilled salmon, corn cakes and strong coffee.

After the meal Greg spread his maps on the table and traced his summer route.

'If I hadn't seen that Vibram design in your boot prints at Tatlatui,' Dan said, 'I'd deny you could have covered that kind of ground.'

'Why did you kill that she-wolf instead of Náhani?'

'You must've come back to know that, huh? That yellow Eugene Charley could've killed Náhani. Had her in his sights and then his liver turned to cloud-milk. She'd already gone over the hill when I got there. Now what?'

'I'm going back next summer,' Greg said. 'I'll spend the winter near here if I can find a cabin for rent. The Chimmesyans say she'll come south for the winter.'

Trapper-Dan's attitude became curiously servile. He explained that he owned a fine cabin near Kitwanga Lake, and he offered to rent Greg the cabin and help haul in winter supplies. He spoke of another empty cabin at Swan Lakes. He was willing to take an oath that Tsimshians had sighted Náhani near both lakes.

It took four trips—two days and one night—for the four of them to pack 800 pounds of supplies and equipment six miles beyond road's end to the Kitwanga Lake cabin. Oddly, Trapper-Dan said he owed the young Chimmesyan an apology for the way he had tried to kill Náhani. If his winter job at Kitimat panned out, he'd give up trapping altogether.

By candlelight Greg wrote in his diary: 'When I let it out that Náhani might come south this winter, all the hostility and meanness vanished from that bastard's ugly face. Why? I wonder what cards he is holding and how I'm playing into his hand.'

The 'fine' cabin proved to be primitive and in bad repair; but its location high above an east beach, and picturesque little food cache on four animal-proof poles, made up for inherent defects. Greg looked forward to uninterrupted weeks of solitude during which he planned to cultivate the friendship of native wildlife, and build the fitness necessary to penetrate the northern Kitiwanga.

On October 10, Trapper-Dan and three husky Tsimshian bandsmen appeared. The big trapper insisted upon leaving a carbine and a box of cartridges. 'Lotta grizzly in here. They break in even if you store your food in the cache house.'

The men ran back down the trail within five minutes of their arrival. Greg sensed in their behaviour an ulterior motive that he failed to decipher. The gun had to be some kind of plant.

As autumn advanced, more unexpected visitors found their way to the cabin. Greg was making repairs to the cabin one morning when a man of about thirty years old and a woman appeared on the trail.

'They call me Peter after my uncle, Buffalo-Bones,' the man said. 'You knew his son, my cousin, No-Guns. This is my wife, Lorna.'

'Peter,' Greg said. 'I thought I was seeing a ghost. You look so much like No-Guns.'

No-Guns, a boyhood friend of Greg's, had lost his life in a lumber-mill accident. Peter and Lorna were a handsome couple, open-faced, easy-smiling, like No-Guns. After coffee, the couple came to the point of their visit.

'News travels fast up here, Greg,' Peter said, as if what he was about to reveal pained him. 'Council smoke around Babine Lake says you'll winter here in Trapper-Dan's cabin. A lot of Indians still depend on trapping in these woods, Mr Wolf-man.' They all laughed, but the mirth was strained. 'I suppose you know what Náhani did to the trap lines the last couple of winters. Arch Aloyet got a close shot at her near Takla Landing. Said his bullet went clean

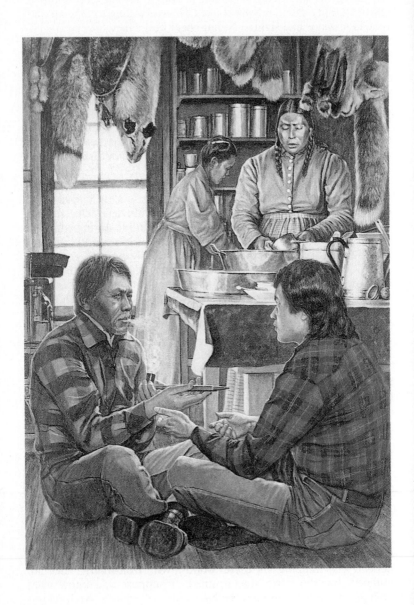

through her as she charged. Before he could shoot again, she threw her weight against him, grabbed his rifle, and ran off with it. The same wolves were seen taking livestock as far south as Burns Lake. I hate to tell you this, Greg, but the reward now stands at a thousand dollars. It'll go fifteen hundred if she comes south this winter.'

'How much of this malarkey do you believe, Peter?'

'Hard to say. The main thing I came to tell you is that a no-good Carrier son of a bitch named Eugene Charley rumours it around that you plan to bring Náhani and her pack to Kitwanga Lake. Talk says the Royal Canadian Mounted Police may take you in. Trapper-Dan thinks Náhani will find you here. Says you know how to talk with wolves. He wants more than that reward. He'll shadow this cabin every moon. And so will Eugene Charley. That's why Dan rented it to you. If Charley gets Náhani first, Dan'll do him in and claim the reward. Don't trust either man, Greg. One of them will break your bowstring . . . once Náhani's dead.'

Three days after Peter's visit an RCMP vehicle stopped at road's end. Constables Larson and McIntyre came up the trail to the cabin.

'Are you the guy that hobnobs with wolves?' Larson asked. He had the eye of a comedian and expected you to laugh either at him or with him. 'Do you realise what stink you've stirred up with this Náhani? Are you really in cahoots with these outlaws?'

Over coffee and a popping log fire, Greg related every detail of the Náhani encounter as well as the reasons why he planned to spend the winter in the cabin—why he planned to carry on the search the following summer.

'Good Lord, Tah-Kloma!' McIntyre exclaimed. 'You're even kookier than we thought. We'll have to keep an eye on this situation. If he shows up, we have only one choice. Too many people stirred up on both sides of the fence. Feuds start that way, don't you know?'

A WEEK WENT BY. Wolves on the ridge behind the cabin had sung for two nights. And then on a Friday afternoon Greg recognised the bent and staggering figure of Eugene Charley trudging up the trail, alpenstock in one hand, carbine in the other. The Carrier was fully equipped with tumpline basket pack for fall hunting.

'Trapper-Dan brought me in the Land-Rover to the trail,' Charley explained.

'Trapper-Dan is working in Kitimat,' Greg said with a smile that accused Charley of a forked tongue.

'We go to work next week. Dan said he'd be here Tuesday with more supplies. Stuff he forgot last time.'

Suddenly Greg had an idea.

'I'm leaving tomorrow morning for the Swan Lakes. You can keep me company. I think we'll meet some wolves. There are two cabins, fifteen miles apart, at the lakes and Cranberry River.'

'Thirty miles!'

'Sixty, round trip.'

'So you made friends with that damned wolf at Nakinilerak. And last summer at Tatlatui?'

'You and Dan know she is coming south, don't you, Charley? You know I spoke her tongue last summer, huh? I found your spear. You were born under a falling star, Charley. I want to see how you act when you come face to face with Náhani at Swan Lakes.'

A catlike grin crept round Charley's weathered lips. 'You'll see.'

Greg was surprised to find Eugene Charley ready the next morning for an early start to the Swan Lakes basin. The route alongside the Cranberry River traversed luxuriant conifer forest. How that Carrier could walk! Greg had to run to keep up with him. Charley was accustomed to long treks. No fifteen-mile jaunt could faze him.

Without difficulty they found an empty cabin at the base of Mount Weber's north shoulder. After his slug of rum that evening, Charley insinuated that Trapper-Dan was cooking up a plot to do away with him as a potential beneficiary of the huge bounty on Náhani. Moreover, he had delved sufficiently into the Náhani mystique to suspect Greg of leading him into a trap. Even as he slept he never relinquished a knuckle-whitening grip on the carbine.

The next day as they crunched along the frosty trail up the Kispiox River valley, Greg felt momentarily sorry for Charley, an Indian so little at peace with himself and the Earth Mother. He had hated the Carrier after seeing him at Tatlatui Lake and knowing the lies he had circulated in order to get the bounty raised, but now he recognised him for what he was, a captive of negative appetites, none of which he could control—rum, greed, and a passion to be someone he never could be.

After crossing a low hogback, the trail swung down a pine-wooded slope to arrive at the eastern shore line of the first Swan Lake. On a slight rise fifty yards from the beach, someone had built a solid cabin, its window shutters properly hinged and hasped.

The two men ate supper without speaking. The ominous silence between them was broken only by the hiss of a rising north wind.

Shortly before midnight, under low-hanging nimbus that screened the waning Fallen-Leaf-Moon, a chorus of wolves sang near the lake shore less than a hundred yards from the cabin. Eugene Charley swigged a whopping draught of rum and cursed Greg for leading him into a trap. He ran to the door and held a flashlight alongside the front sight of his carbine.

'Náhani!' Greg shouted at the top of his lungs.

Charley fired seven times in the direction of the lake. Then he did exactly what Greg hoped he would do. After he had shot at the wolves, he stuffed his belongings into his pack and left.

SOME TIME THAT MORNING Greg fell into deep sleep. He bolted upright when the entire cabin shook with an explosive boom. The blastlike wind had broken a heavy dead limb from an overhanging conifer, and the 'widow maker' had crashed through the cabin's roof ridge. When the droning wind began to drive fish-scale snow horizontally across the basin, Greg hit the trail for the next cabin.

He had climbed to the first hillside, still within snow-veiled sight of the cabin, when he heard the hunting bay of a wolf pack. He turned and listened. Eighteen to twenty-four wolves, using the horseshoe hunting formation, converged upon the cabin and circled slowly as they do when they 'set' a prey animal at bay. Suddenly the leader wolf, a large silver-white animal, discovered Greg's foot-scent trail. The pack followed her across the open savannah.

'Náhani!' Greg shouted as he ran to meet them. They were less than a hundred yards away and racing towards him. Through the swirling snow he saw the wolves thrust forward their long legs in order to stop and sample the air. He called over and over again. For a few moments it looked as if they would allow him to approach. Then they turned in a body and scampered away behind their leader along the frost-hardened shore line.

Greg could not risk becoming snowbound in that cold cabin without supplies or the means of repairing the roof. Reluctantly he resumed his journey, not certain if he had seen Náhani, but apprehensive that he had.

6. A Fragile Image

Wind at first kept the snow from covering the trail, but the storm intensified. When Greg dragged his feet up to the Cranberry River cabin around midnight, a faint glow of orange-red candlelight shone through an unshuttered window.

One glance through the iced south window disclosed the blurred outlines of four people. Three were sitting at the table on which flickered a single candle. The fourth was tending the fire.

'Hello!' Greg shouted and rapped on the windowpane. The four made no move to answer. He walked to the door, knocked and shouted again. Finally the door cracked open and someone muttered in broken English: 'Go away, Chimmesyan Wolf-man!'

'I can't get over that pass in this storm. Let me in.'

'No. Go away, Wolf-man.' The door slammed and was bolted with a drop bar from the inside.

'I'll wring somebody's neck for this!' Greg shouted.

With new flashlight batteries he had no trouble staying on the path near the Cranberry's right bank, but at daybreak, when he reached the north foot of the Kitwanga ridge, he found that the mile-long drifts had buried the trail. He mushed out the day, backtracking from one cul-de-sac to the next. He was too busy and too tired to worry about the four men in the cabin and their intentions.

By the time he broke a route round the east prow of the ridge, he realised that his uncharted wandering had taken him five miles below Kitwanga Lake, so he traipsed out over a frozen marsh to road's end.

There stood Trapper-Dan's Land-Rover. It was locked tight or he would have spent the night inside the vehicle. Could the four in the Cranberry River cabin include Tall-Totem? Did those men expect him to lead them that easily to the queen wolf?

Finally he reached Trapper-Dan's Kitwanga Lake cabin. No one was there. No one had been there. With an extravagant meal in his stomach, Greg fell asleep in a chair in front of the fireplace.

THREE DAYS LATER two RCMP patrolmen with packs and scoped rifles arrived on snowshoes.

'We heard you and Trapper-Dan lugged all your supplies up that trail on your backs,' said the sergeant named Duncan. 'I can't believe Dan Tall-Totem didn't rent a string of mules to do the job, since you were footing the bill.'

'Dan claims the smell of a mule's hind end retches him,' Greg said.

After they had finished dinner and arranged the two sleeping-bags near the fireplace, Greg outlined his trek to the Swan Lakes and return. He omitted only that part where he thought he saw Náhani.

Duncan spoke, 'Tah-Kloma, we are here because of a report that a large wolf pack did pay you a visit at the Swan Lakes cabin. Was the silver-white Náhani in the pack?'

'If she had been, I believe she would have come to me. I called, but they disappeared like thistledown in a snowstorm.'

'We know,' said the corporal named Blakeburn, 'that the four Indians are working for Trapper-Dan. They knew all along about the pack. They suspected the presence of Náhani. They followed Charley and you and were hidden in the forest, hoping for a close-up shot. Under the influence of rum, Charley blew their chances when he rushed out and fired his carbine. The weather also loused up their luck. Of course, now Eugene Charley's been found shot dead.'

346

The two mounties left the next morning for the Swan Lakes. They planned to follow the Nass River trail back to Terrace unless they unearthed 'something interesting'.

DURING NOVEMBER'S Moon-of-the-Storm-Chief, Greg took advantage of a mild spell in order to catch and smoke a hundred pounds of trout and char, which he stored in the weatherproof food cache before December's Moon-of-the-White-Hare freeze.

Autumn was late and mild. Misty rain melted earlier snow, leaving the clearing around the hillside cabin an island of mud for a while. One morning Greg found wolf tracks. The day was clear, so he hounded the prints down the trail. Half a mile before road's end, they led to a bloody blotch and the last of a set of elk tracks. The wolf spoor disappeared towards the hills above the valley of the Kispiox. He slogged along the trail to road's end to check out four distinct sets of boot prints that led to and from the site where the elk had fallen. Men had visited the scene before the wolves. Wolf prints covered boot prints.

He had no sooner returned to the cabin when an RCMP float plane landed on the lake. Corporal Blakeburn and the pilot emerged.

'Anything new?' Blakeburn asked.

'I just got back from road's end,' Greg said.

'Rumour has it that your Náhani is along. The pack killed an elk down about road's end. I thought you said she wintered in the Kitiwanga and chased caribou.'

'Could be she changed her mind.'

When they reached the cabin there was no use trying to conceal the fact that a wolf pack had been there. Blakeburn's suspicions of Greg's integrity surfaced.

'Rendezvous?' His voice was filled with icy insinuation.

'I was asleep. Never knew when they were here. That's why I followed the track to the elk kill.'

'Which way did they head?'

'Into the Kispiox. The only other tracks were made by four game poachers. The elk was dead before the wolves got there.'

'We thought you ought to know about the big weather front moving down from the gulf.'

'That's why the wolves came to the cabin. She tried to warn me. Tomorrow they'll be in the canyon of the Skeena.'

'A hundred fifty miles?'

'No trick under her leadership.'

Blakeburn handed Greg a pound of pipe tobacco, a can of plum pudding and six cans of condensed milk. 'That's for a one-man blow-out,' he said. He smiled for the first time. 'Sorry we have to run. You can pole us off the beach. Carry on!'

For the next five days Greg left the cabin only when necessary. As the wall of Arctic air moved in, the rain turned to snow. Then the lake began to freeze. Growing ice crystals groaned and creaked as they extended from shore line. The temperature dropped to twenty degrees below zero. Soon a plating of snow frosted the surface of the woods, and for two Hunger-Moons the world remained solid white.

Occasionally Greg could see across the lake. At other times visibility was restricted to a few feet. Until the temperature moderated enough for wind to crust the cotton snow, his movements were limited, even on bearpaw snowshoes. For a month he kept two buckets of icicles melting near the fireplace for drinking, cooking, laundry, and the quick once-over he considered a bath.

ALL THROUGH THE DECEMBER and January oestrus period, mating duets of wolf pairs drifted down from the highlands. After breeding, the pairs regrouped to resume organised hunting. They avoided the

cabin vicinity with its painful memories of steel traps, gunshot wounds and the stench of death during Trapper-Dan's occupancy.

One moonlit night when the temperature hovered at forty degrees below zero, Greg heard the leathery crunch of approaching footsteps. Nearby wolves had just finished a ruckus in the forest behind the cabin. Expecting to greet a human visitor, Greg rushed through the storm door, but in the shock of the 110-degree temperature difference he suffered a temporary blackout. As he was recovering he heard a deep-throated woof. It was then he realised that the wolves had discovered and routed out a hibernating bear very near the cabin.

Quickly he put on his down-packed nylon parka hood, attached the fog mask across his mouth and nose, and with gauntlets strapped below the elbows and boots buckled, went outside. A black bear reared and moaned from the cabin's top step and tried to shoulder herself inside, but Greg led the way to a crawl hole under the south side of the cabin floor. He had stuffed the four-foot space with sphagnum moss for insulation. When the bear saw him digging out the dry moss, she plunged through the crawl hole, snarled, and buried herself in the spongy material. Greg plugged the hole with snow and moss so that the bear might sleep undisturbed until spring. Unable now to harass the bear, the wolves pursued their games of tag on the western shore of Kitwanga Lake.

Towards the waning of February's Moon-of-the-Fallen-Antlers, Greg began to feel a physiological and psychological rebellion against the interminable hostility of winter. Restlessness overcame him as he thought of the long months he still must wait before he could resume his search for Náhani.

Under March's Moon-of-Meltwater the wind often howled in concert with meat-craving wolves; for March was also a Hunger-Moon—by then all the easy prey had been taken. Falling snow still kept the land in icy paralysis. When cloud-shafted sunshine finally broke through, Greg rushed to the thermometer.

Ten above! The Old-Man-of-the-North was on the run!

Greg spent most of March and April with the maps, and laid out a day-by-day itinerary for June to September. He worked for hours on every item of equipment, modifying each unit according to what he had learned the previous summer. To regain physical stamina lost indoors he scheduled long hikes uphill and down, with four and a half stones in his pack.

Dark cracks in the frozen lake opened with a saw-toothed roar. April's Moon-of-the-Flowers waned before spring finally seized the land. The old bear dug herself out and headed for meltwater. Greg handed her a smoked trout. She took the fish and headed for the forest trail behind the cabin.

Greg followed her, inhaling the soft scents of spring.

It was there, along the muddy trail, that he saw the fresh boot prints—one Vibram, one British sole rubber. They led to a clump of budding aspens about seventy yards from the cabin. The men had walked back and forth as if trying to reach a decision. The tracks then led up the hill, cut back in a wide arc, and finally re-entered the trail for a return to road's end. Greg had been over the same ground the day before and had seen no human prints.

There remained no doubt as to Tall-Totem's reasons for renting the cabin to Greg. He reasoned that Náhani would lead her pack south in order to take easier prey than herd-guarded caribou in the Kitiwanga. Another incentive for his wintering nearby was the wolf requirement for certain greens after whelping, which would be available only on meadows in the Skeena and Babine river valleys.

Each time fresh wolf tracks showed up at the cabin, Greg discharged the carbine, knowing that if Náhani were nearby and associated the weapon with him, he might never see her again. If gunfire could frighten her away from a situation that endangered her life, however, he had no other choice.

ON MAY 23, 1967, Greg packed his essentials into his car and headed for Hazelton. Twelve hours later, he arrived at the home of his friend Rocky Longspear. After outlining his plans for the summer he drove to Smithers to pick up a four-month supply of freeze-dried and dehydrated staples. He returned to Hazelton at midnight.

'I think one of Trapper-Dan's men was in the trading post and recognised me,' Greg said to Rocky. 'The guy got in one hell of a hurry to leave.'

'This fellow Trapper-Dan Tall-Totem is a bad egg,' Rocky said. 'Never been any good. He has four, five friends he bullies around—drunkards, gamblers, thieves. Dan was fired from the smelter in Kitimat. Mounties have driven to his cabin many times lately.'

'What's the latest?'

'Everybody up and down the Skeena is on tenterhooks because Tall-Totem linked Náhani with an outbreak of rabies. You'll find Tsimshians unfriendly, Greg. Most everybody believes you killed Eugene Charley. That's why Tall-Totem left you a gun at the cabin. He figured you hated Charley enough to kill him. The reward for Náhani now stands at eighteen hundred dollars. Come the Moon-of-Painted-Leaves, don't come back here. Get to the Alaska Highway. And call me on the phone. I'll bring your car. But don't come back here.'

Greg knew his friend well enough to listen attentively. 'One thing's for sure,' Rocky continued. 'Tall-Totem and his trappers will follow you this summer. You'll be lucky to escape them. So don't go up the Skeena

Valley like you did last summer. Go up the Kispiox. I'll drive you as far as the road goes—about forty miles north of here. Don't build fires for two, three days. Stay off the trails. Keep your eyes peeled.'

At 2.00am that night Rocky drove Greg to the road's end about five miles south of the Swan Lakes trail. Greg hiked near the path— but not on it—along the left bank of the Kispiox River. The route led directly to the Swan Lakes cabin, perhaps the area where the trappers would least expect him. To further confuse the Tsimshian trackers, he wore moosehide moccasins over his boots.

When several days and nights dragged by without evidence that Náhani's pack was in the vicinity, Greg climbed the long ridge north along the upper Kispiox basin. After crunching through twenty miles of friable shale in order to stay above the timber line, he descended into the hazy-blue depths of the Nass River gorge. On the shimmering stream's left bank he threw together a comfortable shelter in which to sit out a siege of rough weather.

After a rainstorm he broke camp and plodded upstream, taking sometimes half a day to work out a ford across tributaries, waist-deep, wide, cold and swift. When the cutbank river ran wall-to-wall, costly detours led either along precipices, around mile-long deposits of loose shale, or over massive wickerworks of driftwood. He did not reach the Klappan-Nass headwaters unscathed. When he hobbled onto the beach of the lakelet he was suffering from a badly sprained ankle; lacerated legs, arms and neck; and armpits painfully swollen from tick bites. But his native exuberance and hearty enthusiasm were almost invulnerable to the physical assaults of the Kitiwanga.

'I must confess,' he wrote in his diary, 'I consider my hardest days the ones of greatest gain. When I get to thinking the plateau is hostile, a bear, fox, marten or fisher comes along to share my rations or just sit for a friendly span.'

Following a long rest at No-Name Lake and a slow trek over two Skeena mountain passes, Greg once more undertook the rugged Stikine Plateau. Although spoor and scats indicated that seven major wolf runways crossed the Nass River canyon, it was anything but typical wolf country. Getaway routes were too slow and uncertain for the liking of a wolf, who probably found hunting more to his taste on the highland barrows north and east of the Nass.

At the end of four days on a trail gone cold—without seeing or hearing one wolf—he suddenly stumbled upon fresh spoor. One extra-large set of tracks had been made by a wolf much heavier than other pack members. And from the right front paw prints Greg immediately saw that the wolf had two missing toes!

The fresh tracks mounted a sedgy, seepy hillside that eventually broadened into plateau savannah west of the Ross River.

The wolves made no effort to conceal spoor as they did in regions where scent of trapper, steel and gunpowder meant calamity. Because the latest tracks in the mud pointed downstream, Greg descended the north fork valley of the Ross, then tracked the runway to Cold Fish Lake where he awaited the pack's return. However, with July's Moon-of-Walking-Thunder in the wane, and no new signs of wolves, he left the Stikine Plateau country in favour of the Pitman River valley, where ten-day-old tracks of the two-toed wolf led. For sixty miles between Cold Fish Lake and the Pitman mouth, he walked without encountering serious obstacles.

There was no question about his having picked up a newly established timber-wolf runway.

7. Eyes in the Shadows

Shortly before he arrived at the Stikine–Pitman confluence, fresh spoor and distant wolf song increased Greg's optimism that he was now closing the distance between him and Náhani. In his eagerness he decided to take a chance and cross the river on a driftwood jam.

It was a risky business. The slightest imbalance might cause the jam to collapse. Churning rapids and whirlpools below the jam discouraged the alternative of a raft. Tracks indicated that the wolves had made it over the jam.

The wickerwood held until Greg was within twenty feet of the right bank. Then a log rolled and dumped the young Indian into four feet of water. Fortunately the current allowed him to wade ashore with only minor damage to supplies. It was a sobering lesson.

The broad Pitman Valley soon narrowed and steepened, but a well-beaten game trail paralleled the left bank of the river to the lake of its source. The most recent tracks on the muddy trail had been made by the same wolf pack.

Beyond Pitman Lake, Greg climbed a glacial dike 600 feet high and a mile wide, which separated the Pacific watershed from that of the Arctic. A lake on the east side of the dike founted the Frog River, down whose right bank Greg fought underbrush and wind-downed timber for three days.

One morning after breakfast he sat hunched over the map. For some time there had been no wolf tracks; the wolves must have known that somebody was tailing them. Apparently they preferred to travel in the river, where no tracks would be visible.

Greg packed his rucksack and poured water on the campfire.

When he turned, his eye caught a movement from a granite outcrop to the northwest. Less than a quarter-mile away, a cantering pack of at least twenty-five wolves single-filed along the arête. He jumped to his feet and focused the binoculars.

An extraordinary silver-white female glided effortlessly through space and headed her troop towards the Gataga basin.

TWO EVENINGS LATER Greg reached Denetiah Lake. Could this at last be where Náhani had found some measure of freedom from pursuit? A well-defined wolf runway led to an extensive hillside forest where whelping dens faced the south beach above the lake's outlet, mostly caves beneath stacks of sphagnum-entombed logs.

There was no real clue that the queen wolf was headquartered there. A distinctive manner of movement—and nothing more—suggested that the silver wolf Greg had seen might have been Náhani. A single black wolf with a slight limp had been near the head of the pack.

After removing his pack, Greg hiked to a windy ridge high above timber line south of Denetiah. Here he scanned 250 square miles of forest and barren country. Somewhere in that sprawling hinterland, a silver-white wolf concealed her pack. The basin stretched into a blue-green wonderland of defeating bigness.

He was about to return to the lake in order to prepare a campsite when smoke from seven small fires summoned his attention. Five minutes before, he had scanned that same section and there had been neither movement nor smoke. A warm, dry western down-draught gusted towards the Rockies with consistent force. The seven small fires soon joined and mushroomed into one, exactly as the Indians had planned it. Given that the wind after sundown might change direction and move the holocaust towards Denetiah Lake, Greg had misgivings about setting up camp in the Frog River forest.

For centuries Indians have ignited mature forest sections for access, for improved game forage, and for introduction of new animal populations. Indian-set fires have seldom been known to get out of hand; the Indians are experts not only in gauging the forest acreage they wish to clear, but in prophesying changes in the weather. One could be reasonably certain that a downpour would occur within twenty-four hours of the fires having been set.

With that shaky assurance, Greg descended to the lake. The first early star shone as a tiny yellow spark over the wide sunset. There was something ominous in the air.

The raging fire twenty-five miles to the east reminded Greg of Trapper-Dan Tall-Totem and his accomplices. With a twinge of worry, he sat by the campfire that night and wondered whether or not he had really escaped his pursuers—superior woodsmen in many ways when they weren't drinking. Their cause was far more fundamentally motivated than his; there was a substantial money reward.

With the Indian's knowledge of fire, Trapper-Dan might have encircled the vicinity with a weapon from which neither Náhani nor Greg could possibly escape. The trappers' hatred by now must have reached fever pitch. Whether he found the wolf or not, Greg determined during that sleepless night to find out definitely if the Tsimshian trappers were following him. The uncertainty and interminable waiting gnawed at him. Too often lately he had suffered the disquieting feeling that he was under surveillance.

Towards morning the rain came and extinguished the forest fire. Between two showers Greg climbed to the hilltop in order to assess the burn. A tremendous swath had been reduced to dark grey mineral ash along the riverbank of the Gataga River.

More for rainy-day amusement than necessity, he constructed a driftwood lean-to with a sod and sphagnum roof, about fifty feet from the beach. Then he packed the rucksack and took off on a spying expedition of his own. The feeling that he was under constant scrutiny not only persisted, but grew. One entry in his diary at this time read: 'At times I feel deep physical pain, knowing that somewhere out there in the bush eyes are boring holes through me. When I sleep I see old Trapper-Dan's bloodshot eyes and his boozy toad-eaters squinting down rifle barrels at me.'

He backtracked, pretending to break camp and move on. A mile downstream from the lake the gorge narrowed. After minute examination of both canyon slopes through the binoculars, he removed every unnecessary item from the rucksack, wrapped the excess in his ground cloth, and strung the package from a bear-proof limb. If it was true that he was under observation, he wanted to be seen shouldering his backpack.

Toting a much lighter load, he covered great distances, hid for hours at a time on vantage promontories, and scanned in scrupulous detail the route just travelled. Greg's strategy was to execute wide, converging circles round the Denetiah trough. He avoided all sound and smoke, studied every game trail and open lea where a boot print would make an impression, probed every coppice where several men could hide a camp.

On the second day, in a heavily forested valley five miles west of Denetiah Lake, he dropped quickly into a high-bush cranberry thicket. He sensed that he was being watched, but was unable to locate the source either with the naked eye or with binoculars. Unless he had unwittingly stumbled close to a campsite, he was confident of having exposed himself in no way. Slowly, crouching, he scanned the terrain, looking for the slightest movement.

To relieve a cramped leg muscle, he was about to stand up when a twig snapped some twenty yards behind him. He spun round, whipped out his side knife and prepared for the first fight in his life.

Through a screen of brilliant rhododendron blossoms twelve inches above the ground, four pairs of yellowish-green eyes peered over black muzzles. When the wolves realised they had been discovered, they backed silently and vanished.

Greg sat down and wondered. If sentinel wolves had kept him under surveillance at Nakinilerak before returning to their dens, wouldn't they repeat the performance at Denetiah? He had been scanning the shadows for *human* figures, forms that would have stood between five and six feet tall; the wolves had eyed his movements from a flattened-out position hardly a foot above the ground.

Still not fully convinced, he hiked to the game trailways at the bottom of the Frog River ravine, the only natural migration corridor to Denetiah Lake. It had been Greg's route in; anyone else heading there would utilise the same narrow passage.

In the wet clay, sand and loam of the game trails every northern species on the move, except man, had imprinted his tracks.

8. The Wolves Come Home

For a time after he returned to Denetiah Lake, Greg exposed himself to the scrutiny he felt but could not see. Slow-moving moose foraged the sedge marshes, spiced their bland diet with spruce tips, then ignored the campsite as they waded into the lake. Golden eagles and great horned owls, about to compete for the same hare, disregarded the young man's activities. Once convinced that the shadow men had not followed him, Greg reverted to the serenity of his childhood days, before he knew that men feared other men.

The summer sun as well as wind-sharpened light from the Moon-of-Walking-Thunder intensified the forest depths. The young man frequented the spongy aisles of spruce and hemlock, walking freely.

He had just returned with a harvest of fungi from below the lake's outlet on the afternoon of August 5. The mushrooms had been abundant, and Greg was so preoccupied with the feast to come that it took him some moments to recognise that a change had taken place around him. There were no animals along the lake shore or on the timber-line meadows. Birds exchanged new and strange notes of alarm. He grabbed the binoculars and studied the hillside denning complex. No signs of life there.

But high on a broad, slanted shelf less than six feet below the sky-line at least two dozen timber wolves lay asleep in the sunshine.

After observing and counting the motionless wolves, Greg went to the cook pit and kindled a small fire. Northern Indians do this when they anticipate a change. It is a ceremony akin to prayer. He saw no silver-white queen on the browrock, but his pulse beat wildly at the thought that this might be Náhani's band. Suppose it was? Could he expect, after three years, to meet the same gentle, patrician creature he had known at Nakinilerak Lake?

While he waited at Denetiah, Greg wondered why the wolves had stayed away so long. Undoubtedly, the forest fire had driven them west. Greg's presence had been a disruptive factor, and the four scouts probably had not allowed the pack to return until they had completed their surveillance of the young Indian.

The waxing Moon-of-Walking-Thunder had set. Four or five wolves sang briefly at midnight from a beach half a mile up the shore. Then silence. A curious breeze nosed among the conifers. Greg stoked a small fire. Where was the nightly flute of the great horned owl, the cricket's fiddle, the tree toad's whistle? An atmosphere of expectancy seemed to magnify the solitude of the night. Greg leaned back against the log in front of the shelter. Softly he played the harmonica.

Appearing instantly, almost as if she had materialised from the fragrant campfire smoke, Náhani stood like a statue on the lake side of the log. When she uttered a deep-chested growl, Greg turned slowly and faced her. The campfire light shone in her wide-slanted, greenish-yellow eyes. Each motionless pupil was flecked with gold.

Only because she was there did Greg believe he had found her.

Cautiously, on all fours, he crawled round the end of the log. The huge white wolf growled deeply and chomped her jaws, but not savagely. When she raised her lips and snarled, Greg sat down and began speaking to her. Even from a distance of ten feet, she towered above him. Moving his eyes slightly, he saw twelve pairs of hackled withers as her teammates surrounded the camp. They stood and stared motionlessly, as if awaiting Náhani's orders.

'Náhani,' Greg said, knowing full well she could not recognise the name. But he hoped she would remember the tone of his voice. 'Come sit by the fire. There's nothing to fear.'

She backed away until her hind legs were in the lake. Then she turned momentarily to lap several times at the water before pacing off into the forest. Her legion howled and chomped as they followed her. After several attempts at wolf song—and several answers—Greg threw his sleeping-bag on the sandy beach and retired.

He spent the next day on all fours in and around the camp. Four sentinels, two on the hill north of the creek and two about fifty yards up the side of the denning hill, kept him under constant surveillance. At no time did they attempt to hide. At midafternoon, without ceremony, they changed the guard.

That evening half a dozen wolves trotted onto the beach about a hundred yards west of Greg's camp. They strolled slowly towards the afterglow of an unusually spectacular sunset and yodelled half-minute songs.

After dark the troop became somewhat bolder. Without a sound, they crept to within a few feet of the lean-to, then skittishly kicked up sand and leaves as they rushed away. For an hour and a half all was silent. A warm breeze hummed through the spruce needles and tiny waves clapped against wet sand along the shore line.

At midnight Greg didn't try to hide or control a fit of shaking when he saw once again in the firelight the great silver wolf's eyes even before he could make out the full outline of her body. He decided to sit quietly and, if possible, send a friendship message between his eyes and hers, as they had at Nakinilerak. He felt tears of joy when she finally stepped round the other end of the log and haunched. She never took her gaze from his.

Outside the campfire light he sensed more than saw a seething mass of bodies. An hour later, Náhani whined once. Her pack headed up the lake shore, apparently to hunt. Greg was thrilled that Náhani stayed behind.

When he placed half a dozen small sticks on the embers, the wolf rose slowly and walked to within three feet of his position—walked stiff-legged as a wolf does under circumstances of distrust. For a time she tested the scent his body emitted, then she padded cautiously about camp, sniffing his equipment. The pack rack and canvas rucksack were the only items of his gear that had not been laundered since she had sprinkled them with urine at Nakinilerak. Náhani spent five minutes circling the sweat-laden canvas bag, aluminium frame and webbed nylon straps. Although the pack bag and frame had been rained on many times—including several dunkings at rough river crossings—they still retained enough of her smell for recognition.

There had been no detectable fear as such in her attitude. Indeed Náhani and her phalanx could have shredded Greg in less than a minute. At first there had been a definite aura of distrust. But almost instantly that distrust vanished when Náhani recognised her own smell on the rucksack.

Greg felt he was privileged to participate in one of the Earth Mother's great mysteries when Náhani approached him. She looked him squarely in the eye and wagged her tail. Then she bounded mischievously out of camp and joined her hunting team somewhere up the beach.

To Gregory Tah-Kloma, that one moment made up for a winter fraught with insecurity and uncertainty, for two footsore and disappointing summers, and for an expenditure of more money than the reward offered for her skin.

NÁHANI AND GREG had to get acquainted again—almost like human friends who have been apart for many years. Yet it was soon plain from her ear and lip movements, head shakes, tail wags and the compulsion to press physically close, that Náhani experienced real joy each time they spent an evening together.

When she finally allowed Greg to run his fingers through her gleaming coat, he discovered five gaping scars that looked as though they had been caused by grazing bullets. But a grizzly's claws could inflict similar wounds. Two toes were missing from her right front paw, a graphic explanation of her reputed hatred for traps, if indeed she had been responsible for destroying Tall-Totem's winter lines.

Otherwise, Náhani was in prime physical condition. Her teats still indicated that she had never mothered a litter.

Innate strength, patience, courage and a fierce will to survive accorded the wolf what it took to recover from grievous wounds, and what it took to migrate hundreds of miles across an unfriendly Kitiwanga during the winters. Greg tried to dwell upon her pack's loyalty rather than what she had undergone—how they must have fought off blood-scenting wolverines and other packs, how they fed her and licked her wounds, how they honoured her leadership across some of the most difficult terrain in North America.

Despite twelve-inch back and shoulder scars and the missing toes, Náhani did not limp. Her fluent leap and pace suggested that she probably had to slow down now and then in order for most members of her pack to keep up.

Possibly because a strong leader's authority and decisions are unchallengeable in a permanent troop, they consistently mimicked her moods, even to stance and inflection of voice. There appeared to be instant, direct communication through eyes, ears, tail, paws, ruff, carriage, sounds and emissions from scent glands.

Whenever the wolves prepared for the chase, they assembled and huddled on the beach near Greg's lean-to. They touched noses, wagged tails, vocalised, and sprinkled every upright object in the area. Those designated to stay near the dens assumed their positions before Náhani joined her teammates on the beach.

Each hunter knew his own prearranged duties. Teamwork, whether at chase or in defence, was their formula for survival.

9. The Way of the Northern Wild

On occasion the pack returned with empty bellies. At such times Náhani abandoned the regular runway and led poaching parties into the Gataga and Kechika rangelands. Before leading her team onto territory defended by competing packs, Náhani invariably indicated which wolf would follow her, who would take the third and fourth positions, and so on, so that a chain of command was formed with responsibilities for defence, offence and chase.

Her second in command was a hefty male who directed most routine matters such as assembly, sentry assignments and division of labour at the dens. Greg thought he recognised the big lieutenant as one of those he had observed in the bushes before the pack resumed residence at Denetiah Lake.

The pack accepted Greg's presence because Náhani ordered it. The wolves seemed to view him as a minor annoyance, although he detected a degree of genuine friendliness in three or four individuals.

Greg eventually recognised wolves he had seen at Nakinilerak. He missed three older pairs. Eight new adults, he assumed, were progeny of Náhani's troop, although several could have been admitted from other packs.

Náhani's temperament had undergone a certain mellowing. She no longer browbeat her female subjects as she sometimes had at Nakinilerak. Greg was privileged to study many close conferences she held with her heavyset lieutenant, whom she called on occasion to sit near the campfire log. At Nakinilerak, Greg had never known her to share in decision making.

Following these eyeball confrontations, the big subchief invariably assembled a small group of wolves and disappeared down the canyon for up to three or four hours. During such absences, a messenger would sometimes return, and most of the pack would leave. Greg concluded that the original conference concerned prey to be clawed and fanged away from a weaker neighbouring pack. The wolves generally returned with full bellies, and, more often than not, one of the members would be wounded.

One drowsy afternoon an old doe elk stepped from the forest for a drink about a hundred yards west of camp. Náhani and most of the pack were asleep in the sun on a grassy esplanade above the dens. An alert sentry barked a signal. Within moments the wolf pack had surrounded the unfortunate doe. Greg ran to the scene, but Náhani pounced in front of him to prevent his advance.

He stood on the beach and watched in helpless fascination while the queen wolf's chief deputy organised the team. The big wolf barked a command, lunged, and seized the elk's muzzle for attention. Simultaneously four veteran hunters slashed low at the hind quarters for hamstringing. The old doe plunged towards the underbrush above the lake, but before she could take a dozen steps she simply wilted as ten wolves attacked her back and neck. The kill took four minutes at most.

Within the next half-hour more than four hundred pounds of meat disappeared. Two sentinel guards stood near the remains, but no wolf fed again for four days. During that time, Náhani descended the hillside each evening at dark for a fireside visit with Greg.

On the fourth day after the kill, Greg saw a large wolverine swimming quietly across the lake.

The two sentinels at the carcass may have been a bit slowwitted that morning, or perhaps they believed they could handle the situation without calling for help. The wolverine knocked down one wolf, then gave a sustained war cry not unlike a cougar scream as he headed for the carcass. Of course the cry brought the wildly excited pack within moments. The wounded guard wolf staggered slowly from the scene. Warily, the other wolves trotted in a circle around the carcass where the wolverine stood helping himself to a meal, but no wolf cared to be first to attack. Then Greg saw Náhani's vaulting leap, and the interloper was hurled to the sand. Recovering, the wolverine rushed through the encircling pack to the wounded wolf and delivered a cleaverlike slash to the victim's neck. The wolf died instantly.

Apparently expecting the death of Náhani's confederate to demoralise the kennel, the wolverine underestimated the queen wolf's leadership. She uttered one savage yelp. The entire troop fell upon the invader. Within less than five minutes they had devoured the animal except for the shredded skin, skull and musk glands. The pack proceeded to eat from the putrifying elk carcass as if nothing had happened—except for one female wolf that mourned. Eventually she ran up the beach, and Greg never saw her again. She may have left the region to become a loner, but more than likely she simply returned to the family den where she starved herself to death.

An interesting territorial situation developed in the early evening two days after the wolverine incident. Náhani put in an appearance at Greg's camp. She paced back and forth, knocked over a pot of laundry water, and refused to sit down. As always he stopped what he was doing in order to give full attention to Náhani. Soon, younger wolves came to the log and whimpered, while every adult in the phalanx light-footed continuously between the denning hill and the beach. Náhani tensed.

Then Greg saw a neighbouring pack of wolves slowly advancing from the west end of the lake as if they planned to take over the elk carcass. Suddenly Náhani jumped over the log, issued a squeal like a shrill police whistle and assembled her troop on the beach.

Greg rushed towards the lake, but Náhani immediately headed him off. She reared, placed her two front pads on his shoulders, growled softly, and licked him across the face in a loving but stern warning to keep out of her affairs. She then returned to the lake. The entire pack was silent, motionless, awaiting her next move.

With firm resolution the silver-white queen wolf cantered towards the doe elk's dull-red bones. The rest of the pack followed in a loosely deployed formation. The setting sun touched the distant mountains and sent reddish-copper rays over Denetiah Lake. Although he shielded his eyes with the binoculars, Greg could see only black silhouettes—twenty warriors advancing from the west.

Greg stood on the camp log and awaited the oncoming conflict. Forty feet west of the now fetid carrion, Náhani's command to attack brought a lusty war cry from throats on both sides of the battle line. The fight obviously was a decisive one. Not only could it end Náhani's supremacy among her own wolves but it might cost them their runway, their denning compound, even their confederation as a pack.

One by one the invaders broke and retreated after the initial onslaught, leaving two of their number dead. Náhani's wolves did not pursue. On the way back to the dens to lick their wounds, most of her noisy muster passed close enough for Greg to observe their bleeding slashes. Only a few were unscathed. Náhani threw a single quick glance towards him as she herded her team onto the hill, where they remained and bayed until dawn.

After breakfast the next morning, Greg walked up the beach to bury the two dead wolves, but nothing remained—not even the elk bones. Coyote, fox, fisher and wolverine spoor indicated that he had not been the only spectator.

When he returned to camp, Náhani was sitting near the campfire log. Mustering all his nerve, Greg decided to interfere in Náhani's affairs, and approached her to examine her for wounds. To his surprise she stood rigidly still during the probing, even when he touched a tender spot. She was bruised and swollen along the shoulders and hip, but he found no open cuts. When he knelt and put his arms round her neck and stroked her head and ruff, she licked him across the mouth. Accustomed as she was to most communication through the eyes, she looked for a long moment into his face.

'Let's go, Náhani!' he shouted.

They left the marsh, forded the creek, and climbed through the cool, dark cloud forest, to a gusty alpine terrace that overlooked hundreds of square miles dark with hazy timber, dewy canyons and deep-set lakes. The two sat down on a south-facing granite ledge out of the wind. The big white wolf shone with dazzling brilliance as she flattened out her body and placed her leathery black muzzle on out-stretched paws. While he combed moulting guard hair from her coat, she snoozed with casual indifference.

Greg knew that Náhani was too regal ever to reveal that she hungered for affection.

THE LATE INTERPACK WARFARE stirred general edginess among Náhani's lieutenants. Greg assumed the wolves would carry out a thorough patrol along the full length and breadth of their runway. They would refresh all boundary monuments, re-establishing claim to their forage range against poachers. Greg knew that the runway could conceivably encompass 200 miles and could take them well within the range of Trapper-Dan.

Towards full moon, tension peaked. The pack assembled quickly behind Náhani and headed up the beach. Their voices faded as they crossed the long ridge south. Like Alaskan husky teams, the wolves never changed pace, regardless of terrain. By the time they reached the Frog River watershed, a sense of loneliness descended upon Greg. He played the harmonica by the fire for several hours.

He had often wondered why Náhani had postponed a full range cruise until now. Perhaps it was because the pack had brought down sufficient game near the whelping dens, which led him to believe that a wolf's territorial claim might function as a symbol of status. Perhaps he was thinking in terms that were too human, but he felt quite certain that no wolf pack in the game-rich Kitiwanga actually needed a 200-mile range in order to eat regularly.

Greg also believed that Náhani had some ability to reason. Apparently she had acquired her vast range because she knew she was a hunted wolf and therefore needed a wide variety of terrain in which the pack could hunt, bathe, play, breed and escape. When he had tracked the pack to Denetiah Lake, Greg had been able to follow the travelway with ease. It was the wolves' habit of marking their established runway against intrusion by other wolf packs that led him finally to Denetiah Lake.

He was concerned that Trapper-Dan, who was reputed to be the most astute tracker in western Canada, would also have been able to decipher the runway signs that pointed to a denning complex.

THE EVENING AFTER NÁHANI and most of her pack left on the forage range tour, Greg received a pleasant surprise. Two older brindled females, left behind in the dens, half crawled into camp, whined, slavered, wagged their tails, and fell on their backs. These two had often made friendly gestures from the shadows, but Náhani never permitted them to enter the camp area. While Náhani was away, the two spent most of their time with Greg and became so friendly that he found it difficult not to treat the exuberant wigglers as dogs. He patted and rubbed them, scratched their necks and chins when they finally became accustomed to the human hand near their heads.

At the same time he feared Náhani might expel them from the pack should she return and find them in his company. Nevertheless, he also considered the possibility that the queen wolf may have delegated the visits, because both females raced up the hill nearly every time he gave them cooked fish, straight to a nearby den where an old male was convalescing. He had received serious injuries during the fight over the elk carcass. The two females were his wives, a rare occurrence of bigamy among wolves. Until Náhani returned, Greg caught and cooked a daily combination of trout, char and grayling, which the females took to their mate.

He was fishing for the wolves on the seventh morning after Náhani's departure. Distant yelping and baying drifted throughout the basin long before the troop single-filed down the beach. Náhani led the pack back by ten lengths. As usual, Greg met the wolves on all fours. It was the kind of greeting they could understand. The queen wolf stopped momentarily, wagged her tail, and licked her friend across his mouth, but jumped back and ran up the hill when he tried to put his arms round her neck.

Her first concern, he rejoiced to discover, was the wounded wolf. She showed her satisfaction with the two females by cuffing them playfully and licking their faces. But the two concealed their friendship for Greg when Náhani was in residence.

After careful inspection of their dens, the weary team bathed briefly in the lake, then climbed to the sunning shelf with little more recognition of Greg than a chomp or a tail wag as they trotted past where he sat at the side of their path to the hill.

At dark a tired, but relaxed Náhani slipped quietly behind the camp log. The waning moon projected extra-sharp outlines that night. Forest creatures sang more softly when the wolves were around. For an hour Náhani lay on her back with her head across Greg's lap while he rubbed her belly. He combed out loose hair, gorged ticks, and matted burs. She allowed him to remove clods of pine pitch from between her toes.

Suddenly she jumped to her feet. With her nose pointed towards the beach, she indicated that Greg should follow her. He found it incredible that, despite the mileage she had recently covered, she yearned for a moonlight walk.

Then and later he became convinced that Náhani shared his fascination for exploring the northland by night. At night, the deep-woods lake and its immediate surroundings underwent the most subtle transformation. Changing shadow patterns, even the slightest change in movement or light intensity, triggered Náhani's immediate interest. As a wolf she instinctively registered every change in her environment, but Greg believed she was also attuned to his own emotional nuances. At times she studied his face and wagged her tail or pressed close against his leg.

On most occasions when they left camp, day or night, four to six shadowy outlines moved or stopped as they did. At first Greg resented the background bodyguard, but then he thought of an ever-possible charge by a moose, silvertip grizzly, wapiti or caribou during one of their unguarded moments. Those silent, ghostly shadows—always at a discreet distance—became appreciated.

When Náhani elected to sleep among her own on the rimrock, Greg fished, hiked to the barrens for fresh greens or explored the marsh. With store-bought staples dwindling towards the middle of August, he went on long forays into berry brakes. From rotting logs and subsphagnum leaf mould, he collected daily about three pounds of edible fungi, including morels, agaries, truffles and puff-balls, to bake with trout and grayling. The bog yielded succulent burdock stems, purslane, horsetail tubers, onions and fern fiddle-necks. By experimenting, Greg created a weird bouillabaisse of fish, fungi and fodder.

Greg had finished one of his outback table triumphs one evening and had sat down on the log near Náhani. A swarm of flying squirrels provided a sight and sound spectacle in the forest across the outlet. Suddenly Náhani growled and stood erect on the log.

An adult bull moose sloshed through the creek and displayed an obvious dislike for wolves the moment he saw Náhani. Shaking his rack, and with a terrifying bellow, he kicked up geysers of sand and threatened a head-on charge. Nothing equals a bull moose for noisy rage. Within moments of his appearance the wolves surrounded him in a running circle, nipping at his rear end. The moose set off for the forest, after which Náhani ordered an immediate withdrawal.

In the ensuing silence, Greg wondered why Náhani had ordered her pack away from a ton of red meat on her front doorstep. He concluded that judgment told her that it was too risky to engage in an encounter with a prime moose on open beach where the huge animal could step into three feet of water and kill every wolf that came within range of his sledgehammer hoofs. She would never have allowed her pack to take on even an old, sick or emaciated moose so near the whelping dens. A bear might smell the blood and arrive to feast upon the carcass before the wolves could clean it up. There had been too much trouble earlier when the hunting squad neglected to herd the old elk a mile up the beach before making the kill.

In the sane world of the wolf, adaptability and good judgment so far have saved the remaining packs from extinction; moreover, wherever the wolf has gone—driven on by slings, spears, arrows, guns, traps and poisons—prey species have not only thrived, they have improved. Wolves have weeded out those unfit to reproduce.

After the dark of the Sagamore-Council-Moon, the several families at different times took their yearlings and subyearlings on their own training expeditions, some of which lasted almost a month. Greg and Náhani had walked about five miles up the north-shore beach one night when a baying male, his mate and three offspring overtook them. The farewell scene was touching. They all wagged their tails, licked Náhani over the face and brisket, whined at Greg's feet, then raced away into the night. Although the other families returned for autumn hunting rendezvous, this group apparently wished to establish a pack of its own.

On nights when families or groups of two- and three-year-olds prepared to leave, they came to the lake and sang, perhaps half a dozen wolves in a circle. The five-minute performance always began at the lowest notes, continuing in arpeggios to the highest.

Greg observed that the wolves' various sounds and calls had special meanings for the pack members. There were sounds to soothe, incite and encourage. An entire vocabulary of murmurs governed the gradations of gratitude, pain, pleasure, aggravation, fear, hate, jealousy and suspicion. He became adept at imitating the many snarls, whines, calls and songs. With time and practice he was able to bring forth the desired response from the wolves when he issued a particular signal.

Body language in conjunction with any of the several sounds communicated intensity of mood or intention. At times like these, the atmosphere was heavy with excitement. Greg worried at first, fearing a general breakup of the pack. Perhaps he was to blame because Náhani spent so much time with him. But in her expression he observed a calm and serenity from which he took reassurance. She made no effort to hold back any wolf that was preparing to leave the pack.

One night during the fading Sagamore-Council-Moon as Greg and Náhani sat by the campfire, he realised that not one wolf remained in the denning complex. While the families were away, Náhani never left Greg's side. They ate, drank, sat, walked and slept together. He and Náhani were alone. He shuddered to think what might happen if some misfortune befell the queen wolf during the pack's absence. The returning troop would hunt him down and tear him to shreds.

Could Trapper-Dan have been waiting for this seasonal occurrence?

AT DAWN ONE DAY while several of the paired wolves and their off-spring were still away, Náhani jumped over the camp log and ran, straight for the beach. There she stopped and stood facing the west, with head and tail high, muzzle closed. She emitted a continual hum—deep-throated, ventriloquial in timbre.

Greg peered up the beach and saw a slowly approaching pair of yellowish-grey wolves. With infinite caution, the two strangers padded up to within ten feet of Náhani. All three wolves quickly raised their tails at a right angle to the backbone and pumped musk from the caudal gland on the upper side of the tail near the base. This musk is the wolf's most cordial greeting on the one hand and the most inviolate expression of identity on the other.

Once Náhani satisfied herself with the smell of the two wolves she allowed them the same privilege. Then she snarled viciously at the female. Both strangers fell to their backs and exposed soft under-bellies while she stiff-legged round the pair. Five minutes later she allowed them to follow her towards Greg's camp.

As the strangers got their first scent of the young Indian, instinctively they crouched and froze. When he stepped into full view, the pair whirled and fled. It was late that afternoon before Náhani coaxed them back.

Although Náhani appeared to invite the two wolves to join the pack, when the groups of hunting families returned she did nothing to restrain their hostility towards the newcomers. They were beaten savagely, repeatedly evicted from unoccupied dens, and the other wolves refused to share prey with them. At the same time, Náhani somehow communicated to the newcomers that Greg was an accepted member of the Denetiah Lake ensemble. Eventually, however the pack accepted the newcomers and no longer harried them.

Pair by pair, most mated couples had returned by the end of August. Each wolf resumed its place in the hierarchy. All yearlings and younger wolves returned with their parents, but several unattached individuals never came back. Presumably these had found mates and formed confederations of their own.

All the wolves were gaunt and knotty from late-summer moult, particularly the younger ones, who had undergone a strenuous apprenticeship with their elders.

While other animals were preoccupied with storing up fat for the winter, the wolves feasted upon a bounteous berry crop. They dug rizomes and bulbs, grazed late bunch grass, munched wood sorrel, and gnawed sweetbark and bitterberry branches. From the start of the first quarter of the Sagamore-Council-Moon until far into the Moon-of-Painted-Leaves they became vegetarians. The wolves were densely furred nonhibernators, preying upon nonhibernators, and there was no reason for them to accumulate layers of fat against the winter months.

With the waxing September Moon-of-Painted-Leaves, moaning winds herded sheeplike formations of clouds across the sky and soughed night and day throughout the conifer forest around the choppy lake. When a slow wedge of migrating swans crossed the sky one afternoon, Greg moved into the lean-to and collected a supply of dry firewood. Time was running out.

The first general storm hammered against the Kitiwanga's enormous mass. For three days and nights the tempest raged; rain cascaded over the lake; lightning constantly whittled at sullen crests. Ancient spruce, long overmature, crashed to the forest floor to become tomorrow's nourishing duff. Náhani came to Greg's lean-to day and night. Somewhere, instinctively, she too must have known that time was running out.

On the morning after the storm, the north wind rolled the remaining cloud curtain back towards the Pacific. Most of the pack, led at full canter by the chief hunters, headed down the creek towards the Gataga River canyon. Náhani, on the other hand, indicated that Greg should escort her on an inspection trip along the north shore. For some reason Náhani had sent her bodyguard with the pack. Since the wolves were invading territory defended by other packs, the guards might be sorely needed on the Gataga foray.

Náhani preceded Greg all the way to the north rim of the Denetiah trough. At timber line they came upon an excavation, obviously the den of a coyote family. Toothing bones, scats and other fresh refuse lay scattered about the mound at the tunnel's opening.

Náhani stopped in her tracks. The crest hair on her neck and withers suddenly resembled a mane. A backward flick of one ear signalled that Greg should remain motionless. She spread her feet and barked, as only leader wolves do.

Nothing happened immediately. Then a drowsy male coyote walked slowly from the mouth of the tunnel. He took one look at Náhani and yawned extravagantly. Here was the first creature, Greg thought, to exhibit such a casual attitude towards Náhani. The two animals padded slowly in circles round each other, sniffing rear ends cautiously but with no apparent hostility. Obviously they were more than nodding acquaintances. Náhani was almost twice the size of the coyote and four times his weight. Yet it was clear that the coyote neither owed nor paid homage to Náhani, the queen wolf.

When the coyote scented Greg, he dived deep into his tunnel. As Náhani continued on the inspection trip, Greg paused to compare her six-inch track with the two-inch coyote print.

Náhani quickened her gait along the steep hillside. Long before they reached camp that evening she conveyed a feeling that something was wrong. She kept looking back at Greg, urging greater speed down the north-shore beach. She barked, whined or howled as she ran. She was clearly on edge. Four large males ran to meet them when they were within a mile of the denning complex. Her staff officers reflected distress.

Náhani and her four lieutenants plunged through the outlet flume. Then she inched carefully across the strip of beach, as though afraid and enraged at the same time. The entire pack stood in trembling assembly at the log in front of Greg's camp.

10. A Wolf Betrayed

Náhani shouldered her way to the centre of the group. Her long, white nose lifted above the milling forms; her low moan triggered high-pitched wails from every throat.

As Greg stepped cautiously forward, the wolves' mournful cries became deep, threatening snarls. In the rapidly gathering dusk, the circle of wolves swarmed and shifted so restlessly that he was unable to appraise the situation.

Suddenly Náhani's hackled white back moved away from the centre of the pack. She barked and the wolves slowly separated into groups of twos, threes and fours. With bared, flashing fangs they howled and chomped, seemingly directing their rage towards Greg for something he did not yet understand.

Then he saw the fallen wolf. Panting on the white sand within a few feet of the camp log, lay one of the small mates of the bigamous male that had been injured in the fight over the elk carcass. Greg remembered the times he had fished and cooked for that family while the kennel patrolled its runway. The female's right rear shank was firmly clamped between the jaws of a double-spring steel trap.

Where had she stepped into that trap? How had she managed to unstaple it from its anchoring clog and carry it back to Greg's camp?

The wolves, including Náhani, reached a peak of anger Greg had not believed possible. And now for the first time in his life, he knew—as an animal in danger would know—the meaning of fear.

Instinctively, and from bitter experience, the wolves associated the man smell with the steel smell of traps. Náhani, who at that moment stood at the head of their ranks and glared at Greg, carried a mutilated right front paw as a result of the combination of man and steel.

Greg realised that if he failed to face the wolves down, his life would end in a matter of seconds. Without faltering, he walked rapidly towards the trapped wolf. He never once took his gaze from Náhani's icy stare.

'Náhani!' he shouted. 'I'm coming through!'

At the sound of his voice every wolf between him and the trapped female stepped aside and was instantly silent. But the victim quickly struggled to her feet. She lifted the trapped leg so that nothing but the three-foot chain dragged the ground as she hobbled away to her den. Her mate, the other female, and Náhani disappeared into the same tunnel. Not a wolf remained in sight. Greg stepped over the camp log, sat down, and cupped his hands over his face.

During those first moments after the confrontation, he was too upset to think clearly. He could think of no way to remove that trap before the wolves began to chew away the leg above the steel jaws. It would be no simple task. That female could sever the human jugular vein and tear out the windpipe with a single snap of her jaws.

Deep in the cramped quarters of a den—possibly in the presence of several hostile wolves—the task of removing the trap would be many times more difficult than it would have been on the beach.

All through the long night he waited for Náhani, but she did not come to his camp. He awakened at sunrise. His urgency to remove the trap was spurred by Náhani's serious expression as she looked down at him from the log. He rushed to her and examined her muzzle and brisket. No blood. She licked the stubble of whiskers that covered his chin.

He thanked the Earth Mother that she was still his friend.

The air was warm. He put on a pair of shorts, fixed a quick breakfast, then rushed to the den. He held a flashlight in one hand, a pan of reconstituted milk in the other. Náhani reached the entrance before he did.

From the size of the dirt mound on the hillside below the tunnel entrance, he estimated that the whelping chamber lay about twenty feet beyond the opening. The soil, a light sandy loam, had caved in several times since the family had dug the den.

Greg listened. The faintest whine reached his ears each time he imitated a wolf sound for soothing or calling, but neither he nor Náhani could persuade the wolf to come out.

Greg always felt claustrophobic in dark, close places. He dreaded the thought of crawling into that crumbly tunnel. Yet under the circumstances he had no choice.

He placed his flashlight and a pan of milk in the tunnel beyond the entrance, and tried to squeeze through. His shoulders were too wide. With his knife he enlarged the entrance and cleared away the dirt and rock. The tunnel was slightly larger in diameter than the entrance, but in order to inch along he had to extend his arms full length ahead, pull with his hands and push with his feet.

When he reached the turn in the tunnel, he flashed a beam of light into the whelping chamber at the far end. In a choking explosion of loose hair and dust, the male and the other female shot from the chamber into another tunnel with a secret opening somewhere in the hillside forest. Greg tried to back up but found it physically impossible to move backwards. To make matters worse, Náhani had crawled in right behind him. Perspiration poured from his body as he struggled for oxygen and fought increasing claustrophobia. He was unable to bend either his knees or elbows.

Pulling himself into a cramped sitting position inside the whelping chamber, he handed the milk to the whimpering female. To his surprise, she gulped it down within seconds. Náhani squeezed in alongside her and sniffed the trap briefly. Not waiting for the dust to settle, Greg switched off the flashlight, managed to turn round. He could feel Náhani's hot breath on the soles of his feet as he pulled and pushed himself back towards the circle of light and fresh air that seemed to be a mile away. Twenty-two wolves stood watching when he eventually emerged from the tunnel.

Once outside, he and Náhani rushed to the lake for a five-minute swim. He suddenly became aware that the queen wolf was depending on him to do what she realised no wolf could do, and she appeared anxious for him to return to the den.

When he arrived, the little female had not emerged. If he could only persuade her to face away from him in one of those narrow tunnels, he could grab the trap, depress the springs with both hands, and free her without fear that she would turn and attack him.

The other wolves continued to watch from a distance. They seemed to realise what Greg was trying to do. That day he made three more excruciating trips into the underground chamber, taking a pan of water each time. As long as he imitated certain wolf sounds, the little female allowed him to touch her head and scratch her chin; but if he moved a hand towards the trap, she snarled and chomped.

On the following morning a ruckus among the wolves awakened him. He rushed to the den. The little female sat at the entrance while nearly every male in the pack paced back and forth, growled, and sniffed the female's rear end. False oestrus, a condition sometimes brought on by the shock of a painful accident. When Greg approached with Náhani, the little wolf slunk back into the den.

Still dreading that narrow tunnel, Greg began to build a shield of short branch lengths to place between him and the wolf. She became more friendly with every visit until at last she did not snarl when he picked up the trap. But the presence of oestrous blood caused a

constant tumult among the males. On every trip as Greg shoved the short poles ahead of him, their scrambling back and forth not only filled the passageways with dust and used up precious oxygen but also made the soft, sandy loam more hazardous.

Even before the shield was finished, Greg's flashlight batteries went dead. Total darkness as well as hot, heavy-breathing wolves in the tunnels now caused his claustrophobia to reach panic proportion. He probed under the shield for the trap. The springs were too rusty and too strong for his hands alone. When he tried to get his knee under the trap, the wolf shrieked with pain, knocked the shield apart, and rushed into the auxiliary tunnel where noisy fights ensued. He began to crawl out by the shorter regular tunnel and bumped squarely into Náhani. An inch at a time he was able to push her and persuade her to back out.

Finally, in the open air again, he saw the little female dragging the trap towards the beach, at the same time fighting off her own mate and other males. Although mated for life, a male wolf will try to mount any female in heat unless the oestrus period occurs among all females at the same time in a pack situation.

With large rocks, Greg blocked both entrances to the den, then rushed to camp to get some nylon rope. When the little female finally hobbled back to the den entrance and began to remove the blocking stones, Greg dropped a slip noose round the trap and threw the other end of the rope across an overhead spruce branch. Trusting Náhani to prevent an attack by the other wolves, he lifted the screaming female two feet above the ground by pulling the rope. He stepped quickly behind the tree, reached round with both arms, grabbed the trap, compressed the springs, and freed the wolf in about seven seconds.

Greg ran immediately to the den entrances and cleared away the rocks, but the little female refused to enter. She ran in and out among the trees, shrieked, and slashed at every wolf within reach.

At last, exhausted, she seemed to calm. But there was neither delight nor relief in Náhani's expression. The panting little female moved from wolf to wolf, wagging her tail and whining. She was clearly out of her senses. Then she saw Greg with the roll of rope. Baring her teeth, she dropped her head and tail in the attack attitude and started slowly forwards. Náhani stepped in front of him.

Ignoring the queen wolf's growl, the insane little female attempted to attack. With one mighty lunge, Náhani seized her throat and killed her.

While the other wolves looked on, the big silver-white stared into each face. Gradually the pack dispersed, some to the dens, some to the sunning shelf above timber line.

Greg picked up the lifeless body and the trap. Náhani followed. He buried the wolf near the beach. Then he tied the trap to a low branch above the runway where the other wolves would have to smell it whenever they left the denning complex. He wanted every wolf to remember and hate that instrument for all time.

11. Reconciliation

For most of that day and night Náhani rarely left Greg's camp. Her mane and rump remained hackled. She snarled and chomped every time a wolf passed within hearing distance. A mood of depression had struck the pack after seeing Náhani kill one of their cherished number. In their eyes, the little female was justified in trying to punish her traditional enemy, man, for an unprovoked outrage against her. Their mood expressed itself through confused hostility towards Greg and Náhani.

For a while Greg thought that Náhani was the most inflexible tyrant. She permitted no conferences with the favoured staff officers. She brutally beat every female who dared pass Greg's camp with even a suspicion of a hackled crest. She bobbed the tail of one yearling that answered her snarl in kind.

But no wolf left the pack. On the eighth day after the unfortunate death, Greg noticed a gradual reversal of mood and attitude. Big males that had ignored his existence at Nakinilerak as well as at Denetiah came to the campsite and wagged their tails. They fell on their backs and whined while Náhani watched the young Indian scratch a brisket or rub flanks and belly. Older females were even more demonstrative.

Shortly after sunset on that same day Náhani called for assembly near the outlet flume. The pack milled round her with some of the old adoration. She licked the chins of the dead wolf's sister and mate. There remained traces of uncertainty, confusion and even hostility, yet her wolves were ready to follow her along the runway for the first autumn hunt and conquest of interlopers.

They had hardly crossed into the Frog River watershed when a gusting north wind seized the basin. Within moments the lake writhed under whitecaps. The northland's most outspoken personality was the wind. Every creature bowed down sooner or later before it. When the wind blew, animal activities virtually ceased.

While Greg slept one night, the first autumn blizzard struck. He worried because the wolves were now in moult, unprepared to face frosty nights outside their dens. During the storm, Greg blocked off the open front of the lean-to, using his ground sheet. Following the icy rain, the wind returned. When the gusts subsided at sunset, he walked along the beach. Not a bird, squirrel, frog or insect stirred.

The next day he considered the idea of hiking out before the wolves returned. He studied the maps, but could not bring himself to leave. For several days following the storm, summer seemed to revive. Animal life returned. Waterfowl swam from the reeds and called with renewed vigour, so it seemed. A whisky-jack that lived in a south-shore alder kept every creature advised on large animal movements. Late one afternoon the bird's strident whistle called Greg's attention to distant baying. With deceptively sleepy gait, the wolf pack cantered down the beach.

Greg was elated to see Náhani not only in complete command but also the centre of affection when she stopped the pack at the camp-site before continuing to the dens. At some point along the hunting circuit, four strangers—two males, two females—had joined the pack as mates of unwedded three-year-olds. The new members were happy and playful, but at the same time suspicious and puzzled to find a *man* so close to their new homes. They reacted with seizures of hysteria and stampede, followed by awkward embarrassment when they encountered icy stares from the rest of the pack.

In order to impress the newcomers with the extent of her domin-ion, Náhani resprinkled the uprights of Greg's camp and most of his equipment. The new males and females rolled on their backs, whined, and wagged their tails every time Náhani appeared.

Three affiliates failed to return with the pack. Two unattached younger wolves had left during that first autumn hunt, either to join other packs or to establish a group of their own. The limping old black male, mate of the wolf Trapper-Dan had killed, had almost reached his life expectancy of about twenty years. It was more likely that he died of a heart attack than in a hunting accident.

BECAUSE SEPTEMBER brought clement days and nights, and because of increasing friendly encounters with the pack, Greg decided to stay at Denetiah Lake until the wolves went south, if indeed they did.

The warm night of September 18 was one Greg would never forget. The moon was full. Náhani had slept most of the day on the sunning shelf with her troop. Greg had taken advantage of an espe-cially greedy run of Arctic grayling that rose for every lure that dappled the surface. The wolves had gorged themselves the night before on an early lemming migration, and for that reason Náhani ate only several small bites of a fish Gregg offered her when she stepped round the log. She haunched beside him.

The stars shone with uncommon brilliance that night, a phenomenon that often meant that the vagrant north wind was about to assert itself. After Greg had played the harmonica for about an hour, Náhani pulled at his jeans, her signal that she wanted to walk.

She led the way up the south shore, slowly at first. Instead of lingering behind in the shadows, her bodyguard of four magnificent males joined in the moonlight walk—two at Greg's side, two at Náhani's. How splendid they looked in their new fall coats! By the time the five wolves and the young Chimmesyan had walked a mile, one by one every wolf in the pack had emerged from a different aisle of the forest to join in the walk. Twenty-eight superb denizens of the north woods were escorting Greg. There was some jostling for position, even a few snarls and snaps, because the new wolves were not completely oriented into pack protocol; but at the end of two miles, Náhani, Greg and the four staff officers led the silent procession at a brisk pace for an additional five miles.

After Greg turned back, Náhani and her pack continued for an all-night inspection tour round the lake. He considered that particular walk with the wolves a supreme achievement, second only to the Náhani relationship itself. He gave her full credit for the pack's reconciliation after the little female's death. Gradually she had reconstructed trust that had been seriously shaken. In his diary Greg wrote: 'Náhani had the whole thing planned last night when she came into camp. Every wolf knew what was going to happen. Náhani has shown me how a wolf thinks. There is an old Chimmesyan saying that explains witch doctors' magic: "When anything strengthens a bond of friendship, the friends have walked in the shadow of a rainbow."'

WITH SHORTER DAYS and colder nights towards the end of September, plants as well as animals prepared for winter. Spruce cones, whose clusters Greg had barely noticed, were frosted over with sparkling resin as if they had been given a coat of varnish. Waxed-in crown buds glistened like golden scarabs from every tree-top in the forest. Red and flying squirrels chattered while they cut spruce cones and stashed them in piles of leaf mould.

Responding to some inner signal, the monarch butterflies assembled along an inner-forest trunk. Another signal caused them to flicker like a thousand candles as they rose on a thermal into the exactly correct air current that would bear them to Florida.

The swallows that had swept the air so clean of insects assembled one morning and left for Honduras. Hermit thrushes, grosbeaks and golden eagles left in pairs en route to California. Marsh hawks and ospreys spiralled on Gataga canyon updraughts, on their way to Mexico's warm *lagunas*.

During September, hibernators and nonhibernators alike ate with only one purpose: to store up fat layers for the Hunger-moons ahead. Only the wolves lazed through Indian summer. They knew that fattened prey would soon bog down in snow. Paired and tranquil, they seemed to enjoy their own company more during midautumn than at any other time since Greg had known them.

Wolf serenades in the light of the Fallen-Leaf-Moon occurred with greater frequency than under earlier moons. Although pack members performed with no predictable regularity, on clear nights the wolves dogtrotted to promontories, where they threw back their heads and sang sixty-second solos, two-minute duets and three-minute choruses with effervescent resonance. Younger participants often broke pitch and yodelled. Between wolf songs, Greg played the harmonica for Náhani, but during this time he was never sure she enjoyed that music.

On the sharp, sunny midmorning of October 15, the idyllic autumn atmosphere was abruptly shattered.

Greg and Náhani were sitting face to face on the log, sharing ash-baked trout and grayling. Twelve wolves played tag on the sand between the log and the beach. The rest of the pack lay sprawled out on the rimrock, taking advantage of the last warm sunshine.

Suddenly a float plane stuttered across the deep river gorges to the southeast, swished over the treetops, and landed on the lake surface. A gusting westerly had prevented any warning of the plane's approach.

Every wolf faded into dense forest on the denning hillside. There was no time for organised assembly. Greg saw Náhani lead the pack at full bay towards the Frog River watershed. It was too late for him to douse the fire and try to hide. The men had already seen him, the campfire smoke—and the wolves.

Terror struck the young Indian. The plane turned and taxied rapidly towards the beach in front of the campsite. Two men climbed out of the hatches and onto the pontoons, each clutching a high-power, long-range rifle with telescopic sights.

Greg recognised both men.

12. The Hunters

The bush pilot no sooner killed the engine than one man tied a rope to a strut and signalled to the young Chimmesyan. Trapper-Dan was not aboard, but Greg feared he was closing in from the bush to meet the airborne hunters.

Greg walked slowly to the beach. He caught the painter and pulled the aircraft ashore. Two middle-aged hunters with Mausers jumped to the sand. The pilot followed. They stared at Greg in disbelief. The pilot was first to recover and offer his hand. Greg recognised him and both hunters as the three white men who had accompanied Trapper-Dan and Eugene Charley to Tatlatui Lake in 1966.

'Lex Morgan, Fort St John,' the pilot said. After an awkward silence he pointed to the hunters. 'Jay Spencer, G. Allen Ogilvy. Cheechakos from Seattle.'

In northland jargon the term *cheechako* was used in a derisive way, meaning tenderfoot, greenhorn, and worse. Apparently Spencer and Ogilvy were either ignorant of the inference or too absorbed in the size and number of wolf tracks on the sandy beach to be aware of its rudeness. They were also still recovering from the sight of an Indian in the midst of a pack of timber wolves.

'They call me Gregory Tah-Kloma.' Greg spelled out his name.

'If I hadn't seen you and that big white wolf sitting on that log,' Morgan said, 'I wouldn't have believed it. There must've been a dozen wolves on the beach. At least that many on the hill. Náhani and the phantoms, Tah-Kloma?'

'I'd appreciate it, Mr Morgan,' Greg said, sidestepping the question, 'if the gentlemen would put their rifles back in the plane.'

'We're here to *shoot* wolves, not let them get away—especially Náhani,' Ogilvy said. 'I want that skin. You can have the reward.'

'I'm not interested in any reward,' Greg said.

'Those wolves must be at least ten miles from here by now,' Morgan said. He was studying Greg with curiosity and admiration.

Ogilvy was impatient. 'Let's get a move on. We've got shotguns in the plane and if we take off immediately we can locate the wolf pack from the air and bank in at low altitude for a buckshot kill.' Noting Morgan's hesitation he added, 'Don't forget, we're paying you to take us to Náhani. Are you with us or against us?'

'I'd like to talk to Tah-Kloma first,' Morgan said. 'Meanwhile, do as he says. Put the rifles back on the plane.'

The two hunters cursed but complied. They returned quickly to the beach and walked to the lean-to where Greg was getting into a shirt and jeans. 'What are you doing here at Denetiah, living with wolves?' Spencer asked.

'I'll answer all your questions in a minute,' Greg said. 'Shall we sit on the log by the fire? I'll make coffee provided you have the coffee. I take chinquapin tea.'

'What the hell's chinquapin tea?' Ogilvy asked.

'Indians drink it,' Morgan said. 'Native herb. Tastes like boiled flannel pyjamas. Trapper-Dan was always drinking it. Remember? I'll get the grub box.'

'Where did you come from, Tah-Kloma?' As he spoke, Ogilvy dilated his nostrils. Greg remembered that he had not bathed since the wolves had returned from the last hunt.

'I came from Kitwanga Lake.'

'Where's Kitwanga Lake?' Spencer asked. Instead of looking Greg in the eye, he squatted to examine the white hair shed on Greg's sleeping-bag.

'Southwest of the plateau,' Lex Morgan said as he arrived with the grub box. 'You're the guy the RCMP's yakking about. You're from Prince George. College man. You're the one all right. The wolf-man.'

'I'm a prospector,' Greg said.

Lex Morgan grinned as he made a pot of coffee.

'I'll ask you to excuse the mess around here,' Greg said. 'I've been planning to clean it up.' He removed the pan of fish from the log. 'Náhani and I were having—'

A slip of the tongue. 'I told you that was Náhani sitting on that log with him!' Ogilvy shouted enthusiastically. 'Had to be. Biggest damned wolf in the Kitiwanga. How many in the pack?'

'Twenty-eight,' Greg said.

'That's the killer pack. Killed that Carrier down around Hazelton last fall,' Spencer said.

'Impossible!' Morgan said. 'How long have you been here, Greg?'

'Most of three moons. There's no real proof Náhani southed out of the Kitiwanga in the last three years. This is the second summer I've lived with these wolves. Why didn't they kill *me* . . . if they killed Eugene Charley?'

'How'd you know about Charley?' Ogilvy asked.

'I could ask you the same question,' Greg said with a faint smile.

Morgan laughed and shook his head. 'Spencer and Ogilvy here read about this deadly Náhani and the Indian that lost all his traps, a drunken bum named Trapper-Dan Tall-Totem. When these guys contacted Dan, he wouldn't go on the hunt unless Charley came along too. He said Charley knew more about Náhani than he did. Spencer and Ogilvy footed the tab to bring the Indians to Tatlatui where the white wolf was supposed to have come from. They didn't care about the reward . . . just the trophy. Both Indians said you buddy-buddied with the wolves and would lead them to Náhani sooner or later. You were camped at the upper end of Tatlatui. Dan followed your tracks. Later on after you left, he found where you sat above our camp and watched us through the spyglasses. He was the maddest son of a bitch I ever saw. Too bad about old Dan.'

'What do you mean, "too bad"?' Greg asked.

'He and two or three Tsimshian trappers got crocked one night this summer. At some cabin near Swan Lakes. He shot and wounded a big silver-white wolf. The wolf rushed him and chewed hell out of him before one of the other Indians killed her. They skinned her and took the pelt to Smithers. Everybody swore it was Náhani. Tall-Totem put in claims for the reward but they didn't have enough proof. The wolf was not big enough for Náhani. I think it was about the middle of July when they hauled Tall-Totem to the hospital in Prince Rupert. He died a raving maniac . . . rabies.'

After a long pause, Greg decided to tell the story. He told them about the white wolf he had seen leading a pack at Swan Lakes. He told them of the summer at Nakinilerak, of the long search through the Kitiwanga, of the winter at Kitwanga Lake. He spoke slowly and strung out his experiences with the wolves. Playing for time, he hoped that Náhani would be able to conceal her pack in the dense understorey of the Frog River forest. As Greg talked, the men sat quietly, listening with increased fascination.

It was late afternoon when Greg finished the story. Ogilvy spoke first, respect in his voice. 'The last time we spoke to Trapper-Dan he said, "Náhani won't south again. If she leaves Tatlatui, she'll go to Denetiah. If we follow her to Denetiah, she'll head for the Yukon. No man will ever kill Náhani." That's why we flew here. There were no signs of a two-toed wolf at Tatlatui this summer.'

'There are lots of bush pilots, Greg,' Lex said. 'They've got wives and kids to feed. Plenty of trophy hunters will pay the fee to locate trophy skins. Bounty hunters believe Trapper-Dan killed Náhani.'

Spencer and Ogilvy exchanged glances, they seemed to have reached some decision. 'You can use this extra chow,' Spencer said to Greg. He smiled and emptied the grub box. 'We won't shoot your wolf. Náhani and her legend are already dead. The hunt is over. There's more pleasure in pursuit than in possession. We may even be able to keep your secret.'

'When do you want me to come in and fly you out, Greg?' Lex offered. 'You can't walk out after the end of this month.'

'Thanks, Lex. I know a way out. And thanks for the grub. I was getting low. I appreciate your change of plans. This way we all win, including the big white wolf some people thought was Náhani.'

The hunters and the pilot returned to the plane. Lex Morgan circled the basin twice, dipped his starboard wing on the last pass over Greg's camp, then set his compass on Fort St John.

ON THE THIRD NIGHT following the airborne hunters' visit, Greg sat near the camp log. While he played his harmonica the first ghostly veils of the aurora borealis fluttered across the sky. Náhani walked slowly into camp and sniffed each new item of canned and packaged food. In order to allay her fears of the white-man smell, Greg opened a can of sliced peaches and shared them with her. As they ate, her hackles lowered and she wagged her tail with customary enthusiasm for the things they did together.

'Náhani!' Greg shouted as he put his arm round the startled wolf's neck. 'He's dead! Trapper-Dan is dead! The Náhani myth died with him! We *did* walk in the shadow of a rainbow!'

13. Silence

On October 23, the dawn air had the chilly bite of tinsel rime, and steady breath from the Old Man of the North wheezed across the lake. Greg and Náhani struggled up the gusty slope that had been his 'kitchen garden'. The peaks along the Rocky Mountain horizon were already iced with new snow. Even though her thick winter coat was now fully extended, Náhani tugged at Greg's jeans until he returned to camp and built a fire in the shelter.

Two nights later, frost brought its first magical transformation. Dried stems became elegant banners whose white-fringed outlines did not melt until noon. When evening frost tingled ears and noses, Greg and Náhani sat inside the shelter and leaned close to the fire.

Anxiety permeated the air. Except for mountain goats, jittery herds of animals were on the move. Deer, sheep, elk and caribou retreated into valley meadows far below their windy moorland summer range. Náhani waited until the herds had dispersed over lowland downs. Then she directed two expeditions along Denetiah Creek. After returning 'meat drunk' from both sorties, the troop spent a day chewing at tussocks of dry grama grass on the heath below the rimrock.

On the morning of October 30, all wildlife tracks were rimmed with ice. Frost brought a new glisten to dun-coloured birch and aspen skins. And the frost did not melt. Greg awoke to a grey dawn with a diaphanous veil of ground fog that condensed, then froze, onto evergreen needles. All day the north wind played a brittle, tinkly tune among the fragile crystals. A single grebe that had postponed migration one day too long sat on the lake and called for its mate, who may have been caught by the great grey owl the night before.

At noon, on the last day of October, 1967, Náhani walked into the lean-to. The wind had stopped, but dark clouds seethed over the headland boulders. Greg and the wolf huddled together and listened to the whisper of the first flaky torrent of snow. As softly as the snow, the great grey owl glided to the lake and silenced the remaining grebe's calls. Before sundown a determined south wind folded the clouds back towards the Yukon. The snow on the beach did not melt.

Greg dozed for a few minutes. A whine on the lake side of the log brought him suddenly awake. Náhani hadn't moved, but her entire pack stood with heads and wagging tails lifted high as they faced the lean-to. In twenty-seven pairs of sparkling eyes the young Chimmesyan read the message. For two weeks he and the wolf had delayed that dreaded hour.

Proud and regal, Náhani allowed Greg to embrace her bulky neck. After licking his face and hands, she raised her muzzle and ululated softly. She leapt from the shelter, cleared the log in a single bound, and led her company across the flume and along the north shore. As Trapper-Dan had predicted, Náhani headed for the Yukon.

Greg walked to the runway trail below the dens, cut the hanging steel trap loose, carried it to the beach, and hurled it into deep water.

The last entry in his logbook read: 'Returned to the lean-to. Cut a skein of hair from my temple. Threw it into the fire as my ancestors the Ancient Ones once did. Thanked Gitche Manito for having granted me the privilege of knowing that wolf.'

ROBERT FRANKLIN LESLIE

Throughout his life, Robert Franklin Leslie was passionately interested in wildlife. Sadly, this talented author died in 1990, but his memory is preserved in a number of inspiring novels, among them *In the Shadow of a Rainbow* and *The Bears and I*, which was a hugely popular Condensed Books selection some years ago.

It was from his father, who was one-quarter Cherokee Indian, that Robert Franklin Leslie inherited his profound love of nature in the wild, and an enormous fund of knowledge about plant life, animals and Indian culture. As a boy, he was taken with his brother on numerous expeditions into areas of California and his native Texas, which were, at that time, largely untouched. As an adult, he explored the wilder areas of Canada and Mexico, living for long periods in remote places where he associated closely with wild animals of all kinds.

He is recorded as having told the following anecdote, which encapsulates both his lively character and his lifelong passion: 'When I went camping as a boy, my mother, who was Scottish, used to say that all creatures one-legged, two-legged and three-legged appeared in my sleeping-bag. Once she laughingly threatened to approach my bed with a shotgun because there was always some kind of animal in there with me.'

The author's years spent observing animals in the wild convinced him that men and animals could forge a deeper understanding than many people may realise. 'You'd be surprised how important the eyes can be in communicating with animals,' he once explained. 'All sorts of non-verbal signals can create genuine empathy between us and wild creatures.'

Robert Franklin Leslie spent the last years of his life in California, with his wife Lea. Despite failing eyesight, he continued to write and to impart his knowledge of the wild, right up until his death.

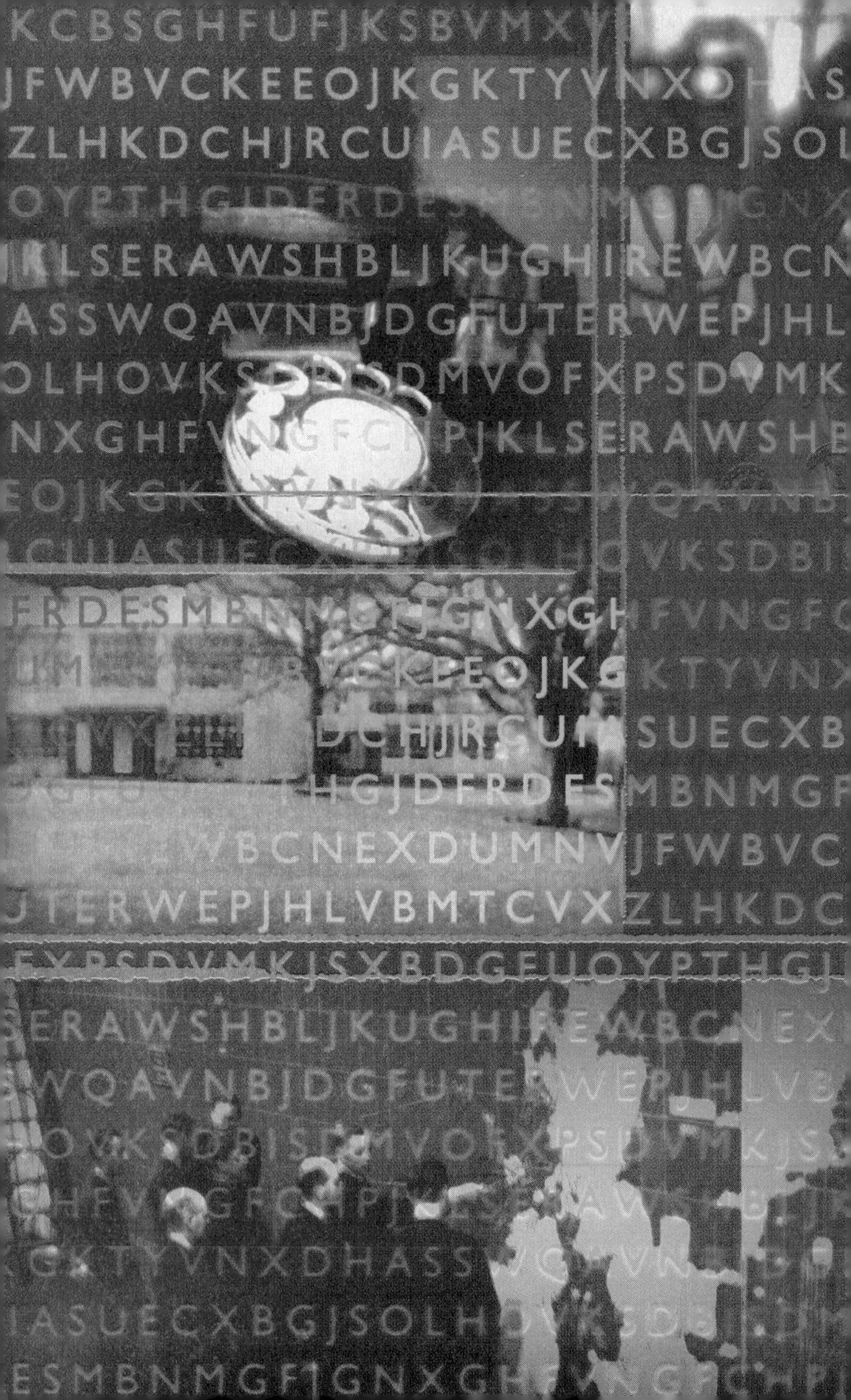

ENIGMA
ROBERT HARRIS

WITH ILLUSTRATIONS BY RAMSAY GIBB

Spring, 1943. At Bletchley Park, teams of men and women are working day and night to decode radio communications picked up from Nazi Germany.

Somewhere in the Atlantic forty-six of Admiral Dönitz's U-boats are lying in wait. Sailing towards them are three Allied convoys laden with 10,000 passengers and a million tons of supplies. Unless Bletchley's code-breakers can crack the enemy's Enigma code, any chance of Allied victory may be lost.

It's time to bring back the brilliant Tom Jericho.

I

Cambridge in the fourth winter of the war: a ghost town.

A ceaseless Siberian wind with nothing to blunt its edge for a thousand miles whipped off the North Sea and swept low across the Fens. It rattled the signs to the air-raid shelters in Trinity New Court and battered on the boarded-up windows of King's College Chapel. It prowled through the quadrangles and staircases, confining the few dons and students still in residence to their rooms. By midafternoon the narrow cobbled streets were deserted. By nightfall, with not a light to be seen, the university was returned to a darkness it hadn't known since the Middle Ages. A procession of monks shuffling over Magdalene Bridge on their way to vespers would scarcely have seemed out of place.

In the wartime blackout the centuries had dissolved.

It was to this bleak spot that there came, in the middle of February 1943, a young mathematician named Thomas Jericho. The authorities of his college, King's, were given less than a day's notice of his arrival—scarcely enough time to reopen his rooms, put sheets on his bed and have more than three years' worth of dust swept from his shelves. And they would not have gone to even that much trouble had not the Provost himself been telephoned by a senior official of His Majesty's Foreign Office, with a request that 'Mr Jericho be looked after until he is well enough to return to his duties'.

'Of course,' replied the Provost, who couldn't for the life of him put a face to the name of Jericho. 'A pleasure to welcome him back.'

As he spoke, he opened the college register and flicked through it until he came to: 'Jericho, T.R.G.; Senior Wrangler, Mathematics Tripos, 1938; Junior Research Fellow at two hundred pounds a year; not seen in the university since the outbreak of war.' Once, perhaps, he would have remembered the name, but the war had shattered the sonorous rhythm of intake and graduation.

'He has recently been engaged upon work of the gravest national importance,' continued the caller. 'We would appreciate it if he were not disturbed.'

'Understood,' said the Provost. 'I'll see to it he is left alone.'

Work of the gravest national importance. The old man knew what that meant. He hung up and looked thoughtfully at the receiver for a few moments, then went in search of the domestic bursar.

A CAMBRIDGE COLLEGE is a village, with a village's appetite for gossip—all the keener when that village is nine-tenths empty—and the return of Jericho provoked hours of analysis among the college staff.

There was, for a start, the manner of his arrival: late on a snowy night, swaddled in a travelling rug in the back of a cavernous official Rover driven by a young chauffeuse in the dark blue uniform of the Women's Royal Navy. Kite, the porter, who offered to carry the visitor's bags to his rooms, reported that Jericho clung to his pair of battered leather suitcases and refused to let go of either, even though he looked so pale and worn out that Kite doubted he would make it up the spiral staircase unaided.

Dorothy Saxmundham, the bedder, saw him next, when she went in the following day to tidy up. He was propped on his pillows, staring out at the sleet pattering across the river, and he never even looked at her, didn't seem to know she was there, poor lamb.

He had only one visitor: the college doctor, who saw him twice and left without saying a word on each occasion.

He took all his meals in his room for the first week—not that he ate very much, according to Oliver Bickerdyke, who worked in the kitchens: he took up a tray three times a day, only to take it away again an hour later barely touched. Bickerdyke's great coup was to come upon the young man working at his desk, wearing a coat over his pyjamas. Normally, Jericho kept the heavy outer door to his study firmly shut, and called politely for his tray to be left outside. But on this particular morning, six days after his dramatic arrival, he had left it slightly ajar. Bickerdyke deliberately brushed the wood inaudibly with his knuckles, and was across the threshold and within a yard of his quarry before Jericho turned round. Bickerdyke just had time to register piles of papers ('covered in figures and circuits and Greek and suchlike'), before the work was hastily covered up and he was sent on his way. Thereafter, the door remained locked.

After listening to Bickerdyke's tale the next afternoon, Dorothy Saxmundham added a detail of her own. Mr Jericho had a small fire grate in his bedroom. In the grate, which she had cleaned that morning, he had obviously burned a quantity of paper.

There was silence while this intelligence was digested.

Bickerdyke suggested he was burning letters. 'Maybe love letters,' he added, with a leer.

'Love letters? Him? Get away.' Kite took off his bowler hat, inspected its frayed brim, then replaced it on his bald head. 'Besides, he ain't had a single letter since he's been here.'

And so they concluded that what Jericho was burning was his work—work so secret nobody could be allowed to see even a fragment of the waste. In the absence of hard fact, fantasy was piled upon fantasy. He was a government scientist, they decided. No, he worked in intelligence. He had had a nervous breakdown. He had friends in high places. He had met Mr Churchill...

In all of which speculation, they would have been gratified to learn, they were absolutely and precisely correct.

THREE DAYS LATER, early on the morning of Friday, February 26, the mystery was given a fresh twist.

Kite was sorting the first delivery of mail when he came across not one but three envelopes addressed to T.R.G. Jericho Esq, originally sent care of the White Hart Inn, Shenley Church End, Buckinghamshire and subsequently forwarded to King's. Kite held one of the envelopes at arm's length and squinted at the postmark.

Bletchley.

There was an old Ordnance Survey map hanging at the back of the lodge, showing the triangle of southern England enclosed by Cambridge, Oxford and London. Bletchley sat astride a big railway junction midway between the two university towns. Shenley Church End was a tiny hamlet northwest of it.

Kite studied the most interesting of the three envelopes. He had been sorting mail for more than forty years and he knew a woman's handwriting when he saw it: clearer and neater, more looped and less angular than a man's. A kettle was boiling on the gas ring at the back of the stove. He glanced round, and within seconds he had stepped into the alcove and was holding the flap of the envelope to the steam. It quickly moistened, curled and opened, and Kite extracted a card.

He had just about read through to the end when he heard the lodge door open. He stuffed the card back into the envelope, dipped his little finger into the glue pot kept ready by the stove, stuck down the flap, then casually poked his head round the corner to see who had come in. He almost had a stroke.

'Good heavens—morning—Mr Jericho—sir . . .'

'Any letters for me, Mr Kite?' Jericho seemed to sway slightly and held on to the counter like a sailor who had just stepped ashore after a long voyage. He was a pale young man, quite short, with dark hair and dark eyes that emphasised the pallor of his skin.

'Not as I've noticed, sir. I'll look again.'

Kite retreated with dignity to the alcove, slipped the damp envelope into the middle of a handful of letters, then came out to the front and performed—even if he said so himself—a virtuoso pantomime of searching through them. 'Ah, yes, here's something. Gracious. And two more.' Kite proffered them across the counter. 'Your birthday, sir?'

'Yesterday.' Jericho stuffed the envelopes into the inside pocket of his overcoat without glancing at them.

'Many happy returns, sir.' Kite watched the letters disappear with a silent sigh of relief. He made another attempt at conversation, remarking on the satisfactory progress of the war in Russia since Stalingrad, but saying that he, Jericho, would surely be more up-to-date about such matters . . .? The younger man merely smiled.

'I doubt if my knowledge about anything is as up-to-date as yours, Mr Kite, not even about myself. Knowing your methods.'

For a moment, Kite was not sure he had heard correctly. He stared sharply at Jericho, who met his gaze and held it with his dark brown eyes, which seemed suddenly to have acquired a glint of life. Then, still smiling, Jericho nodded 'Good morning' and was gone.

That afternoon, when the trio gathered for tea as usual round the coke stove, Kite was able to advance a whole new explanation for Jericho's presence in their midst. Hinting at a man-to-man chat, he asserted with confidence that the young fellow was obviously suffering from a broken heart.

JERICHO DID NOT OPEN his letters immediately. Instead, he squared his shoulders and tilted forward into the wind. After a week in his room, the richness of the oxygen pummelling his face made him feel light-headed. He followed the flagstone path that led through the college and over the little humpback bridge to the meadow beyond. To his left was the college hall; to his right, across a great expanse of lawn, the massive cliff face of the chapel.

He stopped, and a gust of wind forced him half a step backwards. A stone passageway led off from one side of the path. He hesitated, then stepped under the ivy-clad arch into the shadows.

The staircase was just as he remembered it, except that now this wing of the college was closed and the wind had blown dead leaves into the unlit stairwell. But he could still make out the name, one of three painted in white capitals on a wooden board: TURING A.M.

How nervously he had climbed these stairs for the first time in the summer of 1938—a world ago—to find a man barely five years older than himself, as shy as a freshman: the great Alan Turing, the author of *On Computable Numbers*, the progenitor of the Universal Computing Machine. Turing had asked him what he proposed to take as his subject for his first year's research.

'Riemann's theory of prime numbers.'

'But I am researching Riemann myself.'

'I know,' Jericho had blurted out, 'that's why I chose it.'

And Turing had laughed at his outrageous display of hero worship, and had agreed to supervise Jericho's research.

Now Jericho stood on the landing and tried Turing's door. Locked, of course. He tried to remember how the room had looked. Squalor had been the overwhelming impression, with books, notes, letters, dirty clothes and empty bottles strewn across the floor.

Turing had been too shy a man to get to know well. In any case, from the Christmas of 1938 he was hardly ever seen. When, at last, around Easter 1939, not long after the Nazis had marched into Prague, the two men met again, Jericho had nerved himself to say: 'Look, sir, if you don't want to supervise me...'

'It's not that.'

'Or if you're making progress on the Riemann Hypothesis and you don't want to share it...'

Turing had smiled. 'Tom, I can assure you I am making no progress on Riemann whatsoever.' Then he had added, very quietly: 'There are other things now happening in the world, you know, apart from mathematics...'

Two days later, Jericho had found a note in his pigeonhole: *Please join me for a glass of sherry in my rooms this evening. F.J. Atwood.*

Atwood. Nobody refused an invitation from Atwood, Professor of Ancient History, a man with a spider's web of connections in Whitehall. It was tantamount to a summons from God.

'Speak any languages?' had been Atwood's opening question. He was in his fifties, a bachelor, married to the college.

'Only German.' Jericho had learned it to read the great nineteenth-century mathematicians—Gauss, Kummer, Hilbert.

Atwood had nodded and handed over a tiny measure of very dry sherry. 'Do you know the story of Histiaeus, by any chance?'

It was a rhetorical question; Atwood's questions mostly were.

'Histiaeus wished to send a message to his son-in-law Aristagoras, at Miletus, urging him to rise in revolt. However, he feared any such communication would be intercepted. His solution was to tattoo the message onto the shaved head of a trusted slave, wait for his hair to grow, then send him to Aristagoras with a request that he be given a haircut. Unreliable, but effective. Your health.'

Jericho learned later that Atwood told the same stories to all his recruits. Histiaeus and his bald slave gave way to Caesar's letter to Cicero using an alphabet in which *a* was enciphered as *d*, *b* as *e*, *c* as *f*, and so forth. Finally had come the lesson in etymology.

'The Latin *crypta*, from a Greek root meaning "concealed". Hence *crypt*, burial place, and *crypto*, secret. Crypto-communist, crypto-fascist... By the way, you're not either, are you?'

'I'm not a burial place, no.'

'*Cryptogram* . . .' Atwood had raised his sherry to the light and squinted at the pale liquid. '*Cryptanalysis* . . . Turing tells me he thinks you might be rather good...'

As SOON AS JERICHO reached his rooms, he locked the door and laid the three envelopes out on the bed. He considered them for a while, then opened two of them. One was a birthday card from his mother, the other from his aunt. Neither woman had any idea what he was doing, and both, he knew, were guiltily disappointed he wasn't in uniform like the sons of most of their friends.

And the third letter? He turned it over and sniffed it. Was it his imagination, or was there a trace of scent? 'Ashes of Roses' by Bourjois, a minuscule bottle of which had practically bankrupted him just a month earlier. He used his slide rule as a paperknife and slit the envelope open. Inside was a cheap card with a standard message for the circumstances, or so he guessed, never having been in this situation before: *Dearest T . . . always see you as a friend . . . perhaps in the future . . . sorry to hear about . . . in haste . . . much love . . .*

The words blurred before his eyes. He took the card to the grate, knelt and struck a match.

GRADUALLY, HIS DAYS acquired a shape.

He would rise early and work for two or three hours at pure mathematics. Then he would take a nap. He would fill in *The Times* crossword before lunch, timing himself—it never took him more than five minutes to complete it. He managed to solve a series of complex chess problems without using pieces or a board. All this reassured him that his brain had not been permanently impaired.

After the crossword and the chess, he would skim through the war news while trying to eat something at his desk. In the afternoon he would walk, a little further on each occasion—at first confining himself to the college grounds, then strolling through the empty town—before returning, as the light faded, to sit by the gas fire and read

Sherlock Holmes. He began to go into Hall for dinner, although others' attempts at conversation were cut off with a nod. He didn't mind being solitary. An only child, a stepchild, a 'gifted' child—always there had been something to set him apart. At one time he couldn't speak about his work because hardly anyone would understand him. Now he couldn't speak of it because it was classified.

Shark, Enigma, bombe, break, crib—all the weird vocabulary of his secret life—he slowly succeeded in erasing from his conscious mind. Even Claire's image became diffuse. There were still vivid flashes of memory—the lemony smell of newly washed hair, wide grey eyes as pale as water—but increasingly the parts failed to cohere. The whole was vanishing.

'Nurse Time,' the doctor had said, snapping shut his bag of tricks, 'that's who'll cure you, Mr Jericho. Nurse Time.'

Rather to Jericho's surprise, it seemed that the old boy was right. He was going to be well again. 'Nervous exhaustion', or whatever they called it, was not the same as madness after all.

Then, without warning, on Friday, March 12, they came for him.

ON THE DAY IT HAPPENED he had gone, as usual, for his afternoon walk, venturing for once into the frozen countryside. Kite had

gloomily predicted snow, but although it was still cold it was sunny and the sky was a glory—a pure blue dome above the flat landscape of East Anglia. After about an hour he looked at his watch and realised he had better turn back if he was going to reach the college before dark. He strolled back down the darkening lanes and into the town.

Before the war, the 300-yard walk from the college gate to his rooms, at this time of day, at this time of year, had been Jericho's favourite: the footpath running across a carpet of mauve and yellow crocuses, the worn stones lit by ornate Victorian lamps, the spires of the chapel to the left, the lights of the college to the right. But the crocuses were late, the lanterns had not been switched on since 1939, and only one light gleamed faintly in the college. As Jericho walked towards it, he gradually realised it was *his* window.

He stopped, frowning. Had he left his desk light on? As he watched, he saw a movement in the pale yellow square. Two seconds later the light went on in his bedroom.

It wasn't possible, was it?

He started to run. He covered the distance to his staircase in thirty seconds and took the steps like an athlete. 'Claire?' he shouted. 'Claire?' On the landing his door stood open.

'Steady on, old thing,' said a male voice from within. 'You'll do yourself a mischief.'

GUY LOGIE was a tall, cadaverous man, ten years older than Jericho. He lay on the sofa facing the door, a pipe clamped between his teeth, blowing smoke rings at the ceiling. He took his pipe from his mouth and gave an elaborate yawn. 'Hello, Tom.'

'Please, don't get up,' said Jericho sarcastically. 'Please, I insist, make yourself at home. Perhaps I could get you some tea?'

'Tea. What a grand idea.' Before the war Logie had been head of mathematics at a vast and ancient public school. Irony bounced off him like pebbles off an advancing rhinoceros. 'Come here and let me look at you, old thing,' he said. 'You look bloody terrible.'

'I *was* fine.'

'Sorry. We did knock. Your porter chap let us in.'

'Us?'

There was a noise from the bedroom.

'We came in the car with the flag on it. Greatly impressed your Mr Kite.' Logie followed Jericho's gaze to the bedroom door. 'Oh, that? That's Leveret. Don't mind him.' He took out his pipe and called, 'Mr Leveret! Come and meet Mr Jericho.'

A small man wearing a raincoat and trilby appeared at the entrance to the bedroom. 'Good afternoon, sir,' he said.

'What the hell are you doing in there?'

'He's just checking you're alone,' said Logie sweetly.

'Of course I'm bloody well alone!' Jericho threw up his hands in exasperation. 'Guy, for God's sake!'

'I think it's all clear,' said Leveret to Logie. 'I've already closed the blackout curtains in there.' He turned to Jericho. 'Mind if I do the same here, sir?' He didn't wait for permission, but crossed to the small leaded window and drew the curtains.

There was a quarter of a minute's silence. Logie broke it by rubbing his hands and saying, 'Any chance of a fire, Tom? I'd forgotten what this place was like in winter. And tea? You mentioned tea? Would you like some tea, Mr Leveret?'

'I would indeed, sir.'

Jericho opened his mouth to protest, then changed his mind. He got out a box of matches, struck a light and held it to the gas fire. A worm of flame glowed blue and began to spread. He went across the landing to the little kitchen, filled the kettle and lit the gas ring.

Of course they had brought bad news, he thought. What else could it be but bad news? The acting head of Hut 8 wouldn't travel fifty miles across country just to pay a social call. They were going to sack him. *Sorry, old thing, but we can't carry passengers*...Jericho felt suddenly very tired.

He had thought it was her. For about half a minute he had been happy. It was pitiful.

The kettle was beginning to boil. He prised open the tea caddy, unused since 1939, to find age had reduced the tea leaves to dust. Nevertheless, he spooned them into the pot and tipped in hot water.

Logie pronounced it nectar.

THEY SAT in semidarkness, the only illumination provided by the blue glow of the fire. Logie fiddled with his pipe, while Jericho slouched in an easy chair. Leveret had been told to stand guard outside.

'This really is most companionable,' murmured Logie. He made a contented sucking noise through his pipe, then said quietly, 'You know, we've all been terribly worried about you, Tom. I do hope you haven't felt abandoned.'

At this unexpected display of concern, Jericho was surprised and humiliated to find tears pricking at his eyes. He looked down at the carpet. 'I'm afraid I made the most frightful ass of myself, Guy. The worst of it is I can't really remember much of what happened. There's almost a week that's pretty well a blank.'

Logie gave a dismissive wave. 'You're not the first to bust his health in that place, old thing.' He performed a bit more pipe smoker's business, tamping down the tobacco and striking a match.

'It was Shark, wasn't it,' he continued, giving Jericho a shrewd look through a cloud of smoke, 'that did for you?'

'Yes. Perhaps. You could say that.'

Shark nearly did for all of us, thought Jericho.

'But you broke it,' pursued Logie. 'You broke Shark. And then it broke you.'

Jericho had a sudden memory flash of himself on a bicycle, under a starlit sky: a cold night and the cracking of ice. 'Look,' he said, suddenly irritated, 'd'you think we could get to the point here, Guy?'

'This *is* the point, old thing.' Logie stared into the fire, and for the first time Jericho was able to have a good look at his face, ghostly in the blue light. The eye sockets were hollows of darkness. He looked like a man who hadn't slept for a week. 'You know, I was trying to remember, in the car, who decided to call it Shark in the first place.'

'I can't recall,' said Jericho. 'What the devil does it matter anyway? It just emerged. Shark was the perfect name for it. We could tell at once it was going to be a monster.'

'And it was.' Logie puffed on his pipe. 'And it . . . is.'

Something in the way he delivered that last word—some slight hesitation—made Jericho look up sharply.

THE BRITISH NAMED all the German Navy's Enigma ciphers after sea creatures. The main naval cipher they called Dolphin. Porpoise was the Enigma key for Mediterranean surface vessels and shipping in the Black Sea. Oyster was an 'officer-only' variation on Dolphin. Winkle was the 'officer-only' variant of Porpoise.

And Shark? Shark was the operational cipher of the U-boats.

Shark was unique. Every other cipher was produced on a standard three-rotor Enigma machine. But Shark came out of an Enigma with a specially adapted fourth rotor, which made it twenty-six times more difficult to break.

It came into service on February 1, 1942, and it blacked out Bletchley almost completely.

Jericho remembered the months that followed as a prolonged nightmare. Before the advent of Shark, the cryptanalysts had been able to break most U-boat transmissions within a day of interception, allowing ample time to reroute convoys round the German wolf packs. In January, before the blackout, German U-boats destroyed forty-eight Allied ships in the North Atlantic. In February they sank seventy-three. In March, ninety-five.

'The weight of our failure,' said Skynner, the head of the Naval Section, in one of his portentous weekly addresses, 'is measured in the bodies of drowned men.'

Then, on November 24, 1942, nine and a half months into the blackout, came Fasson and Grazier.

Jericho never knew their Christian names: a first lieutenant and an able-bodied seaman. Their destroyer had trapped a U-boat, the *U-459*, in the eastern Mediterranean. They had depth-charged her and forced her to the surface. After the surviving Germans had abandoned the badly holed submarine, the two British sailors had brought off a bundle of secret papers from the radio room, handing them to a boarding party in a boat alongside, and had just gone back for the Enigma machine itself when the U-boat suddenly went bows up and sank. They went down with her—half a mile down, the navy man had said, when he told them the story in Hut 8. *Let's just hope they were dead before they hit the bottom.*

And then he'd produced the code books.

At first glance, they scarcely looked worth the cost of two men's lives: two little pamphlets, the Short Signal Code Book and the Short Weather Cipher, printed in soluble ink on pink blotting paper, designed to be dropped into water by the wireless operator at the first sign of trouble. But to Bletchley they were eventually to be worth more than all the sunken treasure ever raised in history.

U-boats made daily weather reports: air temperature, barometric pressure, wind speed, cloud cover . . . The Short Weather Cipher Book reduced that data to a half-dozen letters. Those half-dozen letters were enciphered on the four-rotor Enigma. The message was then broadcast in Morse code to the German Navy's coastal weather stations, where they used the U-boats' data to compile meteorological reports of their own.

But Bletchley still couldn't break Shark.

Every day the code-breakers, Jericho among them, working from the Short Weather Cipher, fed possible solutions into the bombes—immense electromechanical computers, each the size of a walk-in wardrobe, which made a noise like a knitting machine—and waited. And every day they received no answer. The task was simply too great. Even a message as short as only six letters enciphered on a four-rotor Enigma would theoretically take the best part of a month to decode, as the bombes clattered their way through the billions of permutations.

For three weeks, Jericho worked round the clock, and when he did grab an hour or two's sleep it was only to dream fitfully of drowning men. His brain was beyond tiredness. He began to suffer blackouts.

Curiously enough, the solution, when it came, had nothing to do with mathematics.

It was a Saturday night, the second Saturday in December. At about nine o'clock Logie had sent him home. 'You're going to kill yourself if you go on at this rate, and that won't be any use to anyone, old love, especially you.' So Jericho had cycled wearily back to his digs above the pub in Shenley Church End and had crawled beneath the bedclothes, his mind still churning like a piece of machinery he couldn't switch off.

It had been obvious from the moment Shark had first surfaced that the only long-term solution was to redesign the bombes to take account of the fourth rotor. But that was proving a nightmarishly slow process. If only they could somehow complete the mission Fasson and Grazier had begun so heroically and steal a Shark Enigma machine. But Shark Enigmas were the crown jewels of the German Navy. Only the U-boats had them—and, of course, U-boat communication headquarters in Sainte-Assise, southeast of Paris.

A commando raid on Sainte-Assise, perhaps? A parachute drop? He played with the image for a moment and then dismissed it. Impossible. And, in any case, useless. Even if, by some miracle, they got away with a machine, the Germans would know about it and switch to a different system of communications.

Wait a minute. Jericho sat upright.

If only the U-boats and their controllers in Sainte-Assise were allowed to have four-rotor Enigmas—and Bletchley knew for a fact that that was the case—how the hell were the coastal weather stations deciphering the U-boats' transmissions?

In that instant, Jericho saw the solution.

He seized his dressing gown and pulled it over his pyjamas. He grabbed his overcoat, his scarf, his socks and his boots, and in less than a minute he was on his bike, wobbling down the lane towards the Park. He felt absurdly euphoric, laughing like a madman, steering directly into the frozen puddles along the edge of the road.

He was panting with exertion by the time he reached Hut 8, so much so that he could barely blurt out his discovery and catch his breath at the same time.

His arrival caused a commotion. The night shift all stopped working and gathered in a concerned half-circle round him—and it was clear they thought he had gone mad. They sat him down with a mug of tea and told him to take it again, slowly, from the beginning.

He went through it step by step. Four-rotor Enigmas were restricted to U-boats and Sainte-Assise: correct? Correct. Therefore, coastal stations could only decipher three-rotor Enigma messages: correct? Pause. Correct. Therefore, when the U-boats sent their weather reports the wireless operators must, logically, disengage the fourth rotor, probably by setting it at zero.

After that, everything happened quickly. The best of the weather cribs were laid out on one of the trestle tables. By 4.00am, they had a menu for the bombes. By breakfast, one of the bombe bays was reporting a drop, and a shout went up: 'It's out! It's out!'

It was the stuff of legend.

At midday, Logie telephoned the Admiralty and told the Submarine Tracking Room to stand by. Two hours later, they broke the Shark traffic for the previous Monday, and the teleprincesses, the gorgeous girls in the Teleprinter Room, began sending the translated decrypts down the line to London. By midnight they had broken, translated and teleprintered to the Admiralty ninety-two Shark signals, giving the approximate whereabouts and tactics of half the Germans' U-boat fleet.

Jericho was in the Bombe Hut when Logie found him. Logie clasped Jericho's hand in both of his and shook it vigorously.

'The Prime Minister has just been on the telephone with his congratulations!' he shouted, above the clattering of the bombes.

Logie's voice seemed far away. Jericho bent forward to hear better what Churchill had said, and then the concrete floor melted beneath his feet and he was pitching forward into darkness.

'Is,' said Jericho.

'What, old thing?'

'Just now you said Shark *is* a monster. I know why you've come. You've lost it again, haven't you?'

Logie passed a hand through his thinning hair, and Jericho noticed for the first time that he'd turned quite grey. So it's not just me, he thought; it's all of us, we're all falling to pieces.

'We were still just about ahead of the game when you left,' said Logie. 'You know the drill, of course. You wrote the bloody book. We'd wait for Hut 10 to break the main naval weather cipher, then, by lunchtime, we'd have enough cribs to tackle the day's short weather codes. That would give us three of the four rotor settings, and then we'd get stuck into Shark. The stuff was gold dust, and we were Whitehall's blue-eyed boys.'

Logie glanced at the door and dropped his voice. 'It's an absolute tragedy, Tom. We'd cut losses in the North Atlantic by seventy-five per cent. That's about three hundred thousand tons of shipping a month. The intelligence was amazing. We knew where the U-boats were almost as precisely as the Germans did. Until Tuesday.

'It was about eight in the evening. We got a call from one of the intercept stations: Flowerdown, I think. They'd started picking up something in the early afternoon. A single word, broadcast by Sainte-Assise on the hour, every hour.'

'This word was enciphered in Shark, I take it?'

'No, that's just it. It wasn't in cipher. It wasn't even in Morse. It was a human voice. A man. Repeating this one word: *Akelei.*'

'*Akelei*,' murmured Jericho. '*Akelei* . . . That's a flower, isn't it?'

'Ha!' Logie clapped his hands. 'You are a bloody marvel, Tom. See how much we miss you? We had to go and ask one of the German swots in Hut 3 what it meant. *Akelei*: a five-petalled flower of the buttercup family.'

'*Akelei*,' repeated Jericho. 'A prearranged signal of some sort, presumably? What does it mean?'

'It means trouble, is what it means, old love. We found out just how much trouble at midnight yesterday.' Logie leaned forward, his face grave. '*Akelei* means: "Change the Short Weather Cipher Book." They've gone over to a new one and we haven't a bloody clue what to do about it. They've blacked us out again.'

IT DIDN'T TAKE Jericho long to pack. He'd bought nothing since he arrived in Cambridge. He laid his cases on the bed and moved slowly about the room collecting his possessions, while Logie watched him from the doorway.

'Can I help you with those?' Logie asked, when Jericho had closed the lids on the cases and snapped the locks.

'If I'm well enough to go back to Bletchley, I'm well enough to manage a couple of suitcases.'

He carried them to the door and took a last look round the sitting room: the overstuffed sofa; the scratched chairs; the bare mantelpiece. This was his life, he thought, a succession of cheaply furnished rooms provided by English institutions: school, college, government. He wondered what the next room would be like. Logie opened the door and Jericho turned off the lights.

At the bottom of the dark staircase they could just make out the shape of Leveret, standing guard. He turned round.

'All right, Mr Leveret,' said Logie. 'Mr Jericho's coming with us.'

By the pale beam of Leveret's blackout torch, they made their way through the college. As they passed the porter's lodge and stepped through the gate, Leveret in front of him and Logie behind, Jericho had a curious sensation of being under arrest. This would give Kite something to talk about the next morning, he thought.

The deputy director's Rover was pulled up on the cobbled pavement. Leveret carefully unlocked it and ushered them into the back seat. As Leveret was stowing the suitcases in the boot, Logie said suddenly, 'Who's Claire, by the way?'

'Claire?' Jericho heard his own voice, guilty and defensive.

'When you came up the staircase I thought I heard you shouting "Claire".' Logie gave a low whistle. 'I say, she's not the arctic blonde in Hut 3, is she? You lucky bugger...'

As the big car rocked over the cobbles onto King's Parade and swung left, Logie was still chuckling to himself.

'I bet she jolly well is. You lucky, lucky ...'

2

The night was impenetrable, the cold irresistible. Huddled in his overcoat inside the icy Rover, Tom Jericho reached across and rubbed a porthole in the condensation that had formed on the window beside him. Occasionally, their headlamps flashed on white-washed cottages and darkened inns, but mostly they seemed to travel in a void. There were no streetlights or signposts to guide them; not even a match glimmered in the blackness. They might have been the last three people alive.

Jericho calculated that at Leveret's careful pace they would be lucky to reach Bletchley before midnight. Logie had started to snore within fifteen minutes of leaving King's, his head dropping forward onto his chest each time the Rover hit a bump, but Jericho couldn't sleep. He stuffed his hands deep into his pockets and stared uselessly into the night.

Bletchley, he thought with disgust. Of all the towns in England, why did they have to choose *Bletchley*? Four years ago, he'd never even heard of the place. And he might have lived the rest of his life in happy ignorance had it not been for the glass of sherry in Atwood's rooms in the spring of 1939. How odd it was to trace one's destiny and to find that it revolved around a few sips of pale manzanilla.

Immediately after that first approach, Atwood had arranged for him to meet some 'friends' in London. Thereafter, every Friday morning for four months, Jericho made his way to a dusty office near St James's tube station, where he was initiated into all the secrets of cryptography. And, as Turing had predicted, he was rather good at it.

At the beginning of August 1939, he was formally offered a post at the Government Code and Cipher School at a salary of £300 a year, and was told to go back to Cambridge and await developments. On September 3, the day Britain declared war, a telegram arrived ordering him to report the following morning, with Atwood, to a place called Bletchley Park.

He left King's as soon as it was light, wedged into the passenger seat of Atwood's antiquated sports car. Bletchley turned out to be a small Victorian railway town about fifty miles west of Cambridge. As they rattled down the narrow streets, Jericho had an impression of smoke and soot, of little, ugly terraced houses and the tall black chimneys of brick kilns. They were waved through a pair of high gates by armed sentries. To their right, a lawn sloped down to a lake fringed by large trees. To their left was a mansion—a long, low, late-Victorian monstrosity of red brick and sand-coloured stone.

'Isn't it perfectly hideous?' squeaked Atwood with delight, as he parked outside. 'Built by a stockbroker. *A friend of Lloyd George.*'

Inside, in a panelled drawing room overlooking the lake, sixteen men stood around drinking coffee. Jericho was surprised at how many he recognised. They glanced at one another, embarrassed and amused. *So*, their faces said, *they got you, too.*

Atwood moved among them, shaking hands and making sharp remarks. 'It's not fighting the Germans I object to. It's going to war on behalf of these beastly Poles.' He turned to a handsome, intense-looking young man with a broad, high forehead and thick hair. 'And what's your name?'

'Pukowski,' said the man, in perfect English. 'I'm a beastly Pole.'

Turing caught Jericho's eye and winked.

In the afternoon they were split into teams. Turing was assigned to work with Pukowski on the 'bombe', the giant decryptor which the great Marian Rejewski of the Polish cipher bureau had built to attack Enigma. Jericho was sent to analyse encrypted German radio traffic.

How odd they were, those first eight months of the war, how unreal, how *peaceful*. The staff cycled in each day from their digs. They lunched and dined together in the mansion. In the evenings they played chess and strolled through the grounds, before cycling home to bed.

Jericho's work was pleasantly academic. Three or four times a day, a motorcycle dispatch rider would clatter into the courtyard at the back of the big house, bearing a pouch of intercepted German cryptograms. Jericho sorted them by frequency and call sign, and marked them up on charts in coloured crayons—red for the Luftwaffe, green for the German Army—until gradually, from the unintelligible babble, shapes emerged.

This idyll lasted eight months, until the German offensive in May 1940. Up to then, there had been scarcely enough material for the cryptanalysts to make a serious attack on Enigma. But as the Wehrmacht swept through Holland, Belgium, France, the babble of wireless traffic became a roar. From three or four motorcycle pouches of material a day, the volume increased to two hundred.

It was late one morning, about a week after this had started, that Jericho felt a touch on his elbow and turned to find Turing, smiling. 'There's someone I want you to meet, Tom. Her name's Agnes.'

Jericho tugged his jacket off the back of his chair and walked out into the May sunshine. By this time, the Park had already started to be transformed. Most of the trees at the side of the lake had been chopped down to make way for a series of large wooden huts and a low brick building, outside which a small crowd of cryptanalysts had gathered. Jericho followed Turing through the door. Inside, the noise was deafening, a humming and a clattering, something between a loom and a printing press. A brigadier, an air commodore and two men in overalls were standing round the edge of the room, staring at a large machine full of revolving drums.

'It's the redesigned Polish bombe,' said Turing. 'I thought I'd call her Agnes.' He rested his long, pale fingers tenderly on the metal frame. 'I do hope she works all right...'

Oh yes, thought Jericho, rubbing another porthole into the condensation on the car window; oh yes, she worked all right. And after that the world was different.

DESPITE HIS EARLIER wakefulness, Jericho must have fallen asleep, for when he next opened his eyes Logie was sitting up and the Rover had turned into the road leading to Bletchley's main gate.

'What time is it?' Jericho asked.

'Midnight,' said Logie. 'Shift change.'

Jericho guessed the Park's work force must now be about five or six thousand, toiling round the clock in eight-hour shifts—midnight till eight, eight till four, four till midnight. That meant maybe four thousand people were now on the move, half coming off shift, half going on. Crowds of people had spilled out into the road, most on foot, some on bicycles. A convoy of buses was struggling to get past. Jericho thought, The odds are two to one that Claire's among them. He had a sudden desire to shrink down in his seat, to get away.

Logie was looking at him curiously. 'Are you sure you're up to this, old thing?'

'I'm fine. It's just—it's hard to think it started with sixteen of us.'

'Wonderful, isn't it? And it'll be twice the size next year.'

When they reached the guard post, they had to dig out their identity cards and pass them through the window to an RAF corporal. The sentry studied the cards by torchlight, then directed the beam onto each of their faces in turn. The brilliance struck Jericho like a blow. Behind them, a second sentry was rummaging through the boot. They had tightened up security in the last few weeks.

Their cards were returned. The sentry waved them through. Beside the road was a freshly painted sign showing their new name: 'Government Communication Headquarters'.

The metal barrier came down after them with a crash.

EVEN IN THE BLACKOUT you could sense the size of the place. The mansion and the huts were still the same, but these were now just a fraction of the overall site. Stretching away beyond them was a great factory of intelligence: low, brick-built offices and bombproof bunkers of concrete and steel, tunnels and shelters and guard posts and garages... And more buildings were under construction. There had never been a day when Jericho hadn't heard the racket of mechanical diggers and cement mixers. What was it all for? Sometimes he thought they must be monitoring every radio transmission on the planet.

Leveret drew up the Rover a short distance from the huts. Jericho clambered stiffly from the back seat. A duck splashed somewhere on the lake; its cry made him think of Cambridge, and he had to shake his head to clear the memory.

Logie was explaining that he had a choice: Leveret could take him to his new lodgings and he could have a decent night's kip, or he could come and take a look at things immediately.

'Why don't we start now?' said Jericho. His re-entry into the hut would be an ordeal. He'd prefer to get it over with.

'That's the spirit, old love. Leveret will take your cases round to your new digs.' Logie was fiddling with Leveret's blackout torch. 'What the hell's wrong with this thing? Oh, sod it. Come on.'

He strode away, and after a moment's hesitation Jericho followed. In the darkness, they had to feel their way along the blastproof wall surrounding Hut 8. Logie banged into what sounded like a bicycle and dropped the torch. The impact made it come on. A trickle of light revealed the entrance. There was a familiar smell of lime and damp and creosote. Logie rattled the handle, the door opened and they stepped into the dim glow.

The instant he crossed the threshold, the familiarity of it almost overwhelmed him. A narrow corridor, perhaps twenty yards long, stretched in front of him, with a dozen doors leading off it. The wooden partitions were flimsy, and the noise of a hundred people working at full stretch leaked from room to room: the hum of conversation, the scrape of chair legs on bare boards, the ringing of telephones, the *clack-clack-clack* of the Type-X machines in the Decoding Room. The only tiny difference was that the walk-in cupboard on the right, immediately next to the entrance, now had a nameplate on it: LT KRAMER, US NAVY LIAISON OFFICER.

Familiar faces loomed towards him. Kingcome and Proudfoot were whispering together outside the Catalogue Room and drew back to let him pass. He nodded to them. They nodded in return, but didn't speak. Atwood hurried out of the Crib Room, gawped, then muttered, 'Hello, Tom,' and almost ran towards Research.

Clearly, nobody had expected to see him again.

Logie was oblivious, both to the general astonishment and to Jericho's discomfort. 'Hello, everybody.' He waved to Atwood. 'Hello, Frank. Look who's back! The prodigal son returns!' He stopped outside his office and fiddled with his key for half a minute, then discovered the door was unlocked. 'Come in, come in.'

The room was scarcely bigger than a broom store. It had been Turing's cubbyhole until just before the break into Shark, when Turing had been sent to America. There was a fireproof safe in one corner and a rubbish bin labelled CONFIDENTIAL WASTE. There was a telephone with a red handset. Paper was everywhere—on the desk, on the floor, on the table, on the top of the radiator, in wire baskets and in box files.

'Blast.' Logie had a message slip in his hands and was frowning at it. He took his pipe out of his pocket and chewed on the stem. He seemed to have forgotten Jericho's presence until Jericho coughed to remind him.

'What? Oh. Sorry, old love. The Admiralty's a bit exercised, apparently. Conference in A-Block at eight o'clock with navy brass up from Whitehall. Skynner's in a spin.'

'Does Skynner know I'm back?' Skynner was the head of Bletchley's Naval Section. He'd never cared for Jericho, probably because Jericho had never concealed his opinion of him: that he was a bombast and a bully, whose chief war aim was to greet the peace as Sir Leonard Skynner, OBE, with a seat on the Security Executive.

'Of course he knows you're back, old thing. I had to clear it with him first.' He sat down heavily and looked again at the message. 'Blast.'

Looking at him then, it occurred to Jericho that he knew almost nothing about Logie, though they had worked together for two years and regarded themselves as friends. He didn't even know if Logie was married.

'I'd better go and see him, I suppose. Excuse me, old love.' Logie shouted down the corridor: 'Puck! Puck! Ah, here he comes.'

'So there you are, my dear Guy,' came a familiar voice from outside. 'Nobody knew where to find you.'

Adam Pukowski saw Jericho and stopped dead. He was genuinely shocked. Jericho could almost see his mind struggling to regain control of his features, forcing his famous smile back onto his face. At last he managed it. He even threw his arms round Jericho and hugged him. 'Tom, it's ... I had begun to think you were never returning. It's marvellous.'

'It's good to see you again, Puck.'

Puck was their touch of glamour, their link with the adventure of war. He had arrived in the first week to brief them on the Polish bombe, then flown back to Poland. When Poland fell he had fled to France, and when France collapsed he had escaped across the Pyrenees. When he had popped up again in Bletchley, in the winter of 1940, it was Pinker, the Shakespearean, who had shortened his name to Puck ('that merry wanderer of the night'). His mother was

British, which explained his almost perfect English, distinctive only because he pronounced it so carefully.

'You have come to give us assistance?'

'So it seems.' He shyly disengaged himself from Puck's embrace. 'For what it's worth.'

'Splendid, splendid.' Logie regarded them fondly for a moment, then began rummaging on his desk. He handed Jericho a billeting notice, served on a Mrs Ethel Armstrong, entitling Jericho to lodgings in the Commercial Guesthouse, Albion Street, Bletchley.

'I'm afraid I don't know what it's like. Best I could do.'

'I'm sure it's fine.' Jericho stuffed the chit into his pocket.

'Now don't you go exhausting yourself, my boy,' said Logie. 'We don't expect you to work a full shift. Just come and go as you please. What we want from you is what you gave us last time: insight, inspiration. Isn't that so, Puck?'

'Absolutely.' His handsome face was more haggard, more tired even than Logie's. 'God knows, Tom, we're up against it.'

Logie screwed up the message slip, aimed it at his rubbish bin and missed. 'I'd show you round myself, Tom, but the Skynner waits for no man, as you'll recall. All right with you, Puck? Give him the grand tour?'

'Of course, Guy. As you wish.'

Logie ushered them out into the passage and tried to lock the door behind him, then gave up on it. As he turned he opened his mouth, and Jericho nerved himself for one of Logie's excruciating housemaster's pep talks—something about innocent lives depending on them and the need for them to do their best—but instead his mouth just widened into a yawn.

'Oh, dear. Sorry, old thing. Sorry.'

He shuffled off down the corridor. They heard him mutter something about 'bloody admirals', and he was gone.

HUT 8 WAS THIRTY-FIVE yards long by ten wide, and Jericho could have toured it in his sleep—probably *had* toured it in his sleep, for all he knew. Furnished with trestle tables and folding wooden chairs, it was part of a process that originated somewhere far out in the darkness, maybe two thousand miles away, when the grey hull of a U-boat rose close to the surface and squirted off a radio message to its controllers. The signals were intercepted at various listening posts and teleprintered to Bletchley, and within ten minutes of transmission they were emerging via a tunnel into Hut 8's Registration Room, where they were logged and then passed across the corridor to the Crib Room. Here, the cribsters sifted them for clues: radio-station call signs they recognised (Kiel was JDU, for example), messages whose contents they could guess. Atwood was the champion cribster.

It was in the Big Room next door, whose tables were stacked with cryptograms like ballot papers at an election count, that the cryptanalysts used the cribs to construct possible solutions that could be tested on the bombes. Jericho took in the weak lighting, the fug of tobacco, the college-library atmosphere, and he wondered why— *why?*—he had been so ready to come back. Kingcome and Proudfoot were there, and Upjohn and Pinker and de Brooke, and maybe half a dozen newcomers whose faces he didn't recognise.

Puck was muttering something about back breaks, but Jericho, fascinated by the sight of a young man sitting bold as you please in the seat which had once been his, lost track and had to interrupt him. 'I'm sorry, Puck. What was that?'

'I was saying that from twenty minutes ago we are up-to-date. Shark is now fully read to the point of the cipher change, so now we're going back and picking up the intercepts we missed earlier in the month.' He gave a weak smile and patted Jericho's shoulder. 'Come. I'll show you.'

When a cryptanalyst believed he'd glimpsed a possible break into a message, his guess was sent out of the hut to be tested on a bombe. And if he'd been skilful enough, or lucky enough, then in an hour, or a day, the bombe would churn through half a million permutations and reveal how the Enigma machine had been set up. That information was then relayed to the Decoding Room.

Because of its noise, the Decoding Room was tucked away at the far end of the hut. It contained a dozen British Type-X enciphering machines, which had been modified to mimic the actions of the German Enigma. They were big, cumbersome devices—typewriters with rotors, a plugboard and a cylinder—at which sat young and well-groomed debutantes.

Baxter, who was the hut's resident Marxist, had a theory that Bletchley's work force (which was mainly female) was arranged in what he called 'a paradigm of the English class system'. The wireless interceptors, shivering in their coastal radio stations, were generally working-class and laboured in ignorance of the Enigma secret. The bombe operators, who worked in the grounds of nearby country houses, were petit-bourgeois and had a vague idea. And the Decoding Room girls, in the heart of the Park, were mostly upper-middle-class, and they saw it all: the secrets literally passed between their fingers. They typed out the original cryptogram, and from the cylinder on the right of their Type-X machines a strip of sticky-backed paper, the sort you saw gummed down on telegram forms, slowly emerged, bearing the decrypted plaintext.

'Those three are doing Dolphin,' said Puck, pointing across the room. And this charming young lady here, I believe'—he bowed to her—'has Shark. May we?'

She was young, about eighteen, with curly red hair and wide hazel eyes. She looked up and smiled at him, a dazzling *Tatler* smile, and he leaned across her and began uncoiling the strip of tape from the cylinder. Jericho noticed that as he did so he left one hand resting casually on her shoulder, and he thought how much he envied Puck the ease of that gesture. Puck beckoned him down to read the decrypt:

```
VONSCHULZEQU88521DAMPFER1TANKERWAHRS
CHEILICHAM63TANKERFACKEL . . .
```

Jericho ran his finger along it, translating it in his mind: U-boat commander von Schulze was in grid square 8852 and had sunk one steamship (for certain) and one tanker (probably) and had set one other tanker on fire...

'What date is this?' he asked.

'March the 6th. It's—what?—six days old. Herr Kapitän von Schulze may be five hundred miles away by now. It is of academic interest only, I fear.'

'Poor devils,' said Jericho. *1 DAMPFER1 TANKER* . . . What freezing and drowning and burning were concentrated in that one line! What were the ships called, he wondered, and had the families of the crews been told?

Puck touched Jericho's arm. 'You must be tired. Why don't you go now and rest?'

But Jericho didn't feel like sleeping. 'I'd like to see all the Shark traffic we haven't been able to break. Everything since Wednesday.'

Puck gave a puzzled smile. 'Why? You think we may have missed something, perhaps?'

'Not at all. But...'

'Ah, yes. The celebrated Jericho "intuition".' Puck couldn't conceal his irritation. 'And so from science and logic we descend to superstition and "feelings".'

'For heaven's sake, Puck!' Jericho, too, was becoming annoyed. 'Just humour me, if that's how you prefer to look at it.'

Puck glared at him for a moment, and then, as quickly as they had arisen, the clouds seemed to pass. 'Of course. Forgive me, I'm tired.'

Five minutes later, when Jericho walked into the Big Room carrying the folder of Shark cryptograms, he found that his old seat had been vacated. Someone had also laid out in his place a new pile of jotting paper and three freshly sharpened pencils.

He laid the intercepts out on the table and sat down.

He was back.

IN THE EARLY DAYS at Bletchley, Jericho used to fantasise that some day, when the war was over, he would track down Enigma's German inventor, Herr Arthur Scherbius, and buy him a glass of beer. But then he'd heard that Scherbius had died in 1929, killed—of all ludicrously illogical things—by a runaway horse, and hadn't lived to see the success of his patent.

If he had, he would have been a rich man. By the end of 1942, Bletchley estimated that the Germans had manufactured at least a hundred thousand Enigmas. Every army headquarters had one, as did every Luftwaffe base, every warship, every submarine, every port, every big railway station, and every Gestapo HQ.

In the mansion at Bletchley the cryptanalysts had a roomful of captured Enigmas, and Jericho had played with them for hours. To Jericho, the Enigma machine was beautiful—a masterpiece of human ingenuity. It was small (little more than a foot square by six inches deep), portable and simple to operate. You set up your machine's rotors and plugboard, then typed in your message, and the ciphertext was spelled out, letter by letter, on a panel of small electric bulbs. Whoever received the enciphered message merely had to set up his machine in exactly the same way and type in the cryptogram, and there, spelled out on the bulbs, would be the original plaintext.

The genius lay in the vast number of different permutations even the three-rotor Enigma could generate. You were looking at a machine that had around 150 million million *million* different starting positions. It didn't matter how many Enigma machines you captured, they were useless unless you knew the rotor order, the rotor starting positions and the plugboard connections. And the Germans changed these daily.

The machine had only one tiny—but, as it turned out, crucial—flaw. It could never encipher a letter as itself: an *A* would never emerge from it as an *A*, or a *B* as a *B*, or a *C* as a *C*. *Nothing is ever itself*: that was the guiding principle in the breaking of Enigma.

It was still an immense calculation, one which would have taken a team of human beings several weeks. But Bletchley—and this was what the Germans had never reckoned on—*Bletchley didn't use human beings*. It used calculating machines, or *bombes*. Bletchley had taken espionage into the machine age.

But none of this was of much help to Jericho in breaking Shark.

Shark's four rotors defied every tool he could bring to bear. For a start, Jericho could make only the vaguest guesses at the contents of the cryptograms. In front of him now there were eight long messages originating from Berlin. They would be orders, he supposed, probably directing the U-boats into 'wolf packs' and stationing them in front of the oncoming convoys. The shorter signals—there were

122—had been sent by the submarines themselves. These could contain anything: reports of ships sunk, details of survivors floating in the water, requests for spare parts. Shortest of all were the U-boats' weather messages, but these were encoded with one letter of the alphabet substituting for each piece of information. And then they were enciphered by Shark.

He tapped his pencil against the desk. There was just not enough material to work with. And even if there had been there was still the wretched fourth rotor on the Shark Enigma, the innovation that made U-boat messages twenty-six times more difficult to break than those of surface ships. The engineers had been unsuccessfully struggling to develop a four-rotor bombe for a year.

Hours passed, during which Jericho tried every trick he could think of to prompt some fresh inspiration. This was what it had been like for ten interminable months last year. No wonder he had gone mad. The chorus lines of meaningless letters danced before his eyes. But they were not meaningless. They were loaded with the most vital meaning imaginable, if only he could find it. But where was the pattern? Where was the *pattern*?

IT WAS THE PRACTICE on the night shift for everyone to take a meal break at about four o'clock in the morning. Although the cryptanalysts went off when they liked, the clerks had to leave according to a rota, so that the hut was never short-staffed.

Jericho didn't notice the drift of people towards the door. He had both elbows on the table and was leaning over the cryptograms, his knuckles pressed to his temples.

'"Below the thunders of the upper deep,"' intoned a muffled voice behind him, '"Far, far beneath in the abysmal sea, His ancient, dreamless, uninvaded sleep..."'

'"... The Kraken sleepeth."' Jericho finished the quotation and turned to find Atwood pulling on a purple balaclava. 'Coleridge?'

'Coleridge?' Atwood's face abruptly emerged, wearing an expression of outrage. '*Coleridge?* It's Tennyson, you barbarian. We wondered whether you'd care to join us for refreshment.'

Jericho was about to refuse, but decided that would be rude. In any case, he was hungry. He'd eaten nothing for twelve hours.

'That's kind. Thank you.'

He followed Atwood, Pinker and a couple of the others out into the night. Atwood conducted them past the mansion and through the main gate to the canteen, which lay just beyond the perimeter fence. The dining hall was as big as an aircraft hangar, brightly lit and thunderously noisy, with more than five hundred people sitting down to eat. The din was dreadful, and so was the smell—a blended institutional steam of cabbage and boiled fish and custard, laced with cigarette smoke and damp clothes.

Jericho queued, and didn't pay much attention to the food being slopped on his plate. It was only after he had sat down that he took a good look at it: boiled potatoes and a slab of something ribbed and grey. He stabbed at the lump with his fork, then lifted a fragment cautiously to his mouth. It tasted like congealed cod-liver oil. He winced and put his fork down. 'This is perfectly vile.'

Atwood said, through a full mouth, 'It's whale meat. Don't waste it, dear boy. Don't you know there's a war on? Pass it over here.'

Jericho pushed the plate across the table and tried to swill the taste away with the milk-water coffee.

The pudding was some kind of fruit tart, and that was better, but halfway through it Jericho's appetite finally died. Atwood was giving them his opinion of Gielgud's interpretation of Hamlet, spraying the table in the process with particles of whale, and at that point Jericho decided he'd had enough. He took the leftovers that Atwood didn't want and scraped them into a milk churn labelled PIG SWILL. Then he turned for the door and the salvation of the fresh air.

THIRTY SECONDS LATER, he was picking his way carefully in the darkness towards the guard post, thinking about Shark.

He could hear the *click-click* of a woman's heels hurrying about twenty paces in front of him. The rapid footsteps stopped at the barrier, and a moment later the sentry shone his torch directly into the woman's face. Jericho saw her then, spotlit in the blackout, looking straight in his direction.

It was Claire.

For a fraction of a second, he thought she must have seen him. But he was in the shadows and reeling backwards in panic, and she was dazzled by the light. He couldn't hear what was said, but very quickly the torch was quenched and everything was dark again. And then he heard her moving quickly down the path on the other side of the barrier, *click-click-click*, fading into the night.

He had to catch her up. He stumbled to the guard post, searching for his pass, but he couldn't find the damned thing. The torch came on, blinding him—'Evening, sir', 'Evening, Corporal'—and his fingers were useless, he couldn't make them work. The pass wasn't in his wallet, wasn't in his jacket pockets, breast pocket—he couldn't hear her footsteps now, just the sentry's boot tapping impatiently—and, yes, it *was* in his breast pocket. 'Here you are', 'Thank you, sir', 'Night, sir', 'Night, Corporal', night, night, night...

She was gone.

The sentry's light had robbed him of what little vision he had. He found the edge of the road with his foot and followed its curve. It took him once again past the mansion and brought him out close to the huts. Far away, on the opposite bank of the lake, someone—perhaps another sentry—started to whistle 'We'll Gather Lilacs in the Spring Again', then stopped.

On impulse, he walked down the side of Hut 8, keeping close to the blastproof wall. This brought him to the edge of Hut 6, where the ciphers of the German Army and Luftwaffe were broken. Straight ahead was a narrow alleyway of rough grass, separating Hut 6 from the end wall of the Naval Section. And at the end of that, just visible, was the side of another hut—Hut 3—to which decrypted ciphers were sent for translation and dispatch.

Hut 3 was where Claire worked.

He glanced around. There was no one in sight.

He left the path and started to stumble down the alleyway. The ground was slippery and uneven, and several times he was almost sent sprawling. It took him about a minute to reach Hut 3.

Here, too, was a neck-high concrete wall, designed to shield the flimsy wooden structure from an exploding bomb. He peered over the top. All that was visible were the ghosts of rectangles, where the light seeped round the edges of a row of blacked-out windows.

She must be on duty. She must be working the midnight shift. She might be three feet from where he stood.

He had never been inside Hut 3. For reasons of security, workers in one section of the Park were not encouraged to stray into another without good reason. From time to time, his work had taken him into Hut 6, but Hut 3 was a mystery to him. He had no idea of what she did, but from odd remarks he gathered it was something to do with filing and was 'deadly dull, darling'.

What are you doing, darling Claire? Are you busy with your boring filing, or are you flirting with one of the night-duty officers, or gossiping with the other girls?

Suddenly, about fifteen yards to his left, a door opened. From the oblong of dim light a uniformed man emerged and began to walk towards him. Jericho slid silently to the ground until he was kneeling in the wet earth, and pressed his chest against the wall. The man stopped about ten feet away. He seemed to be listening. Jericho closed his eyes; then he heard a pattering noise, and when he opened them he saw the faint silhouette of the man urinating against the wall. Eventually, the man gave a deep sigh of satisfaction, fumbled with the buttons of his fly and moved away. The door opened and closed again and Jericho was alone.

There was a certain humour in the situation, and later even he was to see it. But at the time he was on the edge of panic. If he were

412

caught, kneeling in the darkness with his ear pressed to a hut in which he had no business, he would have—to put it mildly—a hard time explaining himself. For a moment, he considered simply marching inside and demanding to see her. But his imagination recoiled at the prospect. He might be thrown out. And even if she did appear what did he say? *Oh, hello, darling. I just happened to be passing. You look in good form. By the way, I've been meaning to ask you: Why did you wreck my life?*

He scrambled to his feet. Two minutes later he was back outside the entrance to Hut 8, feeling as if he had been on a cross-country run. Bits of damp grass were sticking to the bottoms of his trouser legs. His knees were sodden. He took out his handkerchief and tried to clean himself up. He had just about finished when he heard the others coming back from the canteen.

He pushed open the door and almost ran down the passage, so that by the time the cryptanalysts appeared in the Big Room he was already seated at his desk, bent over the intercepts, knuckles to his temples, eyes closed.

He stayed like that for three hours. At seven, there was a rattle against the outside wall as the blackout shutters were unfastened. A pale grey light filtered into the hut.

What was she doing, hurrying into the Park at that time of night? That was what he did not understand. Of course, the mere fact of seeing her again was disturbing. But it was the circumstances that troubled him more. She had not been in the canteen, he was sure of that. He had scrutinised every table, every face—had been so distracted he had barely even looked at what he was being given to eat. But if she had not been in the canteen, where had she been? Had she been with someone? Who? And the way she had vanished . . . Could she really have walked the entire distance to the hut in the time it took him to fumble for his pass?

Just before eight o'clock he gathered the cryptograms together and slipped them into the folder. All around him the cryptanalysts were preparing to go off shift—rubbing at tired eyes, briefing their replacements. Nobody noticed Jericho walk quickly down the corridor to Logie's office. He knocked once. There was no reply. He tried the door. As he remembered: unlocked.

He closed it behind him, picked up the telephone and dialled zero. On the seventh ring a sleepy operator answered. His mouth was almost too dry to get the words out. 'Duty officer, Hut 3, please.'

Almost immediately a woman's voice answered, and Jericho asked, 'Do you have a Miss Romilly there?' He didn't need to disguise his voice: it was so strained and quavering it was unrecognisable.

'No, I'm afraid it's Claire's day off. She won't be back on

duty until eight tomorrow morning. Can I help?'

Jericho gently replaced the receiver in its cradle just as Logie threw the door open behind him.

'Oh, *there* you are, old thing. I was looking for you...'

DAYLIGHT DIMINISHED the huts.

The blackout had touched them with a certain mystery, but the morning showed them up for what they were: squat and ugly, with an air of dereliction. A duck waddled across the path from the lake looking for food, and Logie almost kicked it as he strode past.

He had not been in the least perturbed to find Jericho in his office, and Jericho's carefully prepared excuse—that he was returning the Shark intercepts—had been waved away. 'Just dump 'em in the Crib Room and come with me. We've been summoned.'

Across the northern edge of the lake, next to the huts, was A-Block, a long, two-storey affair with brick walls and a flat top. Logie led the way up a flight of concrete steps and turned into a corridor, at the far end of which was a door.

When they reached the door, Logie patted Jericho on the arm. 'Don't say anything when we get inside, Tom. You're only here for show, old love.'

Only here for show, thought Jericho angrily. What the hell does that mean? So that Skynner can put on a good show for the Yanks? But before he could ask, Logie had opened the door and all he could hear was Skynner—'We must expect these setbacks from time to time'—and they were on.

THERE WERE eight men in the room. Leonard Skynner, the head of the Naval Section, sat at one end of the table, with Atwood to his right and Baxter to his left. Gathered round the other end were five officers in dark blue naval uniform, two American and three British, one of them an admiral. They looked grim.

The eighth man, in civilian clothes, had his back to Jericho. He turned as they came in, and Jericho registered a lean face with fair hair.

Skynner stopped speaking. He stood and held out a meaty hand. 'Come in, Guy, come in, Tom.' He was a big, square-faced man, with thick black hair and wide bushy eyebrows. He beckoned to the newcomers eagerly, obviously thankful to see Allied reinforcements. 'This is Guy Logie,' he said to the admiral, 'our chief cryptanalyst, and Tom Jericho, of whom you may have heard. Tom was instrumental in getting us into Shark before Christmas.'

The admiral regarded Jericho blankly through a fog of tobacco, without the slightest interest. Skynner rattled off the introductions, his arm sweeping round the table like the hand of a clock. 'This is Admiral Trowbridge, Lieutenant Cave, Lieutenant Villiers.' One of the British lieutenants had an eye patch. 'Commander Hammerbeck, Lieutenant Kramer, US Navy Liaison. Mr Wigram is observing for the Cabinet Office.' Skynner gave a little bow to everybody and sat down again. He was sweating.

Jericho and Logie each collected a folding chair from a stack beside the table and took up a position next to Baxter.

Almost the whole of the wall behind the admiral was taken up by a map of the North Atlantic. Clusters of coloured discs showed the positions of Allied convoys and their escorts: yellow for the merchantmen, green for the warships. Black triangles marked the suspected whereabouts of German U-boats.

One of the Royal Navy men—Cave, the one with the eye patch—received a nod from the admiral and started speaking. 'Perhaps, if you've finished outlining your problems, it might be helpful for us now to set out the operational situation.' His chair scraped on the bare floor as he rose to his feet.

Jericho passed his hand over his unshaven chin. He couldn't make up his mind whether to keep his overcoat on or take it off. On, he decided: the room was cold, despite the number of people in it. He undid the buttons and loosened his scarf. As he did so, he noticed the admiral glowering at him. They couldn't believe it, these senior officers, whenever they came up to visit: the lack of discipline, the scarves and cardigans, the first-name terms.

The one-eyed naval officer had picked up a pointer and was standing in front of the Atlantic chart, holding a sheaf of notes. 'It must be said, unfortunately, that the news you've given us couldn't have come at a worse moment. No fewer than three convoys have left the United States in the past week and are presently at sea. Convoy SC-122'—he rapped it once with the pointer, hard, as if he had a grudge against it, and read out his notes—'departed New York last Friday. Carrying fuel, oil, iron ore, steel, wheat, bauxite, sugar, refrigerated meat, zinc, tobacco and tanks. Fifty merchant ships.'

Cave spoke in a clipped, metallic voice, without looking at his audience. His one good eye was fixed on the map. 'Convoy HX-229.' He tapped it. 'Departed New York Monday. Forty merchant vessels. Carrying meat, explosives, lubricating oil, refrigerated dairy produce, manganese, lead, timber, phosphate, diesel oil, aviation spirit, sugar and powdered milk.' He turned to them for the first time. The whole of the left side of his face was a mass of purple scar tissue. 'That, I might say, is two weeks' supply of powdered milk for the entire British Isles.'

There was some nervous laughter.

Again the pointer crashed down. 'And Convoy HX-229A. Left New York Tuesday. Twenty-seven ships. Similar cargoes to the others. Three convoys. A total of one hundred and seventeen merchant ships, with a gross registered tonnage of just under one million tons, plus cargo of another million.'

One of the Americans—it was the senior one, Hammerbeck—raised his hand. 'How many men involved?'

'Nine thousand merchant seamen. One thousand passengers, mainly servicemen. Some ladies from the American Red Cross. A party of Catholic missionaries.'

'And whereabouts are the U-boats?'

'Perhaps I might let my colleague answer that.'

Cave sat down and the other British officer, Villiers, took the floor. He flourished the pointer.

'Submarine Tracking Room had three U-boat packs operational as of zero-zero-hundred Thursday—heah, heah and heah.' His accent barely qualified as recognisable English. It was the sort that pronounced 'cloth' as 'clawth' and 'really' as 'rarely', and when he spoke his lips hardly moved.

Hammerbeck leaned forward. 'Zero-zero *Thursday*? You mean more than thirty hours ago?' His hair was the colour and thickness of steel wool, close-cropped to his scalp. 'Where the hell are they now?'

'I'm afraid I've no ideah. I thought that was why we were heah. They've blipped awf the screen.'

Admiral Trowbridge lit another cigarette from the tip of his old one and stared at Hammerbeck through small, rheumy eyes.

Again the American raised his hand. 'How many subs are we talking about in these three wolf packs?'

'I'm sorry to say, ah, they're quite large. We estimate forty-six.'

416

'Let me get this straight,' said Hammerbeck. 'You're telling us that one million tons of merchant shipping, with ten thousand people on board, including ladies of the American Red Cross, is steaming towards forty-six U-boats, and you have no idea where those U-boats are?'

'I'm rather afraid I am, yes.'

'Well, I'll be damned,' said Hammerbeck, sitting back in his chair. 'And how long before they get there?'

'That's hard to say.' It was Cave again. 'The SC convoy is making about seven knots an hour. The HXs are both faster: one ten knots, one eleven. I'd say we've got three days maximum. After that, they'll be within operational range of the enemy.'

Hammerbeck had begun whispering to the other American. He was shaking his head. The admiral leaned over and muttered something to Cave, who said quietly, 'I'm afraid so, sir.'

'Gentlemen, please, if I may?' said Skynner loudly, bringing the meeting back to order. 'I think we should guard against too much pessimism. The Atlantic does cover thirty-two million square miles, you know.' He risked a laugh. 'That's an awful lot of ocean.'

'Yes,' said Hammerbeck drily, 'and forty-six is one hell of a lot of U-boats.'

'I agree. It's probably the largest concentration of hearses we've faced,' said Cave. 'I'm afraid we must assume the enemy will make contact. Unless, of course, we can find out where they are.'

He gave Skynner a significant look, but Skynner ignored it and pressed on. 'And let's not forget these convoys have an escort.'

'Indeed.' That was Cave again. 'They have an escort of'—he consulted his notes—'seven destroyers, nine corvettes and three frigates. Plus various other vessels.'

'Under an experienced commander . . .'

The British officers glanced at one another and then at the admiral. 'Actually, it's his first command,' Cave murmured.

'Good God!' Hammerbeck rocked forward in his chair and brought his fists down on the table.

'How long will this intelligence blackout last?' This was the first time the admiral had spoken and everyone turned towards him. 'Will it be over in four days, d'you think?'

The question was addressed directly to Skynner and now they all turned to look at him. He was an administrator, not a cryptanalyst— he'd been vice-chancellor of some northern university before the war—and Jericho knew he hadn't a clue.

Skynner said carefully: 'It's possible.'

'Yes, well, all things are possible.' Admiral Trowbridge gave an unpleasant rasping laugh. 'Is it likely?'

'We'll give it every priority.'

'I know damn well you'll give it every priority, Leonard. That's not the question.'

'Well, sir, as you press me, sir, yes.' Skynner stuck his big jaw out heroically. In his mind's eye, he was steering his ship manfully into the face of the typhoon. 'Yes, I think we may be able to do it.'

You're mad, thought Jericho.

'And you all believe that?' The admiral stared hard in their direction. He had eyes like a bloodhound's, red-lidded and watery.

Logie was the first to break the silence. He looked at Skynner and scratched the back of his head. 'I suppose we do have the advantage of knowing more about Shark than we did before.'

Atwood nodded judiciously. Jericho inspected his watch.

'And you?' said the admiral. 'What do *you* think?'

Jericho was aware that the room had gone quiet. The civilian, Wigram, was staring at him with particular curiosity. He felt a spasm of irritation.

Afterwards, Jericho was to think about this moment many times. What made him act as he did? Was it tiredness? Was he still ill? Or was he so distracted by the thought of Claire that he wasn't thinking straight? All he remembered for certain was an overwhelming feeling of annoyance. *You're only here for show, old love.* So keep your views to yourself and don't ask questions.

'Actually, I'm not sure I am as optimistic as my colleagues.'

Skynner interrupted him at once. You could almost hear the klaxons going off in his mind, see the big guns swivelling skywards as HMS *Skynner* came under threat. 'Tom's been ill, sir, I'm afraid. He's been away from us for the best part of a month...'

'Why not?' The admiral's tone was dangerously friendly. 'Why aren't you optimistic?'

'...so I'm not sure he's altogether fully *au fait* with the situation. Wouldn't you admit that, Tom?'

'Well, I'm certainly *au fait* with Enigma, ah, Leonard.' Jericho could hardly believe his own words. He plunged on. 'I've just spent the past eight hours reviewing the Shark material, and, ah, forgive me if I'm speaking out of turn, but it seems to me we are in a very serious situation.'

'But you *were* breaking it successfully before?'

'Yes, but we'd been given a key. The weather cipher was the key that unlocked the door. The Germans have now changed the weather cipher. That means we've lost our key. Unless there's been some development I'm not aware of, I don't understand how we're going to...' Jericho searched for a metaphor '...pick the lock.'

The younger American naval officer, Kramer, said, 'And you still haven't gotten those four-wheel bombes. Surely if we had a few of them right now we wouldn't need the weather cribs?'

'Just stop there for a moment,' said the admiral impatiently. 'I'm a sailor, and an old sailor at that. I don't understand all this—*talk*—about keys and cribs and bombs with wheels. Will somebody give me a straight answer to a straight question? Will this blackout definitely be over in four days' time or won't it? Yes or no?'

Skynner's shoulders sagged. 'No,' he said wearily. 'If you put it like that, sir, I can't say *definitely* it will be over, no.'

'Thank you. So, if it isn't over in four days, when will it be over? You. You're the pessimist. What do you think?'

Conscious of everyone watching him, Jericho spoke carefully. 'It's very hard to say. All we have to measure it by is the last blackout.'

'And how long did that go on?'

'Ten months.'

It was as if he had detonated a bomb. Everybody made a noise. The navy men shouted. The admiral started coughing. Logie groaned. Skynner, shaking his head, said, 'That really is defeatist of you, Tom.' Even Wigram, the fair-headed man, gave a snort and stared at the rafters, smiling at some private joke.

'I'm not saying it will definitely take us ten months,' Jericho resumed, when he could make himself heard. 'But I think that four days is unrealistic. I'm sorry. I do.'

There was a pause, and then Wigram muttered, '*Why*, I wonder . . .'

'Mr Wigram?'

'Sorry, Leonard. Thinking aloud. I was just wondering *why* Dönitz should have decided to change this *particular* cipher, and why *now*. Tell me, Leonard, how many people know about this weather cipher and how important it is to us?'

'Really, Douglas,' laughed Skynner, 'what *are* you suggesting?'

'How many?'

'Guy?'

'A dozen, perhaps,' Logie answered.

'Make me a little list, would you? Thanks, Leonard.' Wigram resumed his examination of the ceiling.

The silence that followed was broken by a long sigh from the admiral as he stubbed out his cigarette. 'I think I gather the sense of the meeting. I can't pretend it's the happiest of messages to take back to the First Sea Lord.' He reached for his briefcase and turned to Cave: 'I'd like a report twice a day.'

'Yes, sir.'

'So.' The admiral stood, and immediately they all got to their feet. 'I suggest we reconvene this meeting as and when there are developments to report. Which, with luck, will be within four days.' He paused. 'It's not just one million tons of shipping and ten thousand men, you know. It's one million tons of shipping and ten thousand men *every two weeks*. And it's not just the convoys. It's our chances of invading Europe and driving the Nazis out. It's everything. It's the whole war.' He gave a wheezing laugh. 'Not that I want to put any pressure on you, Leonard.' He nodded. 'Good morning, gentlemen.'

As they mumbled their 'good morning sirs', Jericho heard Wigram say quietly to Skynner, 'I'll talk to you later, Leonard.'

They listened to the visitors clatter down the concrete stairs, and then to the crunch of their feet on the path outside. Skynner's lips were compressed as he gathered up his papers. For what seemed a long time, nobody spoke.

'Well,' said Skynner eventually, 'that was a triumph. Thank you, Tom. I'd forgotten what a tower of strength you could be.'

'It's my fault, Leonard,' said Logie. 'Bad briefing. Should have put him in the picture better. Sorry.'

'Why don't you just get back to the hut, Guy? In fact, why don't you all go back, and then Tom and I can have a little chat?'

The moment the door closed behind the three cryptanalysts, Skynner said, 'I never wanted you back.'

'Logie didn't mention that.' Jericho folded his arms to stop his hands shaking. 'He said I was needed here.'

'You're a wreck. You're ruined. You've cracked once before under pressure and you'll do it again, as your little performance just now showed. You've outlived your usefulness to us.'

'Then why am I here? I never asked to come back.'

Skynner leaned his large bottom against the edge of the table. He spoke in a friendly tone. 'Logie thinks highly of you. And, I'll be honest, after Turing, you probably have—or, rather, *had*—the best reputation of any cryptanalyst on the Park. A little bit of a legend, Tom. Bringing you back, letting you attend this morning, was a way of showing our masters how seriously we take this, ah, temporary crisis. It was a risk. But obviously I was wrong. You've lost it.'

Jericho was not a violent man. He had never hit another person, not even as a boy. But there was a heavy brass ashtray on the table, brimful of cigarette stubs, and Jericho was seriously tempted to ram it into Skynner's smug face.

'It was so much simpler in the old days, wasn't it?' said Skynner, who had begun to pace the floor. 'A country house. A handful of eccentrics. Nobody expecting very much. You potter along. Then suddenly you're sitting on the greatest secret of the war.'

'And then people like you arrive.'

'That's right: people like myself are needed to make sure this remarkable weapon is used properly.' Skynner stopped pacing. He was a big man, nearly a foot taller than Jericho. He came up very close, and Jericho could smell the stale sweat on his clothes.

'You've no conception of this place any more. No idea of the problems. The Americans, for instance. In front of whom you've just humiliated me. We're negotiating a deal with the Americans that—' He stopped himself. 'Never mind. Let's just say that when you— when you *indulge* yourself as you just did, you can't even conceive of the seriousness of what's at stake. I'm going to have you transferred out of Bletchley. You can't return to civilian life, of course, not knowing what you know. Still, I hear the Admiralty's on the lookout for statisticians. Dull stuff, and who knows? Perhaps you'll meet a nice girl. Someone more—how shall we say?—more *suitable* for you than the person I gather you *were* seeing.'

Jericho did try to hit him then, but not with the ashtray, only with his fist, which in retrospect was a mistake. Skynner stepped to one side, the blow missed and he grabbed Jericho's forearm, digging his fingers hard into the soft muscle.

'You are an ill man, Tom. And I am stronger than you, in every way.' Abruptly, he let go of the arm. 'Now get out of my sight.'

JERICHO LEANED against the outside wall of A-Block and waited for his pulse to return to normal. What had he done?

God, but he was tired. He needed to lie down and get some rest. He pulled out the billeting chit and squinted at it. Where was Albion Street? He had a vague memory. He would know it when he saw it.

He pushed himself away from the wall and began to make his way towards the road that led to the main gate. A small black car was parked about ten yards ahead, and as he came closer the driver's door opened and a figure in a blue uniform appeared.

'Hi. Going home? Can I give you a ride?'

Jericho stared with surprise. It was one of the Americans. 'Lieutenant Kramer? Thank you, but it's only a short walk.'

'Aw, come on.' Kramer patted the roof of the car. 'I just got her. It'd be my pleasure. Come on.' Jericho was about to decline again when he felt his legs begin to crumple.

'Whoa there, fella.' Kramer sprang forward and took his arm. 'You're all in. Long night, I guess?'

Jericho allowed himself to be guided to the passenger door and pushed into the front seat. He guessed the little Austin must have been someone's pride and joy until petrol rationing forced it off the road. Kramer clambered in on the other side, slammed the door and started the engine.

The car was carefully inspected at the main gate. The barrier rose and they headed out along Wilton Avenue.

'Which way?'

'Left, I think.'

Kramer turned into the lane that led down to the town. His square-cut, handsome face had a faded tan that suggested service overseas. He was about twenty-five and looked formidably fit.

'I guess I'd like to thank you for that.'

'Thank me?'

'At the conference. You told the truth when the others all talked bullshit. "Four days"—Jeez!'

'They were just being loyal.'

'Loyal? Come on, Tom. D'you mind if I call you Tom? I'm Jimmy, by the way. They'd been fixed.'

'I don't think this is a conversation we should be having . . .' The dizziness had passed, and now it occurred to Jericho that the American must have been waiting for him to emerge from the meeting. 'This will do fine, thank you. Just pull over here, please.'

Kramer swerved into the kerb beside a row of small cottages, braked and turned off the engine.

'Listen, will you, Tom, just a minute? Three months after Pearl Harbor, suddenly we're losing ships like we're going out of business. But nobody tells us why. Finally, it's getting so bad we ask you guys what's happened to all this great intelligence you used to have.' He jabbed his finger at Jericho. 'Only *then* are we told the Germans have brought in Shark.'

'I can't listen to this,' said Jericho. He tried to open the door, but Kramer leaned across and seized the handle.

'I'm not trying to poison your mind against your own people. I'm just trying to tell you what's going on here. After we were told about Shark last year, we started to do some checking. Fast. D'you know how many bombes you guys had by the end of last summer? After two years of manufacture? Fifty! And d'you know how many our people in Washington said they could build within *four months*? Three hundred and sixty!'

'Well, build them then,' said Jericho, staring straight ahead, 'if you're so bloody marvellous.'

'Oh, no,' said Kramer. 'That's not allowed. Enigma is a British baby. Official. Any change in status has to be negotiated.'

Jericho shut his eyes and heard Skynner's voice: *You've no conception of this place any more . . . We're negotiating a deal with the Americans . . . You can't even conceive of the seriousness . . .* Now, at least, he understood the reason for Skynner's anger. His little empire was mortally threatened by Shark. But the threat came not from Berlin. It came from Washington.

'Don't get me wrong,' Kramer was saying. 'I think what you've all achieved is astounding. Brilliant. But things can't go on like this. Not enough bombes. Not even enough typewriters. Those huts. Jeez!'

Jericho felt too tired to argue. Besides, he knew enough to know that it was true, all true: not enough clerks, not enough typists, the factory at Letchworth that made the bombes short of parts, short of manpower. It all came down to money in the end. The Poles had had to give Enigma to the British. Now the Brits would have to share it with the Yanks.

'I can't have anything to do with this. I've got to get some sleep. Thanks for the lift.'

He reached for the handle and was halfway out of the door when Kramer said, 'I heard you lost your old man in the last war.'

Jericho froze. 'Who told you that?'

'I forget. Does it matter?'

'No. It's not a secret.' Jericho massaged his forehead. He had a headache coming on. 'He was wounded by a shell at Ypres, before I was born. He never came out of hospital. He died when I was six.'

There was a moment's silence. Jericho got out of the car.

'My brother died,' said Kramer suddenly. 'One of the first. He was in the merchant marine. Liberty ships.'

Of course, thought Jericho.

'This was during the Shark blackout, I suppose?'

'You got it.' Kramer looked bleak, then forced a smile. 'Let's keep in touch, Tom. Anything I can do for you—just ask.'

He reached over and pulled the door shut with a bang. Jericho stood alone on the roadside and watched Kramer execute a rapid U-turn then head at speed up the hill towards the Park.

Bletchley was a railway town. The great main line from London to Scotland split it down the middle, and then the smaller branch line from Oxford to Cambridge sliced it into quarters, so that wherever you stood there was no escaping the trains.

The Commercial Guesthouse, Albion Street, was about five minutes' walk from Bletchley Park and backed onto the main line. Its owner, Mrs Ethel Armstrong, was, like her establishment, a little over fifty years old, solidly built, with a forbidding late-Victorian aspect. Like the other townspeople, she had no idea of what went on in the grounds of the mansion up the road, and even less interest. It was profitable, which was all that mattered to her. She charged thirty-eight shillings a week and expected her five residents, in return for meals, to hand over all their food-ration coupons. As a

result, by the spring of 1943, she had £1,000 in War Savings Bonds and enough edible goods hoarded in her cellar to open a medium-sized grocery shop.

It was on the Wednesday that one of her rooms had become vacant, and on the Friday that she had been served a billeting notice requiring her to provide accommodation to a Mr Thomas Jericho. Then, late that same night, two suitcases were delivered.

Their owner arrived at nine o'clock on Saturday morning. He wasn't very tall. He was thin, bookish, ill-looking. He hadn't shaved and was as white as—well, she was going to say 'as a sheet', but she hadn't seen sheets that white since before the war, certainly not in her house. He was pleasant enough, though.

She always demanded a month's rent in advance and he paid up without a murmur. When she mentioned his ration book, he looked at her for a moment, very puzzled, and then said, 'Do you mean this?'

Do you mean this? As if he'd never seen one before! He gave her the little brown booklet—the precious weekly passport to four ounces of butter, eight ounces of bacon, twelve ounces of sugar—and told her she could do what she liked with it. 'I've never had any use for it.'

She tucked the money and the ration book into her apron before he could change his mind, and led him upstairs.

Now Ethel Armstrong was the first to admit that the fifth bedroom of the Commercial Guesthouse was not up to much. It was at the end of the passage, overlooking the railway line, and the only furniture in it was a single bed and a wardrobe. It was so small that the door wouldn't open properly, because the bed got in the way. In two and a half years, it must have had thirty different occupants. None had stayed more than a couple of months and some had refused to sleep in it at all. But this one just sat on the edge of the bed and said wearily, 'Very pleasant, Mrs Armstrong.'

'Well, then,' she said, after explaining the rules of the house, 'I'll leave you to get some peace and quiet.'

Two boxes of personal effects and an ancient bicycle were brought round late that morning.

TOM JERICHO sat on the edge of the bed for a couple of minutes after listening to her footsteps descending the stairs.

It was cold in the room and he started to shiver. He felt desperately tired. He opened one of his suitcases, took out a pair of pyjamas and changed into them quickly. He thought about unpacking the rest of his clothes, but decided against it. He might be out of Bletchley by the next morning. That was a point—he passed his hand across his face—he'd just given away over seven pounds, more than a week's salary, for a room he might not need. He drew the curtains, lay down on the lumpy mattress and pulled the blankets up under his chin.

For three years Jericho had led a nocturnal life, rising with the darkness and going to bed with the light, but he'd never got used to it. Lying there listening to the distant sounds of a Saturday morning made him feel like an invalid. He closed his eyes and all he could see was the chart of the North Atlantic. He opened them; the bed shook slightly as a train went by, which reminded him of Claire, and his first glimpse of her on the 15.06 out of Euston.

This must have been—what?—a week after the break into Shark? A couple of days before Christmas, anyway. He and Logie, Puck and Atwood had been ordered to present themselves at the office block near St James's tube station from which Bletchley Park was run. 'C', the boss himself, had made a little speech, and in recognition of their 'vital breakthrough' they had each received an iron handshake from the Prime Minister himself and an envelope containing a cheque for £100. Afterwards, slightly embarrassed, they'd said goodbye to one another on the pavement and gone their various ways: Logie to lunch at the Admiralty, Puck to meet a girl, Atwood to a concert at the National Portrait Gallery—and Jericho back to Euston to catch the train to Bletchley.

There would be no more cheques now, he thought. Perhaps Churchill would ask for his money back.

He turned his face to the wall, and darkness closed around him.

THE DREAM is a memory, the memory a dream.

A teeming station platform—iron girders and pigeons fluttering against a filthy glass cupola. A line of soldiers, bent sideways by the

*weight of kitbags, runs towards the guard's van. A sailor kisses a preg-
nant woman in a red hat. Salesmen in threadbare overcoats, a pair of
thin and anxious mothers in tatty furs, a tall, blonde woman in a well-
cut, ankle-length grey coat, trimmed with black velvet. A prewar coat,
he thinks, nothing so fine is made nowadays...*

*She walks past the window, and he realises with a jolt that she's
noticed he is staring at her. When he looks again, she's actually stepping into his compartment. Every seat is taken. She hesitates. He
stands to offer her his place. She smiles her thanks and gestures to show
there's just sufficient room for her to squeeze between him and the
window. He nods and sits again with difficulty.*

*Doors slam along the length of the train; a whistle blows; they
shudder forward. He's wedged so tightly he can barely move. Such
intimacy would never have been tolerated before the war, but nowadays men and women are always being thrown together, often literally
so. Her thigh is pressed to his, their legs touch. Her stocking rustles
against his calf. He can feel the warmth of her and smell her scent.*

*He looks past her and pretends to stare out of the window at the ugly
houses sliding by. Her face in profile is not conventionally pretty, but
striking—angular, strong—he supposes 'handsome' is the word for it.*

*The compartment is packed. The air smells strongly of cheap ciga-
rettes and unwashed bodies. But gradually, for Jericho, all this begins to
disappear. There are just the two of them, rocking with the train.
Where they touch, his skin is burning.*

*He wonders how far she's going. Each time they stop at one of the
little stations, he fears she might get off. But no: she continues to stare
down at her copy of* The Times, *folded up very small so that she can
hold it in one hand. The hinterland of north London gives way to countryside, dreary in the darkening December afternoon.*

*An hour passes, then she suddenly says, 'German town partly in
French disagreement with Hamelin.'*

He isn't sure if the remark is addressed to him. 'I'm sorry?'

*'German town partly in French disagreement with Hamelin.' She
repeats it, as if he's stupid. 'Seven down. Eight letters.'*

'Ah, yes,' he says. 'Ratisbon.'

*'How do you get that?' She turns her face to him. He has an impres-
sion of large features—a sharp nose, a wide mouth—but it is the eyes
that hold him. Grey eyes, the grey of snow clouds waiting to break.*

'It's a cathedral city on the Danube. Partly in French—well, bon,
*obviously. Disagreement with Hamelin. That's easy. Hamelin—Pied
Piper—rats. Rat is* bon. *Rat is good. Not the view in Hamelin.'*

*He starts to laugh, then stops himself. Just hark at yourself, he
thinks, you're babbling like an idiot.*

'Fill up ten. Nine letters.'

426

'That's an anagram,' he says immediately. 'Plentiful.'

She shakes her head, smiling, filling in the answers. 'How do you get it so quickly?'

'It's not so hard. You learn to know the way they think. May I?'

He reaches over and takes the paper and pencil. Half his brain studies the puzzle, the other half studies her: how she watches him, her head resting slightly to one side. Aster, Tasso, lovage, landau . . . It's the first and only time in their relationship that he's ever fully in control, and by the time he's completed the thirty clues and given her back the paper they're pulling through the outskirts of a small town.

'Bletchley,' calls the guard. 'Bletchley Station!'

He says, 'I'm afraid this is my stop.'

'Yes.' She looks thoughtfully at the finished crossword, then turns and smiles at him. 'Yes. D'you know, I rather guessed it might be.'

'Mr Jericho!' someone calls. 'Mr Jericho!'

'MR JERICHO!'

He opened his eyes. For a moment he was disorientated. The wardrobe loomed over him like a thief in the dim light.

Mrs Armstrong was shouting to him from halfway up the stairs. 'It's a quarter past six, Mr Jericho. Will you be wanting supper?'

A quarter past six? The room was almost dark. To his astonishment he realised he had slept through the entire day.

'That would be very kind, Mrs Armstrong. Thank you.'

The dream had been disturbingly vivid, and as he threw off the blankets and swung his bare feet onto the cold floor he had a peculiar conviction that Claire had been thinking of him, that his subconscious had somehow picked up a message from her. It was an absurd thought for a mathematician, a rationalist, to entertain, but he couldn't rid himself of it. He found his sponge bag, slipped his overcoat over his pyjamas and scuttled down the passage to the bathroom. Standing at the basin, he laid out his toiletries: a sliver of carbolic soap, a safety razor with a six-month-old blade, a wooden toothbrush worn down to a fuzz of bristles, an almost empty tin of pink tooth powder. The taps clanked. He scraped at his chin for ten minutes, until it was red and pricked with blood. This was where the devil of the war resided, he thought: in the details, in the thousand petty humiliations of never having enough soap or baths or clean clothes. Body odour lay over the British Isles like a great sour fog.

There were two other guests downstairs in the dining room, a Miss Jobey and a Mr Bonnyman, and the three of them made discreet conversation while they waited for their food. Miss Jobey was dressed in black, with a cameo brooch at her throat. Bonnyman wore tweeds, with a set of pens in his breast pocket, and Jericho guessed

427

he might be an engineer on the bombes. The kitchen door swung open as Mrs Armstrong brought in their plates.

'Here we go,' whispered Bonnyman. 'Brace yourself, old boy.'

'It's potato pie,' announced Mrs Armstrong defiantly. 'With gravy. And potatoes.'

They contemplated their steaming plates.

'How very, ah, substantial,' said Jericho eventually.

The meal passed in silence. Pudding was stewed apple with powdery custard. Jericho helped Mrs Armstrong clear away the dishes, then went out into the back yard to check his bicycle. There was a sharpness in the air that promised frost. The lights still worked. He pumped up the tyres, then went back to his room.

At half past ten Mrs Armstrong was on the point of laying aside her knitting to go up to bed, when she heard someone coming downstairs. She opened the door a crack, in time to see Mr Jericho hurrying out into the night.

THE MOON DEFIED the blackout, shining a blue torch over the frozen fields, quite bright enough for a man to cycle by. Jericho lifted himself out of the saddle and trod hard on the pedals, rocking from side to side as he toiled up the hill out of Bletchley. Then the road began to level out and he sat back on the saddle, cycling on for about two miles towards the tiny hamlet of Shenley Brook End.

Just before the hamlet, on the left, there was a gap in the hawthorn hedge, where a rutted track led to a little thatched cottage. He turned into it and skittered to a halt, squinting at the cottage. Was it his imagination, or was there a hint of light in the downstairs window? He dismounted and began to wheel his bike towards it.

He felt wonderfully calm. Above the thatched roof, the constellations spread out like the lights of a city: Ursa Minor and Polaris, Pegasus and Cepheus. No glow from earth obscured their brilliance. You can at least say this for the blackout, he thought, it has given us back the stars.

The door was stout and iron-studded. It was like knocking on stone. After half a minute, he tried again. 'Claire?' he called. 'Claire?'

There was a pause, and then: 'Who is it?'

'It's Tom.'

The handle turned and the door opened slightly, just enough to reveal a dark-haired woman, thirtyish. She was wearing spectacles and a thick overcoat and was holding a prayer book.

'Yes?'

For a moment he was speechless. 'I'm sorry,' he said. 'I was looking for Claire.'

'She's not in.'

428

'Not in?' he repeated hopelessly. He remembered now that Claire shared the cottage with a woman called Hester Wallace—*she works in Hut 6, she's a sweetie.* But with her thin face and sharp nose she did not look very sweet. 'I'm Tom Jericho.'

'I'll tell her you called.'

'Will she be back soon?'

'I've no idea. I'm sorry. Now, good evening, Mr Jericho.' She pushed the door closed with surprising force.

Jericho took a step backwards onto the track. This was not a contingency envisaged in his plan. He picked up his bicycle and wheeled it back towards the lane, but instead of going out onto the road he turned left and followed the line of the hedge. He laid the bicycle flat and drew into the shadows to wait.

After about ten minutes, the cottage door opened and closed, and he heard the rattle of a bicycle being wheeled over stone. It was as he thought: Miss Wallace had been dressed to go out because she was working the midnight shift. A pinprick of yellow light appeared, wobbled briefly from side to side, and then Hester Wallace cycled past within twenty feet of him. He waited a full quarter of an hour in case she'd forgotten something, then headed back to the cottage.

There was only one key, ornate and iron and big enough to fit a cathedral. It was kept, he recalled, beneath a flowerpot. Damp had warped the door, and he had to push hard to open it. He replaced the key and closed the door behind him before turning on the light.

He had been inside only once before. There were two rooms on the ground floor: a sitting room with low beams and a kitchen straight ahead. To his left, a narrow staircase led up to a little landing. Claire's bedroom was at the front, looking towards the lane; Hester's was at the rear. The lavatory was a chemical toilet just outside the back door, and there was no bathroom. He wondered how Claire stuck it.

Oh, but darling, it's so much better than having some ghastly landlady telling one what to do...

Jericho took a couple of steps across the worn rug and stopped, feeling uneasy. Everywhere he looked he saw evidence of life being lived quite contentedly without him: blue and white china in the dresser, the vase full of daffodils, the stack of prewar *Vogue*s. He had no business here. All that stopped him leaving was the faintly pathetic realisation that he had nowhere else particularly to go.

Better to make a stand here, he decided, than to run away again. She was bound to be back quite soon.

God, but it was cold! His bones were ice. He sat first in one armchair, then tried the other. Now he was facing the door. To his right was the sofa, covered in frayed pink silk. The springs had gone and when you sat in it you sank almost to the floor. He remembered that sofa and he stared at it for a long time, as a soldier might stare at a battlefield where a war had been irretrievably lost.

THEY LEAVE THE TRAIN together and walk up the footpath to the Park. The December afternoon is raw and misty; the day is leaking into dusk.

She tells him she's been up to London to celebrate her birthday. How old does he think she is?

He hasn't a clue. Eighteen, perhaps?

Twenty, she says triumphantly. And what was he doing in town?

He can't tell her, of course. Just business. Just business.

Sorry, she says, she shouldn't have asked. She still can't get the hang of all this 'need to know'. She has been at the Park for three months and hates it. Her father works at the Foreign Office and wangled her the job to keep her out of mischief. How long has he been here?

Three years, says Jericho. She shouldn't worry, it'll get better.

Ah, she says, that's easy for him to say, but surely he does something interesting.

Not really, he says, but then he thinks that makes him sound boring, so he adds, 'Well, quite interesting, I suppose.'

In truth, he's finding it hard to keep up his end of the conversation. It's distracting merely to walk alongside her. They lapse into silence.

There's a notice board close to the main gate advertising a perform-ance of Bach's Musikalisches Opfer *by the Bletchley Park Music Society. 'Oh, now look at that,' she says; 'I adore Bach,' to which Jericho replies, with genuine enthusiasm, that Bach is his favourite composer. Grateful at last to have found something to talk about, he launches into a long dissertation about the* Musikalisches Opfer's *six-part fugue, which Bach improvised for King Frederick the Great.*

When they reach the huts on the other side of the perimeter fence, they stop and introduce themselves. She offers him her hand—her grip is warm and firm, but her nails are a shock: bitten almost to the quick. Her name is Claire Romilly. He wishes her a merry Christmas and turns away, but she calls him back. She hopes he won't think it too fresh of her, but would he like to go with her to the concert?

She writes down the date and time just above The Times *cross-word—December 27 at 8.15—and thrusts it into his hands. She'll buy the tickets. She'll see him there.*

Before he can say anything, she's gone.

He's due to be on shift on the evening of the 27th, but he calls in a favour he's owed by Arthur de Brooke and waits outside the assembly hall, and waits, and waits. Eventually, after everyone else has gone in, she comes running out of the darkness, smiling her apologies.

The concert is better than he'd hoped. The quintet all work at the

Park and once played professionally. Suddenly the war seems a long way away. As the last notes of the third canon are dying in the air, he risks a glance at Claire, only to discover that she is looking at him. She touches his arm and, as the fourth canon begins, he is lost.

Afterwards, they walk down the hill to the station to have cocoa at the platform buffet.

'So,' she says, as he returns from the counter bearing two cups of brown froth, 'how much am I allowed to know about you?'

'Me? Oh, I'm very boring.'

'I don't think you're boring at all. In fact, I've heard a rumour you're rather brilliant.' She lights a cigarette and he notices again her distinctive way of inhaling—seeming almost to swallow the smoke—then tilting her head back and breathing it out through her nostrils. 'I suppose you're married?' she says.

He almost chokes on his cocoa. 'Good God, no. I would hardly be—'

'Brothers? Sisters?'

'No, no.'

'Parents? Even you must have parents.'

'Only one still alive.'

'I'm the same,' she says. 'My mother's dead.'

'I'm sorry. My mother, I must say, is very much alive.'

And so it goes on, this hitherto untasted pleasure of talking about oneself. Her grey eyes never leave his face, as he finds himself telling her things he's never really spoken of before: about his father's death and his mother's remarriage, about his stepfather (whom he dislikes), about his discovery of astronomy and then of mathematics...

'And your work now?' she says. 'Does that make you happy?'

'Happy?' He warms his hands on his cup and considers the question. 'No, not happy. It's too demanding—frightening, even, in a way.'

'Frightening?' The eyes widen with interest. 'Frightening how?'

'What might happen...' (You're showing off, he warns himself, stop it.) 'What might happen if you get it wrong, I suppose.'

She lights another cigarette. 'You're in Hut 8, aren't you?'

This brings him up with a jolt. He looks round quickly. Four airmen are playing cards. Nobody seems to have heard.

'Talking of which,' he says brightly, 'I think I ought to get back.'

On the corner of Church Green Road and Wilton Avenue, she kisses him, briefly, on the cheek.

The following week, the concert is Schumann, followed by supper at the British Restaurant in Bletchley Road, and this time it's her turn to talk. Her mother died when she was six, she says, and her father trailed her from embassy to embassy. Family has been a procession of nannies and governesses. At least she's learned some languages. She'd wanted to join the Wrens, but the old man wouldn't let her.

431

When they say goodbye, she kisses him again, her lips to one cheek, her cool hand to the other.

In retrospect, it is around this time, in the middle of January, that he should have started keeping a record of his symptoms, for it is now that he begins to lose his equilibrium. He goes for long walks round the lake between shifts, taking bread to feed the ducks—just for the exercise, he tells himself, but really he is scanning the crowds for her.

For their third date she insists they do something different, so they go to the cinema to see the new Noël Coward picture, In Which We Serve. *They sit near the back and she laces her arm through his. The light from the projector high up behind them makes a kaleidoscope of blues and greys in the dust and cigarette smoke. A fanfare of trumpets announces a newsreel, and there, on the screen, long columns of German prisoners are shown trekking through snow, while the announcer talks excitedly about Red Army breakthroughs on the eastern front. Stalin appears, presenting medals, to loud applause. The main film begins—'This is the story of a ship'—with Coward as an improbably suave Royal Navy captain. There's a lot of clipped excitement: 'Vessel on fire bearing green three-oh . . . Torpedo track, starboard, sir . . . Carry on firing . . .' At the climax of the sea battle, Jericho looks round at the rapt faces, and it strikes him that he is a part of all this—a distant, vital part. After the final credits the loudspeakers play 'God Save the King' and they all stand, many of the audience so moved by the film that they begin to sing.*

They've left their bicycles in an alley running beside the cinema. A few paces further on, a shape rubs itself against the wall. As they come closer, they can see it is a soldier with his greatcoat wrapped round a girl. Her back is to the bricks. The movement stops for the time it takes Claire and Jericho to collect their bicycles, then it starts again.

'What very peculiar behaviour,' he says, without thinking.

To his surprise, Claire bursts out laughing.

'What's the matter?'

'Nothing,' she says.

They stand on the pavement holding their bicycles. 'Do come and see my cottage, Tom,' she says. 'I'd love to show it you.'

He can't think of an excuse, doesn't want to think of one.

She leads the way through the town and out past the Park. He begins to wonder how far she's taking him. At last, when they're rattling down the path that leads to the cottage, she calls, 'Isn't it perfect?' She tells him how she found it standing empty, how she charmed the farmer who owns it into letting her rent it. Inside, the furniture is shabby-grand, rescued from an aunt's house in Kensington that was shut up for the Blitz and never reopened.

The place is freezing cold. 'And this is where I sleep,' she says, and he follows her into a room of pinks and creams, crammed full of prewar silks and furs and feathers. A loose floorboard goes off like a gunshot beneath his feet. There's too much detail for the eye to register, so many hatboxes, shoeboxes, bits of jewellery, cosmetic bottles ... She slips off her coat, then lets it fall to the floor and flings herself on the bed, kicking off her shoes and propping herself up on her elbows. She seems amused by something.

'And what's this?' Jericho, in turmoil, has retreated to the landing and is staring at the only other door.

'Oh, that's Hester's room,' she calls.

'Hester?'

'Some bureaucratic beast found out where I was and said if I had a second bedroom I had to share. So in came Hester. She works in Hut 6. She's a sweetie.' He hears the gunshot of the floorboard behind him and looks round. 'Come on,' she says, 'let's make a fire and have a drink.'

Downstairs, he kneels by the hearth and lights the fire. The chimney draws voraciously, sucking up the smoke with a roar.

'Look at you, you haven't even taken off your coat.'

He stands, brushing the dust away, and turns to face her. Grey skirt, navy cashmere sweater, a single loop of pearls at her throat—the unchanging uniform of the upper-class Englishwoman.

'Come here. Let me do it.'

She sets down the drinks and begins to unbutton his overcoat.

'Don't tell me, Tom,' she whispers, 'don't tell me you didn't know what they were doing behind that cinema?'

'Of course I knew ...'

'In London nowadays the girls all call it a "wall job". What do you think? They say you can't get pregnant this way ...'

Instinctively, he draws his coat round her. She wraps her arms about his back.

DAMN IT.

He pitched himself forward out of the armchair, sending his memories scattering and smashing on the cold stone floor. He prowled round the tiny sitting room a couple of times, then went into the kitchen. Everything was clean and swept and put away. That would be Hester's handiwork, he guessed, not Claire's. Where was she? It was a quarter to one. He wandered back into the sitting room, hesitated at the foot of the stairs, then began to climb.

He was quite clear now about what he was going to do, even though conscience told him it was wrong and logic told him it was stupid. He began opening drawers. A letter, a diary, a message—anything that might tell him *why*—he had to see it, he had to, even though the chances of its yielding any comfort were nil. Where was she? Was she with another man?

433

He was suddenly in a rage and he went through her room like a housebreaker, pulling out drawers, sweeping jewellery and trinkets off the shelves, pulling her clothes down onto the floor, throwing off her sheets and blankets. After ten minutes he crawled into the corner and laid his head on a pile of silks and furs.

You're a wreck, Skynner had said. *You're ruined. You've lost it. Find someone more suitable than the person you were seeing.*

Skynner knew about her, and Logie had seemed to know as well. What was it he'd called her? The 'arctic blonde'? Perhaps they all knew: Puck, Atwood, Baxter, everybody.

He had to get out, get away from the smell of her perfume and the sight of her clothes.

And it was that action that changed everything, for it was only when he stood on the landing, leaning with his back to the wall and his eyes closed, that he realised there *was* something he'd missed.

He walked back slowly and deliberately into her room. Silence. The floorboard didn't creak. He got down on his knees. One of Auntie's Kensington rugs covered the floorboards, something oriental, stained. He rolled it up and laid it on the bed. The wooden planks that lay beneath it had been untouched for centuries—except in one place, where a shorter length of the planking was secured by four very modern, shiny screws. He slapped the floor in triumph.

In the mess of her bedroom, he could see no suitable tool. He went down into the kitchen and found a knife. The tip slotted into the head of the first screw and the thread turned easily. So did the other three. The floorboard lifted up to reveal a cavity about six inches deep. He lay on his side and thrust his hand into the space. To begin with he brought out nothing except handfuls of old plaster and small pieces of brick, but he kept on working his way around until at last he gave a cry of delight as his hand touched paper.

HE PUT THE BEDROOM back in place, more or less. He hung the clothes back up from the beams, piled her underclothes back into the drawers, heaped the trinkets of jewellery into their leather case and draped others artfully along the shelves.

Then he sat on the edge of the mattress and surveyed the room. Not bad. Of course, once she began looking for things, then she would know someone had been through it, but at a casual glance it looked the same as before—apart, that is, from the hole in the floor. He didn't know yet what to do about that. It depended on whether or not he replaced the intercepts. He examined them again.

There were four, on cheap wartime paper, the sort Bletchley used by the ton. In the top right-hand corner of each signal was its TOI, Time of Interception. The four had been sent in rapid succession on

March 4, just nine days earlier, beginning at 9.30pm and ending just before midnight. Each consisted of a call sign—ADU—and then about two hundred five-letter groups. That in itself was an important clue. It meant they weren't naval: the Kriegsmarine's signals were transmitted in groups of four letters. So they were presumably German Army or Luftwaffe.

She must have stolen them from Hut 3.

The enormity of the implications hit Jericho for a second time, winding him like a punch in the stomach. He arranged the intercepts in sequence on her pillow and tried very hard to come up with some innocent explanation. A piece of silly mischief? A dare? It was possible. She was capable of anything. But that hole in the floorboards, the cool deliberation of it, mocked his advocacy.

A sound, a footstep downstairs, dragged him out of his reverie and made him jump to his feet.

He said, 'Hello?' in a loud voice that suggested more courage than he felt. He cleared his throat. 'Hello?' he repeated. And then he heard another noise, definitely a footstep and definitely *outside* the cottage now, and a charge of adrenalin snapped in. He moved quickly to the bedroom door and turned the light off. Now he would be able to see anyone coming up the stairs, while remaining hidden himself. But nothing happened. Perhaps they were trying to come round the back? He moved cautiously down the stairs, flinching at every creak. A blast of cold air struck him.

The front door was wide open.

He threw himself down the last half-dozen steps and ran outside, just in time to see the red rear light of a bicycle vanish down the lane.

There was a heavy frost. In every direction the ground shone a dull and luminous blue. Two sets of tyre tracks were imprinted in the glittering ice: incoming and outgoing. He followed them back to the door, where they ended in a series of sharp footprints.

Sharp, large, *male* footprints.

Jericho hurried back into the cottage.

Upstairs, he rolled the intercepts very tightly into a cylinder. He used his teeth to tear a small hole in the lining of his overcoat and pushed the signals into it. Then he quickly screwed down the floorboard and replaced the rug. He turned off the lights, locked the door, replaced the key.

At the entrance to the lane, he stopped and looked back at the darkened cottage. He had a strong sensation—foolish, he told himself—that he was being watched.

Jericho shivered again, retrieved his bike and pointed it down the hill, towards Orion and the constellation of Hydra, which hung suspended in the night sky above Bletchley Park like a knife.

He doesn't know what wakes him: some faint sound, some movement that hooks him in the depths of his dreams and hauls him to the surface.

At first, his darkened room seems entirely normal, but then he realises that a faint light is rising from the foot of his bed.

'Claire?' he says, propping himself up. 'Darling?'

'It's all right, darling. Go back to sleep.'

'What on earth are you doing?'

'I'm just going through your things.'

'You're what?'

His hand fumbles across the bedside table and switches on the lamp.

'That's better,' she says, and she turns off the blackout torch.

And she is doing exactly what she says. She is naked except for his shirt, she is kneeling, and she is going through his wallet. She removes a couple of pound notes, turns the wallet inside out and shakes it.

'No photographs?' she says.

'You haven't given me one yet.'

'Tom Jericho,' she smiles, replacing the money, 'I do declare, you're becoming almost smooth.'

She checks the pockets of his jacket and his trousers, then shuffles on her knees across to his chest of drawers. He laces his hands behind his head and leans back against the iron bedstead and watches her. It is only the second time they have slept together—a week after the first—and at her insistence they are not in her cottage but in his room at the White Hart Inn. His books are lined up on the top of the chest of drawers and she picks up each in turn, flicking through the pages.

Does he see anything odd in all this? No, he does not. It merely seems amusing, flattering, even—one further intimacy, a continuation of all the rest. Besides, he has no secrets from her—or, at least, he thinks he hasn't. She finds a paper by Turing and studies it closely.

'And what are computable numbers with an application to the Entscheidungsproblem, when they're at home?'

Her pronunciation of the German, he registers, is immaculate.

'It's a theoretical machine, capable of an infinite number of numerical operations. Come back to bed, darling.'

'This Turing, does he work at the Park?'

He sighs and makes no reply. She leafs through the paper, squinting with disgust at the mathematics, then replaces it with the books and opens one of the drawers. As she leans forwards the shirt rides higher. He stares, mesmerised, at the soft white triangle at the base of her vertebrae as she rummages among his clothes.

'Ah,' she says, 'now here is something.' She withdraws a slip of paper.

'*A cheque for a hundred pounds, drawn on the Foreign Office Contingency Fund, made out to you—*'

'*Put that back.*'

He is across the room and standing beside her within a couple of seconds, but she is quicker than he is. She is on her feet, on tiptoe, holding the cheque aloft, and she—absurdly—is just that half-inch taller than he. The money flutters like a pennant beyond his reach. He should have banked it weeks ago. '*You must have done something frightfully clever in that Naval Hut of yours. A new code? Is that it? You broke some new important code, my clever, clever darling?*'

She may be taller than he is, but he has the advantage of desperation. He seizes her arm, pulls it down and twists her round. They struggle for a moment, and then he throws her back on the narrow bed. He prises the cheque out of her fingers and retreats with it across the room.

'*Not funny, Claire. Some things just aren't that funny.*'

He folds the cheque and slips it into his wallet, puts the wallet into his jacket and turns to hang the jacket in the wardrobe. As he does so, he is aware of a peculiar noise coming from behind him—a frightening, animal noise, something between a rasping breath and a sob. She has curled herself up tight on the bed, her knees drawn up to her stomach.

My God, what has he done?

He starts to gabble his apologies. He hadn't meant to frighten her, let alone to hurt her. He goes across to the bed and sits beside her. Tentatively, he tries to pull her towards him, but she has become as rigid as a corpse. The sobs are shaking the bed. It is like a fit, a seizure. She is somewhere beyond grief, somewhere far away from him.

'*It's all right,*' *he says.* '*It's all right.*'

He can't tug the bedclothes out from under her, so he fetches his overcoat and lays that across her, and then he lies beside her, shivering in the January night. They stay like that until she is calm again; then she gets up and begins to dress. He cannot bring himself to look at her as she collects her scattered clothes. Then the door closes quietly. A minute later he hears the click of her bicycle being wheeled away.

And now his own nightmare begins.

First, there is guilt, that most corrosive of emotions. Why did he respond so dramatically to so small a provocation? The cheque could, after all, have been a reward for anything. He didn't have to tell her the truth. What had he done to provoke such terror in her? What awful memory had he reawakened?

He groans and draws the blankets over his head.

The next morning he takes the cheque to the bank and exchanges it for twenty large, crisp, white five-pound notes. Then he searches out the dreary little jewellery shop on Bletchley Road and buys a ring.

He will make it up to her. He will apologise. It will all be right.

But luck is not with Jericho. A Shark decrypt discloses that a U-boat tanker is to rendezvous with and refuel the Italian submarine Kalvi *300 miles east of St Paul's Rock, in the middle of the Atlantic. And some fool at the Admiralty, forgetting that no action, however tempting, must ever be taken that will endanger the Enigma secret, orders a squadron of destroyers to intercept. The attack is made. And Dönitz is immediately suspicious. In the third week of January, Hut 8 decrypts signals ordering the U-boat fleet to tighten its cipher security. Shark traffic dwindles. There is barely enough material to make a menu for the bombes. At Bletchley, all leave is cancelled. Eight-hour shifts drag on to twelve hours, to sixteen hours . . . The daily battle to break the codes is almost as great a nightmare as it was in the depths of the Shark blackout, and Skynner's lash is felt on everyone's back.*

Jericho's world has gone from perpetual sunshine to bleak midwinter in the space of a week. His messages to Claire, of entreaty and remorse, vanish, unanswered. He can't get out of the hut to see her. He can't work. He can't sleep. And there's no one he can talk to.

On the final day of January, collecting a copy of The Times *from the newsagent in Victoria Road, he spots her, at a distance, with another man, and he shrinks into a doorway to avoid being seen. Apart from that, he never meets her: the Park has become too big. Eventually, he's reduced to lying in wait in the lane opposite her cottage, like a peeping Tom. But she seems to have stopped coming home.*

And then he almost walks right into her.

It is February 8, a Monday, at four o'clock. He's walking wearily back to the hut from the canteen; she is part of a flood of workers streaming towards the gate at the end of the afternoon shift. He has rehearsed for this moment so many times, but in the end all he manages is a whine of complaint: 'Why don't you answer my letters?'

'Hello, Tom.'

She tries to walk on, but he catches her arm. 'I need to talk to you.'

'Tom,' she hisses, 'for God's sake, you're making a scene.'

'Good. Let's get out of here.' He is pulling at her arm. His pressure is insistent, and reluctantly she surrenders to it. The momentum of the crowd sweeps them through the gate and along the road. He doesn't know how long they walk for—fifteen minutes, perhaps, or twenty—until, at last, the pavements are deserted and they are passing through the hinterland of the town, near a derelict brickworks. She shakes her arm free.

'There's no point in this.'

'You're seeing someone else?' He hardly dares to ask the question.

'I'm always seeing someone else.'

He stops, but she walks on. He lets her go for fifty yards, then hurries to catch her up. 'What do you want to know?' he says. 'I'll tell you everything you want to know.'

438

And he will, if she wants it. He doesn't care about security or the war. He'll tell her about Shark and Dolphin and Porpoise. He'll draw her a diagram of how the bombe works, if that's what she wants. But all she says is: 'I do hope you're not going to be a bore about this, Tom.'

A bore. Is that what he is? Is he being a bore?

'Wait,' he calls after her, 'you might as well have this.'

He gives her the little box with the ring in it. She opens it and tilts the stone to catch the light, then snaps the lid shut and hands it back.

'Not my style.'

By the end of the week, he's in the deputy director's Rover, being borne through the snow to King's College.

SUNDAY BREAKFAST was a ritual at the Commercial Guesthouse in Albion Street. The meal was served up with appropriate solemnity by Mrs Armstrong, on plain white utility crockery: one piece of fried bread, as thick as a hymnbook, with two spoonfuls of powdered egg scrambled and slopped on top.

It was not, Jericho had to acknowledge, a great meal, nor even a particularly edible one. Yet such was his appetite after the excitements of the night that he ate every scrap of it, washed it down with two cups of greyish tea and even complimented Mrs Armstrong on the quality of her cooking—a gesture which caused her to search his features for a trace of irony. She found none.

By seven forty-five he was back in his room. He had unpacked his suitcases and his books were lined up along the mantelpiece. Balanced on the top of them was his print of King's College Chapel.

He sat on the edge of the bed and stared at the picture. It was not a skilful piece of work. But even bad art can have its uses. Behind the cheap mezzotint, laid flat and carefully secured, were the four intercepts he had removed from Claire's bedroom.

Jericho should have returned them to the Park, of course. He should have sought out Logie, or some other figure of authority, and handed them in. Even now, he couldn't disentangle his motives for not doing so, couldn't sort out the selfless (his wish to protect her) from the selfish (his desire to have her in his power). He only knew that he could not bring himself to betray her, and he told himself there was no harm in giving her the chance to explain.

For the hundredth time, he ran through all the possibilities: she was crazy; she was being blackmailed; she was a spy.

A spy? The notion seemed melodramatic to him, illogical. For one thing, why steal cryptograms? A spy would be after decodes, surely: the hard proof that Enigma was being broken.

He checked the door, then gently took down the picture and lifted away the cardboard backing. Now he thought about it, there *was* something distinctly odd about these cryptograms. They should have had the thin paper strips of decode produced by the Type-X machines gummed to them. But there were no strips, and no marks to show where any strips had been torn off. By the look of them, these signals had never even been broken. Their secrets were intact.

He looked at his watch. It was time to go. He slipped the cryptograms behind the picture and replaced it on the mantelpiece.

From Albion Street to Bletchley Park was a walk of less than half a mile. The sentry, raw-faced from the cold, barely glanced at his pass before waving him into the grounds.

Past the mansion he went, keeping his head down to avoid having to speak to anyone, past the lake and into Hut 8. He caught a glimpse of Logie's tall figure at the end of the corridor, and darted into the Registration Room. There, to his surprise, was Puck, sitting in a corner, watched by a pair of love-struck Wrens. His face was grey and lined, his head resting against the wall. Jericho thought he might be asleep, but then he opened a piercing blue eye.

'Logie's looking for you.'

'Really?' Jericho took off his coat and scarf and hung them on the back of the door. 'He knows where to find me.'

'There's a rumour going around that you hit Skynner. For God's sake tell me it's true.'

One of the Wrens giggled.

Jericho had forgotten all about Skynner. He passed his hand through his hair. 'Do me a favour, Puck, will you?' he said. 'Pretend you haven't seen me?'

Puck regarded him closely for a moment, then shut his eyes. 'What a man of mystery you are,' he murmured sleepily.

Jericho trotted back into the fresh air, then walked briskly round the corner, past Hut 6, towards the entrance to Hut 3. Only when he was within twenty paces of it did his footsteps slow, then stop.

The truth was, he knew very little about Hut 3, except that it was the place where the decoded messages of the German Army and Luftwaffe were processed. It was about twice the size of the other huts, and where exactly Claire worked within its warren of rooms, let alone what her 'boring' job entailed, was a mystery to him.

Jericho did his best to look as if he had a right to be there. He pulled out a pen and set off down the central corridor, thrusting past airmen and army officers, glancing officiously from side to side into the busy rooms. He had barely gone halfway down the passage when a colonel with a large moustache stepped smartly out of a doorway and blocked his path. 'Hold on, stranger. Who are you?'

On impulse, Jericho stuck out his hand. 'Tom Jericho, Naval Section, Hut 8,' he said. 'Who are you?'

'Never mind who the hell I am.' The colonel ignored the proffered hand. 'State your business here.'

'I'm looking for Dr Weitzman.'

An inspired lie. He knew Weitzman from the Chess Society: a German Jew, naturalised British.

The colonel looked Jericho up and down. 'Haven't you navy people ever heard of the telephone? You'd better come with me.'

Jericho followed the colonel's broad back along the passage and into a large room. Two groups of about a dozen men sat at tables arranged in a pair of semicircles, working their way through wire baskets stacked high with decrypts. Walter Weitzman was perched on a stool in a glass booth behind them.

'I say, Weitzman, d'you know this chap?'

Weitzman was bent over a German weapons manual. He looked up, and when he recognised Jericho his melancholy face brightened into a smile. 'Hello, Tom. Yes, of course I know him.'

'"*Kriegsnachrichten für Seefahrer*",' said Jericho, a fraction too quickly. 'You said you might have something by now.'

For a moment Weitzman didn't react, but then the old man said slowly, 'Yes. I believe I have that information for you.' He lowered himself carefully from his stool. 'You have a problem, Colonel?'

The colonel thrust his chin forward. 'Yes, actually, Weitzman, I do. "Interhut communication, unless otherwise authorised, must be conducted by telephone or written memorandum." Standard procedure.' He glared at Weitzman. 'Remember that in future.'

'Arsehole,' hissed Weitzman, as the colonel moved away. 'Well, well. You'd better come over here.'

He led Jericho to a rack of card-index files, selected a drawer, pulled it out and began riffling through it. Every time the translators came across a term they couldn't understand, they consulted Weitzman and his famous index system. Very few phrases defeated him.

'"*Kriegsnachrichten für Seefahrer*"—"War notices for Marines". First intercepted and catalogued on the 9th November last year. As you knew perfectly well already.' He studied the card through his thick spectacles. 'Tell me, is the good colonel still looking at us?'

Jericho risked a look at the colonel. 'He's going out of the door... now. It's all right. He's gone.'

Weitzman slipped the card back among the rest and closed the drawer. 'So. Why are you asking me questions to which you already know the answers?' His hair was white; his small brown eyes were wrinkled at their edges, suggesting a face that had once creased readily into laughter. But Weitzman didn't laugh much any more. He was rumoured to have left most of his family behind in Germany.

'I'm looking for Claire Romilly. Do you know her?'

441

'Of course. The beautiful Claire. Everyone knows her.'

'Where does she work?'

'"Interhut communication, unless otherwise authorised, must be conducted by telephone or written memorandum. Standard procedure."' Weitzman clicked his heels. 'Heil Hitler!'

'Walter. Please. It's important.'

'And it can't wait until the end of the shift?' He gave Jericho a careful look. 'Obviously not. All right, follow me.'

Weitzman led Jericho almost to the other end of the hut, past the translators, through a room lined with teleprinters and down a short length of passage, at the end of which was a closed door bearing the sign GERMAN BOOK ROOM.

Weitzman knocked on the door, opened it and went inside. Jericho followed. His eyes registered a large room; shelves stacked with ledgers and files; half a dozen trestle tables pushed together to form one big working area; six or seven women, two typing very fast, the others moving back and forth arranging sheaves of paper into piles.

Before he could take in any more, a plump, harassed-looking woman in a tweed jacket and skirt advanced to meet them. Weitzman was beaming now, exuding charm as he took her hand and bowed to kiss it.

'*Guten Morgen, mein liebes Fräulein Monk. Wie geht's?*'

'*Gut, danke, Herr Doktor. Und dir?*'

'*Danke, sehr gut.*'

It was clearly a familiar routine between them. She flushed pink with pleasure. 'And what can I do for you?'

'My colleague and I, my dear Miss Monk'—Weitzman patted her hand, then released it and gestured towards Jericho—'are looking for the delightful Miss Romilly.'

At the mention of Claire's name, Miss Monk's flirtatious smile evaporated. 'In that case, you must join the queue, Dr Weitzman. We are all trying to find Claire Romilly. Perhaps you, or your colleague, have an idea where we might start?'

For an instant, Weitzman's expression became a mask of bafflement, and he gave Jericho a peculiar look, as if to say, What have you got me into? As his brain tried to compute the implications, Jericho could hear his own voice say, 'But I thought she was supposed to be on duty at eight this morning...'

'Quite right,' Miss Monk was saying. 'It really is most thoughtless of her.'

'Perhaps she's ill?' Weitzman suggested.

'Then surely a note would have been considerate? We can barely cope when there are eight of us. When we're down to seven...' She started to prattle on about all the staffing memos she'd written.

442

Jericho cut in: 'I wonder, could I ask you, has she done this before? Failed to turn up, I mean, without telling you?'

'Oh no. Never. I will not tolerate slacking in my section. Dr Weitzman will vouch for that.'

'Indeed,' said Weitzman gravely. 'No slacking here.'

Miss Monk was of a type that Jericho had come to know well over the past three years: mildly hysterical at moments of crisis; jealous of her precious rank; convinced that the war would be lost if her tiny fiefdom were denied a gross of lead pencils. She would hate Claire, he thought—hate her for her prettiness and her confidence and her refusal to take anything seriously.

'When did you last see her?'

'That would be midnight on Friday.' Miss Monk obviously prided herself on her memory for detail. 'Yesterday was her rest day.'

'So I don't suppose it's likely she came back into the hut, say, early on Saturday morning?'

'No. I was here. Anyway, why should she do that? Normally, she couldn't wait to get away.'

I bet she couldn't. He glanced again at the girls behind Miss Monk, and tried to imagine Claire here, in this drab room. It was like picturing some gorgeous parakeet in a cage full of sparrows.

'What will you do now?' he asked.

'Obviously—because of the level of classification—there's a certain procedure we have to follow. I've already notified Welfare. They'll send someone round to her room to turf her out of bed.'

'And if she isn't there?'

'They'll contact her family to see if they know where she is. But it never gets that far. I'm sure there's a *man* at the bottom of this. There usually is.'

Weitzman touched Jericho on the arm. 'We ought to go now.'

'Do you have an address for her family?'

'Yes, but I'm not sure I should . . .' She turned towards Weitzman. He hesitated fractionally. 'I can vouch for him.'

'Well,' said Miss Monk, 'if you think it's permissible . . .' She went over to her desk. 'The curious thing is,' she went on, 'she'd really become much more *attentive* of late. Anyway, this is her card.'

Next of kin: Edward Romilly. Relation: Father.
Address: 27 Stanhope Gardens, London SW.
Telephone: Kensington 2257.

Jericho glanced at it for a second and handed it back.

'I don't think there's any need to trouble him, do you?' asked Miss Monk. 'Certainly not yet. No doubt Claire will arrive at any moment with some silly story about oversleeping—'

'I'm sure,' said Jericho.

'— in which case, who shall I say was looking for her?'

'*Auf Wiedersehen, Fräulein Monk.*' Weitzman had had enough. He was already half out of the room, pulling Jericho after him. Jericho had a last vision of Miss Monk, standing bewildered and suspicious, before the door closed on her schoolroom German.

'*Auf Wiedersehen, Herr Doktor, und Herr ...*'

WEITZMAN DIDN'T LEAD Jericho back the way they had come. Instead he bundled him out of the rear exit. He shook a cigarette out of a crumpled pack and lit it, then leaned against the wall of the hut and exhaled a sigh of steam and smoke. 'What's going on, Tom?'

'You don't want to know, Walter. Believe me.'

'Troubles of the heart?'

'Something like that. Walter, what's the German Book Room?'

'I'd better get back,' said Weitzman.

'Please, Walter ...'

'Ach!' Weitzman began making his way down the side of the hut towards the path. Jericho had to scramble to keep pace with him.

'You ask too much, you know.'

'I wouldn't ... it's just ... there's nobody else ...'

A pair of sentries with rifles rounded the corner and strolled towards them. Weitzman abruptly turned right off the path towards the tennis court. Jericho followed him. Weitzman opened the gate and they stepped onto the asphalt. Weitzman closed the gate after them and walked towards the net post.

'Is she in trouble, then, your girl?'

'I think so. I mean yes—yes, she is.'

'I'm sorry to hear it. I like her. She laughs at my jokes. Pretty young women who laugh at my jokes must be cherished ...'

'Walter ...'

Weitzman turned towards Hut 3. He had chosen his ground well. Nobody could come up behind them without entering the tennis court. Nobody could approach from the front without being seen. And if anyone was watching from a distance—well, what was there to see but two old colleagues having a private chat?

'It's organised like a factory line.' He curled his fingers into the wire netting. His hands were white with cold. 'The decrypts arrive by conveyor belt from Hut 6. They go first to the Watch for translation—you know that, that's my post. Translated Luftwaffe signals are passed to 3A, army to 3M. A for air, M for military. God in heaven, it's cold.' He pulled out a filthy handkerchief and blew his nose. 'The duty officers decide what's important and give it a Z priority. A single Z is low grade; five Zs is pure gold. The intelligence is summarised,

444

then three copies are dispatched—one to the Secret Intelligence Service, one to the appropriate service ministry in Whitehall, one to the relevant commander in the field.'

'And the German Book Room?'

'The German Book Room is the very end of the process. All this paper—the intercept, the decode, the translation, the Z signal, the list of cross-references—all these thousands of pages—it all comes together at the end to be filed. The German Book is a verbatim transcription of all decoded messages in their original language.'

'Is that an important job?'

'In intellectual terms? No. Purely clerical.'

'But in terms of access? To classified material?'

'Ah. Different.' Weitzman shrugged. 'In theory, on an average day, a girl like Claire would probably see more operational detail about the German armed forces than Adolf Hitler.' He glanced at Jericho and smiled. 'Absurd, isn't it? What is she? Nineteen?'

'Twenty,' muttered Jericho. 'She told me her job was boring.'

'Twenty! I swear it's the greatest joke in the history of warfare. Look at us: the harebrained debutante, the weakling intellectual and the half-blind Jew. If only the master race could see what we're doing to them—sometimes the thought of it is all that keeps me going.' He held his watch up very close to his face. 'I must get back. I fear I have talked too much.'

He turned towards the gate. Jericho made a move to follow, but Weitzman held up a hand to stop him. 'Why don't you wait here, Tom? Just for a moment. Let me get clear.' Then he said softly, 'And if you think I can help you again—please, don't ask me.'

Before Jericho could answer, he had crossed the path and disappeared round the back of Hut 3.

WITHIN THE GROUNDS of Bletchley Park, just beyond the mansion, stood an ordinary red telephone box. Inside it, a young man in motorcycle leathers was finishing a call. He pushed open the door.

'All yours, pal.'

Jericho waited until the dispatch rider had moved away before dialling zero.

A woman's voice said, 'Operator speaking.'

'Good morning. I'd like to make a call, please, to Kensington double two five seven.'

She repeated the number. 'That'll be fourpence, caller.'

He pressed four pennies into the slot, and after a series of clicks he heard a ringing tone.

It took fifteen seconds for a man to answer. 'Ye-es?'

It was exactly the voice Jericho had always imagined for Claire's

father: languid and assured. Jericho pushed the A-button. His money tinkled into the coin box.

'Mr Romilly?'

'Ye-es?'

'I'm sorry to trouble you, sir, especially on a Sunday morning, but I work with Claire . . .' There was a faint noise, and then a pause, during which he could hear breathing. 'Are you still there, sir?'

The voice, when it came again, sounded hollow, as if emanating from an empty room. 'How did you get this number?'

'Claire gave it to me.' It was the first lie that came into Jericho's head. 'I wondered if she was with you. She hasn't turned up for her shift this morning. Yesterday was her day off. I wondered if she might have gone down to London.'

'Who is this speaking?'

'My name is Tom Jericho. She may have spoken of me.'

'I don't believe so.' Romilly's voice was barely audible. 'I'm afraid I can't help you, Mr Jericho. My daughter's movements are as much a mystery to me as they seem to be to you. Goodbye.'

'Hello?' said Jericho. He thought he could still hear somebody breathing on the line. 'Hello?' He held on to the receiver for a couple of seconds, straining to hear, then carefully replaced it.

He leaned against the side of the telephone box and massaged his temples. *My daughter's movements are as much a mystery to me as they seem to be to you.* Was that the reaction one would expect of a father on being told his only child was missing?

Jericho dialled zero again.

'Operator speaking.'

'Kensington double two five seven.'

Once again, Jericho inserted four pennies into the metal slot. He tightened his finger on the button. But this time there was no ringing tone, only the *blip-blip-blip* of an engaged signal, pulsing in his ear like a heartbeat.

St Mary's Parish Church, eight solid centuries of hard white stone and Christian piety, lay at the end of an avenue of yew trees, less than a hundred yards beyond Bletchley Park. As Jericho walked through the gate, he heard the piping of the organ and the mournful lilt of a Church of England congregation in mid-hymn.

He considered slipping inside and standing at the back of the nave until the service ended, but experience had taught him there was no such thing as a quiet entry into a church. Instead, he buttoned his jacket against the cold and pretended to study the tombstones in the graveyard. Frosted cobwebs of improbable size and delicacy shone like ectoplasm between the memorials: marble monuments for the well-to-do, slate for the farm workers, weathered wooden crosses for the poor and infants. All the time, he kept listening to the service.

At last it was over. Jericho stationed himself behind a large bush, from where he had a clear view of the porch. He had picked up a few details about Hester Wallace from Claire—that before the war she'd been a teacher at a girls' private school in Dorset, that she played the organ and was a clergyman's daughter—just sufficient clues to suggest the sort of woman who might go straight from an eight-hour night shift to Sunday matins.

The door opened and the elderly priest stationed himself to say farewell to his parishioners. One by one the worshippers stepped into the daylight. Jericho didn't recognise any of them. He began to think he might have come to the wrong conclusion. But then, sure enough, a small, lean young woman appeared, holding her prayer book.

She shook hands briefly, even curtly, with the vicar, looped her carpetbag over the handles of her bicycle and wheeled it towards the gate. She walked quickly, with short, rapid steps. Jericho waited until she had gone past him, then stepped out and called, 'Miss Wallace!'

She stopped and glanced back in his direction. 'Why, Mr Jericho. The stranger in the night.' The cold had reddened the sharp point of her nose and painted two neat discs of colour, the size of half-crowns, on her white cheeks. She had long, thick black hair, which she wore piled up, secured by an armoury of pins. 'What did you make of the sermon?'

'Uplifting?' he said tentatively.

'Did you really? I thought it the most frightful rot I've heard all year. "Suffer not a woman to teach, nor to usurp authority over the man, but to be in silence..."' She shook her head furiously.

She resumed her brisk progress towards the lane. Jericho fell in beside her. 'Do you attend most Sundays?'

'Always. Although increasingly one wonders why. And you?'

He hesitated. 'Occasionally.'

'Whereabouts do you sit? I don't recall ever seeing you.'

'I try to keep at the back.'

'So do I.' She gave him a second look, her spectacles flashing in the winter sun. 'Really, Mr Jericho—a sermon you obviously didn't hear, a pew you never occupy: one might suspect you of laying claim to a piety you don't possess. I'll bid you good day.'

They had reached the gate. She swung herself onto the saddle of her bicycle with surprising grace. Jericho had to reach out and hold on to the handlebars to stop her pedalling away.

'I wasn't in church. I'm sorry. I wanted to talk to you.'

She glared at him angrily. But there was curiosity as well as anger in her eyes, and curiosity won. She sighed and dismounted.

'Thank you.' He tried to think of some way of broaching the subject. 'Claire tells me you work in Hut 6. That must be interesting.'

'Claire has no business telling you where I work. Or anyone else, for that matter. And no, it is not interesting. Everything interesting seems to be done by men. Women do the rest.'

She could be pretty, he thought, if she put her mind to it. Her skin was smooth and white. Her nose and chin, though sharp, were delicate. But she wore no make-up, and her expression was permanently cross, her lips drawn into a thin, sarcastic line.

'Claire and I, we were . . .' He searched for the word. He was so hopeless at all this. ' "Seeing one another" I suppose is the phrase. Until about a month ago. Then she refused to have anything more to do with me.' His resolution was wilted by her hostility, but he pressed on. 'To be frank, Miss Wallace, I'm worried about her. She hasn't turned up for her shift this morning. I think she's disappeared.'

She sniffed. 'Nonsense. An hour late for work hardly constitutes a disappearance. She probably overslept.'

'I don't think she went home last night.'

'Then perhaps she overslept *somewhere else*,' said Miss Wallace, maliciously. 'Incidentally, *how* do you know she didn't come home?'

He had learned it was better not to lie. 'Because I let myself in and waited for her.'

'So. A housebreaker as well. I can see why Claire wants nothing more to do with you.'

To hell with this, thought Jericho.

'There are other things you should know. A man came to the cottage last night while I was there. He ran away when he heard my voice. And I just telephoned Claire's father. He claims he doesn't know where she is, but I think he's lying.'

That seemed to impress her. She chewed on the inside of her lip and looked away. 'None of this is my concern,' she said at last.

'She hasn't seemed odd to you lately? Under any sort of strain?'

'Mr Jericho, we could probably fill an entire double-decker bus with young men who are worried about their relationships with Claire Romilly. Now, I'm really very tired. Excuse me.'

She mounted her bicycle, and this time Jericho didn't try to stop her. 'Do the letters ADU mean anything to you?' he shouted after her, remembering the stolen documents. 'It's a call sign. Probably German Army or Luftwaffe.'

She applied the brakes with such force that she slid off the saddle, her flat heels skittering in the gutter. She looked up and down the empty road. 'Have you gone utterly mad?'

'You'll find me in Hut 8.'

'Wait a moment. What has this to do with Claire?'

'Or, failing that, the Commercial Guesthouse in Albion Street.' He nodded politely. 'ADU, Miss Wallace. Angels Dance Upwards. I'll leave you in peace.'

'Mr Jericho . . .'

But he didn't want to answer any of her questions. He hurried down the avenue towards the main gate. When he glanced back, she was still where he had left her, her thin legs planted either side of the pedals, staring after him in astonishment.

LOGIE WAS WAITING for him when he got back to Hut 8. He was prowling round the Registration Room, the bowl of his pipe jerking around as he chomped furiously on its stem.

'This your coat?' was his only greeting. 'Bring it with you.'

'Hello, Guy. Where are we going?' Jericho unhooked his coat from the back of the door.

'*We're* going to have a chat, old cock. Then *you're* going home.'

Once inside his office, Logie threw himself into his chair and swung his immense feet up onto his desk. 'Close the door then, man. Let's at least *try* and keep this between ourselves.'

Jericho did as he was told. He felt surprisingly calm. 'I don't know what Skynner's been telling you,' he began, 'but I didn't actually land a punch.'

'Oh, well, that's fine then.' Logie raised his hands in mock relief. 'I mean to say, as long as there are no *broken bones*—'

'Come on. I never touched him. He can't sack me for that.'

'He can do whatever he likes.' Logie picked up a brown folder and flicked it open. 'Let us see what we have here. "Gross insubordination," it says. "Attempted physical assault," it says. "Latest in a long series of incidents which suggest the individual concerned is no longer fit for active duties."' He tossed the file back on his desk. 'Not sure I disagree, as a matter of fact. Been waiting for you to show up since yesterday afternoon. Where've you been? Admiralty? Taking a swing at the First Sea Lord?'

'You said not to work a full shift. "Just come and go as you please." Your very words.'

'Don't get smart with me, old love.'

Jericho was silent for a moment. Then he asked, 'When does he want me to go?'

'Now, you idiot.' He sighed and shook his head. 'You shouldn't have made him look a fool, Tom. Not in front of his clients.'

'But he *is* a fool.' Outrage and self-pity were welling in him. 'Come on, Guy. Do you honestly believe, for one minute, that we can break back into Shark within the next three days?'

'No. But there are ways of saying it and there are ways of saying it, especially when our American brethren are in the same room.'

Someone knocked, and Logie shouted, 'Not now, old thing.'

He waited until whoever it was had gone and then said, 'I don't think you appreciate how things have changed here.'

'That's what Skynner said.'

'Well, he's right. For once. Just look at the map, man. The convoys embark from *New York*. A quarter of the ships are American. The cargo's *all* American. American troops. American crews.' Logie suddenly covered his face with his hands. 'My God, I can't believe you tried to hit Skynner. You really are potty, aren't you?' He lifted his feet off the desk and picked up the telephone. 'I'll arrange for you to be taken back to King's.'

'No!' Jericho was surprised at his own vehemence. 'No,' he said, more calmly. 'Give me a couple of days. Tell Skynner you want to give me a couple of days to see if I can find a way back into Shark.'

Logie stared at Jericho, then started to laugh. 'Yesterday you're telling us Shark can't be broken in three days. Now you're saying you might be able to do it in two.'

'Please, Guy. I'm begging you.' And he was. He had his hands on Logie's desk and was leaning over it, pleading for his life. 'Skynner doesn't just want me out of the Park, he wants me locked up in some garret in the Admiralty, doing long division.'

'I have already stuck my neck out so far for you, my lad.' Logie jabbed his pipe into Jericho's chest. '"Jericho?" they said. "We're in a crisis and you want *Jericho*?"' He jabbed his pipe again. 'So I said, "Yes, I know he's half bloody cracked and keeps on fainting like a maiden aunt, but he's got something, got that extra two per cent. Just trust me." So I beg a bloody car—no joke round here, as you've gathered—and I come and drink stale tea in King's and plead with you, bloody *plead*, and the first thing you do is make us all look like idiots, and then you slug the head of section—all right, all right, *try* to slug him. Now, I ask you: who's going to listen to me?'

'Skynner will have to listen if you insist you need me.'

There was another knock, louder this time. 'For God's sake,' yelled Logie, 'get lost!' The handle started to turn. Jericho moved out of the way, the door opened and Puck appeared.

'Sorry, Guy. Good morning, Thomas.' He gave them each a grim nod. 'There's been a development, Guy.'

'Good news?'

'Frankly, no, to be entirely honest. You had better come.'

'Hell, *hell*!' muttered Logie. He gave Jericho a murderous look, grabbed his pipe and followed Puck out into the corridor.

Jericho hesitated for a second, then set off after them down the passage and into the Registration Room. He had never seen it so full. Lieutenant Cave was there, along, it seemed, with almost every cryptanalyst in the hut—Baxter, Atwood, Pinker, Kingcome, Proudfoot, de Brooke—as well as Kramer, like a matinée idol in his American naval uniform. He gave Jericho a friendly nod.

Logie glanced round the room with surprise. 'What's up, Puck? Holding a rally? Going on strike?'

Puck picked up the familiar yellow log sheet as if he were about to perform a conjuring trick. 'I happened to show this to Lieutenant Cave,' he said. 'Two long signals intercepted in the last twelve hours, coming out of the Nazis' new transmitter near Magdeburg. One just before midnight, one just after, rebroadcast twice over both the Diana and Hubertus radio nets.'

'Oh, do get on with it,' said Atwood, under his breath.

Puck affected not to hear. 'In the same period, the total number of Shark signals intercepted from the North Atlantic U-boats up to oh-nine hundred this morning: only five.'

'Five?' repeated Logie. 'Are you sure, old love?' He took the log sheet and ran his finger down the neatly inked columns.

'Yes. I rang the Intercept Control Room ten minutes ago. They say there's no mistake.'

An excited murmur of conversation broke out.

Puck said, 'Lieutenant Cave believes there's a pattern.'

'We've been interrogating captured U-boat crew about tactics.' Lieutenant Cave leaned forward, and Jericho saw Atwood flinch at the sight of his scarred face. 'When Dönitz sniffs a convoy, he draws his hearses up line abreast across the route he expects it to take. Twelve boats, say, maybe twenty miles apart. Possibly two lines, possibly three—nowadays he's got enough hearses to put on a pretty big show. Our estimate was forty-six operational in that sector alone.' He broke off, apologetically. 'Sorry,' he said, 'do stop me if I'm telling my grandmothers how to suck eggs.'

'Our work's rather more theoretical,' said Logie. He looked round and several of the cryptanalysts nodded in agreement.

'All right. Once the lines are established, there's one golden rule: absolute radio silence until the convoy's sighted. My hunch is that that's what's happening now. The two long signals coming out of Magdeburg—those are most likely Berlin ordering the U-boats into line. And if the boats are now observing radio silence . . .' Cave shrugged: he was sorry to have to state the obvious. 'That means they must be on battle stations.'

Nobody said anything. The intellectual abstractions of cryptanalysis had taken solid form: 2,000 German U-boat men, 10,000 Allied seamen and passengers, converging to do battle in the North Atlantic winter, 1,000 miles from land.

Someone asked what would happen next.

'If one of the U-boats finds the convoy? It'll shadow it. Send a contact signal every two hours—position, speed, direction. That'll be picked up by the other hearses and they'll start to converge. Usually, they try to get right inside the convoy, in among our ships. They'll wait until nightfall to attack. Fires from the ships that have been hit illuminate other targets. Also, night-time makes it harder for our destroyers to catch them.'

'Of course, the weather's appalling,' added Cave, his sharp voice cutting into the silence, 'even for the time of year. Snow. Freezing fog. But that's actually in our favour.'

Kramer said: 'How long do we have?'

'Well, the U-boat is a slow beast. On the surface it moves at the speed of a bicycle, underwater it's only as fast as a man on foot. And the bad weather will give them visibility problems. But if Dönitz knows about the convoys? I'd guess a day and a half, at the outside.'

CAVE EXCUSED HIMSELF to go and phone the bad news to the Admiralty. The cryptanalysts were left alone. At the far end of the hut a faint clacking noise began as the Type-X machines started their day's work.

452

'If only we had a four-wheel bombe,' moaned Proudfoot.

'Well, we ain't got one, old love, so don't let's waste time on that,' Logie replied.

Kramer had been leaning against one of the trestle tables. Now he pushed himself onto his feet, smacking his fist into the palm of his left hand. 'Goddamn it, I feel so *helpless*. A measly *day and a half*. There must be *something*.'

Jericho wasn't listening. Something was stirring in his mind, some tiny shift in the depths of his subconscious, beyond the reach of any power of analysis. What was it? A memory? A connection? The more he tried to concentrate on it, the more elusive it became.

De Brooke began to talk about some theory of his which had been running on a pair of bombes for the past nine hours, but Jericho had stopped listening. He was searching back through his mental record of the past ten minutes to find the word, the phrase, that could have stirred the phantom in his mind. Diana, Hubertus, Magdeburg, radio silence, contact signal . . .

Contact signal. The scouting U-boat's regular contact signal.

'Guy, where d'you keep the keys to the Black Museum?'

'What, old thing? Oh, in my desk. Top drawer. Hey, where're you going? I haven't finished talking to you yet . . .'

IT WAS A RELIEF to get out of the claustrophobic atmosphere of the hut and into the fresh air. He trotted towards the mansion.

He seldom went into the big house these days. He was hazy about what went on there now. Upstairs, all sorts of mysterious things were done: he'd heard rumours they were breaking the ciphers of the German secret service.

He walked quickly across the hall. An army captain was pretending to read the *Observer* while listening to a middle-aged man in tweeds trying to chat up a young RAF woman. Nobody paid any attention to Jericho. At the foot of the elaborately carved oak staircase, a corridor led off to the right and wound round the back of the house. Midway along it was a door which opened onto steps down to the cellar, where the cryptanalysts stored their stolen treasures.

Jericho felt along the wall for the light switch.

The larger of the two keys unlocked the door to the 'museum'. Stacked on metal shelves along one wall were a dozen or more captured Enigma machines. The smaller key fitted one of a pair of big iron safes. Jericho knelt and opened it and began to rummage through the contents. Here they all were, their precious pinches: each one a victory in the long war against Enigma. He pulled out armfuls of papers and charts.

Finally, from the bottom shelf at the back, he withdrew a small package wrapped in brown oilcloth. This was the haul for which Fasson and Grazier had died, still in its original covering, as it had been passed out of the sinking U-boat. He never saw it without thanking God that they'd found something waterproof to wrap it in. The smallest exposure to water would have dissolved the ink . . . It was enough to make even a mathematician believe in miracles. Jericho removed the oilcloth tenderly, to reveal two little pamphlets, printed in Gothic lettering on pink blotting paper: the second edition of the U-boats' Short Weather Cipher, now useless, following the code-book change, and the Short Signal Code Book.

A typed notice was stuck on the back of the safe door: 'It is strictly forbidden to remove any item without my express permission. (Signed) L.F.N. Skynner, Head of Naval Section.'

Jericho took particular pleasure in slipping the Short Signal Code Book into his inside pocket and running with it back to the hut.

JERICHO TOSSED the keys to Logie, who just caught them.

'Contact signal.'

'What?'

'Contact signal,' repeated Jericho.

'Praise the Lord!' said Atwood, throwing up his hands like a revivalist preacher. 'The Oracle has spoken.'

'All right, Frank. Just a minute. What about it, old love?'

Jericho could see it all much faster than he could convey it. Indeed, it was quite hard to formulate it in words at all. He spoke slowly, reordering it in his mind, turning it into a narrative.

'Do you remember, in November, when we got the Short Weather Cipher Book off the *U-459*? When we also got the Short Signal Code Book? Only we decided not to concentrate on the Short Signal Book at the time, because it never yielded anything long enough to make a worthwhile crib? I mean just five letters, once in a blue moon.' Jericho withdrew the little pink pamphlet carefully from his pocket. 'One letter for the speed of the convoy, a couple for its course, a couple more for the grid reference . . .'

Baxter stared at the code book as if hypnotised. 'You've removed that from the safe *without permission?*'

'But if Lieutenant Cave is correct, and whichever U-boat finds the convoy is going to send a contact signal every *two hours*, and if it's going to shadow it till nightfall, then it might send as many as four, or even five, signals in a day. And if other U-boats attach themselves to the same convoy, on the same day, and *they* all start sending contact signals every two hours . . .'

Logie, at least, could see what he was driving at. He withdrew his pipe slowly from his mouth. 'Bloody hell!'

'If it's an attack by eight boats, let's say, we could easily get a hundred letters. Enough to work with. It's just as good as the weather crib.' Jericho felt as proud as a father, offering the world a glimpse of his newborn child. 'It's beautiful, don't you see? It wasn't possible till this moment, because the Germans have never been able to throw so many U-boats against such a mass of shipping. The very scale of the Germans' achievement breeds such a mass of material for us that it'll sow the seeds of their eventual defeat.'

He paused.

'Aren't there rather a lot of *ifs* there?' said Baxter drily. '*If* the U-boat finds the convoy early enough in the day, *if* it reports every two hours, *if* the others all do the same...'

'And *if*,' said Atwood, 'the Short Signal Code Book we pinched in November wasn't changed last week at the same time as the Weather Cipher Book...'

That was a possibility Jericho hadn't considered. He felt his enthusiasm crumble slightly.

Now Puck joined in the attack. 'I agree. The concept is quite brilliant, Thomas. But your strategy depends on failure, does it not? We will break Shark only if the U-boats find the convoy, which is exactly what we want to avoid. And suppose we do come up with that day's Shark settings—so what? Marvellous. We can read all the U-boats' signals to Berlin, boasting to Dönitz about how many Allied ships they've sunk. And twenty-four hours later the settings change and we're blacked out again.'

'No, no.' Jericho shook his head emphatically. 'We hope, obviously, that the U-boats *don't* find the convoys. Yes—that's the whole point of the exercise. But, if they do, we can at least turn it to our advantage. If we break the Shark settings for twenty-four hours, then we'll pick up the encoded weather messages for that entire period. And, remember, we'll have our own ships in the area, able to give us the precise weather data the U-boats are encoding. So we'll be able to make a start on constructing the new Weather Cipher Book. We could get our foot back in the door again. Don't you see?'

He ran his hands through his hair and tugged at it in exasperation. Why were they all being so dim?

Kramer had been scribbling furiously in a notebook. 'He's on to something, you know. Come on. It's worth a try. At least it puts us back in the fight.'

'I still don't see it,' said Baxter, and Puck grunted in agreement.

'Enough!' Logie banged his pipe on one of the trestle tables. 'It's quite right we should be cautious, Puck. But we've also got to face facts. We've been blacked out for four days, and Tom's is the only decent idea we've got. So good work, Tom.'

Jericho stared at an ink stain on the floor. Oh, God, he thought, here comes the housemaster's pep talk.

'Now, there's a lot resting on us here, and I want every man to remember he's part of a team. And if ever any of us—any of us—is tempted to forget it, just think of those convoys, and all the other convoys this war depends on. Got it? Right, back to work.'

Baxter and Puck exchanged grim glances on their way out. Jericho watched them go and wondered why they were so determinedly pessimistic. What was it? Resentment that he had come in after all their hard work and made them look like fools?

Logie was shaking his head. 'What are we to do with you, old love?' He tried to look stern, but he couldn't hide his pleasure.

'Give me my job back.'

'I'll have to talk to Skynner.' He held the door open and ushered Jericho out into the passage. 'He's going to love it, isn't he, having to tell his friends the admirals that the best chance of getting back into Shark is if the convoys are spotted? Oh, hell, I suppose I'd better go and call him.' He went halfway into his office, then came out again. 'And you're quite sure you never actually hit him?'

'Quite sure, Guy.'

'Pity,' said Logie, half to himself. 'In a way. Pity.'

HESTER WALLACE couldn't sleep. The blackout curtains were drawn against the day. Her tiny room was a study in monochrome. A nosegay of lavender sent a soothing fragrance filtering through her pillow. But, even so, oblivion eluded her.

ADU, Miss Wallace. Angels Dance Upwards . . .

The mnemonic was infuriatingly effective. She couldn't get it out of her brain, even though the letters meant nothing to her.

It's a call sign. Probably German Army or Luftwaffe . . .

No surprise in that. It was almost bound to be. After all, there were so many of them: thousands upon thousands.

ADU . . . ADU . . . She couldn't place it.

She thought about the two men who had been waiting for her when she returned from church. They had Bletchley passes and they were looking for Claire. Hester couldn't help them. Had anyone else been asking after her? Hester mentioned Jericho's visit of the previous night. Other questions followed. Finally, they told her there was nothing to worry about, and went away.

'Oh, Claire,' she said aloud, 'you silly girl. What *have* you done?'

She turned on her side and tried to fill her mind with soothing thoughts. But no sooner had she rid herself of the intense, pale face of Tom Jericho than the Brylcreemed head of Miles Mermagen, her head of section, rose greasily before her inner eye. He had been a manager at Barclays Bank before the war, and liked to come up behind the girls as they worked and massage their shoulders. At the Hut 6 Christmas party, he had manoeuvred her under the mistletoe and clumsily taken off her glasses. ('Thank you, Miles,' she'd said, trying miserably to make a joke of it, 'without my spectacles you look almost tolerably attractive . . .') His lips on hers were unpleasantly moist, and tasted of sweet sherry.

In a way, it was all Miss Smallbone's fault. If Angela Smallbone hadn't pointed out in the common room that the *Daily Telegraph* was holding a crossword competition, then Hester Wallace's life would have gone on undisturbed. It was not a particularly thrilling life—as a teacher of divinity at a remote girls' preparatory school near Beaminster—but it was not much touched by war, either.

Hester had a gift for crosswords and when Angela read out that night that the prize money was twenty pounds . . . Well, she thought, why not? The first hurdle, an abnormally difficult puzzle printed in the next day's paper, she passed with ease. She sent off her solution, and a letter arrived by return post inviting her to the final, to be held in the *Telegraph*'s staff canteen, a fortnight hence. Hester caught the train up to London, joined fifty other finalists—and won. She put the money in her Post Office savings account.

It was on the Thursday that the second letter had arrived, this one very different: registered post; On His Majesty's Service.

Afterwards, she could never quite decide. Had the *Telegraph* held the competition at the instigation of the War Office, as a way of trawling the country for men and women with an aptitude for word puzzles? Or had some bright spark at the War Office merely seen the results of the competition and asked the *Telegraph* for a list of the finalists? Whatever the truth, five of the most suitable finalists were interviewed in a grim Victorian office block south of the Thames, and three of them were ordered to report to Bletchley. She had picked up enough clues at the interview to guess that the work would be on codes, and her fantasies were all of quiet, book-lined libraries and the pure, clear air of the intellect.

Arriving at Bletchley Station on a soaking Monday morning, she was driven straight to the mansion and given a copy of the Official Secrets Act to sign. Then they were assigned. The two male finalists became cryptanalysts, while she, the woman who had beaten them, was dispatched to a bedlam called Control.

'You take this from here, see, and in this first column you enter the code name of the intercept station. Chicksands, right, that's CKS, Beaumanor is BMR, Harpenden is HPN—don't worry, dear, you'll soon get used to it . . .'

Her fantasies were dust. She was a glorified clerk, Control a glorified funnel between the intercept stations and the cryptanalysts, a funnel down which poured the output of some forty thousand different radio call signs. Sitting in the freezing hut that winter, filling in endless charts they called 'blists', Hester had a sense of Nazi Germany only as an endless, darkened plain, with thousands of tiny, isolated lights flickering at one another in the blackness.

She grimaced at the memory and shifted her position in the bed again. It was quite hopeless. She reached out and switched on the little bedside lamp, fumbling around its base for her glasses.

She propped herself up in bed and tried to focus on her copy of *Abelman's German Primer*.

Ich lerne Deutsch, ich lernte Deutsch, ich habe Deutsch gelernt ...

German, she thought: German would be her salvation. A working knowledge of written German would lift her out of the grind of the Intercept Control Room and propel her into the rarefied air of the Machine Room, where the *real* work was done—where she should have been put in the first place.

FOR THE FIRST TIME in more than a month, Tom Jericho found that he was busy.

He had to supervise the copying of the Short Signal Code Book, six typewritten transcripts of which were duly produced and stamped MOST SECRET. Every line had to be checked, for a single error could spell the difference between a successful break and days of failure. The intercept controllers had to be briefed. Teleprinted orders had to be sent to all the duty officers of every Hut 8 listening post. Their brief was simple: concentrate everything you have on the known Atlantic U-boat frequencies, cancel all leave and pay even greater attention than usual to very short bursts of Morse preceded by 'E-bar'—*dot dot dash dot dot*—the Germans' priority code, which cleared the wavelength for convoy contact reports.

That afternoon, sitting in his old place by the window in the Big Room, Jericho proved by slide-rule calculation what he already knew by instinct: that seventeen convoy contact reports, if harvested in the same twenty-four-hour stretch, *might*—if the cryptanalysts had the requisite percentage of luck—give them a break into Shark, provided they could get at least ten bombes working in relay for a minimum of thirty-six hours ... And all the time he thought of Claire.

There was very little, practically, he could do about her. Twice during the day he managed to get out to the phone box to try to call her father: once as they all went off to lunch, and the second time in the late afternoon, when he pretended he needed to stretch his legs. On each occasion, the phone rang unanswered. He had a vague but growing feeling of dread, made worse by his powerlessness.

458

He couldn't return to Hut 3. He didn't have the time to check out her cottage, or to rescue the intercepts from his room.

In the event, it was to be well past seven before he got away. Logie was passing through the Big Room when he stopped off at Jericho's table and told him to get some rest. 'There's nothing more to do here, old love. Except wait.'

Jericho reached thankfully for his coat. 'Did you talk to Skynner?'

'Not about you. There's some other flap on that seems to have taken his mind off things. Now you just make sure you get some kip.'

Jericho returned the Shark intercepts to the Registry and went outside. The March sun, which had barely risen above the trees all day, had sunk behind the mansion, leaving a fading streak of primrose and pale orange at the rim of an indigo sky. He had almost passed the telephone box before he realised that it was empty.

One last try? Why not?

The Kensington number still wasn't answering, so he decided, on a whim, to try the Foreign Office. The operator put him through to a duty clerk, and he asked for Edward Romilly.

'Which department?'

'I don't know, I'm afraid.'

The line went silent. The chances of Edward Romilly being at his desk on a Sunday night were slim. He rested his shoulder against the glass panel of the booth and waited. Presently there was a click, and a cultured female voice said, 'German Desk.'

German Desk? He was momentarily disconcerted. 'Ah, Edward Romilly, please.'

'And who shall I say is calling?'

My God, he *was* there. 'A friend of his daughter.'

'Wait, please.'

His fingers were clamped so tightly round the receiver that they were aching. He made an effort to relax. There was no good reason why Romilly *shouldn't* work on the German Desk. Hadn't Claire told him once that her father had been a junior official at the Berlin Embassy just as the Nazis were coming to power?

'I'm afraid, sir, Mr Romilly's already left for the evening.'

'Thank you. It doesn't matter. Good night.'

He hung up quickly. He didn't like the sound of that. He came out of the telephone box and walked rapidly through the main gate and down the hill towards the town.

He had almost reached the guesthouse, which was about halfway down Albion Street, when he noticed a car. He slowed his pace. When he was almost level with it, one of the occupants struck a match. As the driver leaned over to cup his hand to the light, Jericho saw on his sleeve the three white stripes of a police sergeant.

459

He let himself into the guesthouse and prayed he could make the stairs before Mrs Armstrong rose like a night fighter to intercept him in the hall. But at the sound of his key in the latch she appeared from the kitchen, drying her hands on her apron. 'You've got a visitor. It's a very nice-looking young gentleman. I've put him,' she added, with heavy significance, 'in the parlour.'

The parlour! Open nightly to any resident from eight till ten, as formal as a ducal drawing room with its matching three-piece suite and antimacassars, and its mahogany standard lamp with tasselled shade. Who had come to see him, wondered Jericho, who warranted admission to the *parlour*?

At first, he didn't recognise him: golden hair, a pale and freckled face, pale blue eyes, a practised smile, advancing across the room to meet him, right hand outstretched, fifty guineas' worth of Savile Row coat draped over manly shoulders.

'Wigram. Douglas Wigram. Foreign Office. We met yesterday but weren't introduced properly.'

He took Jericho's hand lightly and oddly, a finger crooked back into his palm, and it took Jericho a moment to realise he had just been the recipient of a Masonic handshake.

'Digs all right? Super room, this. Super. Mind if we go somewhere else? Whereabouts are you based? Upstairs?'

He held out his arm, still smiling, and Jericho found himself being ushered up the stairs. He felt as though he had been tricked somehow. On the landing, he rallied sufficiently to turn and say, 'It's very small; there's barely room to sit.'

'That's perfectly all right, my dear chap. As long as it's private.'

Jericho switched on the dim light and stood back to let Wigram go in first. The picture of the chapel, he was relieved to note, looked undisturbed. He closed the door and stood by it.

'See what you mean about the room,' said Wigram, cupping his hands to the glass to peer out of the window. 'The hell we have to go through, what?' He closed the curtains. 'We're rather worried about a girl called Claire Romilly. Mind if I sit down?'

He shrugged off his overcoat and laid it on the bed, then sat on the edge of the mattress and patted the eiderdown beside him. 'Let's talk.' He didn't seem in the least put out when Jericho stayed where he was. He merely folded his hands contentedly in his lap.

'All right,' he said, 'we'll make a start, then, shall we? Claire Romilly. Twenty. Clerical-grade staff. Officially missing for'—he looked at his watch—'twelve hours. Failed to show for her morning shift. The girl she lives with swears she hasn't seen her since Thursday. Her father says he hasn't seen her since before Christmas. Nobody else—girls she works with, family, so forth—nobody seems to have the foggiest. Vanished.' Wigram snapped his fingers. 'Just like that. Rather a good friend of yours, I gather?'

'I haven't seen her since the beginning of February.'

'But good enough? Good enough that you've *tried* to see her? Out to her cottage last night, according to Miss Wallace. Questions, questions. Then, this morning, into Hut 3: questions, questions, again. Phone call to her father—oh, yes,' he said, noticing Jericho's surprise, 'he rang us straight away to say you'd called. You've never met Ed Romilly? Lovely bloke. But rather lost the plot after his wife died. Tell me, Mr Jericho, why the interest?'

'I'd been away for a month. I hadn't seen her.'

'But surely you've got plenty more important things to worry about, especially just now?' Receiving no answer, he changed tack. 'Ever talk to the girl about your work?'

'Of course not.'

'Of course not. Strike you as odd, though—possibly even sinister—that one day the Germans black us out in the North Atlantic, and two days later the girlfriend of a leading Hut 8 cryptanalyst goes missing? Actually on the same day as he comes back?'

Jericho's gaze flickered involuntarily to the print of the chapel. 'I told you. I never talked to Claire about my work. I hadn't seen her for a month. And she wasn't my girlfriend.'

'No? What was she then?'

What was she then? A good question. 'I just wanted to see her,' he said lamely. 'I couldn't find her. I was concerned.'

'Got a photo of her? Something recent?'

'No. Actually, I don't have any pictures of her.'

'Really...Can you fire a gun, Mr Jericho?'

'I couldn't hit a duck at a funfair.'

'Now that's what I would have thought, though one shouldn't always judge a chap by his looks. Only the Bletchley Park Home Guard had a little burglary at their armoury on Friday. Two items missing. A Smith & Wesson .38 revolver, issued by the War Office. And a box containing thirty-six rounds of ammunition.'

Jericho said nothing. Wigram looked at him for a while, as if he were making up his mind about something. 'No reason why *you* shouldn't know, I suppose. Trustworthy fellow like you. Come and sit down.' He patted the eiderdown again.

Reluctantly, Jericho sat down. Wigram leaned forward. As he did so, his jacket parted slightly, and Jericho glimpsed a flash of leather and gunmetal against the white shirt.

'Five days ago,' he said softly, 'Hut 6 decoded a German Army signal from the Middle East. General Rommel's becoming a bit of a bad sport. Seems to think the only reason he's losing is that somehow, by some miracle, we always appear to know where exactly he's going to attack. Suddenly, the Afrika Korps want an enquiry into cipher security. Oh, dear. *Ding-dong*, bells start ringing. Twelve hours later, Admiral Dönitz suddenly decides to tighten Enigma procedure by changing the U-boat weather code. *Ding-dong* again. Today, it's the Luftwaffe. Four German merchant ships loaded with goodies for Rommel were recently "surprised" by the RAF and sunk halfway to Tunisia. This morning, we read that the German C-in-C, Mediterranean, is demanding to know whether the enemy could have read his codes.'

Wigram patted Jericho's knee. 'Peals of alarms, Mr Jericho. And in the middle of them all, your lady friend disappears, at the same time as a shiny new shooter and a box of bullets. Now, exactly who or what are we dealing with here?' Wigram had taken out a small black leather notebook. 'Claire Alexandra Romilly. Born: London, 21st of the 12th, '22. Father: Edward Arthur Macauley Romilly, diplomat. Mother: the Honourable Alexandra Romilly, *née* Harvey, deceased in motor accident. The child is educated privately abroad. Father's postings: Bucharest, Berlin, Washington, Athens, then London. The girl by now is at some fancy finishing school in Geneva. She returns to London on the outbreak of war, aged seventeen. Some voluntary civil-defence work. Nothing too arduous. August '42: applies for clerical position, Foreign Office. Good languages. Recommended for position at Bletchley Park. See attached letter from father, blah blah. Interviewed September the 10th. Accepted, cleared, starts work the following week.' Wigram flicked the pages back and forth. 'That's the lot. Not exactly a rigorous process of selection, is it? But then she does come from a *frightfully* good family. Care to add anything to the record?'

'I don't think I can.'

'How'd you meet her?'

For the next ten minutes, Jericho answered Wigram's questions. He did this carefully and—mostly—truthfully. Where he lied, it was only by omission. They had gone to a concert for their first date. After that, they had gone out in the evening a few times. She had never talked about politics. She had never discussed her work. She had never mentioned other friends.

'Did you sleep with her?'

'Mind your own bloody business.'

'I'll put that down as yes.'

More questions. No, he had noticed nothing odd about her behaviour. No, she had not seemed tense or nervous, secretive, silent, inquisitive, depressed or elated—no, none of these—and, at the end, they hadn't quarrelled. Really? No. So they had—what, then?

462

'I don't know. Drifted apart.'

'She was seeing someone else?'

'Perhaps. I don't know.'

'Perhaps. You don't know.' Wigram shook his head in wonder. 'Tell me about last night.'

'I cycled over to her cottage at about ten thirty. She wasn't there. I talked with Miss Wallace for a bit. Then I came home.'

Wigram gazed down at his notes, tapping the side of his nose. 'Not right, Mr Jericho. Can't quite put my finger on it, but definitely *not right*. Still'—he snapped the notebook shut—'time to go into all that later, what?' He put his hand on Jericho's knee and pushed himself to his feet. 'First, we must catch our rabbit. You've no idea where she might be, I suppose? No? Thought not.'

By the time Jericho felt he could trust himself to look up, Wigram was draping his overcoat back round his shoulders.

'It could all be a coincidence,' said Jericho. 'You do realise that? I mean, Dönitz always seems to have been suspicious about Enigma. That's why he gave the U-boats Shark in the first place.'

'Oh absolutely,' said Wigram. 'But let's look at it another way. Let's imagine the Germans *have* got a whisper of what we're up to here. What would they do? They couldn't exactly chuck out a hundred thousand Enigma machines overnight, could they? No. They'd start checking every suspicious incident. And in the meantime they'd try and find hard proof. A person with documentary evidence, perhaps. God, there are enough of them about.' He withdrew a sheet of paper from his inside pocket and unfolded it. 'This is the list I asked for yesterday. Eleven people in the Naval Section knew about the importance of the Weather Cipher Book. Skynner we can exclude, I suppose. And Logie. But Baxter? Baxter's a communist, isn't he?'

'Communists don't have much time for Nazis. As a rule.'

'What about Pukowski?'

'Puck lost his father and his brother when Poland was invaded. He loathes the Germans. Really, Mr Wigram, this is ridiculous...'

'Atwood. Pinker. Kingcome. *You* . . . Who *are* you all, exactly?' Wigram looked round the tiny room with distaste. For the first time, he seemed to notice the print on the mantelpiece. 'I mean, just because a bloke's been to King's College, Cambridge ...'

He picked up the picture and held it at an angle under the light. Jericho watched him, transfixed.

'E.M. Forster,' said Wigram thoughtfully. 'He's still at King's, isn't he? What was that essay of his? The one about choosing between your friend and your country?'

'"I hate the idea of causes,"' Jericho quoted, '"and if I had to choose between betraying my country and betraying my friend, I hope I should have the guts to betray my country." But he did write that before the war.'

Wigram set the print carefully back on the top of Jericho's books.

'So I should hope,' he said, standing back to admire it. He turned and smiled at Jericho. 'So I should damn well hope.'

AFTER WIGRAM had gone, it was some while before Jericho felt able to move. He lay full length on the bed, still wearing his overcoat, and listened to the sounds of the house. There were footsteps on the landing. A whispered conversation ensued, which ended with a woman having a fit of the giggles. Then silence again.

When he did move, after about a quarter of an hour, his actions had a frantic, fumbling haste. He took the print and laid it face down on the threadbare carpet, lifted off the back, rolled the intercepts into a tube and took them over to the grate. Beside the hearth was a matchbox. He struck a match, and when the yellow flame caught he applied it to the bottom of the intercepts. He held on to them as they writhed and blackened, until the pain obliged him to drop them in the grate, where they disintegrated into tiny flakes of ash.

The wartime lipstick was hard and waxy: it was like trying to colour your lips with a Christmas candle. When, after several minutes of hard rubbing, Hester Wallace replaced her glasses, she peered into the mirror with distaste. Make-up had never featured much in her life, not even before the war, when there had been plenty in the shops.

The shortage of cosmetics seemed to have caught up at last even with Claire. Although there was a profusion of pots and bottles all over her little dressing table—Max Factor, Coty, Elizabeth Arden, each name redolent of prewar glamour—most of them turned out on closer inspection to be empty. Nothing was left except a trace of scent. Eventually, Hester found a half-full pot of mascara and a glass-stoppered jar with an inch of rather lumpy face powder, and set to work with those.

She had no qualms about helping herself. Hadn't Claire always told her she should? Make-up was fun, that was Claire's philosophy, and, besides, *If this is what it takes, then, darling heart, this is simply what one does*. Very well—Hester dabbed grimly at her pallid cheeks—if *this* was what it took to help persuade Miles Mermagen to approve a transfer, this was what he'd *get*.

She regarded her reflection without enthusiasm, then went

downstairs. She had made a carrot flan earlier in the evening, with ingredients she had grown herself in their little vegetable patch, and now she laid a place for Claire and left a note telling her where to find the flan and how to heat it. She hesitated, then added at the end: *Welcome back—from wherever you've been!—much love, H.*

Of course Claire would come back. It was all a stupid panic, too absurd for words.

As her bicycle bounced along the track towards the lane, she startled a white owl, which rose like a ghost in the moonlight.

She parked her bicycle outside the canteen, and was borne along by the stream of workers to the entrance to Hut 6. Control was already in a fine state of uproar, Mermagen bustling self-importantly between the desks. Fourth Panzer Army was reporting the successful recapture of Kharkov from the Russians, and the ninnies in Hut 3 were demanding that every frequency in the southern sector, eastern front, be double-backed *immediately*.

'Hester, Hester, just in time. Will you talk to Chicksands, there's a good girl, and see what they can do? And, while you're on, the Machine Room reckon they've got a corrupt text on the last batch of Kestrel—the operator needs to check her notes and resend. Oh, and the Index could do with a sorting out.'

All this before she had even taken off her coat.

It was two o'clock before she could talk to Mermagen in private. He was in his broom-cupboard office, studying papers through half-closed eyes in a terrific man-of-destiny pose she guessed he'd copied from some actor in the pictures. He was trying to grow a Clark Gable moustache, but it was slightly too long on the left-hand side.

'Might I have a word, Miles? My request for a transfer—'

He groaned and flicked over a page. 'Not again.'

'I've been learning German—'

'How brave.'

'You did say that *not* having German made a transfer impossible.'

'Yes, but I didn't say that *having* it made a transfer *likely*. Oh, well, come in, then.' With a sigh, he put aside his papers and beckoned her over the threshold.

'Transfers of personnel from section to section are, as I've told you before, extremely rare. We —'

Suddenly he was staring at her intently, and she realised he had noticed the make-up. He couldn't have looked more startled if she'd painted herself with woad.

'Look here, Hester, the last thing I want to be is difficult. What you need is a change of scene for a day or two. Why don't you take a look round one of the intercept stations, get a feel for where you fit into the chain? I know,' he added, touching his moustache, 'I could do with a refresher myself. We could go up together.'

'Together? Yes... Why not? And find a little pub somewhere—with rooms, so we could stay overnight if it got late?'

He laughed. 'I still couldn't guarantee a transfer, you know.'

'But it would help?'

'Your words.'

'I'd rather die.'

'Frigid little bitch.'

SHE FILLED THE BASIN and splashed her face furiously. The icy water numbed her hands and stung her face. She welcomed the shock and the discomfort: it was a punishment for her folly and delusion.

She felt a pricking of self-pity in the corners of her eyes and immediately lowered her head back over the basin and scrubbed at her cheeks and mouth with a sliver of carbolic soap.

She wished she could talk to Claire.

ADU, Miss Wallace . . .

Behind her, in the cubicle, the toilet flushed. Hurriedly, she dried her face and hands and returned to her desk.

At four o'clock the first half of the night shift began drifting off to the canteen.

Hester bent her head lower over her desk and continued to write in her careful schoolmistress copperplate. She watched the other women putting on their coats and filing out. Ah, but Claire had been so *funny* about them. It was one of the things Hester loved in her the most, the way she mimicked everyone: Anthea Leigh-Delamere, who liked to come on shift in jodhpurs; Binnie, who wanted to be a Catholic nun; the girl from Solihull, who held the telephone a foot away from her mouth because her mother had told her the receiver was full of germs... The ghastliness of Bletchley had been their private joke, their conspiracy against the bores.

Bores. Boring. Claire's favourite words. The Park was boring. The war was boring. The town was *terrifically* boring. And the men were the biggest bores of all. There were always two or three of them, at least, hanging round her like tomcats. And how she mocked them, on those rare evenings when she and Hester were alone together. She mocked their clumsy fumblings, their corny dialogue, their absurd self-importance. The only exception, now Hester came to think of it, was the curious Mr Jericho, whom she had never even mentioned.

ADU, Miss Wallace...

Now that she had made up her mind to do it—and hadn't she always *known* that she was going to do it?—she was astonished at how calm she felt. She even had the perfect excuse to slip across to the Index, for hadn't Miles, in everybody's hearing, commanded her to ensure the volumes were all in order?

She finished the blist, slotted it into the rack and then moved as casually as she could towards the Index Room.

JERICHO DREW BACK the curtains to unveil another cold, clear morning. It was only his third day in the Commercial Guesthouse, but already the view had acquired a weary familiarity. First came the long and narrow garden (concrete yard with washing line, vegetable patch, bomb shelter). Then there was a broad expanse of railway lines, a dozen or more, which led the eye, at last, to the centrepiece: a huge London, Midland & Scottish engine shed.

What a day in prospect: the sort of day one waded through with no aim higher than to reach the other end intact. He looked at his alarm clock. It was a quarter past seven. By his reckoning, there would be nothing for him to do until about midnight, British time, when the first elements of the convoy would begin to enter the U-boat danger zone. Nothing to do except wait and brood.

There had been occasions during the night when Jericho had made up his mind to seek out Wigram and make a full confession. But in the end the judgment was too fine a one to call. On the one hand, yes, it was his duty to tell Wigram all he knew. On the other, what he

467

knew would make little practical difference to the task of finding her, so why betray her? And, anyway, she might have turned up by now, wondering what on earth the fuss was all about.

He was on the point of turning away from the window when his eye was caught by a movement at the far end of the engine shed. Was it a large animal of some sort, or a big man crawling on all fours, sniffing under the wheels of a goods wagon? He looked more closely and saw a little group of two policemen and two dogs on leashes, searching an empty train.

Two men and two dogs for the railway yard. How many in the town? Twenty? And in the surrounding countryside?

What would they do if they caught her?

Hang her?

Come on, Jericho. He could practically hear the housemaster's voice at his elbow. *Brace up, boy.*

Get through the day, somehow.

Wash. Shave. Dress. Go downstairs. Endure attempts to make polite conversation with Bonnyman. Be introduced to two of the other guests: Miss Quince, rather pretty, a teleprincess in the Naval Hut, and Noakes, a cryptanalyst in the Weather Section. Chew stale toast. Drink tea as grey and watery as a February sky.

At ten to eight, Mrs Armstrong came in with the morning post. Two letters for Miss Jobey, a postcard for Miss Quince—oh, and this for Mr Jericho, which must have been put through the door at some time in the night.

He held it carefully. His name was printed on the envelope in blue ink, with 'By hand, Strictly Personal' added underneath.

He took it into the hall to open, Mrs Armstrong at his heels.

> *Dear Mr Jericho,*
>
> *As you expressed such a strong interest in medieval alabaster figurework when we met yesterday, I wondered if you might care to join me at the same place at 8 this morning to view the altar tomb of Lord Grey de Wilton?*
>
> *H.A.W.*

'Bad news, Mr Jericho?' Mrs Armstrong couldn't quite suppress the note of hope in her voice.

But Jericho was already dragging on his overcoat and was halfway out of the door.

HE HADN'T BEEN in a church for years, and the chilly stink of candle wax and damp and incense brought memories of childhood crawling back. He was five minutes late, yet there was no sign of anyone else in the cold, dark, cavelike interior.

He began to walk up the nave. To the left of the altar was a stone coffin with an inscription; next to it, the smooth white effigy of Richard, Lord Grey de Wilton, dead these past five hundred years, reclining in full armour, his head resting on his helmet.

'The armour is especially interesting. But then warfare in the fifteenth century was the highest occupation for a gentleman.' He wasn't sure where she'd come from. She was simply there when he turned round, about ten feet behind him.

'You weren't followed, I trust?'

'No. I don't think so, no.'

She took a step towards him and held out her hand. 'May I have my note back, please? I'd prefer to leave no trace. Thank you.' She took it and stowed it away at the bottom of her voluminous carpet-bag. Her hands were shaking.

He knew it would be wise to let her come to it in her own time, but he couldn't help himself. 'You've checked it?' he said. 'The call sign?'

She snapped the bag shut. 'Yes. I've checked it.'

'And is it army or Luftwaffe?'

She held up a finger. 'Patience, Mr Jericho. Patience. First, there's some information I'd like from you, if you don't mind. We might begin with what made you choose those three letters.'

'You don't want to know, Miss Wallace. Believe me.'

She raised her eyes to heaven. 'God preserve me. I seem to move in an endless round, Mr Jericho, from one patronising male to another, forever being told what I am and am not allowed to know.'

His shoulders sagged. 'I'm sorry. ADU was the call sign on a series of four intercepts our mutual friend . . . stole from Hut 3.'

'How do you know she stole them?'

'They were hidden in her bedroom. Under the floorboards. As far as I know, we're not encouraged to take our work home.'

'Where are they now?'

'I burned them.'

They sat down in the second row of pews then, side by side. It was almost like a confession—she playing the priest and he the sinner.

'Do you think she's a spy?' Hester asked.

'I don't know. But a man from the Foreign Office called Wigram does, for one.'

'Why? I mean, why all this fuss for one missed shift?'

He ran his hand nervously through his hair. 'There are . . . indications that the Germans may suspect Enigma is being broken.'

A long pause.

'But why would our mutual friend wish to help the *Germans*?'

'If I knew that, Miss Wallace, I wouldn't be sitting here with you, passing the time of day by breaking the Official Secrets Act.

Now really, please, have you heard enough?'

Another pause. A reluctant nod of the head.

'ADU is the call sign of a motorised German Army signals unit,' she said. 'Its transmissions are on wavelengths monitored by the Beaumanor intercept station in Leicestershire. Since October, unit number five-three-seven has been based in the Smolensk military district of the Ukraine, presently under the command of Field-Marshal Gunther von Kluge.'

Jericho had been leaning forward in anticipation. Now he drew back in surprise. 'A signals unit?' He felt disappointed. He had been expecting something a little more... *exotic*, he supposed.

'Five-three-seven,' he said. 'Is that a front-line unit?'

'The line in that sector is shifting every day. But according to the situation map in Hut 6, Smolensk is still about a hundred kilometres inside German territory: a standard, rear-echelon, low-priority target. But there are several... complications.'

SHE TOLD IT like a story, in a low voice, without looking at him. She used her hands a lot, he noticed. They fluttered like tiny white birds: now pecking at the hem of her coat, now perching on the back of the pew in front, now describing, in rapid, circling motions, how she had gone about her crime.

After identifying the call sign from the row volume in the Index Room, it is the work of less than a minute to pull down the appropriate column book and make a note of the intercept serial numbers, so that she can look them up in the Registry. Then she collects her coat, clicks on her blackout torch and steps out into the night.

A gust of wind swirls down the alley between the huts and buffets her face. At the far end of Hut 8 the path forks: right will take her to the main gate and the warm bustle of the canteen, left leads into the blackness along the edge of the lake, towards the big, squat, bunkerlike building that houses Bletchley's central Registry. Her torch flashes on steel-shuttered windows, then finds the heavy door.

Thou shalt not steal, she tells herself, reaching for the handle.

No, no. Of course not. Thou shalt not steal, merely take a quick look and then depart.

The rawness of the white neon is a shock after the gloom of the hut. The duty clerk, a friendly corporal in the Women's Auxiliary Air Force, leans across the counter as if she is serving in a shop.

'Cold night?'

'Rather.' Hester manages to smile and nod. 'I've got some serials to check, for Hut 6 Control.'

'Pass?'

The woman takes the pass and the list of numbers and disappears into a back room. Through the open door, Hester can see stacks of metal shelving, infinite rows of cardboard files. A man strolls past the doorway and takes down one of the boxes. He stares at her. She looks away.

There is nowhere to sit. Behind the counter is a large clock with 'RAF' stamped on its face—so large, in fact, that Hester can actually see the big hand moving. Four minutes pass. Five minutes. The Registry is unpleasantly hot. She can feel herself starting to sweat. Seven minutes. Eight minutes. She would like to flee, but the corporal has taken her identity card. Dear God, how could she have been so utterly stupid? What if the clerk is now on the phone to Hut 6, checking up on her? At any instant, Miles will come crashing into the Registry: 'What the hell d'you think you're doing, woman?' Nine minutes. Ten minutes. ·

She's in such a state that she actually fails to hear the clerk come up behind her. 'I'm sorry to have been so long, but I've never come across anything like this...'

The girl, poor thing, is rather shaken.

'Why?' asked Jericho.

'The file,' said Hester. 'The file I'd asked for was empty.'

JERICHO CONTEMPLATED the stained-glass window above the altar and made a steeple of his fingers. 'So what exactly are we to make of this? That Claire must have stolen the entire contents of the file? No, no, that can't be right, because what she had in her room were four of the original cryptograms, not the decodes...'

'Precisely,' said Hester. 'There was a typewritten slip in the Registry file, which the clerk showed me: words to the effect that the enclosed serial numbers had been withdrawn, and that all enquiries should be addressed to the office of the director-general, that's the chief of the Secret Intelligence Service.'

'What was the date on the slip?'

'March the 4th.'

Jericho massaged his forehead. It was the oddest thing he'd ever heard. 'What happened after the Registry?'

'I wrote my note to you. Delivering that took the rest of my meal break. Then it was a matter of getting back into the Index Room. We keep a daily log of all intercepts.' Once again she rummaged in her bag and withdrew a small index card with a list of dates and numbers. 'I wasn't sure where to start so I simply went right back to the beginning of the year and worked my way through. Nothing recorded from five-three-seven till February the 6th. Only eleven ADU interceptions altogether, four of which came on the final day.'

'Which was what?'

'March the 4th. The same day that the file was removed from the Registry. What do you make of that?'

'Nothing. Everything. I'm still trying to imagine what a rear-echelon German signals unit could possibly say that would warrant the removal of its entire file.'

She handed him the list of interceptions. It certainly made a bizarre pattern. Following the initial interception, just after noon on February 6, there had been two days of silence. Then there had been another signal on the 9th, then a gap of ten days. Then a broadcast on the 20th, and another long gap, followed by a flurry of activity: two signals on March 2nd, two on the 3rd, and finally four signals, in rapid succession, on the night of the 4th. These must have been the cryptograms he had taken from Claire's room.

There was no shape to it at all.

He said, 'What Enigma key were they transmitted in? They *were* enciphered in Enigma, I take it?'

'In the Index they were catalogued as Vulture, the standard Wehrmacht Enigma key for the Russian front.'

'And the signals—how were they sent? They were what, just carried on the usual military net?'

'I'd say almost certainly not. The frequency's not one I recognise. It feels to me like something rather more special—a private line, as it were. Just the two stations: a mother and a lone star. But we'd need to see the log sheets to be certain, and they've all been removed from the Registry as well.'

'My, my,' murmured Jericho, 'they really have been thorough.'

He rested his head on the back of the pew and stared up at the vaulted ceiling. Special? he thought. I'll say it was special, more than special for the director-general himself to palm the entire bloody file, plus all the log sheets. There was no sense to it.

He slowly let his gaze descend to take in the rest of the church: the saints in their windows, the marble angels, the stone memorials to the dead of Bletchley parish. He closed his eyes.

Claire, Claire, what have you done? Did you see something you weren't supposed to in that 'deadly dull' job of yours? Did you rescue a few scraps from the confidential waste when nobody was looking and spirit them home? Is that why Wigram's after you?

He saw her on her knees in the darkness at the foot of his bed, heard his own voice—*What on earth are you doing?*—and her ingenuous reply: *I'm just going through your things . . .*

You were always looking for something, weren't you? And when I couldn't provide it you just went on to someone else. (*I'm always seeing someone else*, you said: almost the last words you ever spoke to me.) What is this thing you want so badly?

'I need some air,' he said.

She gathered her bag and followed him down the aisle. Outside, they pretended to study the tombs. A motorcycle passed noisily down the lane towards the town. Jericho waited until the crackle of its engine had dwindled to a drone in the distance and then said, 'The question I keep asking myself is why did she steal *cryptograms*, given what else she could have taken? If she was a spy, surely she would steal proof that Enigma was being broken? What earthly use is an intercept?' He lowered himself to his haunches and ran his fingers over an inscription that had almost crumbled away. 'If only we knew more about them . . . To whom they were sent, for instance.'

'We've been over this. They've removed every trace. What a pity,' she said, with some asperity, 'that you burned our only clues.'

'Keeping them was too much of a risk. For all I knew, you might have told Wigram I'd asked you about the ADU call sign.' He looked up at her uneasily. 'You didn't, I take it?'

'Credit me with some sense, Mr Jericho. Would I be here talking to you now?' She stamped off down the row of graves and began furiously studying an epitaph.

She regretted her sharpness at once. She was jealous, that was the truth of it. She had thought she knew Claire well, but it was fast becoming apparent that she knew her hardly at all. She shivered.

Jericho was back on his feet now, moving between the graves. She wondered whether she might have been like him if she'd been allowed to go to university. But her father wouldn't stand for it, and her brother George had gone instead. Men go to university, men break codes; women stay at home, women do the filing.

Hester, Hester, just in time. Will you talk to Chicksands, there's a good girl, and see what they can do? And, while you're on, the Machine Room reckon they've got a corrupt text on the last batch of Kestrel: the operator needs to check her notes and resend.

She had been standing slack with defeat, gazing at a tombstone, but now she felt her body slowly coming to attention.

The operator needs to check her notes . . .

'Mr Jericho!' He turned at the sound of his name, to see her stumbling through the graves towards him.

'We must go to the intercept station, Mr Jericho—go to Beaumanor and get hold of the operator's handwritten notes. They'll never have dreamed of removing those. Only we poor drones have anything to do with them.'

IT WAS ALMOST TEN O'CLOCK and Miles Mermagen was combing his hair in his office, preparatory to returning to his digs, when Hester Wallace appeared at his door.

'No,' he said, with his back to her.

'Miles, listen, I've been thinking: you were right, I've been a fool.'

He squinted suspiciously at her in the mirror.

She forced a smile. 'I was thinking about what you said, about needing to know where one fits into the chain . . .' He finished his grooming and turned his profile to the mirror, trying to look at his reflection sideways on. 'If you remember, we talked about my possibly going to an intercept station, and, well, as I'm not due on shift till tomorrow afternoon, I thought I might go today. Beaumanor, perhaps.'

'Today?' He looked at his watch. 'Actually, I'm tied up, rather.'

'I *could* go on my own, Miles. And report my findings'—behind her back she dug her nails into her palm—'one evening.'

He gave her another narrowed look and then shrugged. 'Why not? Better call them first.' He waved his hand grandly. 'Invoke my name.'

'Thank you, Miles.'

On her way out, he patted her bottom.

THIRTY YARDS AWAY, in Hut 8, Jericho was knocking on the door marked US NAVY LIAISON. A loud voice told him to 'come on in'.

Kramer didn't have a desk—the room wasn't big enough—just a card table with a telephone on it and wire baskets filled with papers stacked on the floor. He saw Jericho and grinned.

'Got something to show you.' He opened his attaché case and pulled out a wad of papers marked MOST SECRET: ULTRA. 'Skynner finally got the order to give them me this morning. I'm supposed to get them off to Washington tonight.'

Jericho flicked through them: a mass of calculations and some complex drawings of what looked like electronic circuitry.

Kramer said, 'The plans for the prototype four-wheel bombes.'

Jericho looked up in surprise. 'They're using valves?'

'Sure are. Gas-filled triode valves.'

'Good God.'

'They're calling it Cobra. The first three wheel settings will be solved in the usual way, on the existing bombes. But the fourth—the *fourth*—will be solved purely electronically, with valves linked to the bombe by this fat cable. Using valves in sequence—that's a revolution. Never been done before. Your people say it should make the calculations a hundred times, maybe a thousand times, as fast.'

'And when will this happen?'

'That's the bad news. It won't be operational till June. Same old goddamn story. No components, no workshops, not enough technicians.' He stuffed the papers back into his case. 'Got to get something moving on this. I'm going to London right now.'

Jericho winced. 'I suppose you're taking your car?'

'Are you kidding? With this?' He patted the case. 'Skynner's making me go with an escort. Why?'

'I know this is an awful cheek, but you said if I had a favour to ask—well, I was wondering if I might possibly borrow it?'

'Sure.' Kramer pulled on his overcoat. 'I'll probably be gone a couple of days. I'll show you where she's parked.'

They went out into the corridor, and by the entrance to the hut they ran into Wigram. Jericho was surprised at how unkempt he looked. He had obviously been up all night.

'Ah, the gallant lieutenant and the great cryptanalyst. I heard you two were friends.' He bowed with mock formality and said to Jericho, 'I'll need to talk to you again later, old chap.'

'Now there's a guy who gives me the creeps,' said Kramer, as they walked up the path towards the mansion. 'Had him in my room this morning, asking me questions about some girl I know.'

Jericho almost trod on his own feet.

'You know Claire Romilly?'

'There she is,' said Kramer, and for an instant Jericho thought he meant Claire, but actually he was pointing to his car. 'The tank's full and there's a can in the back.' He fished in his pocket for the key and threw it to Jericho. 'Sure, I know Claire. Hell of a girl.' He patted Jericho on the arm. 'Have a nice trip.'

IT WAS ANOTHER half-hour before Jericho was able to get away. He went in search first of Logie, who dismissed him with a wave of his pipe ('Fine, old love, you rest up, curtain rises twenty hundred'), and then of Atwood, who eventually agreed to lend him his AA touring atlas of the British Isles. After that he was ready.

He sat in the front seat of Kramer's Austin and ran his hands over the unfamiliar controls, and it occurred to him that he'd never quite got round to learning how to drive. He knew the basic principles, of course, and at least he wasn't doing anything illegal: for some reason, in a country dominated by wartime regulations, it was no longer necessary to have a driving licence.

He took several minutes trying to sort out clutch pedal from accelerator, handbrake from gear lever; then he pulled out the choke, switched on the ignition and pressed the starter. Miraculously, as his left foot lifted off the clutch, the car crawled forward.

At the main gate he had to climb out while one of the sentries searched the interior.

Half a minute later, he was driving at a cyclist's pace along the narrow lanes towards Shenley Brook End. He had arranged with Hester Wallace to pick her up from the cottage—assuming he could get Kramer's car—and he was just rounding the bend a quarter of a mile before the turning when something flashed dark in the field up ahead. Immediately, he swerved up onto the verge and braked.

Policemen again. One moving stealthily round the edge of the field. Another half hidden in the hedge, apparently watching the road outside the cottage.

Jericho wasn't sure whether he had been seen, but the sooner he got out of their range of vision the better. He jammed the gear lever into reverse. The engine clanked and whined. First he nearly backed into the ditch, then he overcorrected, and the car went weaving drunkenly across the road, mounted the opposite bank and stalled. Now, at least, he was out of sight.

They had to have heard him, surely? At any moment one of them would come strolling down the lane to investigate, and he tried to think up some excuse for his lunatic behaviour.

Suddenly, the scale of the odds stacked against them struck him as so overwhelming that he was seriously tempted to jack in the whole damn-fool project. Indeed, he might well have turned the car round that very minute, if there hadn't been a loud tapping noise at the window to his left. He jumped a full inch in his seat.

It was Hester Wallace. She had exchanged her skirt and blouse for a heavy tweed jacket, a thick sweater and a pair of corduroy trousers. She hefted her carpetbag into the back and sank down low in the passenger seat. She closed the door and gave a sigh of relief.

'Thank God. I thought I'd missed you.'

'How many are there?'

'Six. Two in the fields opposite. Two going from house to house in the village. Two in the cottage—one upstairs dusting for fingerprints and a policewoman downstairs. She tried to stop me going out, but I said it was my day off and I'd do as I pleased. I left by the back door and worked my way round to the road.'

'Did anybody see you?'

'I don't think so.' She blew warmth on her hands and rubbed them. 'I suggest we drive, Mr Jericho. And don't go back into Bletchley, whatever you do. I overheard them talking. They're stopping all cars on the main road out of town.'

Jericho started the engine and the Austin rolled forward. As they came level with the cottage, a policeman suddenly stepped out from the hedge opposite and held up his hand. Jericho hesitated and then pressed his foot down on the accelerator. The policeman stepped smartly out of the way and Jericho had a momentary impression of an outraged brick-red face. Then they were dropping down into the hollow and passing through the village.

A few minutes later, Jericho glanced in his mirror to check there was no one behind them. It seemed safe enough. He said to Hester,

476

'You can get up now.' He was in a daze. He couldn't believe what he was doing. The road ran straight and true ahead of them, northwest, for as far as they could see. Jericho changed up a gear, the Austin gathered speed, and they were clear.

WARTIME ENGLAND opened up before them—still the same, but somehow subtly different: a little bit smudged, a little bit knocked about, like a prosperous estate going to ruin. Fences beside the road were sagging or collapsed. The houses were shabby, unpainted since 1940. Broken windows were boarded over, ironwork rusted. Even the inn signs were blistered. The country was degraded.

Beside him, Hester Wallace was silent, monitoring their progress on Atwood's atlas. Good, he thought. With all the signposts and place names taken down, they would have no idea where they were if they once got lost. He didn't dare drive quickly. The Austin rolled on steadily across a bleak, flat landscape for more than an hour, until, just before a market town she declared was Hinckley, she told him to turn off right onto a narrower road. Soon they were climbing into much more hilly country, thickly wooded, with outcrops of bare rock striped white by snow.

'This is Charnwood Forest. We're almost there. You'd better pull over in a minute. Here,' she said, pointing to a deserted picnic area set just off the road. 'Here will do. I shan't be long.'

She hauled her bag from the back seat and set off towards the trees. He watched her go. It struck him that she was almost the exact physical opposite of Claire, that where Claire was tall and blonde and voluptuous, Hester was short and dark and skinny. Rather like himself, in fact. A few minutes later she emerged from the dark woodland, having changed into an olive-green dress.

'Drive on, Mr Jericho,' she said, as she got back into the car.

His hand paused on the ignition key. 'Do you think, Miss Wallace,' he said hesitantly, 'in view of the circumstances, we might now risk first-name terms?'

She gave him a faint smile. 'Hester.'

'Tom.'

They shook hands.

BEAUMANOR HALL was another of those huge, secluded country houses that had been commandeered by the military from their grateful, almost bankrupt owners, and that would never, Jericho guessed, return to private use. It was early Victorian, with an avenue of dripping elms. Hester told the guard at the lodge gates they were expected; he checked her name on a clipboard and directed them into the courtyard. As Jericho parked, a uniformed man hurried over to them, carrying a vast umbrella to ward off the rain.

'Heaviside,' he said, 'Major Heaviside. And you must be Miss Wallace, and you must be...?'

'Tom Jericho.'

'Mr Jericho. Excellent. Splendid.' He shook their hands vigorously. 'This is a treat for us, I must say. A visit from head office. Commander sends a thousand sorrows and says d'you mind if I do the honours? He'll try and catch us later. *Filthy* weather...'

Jericho had been braced for some suspicious questions, but the major merely ushered them into the house. He was young, tall and balding, with spectacles so smeared it was a wonder he could see through them. He took them into a musty drawing room and ordered tea.

By now, he'd finished his potted history of the house and was well embarked on a detailed history of the wireless interception service. Jericho glanced impatiently round the empty walls. Grimy shadows traced the outlines of large pictures, now removed.

Hester noticed he was fidgeting. 'Perhaps,' she said, in a brief lull in the major's monologue, 'we could look around?'

Heaviside looked startled and clattered his teacup into his saucer. 'Oh, crumbs, sorry. Right. We'll make a start.'

The rain was mixed with snow now. It lashed their faces as they came round the side of the big house and picked their way through the mud of a flattened rose garden. There was an odd keening, howling noise coming from beyond a wall.

'What the devil's that?'

'The aerial farm,' said Heaviside.

They went through a gate in the wall and there it was—dozens of radio masts laid out in odd patterns, like the stone circles of the Druids, across several acres of fields. The metal pylons were bound together by thousands of yards of cable. Some of the taut steel hummed in the wind, some screamed.

'We're about three hundred feet up here, hence this bloody wind,' shouted the major above the racket. He spread his arms wide and bellowed, 'Beautiful, isn't it? We can pick up everything for the best part of a thousand miles.' He laughed and waved his hands as if he were conducting an imaginary choir.

The wind slashed sleet in their faces, and when another gust of wind knocked them backwards Heaviside yelled, 'Let's get out of here.' Once they were on the other side of the wall, they had some shelter from the wind. An asphalt road girdled what looked, at a distance, to be an estate village nestling in the grounds of the big house: cottages, farm sheds, a greenhouse, even a cricket pavilion. All dummy frontages, explained Heaviside cheerfully, designed to fool

German air reconnaissance. This was where the work of interception was done. Was there anything they were especially interested in?

'How about the eastern front?' said Hester.

'Eastern front?' said Heaviside. 'Yes. Fine.'

The rain worsened, and their fast walk turned into a run as they sprinted for the hut. The door banged shut behind them.

'We rely on the feminine element, as you can see,' said Heaviside, taking off his spectacles and drying them on the corner of his tunic. 'Good afternoon,' he said to a stout woman with sergeant's stripes. 'The supervisor,' he explained.

Jericho counted twenty-four wireless receivers, arranged in pairs, on either side of a long aisle, each with a woman hunched over it wearing headphones. The room was quiet, apart from the hum of the machines and the rustle of intercept forms.

'How many people d'you have working here?' asked Hester.

'Couple of thousand.'

'And you intercept absolutely everything?'

'Absolutely. Unless you tell us not to.'

'Which we never do.'

'Right, right.' Heaviside's bald head was glistening with rainwater. He bent forward and shook himself vigorously, like a dog. 'Except that time the other week, of course.'

AFTERWARDS, WHAT JERICHO would remember most was how coolly she handled it. She didn't even blink. Instead, she actually changed the subject and asked Heaviside how fast the girls had to be ('We insist on a speed of ninety Morse characters a minute'), and then the three of them began to stroll down the central aisle.

'These sets are tuned to the eastern front,' said Heaviside, when they were about halfway down.

'Are the nets particularly active at the moment?' Jericho felt it was time he should say something.

'Very much so, since Stalingrad. Retreats and counterattacks all along the front. These Reds, you know, they can't half fight.'

Hester said casually, 'It would have been a Vulture station you were told not to intercept?'

'That's right.'

'And this would have been around on March the 4th?'

'Bang on. Oddest damn thing I ever heard. About midnight your chap Mermagen comes on the blower in a frightful panic and says, "No more of *that*, thanks very much: not now, not any more."'

'Perhaps,' suggested Jericho, 'knowing you were busy, they wanted to knock out low-priority traffic.'

'Balls!' said Heaviside. His professional pride was wounded. 'Nothing we couldn't handle, was it, Kay?' He patted the shoulder of a pretty ATS operator, who took off her headphones. 'No, no, don't get up. We were just discussing our mystery station.' He rolled his eyes. 'The one we're not supposed to hear.'

'You mean it's still broadcasting?' Jericho asked.

'Yes, sir.' Kay had a rather melodious Welsh accent. 'Not so often now, sir, but he was awful busy last week.' She hesitated. 'I don't try to listen, sir, but he does have the most beautiful fist. Real old school. Fist like a concert pianist he has.'

'A man's style of Morse,' said Heaviside pompously, 'is as distinctive as his signature.' He gave the operator's shoulder another pat. 'All right, Kay. Good work. Back to it.'

They moved on. 'One of my best,' he confided. 'Can be pretty ghastly, you know, eight hours listening at a stretch, just taking down gibberish. Ah, now here, look: here's one coming in.'

They stood behind an operator who was frantically writing. With her left hand she kept fractionally adjusting the dial on the wireless set; with her right she was taking down the message.

'Two forms,' said Heaviside. 'Log sheet, on which she records the whispers: that's tuning messages and so forth. And then the red form which is the actual signal. Top copy of each goes to the Teleprinter Hut for transmission to your people. Other copies we keep here, just for a couple of months, in case there's a garble or something goes missing.'

'Can we see?'

'If you want. Not much to it, though.'

Heaviside led them to the far end of the hut, opened a door, turned on the light and stood back to show them the interior: a walk-in cupboard and about a dozen filing cabinets. And not locked, noted Jericho. He could feel his heart beginning to thump.

'Major Heaviside, sir!'

They turned to see Kay beckoning to them. 'My piano player, sir. He's just started doing his scales again, if you're interested.'

Heaviside took the headset first. He listened with his eyes focused on the middle distance, like an eminent doctor with a stethoscope being asked to give a second opinion.

When it was Jericho's turn, he removed his scarf and placed it carefully on the floor. Through the headphones came a strange howling sound that reminded him of the wind in the aerial farm.

'I can't hear anything. Must have drifted off frequency.'

Kay turned the dial minutely anticlockwise; the sound wowed up and down an octave, and then, like stepping into an open space, came a rapid, staccato *dah-dah-dee-dah-dah* of Morse, pulsing clearly and urgently somewhere in German-occupied Ukraine.

THEY WERE HALFWAY to the Teleprinter Hut when Jericho raised his hand to his throat and said, 'My scarf.'

'I'll get one of the girls to bring it over,' Heaviside offered.

'No, no, I'll fetch it. I'll catch you up.'

Hester took her cue. 'And how many machines did you say you have?' She began to walk on. Heaviside hesitated between the two of them, then hurried after Hester. Jericho could have kissed her.

He went back into the hut, walked swiftly down the central aisle and let himself into the storeroom. He closed the door behind him.

How long did he have? Not long.

He tugged at the first drawer of the first filing cabinet and it slid open. Brown cardboard folders. Bundles of smudged carbons. Log sheets and W/T red forms. Day, month and year in the top right-hand corner. Meaningless jumbles of handwritten letters. This folder was for January 15, 1943.

He stepped back and counted quickly. Fifteen four-drawer cabinets. Sixty drawers. Two months. Roughly a drawer a day.

He strode over to the sixth cabinet and opened the third drawer down. February the 6th. Bingo.

It would have helped if his fingers hadn't swollen to the size of sausages, if they weren't shaking and slippery with sweat.

Someone must come in, he thought. Someone must hear him opening and closing the metal drawers like organ stops, pulling out two, three, four cryptograms and the log sheets, too (Hester had said they'd be useful), stuffing them into his inside coat pocket, five, six— dropped it, damn—seven cryptograms.

A footstep outside the storeroom. He grabbed the last four cryptograms, the four Claire had hidden in her room, and had just about got them into his pocket and the drawer shut when the door opened to silhouette the trim figure of Kay, the intercept girl.

'I thought I saw you come in,' she said, 'only you left your scarf, see?' She held it up and closed the door behind her. Jericho stood paralysed, with an idiot grin on his face.

'I don't mean to bother you, sir, but it is important, what we do, isn't it?' Her dark eyes were wide.

'I'm sorry?'

'I know I shouldn't ask, sir—but, well, *is it*? Rubbish, that's all it is to us, just rubbish, all day long. Drives you barmy after a bit.' She had come up very close to him. 'You *are* making sense of it? I won't tell,' she added solemnly, 'honest.'

'Yes,' said Jericho. 'We are making sense of it, and it is important. I promise you.'

She smiled, looped his scarf round his neck, then walked slowly out of the storeroom. He gave it twenty seconds, then walked out through the hut and into the rain.

HEAVISIDE DIDN'T WANT them to leave. Jericho tried feebly to protest—they had a long journey ahead, they had to beat the black-out—but Heaviside insisted they at least take a look at the high-speed Morse receivers. And so they trailed meekly after him to another fake cottage. Hester pretended heroically to be interested and carefully avoided meeting Jericho's eye, but Jericho walked around unhearing. Never had he been more desperate to get away from anywhere.

When they finally said goodbye, an interminable half-hour later, Heaviside shook hands with them and saluted as they got into the Austin. He turned as if to go, then froze, and suddenly ducked down to the window.

'What was it you said you did again, Mr Jericho?'

'Actually, I didn't.' Jericho smiled and turned the engine on. 'Cryptanalytic work.'

'Which section?'

'Can't say, I'm afraid.'

As they pulled away, he could see Heaviside in the rearview mirror, standing in the rain watching them. The curve took them off to the left and the image vanished. 'Pound to a penny,' muttered Jericho, 'he's on his way to the nearest telephone.'

'You got them?'

He nodded. 'Let's wait till we get clear of here.'

Out through the gates, along the lane, past the village, towards the forest. He started to tell her about the storeroom, but then he noticed a track coming up, leading into the privacy of the wood. Perfect.

They bounced along the rough trail for about a hundred yards, plunging into puddles that turned out to be potholes a foot deep. When at last the headlights showed a patch of bog too wide to negotiate, Jericho turned off the engine.

Overhanging branches blotted out the sky. It was almost too dark to read. He turned on the interior light.

'VVVADU QSA? K,' said Jericho, reading off the whispers on the first log sheet. 'Which, if I remember my days in traffic analysis, roughly translates as: *This is station call sign ADU requesting reading of my signal strength, over.*' He ran his finger down the carbon copy. Q-code was an international language, the Esperanto of wireless operators; he knew it off by heart. 'And then we get VVVCPQ BT QSA4 QSA? K. *This is station call sign CPQ, break, your signal strength is fine, what is my signal strength? Over.*'

'CPQ,' said Hester, nodding. 'I recognise that call sign. That has something to do with Army High Command in Berlin.'

'Good. One mystery solved, then.' He returned his attention to the log sheet. 'Smolensk is saying to Berlin: *Your signal strength is reasonable. I have one message for you. My message consists of a hundred and nine cipher groups.*'

Hester fluttered the first cryptogram triumphantly. 'Here it is. One hundred and nine exactly.'

'OK. Fine. So that goes through—straight away, presumably, because Berlin replies: VVVCPQ R QRU HH VA. *Message received and understood. I have nothing for you.* Right out of the manual.'

'That girl in the Intercept Hut said he was precise.'

'What we don't have, unfortunately, is Berlin's replies.' He riffled through the log sheets. 'Easy contact on the 9th as well, and again on the 20th. Ah,' he said, 'now on the 2nd of March it looks to have been more tricky.' He held the form up to the light. Smolensk to Berlin: QZE, QRJ, QRO. (*Your frequency is too high, your signals are too weak, increase your power.*) And Berlin snapping back: QWP, QRX10. (*Observe regulations, wait ten minutes.*) 'Now this is interesting. No wonder they suddenly start to sound like strangers.' Jericho squinted at the carbon copy. 'The call sign in Berlin has changed. It's changed to TGD.'

'*What?* Let me see that.' She snatched the form out of his hand. 'That's not possible. No, no. TGD isn't a Wehrmacht call sign at all. It's Gestapo headquarters in Berlin.'

'Gestapo?' Jericho fumbled through the remaining log sheets. 'But all the messages from March the 2nd onwards are addressed to that call sign.' He gave the forms to her so that she could check for herself, and sat back in his seat.

After a minute or two he said, 'Let's try and construct a thesis. Up to March the 4th, everything is proceeding normally. A signals unit hibernating for the winter in the Ukraine has come to life in the warmer weather. First, a few signals to Army HQ in Berlin, and then a burst of longer traffic to the Gestapo—'

'That's not normal,' said Hester scathingly. 'An army unit transmitting reports in a Russian-front Enigma key to the headquarters of the secret police? That's unprecedented.'

'Quite. In fact, it's so unprecedented that someone at Bletchley wakes up to what's happening and starts to panic. All previous signals are removed from the Registry. And just before midnight on that same day your Mr Mermagen telephones Beaumanor and tells them to stop interception. Ever happen before?'

'Never.' She paused, then moved her shoulder slightly in concession. 'Well, all right, *maybe*, when traffic's very heavy, a low-priority target *might* be neglected for a day or so. But we're always being told that the whole point of the exercise is to monitor *everything*.'

'So he wouldn't have told them to stop on his own authority?'

'Miles? God, no. His orders usually come from Hut 6 Machine Room. They decide priorities.'

'Could he have made a mistake?'

'In what sense?'

'Well, Heaviside said Miles called Beaumanor just before midnight on the 4th in a panic. I was wondering: what if Miles had been told earlier in the day that this unit was no longer to be intercepted, but forgot to pass on the message.'

'Eminently possible, knowing Miles. Yes, yes, *of course*.' Hester turned round to face him. 'I see what you're driving at. In the time between Miles being told to pull the plug and the order reaching Beaumanor, four more messages had been intercepted.'

'Exactly. Which came into Hut 6 late on the 4th. After the order had been issued that they weren't to be decoded.'

'So they just got caught up in the bureaucracy and were passed along the line. Until they ended up in the German Book Room.'

'In front of Claire.'

'Undecrypted.'

Jericho nodded slowly. Undecrypted: that was the crucial point. That explained why the signals in Claire's bedroom had no strips of Type-X decode gummed to their backs. They had never been broken.

He remembered what Weitzman had said: *In theory, on an average*

*day, a girl like Claire would probably see more operational detail about
the German armed forces than Adolf Hitler.*

Ah, but they weren't supposed to *read* it. Well-bred young ladies
wouldn't dream of reading someone else's mail. That was the reason
why Bletchley employed them.

But what was it Miss Monk had said of Claire? *She'd really
become much more attentive of late . . .* Naturally. She had begun to
read what was passing through her hands. And at the end of
February she had seen something that had changed her life, something to do with a German rear-echelon signals unit. So when
Bletchley had decided they couldn't bear to read the traffic any more,
she had felt compelled to steal the last four intercepts herself.

And why had she stolen them? Hester reached the answer ahead of
him, although her voice was faint and almost drowned out by the rain.

'She stole them to decrypt and read them.'

Oh, the nerve of it, thought Jericho. 'But she couldn't have
managed it on her own,' he said. 'She'd have needed help.'

'Who?'

He raised his hands hopelessly. It was hard to know where to
begin. 'Someone with access to Hut 6. Someone who could look up
the Enigma settings for German Army key Vulture on March the
4th. Then that person would have to get access to a Type-X machine,
set it up, type in the cryptograms and tear off the plaintext.'

'Could Claire have done that?'

'Almost certainly not. She'd never have been allowed anywhere
near the Decoding Room. And, anyway, she wasn't trained.'

'So her accomplice would have needed some skill?'

'Skill, yes. And time. Even an expert operator would need the best
part of half an hour to decode that much.'

The events of Saturday night began to drift into his memory: the
sound downstairs in the cottage, the big male footprints in the frost,
and the bicycle shooting away from him into the darkness.

If only I'd been quicker, he thought, I'd have seen his face. And
maybe got a bullet in my own, from a stolen Smith & Wesson .38.

Shark.

He realised guiltily that he had nearly forgotten it.

'What's the time?'

'Almost five.'

'We should be getting back. I'm due on at eight.'

He reached for the ignition.

THE CAR WOULDN'T START. Jericho pressed the starter button and
pumped the accelerator, but all he managed to coax from the engine
was a dull turning noise.

'Oh, hell!'

He got out and went round to the boot. There was a starting handle under the spare can of petrol, and he inserted that into the hole in the front bumper and gave the handle a hopeful tug. It was horribly stiff.

'Pull out the choke,' he shouted to Hester, 'and press your foot down on the third pedal if she starts to fire.'

As she slid across into the driver's seat, he bent to his task again. The forest floor was only a couple of feet from his face, a pungent brown carpet of decaying leaves and fir cones. He heaved a couple more times, until his shoulder ached. He was beginning to sweat now, perspiration mingling with the rainwater trickling down his neck. The insanity of their whole undertaking seemed encapsulated in this moment. The greatest convoy battle of the war was about to start, and where was he? In some forest in the middle of nowhere with a woman he barely knew. He must be—he tightened his grip— *crazy* . . . He jerked viciously on the starting handle; suddenly the engine caught, spluttered and nearly died, then Hester revved it loudly. It was the sweetest sound he'd ever heard.

DROPPING SOUTHWARDS, heading for home. The sky over the distant pale hills brightened from black to grey as they crossed the county border into Northamptonshire. The rain slowed, then stopped.

Why had Claire run? That was what Hester said she couldn't understand. Everything else seemed logical enough: how she would have got hold of the cryptograms in the first place, why she might have wanted to read them, why she would have needed an accomplice. But why then commit the one act guaranteed to draw attention to yourself? Why fail to turn up for your morning shift?

'It must be you,' she said, after she had thought it over for a few more miles. There was a hint of accusation in her voice.

Like a prosecuting counsel, she took him back over the events of Saturday night. He had gone to the cottage and discovered the intercepts, yes? A man had arrived downstairs, yes? 'Did he see you?'

'No.'

'Did you *say* anything?'

'I may have shouted, "Who's there?" or something of the sort.'

'So he could have recognised your voice?'

'It's possible.' But that would mean I knew him, he thought.

'There you are,' she said. 'It *is* you. Claire returns to the cottage after you've gone. She discovers the intercepts are missing. She realises that you must have them, because this mysterious man has told her you were there. She believes you'll take them straight to the authorities. She panics. She runs...'

486

'But that's madness. I'd never have betrayed her.'

'So *you* say. But did *she* know that?'

No, he realised, she did not know that. Indeed, on the basis of his behaviour on the night she found the cheque, she had good reason to assume he was a fanatic about security.

'Who were her boyfriends? Apart from me?'

'You don't want to know. *Believe me.*' There was relish in the way she threw back at him the words he had used to her in the church. He couldn't blame her for it.

'Come on, Hester.' He gripped the steering wheel grimly and glanced into the mirror. A car was coming up behind them. 'Don't spare my blushes.'

Well, they were impressions, she said, rather than names. The first one she'd encountered had been young, with reddish hair, clean-shaven. She'd met him on the stairs with his shoes in his hand one morning in early November. A week later, she'd cycled past a colonel parked in the lane in an army staff car. And then there was an air-force man called Ivo, with a weird vocabulary of 'prangs' and 'crates' and 'shows' that Claire used to mimic fondly. There was an older man, who Hester thought had something to do with the navy. And there was an American: he was definitely navy.

'That would be Kramer,' said Jericho. 'He's the man who lent me the car. How recent was that?'

'About a month ago. But I got the impression he was just a friend. A source of Camels and nylons, nothing special.'

'And before Kramer there was me.'

'She never talked about you.'

'I'm flattered.'

'Given the way she used to talk about the others, you should be.'

'Anyone else?'

She hesitated. 'There may have been someone new in the last month. She was certainly away a good deal.'

'That's seven, then, by my count. Including me. And leaving out any others you've forgotten or don't know about.'

'I'm sorry, Tom.'

'It's quite all right. If anything, it's rather fewer than I'd thought.' He was lying, of course, and he guessed she knew it.

He checked the road behind them. Still empty, apart from the same solitary car. It was lying about a hundred yards back, low and wide and dark. He squeezed his foot harder on the accelerator and was relieved to see the gap between them widen, until at last the road dipped and turned and the big car disappeared.

A minute later it was back, maintaining the same distance.

'How far is it to Bletchley?'

'Stony Stratford coming up, then about six miles. Why?'

He looked again in the mirror and had just begun to say, 'I fear—' when a bell started to clamour behind them. The big car was flashing its headlights, ordering them to pull over.

Until this moment, Jericho's encounters with the police had been rare, brief and respectful. But this one would be different, he saw that at once. An unauthorised journey between secret locations, without proof of ownership of the car, at a time when the country was being scoured for a missing woman: what would that earn them? A trip to the local police station, for sure. A lot of questions. A telephone call to Bletchley. A body search.

It didn't bear contemplating.

And so, to his astonishment, he jammed his foot down hard.

The speedometer climbed past forty to nearly sixty, as the countryside flashed by narrowly on either side of them. A main road appeared ahead. Jericho hesitated, until there was nothing he could do but brake as hard as he dared, change down into second gear and yank the steering wheel hard left. They cornered on two tyres, he and Hester pitched sideways by the force. The clanging bell was drowned by the roar of an engine and suddenly the radiator grille of a tank transporter was rushing to fill the rearview mirror. Its bumper touched them. An outraged blast from its hooter, as loud as a foghorn, seemed to blow them forward. They shot across the bridge over the Grand Union Canal and then through the market town— right, left, right, shuddering over cobbled alleys—until the houses receded and they were out in open country again.

'Left here,' said Hester, and they swung into a lane that was not much better than the forest track. Hester turned and stared out of the back window for any sign of the police, but the lane had closed behind them like a jungle. They passed through a tiny hamlet. A mile the other side of it, a space had been dug out to allow cars to pass one another. He drove into it and switched off the engine.

JERICHO KEPT WATCH on the lane, while she changed back into trousers, sweater, jacket and boots in the back seat of the Austin. They were only about a mile due west of Shenley Brook End, and she was insistent she could make it back to the cottage on foot across open country before dark.

'Can't we read them?' Hester had asked, after they had parked. He had taken the cryptograms from his pocket so that they could decide what to do with them. 'Come on, Tom. We can't just burn them. If she thought she could read them, why can't we?'

'For a start, we'd need the Vulture settings that were in use on the days the signals were sent.'

'I can try to get those. They must be in Hut 6 somewhere.'

'Well, maybe you could, but we'd still need several *hours* on a Type-X machine—and not one of the Type-Xs in Hut 8, either, because naval Enigmas are wired differently from army ones.'

She made no answer to that.

There was a movement in the hedge about thirty yards ahead of him. A fox came nosing out of the undergrowth and stepped into the lane. Halfway across, it stopped and sniffed the air, then slouched off into the opposite hedgerow. Jericho let out his breath.

And yet . . . Even as he ticked off all the objections, he knew that they couldn't simply destroy the cryptograms, not after all they had gone through to get them. The only logical course was to try to break them. Hester would have to steal the settings somehow, while he looked for a way of gaining access to a Type-X machine. But it was dangerous: the previous person to have stolen these cryptograms was Claire, and there was no telling what had happened to her. And somewhere—maybe looking for them now, for all they knew—was a man who knew that Jericho had been in Claire's room and had taken away the signals: a man apparently armed with a stolen pistol.

The car door opened and Hester emerged. He took her bag and stowed it in the Austin's boot.

'For God's sake, be careful,' he said.

'You should worry about yourself.' The air was milky with the approaching dusk—damp and cold. Her face was beginning to blur. She said, 'I'll see you tomorrow.'

She swung herself easily over the gate and set off directly across the field. He watched her until she safely reached the far side, where she vanished in a gap in the hedge, like the fox.

WITHIN FIVE MINUTES he was entering the outskirts of the town. He drove on past the suburban villas then left up the hill towards Bletchley Park. He turned into Wilton Avenue and immediately braked. Parked at the end of the street beside the guard post was a police car. An officer was talking earnestly to the sentry.

Short of flying a swastika the Austin could hardly have looked more suspicious. Mud was spattered over it to the height of the windows. The back bumper was buckled where the tank transport had struck it. He wondered what on earth he would say to Kramer.

Jericho reversed into Church Green Road. Then he drove on up the hill and parked the car in a residential street. Where to hide the cryptograms? Albion Street? Too likely to be searched. A process of elimination brought him to the answer. Where better to hide a tree than in a forest? Where better to conceal a cryptogram than in a code-breaking centre? He would take them into the Park.

He transferred the papers from the inside pocket of his overcoat to the hiding place in the lining. Having retrieved Atwood's atlas, he closed the door quietly and set off at a brisk walk for the Park.

INSIDE HUT 8, there was a crowded, nervous atmosphere, like the greenroom of a theatre on opening night.

Jericho found his usual place next to the window. To his left was Atwood, leafing through Dilly Knox's edition of Herodas. Kingcome and Proudfoot were playing with a pocket chess set. Baxter was rolling a series of spindly cigarettes with a little tin contraption that didn't work properly. Puck had his feet up on the desk. Jericho nodded a general 'Good evening', gave Atwood back his atlas and draped his overcoat over the back of his chair. He was just in time.

'Gentlemen!' Logie appeared in the doorway and clapped twice to draw their attention, then stepped aside to allow Skynner to precede him into the room.

There was a general clatter and scraping of chair legs as they all clambered to their feet.

'Easy, everybody,' said Skynner and waved them back into their seats. Jericho leaned back against the stolen cryptograms. 'Just stopped by to wish you luck.' Skynner's heavy body was swathed like a Chicago gangster's in a prewar double-breasted pinstripe. 'I'm sure you're all aware of what's at stake here as well as I am.'

'Shut up, then,' whispered Baxter.

But Skynner didn't hear him. This was what he loved. He stood with his feet planted firmly apart, his hands clasped behind his back. 'I don't think I'm exaggerating when I say this could be one of the most decisive nights of the war.' His gaze sought out each of them in turn, coming last of all to Jericho and sliding away with a flicker of distaste. 'A mighty battle—probably the greatest convoy battle of the war—is about to start.' He nodded abruptly. 'Go to it.'

After Skynner had gone, Logie handed out copies of the convoy contact section of the Short Signal Code Book. To Jericho, as a mark of recognition, he gave the precious original.

'We're after convoy contact reports, gentlemen: as many of them as possible in the twenty-four hours between midnight tonight and midnight tomorrow—in other words, the maximum amount of crib covering one day's Enigma settings.'

Jericho had calculated the day before that they would need at least thirty contact reports for the scheme to succeed. The instant an E-bar signal was heard, the receiving station would telephone to alert them. When the contact report arrived by teleprinter, a minute later, ten copies would be made and distributed. No fewer than twelve bombes would be placed at their disposal the moment they had a worthwhile menu to run.

The blackout shutters were fixed to the windows, and the hut was battened down for the night.

MIDNIGHT CAME and went without a sound from the North Atlantic, and the tension began to slacken.

By 2am, the fumes from the paraffin heater were casting a soporific pall over the naval cryptanalysts in Hut 8. Atwood was the first to succumb. His mouth dropped open. Puck, too, fell asleep, his body bent forward, his left cheek resting on his forearms on the table. Even Jericho, despite his determination to stand guard over the cryptograms, found himself slipping over the edge into unconsciousness. He pulled himself back a couple of times, but finally he couldn't fight it any longer and he slid into a turbulent dream of drowning men, whose cries sounded in his ears like the wind in the aerial farm.

At 5am GMT on Tuesday, March 16, just one week after Shark was blacked out, *U-653*, under the command of Kapitänleutnant Gerhard Feiler, was heading due east on the surface, returning to France.

After ten days on station, with no sign of any convoy, Feiler had finally decided he had no choice but to head for home. The starboard diesel was giving trouble. Provisions were running low. And, after a successful attack on a steamship three weeks before, only one torpedo remained, and that was defective. Feiler lay on his bunk, wincing at the irregular beat of the engine, and tried to sleep.

Up on the bridge, where the wind was a steel attack, four men made up the night watch: one for each point of the compass. They were cowled like monks in dripping black oilskins, lashed to the rail by metal belts, and each had a pair of Zeiss binoculars clamped to his eyes and was staring into his own sector of darkness.

Facing directly ahead, towards the invisible prow, was a young Obersteurmann, Heinz Theen. He was peering into such blackness that it was possible to imagine they might have fallen off the edge of the world, when suddenly he saw a light, several hundred yards in front of him. It winked for two seconds, then disappeared.

Astonishing though it seemed, he realised he had just witnessed an Allied seaman lighting a cigarette in the middle of the North Atlantic. He called down the conning tower for the captain.

By the time Feiler had scrambled up to the bridge, thirty seconds later, the cloud had shifted slightly in the high wind and shapes were moving all around them. Feiler swivelled through 360 degrees and counted the outlines of nearly twenty ships.

A whispered cry, as much of panic as command: 'Dive!'

Minutes later, the *U-653* hung motionless in the calmer water beneath the waves.

Feiler's task under standing orders was not to attack—impossible in any case, given his lack of torpedoes—but to keep his quarry in sight while drawing in every other U-boat within a radius of 100 miles. 'Convoy steering oh-seven-oh degrees,' he announced. 'Naval grid square BD one-four-nine-one.'

The first officer made a scrawled note in pencil, then dripped down the conning tower to collect the Short Signal Code Book. In his cubbyhole next to the captain's berth, the radio man pressed his switches. The Enigma came on with a hum.

AT 7.25AM, Logie stepped into the Big Room, with the queasy expression of guilty excitement which would characterise the whole of the day. 'It looks like it may have started.'

St Erith, Scarborough and Flowerdown had all reported an E-bar signal followed by eight Morse letters, and within a minute one of the Wrens from the Registration Room was bringing in the first copies. Jericho placed his carefully in the centre of his trestle table.

RGHC DMIG. His heart began to accelerate.

'Hubertus net,' said Logie. 'Four-siz-zero-one kilocycles.'

Cave was listening to someone on the telephone. He put his hand over the mouthpiece. 'Direction finders have a fix. Pencil. Quick.' Baxter threw him one. 'Forty-nine point four degrees north,' he repeated. 'Thirty-eight point eight degrees west. Got it. Well done.' He hung up.

Cave had spent all night plotting the convoys' courses on two large charts of the North Atlantic, one issued by the Admiralty, the other a captured German naval grid. The cryptanalysts gathered round him. Cave's finger came down on a spot almost exactly midway between Newfoundland and the British Isles. 'There she is. She's shadowing convoy HX-229.'

Jericho said, 'What grid square is that?'

'BD one-four-nine-one.'

'And the convoy course?'

'Oh-seven-oh.'

Jericho went back to his desk, and in less than two minutes, using the Short Signal Code Book and the current Kriegsmarine address book for encoding naval grid squares, he had a crib to position under the contact report.

```
RGHC DMIG
DDFG RX??
```

The first four letters announced that a convoy had been located steering 070 degrees, the next two gave the grid square, the final two represented the code name of the U-boat, which he didn't have. He circled R–D and D–R. A matching pattern on the first signal.

'I get D–R/R–D,' said Puck a few seconds later.

'Me too,' said Baxter.

Jericho nodded. 'A good omen.'

AFTER THAT, the pace of events began to quicken. At 8.25, two long signals were intercepted emanating from Magdeburg, which Cave at once surmised would be U-boat headquarters ordering every submarine in the North Atlantic into the attack zone. At 9.27, Flowerdown intercept station rang again: a second E-bar flash from almost the same location as the first. The Wrens hurried in with it: KLYS QNLP.

'The same hearse,' said Cave. 'following standard operating procedure. Reporting every two hours, or as near as damn it.'

'Grid square?'

'The same.'

'Convoy course?'

'Also the same. For now.'

Jericho went back to his desk and manipulated the original crib under the new cryptogram.

```
KLYS QNLP
DDFG RX??
```

Again, there were no letter clashes. The golden rule of Enigma, its single, fatal weakness: *nothing is ever itself—A can never be A, B can never be B...* It was working.

An hour later, Logie came through to say that a second U-boat had just sent a contact signal. At 11.40, a third U-boat began to shadow the convoy, at 12.20 a fourth, and suddenly Jericho had seven signals on his desk. He was conscious of people coming up and looking over his shoulder. He didn't look round. He didn't talk. The outside world had melted for him. Even Claire was just a phantom now. There were only the loops of letters, forming and stretching out towards him from the grey Atlantic, multiplying on his sheets of paper, turning into thin chains of possibility in his mind.

THEY DIDN'T STOP for breakfast, nor for lunch. Minute by minute, throughout the afternoon, the cryptanalysts followed, at third hand, the progress of the chase some two thousand miles away.

Two signals came at 13.40: both were for the first time close enough to be fixed by direction finders on board the convoy's own escorts. Cave listened gravely for a minute, then announced that HMS *Mansfield*, a destroyer, was being dispatched from the main body of merchantmen to attack the U-boats.

'The convoy's just made an emergency turn to the southeast. She's trying to shake off the hearses, while *Mansfield* forces them under.'

Jericho looked up. 'What course is she steering?'

Cave spoke into the telephone. 'Yes. Thank you. Convoy steering one hundred and eighteen degrees.' Jericho reached for the Short Signal Code Book.

'Will they manage to get away?' asked Baxter.

Cave bent over his chart with a ruler and protractor. 'Maybe. It's what I'd try to do in their place.'

A quarter of an hour passed and nothing happened.

'Perhaps they have done it,' said Puck. 'Then what do we do?'

Jericho counted through the signals. 'We've got nine. We need another twenty. Another twenty-five would be better.'

'Good God!' Cave regarded them with disgust. 'It's like sitting with a flock of carrion crows.'

Somewhere behind them, a telephone managed half a ring before it was snatched out of its cradle. Logie came in a moment later, still writing. 'That was St Erith reporting an E-bar signal at forty-nine point four degrees north, thirty-eight point one degrees west.'

'New location,' said Cave, studying his charts. He made a cross, then threw his pencil down and leaned back in his chair, rubbing his scarred face. 'All the convoy's managed to do is run straight from one hearse into another.'

'She isn't going to get away,' said Puck, 'is she?'

'Not a chance. Not if they're coming in from all round her.'

A Wren moved among the cryptanalysts, doling out the latest cryptogram: BKEL UUXS.

Ten signals. Five U-boats in contact. Then a sixth.

HESTER WALLACE was not a poker player, which was a pity, as she had been blessed with a poker face that could have made her a fortune. Nobody sitting with her in Intercept Control that afternoon would have guessed the turmoil in her mind.

Her fingers moved across the blist in a short, staccato pecking motion. *Name of intercept station, time of interception, frequency, call sign, letter groups . . .*

She and Jericho needed the record of settings. Where was it kept? That was the first matter to determine. Not in Control, obviously. Not in the Index Room. Not in the Registry.

The only conclusion was that it had to be kept where the cryptanalysts worked, in the Machine Room, or else close by.

She finished blisting Chicksands, noon till three, and moved towards the door.

There was no machinery in the Machine Room—the origin of its name was lost in the glorious mists of 1940—just desks, cryptanalysts and shelf after shelf of files. She stopped and looked around distractedly, as if searching for a familiar face. The problem was she knew nobody. But then her gaze fell upon a bald head with a few long ginger hairs combed pathetically across a freckled crown, and she realised that wasn't entirely true. She knew Cordingley.

Dear old, dull old Donald Cordingley. Ineligible for military service owing to a funnel chest. By profession: actuary. Ten years' service with the Scottish Widows Assurance Society, until a lucky third place in the *Daily Telegraph* crossword competition won him a seat in the Hut 6 Machine Room.

Her seat.

She watched him for a few more seconds, then moved away.

When she got back to Control, Miles Mermagen was standing at her desk. 'How was Beaumanor?' he asked.

'Engrossing.'

'How'd you get there?'

'A friend gave me a lift.'

'A male friend, I gather.' Mermagen's smile was unfriendly.

'How do you know that?'

'I have my spies,' he said.

THE OCEAN WAS ALIVE with signals. They were landing on Jericho's desk at the rate of one every twenty minutes.

By 18.00, Jericho had a pile of nineteen contact signals, out of which he had conjured a mass of half-sketched bombe menus that looked like the plans for some complex game of hopscotch. His shoulders were so knotted with tension he could barely straighten up.

A Wren with a tray offered Jericho a curling Spam sandwich and an enamel mug of tea, and he took them gratefully.

Logie came up behind him. 'How are you feeling, old love?'

'Wrecked, frankly.'

'Come into my office and I'll give you something. Bring your tea.'

The 'something' turned out to be a large yellow Benzedrine tablet, of which Logie had half a dozen in a hexagonal pillbox.

Jericho hesitated. 'I'm not sure I should. These helped send me funny the last time.'

'They'll get you through the night, though, won't they? Come on, old thing.' He rattled the box under Jericho's nose. 'So you'll crash out at breakfast? So what? By then we'll either have this thing beaten. Or not. In which case it won't matter, will it?' He took one of the pills and pressed it into Jericho's palm. He closed Jericho's fingers round it and said quietly, 'Because I can't let you go, you know, old love. Not tonight. Not you. Some of the others, maybe, but not you.'

'Well, since you put it so nicely.' Jericho swallowed the pill.

'That's my boy.' Logie put the box back in his desk drawer and locked it. 'I've been protecting your bloody back again, incidentally. I had to tell him you were too important to be disturbed.'

'Tell who? Skynner?'

'No, Wigram. For such a quiet bloke, you don't half make some enemies. I told him to come back at midnight. All right by you?'

Before Jericho could reply, the telephone rang and Logie grabbed it.

'Yes? Speaking.' He grunted and stretched across his desk for a pencil. 'Time of origin nineteen-oh-two hours, fifty-two point one degrees north, thirty-seven point two degrees west. Thanks, Bill. Keep the faith.'

He replaced the receiver. 'And then there were seven . . .'

IT WAS DARK AGAIN and the lights were on in the Big Room. The sentries outside were banging the blackout shutters into place, like prison warders locking up their charges for the night.

Jericho hadn't set foot out of the hut for twenty-four hours, hadn't even looked out of the window. As he slipped back into his seat, he wondered vaguely what Hester was doing.

Don't think about that now.

Already he could feel the Benzedrine beginning to take effect. When he glanced at his notes, what had seemed inert and impenetrable a half-hour ago was suddenly full of possibility.

Logie said, 'A message from Mr Skynner. A bottle of Scotch for the first man with a menu for the bombes.'

Twenty-three signals received. Seven U-boats in contact. Two hours to go till nightfall in the North Atlantic.

THE CONTROL ROOM girls took a table near the serving hatch for their evening meal. Celia Davenport showed them all some pictures of her fiancé, who was fighting in the desert. Hester passed on the photographs without looking at them. Her eyes were fixed on Donald Cordingley queuing for his meal.

She was cleverer than he, and he knew it. She intimidated him.

Hello, Donald, she thought. *Hello, Donald . . . Now, listen, Donald, there's this funny little wireless net in the southern Ukraine. Nothing vital, but we've never quite broken it, and Archie—you must know Archie?— Archie has a theory it may be a variant on Vulture . . . Traffic runs through*

February and the first few days of March . . . That's right . . .

She watched him as he sat alone and picked at his lonely supper. And when, after fifteen minutes, he rose and scraped the leftovers from his plate into the swill bins, she followed him.

She was vaguely aware of the other girls staring after her in astonishment. She ignored them.

She tracked him all the way back to Hut 6, gave him five minutes to settle down, then went in after him.

'Hello, Donald.'

He turned round and blinked up at her in surprise. 'Oh, hello.' The effort of memory was heroic. 'Hello, Hester.'

'IT'S ALMOST DARK out there,' said Cave, looking at his watch. 'Not long now. How many have you had?'

'Twenty-nine,' said Baxter.

'I believe you said that would be enough, Mr Jericho?'

'Weather,' said Jericho, without looking up. 'We need a weather report from the convoy. Barometric pressure, cloud cover, wind speed, temperature. Before it gets too dark.'

'They've got ten U-boats on their backs and you want them to tell you the *weather*?'

'Yes, please. Fast as they can.'

The weather report arrived at 21.31.

There were no more contact signals after 21.40.

THUS CONVOY HX-229 at 22.00:

Thirty-seven merchant vessels, ranging in size from the 12,000-ton British tanker *Southern Princess* to the 3,500-ton American freighter *Margaret Lykes*, making slow progress through heavy seas, steering a course of 055 degrees towards England. Five escort vessels, including two slow corvettes and two elderly ex-American destroyers, one of which—HMS *Mansfield*—had lost touch with the convoy after charging the U-boats, because the convoy commander had forgotten to signal her with his second change of course. No rescue ship available. No air cover. No reinforcements within a thousand miles.

'All in all,' said Cave, lighting a cigarette and contemplating his charts, 'what you might fairly call a bit of a cockup.'

The first torpedo hit at 22.01.

At 22.32, Tom Jericho was heard to say, very quietly, 'Yes.'

THE BOMBE WAS HEAVY—Jericho guessed it must weigh more than half a ton—and even though it was mounted on castors it still took all his strength, combined with the engineer's, to drag it away from the wall. The Wrens moved in at once to strip it.

The decryptor was a monster, like something out of an H.G. Wells fantasy of the future: a black metal cabinet, eight foot wide and six foot tall, with scores of five-inch-diameter drum wheels set into the front. The back was hinged and opened up to show a bulging mass of coloured cables and the dull gleam of metal drums.

Jericho retreated to watch from a corner. One Wren went round to the back of the cabinet and began disconnecting and replugging the cables. The other moved along the front, pulling out each drum in turn and checking it for wiring faults.

Jericho's menu was at that moment being rushed into the promised dozen bombe bays all across the Bletchley area.

Here in Hut 11, having completed the mechanical check, the Wren went back to the first row of drums and began adjusting them to the combination listed on the menu. When all the drums had been set, the bombe was trundled back into place and the motor started.

The engineer began dragging out the other bombe and Jericho moved forward to help, but was stopped by a tugging on his arm.

'Come on, old love,' shouted Logie above the din. 'There's nothing more we can do here.' He pulled at his sleeve again.

Reluctantly, Jericho turned and followed him out of the hut.

Maybe tomorrow evening, or maybe on Thursday, the bombes

would give them the Enigma settings for the day now ending. Then the real work would begin, the laborious business of trying to reconstruct the new Short Weather Cipher Book: taking the meteorological data from the convoy, matching it to the weather signals already received from the surrounding U-boats, making some guesses, testing them, constructing a fresh set of cribs... It was a chess tournament of a thousand rounds against a player of prodigious defensive strength.

'I've sent the others home to their digs for some kip,' Logie was saying, 'which is where I'm going. And where you ought to go, too, if you're not too high to sleep.'

'I'll just clear up here for a bit, if that's all right. Take the code book back to the safe in the Black Museum.'

'Do that. Thanks.'

'And then I suppose I'd better face Wigram.'

'Ah, yes. Wigram.'

They went into Hut 8. In his office, Logie tossed Jericho the keys to the Black Museum. 'And your prize,' he said, holding up a bottle of Scotch. 'Don't let's forget that.'

Jericho smiled. 'Give it to the others.'

'Oh, don't be so bloody pious.' Logie produced a couple of enamel mugs. 'What shall we drink to?'

'The end of Shark? The future?'

Logie splashed a measure of whisky into each mug. 'How about,' he said, offering one to Jericho, 'how about *your* future?'

They clinked mugs and sat in silence, drinking.

'I'm defeated,' said Logie at last, using the desk to pull himself to his feet. 'I couldn't tell you the year, old love, never mind the day.' He had three pipes in a rack and he slipped them all into his pocket. 'Now don't forget your Scotch.'

'I don't want the bloody Scotch.'

'Take it. Please. For my sake.'

In the corridor, he shook Jericho's hand, and Jericho feared Logie was going to say something embarrassing. Instead, he gave a rueful salute and lurched along the passage, banging the door behind him.

THE BIG ROOM, in anticipation of the midnight shift, was almost empty. A little desultory work was being done on Dolphin and Porpoise at the far end. Only Cave was still there, bent over his charts. He looked up as Jericho came in.

'Well? How's it going for you?'

'Too early to tell,' said Jericho, retrieving his coat. He found the code book and slipped it into his pocket. 'And you?'

'Three hit so far. A Norwegian freighter and a Dutch cargo ship.

They just went straight to the bottom. The third, a liberty ship, is on fire and going round in circles. Half the crew lost, the other half trying to save her. It's absolute bloody slaughter. And it's going to go on and on like this for days. They're going to be chased and harried and torpedoed right the way across the bloody North Atlantic. Can you imagine what that feels like? Watching the ship next to you blow up? Waiting for your turn?' He touched his scar, then seemed to realise what he was doing and let his hand fall. There was a terrible resignation in the gesture. 'And now, apparently, they're picking up U-boat signals swarming all round convoy SC-122.'

His telephone began to ring, and he swung away to answer it. While his back was turned, Jericho quietly placed the bottle of Scotch on his desk, then made his way out into the night.

HE CLIMBED THE SLOPE towards the big house. His mind, on a fuel of Benzedrine and Scotch, seemed to be churning like the bombes in Hut 11, making bizarre and random connections—Claire and Hester and Skynner and Wigram, and the tyre tracks in the frost outside the cottage, and the blazing liberty ship going round and round over the bodies of her crew.

In the labyrinth of the house, he nodded cautiously to the few people he passed: an elderly man in a dark grey suit, an army captain, a Waaf. They appeared seedy in the dingy light, and he guessed he must look pretty odd himself. Benzedrine could do funny things to the pupils of your eyes, he seemed to remember, and he hadn't shaved or changed his clothes for more than forty hours. But nobody in Bletchley was ever thrown out for simply looking strange, or the place would have been empty from the start.

He opened the door to the cellar passage. The bulb must have blown since his last visit, and he found himself groping his way down towards a faint gleam at the foot of the stairs. It was the keyhole to the Black Museum, traced in luminous paint: a trick they had learned in the Blitz.

Inside the room, the light switch worked. He unlocked the safe and replaced the code book, and for a moment he was seized by the crazy notion of hiding the cryptograms inside it as well. They might pass unnoticed for months. But one day they would be discovered.

He closed the steel door.

Still he couldn't quite bring himself to leave. So much of his life was here. He contemplated the row of Enigmas on the metal shelf. They were far more than mere machines, he thought. These were the synapses of the enemy's brain—mysterious and complex.

He began to turn away, then stopped.

'Tom Jericho,' he whispered. 'You bloody fool.'

The first two Enigmas he lifted down and inspected turned out to be badly damaged and unusable. The third had a label attached to its handle: 'SIDI BOU ZID 14/2/43'. An Afrika Korps Enigma, captured by the 8th Army during their attack on Rommel last month. He unfastened the clasps and opened the lid.

This one was in perfect condition: a beauty. The letters on the keys were unworn, the glass bulbs clear and gleaming. He pushed a key. When he had depressed it far enough, the machine emitted a clunk and the right-hand rotor moved on a notch. At the same time, one of the bulbs lit up.

Hallelujah! The battery was charged. The Enigma was alive, ready to decode the cryptograms. All he needed was the settings.

He looked at his watch. Two minutes to twelve.

He hoisted the Enigma back up on its shelf.

To the people whom he ran past in the mansion's corridors, who was he? Nobody. Just another peculiar cryptanalyst in a flap.

HESTER WALLACE, as she and Jericho had agreed, was in the telephone box at midnight, the receiver in her hand, feeling more foolish than afraid as she pretended to make a call. Beyond the glass, one shift streamed in from the main gate and the other ebbed towards it. In her pocket was a sheet of Bletchley's wood-flecked, brownish notepaper, on which were jotted six entries.

Cordingley had swallowed her story whole—indeed, he had been, if anything, a little *too* eager to help. The file had been procured and a space cleared in the corner, and never had Miss Wallace made a pencil move more quickly. The worst part had been at the end: keeping her nerve and not fleeing when she'd finished, but checking the figures, returning the file to Donald and observing the normal code.

We really must have a drink one of these evenings.

Yes, really we must. I'll be in touch—neither, of course, having the slightest intention of ever doing so.

Come on, Tom Jericho.

Midnight passed. Then, just as she was beginning to give up hope, a blur of white; a hand tapped softly on the glass. She shone her torch onto the face of a lunatic pressed close to the pane: dark wild eyes and a convict mask of shadowed beard. 'There's no need to scare me half to death,' she muttered, but that was in the privacy of the phone booth. As she came out, all she said was, 'I've left your settings on the telephone.'

She held the door open for him. His hand rested on hers. A brief moment of pressure signalled his thanks.

'Meet me here at five,' he whispered.

EXHILARATION GAVE fresh energy to her tired legs as she pedalled up the hill towards the cottage.

He needed to see her at five. How else could one interpret that, except as meaning that he had found a way to interpret the numbers? A victory! A victory against the Mermagens and the Cordingleys!

She was bouncing along the potholed track, just six feet from the door, when headlights came on behind her—slitted blackout headlights, but dazzling enough to splash her shadow against the whitewashed wall. She heard the engine cough, and turned, shielding her eyes, to see the big car coming towards her—calm, unhurried, implacable, nodding over the bumpy ground.

JERICHO TOLD HIMSELF to take his time. There's no hurry. You've given yourself five hours. Use them.

He locked himself into the cellar room, leaving the key half turned in the keyhole, so that anyone trying to insert *their* key from the other side would find it blocked. He knew he'd have to open up eventually—but at least he would now have thirty seconds' warning, and to give himself a cover story he reopened the safe and spread a handful of code books across the table.

Then he lifted down the Enigma.

He would work backwards, he decided, deciphering the last cryptogram first, on the theory that whatever had caused Claire's disappearance was contained somewhere in those final messages.

He ran his finger through Hester's notation to find the Vulture settings for March 4—panic day in the Bletchley Registry.

```
III V IV GAH CX AZ DV KT HU LW GP EY
MR FQ
```

The Roman numerals told him which of the machine's rotors were to be used that day, and in what order they were to be placed. GAH gave him the rotor starting positions. The next ten letter-pairs represented the cross-pluggings he needed to make on the plugboard at the back of the Enigma.

He did the plugging first, then the rotors. The machine was now primed, just as its twin had been in Smolensk on the evening of March 4.

He was ready.

DECODING SHOULD HAVE been easy. Jericho realised quite quickly, though, that something was going wrong. This was no German language he recognised. Still he went on, in the increasingly desperate hope that it would start to come right. Only after thirty-seven letters did he give up.

HYCYKWPIOROKDZENAJEWICZJPTAKJHRUTBPYS

He ran his hands through his hair and groaned.

There were two possibilities, both equally unpleasant. One: the message had been super-enciphered, its plaintext scrambled once and then again, to make its meaning doubly obscure. Two: Hester had made a mistake in transcription—had got, perhaps, just one letter wrong—in which case he could sit here, literally for the rest of his life, and would still never make the cryptogram disgorge its secrets.

Of the two explanations, the latter was the more likely.

He paced around his cell for a while, trying to get some circulation back into his legs. Then he set the rotors back at GAH and attempted to decipher the second message from March 4. All the Enigma gave him was more gobbledygook.

FOUR IN THE CAR. Hester in the back seat next to Wigram. Two men in the front. The heater on, a stench of cigarette smoke and sweat so strong that Wigram had his paisley scarf pressed delicately to his nose. He didn't say a word. She hadn't spoken, either—it was her single, token gesture of defiance.

After a couple of minutes they stopped somewhere and Wigram sat motionless while the men in the front seats scrambled out. One of them opened his door. Torches flashed in the darkness. Shadows appeared. A welcoming committee.

'Get the generator going for the lights yet, Inspector?' asked Wigram.

'Yes, sir.' A deep male voice; a Midlands accent. 'A lot of complaints from the air-raid people, though.'

'Well, they can frig off for a start. Jerry wants to bomb this place, he's welcome. Got statements from the lovebirds who found it?'

'Yes, sir.'

'Good-oh.' Wigram grabbed the roof and hoisted himself out. He waited a second or two, and when Hester didn't move he ducked back inside. 'Come on. D'you expect me to carry you?' he said irritably.

She slid across the seat.

Two other cars—no, *three* other cars—with their headlights on, showing a small army truck and an ambulance. The ambulance shook her. Its doors were open, and as Wigram guided her past it, his hand lightly on her elbow, she caught the smell of disinfectant.

'Been here before?' said Wigram.

'Where are we?'

'Lovers' lane. Not your scene, I fancy.'

He was holding a flashlight, and as he stood aside to usher her through a gate she saw a sign: DANGER: FLOODED CLAY PIT—VERY

DEEP WATER. She could hear a guttural engine somewhere ahead, and the cry of sea birds. She started to shake.

The engine noise was louder now, and seemed to be coming from inside a brick building to her left. A white light shone up through the gaps in its roof to reveal a tall, square chimney, its lower part engulfed by ivy.

'Mind yourself here,' warned Wigram, pulling on a pair of light brown calfskin gloves. 'Got something to show you.'

Inside the building, a police sergeant stood beside a rumpled heap of sacks. Hester had to will her legs to move forward. *Please, Lord, don't let it be her.*

'Get your notebook out,' said Wigram to the sergeant. He squatted on his haunches. 'I am showing the witness, first, one lady's coat, ankle length by the look of it, colour grey, trimmed with black velvet.' He drew it completely out of the sack and turned it over. 'Quite badly stained. Probably blood. Collar label: "Hunters, Burlington Arcade". And the witness responded?' He held it up.

'It's hers.'

'Good. OK. Next. One lady's shoe. Left foot. Black. High heel. Heel snapped off. Size seven. What size did she take?'

A pause, then Hester, quietly: 'Seven.'

'We've found the other one outside, sir,' said the inspector. 'Near the water's edge.'

'And a pair of knickers. White silk. Recognise these, Miss Wallace?' He let them drop and rummaged in the bottom of the sack. 'Final item. One brick.' He shone his flashlight onto it; something glinted. 'Bloodstained. Blonde hairs attached.'

They moved out to the spot where the second shoe had been found. 'Local fishing club use a shed here,' said the inspector. 'Three rowing boats stowed here, but one's missing.'

'Since?'

'Well, there was some fishing on Sunday. That was the last day of the season. Everything was all right then.'

'Sunday. And we're now into Wednesday.' Wigram sighed and shook his head. 'And how big's the lake?'

'About a quarter of a mile across. Sixty or seventy feet deep. They built the town with what they dug out here.'

'Did they really?' Wigram flashed his light across the lake. 'Makes sense, I suppose. Making one hole out of another.' Mist was rising, swirling like steam above a cauldron. 'So, what happened here?' he said softly. 'Our man lures her out on Sunday night. Kills her, probably with that brick. Drags her down here . . .' The beam of light traced the path from the kilns to the water. 'Then what? Gets a boat. Stuffs the body in a sack, maybe. Weights it down with bricks. That's

504

obvious. Rows it out. Dumps it . . . Something made him leave the clothes. Perhaps the next pair of lovebirds had arrived.'

'May I go now?' said Hester. She had kept herself very quiet and composed so far, but now the tears had started.

Wigram aimed the beam at her wet face. 'No,' he said sadly. 'I'm rather afraid you can't.'

JERICHO WAS REPLUGGING the cipher machine as quickly as his numb fingers would permit.

He would begin again, this time with the first signal. Enigma settings for German Army key Vulture, February 6, 1943.

He lifted the lid, unfastened the spindle, slid off the rotors. Above his head, the great house was silent. He wondered what they were doing up there. Looking for him? Probably. He slid the rotors into place—first, fifth, third—and clicked them round.

Almost at once, he began to sense success. First C and X, which were nulls, and then A, N, O, K, H.

An OKH . . . He translated: To OKH. To the Army High Command. A miracle.

His finger hammered away at the keys. The lights flashed.

Just before three o'clock he succeeded in deciphering and translating the first message:

```
TO THE OFFICE OF THE COMMANDER IN
CHIEF.  URGENT.  DISCOVERED  TWELVE
KILOMETRES  WEST  SMOLENSK  EVIDENCE
HUMAN  REMAINS.  BELIEVED  EXTENSIVE,
POSSIBLY THOUSANDS. HOW AM I TO PRO-
CEED? LACHMAN, OBERST, FIELD POLICE.
```

Jericho sat back and contemplated this marvel. Well, yes, Herr Oberst, how are you to proceed? I die to know.

Once again, he began the tedious procedure of replugging and re-rotoring the Enigma. The next signal had been sent from Smolensk three days later, on February 9. Letter by letter, the whole ghastly story unfolded before him:

```
PRELIMINARY EXCAVATION UNDERTAKEN IN
FOREST  NORTH  DNIEPER  CASTLE.  SITE
APPROXIMATELY  TWO  HUNDRED  SQUARE
METRES. TOPSOIL COVERING TO DEPTH OF
ONE  POINT  FIVE  METRES  PLANTED  PINE
SAPLINGS. FIVE LAYERS CORPSES. TWENTY
BODIES  RECOVERED.  DEATH  CAUSED  BY
SINGLE  SHOT  HEAD. MILITARY  UNIFORMS,
HIGH  BOOTS  AND  MEDALS  INDICATE  VIC-
TIMS  POLISH  OFFICERS.  SEVERE  FROST
OBLIGES US SUSPEND OPERATIONS PENDING
THAW.  I  SHALL  CONTINUE  MY  INVESTIGA-
TIONS. LACHMAN, OBERST, FIELD POLICE.
```

Jericho took a tour round his little cell, flapping his arms and stamping his feet. It seemed to him to be peopled with ghosts, grinning at him with toothless mouths. He was walking in the forest himself. And when he stopped and listened he could hear the sound of spades and pickaxes ringing on frozen earth.

Polish officers?

The third signal, after a gap of eleven days, had been sent on February 20.

```
FOLLOWING  THAW  KATYN  FOREST  EXCAVA-
TIONS   RESUMED.   FIFTY-TWO   CORPSES
EXAMINED. QUANTITIES OF PERSONAL LET-
TERS, MEDALS, POLISH  CURRENCY  RECOV-
ERED. INTERROGATION  LOCAL  POPULATION
```

ESTABLISHES ONE: EXECUTIONS CON-
DUCTED NKVD DURING SOVIET OCCUPATION
MARCH AND APRIL NINETEEN HUNDRED AND
FORTY. TWO: VICTIMS TAKEN INTO FOREST
AT NIGHT IN GROUPS. SHOTS HEARD.
THREE: TOTAL NUMBER VICTIMS ESTIMATED
TEN THOUSAND REPEAT TEN THOUSAND.
ASSISTANCE URGENTLY REQUIRED IF FUR-
THER EXCAVATION DESIRED.

Jericho sat motionless for fifteen minutes, gazing at the Enigma, trying to comprehend the scale of the implications. Ten thousand Poles—our gallant allies—shot by our other, more recent, gallant allies, the Soviet Union? No wonder the Registry had been cleared.

An idea occurred to him and he went back to the first meaningless cryptogram. If one rearranged it thus: HYCYK, W., PIORO, K., DZENAJEWICZ, J., PTAK, J., HRUT, B.,... then out of the chaos was conjured order: names, Polish names.

He had enough now. He could have stopped. But he went on anyway, for he was never a man to leave a mystery partially solved. He set the Enigma for German Army Vulture, March 2, 1943, and began decoding. He knew what he was looking for and he found it after an hour, buried in a babble of other names sent to the Gestapo on March 3: PUKOWSKI, T ....

A few minutes after 5am, Jericho surfaced, molelike, from his sub-terranean hole, and stood in the passage of the mansion, listening. The Enigma had been returned to its shelf, the safe locked. The cryptograms and the settings were in his pocket.

He moved cautiously, keeping close to the wall. If Wigram had gone looking for him in the hut at midnight and failed to find him, he might by now have roused a considerable search party. And Jericho didn't want to be found, not yet. There were too many questions he had to ask, and only one man had the answers.

You became her lover, didn't you, Puck? The next after me in the great revolving door of Claire Romilly's men. And somehow—how?—you knew that something terrible was going on in that ghastly forest. Wasn't that why you sought her out? Because she had access to information you couldn't get to? And she must have agreed to copy out anything that looked of interest. (*She'd really been much more attentive of late . . .*) And then there came the nightmare day when you realised—who? your father? your brother?—was buried in that hideous place. And then, the next day, all she could bring you was cryptograms, because the British—your trusty allies, your loyal protectors—had decided that in the higher interest they simply didn't want to know any more.

Puck, Puck, what have you done with her?

There was a sentry in the Gothic entry hall, a couple of cryptanalysts talking quietly on a bench. Jericho opened the door and walked towards the morning star and the main gate. The sky was black, the telephone box almost invisible in the shadows. It was empty. He walked straight past it and pushed his way into the vegetation, where he squatted on the dry earth and waited for Hester Wallace.

By five fifteen, it was clear to him she wasn't coming, which suggested she had been detained. In which case, they were almost certainly looking for him.

He had to get out of the Park, and he couldn't risk the main gate.

He began to move back towards the house. He could still feel the effects of the Benzedrine—a lightness in his muscles, an acuteness in his mind, especially to danger—and he offered a prayer of thanks to Logie for making him take it.

By now, a faint blue stain had begun to seep up from the rim of the sky. Night—his friend and ally—was preparing to desert him. Ahead, he could begin to make out the contours of a building site: pyramids of earth and sand, squat rectangles of bricks.

Jericho had never before paid much notice to Bletchley's perimeter fence, which turned out, on inspection, to be a formidable stockade of seven-foot-high iron stakes, tapering at their tips into triple spears, bent outwards to deter incursion. It was as he was running his hands over the metal that he heard a movement in the undergrowth to his left. He retreated behind a stack of steel girders. A moment later, a sentry ambled past, in no great state of alertness to judge by the shuffle of his step.

Jericho crouched lower, listening as the sounds faded. The perimeter was perhaps a mile long. Say fifteen minutes for a sentry to complete a circuit? Say two sentries patrolling, possibly three?

If there were three, he had five minutes.

He looked round to see what he could use. There were planks and some sections of concrete drainage pipe, both of which he was able to drag over to the fence.

He upended the pipes and stood them about five feet apart. He laid a plank on top. Then he hefted a second set of pipes onto the first, picked up another length of timber and set it down carefully, making a platform with two steps—about the first practical thing he had made since boyhood. He climbed onto the rickety structure and seized the iron spears. The fence was designed to keep people out, not in, and, fuelled by chemicals and desperation, Jericho was able to pull himself astride it, twist and lower himself down the other side. He stayed there, recovering his breath. His final act was to put his foot through the railings and kick away the planks.

He didn't wait to see if the noise had attracted attention. He set off across the field, sliding and skidding over the dewy grass. He looked back only when he reached the road, and that was his last impression of Bletchley Park: a thin line of low black buildings—mere dots and dashes along the horizon—and above them in the eastern sky an immense arc of cold blue light.

HE HAD BEEN to Puck's digs once before, on a Sunday afternoon a year ago, for a game of chess. He had a vague memory of an elderly, doting landlady pouring them tea in a cramped front room.

Alma Terrace. That was it. Alma Terrace. Number nine.

He was moving quickly—long strides and an occasional loping run—down the hill, under the railway bridge. On the opposite side of the road was Albion Street, and another twenty yards on the turning into Alma Terrace.

It was a street like so many others: a double row of tiny, red-brick houses running parallel with the railway. Number nine was a clone of all the rest: two little windows upstairs and one downstairs. Jericho tried the front door—locked—and hammered on it with his fist.

A short while later, he heard a bolt being worked and drawn back. The door opened a crack. An old woman peered out.

'I'm so sorry,' said Jericho, 'but it's an emergency. I need to speak to Mr Pukowski.'

She hesitated, then let him in. She was less than five foot tall, a wraith in a pale blue quilted housecoat. 'He's in his room.'

'Could you show me?'

She shuffled down the passage and he followed.

'Mr Puck?' She tapped on the door. 'Mr Puck?' She said to Jericho, 'He must be still asleep. I heard him come in late.'

'Let me. May I?'

The little room was empty. Jericho was across it in three strides, pulling back the curtains. Grey light lit the kingdom of the exile: a single bed, a washstand, a wardrobe, a wooden chair. The bed had been lain on rather than slept in, and a saucer by the bedhead was filled with cigarette stubs.

He turned back to the window. The inevitable vegetable patch and bomb shelter. A wall.

'What's on the other side of the wall? What's over there?'

She looked aghast. 'The station.'

He tried the window. It was jammed shut.

'Is there a back door?'

She led him through a kitchen that couldn't have altered much since Victorian days. A mangle. A hand pump by the sink . . .

The back door was unlocked.

'He's all right, isn't he?'

'I'm sure he is.'

Footprints led across the vegetable patch. A tea chest stood against the wall. It splintered as Jericho mounted it, but he was just able to fold himself over the top of the sooty brickwork.

In the distance, the whistle of a train.

He hadn't run like this for fifteen years, not since he was a schoolboy being screamed at on a five-mile steeplechase.

He tore through the back entrance into Bletchley Station and flailed round the corner onto the platform. His feet rang on the ironwork of the footbridge. He took the stairs two at a time and ran across the gantry. A fountain of white smoke spurted up to his left, to his right, as the locomotive passed slowly underneath.

Jericho was halfway down the steps to the northbound platform when he spotted Puck about fifty yards away, standing close to the tracks. Jericho stopped and clutched the handrail, struggling for air. The Benzedrine, he realised, was wearing off. When the train at last jolted to a stop, Puck walked casually towards the front, opened a compartment door and disappeared.

Using the rail for support, Jericho picked his way down the last few steps and toppled breathlessly into an empty compartment.

He must have blacked out for several minutes, because he never heard the whistle blow. The next thing he was conscious of was a rocking motion. The seat was warm and dusty to his cheek, and through it he could feel the soothing rhythm of the wheels. He opened his eyes, recollecting vaguely that there was something he was supposed to be afraid of, and then he remembered.

Levering himself up, he pushed down the window and thrust his head into the rushing air. No sign of any town. Just flat, hedged countryside, interspersed with barns and ponds that glinted in the morning light. They were heading north on the main west-coast line, which meant—he tried to recall—Northampton next, then Coventry, Birmingham, Manchester, Liverpool...

Liverpool. And the ferry across the Irish Sea.

He was stunned by the unreality of it all, yet at the same time by its simplicity, its obviousness. His immediate reaction was to pull the communication cord. But then what? *Think.* He would be left, ticketless, drug-eyed, trying to convince some sceptical guard that there was a traitor on board, while Puck would climb down from the train and disappear. Jericho suddenly saw the absurdity of his own situation. He didn't even have enough money to buy a ticket. All he had was a pocketful of cryptograms.

Get rid of them.

He pulled them from his pocket, tore them into fragments, then released them out of the window into the slip-stream. Craning his head the other way, he tried to guess how far up the train Puck was. Three carriages? Four? He pulled his head back in and closed the window, then crossed the compartment and slid open the door to the corridor.

Jericho lurched towards the head of the train, glancing into each compartment as he passed. Here were a pair of sailors playing cards, there a young couple asleep in one another's arms, there again a family sharing sandwiches and a flask of tea.

He opened the door leading to the next carriage and stepped through. There was no sign of Puck in this carriage, or in the next, and by the time he'd reached the third he could sense the train beginning to slow. He moved on down the corridor.

Two compartments filled with sullen-looking soldiers.

Then one empty compartment.

Then Puck.

HE WAS SITTING with his back to the engine, leaning forward—the same old Puck, handsome, intense, engrossed in conversation with someone just out of Jericho's line of sight.

It was Claire, thought Jericho. It had to be Claire.

He turned his back on the compartment and moved discreetly crabwise, pretending to look out of the window. His eyes registered an approaching town—scrubland, goods wagons, warehouses—and then an anonymous platform.

'Northampton!' shouted a man's voice, as the train crawled to a halt. 'Northampton Station!'

And if it was Claire, what would he do?

But it wasn't her. He looked and saw a young man—neat, dark, aquiline: in every essence *foreign*—saw him smiling and nodding—some transaction had been completed—and then the man was up on his feet and stepping out of the compartment. Puck watched him, then pulled the door shut and sank back into his seat.

Jericho jerked his gaze away.

Suddenly he saw what must have happened. Puck cycling over to the cottage on Saturday night to retrieve the cryptograms—and instead finding Jericho. Puck returning later to discover the cryptograms were missing. And Puck assuming, naturally, that Jericho would run straight to the authorities and turn Claire in.

But you couldn't allow that, could you, Puck, because she was the only link between you and the stolen papers? And you needed time to plan this escape with your foreign friend.

So what have you done with her?

A whistle. A frantic working-up of steam. The platform began to slide away. Jericho barely noticed, unconscious of everything except the inescapable sum of his calculations.

WHAT HAPPENED NEXT happened very quickly, and if there was never a coherent explanation of events that was owing to a combination of two factors: amnesia induced by violence, and the bureaucratic fog machine of the Official Secrets Act.

But it went something like this.

About two miles north of Northampton Station, a set of points connected the west-coast main line with the branch line to Rugby. With five minutes' notice, the train was diverted westwards down the branch line, and very shortly afterwards a red signal warned the driver of an obstruction on the tracks ahead.

The train was already slowing, although he didn't recognise it, when Jericho slid open the door to Puck's compartment.

Puck was pushing down the window—presumably because he had noticed the loss of speed and was suspicious. He heard the door behind him and turned, and his eyes flickered from Jericho to the corridor to the window and back to Jericho, computing odds, angles, trajectories. 'Why are we stopping?'

Jericho said, 'What have you done with her?'

Puck had the stolen Smith & Wesson in his hand, safety catch off. He brought it up and waved him back with it, but Jericho didn't care what happened now. He took a step closer.

Puck began to say something like 'Please don't make me—' and then farce, as the guard came in to inspect their tickets.

For a long moment they stood there, this curious trio—the guard, face creasing with surprise; the traitor, with his wavering pistol; the cryptanalyst between them—and then several things happened at once. The guard said, 'Give me that,' and made a lunge at Puck. The gun went off. The noise of it was like a physical blow. The guard looked down, puzzled, at his stomach, as if he had a bad twinge of indigestion. The wheels of the train locked and suddenly they were all on the floor together. It may have been that Jericho was the first to crawl free. Certainly he had a memory of pulling Puck out from beneath the guard, who was leaking blood everywhere. Jericho knelt over him and said, rather fatuously, 'He needs a doctor.' There was a commotion in the corridor. He turned to find that Puck had the outside door open and the gun pointed at him again. Jericho closed his eyes for the bullets and Puck said—and this Jericho was sure of, because he spoke the words very deliberately, in his precise English, 'I killed her, Thomas. I am so terribly sorry.'

Then he vanished.

THE TIME BY NOW was just after a quarter past seven. Jericho stood on the threshold of the carriage and watched, as all along the train doors banged open in the sunshine and people jumped out. Beyond the locomotive, a group of soldiers was scrambling down the slight embankment, led—Jericho was surprised to see—by Wigram. More soldiers were deploying from the train itself. Puck was only about twenty yards away. Jericho jumped down to the grey stones of the track and set off after him.

Someone shouted, directly behind him, 'Get out of the way, you idiot!'—wise advice, which Jericho ignored.

It couldn't end here, he thought, not with so much still to know.

He was all in. His legs were heavy. But Puck wasn't making much progress either. He was hobbling across a meadow, trailing a left ankle which autopsy analysis would later show had a hairline fracture—whether from his fall in the compartment or his leap from the train no one would ever know.

Jericho was very close to him when Puck turned and fired his pistol. He couldn't have been aiming at Jericho: the shot went wide of anything. It was just a parting gesture. His eyes were dead now, blank. There was an answering crackle of fire from the train.

Five bullets hit Puck and two hit Jericho. Jericho felt as though he had been struck from behind by a car—not painfully, but terrifically hard. It winded him and pitched him forward. He somehow kept on going, and then a second blow—irresistible this time—spun him from his right shoulder round in a graceful arc.

The apple trees wept blossom in the wind. It drifted across the graveyard and piled like snow against the marble tombs.

Hester Wallace leaned her bicycle beside the low brick wall, straightened her shoulders and strode on up the flagstone path towards the church porch.

The truth was if it hadn't been for her there would never have been a memorial service. It was she who persuaded the vicar to open the doors of St Mary's, Bletchley, even though she had to concede that Claire was not a believer. It was she who booked the organist and told him what to play. It was she who chose the hymns and the readings and had the service cards printed, she who lay awake the night before, worrying in case nobody bothered to come.

But they came all right.

Lieutenant Kramer came in his American naval uniform, and old Dr Weitzman came from the Hut 3 Watch, and Miss Monk and the girls from the German Book Room, and various rather sheepish-looking young men in black ties, and many others whose names Hester never knew.

Hester sat in the front pew, with her Bible marked at the passage she intended to read (I Corinthians 15.lLI–LV: 'Behold, I show you a mystery…'), and every time someone new came in she turned to see if it was *him*, only to glance away in disappointment.

'We really ought to begin,' said the vicar, fussing with his watch. 'I've a christening due at half past.'

'Another minute, Vicar, if you'd be so good.'

It was a long time since she had seen Tom Jericho. In fact, she had only Wigram's word that he was still alive, and Wigram wouldn't even tell her which hospital he was in, let alone allow her to visit. He had, though, agreed to pass on an invitation to the service, and the following day he announced that Jericho would love to come. 'But the poor chap's still quite sick, so don't count on it.'

By five past ten, the organist had run out of music to play and there was an awkward hiatus of shuffling and coughing.

'Hymn number four hundred and seventy-seven,' said the vicar, with a glare at Hester. '"The day thou gavest, Lord, is ended."'

The congregation stood. The organist hit a shaky D. They started to sing. From somewhere near the back, she could hear Weitzman's rather beautiful tenor. It was only as they reached the fifth verse that Hester heard the door scrape open behind them. She turned, and there, beneath the grey stone arch—thin and frail and supported by the arm of Wigram, but indisputably alive—was Jericho.

THE FIRST BULLET had struck him in the lower left-hand quadrant of his back, nicked his eleventh rib and exited through his side. The second had buried itself deep in his right shoulder, and that was the bullet they had to cut out surgically. He lost a lot of blood. There was an infection.

He lay in isolation, under guard, in some kind of military hospital just outside Northampton—isolated in case, in his delirium, he babbled about Enigma; guarded in case he tried to get away.

The first morning he woke up, he asked to see a doctor. He wanted to know what had happened. The doctor told him he had been involved in a shooting accident. Apparently he had wandered too close to an army firing range and was lucky he hadn't been killed.

No, no, protested Jericho. It wasn't like that at all. He tried to struggle up, but they gave him an injection and he went back to sleep.

Gradually, as he started to recover both mentally and physically, he almost looked forward to the daily agony of the changing of his dressing, as an opportunity to ask about what had happened. He had part of the picture, but not all of it. But at any attempt to ask questions, any behaviour that might be construed as 'difficult', out would come the needle with its cargo of oblivion.

He learned to play along.

He passed the time by reading mystery stories, Agatha Christie mostly, which they brought him from the hospital library. He got through two, sometimes three, a day. By the end of the first week, he was strong enough to take a few steps down the corridor and visit the lavatory unaided.

Logie must have come to see him some time at the beginning of April. It was early evening, but still quite light, with shadows dividing the little room. Logie perched uneasily on the edge of the bed and told him that everyone sent their best.

'Even Skynner?'

'Well, no, maybe not Skynner. But then I haven't seen much of Skynner, to be honest. He's got other things on his mind.'

Logie talked for a bit about what everyone was doing, then started telling him about the convoy battle: twenty-two merchantmen sunk by the time the convoys reached air cover and the U-boats could be driven off, 150,000 tons of Allied shipping destroyed and 160,000 tons of cargo lost.

'How many died?'

'About four hundred. Mostly Americans.'

Jericho groaned. 'Any U-boats sunk?'

'Only one. We think.'

'And Shark?'

'Going great guns, old love.' He patted Jericho's knee through the bedclothes. 'You see, it *was* worth it in the end, thanks to you.'

It had taken the bombes forty hours to solve the settings, from midnight on Tuesday until late on the Thursday afternoon. But by the weekend the Crib Room had made a partial recovery of the Weather Cipher Book—or enough of it to give them a toehold—and now they were breaking Shark six days out of seven.

After a while, Logie said quietly, 'Skynner's had to hand over the plans for the four-wheel bombes to the Americans.'

'Ah.'

'Well, *of course*,' said Logie, folding his arms, 'it's all *dressed up* as cooperation. From now on, we're to teleprinter a copy of all Atlantic U-boat traffic to Washington the moment we receive it, then it's two teams working in friendly consultation. Blah, blah, blah. And when they've got ten times the bombes we have—which I reckon will be in six months at the outside—what chance do we stand? We'll just do the interception and they'll do all the breaking.' He sighed and stretched out his legs, contemplating his vast feet. 'Still, there is one bright side, I suppose.'

'What's that?' Jericho looked at him, then saw what he meant, and they both said, 'Skynner!' simultaneously, and laughed.

'He is *bloody* upset,' said Logie contentedly. 'Sorry about your girl, by the way.'

'Well...' Jericho gestured feebly with his hand and winced.

There was a difficult silence, mercifully ended by the nurse coming in and telling Logie his time was up. He got to his feet with relief and shook Jericho's hand. 'Now you get well, old love, d'you hear what I'm saying, and I'll come and see you again soon.'

'Do that, Guy. Thank you.'

But that was the last time he saw him.

Wigram's visits, on the other hand, had been frequent and solicitous. He would plump his pillows, pour his water, fuss with his sheets. Oh, yes, Wigram was charming.

In the beginning, it was Jericho who did most of the talking, answering Wigram's questions. Why hadn't he reported the cryptograms in Claire's room to the authorities? What had he taken from Beaumanor? How had he broken the intercepts?

Jericho tried to mix in some questions of his own, but Wigram always brushed them away. All in good time, he would say.

And then one afternoon he came in beaming even more broadly than usual to announce that he had completed his enquiries. A little web of wrinkles appeared at the edges of his blue eyes as he smiled down at Jericho. 'So, my dear chap, if you're not too exhausted, I suppose I should tell you the story.'

'ONCE UPON A TIME,' said Wigram, settling himself at the bottom of the bed, 'there was a man called Adam Pukowski, whose mother was English and whose father was Polish, who lived in London until he was ten, and who, when his parents divorced, went away with his father to live in Krakow. The father was a professor of mathematics; the son showed a similar aptitude, and in due course found his way into the Polish cipher bureau. War came. The father rejoined the Polish Army. Defeat came. Half the country was occupied by the Germans, the other half by the Soviet Union. The father disappeared. The son escaped to France to become one of the fifteen Polish cryptanalysts employed at the French cipher centre. Defeat came again. The son escaped via Vichy France to neutral Portugal, where he made the acquaintance of one Rogerio Raposo, a junior member of the Portuguese diplomatic service and an extremely dodgy character.'

'The man on the train,' murmured Jericho.

'Indeed. The man on the train.'

'From Portugal, Pukowski made his way to England. Nineteen

forty passed with no news of Pukowski's father or, indeed, of any of the other ten thousand missing Polish officers. In 1941, after Germany invaded Russia, Stalin became our ally. Representations were duly made about the vanished Poles. Assurances were duly given: there were no such prisoners in Soviet hands.

'Anyway,' Wigram continued, 'to cut a long story short, it appears that at the end of last year rumours began to circulate among the Poles in exile in London that these officers had been shot and then buried in a forest near Smolensk.' He smiled. 'Tell me, was it you who introduced Pukowski to Claire?'

Jericho shook his head.

'Ah, well,' sighed Wigram, 'I don't suppose it matters. We don't know how they met, or why she agreed to help him. But I think we can guess what must have happened. She'd make a copy of these signals from Smolensk and sneak them out. Hide them under her floorboards. Lover-boy would collect them. This may have gone on for a week or two, until the day when Pukowski saw that one of the dead men was his own father. And then the next day Claire had nothing to bring him but the undecoded intercepts, because *someone*, someone very senior *indeed*, had decided they just didn't want to know.'

He suddenly picked up one of Jericho's discarded mystery stories, flicked through it, smiled, replaced it.

'You know, Tom,' he said thoughtfully, 'there's never been a time in the history of the world when one side knew so much about its enemy. In fact, sometimes, I think, it's possible to know too much. Take the U-boat tankers, for example. Thanks to Shark, we know where they're going to be, and when, and if we knocked them out we might save hundreds of Allied lives—in the short term. But we'd jeopardise Enigma, because if we did that Dönitz would know we must be reading his codes. You see what I'm driving at? So Stalin has killed ten thousand Poles? I mean, *please*, Uncle Joe's a national hero. He's winning the war for us. What's that Hebrew proverb? "My enemy's enemy is my friend"? Well, Stalin's the biggest enemy Hitler's got, so as far as we're concerned he's a bloody good friend of ours. Katyn massacre? Thanks awfully, but do shut up.'

'I don't suppose Puck would have seen it quite like that.'

'No, old chap. Shall I tell you something? I think he rather hated us. After all, if it hadn't been for the Poles we might not even have broken Enigma in the first place. But the people he really hated were the Russians. And he was prepared to do anything to get revenge. Even if it meant helping the Germans. And how could he help the Germans? By warning them Enigma wasn't safe. And how could he do *that*?' Wigram smiled and spread his hands. 'Why, with the assistance of his old friend from 1940, Rogerio Raposo, recently transferred from Lisbon and now employed at the Portuguese legation in London. The same Senhor Raposo who is now residing in His Majesty's Prison, Wandsworth. Who has confessed to everything.'

On March 6, Pukowski had gone to see Raposo in London, handed him a thin sealed envelope and told him he could make a great deal of money if he delivered it to the right people. The following day, Raposo flew to Lisbon carrying the said envelope, which he passed to a contact of his on the staff of the German naval attaché.

Two days after that, the U-boat service changed its Short Weather Cipher Book, and a review of cipher security began—Luftwaffe, Afrika Korps . . . But the Germans weren't about to abandon Enigma on the basis of one letter. They suspected a trick. They wanted proof. They wanted this mysterious informant in Berlin, in person.

On March 14, two days before the start of the convoy battle, Raposo made his next trip to Lisbon and returned with instructions for Pukowski. A U-boat would be waiting to pick him up off the coast of northwest Ireland on the night of the 18th.

'That was what they were discussing on the train,' said Jericho.

'Quite right. Our man Puck was collecting his ticket, so to speak. And if it hadn't been for you he might just have got away with it.'

'But Claire would never have gone along with this,' protested Jericho. 'Passed on a few intercepts—yes. For a lark. For love, even. But she wasn't a *traitor*.'

'Lord, no.' Wigram sounded shocked. 'No, I'm sure Pukowski didn't tell her what he was planning to do. But she was the weak link. She could have given him away at any moment. So imagine how he must have felt when he saw *you* walk back through the door, recalled from Cambridge on that Friday night.'

Jericho remembered the look of horror on Puck's face, that desperate attempt to force a smile. He had already seen what must have happened: Puck leaving a message at the cottage that he needed to talk to her, Claire hurrying back into the Park at four in the morning—*click-click-click* on her high heels in the darkness. He said quietly, almost to himself, 'I was her death warrant.'

'I suppose you were. He must've known you'd try and get in touch with her. And then, the next night, when he went round to the cottage to get rid of the stolen cryptograms and found you there—well . . .'

Jericho lay back and stared at the ceiling as Wigram rattled through the rest of the story. How, on the night the convoy battle had started, he'd been called by the police and told that a woman's clothing had been found. How he'd tried to find Jericho, but Jericho had disappeared, so he'd grabbed Hester Wallace instead and taken her down to the lakeside. How it had been obvious that Claire had been bludgeoned, and her body rowed out onto the lake and dumped.

'Mind if I smoke?' He lit up without waiting for a reply. Well, Hester had refused to talk at first, but eventually she'd told him everything, at which point Wigram had realised that Jericho wasn't a traitor—realised, in fact, that Jericho was probably closer to discovering the traitor than *he* was.

So he had deployed his men. And watched.

First, Jericho was seen hurrying down Church Green Road into the town. Then he was observed going into the house in Alma Terrace. Then he was identified boarding the train. 'After that, the three of you were just flies in a jam jar, frankly.'

All passengers alighting at Northampton were stopped and questioned, and that took care of Raposo. By then, Wigram had arranged for the train to be diverted onto a branch line, where he was waiting to search it at leisure. His men had orders not to shoot unless they were shot at first. Pukowski had used his pistol. And fire had been returned.

'You got in the way. I'm sorry about that.' Still, as he was sure Jericho would agree, preserving the Enigma secret had been the most important objective. And that had been accomplished. The U-boat that had been sent to pick up Puck had been intercepted and sunk off the coast of Donegal, so the Germans probably now thought that the whole business had been a set-up all along.

'And Raposo?' Jericho was still staring at the ceiling. 'What will happen to him?'

'He'll hang,' said Wigram pleasantly. 'Poor little sod. He really was only in it for the money. We found two thousand dollars the Germans had given him in his flat, stuffed in a shoebox on top of his wardrobe. Two grand! Pathetic. But never mind about him. The question is, what are we going to do with *you*?'

After Wigram had gone, Jericho lay awake for a long time, trying to decide which parts of his story had been true.

AFTER THE SERVICE, Hester found him waiting for her outside the church. He had his face raised to the sun, and she guessed from the way he seemed to be drinking in the warmth that he hadn't seen it for a long while. As he heard her approach, he turned and smiled, and she hoped her own smile hid her shock. His cheeks were concave, his skin as waxy as one of the candles in church.

'Hello, Hester.'

'Hello, Tom.' She hesitated, then held out her gloved hand.

'Super service,' said Wigram, arriving at a gallop. 'Absolutely super. Everybody's said so, haven't they, Tom?'

'Everybody. Yes.' Jericho closed his eyes for a second, and she understood immediately what he was signalling: that he was sorry

Wigram was there, but that he couldn't do anything about it. He released her hand. 'I didn't want to leave,' he said, 'without seeing how you were.'

'Oh, well,' she said, with a jollity she didn't feel, 'bearing up. Still blisting away.'

'And still in the cottage?'

'For now. But I think I'll move out, as soon as I can find myself another billet.'

She suddenly found herself loathing the banality of the conversation, but she couldn't think of anything better to say.

'Leveret's waiting,' said Wigram. 'To run us to the station.'

Through the gate Hester could see the long black bonnet. The driver was leaning against it, watching them.

'I'm going back to Cambridge,' explained Jericho. 'For a few months' rest.'

'In fact, we ought to push off,' continued Wigram, looking at his watch. 'There's always a *chance* the train may be on time.'

Jericho said irritably, 'Will you excuse us for just one minute, Mr Wigram?' Without waiting for a reply, he guided Hester away from Wigram, back towards the church. 'This bloody man won't leave me alone for a second,' he whispered. 'Listen, if you can bear it, will you give me a kiss?'

'What?' She wasn't sure she could have heard him correctly.

'A kiss. Quickly. Please.'

'Very well. It's no great hardship.'

As her lips brushed his cheek, he held her shoulder and said softly in her ear, 'Did you invite Claire's father to the service?'

'Yes. Of course I did. But he didn't reply.'

'I knew it,' he whispered. She felt his grip tighten. *'She isn't dead . . .'*

'How touching,' said Wigram loudly, coming up behind them. 'I hate to break things up, but you'll miss your train, Tom.'

Jericho released her and took a step back. 'Look after yourself,' he said. He gave her a final smile and a shrug, then allowed himself to be led away.

She watched him walk painfully up the path and through the gate. Leveret opened the car door, and, as he did so, Jericho turned and waved. She raised her hand in return.

She stayed there for several minutes, long after the big car had pulled away, then she went back into the church.

'I ALMOST FORGOT,' said Wigram, as the car turned down the hill. 'I bought you a paper. For the journey.'

He unlocked his briefcase and took out a copy of *The Times*, opened it at the third page and handed it to Jericho.

MISSING POLISH OFFICERS:
GERMAN ALLEGATIONS

The Polish Minister of National Defence, Lieutenant-General Marjan Kukiel, has issued a statement concerning some 8,000 missing Polish officers who were released from Soviet prison camps in the spring of 1940. In view of German allegations that the bodies of many thousands of Polish officers had been found near Smolensk and that they had been murdered by the Russians, the Polish Government has decided to ask the International Red Cross to investigate the matter...

'I particularly like that line,' said Wigram, '"released from Soviet prison camps". Don't you?'

'That's one way of putting it, I suppose.' Jericho folded the paper and slipped it into his pocket, then stared firmly out of the window to forestall any further conversation. He'd had enough of Wigram and his lies.

At the station, Wigram insisted on seeing him onto the train. That peculiar handshake again, the little finger somehow tucked up into the palm.

'Goodbye, Mr Wigram.'

He settled his aching back into a seat facing the engine. Wigram closed the door. There were three other passengers in the compartment: a fat man in a fawn raincoat, an elderly woman in a silver fox and a dreamy-looking girl reading a copy of *Horizon*. They all looked innocent enough, but how could one tell?

'We'll be in touch when you're fit again, all right? You know where to get hold of me if anything comes up,' Wigram shouted through the open window.

'I certainly do,' said Jericho, and slid the window up with a bang.

THIRTY-FIVE MINUTES after boarding the train at Bletchley, Jericho disembarked at Bedford, bought a one-way ticket to London, then waited in the sunshine at the end of the platform. A crowd of passengers was beginning to build up and he scanned each face automatically, even though logic told him it was unlikely he was being followed. If Wigram had feared he might abscond, he would surely have arranged for Leveret to drive him all the way to Cambridge.

The tracks began to whine, and soon afterwards the London express pulled in. By 2.30, he was at St Pancras Station, moving awkwardly through the mass of people towards the underground.

WITH THE SOLUTION in his pocket, Tom Jericho left Somerset House and made his slow way westwards along the Embankment, until he managed to find a taxi for hire and directed the driver to Stanhope Gardens in South Kensington.

The house was big enough to be an embassy, wide and stucco-fronted, with a pillared entrance. It must have been impressive once, but now the plasterwork was flaking, and in places great chunks of it had been blasted away by shrapnel. Jericho climbed the steps and pressed the bell. Silence. He tried again, even though he knew it was useless, then retreated across the road to wait.

Fifteen minutes passed; then, from the direction of Cromwell Place, a tall, skeletal man appeared, and Jericho knew at once it must be he. Black jacket, grey-striped trousers, a grey silk tie: all that was needed to complete the cliché was a bowler hat and a rolled umbrella. Instead, incongruously, he carried, as well as his briefcase, a string bag full of groceries. He approached his vast front door wearily, unlocked it and vanished inside.

Jericho followed. He rang the doorbell again; again, nothing happened. He tried a second time, and a third, and then, with difficulty, got down on his knees and opened the letter flap.

Edward Romilly was standing at the end of a gloomy passage, with his back to the door, perfectly still.

'Mr Romilly?' Jericho had to shout through the flap. 'I'm Tom Jericho. We spoke once on the telephone. Bletchley Park.'

Romilly's shoulders sagged. 'For God's sake, will you people just *leave me alone!*'

'I've been to Somerset House, Mr Romilly,' said Jericho. 'I have her death certificate here.' He pulled it out of his pocket. 'Claire Alexandra Romilly. Your daughter. Died on June the 14th, 1929. Of spinal meningitis. At the age of six.' He propelled it through the letter flap and watched it slither across the black and white tiles. 'I'm going to have to stay here, sir, I'm afraid, for as long as it takes.'

He let the flap snap shut. Wearily, he turned away and leaned his good shoulder against one of the pillars. He wasn't sure how long he knelt there, until at last, behind him, Romilly unlocked the door.

HE WAS FIFTY or thereabouts, with an ascetic, almost monkish face. He led Jericho up a wide staircase and through a doorway into darkness. As he tugged open a pair of heavy curtains, light spilled into a drawing room full of furniture draped in white sheets. Only a sofa was uncovered, and a table, pushed up close to a marble fireplace. On the mantelpiece was a pair of large silver photograph frames.

'One lives alone,' said Romilly apologetically, fanning away the dust. 'One never entertains.' He hesitated, then walked over to the fireplace and picked up one of the photographs. 'This is Claire,' he said quietly. 'Taken a week before she died.'

522

A thin girl with dark ringlets smiled up at Jericho.

'And this is my wife. She died two months after Claire.'

The mother had the same dark hair as her daughter. Neither looked remotely like the woman Jericho knew as Claire.

'She was driving alone in a motor car,' went on Romilly, 'when it ran off an empty road and struck a tree. The coroner was kind enough to record it as an accident.' His Adam's apple bobbed as he swallowed. It was a minute before he could speak again. 'What exactly do you want from me, Mr Jericho?'

ROMILLY FOUND a bottle of whisky and a pair of tumblers. They sat on the sofa together, staring at the empty fire.

What exactly do you want from me?

The truth, at last, perhaps? Peace of mind? An ending...

And Romilly seemed to want to give it, as if he recognised in Jericho a fellow sufferer.

It had been Wigram's bright idea, he said, to put an agent into Bletchley Park. A woman. Someone who could keep an eye on this peculiar collection of characters, so essential to the defeat of Germany, yet so alien to the gentlemanly tradition of intelligence.

No one at Bletchley was to know she was an agent, not even the commander. And it was vital that she came from the right kind of background, otherwise she might have been dumped at some wretched outstation somewhere.

Well, he said, sighing, it was harder than one might think to manufacture such a person: to conjure her into life complete with identity card and ration books and all the other paraphernalia of wartime life, to give her the right background, without at the very least dragging in the Home Office and half a dozen government agencies who knew nothing of the Enigma secret.

But then Wigram had remembered Edward Romilly.

Poor old Edward Romilly. The widower. Barely known outside the Office, abroad these past ten years, with all the right connections, initiated into Enigma—and, more importantly, with the birth certificate of a girl of exactly the right age. All that was required of him, apart from the use of his daughter's name, was his signature on a letter of introduction to Bletchley Park.

Jericho said, 'You never met her, I suppose? The girl who took your daughter's name?'

'Good God, no. In fact, I made that a condition. And I didn't hear another word about it for six months. Until you called on Sunday morning and told me my daughter had disappeared.'

'And you got straight on the telephone to Wigram to report what I'd said?'

'Of course. I was horrified.' Romilly drained his Scotch and frowned. 'The memorial service was today, I think?'

Jericho nodded, and looked away from the photograph above the fireplace. 'Except that Claire—my Claire—isn't dead, is she?'

AFTERWARDS, HE REALISED he never actually told Romilly how he had worked it all out: that host of inconsistencies that had made a nonsense of the official version.

The oddity of her behaviour, for a start; the failure of her supposed father to react to her disappearance, or to show up at her memorial service; the puzzle of why her clothes had been so conveniently discovered, when her body had not . . . All these had clicked and turned and rearranged themselves into a pattern of perfect logic.

Once one accepted she was an informer, everything else followed. The material which Claire—he still called her Claire—had passed to Pukowski had been leaked with Wigram's approval, hadn't it? Where was the harm?

'It was nothing compared with what Puck already knew about naval Enigma. And Wigram wanted to see what Puck would do with it. See if anyone else was involved. Am I right?'

Romilly said nothing.

It was only later that Wigram had realised he'd made the most almighty miscalculation: that the decision to stop monitoring Katyn had tipped Puck over the edge into treason, and that somehow he'd managed to tell the Germans about Enigma. From that point on, Puck must have been under twenty-four-hour watch, to find out who his contact was and to catch them both red-handed.

'Now, when Puck discovered I had the cryptograms, he knew Claire would have to disappear, otherwise she'd be questioned. She had to vanish for at least a week, so he could get away. So between them they *staged* her murder—stolen boat, bloodstained clothes beside the lake. He guessed, correctly, that would be enough to make the police call off their hunt. He never suspected she was betraying *him* all the time.'

Jericho took a sip of whisky. 'Do you know, I really think he may have loved her—that's the joke of it. So much so that his last words, literally, were a lie—*I killed her, Thomas, I'm so very sorry*—a deliberate lie, to give her a chance to get away.

'And that, of course, was the cue for Wigram, because, from his point of view, that confession neatly tied up everything. Puck was dead. Raposo would soon be dead. Why not leave "Claire" at the bottom of the lake as well? All he needed to do to round the story off was to pretend that it was *me* who led him to the traitor.

'So to say that she's still alive is not an act of faith, but merely logical. She *is* alive, isn't she?'

A long pause. 'Yes,' said Romilly, hopelessly. 'I understand that to be the case.' He looked up. 'Will you try to find her?'

'I don't know,' said Jericho. 'Perhaps.'

The death certificate was still lying on the table beside him. 'Then you'll need this,' said Romilly, picking it up. 'You must show it to Wigram. If you like, you can tell him you've seen me. In case he tries to deny everything.'

'Wouldn't that get you into trouble?'

'Trouble?' Romilly gave a laugh. He gestured behind him, at his mausoleum of a house, at the photographs on the mantelpiece. 'D'you think I care about *trouble*? Come on, Mr Jericho, take it.'

Jericho hesitated, and in that moment he had a vision of himself: a few years older, another Romilly, struggling vainly to breathe life into a ghost.

'No,' he said at last. 'You're very kind. But I think I ought to leave it here.'

He left the silent street with relief, and walked towards the sound of traffic. On Cromwell Road, he hailed a cab.

The spring evening had brought out the crowds. Along the wide pavements of Knightsbridge it was almost like a festival: a profusion of uniforms—dark blue, khaki, grey—with everywhere the splashes of colour from the summer dresses.

She is probably here, he thought, tonight, somewhere in the city. Or perhaps that would have been considered too risky, and she had been sent abroad by now, to lie low until the whole business had been forgotten.

He pulled down the window and felt the warm night air on his face. And here was something very odd. Staring out at the teeming streets, he began to experience a sense of—well, he could not call it *happiness*, exactly. *Release*, perhaps, would be a better word.

He remembered their last night together, lying beside her as she wept. What had that been? Remorse, was it? In which case, perhaps she *had* felt something for him.

She never talked about you, Hester had said.

I'm flattered.

Given the way she used to talk about the others, you should be . . .

At King's Cross Station, he bought a postcard and a book of stamps and sent a message to Hester, asking her to visit him in Cambridge as soon as she could.

On the train he found an empty compartment and stared at his reflection in the glass, an image which gradually became clearer as the dusk gathered, until he fell asleep.

THE MAIN GATE to the college was closed. Only the little doorway cut into it was unlocked, and it must have been ten o'clock when Kite, dozing in the porter's lodge, was woken by the sound of it opening and closing. He lifted the corner of the blackout curtain in time to see Jericho walking into the great court.

Kite quietly let himself out of the lodge to get a better view.

It was unexpectedly bright—there were a lot of stars—and he thought for a moment that Jericho must have heard him, for the young man was standing at the edge of the lawn and seemed to be listening. But then he realised Jericho was actually looking up at the sky. The way Kite told it afterwards, Jericho must have stood that way for at least five minutes, turning first towards the chapel, then the meadow, and then the hall, before moving off purposefully towards his staircase, passing out of sight.

ROBERT HARRIS

Although he was born more than a decade after the end of the Second World War, Robert Harris has a remarkable ability to re-create the atmosphere of the war years, as revealed in *Fatherland*, his first novel, which sold more than four million hardback copies, and now in *Enigma*.

Of course, none of this success happened by accident, and Harris's meticulous research—two years' worth went into *Enigma*—is largely responsible for the accuracy and extraordinary vividness of his settings.

The original source of inspiration for *Enigma* was a documentary that Harris saw about Alan Turing, the pioneer in computer theory who played a key role in unscrambling the torrent of radio messages transmitted by the 200,000 Enigma machines manufactured by the Third Reich. 'I knew that Enigma was important,' the author explains, 'but what was it like at Bletchley Park? Ten thousand people worked there. I felt curious about how they lived. I like novels that take you inside another world.'

Formerly a BBC researcher and reporter, and later a political columnist for the *Observer* and the *Sunday Times*, Robert Harris does not regret turning his back on either politics (which he almost entered) or journalism. The success of his novels has given him the freedom to become a full-time writer, and to explore in-depth the Second World War, a subject that has fascinated him since he was a boy of thirteen and first read *The Rise and Fall of the Third Reich*. 'I just found it all riveting. Those twelve years are the crucible of the modern world, possibly the most important in human history, in what they tell us about what human beings are capable of.'

His first book, *Selling Hitler*, about the Hitler Diaries fiasco, was nonfiction written in fictionalised style. While writing it, Harris realised that he enjoyed the process of blending fictional narrative with facts. It has proved to be a lucrative combination, enabling him to move with his wife, a BBC producer, and their two children, to a beautiful Berkshire vicarage with a garden that slopes down to the Kennet and Avon canal. 'As my publisher says,' the author comments wryly, '"You can say what you like about Adolf, but he's been good to Robert."'

PICTURE CREDITS: page 4, Bruce Coleman; pages 6 and 7, Images Colour Library; page 129, © Patti Thayer; pages 130/131 main picture: the publishers have made all possible efforts to trace the copyright holder, but if any omission has occurred, please let us know; page 313 © *People Weekly* © 1995 Stephen Ellison; pages 314/315 Ardea, London; map on page 318: Malcolm Porter; pages 384 and 385, top left: British Telecommunications Plc, bottom left: Imperial War Museum; page 527, *Publishing News*. The publishers would like to thank the following organisations for their help in providing art reference: page 416, Imperial War Museum; page 446, British Telecommunications Plc.